Outer Realm:
Advent of Fire

Part One

Abdul-Azeez Ayodele Azeez

Outer Realm: Advent of Fire
Part One
Copyright © 2025 by Abdul-Azeez Ayodele Azeez
Contact #: 1-347-971-8430
Email: abdulartist@yahoo.com

ISBN-13: Paperback: 979-8-9999096-0-2
          Hardback: 979-8-9999096-1-9
          ePub: 979-8-9999096-2-6

Printed in the United States of America

CONTENTS

DEDICATION

This book is dedicated in the memory of my grandmother, Alhaja Rafat Amoke Hameed, to my mom, Hadrat Adejoke Azeez, my sisters Azeezat and Hafeezat, and to other family members and friends that are too numerous to mention.

Your support and encouragement were highly appreciated.

PROLOGUE

Our tale takes place in another universe on another planet. This planet is called Mirthadine (*merth-a-dyne*). The inhabitants of this planet are stronger, faster, and more durable than the inhabitants of Earth from the 21st century. This is the result of the greater force of gravity on Mirthadine, which is five times the gravity on Earth. In addition, their planet's ozone layer is thinner than it is on Earth. This means the inhabitants are constantly exposed to ultraviolet radiation; their bodies get used to it, thus they are more resistant to free radicals and carcinogens. In addition, because of the frequency of ultraviolet rays and other particles bombarding these beings, they build resistance in the form of denser bones, tougher skin, and faster platelet production for faster healing. Their muscles are made of a different kind of fiber that allows these beings to allocate more strength. With this kind of strength, an individual from Mirthadine could lift the earthly equivalent of a car. Compared to earthlings, these beings have more twitch fibers that gives them superhuman reflexes allowing them to both stop and perceive objects moving at light speed within a limited vicinity. These unique twitch fibers allow individuals to perform feats such as stopping a bullet mid-flight, and run long distances, like twenty miles, without a break. If an object approaches a being from Mirthadine at light speed, their brains can slow down the perception of this speed, allowing the individual to react, thus giving the individual enough time to notice the object. The reason for this is unknown, but many scholars believe that neurons fire at an incredible rate, allowing an individual from Mirthadine to think faster. As for the reflexes, many believe that the anatomy of the twitch fibers allows certain body parts to move at light speed but not simultaneously in the way a speedster (someone who can at least break the sound barrier) does. Not everyone in Mirthadine can run at the speed of light, but everyone in Mirthadine can evade or block objects at the speed of light, except for those with neurological disorders.

Additionally, non-speedsters can only react to something traveling at the speed of light provided the object is large enough to see (tiny particles do not count). Furthermore, when not in the presence of something traveling the speed of light in other words normal speed or less than the speed of sound, their reflexes are relatively normal. Many scholars believe objects travelling at the speed of light activates the central nervous system, enabling the individual to siphon speed temporarily from the object in an albeit limited fashion. How this is done is unclear. It is important to note that the dynamic force (more on that later) produces a similar effect on non-speedsters when used in motion at preternatural speeds.

This is not the only mystery of their anatomy. For some unknown reason, their muscle and bones do not atrophy at the rate an earthling does. In addition, their blood can acclimate to whatever environment they are in, regardless of force of gravity. However, these spectacular attributes are most prominent on Earth or other planets with significantly less gravity than Mirthadine. Additionally, such traits are not as expressed on Mirthadine. Nevertheless, individuals on Mirthadine are still significantly stronger than your average human from Earth in the 21st century. These qualities apply to animals as well. Inorganic objects are often denser; sometimes they are up to seven times as dense as their earthly equivalents while still maintaining their properties.

Mirthadine is a world where magic, monsters, and the supernatural exist. Furthermore, all beings in Mirthadine possess some type of abilities. There are four types of abilities. The supernatural, magical, any form of soul manipulation (relating to chi, or chakra manipulation, this includes the control of the elements) and simple mutation. Before we go over these abilities, we must first discuss the different races in relations to these abilities. Let us first discuss the most familiar of races, at least to you, reader, humans sometimes known as man. The race man, like many other races on Mirthadine, has a soul. A typical soul is an invisible sphere that resides in the center of the stomach. The soul has two parts - the core, which is the life force, and the corona. In this sense, the soul resembles a miniature sun. Although there is great debate on whether there is a soul in our Earth on Mirthadine, the soul is a crucial part of one's existence. In other words, if the soul were to get damaged or depleted, that individual would die a horrible death or, worse, experience endless suffering. This, however, will only occur if the soul were prematurely extracted or tampered with.

Now that we discussed both the anatomy of the soul and its importance, we can then move on to its properties. Reader, if you have read this far, then I take it you have heard of the term "soul manipulation." Well, *soul manipulation* pretty much defines itself. Soul manipulation entails the production of chakra/chi. It is sometimes known in Mirthadine as halo-soul manifest and core-soul manifest. The suffix-*soul manifest* simply means harnessing the soul's energy to create several things, such as auras, makeshift weapons, and shields. The number of objects, their density, and how well they can be manipulated depends on the amount of soul energy one has. Soul energy is equivalent to chakra or chi.

It is important to note that when the energy is emitted by the soul, the soul manifest departs from the body and is no longer colorless. It can come in a variety of colors. The colors do not represent anything. There are exceptions, however, there is the pure spectrum of colors and the impure spectrum. Now getting into this is quite complicated, so I will gloss over it for now. The halo-soul manifest is the energy coming from the corona.

To create things out of soul, one must first use the soul's energy. Unfortunately, this energy is somewhat limited. Although the energy from halo-soul manifest can be regenerated, if it is depleted, it is advised not to attempt to garner any more energy because then you'll take energy from the core-soul manifest, which is the life force. In addition, the core-soul manifest cannot be regenerated. So how does one know when they consumed too much halo-soul manifest? Well, once the corona energy is depleted, the smell of Sulfur will follow. For those who are unaware of the significance of Sulphur on Earth, it is usually used to identify demons according to the lore. The Sulphur described here, however, has nothing to do with demons.

Now let's talk about the elementals, individuals who can use elements. It is important to note that not every natural being can utilize the elements, but every natural being can utilize soul energy in its raw form, apart from magic wielders (we will get into that later). The elementals can control elements, such as lightning, fire or both, terrain (otherwise known as earth on Earth), metal, wind, light, water, and others. Some people can utilize all elements, some cannot use any, while others can use multiple, some only one. The usage of elements all depends on one's genetics. For instance, if your genes code for two incongruous elements like fire and water, then you will not be able to wield the elements. If your genes code for two complementary elements such as terrain and metal, then you will be able to utilize those elements. Then there are the previously mentioned wielding all elements. In that instance, all genes code for all elements in which case the incongruous elements do not matter. So how do the elementals work? Well, as you already know, the soul powers every single cell in the body, including organelles such as the mitochondria (referring to beings in Mirthadine). The mitochondria are interesting organelles in the fact they are deemed by many as the powerhouse of the cell. They already produce energy in the form of ATP with an electron transport chain in the inner mitochondrial membrane. A high-energy electron is passed along with an electron transport chain. The energy released pumps hydrogen out of the matrix space. Then the gradient created by this drives hydrogen (protons) back through the membrane through ATP synthase. That's the complicated explanation, but an accurate one necessary to understand the production of ATP.

The simpler explanation is that the mitochondria turn the energy from food into ATP and then distributes it to the rest of the cells. Beings from Mirthadine, at least those that can utilize the elements, can convert that ATP into energy (Soul Energy) willingly and convert that same energy into the elements. It is important to note that both utilizing soul and to an extension the elements is taxing on the body because it interferes with the production of ATP that the body produces naturally. In other words, the energy from the food one eats can be depleted because the energy used to fuel the cells that comes from food are no longer used to enrich the cells and it is instead wasted and is propelled outside the body in the form of soul manifest.

Now let's talk about magic and its wielders. Not all beings in Mirthadine can produce magic, at least in the natural sense. Man, elves, rhodeac (the term goblin is used, but it is a slur, there are various slurs for other races, but we will get into that later; mainly because they are numerous), dragons, and snake people (a colloquial but inaccurate term to describe a race known as sison (PSY-SON). They are often called snake people because, like a snake, they possess a fork tongue, retractable fangs that often but not always contain venom. Some even have thermal vision. Despite this, they share no evolutionary link with snakes. It is important to note that both rhodeac and sison are called by mainly human and elf bigots, as the demon races because of features such as a fork tongue and horns, even though they share no inherent link to demons). Most races have at least one individual capable of producing magic. However, not all the races have the same affinity to magic. For instance, both the rhodeac and elves have an affinity of 98% towards magic, sison have a 53% affinity towards magic, humans have 50%, dragons have 14%, angels and djinn have 84%. There are other races that can produce magic, but that would make this section too numerous and ultimately boring. You may be wondering how the percentages came about, well a census was taken with a population of a hundred thousand by Nadarc Sismoot - a half rhodeac half sison (this means he possessed both horns and a fork tongue, because those are dominant traits) in the year 1221 (NEEOT, New Era, End of Time). This means the data collected is not always accurate, but it's the closest we are going to get. There are races that cannot produce magic naturally, such as giants, dwarfs and the supernatural.

Now that we have established the races that can and cannot use magic, we can now explore both its anatomy and origin. Magic comes in many forms, but traditional magic, or as it is sometimes known in Mirthadine as athenuit (*a-theyn-nuit*), which is the old tongue for coming from another place, is the most prevalent form. Athenuit simply means that an actual hex is from another dimension.

There are ten to eleven known dimensions, and it is unclear which dimension the hexes come from. It is believed that athenuit magic comes from other dimensions because the hexes often do not obey standard laws of physics. It is alleged that athenuit spells can only be utilized in old tongue. Old tongue is thought to be the oldest language in all Mirthadine. Although the legitimacy of this claim has been disputed, supporters of the claim, nevertheless, continue to acquire growing evidence for it.

An example of how magic works is if one is capable of wielding magic, and they want to summon lightning, they will simply say, "*Uthra* [summon] *Thragaa* [lightning/thunder]," and lightning will appear. But there is a catch: one cannot just summon any object. Some objects have anti-magic properties and cannot be summoned. In addition, like the elementals (those who practice a type of soul manipulation involving the elements), the number of objects that can be summoned is limited to the size of one's corona or core. We will discuss this in detail later when we discuss the anatomy of the magic soul. So far, we have only discussed one aspect of magic that is summoning. Although it is the most common form of magic, it is not enough to be proficient. It is believed that speaking old tongue is the only method to perform traditional magic, which means magic wielders must study old tongue to practice magic. However, that is a bit of a fallacy, magic does not need to be spoken, it can be thought. Thinking of spells in your head is quite difficult because it requires total concentration. Meaning you must only think of the one spell to cast it. If you are distracted by other thoughts, it will not work. Magic also requires eye contact or some sort of focus point, so spells know exactly where to go. Not all magic begins with "*Uthra.*" Magic involving energy projection/alteration of one's own soul is known as *kiklu* old tongue for gambit magic. This is different from soul manipulation because the energy the magic wielder generates is not controlled by them hence it is uniform for every magic wielder only varying in the time the spell lasts. In addition, an utterance must be said or thought.

Reader, you may be asking, if magic is the result of summoning things from another dimension or using one's own magic soul, how come there are hexes that cause disease, pain, death, and reanimating corpses? Surely these things have little in the way to do with summoning. This is true. Not all magic involves summoning. There is a type of magic that is known as *hokraft* which is old tongue for "negative magic." Hokraft is an umbrella term for atypical magic. It is referred to as negative magic because it involves risky things. It includes, although not limited to, necromancy, bad juju, and possession. Some forms of summoning are considered hokraft, such as the summoning of demons or other supernatural creatures or the marking of such creatures. (*Marking* means claiming an object or being through magic. It involves a sacrifice, either blood or soul exchange. Soul exchange involves a longer union, possibly even permanent.) I know this all seems complicated, but I'll explain this in detail later. There is also another type of magic known as faux magic, also known in our world as manifesting illusions or genjustu. It involves the summoning of false images or delusions into an individual or individuals mind.

Now that we've discussed the function of magic, we can now discuss its anatomy. So magic wielders have a soul just like everyone else; they have a core and corona, but they cannot utilize the elements, only summon them. On the surface, the soul of an elemental and the soul of magic wielders may look the same, but fundamentally they are different. You see, when we get down to the subatomic level, we can see that they are vastly different. Subatomic particles include electrons, neutrons and protons but as you may know scientists have discovered even more particles such as quarks, leptons, and bosons. There are, however, particles that are not discovered at least in our world. These particles, which are even smaller than quarks, are known as *ruda* (the source of magic) and *dorah* (the source of soul). Ruda makes up a magic wielder's soul, and as you'd expect, dorah makes up the soul of soul manipulators. Dorah and ruda have many similarities and differences. Such similarities include size and excitation rate. When it comes to size, both ruda and dorah are relatively the same size, about 1/10000th the size of an electron. Both ruda and dorah are particles that are in the electron cloud, but they only reside in the center of the stomach, where the soul is.

Reader, you must be wondering how the soul can be located if it is invisible. Well, the response to that is the soul is invisible at least while contained in its shell (the being it resides in) but with a powerful electron microscope one can see a small outline of the soul, the core and the corona located at the center of the electron cloud. Note as mentioned prior, the existence of the soul is heavily debated, at least amongst modern-day humans (our Earth). The reason being is the outline of the soul in the electron cloud is difficult to find being it only appears in the exact center of one's anatomy furthermore even if it is found, modern scientist either call it an error or simply empty space as you can imagine the soul is not very large, but it is compact. Both ruda and dorah make up 99% of the soul of their respective wielders. The other 1% is unknown possibly smaller particles or energy.

The soul consisting of dorah is made up of 46.5 billion particles. The soul consisting of ruda is made up of 34.3 billion particles (these numbers are averages depending on the person). Although a single ruda particle and a single particle dorah are relatively the same size, their souls are not. When ruda particles aggregate, they are smaller than dorah particles. The reason for this is that ruda particles have a greater attraction towards each other. This attraction causes ruda particles to contract. It also brings the corona closer to the core. Note if the halo touches the core, depending by how much, it could result in soul sickness. Soul sickness is a term for anything hazardous involving the soul. Someone who is an infected soul is often called a demon even though this term is wrong and bigoted; wrong because in Mirthadine, demons are mindless forms of erratic energy. Bigoted because infected people (a shorthand for infected soul) are often looked at as less than and many people erroneously believed infected people are automatically evil. Evil is a point of view, but that is for another discussion.

I know I stated earlier that the supernatural were incapable of magic, well some powerful infected can possess individuals but not through magic. Possession through magic usually involves swapping consciousness with the one being possessed and the conscious of the one being possessed will be placed in another dimension. [When a consciousness is placed in another dimension, the distance between the body and the consciousness is so great that by the time it returns to the body, its memory is lost.] Sometimes the possessor only swaps part of their consciousness so they can have control of their own body when possessing another. When infected possession or, in colloquial/erroneous terms, demonic possession occurs, the possessor forces his/herself into the possessed body and shuts down their conscious like a virus infecting a cell.

Reader, you may be wondering how individuals on Mirthadine discovered these particles. Surely, they don't have electron microscopes, or even telescopes for that matter. What Mirthadinelings (residents of Mirthadine) lack in technology, they have in magic. Through a device known as the resonance divider invented by a great sorcerer by the name of Rawlin the Bold (651-748 NEEOT), who was able to discover these particles. A resonance divider was created through magic and crafted in technology through a practice known as Magi-technology. It uses sounds to identify the subatomic particles. Each particle resonates at a specific frequency. The resonance divider helps to separate these frequencies to determine which particle is which. As for the number of particles, the resonance divider can also count the number of frequencies from each resonance. In addition, given the nature of the sound, one can determine particle size as well.

Given this recent information, one may believe that magic wielders are more susceptible to soul sickness, because the corona is closer to the core. However, that is not the case. You see, surrounding the core is this energy that forms a type of force field that neutralizes any wayward ruda particle. This is one of the reasons there are fewer ruda particles than dorah particles. This neutralizing force field is called Mytar (Mia-Tar) or the purifier. (Mytar is part of a subatomic theory known as the purifiers devised by a scientist named Albert Watts (1215-1275 NEEOT) There are some souls consisting of dorah particles that have a type of force field. Because of their rarity, individuals with this force field around their core are called pure souls. This does not mean they are pure in personality. There have been several terrible people with pure souls and likewise several good people with infected souls. There are two advantages to having a pure soul. For one, it means that one's soul cannot get infected. The second advantage is not proven, but some scholars have stated the individuals with pure souls have more control over soul manifest. Of course, there are very few people with pure souls except for all magic wielders, as aforementioned. (It is possible pure souls have white color.) The reason being is it's nearly impossible to keep dorah particles from the halo from reaching the core without some sort of barrier. As a result, most people on Mirthadine are infected slightly. However, to be considered infected by the public, at least 40% of dorah particles from the halo must infiltrate the core or vice versa. For this reason, magic wielders are sometimes considered holy and powerful. Magic wielders are sometimes even worshiped. Of course, this is a fallacy. Magic wielders are not holy because there is no proof of heaven, hell, gods, God, or the afterlife for that matter. These things only exist in religious doctrine, which is often unreliable. However, this does not stop individuals from believing they are the chosen race. For instance, since rhodeac and elves have an almost

100% affinity towards magic some, not all, often believe they are the chosen race (note they don't consider each other holy, there is a lot of animosity between the two races, but that is a tale for another time). Angels, despite the name, are not any closer to God (not proven) than your average land dweller, but some believe they are because they live on a floating continent known as Erthria. In summation, everyone thinks they're special. It is important to note that since magic wielders rely on ruda particles, they cannot produce auras but can still use protection spells and summon things to aide them in a fight.

Well, now that we've exhausted soul manipulation and magic, we can now move on to the supernatural. The supernatural cannot be explained precisely, instead it breaks down into theories. Now let's start with something simple—werewolves/lycanthropes and vampires. These conditions are known as human maladies because they don't exist in other species. That is why other races, especially some rhodeac, believe humans to be the cursed race. The terms lycanthrope and werewolves are nearly analogous. However, some theologians on planet Earth seem to think that they are distinctly different. In Mirthadine, a werewolf is simply a lycanthrope that cannot willingly transform into *wolf beast man hybrid* (Wolf beast man hybrid can refer to a lycanthrope or werewolves.) This is not to discredit the claim that there are differences between the lycanthrope and the werewolf, but rather they are the same species with different behaviors. Lycanthropes are generally saner and less beast like in behavior than their werewolf counterpart. They are said to be better at communication, forming packs, organizing armies and some can even talk as well as comprehend humanoid languages. This does not mean that a lycanthrope is smarter than a werewolf, but rather they have more control. You see, a werewolf experiences a type of madness during transformation. This due to either the shock of transforming into a beast or the mind not being able to handle the brain of a wolf and man simultaneously. For this reason, werewolves are sometimes in a constant state of fear, stress, or rage. They are not, however, limited to these emotions. In fact, some werewolves become manic, lustful, or megalomaniacal. Werewolves attack for three reasons. The first reason is fear. They believe that a group or individual is trying to kill or physically harm them, hence they act like a cornered animal going on the offensive launching a preemptive attack. The second reason is rage. The werewolf believes that their dominance is being challenged. This usually occurs in male werewolves when they are in contact with a large beast or another male. The third reason is hunger. When werewolves transform, they become an apex predator and sometimes they no longer fear humans like regular wolves, hence they prey on them.

The description of a werewolf/lycanthrope goes as follows: a creature that averages at ten feet in height for males and is completely covered in fur, eight feet for females. The color of the fur are your typical wolf colors, although there are some rare colors like blood red/crimson and gold. The beast is described as having a very muscular humanoid torso with a head resembling a wolf's head except for the scalp resembling a human and the teeth larger and sharper than any wolf or human, with canines measuring about 3 inches. Both werewolves and lycanthropes possess retractable claws that measure on average 5.5 inches. In addition, they have exceptionally long hands that resemble the mix between a wolf and a human palm. With a length of 22.3 inches and a breadth of 4.0 inches for a male. For females, 20.3 inches and 3.5 inches, respectively. For comparison's sake, the length of the beast hand is about three times of a normal hand and nearly twice the breadth. For this reason, it is difficult although not impossible to grasp things since the human hand is ideal for grasping and clubbing. Both werewolves and lycanthropes sometimes stand on their hind legs. More on that later, they are digitigrade like most canine species. The spine grows during transformation, causing the vertebrate to push against the skin, thus giving them a hunched-over look. They can be bipedal, usually to portray dominance but often remain on all fours when running.

Now that we've discussed the physical traits of a werewolf/lycanthrope, we can now explore their abilities, some fallacies about them, their soul anatomy and their highly disputed origins. Lycanthropes and werewolves both run at speeds greater than any regular wolf or regular human, usually clocking in at speeds up to 60 mph, they also possess great feats of strength, near invulnerability (the only way to kill a lycanthrope/werewolf is through decapitation with steel equal to or greater than the strength of Mylecan steel, not silver bullets, that is a fallacy), enhanced senses, enhanced durability, shape-shifting, enhanced agility, night vision and a healing factor which can be nullified when in contact with certain metals. It is also important to note that both lycanthropes and werewolves can, through training, possess these abilities in human form, albeit in a limited capacity. There are also some ancient manuscripts that claim that some werewolves/lycanthropes are immortal. A man by the name of Gaius Bennett (200 -140 WEBOT, Wild Era, Beginning of Time), claimed that the first lycanthrope lived to be 800 years old before being slain by a warrior by the name of Lucius Clodius Allectus (unknown time or origin but suspected to be during the wild era) who is speculated to be the first human werewolf. However, these claims are speculative because no one has found an immortal lycanthrope or werewolf. In addition, werewolves or lycanthropes sightings are rare so there is little evidence to back up this claim.

The main fallacy about werewolves is that they transform during the full moon. This couldn't be further from the truth. Werewolves transform at random, and no one knows why. There are many theories, but one remains most prevalent—soul sickness. The *demon theory*, as it is colloquially and inaccurately named, was proposed by a monk by the name of Charles Richfeather (1100-1165 NEEOT). It states that the werewolf is suffering from soul sickness. When an individual suffers from soul sickness, they become unstable, meaning they are trapped between two states—man and the beast. This leaves the individual with an ultimatum to become the monster or remain the man. This choice is not done consciously, rather it is made for the individual. If a choice is not made, then the werewolf/man will die a horrible death. The idea that a werewolf is an individual with an infected soul is not a new one. There is evidence to back it up. For instance, an individual with an infected soul and a werewolf share similarities, such similarities include their hybrid beast monstrous appearance. Another interesting similarity is the phenomenon of multiple souls or polysoul, as it is known in Mirthadine. Polysoul, as you may have guessed, means a single vessel containing more than one soul; dual soul (two souls) in the case of the werewolves/lycanthropes. Polysoul is a common occurrence amongst those with soul sickness, but not everyone with soul sickness has a polysoul. All werewolves and lycanthropes, however, have at least dual souls, the soul of the beast and the soul of a man (using magical tools allows individuals in Mirthadine to analyze the soul. Hence, individuals know how many souls a lycanthrope/werewolf has). Having multiple souls as you can imagine can almost certainly result in soul sickness but not necessarily. Sometimes individuals can live with two souls but it's a precarious situation. What usually happens is that the coronas get entangled and often the cores collide. The soul is like an organism. It has a symbiotic relationship with its vessel, neither can survive without the other. When a soul is infected, it wants to escape the vessel because the relationship is no longer beneficial, but it cannot escape, so instead it poisons the vessel until the vessel is destroyed, thus the soul can escape and find a new vessel. Sometimes, the vessel remains intact but in agony and since the soul is often unsuccessful in its flight, it remains in the vessel indefinitely. As a result, the vessel is in a constant state of agony sometimes to the end of days, this however, is not what happens to all those suffering from soul sickness. Some are lucky enough to die with their own soul destroying them, eventually. The life expectancy for the infected ranges from 2 days to forever. The infected feel excruciating pain and those with two or more souls feel even more pain. Soul sickness can greatly extend an individual's life. That is why several concluded that werewolves and lycanthropes are immortal. Like someone suffering from soul sickness werewolves and lycanthropes feel agonizing pain during transformations. In addition, like lycanthropes, some infected can control the unstableness of their condition, granted they cannot stop the pain entirely, however, they can be treated with potions and items though not cured.

You see, both werewolf/lycanthrope and infected often transform into monstrous beings. This is the direct result of having multiple souls. An example of this is having the soul of a goat, a frog, and a human. Yes, there are souls specific to species, anyone who has all three souls needs a physical body that can adapt to its needs hence the body of the vessel will change it to something more fitting like a frog-goat human hybrid. It is not only animals an infected can transform into, sometimes it can be a cloud of smoke, but this usually occurs when only one soul is infected.

The demon theory has its inconsistencies and holes. One such thing is the fact that werewolves do not exhibit any type of infected aura. Auras are the energy that surrounds a being after using soul manifest in beings capable of producing them. These auras emit a certain signature either by color or smell. I recall rambling on about the impure and pure spectrums. Well, an infected aura falls within the impure spectrum of color. To explain this right now would be cumbersome and tedious, so instead I will just leave it here. As for smell, it is the noxious smell of gas that can cause respiratory damage and even death to all except the infected. This smell can only be combated with a soul manifest from a pure soul (any other soul manifest would result in soul sickness) and anti-infection tools colloquially known as anti-demon weapons. Since neither werewolf nor lycanthropes have an infected aura (it is not even clear if they can produce auras, something every recorded infected can do) it is assumed by some that they are not infected but rather just monsters. It is important to note that an infected aura, or any aura for that matter, is not generated all the time but can always be emitted except during death resulting from the soul completely leaving the body. Lisput (*lyes-put*) Mordath, a sison (1135-1185 NEEOT) was the first to dispute the demon theory and came up with the *monster theory*. The monster theory claims all beasts share a common ancestor and some individuals are more beastly than others which is by no means their own fault, rather the result of overactive genes (at the time individuals in Mirthadine had a primitive concept of genes), genes from the time of old. These genes become active when scratched or bitten by a lycanthrope or werewolf, thus concluding werewolves and lycanthropes are monsters. The proof lies in the fact that not everyone bitten or scratched by the werewolf or lycanthrope turns into one, most actually just die. But the problem with the monster theory is it does not explain what caused the first werewolf to transform. It could not have been bitten or scratched by another werewolf. Did the beast transform or was it bitten? Some claim transformation others claim it was bitten. This circular logic is why the theory remains highly contentious to this day.

The beast theory could not explain the origins of the werewolf and lycanthrope, but one theory does—it is known as the *hellhound theory.* Although, it is more of a myth than a theory. It is known as *The Curse of Oatblight,* and its author is unknown, but before we get into that, we must first explain what a hellhound is. To explain that, we must first explain what a hellhole is. Now there is no proof of an afterlife, heaven, or hell in Mirthadine, but individuals, mainly the magic wielders, create artificial heavens and artificial hells.

A hellhole is an artificial hell. It was designed to torture, punish, or get information from what governments deemed criminals. It is called a hellhole because the first artificial hell created by King Simon the Cruel (314-278 WEBOT) was a hundred-foot chasm, and ever since, the name has stuck. A hellhole is created with hokraft, and it is imbued with dark energy—the type of erratic energy that creates the infected. It is believed that a man by the name of Walter Oatblight (no one knows when he lived or died or if he even existed, but many scholars swear that he lived sometime during the wild era also known as the godless era) was transformed into a dog permanently through powerful magic. He had the mind of a man and a body of a beast. He spent the equivalent of eighty years in that hole. (Time passes differently in a hellhole.) It not only altered his body because of the negative energy, but his mind as well. He became obsessed with revenge on the house of Lyca and Were—the two houses that placed him in this hell; with the help of a wizard by the name of Alduit the cunning (no one knows if he existed either). He was able to hex his teeth and escape with a magical device known as the devil's rope (its existence is speculative).

When Oatblight escaped the hellhole, he became the first hellhound in existence. He was not just an ordinary dog; he was as big as an elephant and had wings. His hide was a hellish red, and his eyes completely yellow. Tendrils of smoke radiated from his body, especially his nostrils. (Modern hellhounds can be as small as house cats or as large as mountains.

Some have wings, some do not. Others can even have multiple heads.) Oatblight attacked anything that came near which were mostly common forest creatures—deer, squirrel, moose. He had not felt full in eighty years, so he ravaged these beasts.

Oatblight was careful though. He stayed out of sight of humans. He came upon a large wolf or as it is known in Mirthadine an *ora-wulf* (not to be confused with dire wolves. Ora-wulfs are usually comparable in size to fully grown horses. Although Fenra, a female ora-wulf, was rumored to be as large as a mammoth. She is said to exist during the early wild era before civilization. Some cultures even worship the mythical beast.) Ora-wulfs are said to be noble and gentle creatures that only attack when provoked. Despite this, Oatblight viciously attacked the poor beast— ripping, tearing, and gnashing at the beast. The ora-wulf fought back, but the effort was futile. Oatblight outmatched the wolf in size and speed. Eventually it lay dead in a pool of its own blood.

This attack was deliberate. Oatblight was planning something, he used his powerful jaws to clamp down on the wolf's neck. Oatblight then dragged the carcass to a nearby hut. Inside the hut was an old friend of Oatblight, Alduit the cunning. It is said that in the hut they performed experiments on the corpse akin to genetic engineering only with the use of alchemy and magic. They were eventually able to resurrect the ora-wulf, only it was hardly the same beast. What Oatblight and Alduit did to the ora-wulf was both horrifying and repugnant. They created an undead monster that was rabid and malicious. Its fur was disheveled, its eyes were completely black, and it had a thirst for blood especially those of house Lyca and Were. Alduit the cunning placed a hex on the beast. Its bite and claw would curse all descendants of house Lyca and Were with a terrible affliction, a fate worse than death, for they would be forever trapped in a limbo state between man and beast. This beast would later be known as the werewolf, and it would unleash hell on any one unfortunate to cross its path. And so Alduit the cunning and Walter Oatblight unleashed this blight unto the world. When they eventually released the undead ora-wulf, it killed forty people in the town of Graca (actual village in the Arcadiem continent) where descendants of Lyca and Were resided. One man was scratched by the beast, his name was Lucien Were, and he became the first human werewolf after slaying the undead ora-wulf. (It was previously stated that Lucius Clodius Allectus was the first werewolf. But remember, this is all speculation. No one knows for sure who the first werewolf was. The records that were being kept at the time were unreliable.)

Just like the curse stated, in the successive days, members of house Lyca and Were transformed into werewolves through bite or scratch, if not outrightly killed by Lucien. Soon werewolves were rampant in the town, and people started to take notice that the werewolves only came from house Lyca and Were, so naturally they were blamed for this catastrophe. It is said that during this time, not including the forty killed by the ora-wulf, a total of 113 people were slain.

Those who believe in the myth no longer allow ora-wulfs in the town Graca. They are viewed as hell beasts and are hunted for sport and as for house Lyca and Were, they were said to have been disbanded and several were murdered by an angry mob who blamed them for the curse of the beast whom they fittingly named werewolf/lycanthrope (lycanthrope later came to mean something different today but at the time it was another word for werewolf).

The hellhound theory has its merits. Garca is a town that historically has the highest density of werewolf sightings, and both Lyca and Were are actually houses, although these days few people bear the surname Lyca or Were, most likely because of this myth. However, the point of contention lies in the undead ora-wulf, and the magic, alchemy, or maybe even science used to create the beast, is quite advanced. There is currently no known magic that can resurrect a being in a natural state even when you look at hokraft. This does not include man-eating roamers (zombies), roamers for short, and vampires, which are not resurrected through magic but rather a parasite and blood sickness, respectively. In other words, as far as we know, one cannot manufacture blood sickness or somehow manipulate the parasite that creates roamers to specifically transmit a curse to a certain set of people. The idea is quite far-fetched. In addition, the curse Alduit placed on the ora-wulf is a spell so advanced and potent that its effects are still apparent that till this day it is difficult to be believed. Most potent curses only last months and are reversible. Furthermore, a hex that powerful would have to take the work of at least three hundred magic wielders, and Alduit is said to have acted alone. Furthermore, spells, even those using hokraft, require upkeep to last. In other words, someone must constantly cast it and there is no guarantee it will still be effective; there is no guarantee with hokraft in general. In the case of necromancy, the corpses being brought back do not have a mind of their own, not even a stem, and are reliant on the magic wielder. Hence, they cannot act independently.

There is a reason this theory is considered myth in most circles, but it does answer the question as to why some people who are bitten or scratched by a werewolf or lycanthrope die while others survive. It also explains why there are no werewolf/lycanthrope sightings outside of Arcadiem.

Now let's move on to another supernatural being with an albeit simpler origin: vampires. Vampires are part of a group known as the undead, which include roamers, both brain dead and sentient. The first case of vampirism occurred in the large country of Yetic 2345 WEBOT. It happened in the small province of Siamu (*psy-ya-mu*). A giant hornet infestation had plagued the land. This is likely due to the decrease in numbers of the hornet's natural predator's spiders and birds. These hornets were erratic, and their behavior was unusual. For instance, several of them died off haphazardly and the ones that survived were not the same. They had a version of a disease that affected their wellbeing. This disease was known as Aggressive Deadly Hornet Syndrome (ADHS), discovered by a man name Pei Chi (2413-2346 WEBOT). As you may have known, giant hornets are already an aggressive breed, especially when provoked. Their venom can alter blood chemistry in red blood cells, causing kidney failure. The venom has also been attributed to other types of organ failure as well. In addition, those with allergies to bug bites in general can suffer anaphylactic shock that may cause death. With this information in mind, one can deduce that the giant hornets suffering from ADHS would have these traits tenfold. And as you expect, the giant hornets became more aggressive attacking other animals such as squirrels, rats, bats; most people associate bats with vampires, particularly vampire bats, but it's been highly debated whether vampire bats are the origin of human vampires. Some scholars believe another sanguinivore is responsible. It is known as the mosquito. This theory is referred to as the *mosquito theory* proposed by a noblewoman Sun Jie (2212-2132 WEBOT). However, the problem with this theory is that the largest mosquito, the tiger mosquito, is only one inch. Surely, the giant hornet would have crushed the mosquito with its stinger (0.24 inches) being about a quarter of the biggest mosquito body length. In addition, the giant hornet is about twice the size of the tiger mosquito. It is more likely the mosquito would be consumed by the giant hornet rather than be stung by it. Still, the theory has its merits. It would seem the mosquito is more likely to spread ADHS more effectively than a vampire bat, especially since bats are nocturnal and most people do not go out at night. Although proponents of the *vampire bat theory* proposed by Yin Chen (2366-2301 WEBOT) will tell you that vampires resemble vampire bats more than they do mosquitos (they are referring to their retractable fangs). The giant hornets stung house pets and humans. Most of these attacks were unprovoked.

The animals stung by the mad bug suffered great multiple organ failure, cardiac arrest, skin hemorrhaging, and necrosis. Suddenly, rare side effects of the giant hornet's venom became regular occurrences. What was worse was the birth of a new disease—a type of blood sickness that affected red blood cells in such a way that it mutated them, causing them to cannibalize each other, requiring those infected (not to be confused with the infected; soul sickness) to constantly replenish blood or else run the risk of permanently turning into a mindless roamer (a variation). Yes, this is what happens to vampires who do not feed in time. The disease also renders the victim relatively immortal, but in an endless state of hunger, even when blood is consumed. (Many vampires, however, believe they can satiate the endless hunger by consuming enough human blood thereby, or as they deem it, ascend, this information was taken from the vampire scriptures, date unknown). Furthermore, the only way to end the suffering of said victim is to behead them. This disease would later be known as vampirism (the word "vampirism," 256 NEEOT, is a modern iteration of the ancient word *va-impism* 2405 WEBOT).

While werewolf/lycanthrope origins are shrouded in mystery and myth, vampire origins are clearly recorded in history. As stated previously, the first case of human vampirism (vampirism like lycanthropy is a human affliction) was in 2345 WEBOT. In the province of Siamu, A noblewoman by the name of Su Fu (2363- WEBOT) was frolicking in her garden when the creature bit her. What creature exactly is unknown, but many scholars believe it was either a mosquito or vampire bat that was suffering from a transmitted form of ADHS, also called blood sickness. A name coined by a hunter by the name of Kong Delan (2134-2079 WEBOT). It is said that he came up with the term when hunting rabbits exhibiting ADHS behavior. When he killed and gutted the beast, he noticed they had little to no blood hence the term blood sickness was born. Before the condition was called the bloodless state, no one knows who or when that term came about. Su Fu is said to have gone into a coma. In her comatose state she is said to have change physically, her skin was paler, her irises when opened were red and when her nursemaids came to feed her, they noticed that every time they opened her mouth a pair of retractable fangs would come out (note lady Su Fu was not a sison. Sison fangs are longer and thinner, averaging 1.5 inches, whereas vampire fangs are shorter and sharper, averaging 1inch, more suitable for digging into and tearing flesh). She was in this state for three years. The most troubling aspect of all this is that during the three-year coma the nursemaids and doctors fed her with primitive tubes, funnels and liquified food, but she seemed to get gaunter, it was as though the food provided no nourishment. Which might be expected given the technology they had at hand, but what was peculiar was that when they started feeding her blood, her body seem to replenish itself.

The idea to feed her blood was an accident, a serendipitous event it would seem, until another event happened. The seemingly serendipitous occasion came in the form of a butcher. He was a friend of Su Fu, though some sources say he was her lover. The butcher, whose name was not mentioned in the text, maybe for the reason of not making Su Fu look like an adulterer, since she is seen as a tragic figure. Her supposed clandestine actions with the butcher might make people less sympathetic to her plight. The butcher came to visit her. He had some dead rabbits in his pocket. They had been gutted and their entrails removed, but the smell of blood was still there on the butcher's hands, on the rabbits, and in the air. He was at first scolded by the servants and doctors for his carelessness, coming to his lady looking disheveled and covered in blood. At first, he was turned away, but then one of the doctors noticed Su Fu's response to the blood. She was salivating, her nostrils flared, and she was breathing heavily. At this point, a connection was made that Su Fu favored blood as opposed to liquified grains. So, they continued to feed her with rabbit's blood. It was a taxing task because a vampire can never be satiated. Hence, she constantly needed blood. But even though the color in her cheeks returned and her body became plumper, her fangs and eyes remain the same. There were even reports of her smiling, like she was having a nice dream. More likely this was the result of bloodlust, a type of madness a vampire suffers while consuming blood. There is literally a lust for blood, particularly human blood. Think of it this way, bloodlust can be compared to an addict experiencing euphoria from a certain drug, thus wanting more, but that euphoria will be experienced less every time they take the drug. In the case of vampires, they move on to another more satisfying drug: human blood. After weeks of feeding Su Fu animal blood, she seemed to regress, and she remain more comatose (you see vampires can feed on animal blood without turning into a mindless roamer variant, but it's not potent enough to come out of a coma.) Fearing the worse, many of the noblemen, including her own husband, marquess Yi Yong (2370-2345 WEBOT) thought precious resources were being wasted on Su Fu who he deemed was a lost cause. Copious amounts of livestock were being sacrificed, and they did not have enough food to feed their armies which they were in desperate need of now that there was an upcoming attack from the war lord, Tao Fang (2414-2345 WEBOT), and they had lost three quarters of their garrison to the giant hornet infestation. Many even feared she was turning into a demon because of the fangs and red irises. The truth is these men feared Su Fu. She was consuming blood at an alarming rate, escalating from rabbits to pigs to cows to eventually horses. A quarter of the livestock had been wiped out due to the giant hornets. It was deemed unwise to consume the dead meat of the animals inflicted by the hornet's potent venom, as it would most likely spread disease. This was also the recommendation for the animals Su Fu drank the blood from. It was put to a vote and by majority ruling, the men agreed to put Su Fu out of her misery.

She awoke as one of the men drove a dagger into her chest. She let out a bloodcurdling shriek.

That silenced everyone. She then turned to her husband, who was petrified. She stared at him with a seemingly innocuous look on her face. However, her traits betrayed her. Those red eyes and fangs vexed him; it was at that moment that he realized he wasn't looking at his wife anymore but a monster. The following is an excerpt of a conversation taken directly from the vampire scriptures *chapter 1 Su Fu the first vampire author unknown*. It described the events that happen when Su Fu awoke.

"She-she she's alive!" shouted one of the servants.

"Impossible," said one of the noblemen named Ling Yong (2398-2345 WEBOT). He looked straight at the doctor, his countenance suggested he wanted an explanation. After a few minutes, Su Fu lost consciousness and all eyes were on the doctor. The doctor was nervous. He was sweating profusely.

"I-I-I," he stammered before he was interrupted by another noble man, Shi Yong (2410- 2345 WEBOT).

"Stop yammering and explain yourself!" he said angrily. "I don't know!" the doctor responded.

"You don't- why you troublesome no good rotten cur." Shi then seized the doctor by the collar so forcefully that the doctor nearly fell. "Listen you villain, you're going to tell me what happened or by the gods I'll have you castrated. You're going to fix it because if you don't-" Shi said through gritted teeth in a low menacing voice that further frightened the poor doctor.

"Let him go, you ruffian. He didn't do anything!" interrupted one of the female servants.

Shi met the gaze of this woman and he recognized her. He was furious, then he said with his voice getting progressively louder, "How dare you, a servant woman, address me in such a way. Do you have any idea who I am?"

"Yeah, a pathetic little coward who takes pleasure in beating women and children," the woman said brusquely.

"What did you say to me, you temptress bitch? A whore who spreads her legs for anyone is talking to me in such a way, such insolence! Woman, you best watch your tongue or else—"

"Or else what? You'll kill me like you did your wife and daughter?"

Shi looked as if he was ready to strike the woman, but there was no fear in her eyes. The doctor stepped between them in an attempt to deescalate the situation. He said with a nervous laugh, "Please, noble one, she didn't mean it. She is fatigued from working all day." His words did not ease tensions at all. Instead, he received a blow from Shi's backhand across the face. The blow caused him to stumble, but he remained on his feet.

"Shut up, you worthless sycophant, pandering to me to save this vile woman. How pathetic!"

"Are you all right, Jian (2410-2345 WEBOT)?" said the female servant, arguing with Shi.

"I'm fine," the doctor said while massaging his cheek.

The servant woman turned her attention to Shi and scowled at him, but before she could do anything, Jian stopped her.

"Please Jia (2366-2345 WEBOT). He is a nobleman."

Shi started to laugh derisively. "So the whore finally knows her place."

"I'm no whore. Your dogs of war . . ." she began. (The Dogs of War refers to the militia granted to Shi Yong by the emperor Cai Yong (2406- 2308 WEBOT) during the Yong dynasty (2515-2186 WEBOT). They were to be dispatched during war to fend off invaders or during public strife such as rebellion. In a way, they were like a police force. Of course, they often abused their power and were prone to violence, bribery, rape, and even murder. Their misdeeds did not end there. It was said they often tortured those who refuse to stoop to their level.)

"They raped me!" retorted Jia.

"What do you expect, dressing so loosely around men then prancing about in front of them with your voluptuous body? A man can only show so much restraint. You were *asking for it*," said Shi with a smirk.

"That's enough!" cried a stern voice. A silhouette of a large figure entered the room.

Shi's smile quickly turned to a fearful expression. He began to stutter, "D-d-Duke Jin Yong (2370-2308 WEBOT). I-I-I was teaching this insolent woman respect."

"No, you weren't. You were just being an idiot as usual," said Jin. Shi's expression sank. The duke had a scowl on his face. "Now, what is the meaning of this noise? Please, someone answer at once."

"Yes, Duke Jin Yong. After our deliberation, we put it to vote that Su Fu should be put to death," said nobleman Huan Chen.

"To death!" the duke exclaimed.

"Yes, she was in a coma and was not getting better—"

"Uh, she was getting better," Jia interrupted. Realizing she made a mistake interrupting Huan Chen, she averted the gaze of the duke and said, "Sorry."

"Don't be. I'm sure the woman who took care of Su Fu would know what happened. As you were saying," said the duke calmly.

"Right, you see, when we fed her blood, she started to recover, albeit slowly, but she became more responsive."

"Is this true, doctor?" asked the duke. The doctor confirmed this by nodding his head. "What about the fangs and eyes?" asked the duke.

"She's been that way since she was bitten," said Jia "So they are symptoms of ADHS?" said the duke. "Correct," replied Jian.

"I see," said the duke.

"But this still doesn't explain how she survived a fatal wound without much blood loss," said Huan Chen.

"Ming Zheng (2430-2345 WEBOT) probably missed her vitals, you know his right arm has been shaking ever since he received the blow to the back of the head from Xue Wei's (2436-2391 WEBOT) chui, his coordination has suffered greatly," said Lu Fu (2362-2345 WEBOT), Su Fu's younger brother.

"My coordination is just fine, boy. If you don't believe me, have your doctor inspect her. I drove that dagger straight through her heart!" retorted Ming Zheng.

"Come on, you expect us to believe that you delivered the fatal blow, yet my sister is still breathing. Maybe the years have dulled your senses," said Lu Fu.

"Why, you insolent little pup!"

"There appears to be no exit wound. It's quite possible the heart was only punctured, but still with this amount of damage, she is lucky to be alive," said Jian after inspecting the body by laying it on its side.

"Hmm, what do you make of all this... huh, brother?" the duke asked. The duke was referring to Yi Yong, who was his brother from the same mother. "Yi, Yi!" the duke said with great concern for his younger brother, but Yi was transfixed on Su Fu's unconscious body.

He repeated in an almost inaudible whisper, "She's my wife, but she's not. We killed her, but we didn't." It was almost as if he were in a trance. "Get it together, Yi" the duke said while seizing his brother by the shoulders and shaking him.

When Yi's speech finally became lucid, he looked at his brother and said, "She's a monster and she means to kill us all. I saw hell in her eyes."

"She is not a monster. She is your wife, and she is very ill," the duke said slowly and methodically.

"No, she is not my wife. She is a monster, and I must finish the job." He was referring to the dagger stuck in Su Fu's breast. Before the duke could do anything, Yi pulled the dagger from his wife's breast. She awoke with a large exhale, then she looked up at Yi, whose hands were shaking. Tears were streaming down his face. His voice quavered as he said, "I'm sorry."

"Yi, don't!" cried the duke.

"I'm so sorry, but you're not her."

It is believed that when vampires turned their former selves die, they still possess the memories of their former self, but they are ultimately a different person supposedly. It is even believed that you can see their true intentions in their eyes—what they have done and what they are going to do. This is all, however, not proven, only what was said and thus cannot be taken as fact.

Su Fu caressed his cheek and said, "I'm sorry. I'm not her, do what you must."

Yi held her hand on his cheek and began weeping profusely. "Yi, think about this. She is still your wife, no matter what she says. Let's be rational, she was bitten but now she's here alive, breathing. She's back. We don't need to end her. This is a joyous occasion," said Huan Chen.

"Listen to him!" the duke said.

As Yi contemplated what to do, Su Fu gently placed her hand at the back of his neck and gently drew him closer to her as she whispered, "So cold. Always, so cold. The hunger . . . it never stops. Please end me."

Yi was about to stab Su Fu with the dagger but stopped midway with the point being only two centimeters from her chest.

"Do it. I want to die! End my suffering!" Su Fu said as she began sobbing.

Yi, also sobbing, said, "I can't! You look too much like her, in a way I still see her in your eyes."

"You don't understand. People are going to die if you don't do it. I want to kill everyone; I want to rip out their throats and suck them dry. I want to lick the marrow from their bones until it satiates me even though I know it never will!"

"We'll find you more blood. We'll find a way to stop the hunger," Yi said while gently moving the hair on her forehead to behind her ear. He then proceeded to kiss her. Yi then closed his eyes and placed his forehead on Su Fu's. He whispered, "By the gods, you will be cured from this disease, and my Su will return to me. Please, oh great Yaga, return her to me. I will do anything you ask of me. Just cure my beloved Su."

(Yaga is the main deity in the polytheistic religion of Yetic, known as Yagaism. Yagaism was practiced in Yetic during the wild era, WEBOT. It has since been replaced with less concrete religions such as Polarism, Orderism, and the foreign religion Yamaism.)

After he finished praying, Yi noticed Su Fu was looking up at him, smiling. "I can see why she loves you. You're a good man. You were so adamant about being the one to kill her, so you could end her suffering, so you could be the last thing she sees before she dies, but there was a change of plan once you saw her in my eyes, you were desperate to save her, it's almost sweet but ultimately foolish and futile." He could see the smile vanish from her face as she averted his gaze.

"What are you saying, Su?" said Yi with a perplexed expression on his face.

"Su Fu is dead, yes there are remnants of her within me, but I am not her. You said it yourself."

"If this is about acceptance, I will accept you along with Su Fu and with the power of prayer we can cure this affliction," said Yi as he gently grasped Su Fu's hand.

"It's not a disease. It's a transformation and if you think prayer will solve anything, then you're a bigger fool than I thought."

"I know you're ill, but don't turn your back on the gods," said Yi. "No, the gods turned their backs on us. I'm sorry, I've upset you," said Su Fu. "No, you haven't. You have every right to be upset. I'm just glad you're here." Su Fu sat up and extended her hand to Yi who held it. Their fingers interlocked. Yi was smiling but Su Fu was not. Instead, she had a very somber expression. This caused Yi's smile to fade and it was replaced with a befuddled expression. "Is something the matter?" "Everything!" Su Fu burst into tears. She said with a quavering voice

"I don't want to hurt you, but I know I will. I just want to remember this… this moment with you. Hold me!" she cried and the two embraced. "You're a good man but good men always die. I truly am sorry!" said Su Fu. What happened next can only be described as pure carnage. Su Fu bit Yi with her fangs. As her fangs dug into his flesh, she sucked the blood from his body as he flailed about helplessly and screamed in agony. It only took a total of 30 seconds to drain Yi of all his blood, but to the people unfortunate to watch this macabre display, it felt like an eternity. It didn't take long for Su Fu to kill everyone in the room except for the duke, who managed to escape. It is said that she displayed some prowess moving at supernatural speeds and displaying feats of supernatural strength. (This is consistent with the traits of the modern-day vampires.) The rest of the unlucky people had their throats ripped out and there was blood splatter everywhere. The dogs of war came to inspect the room and they found Su Fu curled up in a ball sobbing. She was surrounded by about fifteen blood-stained corpses.

"What happened here, madam?" said one of the men.

"They were my family, and I loved most of them, yet I murdered them." One of the men pointed to Su Fu's mouth, which was still covered in blood. He turned to his fellow man and whispered something inaudible. Su Fu looked at her hands and to her horror they were covered in blood.

"What have I done?" she said.

"She ate them!" shouted one of the men.

"Cannibal!" said another. All ten men drew their swords and surrounded Su Fu.

"Still hungry, still hungry, must feed," said Su Fu.

All ten men became deceased in a gory fashion, their throats ripped out. In his dying breath, one of the men asked, "What are you?"

"I am a monster, I am a parasite, a bloodsucker, an agent of the devil, a plague upon this world, I am a vampire."

She then proceeded to drain the man of his blood. (It is important to note that vampires are not connected to the devil, but because of this statement, people assume this.)

Eventually word got out about what happened in Siamu palace thanks to the duke, and the emperor dispatched an elite force of warriors to deal with Su Fu. Only Su Fu was no longer at Siamu and no one knew where she went. Some say she hid in Temit mountains (a mountain range that separates Yetic from the neighboring country Oglire (AUG-LEE-RE)) and fed on unsuspecting travelers and animals. Some even think that she is alive today, which, if true, would make Su Fu the oldest vampire in existence. Still others believed she died. Nonetheless, she left her mark because after 200 years the prevalence of vampires in Yetic went from one to twenty and has been increasing ever since. As for Tao Feng, he and his men were butchered at Siamu palace sometime during 2345 WEBOT, the same year of Su Fu's massacre. He narrowly missed the blood shed but was soundly defeated by the emperor's elite troops that were intended to slay Su Fu. It was a thousand to three hundred. Tao Feng was ill prepared. He heard of the massacre and suspected Siamu's forces to be weak. It was quite the contrary. Thus, Tao Feng and his rebellion were crushed. This, however, did not please the emperor, for he had a bigger problem than a defective warlord. If Su Fu was still out there, no one in Yetic possibly the world was safe.

This grisly anecdote is mostly true, most of the people in the tale are all real people. Now that we covered a little of vampire history, we can now talk about vampire abilities, both founded and unfounded. Most of their abilities are the same as lycanthropes/werewolves. While not quite as strong as the werewolf/lycanthrope, they possess supernatural strength. As for speed, at their max they can clock in at about 80mph. They, as you would have guessed, have a healing factor. They possess supernatural agility, durability, endurance, and enhanced senses. Although their senses are not as good as werewolves/lycanthropes, they can still smell blood from 10 miles away. Vampires are functionally immortal (the only way to kill them is to behead them). Now, for the unfounded abilities, the most popular supposed ability has to do with bats. Many claim that vampires can turn into bats, which is false. Three of the most unfounded abilities are the ability to see the future, the past, and place people under trances just by looking into their iconic red eyes. These abilities have more merit than the bat ability. They are believed by many to be true, in fact some believe that Yi Yong was placed under a trance by Su Fu, that is why he changed his opinion of Su Fu so abruptly. He went from kill the monster to do everything possible to save her. Because he originally saw the massacre in Su Fu's eyes. Though this may have not been the future but rather Su Fu's true intentions, some suggest he either ignored the vision or forgot about it. Others argue that it was love that caused the abrupt change and that there were no visions in Su Fu's eyes. Some further postulate that if there were visions, how come only Yi saw them? This is a heated debate among certain circles and even some vampires doubt the ability since few amongst them claim to possess it. Another unfounded ability is *the stronger with blood ability*. The stronger with blood ability states that vampire's abilities increase the more human blood they consume. In addition, the more human blood they consume, the closer they are to ascension. Ascension is a state of being for a vampire, where they are completely satiated. Most people consider stronger with blood to be nonsense and claim ascension is impossible. However, many vampires state that when they drink copious amounts of human blood, they feel more powerful. Many consider this to be a psychological effect rather than a physical one. Another unfounded ability is that vampires can levitate. This has mostly been debunked as vampires themselves have not claimed to have this ability.

The next two sections are going to be short, mainly because little is known about them. Behemoths and interlopers are beings shrouded by mystery and speculation. When it comes to behemoths, what is certain is that they are monsters not infected, although they are susceptible to soul sickness, just like anyone else without a pure soul. Behemoths are very large monsters that often take up human/humanoid forms for reasons unknown. In their human/humanoid form, they draw their strength and abilities from the beast. This gives them abilities unique to the behemoth. Usually but not limited to supernatural strength, supernatural agility, supernatural speed, and a healing factor. The abilities taken from the beast are limited in human/humanoid form, which is why it's perplexing for behemoths to have a lesser form in the first place. Some speculate that it is to blend in with the regular populace. Like vampires and lycanthropes, the only way to kill a behemoth is to decapitate one. It is known that behemoths don't have two souls. Behemoth Laka (giant whale) was slain by a fisherman, Peter Dagort, using explosives and a giant glaive attached to a motor. After the death of Laka, 1230 NEEOT scientist (a new field with little members in Mirthadine. Few people even know what a scientist is. The term science officially came about during the 11th century NEEOT, although, some believe it was practiced hundreds of years prior), alchemist (Alchemy is a much more known profession than science, it has origins that date back to the 2nd century NEEOT. Alchemy, however, is shrouded in mystery and mysticism, not facts and reason, like science. Hence, there is often a rivalry between the two groups) and magic wielders studied the beast remains. The scientist discovered that the humanoid/human body was nowhere to be found. Now some claim that the corpse was lost in the deep waters of the Balmus ocean, but there is another explanation. This explanation, known as the extension theory by a rhodeac by the name of Rolac Fimar (1212-1282 NEEOT) states that the behemoth is the main entity, and the human/humanoid is an extension of it, hence Laka had no human body when it died.

Reader, I take it you're wondering how the scientist, alchemist and magic wielders knew Laka only had one soul, well the answer is quite simple: they extracted it. Extracting a soul is a dangerous process because you run the risk of creating a demon, but with some magic and a device aptly named the extractor, it can be done safely. The extractor is like a magnet except it attracts both ruda and dorah particles. In case you were wondering why they couldn't just wait until Laka's soul left its body, the reason is that a soul does not leave the body immediately after the body dies. It can remain in its vessel for as long as 2 years. In addition, when the soul leaves the body, it is hard to locate because it's so small, microscopic even though it travels slowly. With the extractor one does not usually see the soul but feels its presence. You see the extractor has a code, a certain language consisting of clicks and beeps. A beep means an infected soul, two beeps mean a pure soul, and one click means one soul, two clicks mean two souls, and so on.

It is said that the beast is immortal, but the humanoid/human is not. That begs the question are the beast and the human/humanoid one or are they separate? The answer to that question is difficult. There are two schools of thought for this question. The first theory known as the *memory theory* was proposed by a sison named Aggar Leptar (1234-1286 NEEOT). The memory theory states that the beast is immortal, but it has limited memory due to immortality and a smaller, less complex brain, hence it takes the form of a human/humanoid to rectify the situation. This would imply that beast and the human/humanoid are one, because the beast created the human/humanoid to make things easier for itself. Another theory known as the *movement theory* was proposed by an elf by the name of Heland Poiter (1351-1401 NEEOT). The movement theory says since the behemoth is so large, it has trouble moving around hence it adopts a human/humanoid body. Most people believe that the behemoth and the human/humanoid are one and that the human/ humanoid is an extension of the behemoth. However, there are others who believe that they are separate entities. The *separate entity theory* was proposed by Deryk Grayhelm (1210-1270 NEEOT). It suggests that the mind is responsible for the humanoid/human's relationship with the behemoth. Grayhelm claimed that they had a psychic link with each other and that they had separate souls. Furthermore, Grayhelm claimed that when the behemoth is in its beast form, the human/humanoid fades into the subconscious plane likewise for its human form. Greyhelm explained why the humanoid/human soul was absent during Laka's death. The explanation is that it was stuck in the beast's subconscious. Many people dispute Grayhelm's theory because little is known about the subconscious. In addition, those who consider the subconscious a legit concept, don't believe behemoths are capable of such advanced thought. The separate entity theory does have its supporters. They believe that one can disappear into the subconscious mind without being traced. While many consider this a ludicrous notion, Grayhelm supporters believe the theory was simply ahead of its time. Little is known about behemoths, Laka was the only one discovered and its human/humanoid vessel was nowhere to be found. Before Laka, people doubted the existence of behemoths, they were only referred to in the scriptures for Arda worshippers in *the book of Noga*. They are described as *beings capable of tearing the world asunder; they walk amongst us as mere mortals but in their beast form, they bring death and destruction in their wake. They are the oldest creatures on*

Mirthadine, save Arda himself, and the monstrosities will soon destroy the world during the end of days.

Interlopers are beings from other universes, even other planets that supposedly reside in Mirthadine. Most people doubt their existence, but there have been people who claim to have seen giant spider men and technology more advance than anything seen on Mirthadine. Some people even worship interlopers like gods. There is even a cult still active today known as the cult of Oaken. Oaken Thragfoot (1289-1377 NEEOT) was a dwarf who is said to have found a piece of interloper technology, what technology no one knows. Since then he has considered himself a type of prophet, emissary if you will, of all things relating to interlopers. His follower's, beings of all races, believe Thragfoot to be some sort of messiah that was going to help all races of Mirthadine ascend and meet their creators, the interlopers. There are other examples of worshipping interlopers, for instance, on the continent of Odun-mar in the country of Gin-hausba, there is an established albeit small religion of Spider-God worshippers. Not everyone, however, was endeared by interlopers. Many people saw them as extra-terrestrial threats. In fact, in the 14th century NEEOT, a human, from the continent Arcadiem, country unknown, named Jarin Stormwalker (1330-1355 NEEOT), gathered up a sizable militia to kill these interlopers. He did not find any interlopers, he instead targeted any being that did not resemble humans, race man. In other words, any being with atypical features when compared to men, such as rhodeac horns, elf pointed ears, sison forked tongue and several others. To avoid a possible war, the king, King Kenelm the second (1329-1379 NEEOT), ordered Jarin to disband his militia but Jarin refused thinking he was doing God's work *by rebuking the interloper devil's ideas and in turn slaying them* as he called it. Because of Jarin's madness and fervor to his ludicrous crusade, King Kenelm sent an army of 1000 to dispatch a militia of 800. Jarin was ordered to be kept alive and captured. Jarin's forces were decimated in the battle of Hilegger hill 715 of his men were killed; the rest surrendered. Those who surrendered were hung for treason. As for Jarin, he was beheaded with his head placed on a pike where he gained the epithet Jarin the fool.

Reader, recall I mentioned individuals being able to move at the speed of light. Well, how do they do that exactly? Mirthadine technology is primitive when compared to earthling technology and no amount of magic could protect one from the impact of traveling that fast. I'm sure you already know traveling at that velocity would burn an individual up without a special suit or vessel to travel in. What if I told you that there are certain individuals with pure souls that could achieve such a feat without magic and technology? It's called having a dynamic soul. A dynamic soul is a soul that can change form, a type of soul shape shifting. Recall the mystery of the behemoth soul. The reason behemoths don't have dynamic souls is because they don't have pure souls, only a pure soul can be dynamic. Remember the extractor device test for pure souls as well. The dynamic souls of these speedsters can shift from human to animal and the vessels change form as well. They are faster in animal form naturally; the animals they change to are typically quick animals, which include but are not limited to rabbits, hares, dogs, stallions, hawks, falcons, wolves, foxes, cheetahs, and wingless serpent-type dragons.

Now there are two forms of shapeshifting that these Mirthadine speedsters are capable of. One is normal shapeshifting which is limited to one animal. Normal shapeshifting involves turning into the animal designated to that speedster without using the dynamic force. The dynamic force is a medium that speedsters travel through, like a wormhole. It has several branching paths. Think of it like getting on a train. The railway tracks and tunnels are all part of the dynamic force. It's sometimes referred to as, in colloquial speech, the road. The dynamic force is a force that protects speedsters from burning up when traveling at high velocities while simultaneously allowing them to lose mass, so they can travel at said velocities. At a near massless state, they can move through solid walls. In addition, being near massless allows one to travel at great velocity and if one has no mass, they can travel at light speed. This is, however, an impressive feat even for a speedster because traveling at light speed is risky. You see, speedsters can only be massless for twelve nanoseconds. If they are even a nanosecond longer, they will dissolve into nothingness. Therefore, it is recommended when traveling that fast to go near light speed. Even so, traveling at high speeds is still risky because a speedster can only travel a maximum of 500 hours in the dynamic force before it will dissipate for that speedster, and then they will burn up.

The second form of shapeshifting is dynamic. You see, for a speedster to use the dynamic force, they must hit an initial velocity on foot of 35mph. After they hit the initial velocity, the dynamic force will be activated. When this happens, they will be transformed into a near massless humanoid state where they can remain or shapeshift into a near massless animal form for even greater speeds. It is important to note that they can hit this initial velocity quicker if they normal shapeshift into their animal form prior. So how exactly is this done and what does this have to do with the soul? Well, the dynamic force only reacts to those with a dynamic soul, and a dynamic soul can move and transform while taking its vessel with it. It is important to know that people who can use the dynamic force can temporarily grant access to those who do not. Additionally, non-speedsters cannot view the dynamic force unless granted access to it. In other words, if they are even able to see speedsters, they will only appear as a blur. The dynamic force is a complex series of tunnels that exist within every plane of existence and can only be access by speedsters with dynamic souls unless granted access by said individuals. A speedster does not have to enter the dynamic force to utilize it but rather be adjacent to it, a max distance of 400,000 miles. However, outside the dynamic force a speedster is not protected, and non-speedsters may be able to see them, the blur I alluded to earlier. In addition, non-speedsters may be able to counter act their attacks now that the speedster is visible. Remember reader the dynamic force may not react to non-speedsters but non-speedsters can react to it.

Pure souls can be quite interesting. Dynamic souls are part of a larger branch of shapeshifting pure souls known as the *splythe*, which is old tongue for altering animal souls. There are, as you may already know, two types of shape shifting. One that involves altering one's appearance into virtually anything but only at the surface level, otherwise known as shapeshifting. Shapeshifting only entails changing the appearance of the vessel, not the soul. Shapeshifting usually, but not always, involves some type of magic. Splythe shapeshifting is only regulated to a specific animal. Splythe shapeshifting involves altering of the soul as well as the vessel. This explains how people can turn into wolves, dragons, bears, and so on for limitless periods of time. The key difference besides the soul between a shapeshifter and splythe is the duration of time. Shapeshifters can only shape shift for an allotted amount of time and it varies for each person, whereas splythe shapeshifters are the animal they are shape shifting into; therefore, they can stay as that animal for an indefinite amount of time. Another small difference between the two is that shapeshifters are not limited to shape shifting into animals, they can turn into inanimate objects. This is all provided the thing they want to turn into is a solid thing hence they cannot turn into wind or smoke (skilled elementals can sometimes transform into their element, but this is known as elemental transfer not shape shifting). In addition, the thing they are transforming into must exist or had to have existed. Another slight difference between shapeshifting and splythe shapeshifting is that splythe shapeshifters can use traits of their soul animal in human/humanoid form while shapeshifters cannot. It is important to note that not every splythe shapeshifter is a speedster or can use dynamic force.

Earlier, we mentioned simple mutation. Reader, I'm sure you are familiar with the term mutation. An alteration of one's genetic sequence that can be attributed to external factors such as radiation or simply nature. In Mirthadine, mutations are less common but they do occur. Mutations were discovered by using magi-technology. The father of all thing's mutation was an elven scientist by the name of Eldar Falen (1245-1305 NEEOT). The most common mutation is superhuman strength and durability. Now there are plenty of ways one can possess these abilities, as discussed earlier. Supernatural methods include but are not limited. to vampirism and lycanthropy. However, mutation based superhuman strength and durability is due to a change in DNA not supernatural diseases. This alteration results in individuals possessing strength tenfold even a thousandfold that of your average Mirthadineling. (It is important to note that such strength is retractable, meaning the being possessing it must actively harness it to use it.) Other types of mutations that are even rarer are soul oriented mutations. These mutations include things such as having multiple coronas, an enlarged corona, or no corona. (Those that have soul-oriented mutations are more susceptible to soul sickness and sometimes soul sickness is caused by mutation. Having multiple or an enlarged corona would place it precariously close to the core. It is important to note the corona vibrates and expands slightly when soul manifest is utilized.) One of the rarest forms of soul-oriented mutations are the ones involving the core, such as having multiple cores or an enlarged core. Arguably, the rarest form of soul-oriented mutation is the illustrious infinite soul. Discovered by Falen in 1266 NEEOT, infinite soul is a soul with multiple cores only it is unique in the fact that the cores are not separate entities nor are they the same size. You see, one of the cores is attached to the other like a parasite and is usually significantly smaller than the other. The smaller core is known as a bud. (There can be multiple buds attached to one core.) Despite the name, individuals who possess infinite souls do not possess infinite soul manifest, such a thing is impossible, instead the bud or buds attached to the core somehow allows the core to regenerate like a corona during soul manipulation. The bud or buds can only be used a limited amount of times. In addition, when the buds are used, it can have adverse effects on the body, such as impairing the central nervous system, temporary blindness, delirium, and hemostasis, which can result in death. Yet being able to access soul manifest directly from the core can result in powerful soul manipulation. There are, of course, other types of mutations in Mirthadine— some beneficial, some harmful, but they are all too numerous and that is a discussion for another time. This concludes the prologue section of this novel. I know it was quite lengthy, but hopefully it will make understanding things easier when moving forward.

CHAPTER ONE
KRAAG

The year was 1548 NEEOT (New Era End of Time), and it was raining at dawn with the low rumbling of thunder in the distance, the rain poured down intensely; the horses neighed, frighten of the approaching storm, the riders seized the reigns to calm them. They trudged through the mud and grass until they came upon a grotesque sight. There was an irritating buzzing noise from the flies that seem fixated with some hundred dead bodies on the ground. The sound of squawking crows in the distance circling the corpses indicated that the situation was grim. The air smelled repugnant amidst the fallen, both men and steed sprawled on the ground with their blood spread out across the marshes, staining it crimson. Despite the apparent disarray, there seemed to be some haphazard attempt to divide the bodies into heaps. It was almost as though the butchers were attempting to dispose or display them. There were two distinct piles for reasons unknown and they comprised primarily of men. Based on the condition of the corpses, they were no more than 12 days deceased. Putrefaction, although blackened with discoloration, you could still make out some of their faces.

They told a story of anguish, fear, and shock. The frozen expressions revealed their final moments, their relationship with death. Some were prepared for it while others it crept up on. The mangled decaying bodies of the deceased revealed how they were killed, impaled, mutilated or both. The faceless ones, both bludgeoned and charred, had their stories lost forever. In a way they were blotted out of existence, who they were, who they would become was robbed from them by the cold hands of death and that was the greater tragedy. The sound of the horses' hooves trotting ceased, and the riders came to a halt.

Leading them was Lord Albert Franklin, leader of house Franklin, a man in his sixties, healthy from years of moderate to intense exercise and strict dietary discipline. Lord Albert Franklin rarely drank or over indulged. Though this was most likely due to dislike of drunkenness and wanting to appear capable in front of his men, rather than for vanity purposes. *"A king not fit to lead his men in battle is not fit to be a king."* Words of his father, Lord Franklin often wondered how practical they were, after all kings ruled for life ideally anyway, decline in physicality and sensibilities was inevitable. With age came decay, which in Lord Franklin's mind was worse than death. An extreme and perhaps even juvenile take on a natural process. Nonetheless, Lord Franklin still obsessed over it. Dying young meant one would be remembered even immortalized that way by everyone who knew them and those who remembered would, in turn, instill their memories upon their descendants. Dying old meant one would be remembered as decrepit and frail as opposed to being in one's prime, strong, and capable. The juxtaposition of thoughts made Lord Franklin uneasy. He was no longer young that much was apparent and now he was faced with the nebulous task of how to spend the rest of his fleeting existence. How would he be remembered if at all? The glory days were over and his window for making a mark on this world was narrowing. But was it all futile… was it too late? Death of the memory of one's greater self in the eyes of others is a greater death than death itself. Perhaps he had missed his shot… perhaps he had already died in their eyes.

These were the type of insidious thoughts that often plagued Lord Franklin's mind. He never spoke of them, for fear of sounding vain and childish, because that's how he felt as they manifested in his head. Ashamed and angry with himself, he did what most people do with negative thoughts, suppress them. As you can imagine, this only made them stronger.

Like all thoughts in a rational mind, there is some element of truth in them. That's what makes the harmful ones so dangerous. As superficial as it seems, worrying about something you have no control over, such as aging or how people see you, is a problem. Which is why the mind attempts to find a solution by ruminating on it. It is only when one addresses the problem and implements a solution that rumination ceases. Implementing a solution requires communicating with the mind and convincing it why energy is wasted on such thoughts. Only then will they begin to dissipate. But this strategy is often never executed, instead most ignore or suppress negative thoughts, which only aggravates the condition. However, the unfortunate are conditioned to employ such techniques. The fact is most of us are aware of our maladaptive coping mechanisms but simply don't do anything about it. Why? Well because we fall into patterns, and we are hard-wired to prefer patterns over the chaos of the unknown. Even if that pattern is harmful, it's how we survived evolutionarily. Taking risk meant death, but the world has changed. Those tools don't work anymore they've become detrimental. Pain is not an adversary; it is a guide. If you ignore it, it will lead to suffering. Acknowledge it and you will regain control of the mind, for you are its rightful master.

Appearance wise, Lord Franklin looked his age. His hair was gray and he was bald from his crown to the rest of his entire scalp. He had a steely-eyed look about him. He stood about six feet tall, wore plated armor with chain mail underneath. The armor covered his entire body except for his face, because his visor was lifted. Engraved on his chest plate was a white circle surrounded by lightning bolts. The circle represented the sun and the Franklin's house talent to manipulate light energy; the lightning bolts that replaced sun rays represented the Franklin's house ability to manipulate lightning. He wielded an arming sword known as the Great Divider and a buckler.

Lord Franklin dismounted from his steed to analyze the heap of dead bodies next to him.

He covered his mouth to prevent himself from inhaling the foul stench of the fallen. "My God, this is a bloody massacre!" Lord Franklin said with a disgusted look on his face. "How did this happen? Our army was twice the size of Hector's at the battle of Rilek," Lord Franklin said with frustration in his voice.

"I believe they out flanked us from the north, my lord," said Sir Cedric Oak, one of Lord Franklin's finest knights. He was knighted after he rescued Lord Franklin from an assassination attempt as well as proving himself a capable warrior and tactician. As a result, he was promoted to the rank commander. Oak was a man in his forties. He stood about five-foot ten, slim build with short straight brown hair, blue eyes, and a stubble beard.

"How exactly did they out flank us?" Lord Franklin said with an inflection of anger in his voice.

Sir Oak, sensing this spoke slowly and methodically. "Hector's army initially met ours at the center of the marshland, then his reinforcements came from the north through the woods." Sir Oak kneeled down and traced an invisible pathway with his index and middle finger, from the woods to the pile of corpses, his gaze was drawn downwards at the peculiar tracks on the ground. "You can see this through the tracks-"

3

Sir Oak paused as something disturbed him and his pupils widen, his body trembled.

"What is it?" Lord Franklin said impatiently. Sir Oak turned towards Lord Franklin, with a petrified expression on his face.

Lord Franklin responded with a befuddled expression. Sir Oak's voice quavered when he said, "These tracks aren't human. They belong to some type of monsters; like the monsters of old."

"Monsters of old?" Lord Franklin said still perplexed as to what was being said.

"The monsters of old. Surely you heard of them there in the sacred texts my lord," said Sir Ulric Edwards, a portly, balding man who stood about five-foot six. He had blue eyes and was the advisor to King Franklin. Of course, Lord Franklin was not king yet. Lord Albert Franklin was the younger brother of the late king, Gavin Franklin (1481-1536 NEEOT), a large ginger with a medium size beard, he would have been in his late 60s. He had a misshapen nose, probably due to a fight. He had stood about six-foot five and had green eyes. The circumstances of Gavin's death were suspicious, at one moment he was hale and hearty the next, he was bleeding from the eyes and coughing up blood, he cried out in agony and started contorting on the ground, his skin turned a yellowish hue and the veins on his faced continued to protrude as he thrashed about wildly. Albert Franklin seized him by the shoulders, calling out Gavin's name, but it was too late. The light had already left Gavin's eyes. These events led to people speculating that Albert was responsible for King Gavin's death with some going as far as accusing Albert of king slaying and kin slaying. It was believed that his weapon of choice was poison, a poison known as yellow death. It grows outside Arcadiem near the border of Yetic. Yellow refers to the yellowing of the skin and eyes of the victims. Albert was thought to have poisoned Gavin to claim the throne since Gavin did not have any sons. Sir Ulric helped to invalidate those suspicions, claiming that Albert had no knowledge of poisons, and he loved his brother. There was a trial to determine Albert Franklin's fate. Sir Ulric defended Albert and eventually cleared Albert of any wrongdoing. This did not, however, quiet those who still believed Albert was guilty nor did it solve the mystery of King Gavin's death. This wasn't the end of Albert's troubles. There was another claim to the throne, a man by the name of Hector Everard. Allegedly, Hector was initially believed to be an Everard, but it was later revealed to him by his supposed adoptive father Rowan on his deathbed that his real father was Gavin Franklin and that his mother was a noble woman. This woman whose name is unknown was allegedly King Gavin's bride. They married in secret because Lord

Hadrian Baudry was not to be trifled with and Gavin was promised to his daughter Elizabeth, Gavin's current widow.

The Baudry's held the purse strings for everything in Iiadec (EYE-YA-DECK). Everyone owed them money. They funded wars, rebellions, marriages, protection, and taverns. In addition, they resorted to kidnapping and holding relatives and love one's to ransom if debt was not paid and Hadrian was a particularly ruthless man who was not above torture, maiming, even murder. High born or low born; it was of no consequence to him. If he did not get his way, there was a price to pay. The Baudry's kept their unscrupulous deeds hidden from the public eye, but those within their certain circles were fully aware.

Some believed Hector's tale to be complete fabrication and amongst those people was Sir Ulric Edwards. Ulric was one of the first people to advocate for Albert Franklin's legitimacy to the throne. Soon others joined as well, and soon Albert had a sizeable army. Hector also had supporters that rallied behind those who believed in Hector's tale and others who believed Albert to be a kin and king slayer. This led to the current conflict between Hector and Albert.

"I must apologize. I'm not too versed on the sacred text," said Lord Franklin disingenuously.

Sir Ulric responded with a reflexively annoyed look on his face, which he quickly tried to hide upon realization. Lord Franklin took notice of Sir Ulric's frustration but was quite indifferent, nonetheless. A part of him thought he should employ more tact, after all, religion was important to most people in Iiadec. Disinterest or lack of knowledge in it would run the risk of being labeled a pariah or worst a heretic, that was the last thing that he needed. He had also been ambivalent about the existence of God and thought religion was trivial ceremony but unfortunately for him it had a stranglehold on the people's allegiance. This was one of the reasons Sir Ulric was here in the first place so Lord Franklin could appear God fearing. The efficacy of this stratagem was too early to tell.

Sir Ulric sighed. "The monsters of old are the original beings of Mirthadine, created by our God, Arda; the lord of all things and the lord of nothing," Sir Ulric Franklin and Sir Oak said in unison. Such a phrase was often spoken before or after Arda's name, though this was by no means compulsory. It is common for believers of the book of Noga or Ardinians as they're called, to say this. The phrase lord of all things means everything in creation was created by Arda. The phrase lord of nothing means Arda was there when there was nothing, a single entity in a realm of emptiness. Ardinian's believe Arda created the nothingness as a template in which to create all things.

Most people will define nothingness as an absence of everything, but this definition is a contradiction because everything is everywhere, so by default the nothingness is a part of everything, which means that even the voids of endless space and time are entities onto themselves. Additionally, there cannot be an absence of everything since everything implies all things, that leads to the only logical explanation is that the word nothingness, null, oblivion is simply used to describe that which cannot be seen in the grand tapestry that is life. Matter is defined as a substance of the universe that has mass, occupies space, and is convertible to energy. Dark matter is simply matter that cannot be seen, but one knows exists. In essence, darkness is the true meaning of nothingness; that which is hidden. The darkness has been associated with several words, many of which are not in the actual definition of darkness but are nonetheless related to it; fear and unknown comes to mind. People fear the darkness because they cannot see it, they cannot feel it, and they cannot understand it; these three reasons lead to an unparalleled fear of it. People fear what is unknown because they believe there is more danger in obscurity than what is known. The reality, however, is that the unknown and the known are one and the same just like darkness and light or nothing and everything. Not everything in light can be seen, and not everything in darkness is obscure. Not every danger that is known can be dealt with and not every unknown danger is an immediate threat. For these reasons, people should fear the known as much as they fear the unknown.

Sir Ulric continued. "They are an unnatural amalgamation of mismatched animal, plant, and humanoid parts. It is said some even have a hundred heads or a thousand arms."

"So, like a chimera," Lord Franklin deduced.

"Not quite. Unlike chimeras, these creatures are intelligent-," said Sir Ulric.

"You mean intelligent enough to lead an army," said Lord Franklin. "Exactly. They even have ranks and can communicate with each

other telepathically," said Sir Ulric.

"So, how do we stop this army of monsters?" asked Lord Franklin. "It's impossible. They can't be killed. They're indestructible," said

Sir Ulric.

"Then how did they disappear in the first place?" Lord Franklin asked with a tinge of incredulity in his voice.

Sir Ulric responded, "No one knows, but they are thought to be made out of the very nothingness itself."

"So, Hector managed to raise an army of invincible monsters right under our noses," Lord Franklin said in disbelief. Sir Ulric and Sir Oak remained silent, for even they understood how ludicrous their claims sounded to Lord Franklin.

Sir Oak finally broke the silence. "We know there were monsters here. You can see the footprints," Sir Oak said while pointing to the peculiar tracks on the ground. The tracks were wildly different from each other. Some resembled bear tracks, goat, bird and even the unrecognizable; others did not come in pairs.

"How do we know those tracks don't belong to lycanthropes or centaurs?" said Lord Franklin.

"Those beasts don't leave such inconsistent tracks," said Sir Oak.

Lord Franklin sighed and asked with frustration, "What does this all mean?"

"Well, the return of the monsters of old is a sign," said Sir Ulric. "Sign of what?" said Lord Franklin.

Sir Ulric recited the sacred text, *"Everything in the light will return to the shadow, everything that ever was, will return to the void from whence it came. Everything will become nothing, and nothing will become everything again. And when the monsters of old return, they will be the precursor to the end of days."*

"End of days," Lord Franklin said dubiously.

Sir Oak knew with Lord Franklin this discussion was going in circles. You see, he knew Lord Franklin to be a pragmatist. Talk of mysticism was bound to elude or frustrate him. Sir Oak thought it was best to transition. After all, Sir Ulric was getting irritated explaining everything Lord Franklin should have probably known. He deduced this by the subtle micro-expressions on Sir Ulric's brow and cadence in the way he spoke, monotonous as though his words had been said before. It was not a good look for their leader to be ignorant of religious text, though he did not fault his Lord. The scriptures where lengthy and convoluted to put it lightly. Sir Oak thought it would be best to highlight his Lord's strength as opposed to weakness, as it would increase overall morale amongst the men. Something they desperately needed, omen or not this was a frightening and unusually macabre scene.

"We don't know that these are the monsters of old. For all we know this could be a trick by some magic wielder," said Sir Oak to alleviate tension but mostly calm himself.

"Or wielders," said Lord Franklin.

It was certainly a possibility, thought Sir Oak. The bodies greatly resembled corpses. That level of detail would be difficult to pull off with just one person, even if it was just an illusion. He began to question, however, the rationale. If Hector had such powerful magic wielders at his disposal, logistically, it would make more sense to allocate such resources in battle rather than stage a fake massacre. Sir Ulric questioned this theory as well. He had studied faux magic and, although not impossible, it would be unlikely a magic wielder or wielders would be able to replicate the smell and appearance of corpses. Smell especially was difficult, since corpses had a distinct smell and individuals would know if the corpses were real. Faux magic worked best when manipulating one's vision. As far as he knew, there was not many spells affecting olfactory receptors

"It's no trick," said a voice that sounded anemic and pained. It seemed to be originating from one of the heaps.

"Who said that?" Lord Franklin asked. All three men looked at the corpses and saw a pair of legs underneath, just barely moving. Lord Franklin's men helped to lift the bodies that were crushing this poor individual and carried him to a nearby tree. The man appeared to be in his thirties with brown hair and brown eyes; he was so enervated that he barely had the will to move. They managed to sit the man up with his back slumped against a tree and his legs stretched out on the ground languidly.

"What's your name?" said Lord Franklin.

"Tristian Ben-" the soldier said, stopping abruptly as he coughed up blood in Lord Franklin's face. "Sorry milord I-"

"It's alright, take your time," Lord Franklin said as he wiped the blood from his face with a handkerchief.

"My name is Tristian Bennett." His breaths were slow and heavy, he was grasping his gut where he had been wounded, the warm blood oozed through his fingers; his eyes drooped, and his skin was pale. The loss of blood caused him to slip in and out of consciousness. His eyes constantly rolled to the back of his head, leaving Lord Franklin to constantly restrain him.

"Hey Tristian, stay with me. What did you mean by it's not a trick?" Lord Franklin said as he tapped Tristian's cheeks.

Tristian's gaze was directed towards the woods instead of Lord Franklin's face. His eyes widened, his breaths became shallow and there was a terrified expression on his face. He pointed towards the woods and bellowed out, "Monster! Monster!"

The men turned away towards the woods but saw nothing. "There's nothing there my lord," Sir Ulric whispered.

"I can see that," Lord Franklin said sarcastically.

"He is suffering from delirium due to loss of blood," said Sir Oak while Tristian still screamed.

"No, I can see him, he's in my head. Arrgh!" Tristian screamed as he writhed about while Lord Franklin struggled to restrain him.

"Who, who can you see?" Lord Franklin shouted.

"I can feel him burrowing through my veins and searing my flesh from my bones; AAArgh it burns! It burns! It burns! It BURNS!!" screamed Tristian.

"What burns?" said Lord Franklin.

"We need to tend to his wound, he's bleeding out!" said Sir Oak. "Right, you two hold down his legs and arms," Lord Franklin said referring to two knights in his calvary.

Two knights came forward and seized Tristian by the legs and arms, thus preventing him from thrashing about. "Help, help I can see him with my waking eyes, my insides are burning, oh it hurts so bad!"

Sir Oak knelt down beside Tristian and said in a calming voice, "I know it hurts but you're going to have to calm down, you're bleeding out."

Tristian started wailing profusely, his face turned red and the veins on his forehead started to protrude. "The pain, the pain is unbearable," he said with a muffled cry. While trying to fight back tears, he whispered, "Please. Just kill me, just kill me."

"I will do no such thing," said Sir Oak firmly.

"Please just kill me," said Tristian in a quavering voice.

"You're going to live. Now stop that talk and hold still. Fetch me my pouch," Sir Oak said to one of the knights. The knight quickly unhooked a black leather pouch from the saddle of Sir Oak's steed and handed it to him. Sir Oak rummaged through his bag until he pulled out a brown leather bottle made of animal skin. The bottle was filled with vinegar. Sir Oak poured the vinegar over Tristian's wound. Tristian, who had lost consciousness, was no longer restrained. Sir Oak took out myrrh a herb found on the Groli continent. He used the myrrh as an antiseptic, spreading bits and pieces of it over the wound. Next, he took some bandages from his pouch and wrapped them around Tristian's lower abdomen. "There that should do it, now carry him-" But before he could finish speaking, Tristian grabbed a hold of Sir Oak's arm, he was shaking with trepidation and his eyes widen.

"You must kill me, he means to send me to the void, into the darkness where it is so cold, he wants to kill us all so we can become a part of them. They collect the parts of the things they have slain and make those parts a part of them but you can stop him. Kill me, kill me please, you have to kill me before-"

9

Then, abruptly, Tristian fainted. Something happened to Tristian when he awoke. Something caused Lord Franklin and all members of his cavalry to gasp, for Tristian's eyes were pitch black, a symptom of possession. Black-eyed Tristian sprang to his feet with such vigor that it was hard to believe he was ever even injured. Tristian's eyes vexed Lord Franklin so much that he unsheathed his blade. The members of the calvary drew their blades as well. With all swords pointed at a possessed Tristian, Lord Franklin asked, "Who or what are you?"

"I am Kraag, leader of the Horridus, what you people referred to in your sacred text as the monsters of old." Kraag's voice was guttural for the most part but there were also other noises that echoed in the distance; a combination of different distorted sounds layered on top of each other. Some of the sounds were animal in origin, some humanoid and others unrecognizable, thus creating an erratic and unstable voice.

"Are you a demon?" asked Lord Franklin.

"We were there before the demons, before the trees, before the wind, before this very world in which you stand. We are the nothingness, the darkness, oblivion, the void, we are the originals, the progenitor of God itself."

"What have you done with Tristian?!" asked Lord Franklin angrily. "I'm merely commandeering this vessel to deliver a message to you, Albert Franklin."

Lord Franklin was taken aback. "How do you know my name?" Lord Franklin asked.

"I've been watching you since you were a boy, Albert Franklin, son of Aiken and Alice Franklin. You are also the younger brother of Gavin Franklin the recently deceased king. I know you're envious of your brother Gavin. He was bigger and stronger but stupid, you were the far more intelligent and sophisticated one, but your parents never noticed you. No they only cared about Gavin, they never loved you like they loved him. So, when he died-"

"I don't know what you heard or who you're working for, but I will not be fooled by such deception," interrupted Lord Franklin.

"There can be no deception in truth, and you have to admit a part of you was happy when he died. It gave you opportunity," said Kraag.

"Opportunity?!" Lord Franklin said crossly.

"The opportunity to take center stage in your life and no longer run the risk of fading in obscurity. You knew you'd be a better king than Gavin and history would remember you as the great king," Kraag said nonchalantly.

Sir Ulric shouted, "Uthra Manaca-la!" (a powerful binding spell said in old tongue translation: summon the restraints to bind, it prevents any magic or soul manifest from being used by the captured). Suddenly, Kraag was restrained by organic looking chains composed of an amalgamation of rocks, stone, plants, and unrefined metal. Kraag found this amusing, yet his whole body except his head seemed to be immobile.

"Kraag, what exactly do you and the Horridus intend to do with our world?" asked Sir Oak.

"Ah always straight and to the point Sir Cedric Oak or should I say Hadrian Baudry's bastard," said Kraag. Lord Franklin and several of the men where bemused. "I take it you didn't know; Sir Cedric Baudry is a bastard. His mother was a common tavern whore named Mary. He knew you would never knight him with the Baudry name because you disliked the Baudry's for their immoral ways and rightfully so. They are rapists, murderers, megalomaniacal and extremely apathetic when causing others harm. Hence, Cedric Baudry chose the name Oak because he didn't want to be associated with them, he even came up with the ludicrous surname Oak after the tree," said Kraag. The men were perplexed. They thought surely to accuse a house such as Baudry with crimes such as these was preposterous. The Baudry house has been loyal to the Franklins for decades, providing mostly monetary support and the occasional defense of the people during times of war. To besmirch the name of a good lord with such outrageous and seemingly baseless accusations, was unforgivable.

Sir Avery stepped forward. Gripping his sword tightly, he transitioned into Ochs guard preparing to perform and undercut. The other knights appeared ready to attack as well. "Let's not mince words, tell us who you really are, no more lies."

Kraag paused for a moment. He seemed genuinely perplexed. He said rather absently under his breath, "Another was supposed to say those words to me...."

He chuckled slightly. "Never mind, it is of no consequence."

Sir Avery and the other knights were bemused by Kraag's words but were nonetheless too determined to fight than to ponder a seemingly offhand remark. Lord Franklin looked around. It was quite clear that whether or not this Kraag was telling the truth, he was skilled at magic. Rushing into battle blindly could mean they would end up like the pile of corpses. Additionally, what Kraag said about the Baudrys was true. He had witnessed house Baudry's cruelty firsthand.

It was several years ago, Lord Franklin and his brother Gavin had been guests at Lord Baudry's castle, Dae le Maut. It was the spring of

11

1533 NEEOT and there had been relative peace in Iiadec. The Franklins were discussing the tricky concept of allegiance after a long, grueling war. Lord Baudry was more concerned with status. He felt he earned it in the war. He wanted to be like Lord Fowler and be in the pocket of the Franklins, the royal dynasty. Wealth was something the Baudrys had in abundance, but what was wealth without status? It was the reverence he desired.

Lord Franklin and King Gavin entered the great hall. It was quite spacious despite the copious amount of people vacating it. They were an unruly bunch gathered around wooden tables drinking, dancing and highly inebriated. This was to be expected. The war was over and they were victorious. Still, the lack of control some of these men displayed, as well as the sheer amount of people, made Lord Franklin uneasy. They consisted mainly of highborn or the very wealthy. This was evident in the way they dressed adorned with jewelry, shimmering necklaces, colorful rings, embroidered clothing. They drank wine from expensive flagons and ate with the finest cutlery.

Lord Franklin's eyes gravitated toward the ceiling, a tapestry. On it, paintings of angels playing various string instruments ranging from but not limited to, the harps, lutes, and citoles. Bordering the art were extravagant golden carvings of foliage and flowers. Opulence, unnecessary and careless, thought Lord Franklin. It seems Hadrian Baudry could afford frivolous luxuries, despite the recent war. Although the Baudrys did their part providing financial backing, Lord Franklin wondered perhaps they could've done more. He wondered where they got all this gold. His thoughts were interrupted by an unusually reserved Gavin. *"Ahem, brother, we're here. Try not to act lost were in the presence of Lord Hadrian Baudry after all,"* he smiled weakly. Lord Franklin was not amused. Gavin was acting strangely. What was he hiding? He was usually not one for courteousness. It suddenly occurred to him that he never entered Dae le Maut until now, but Gavin had frequented once or twice no doubt to beg for money, he had foolishly wasted on drinking, gambling, and parties. *Is that what this was?*

Lord Franklin groaned. *"How long will we be in debt to these people?"* thought Lord Franklin.

When the Franklins entered the room, there was silence. Then Lord Baudry got up from his chair, raised a silver cup and said, *"Hail King Gavin Franklin!"* Others followed suit. Lord Franklin found it irksome that he was not even properly addressed, as though he was a mere servant following his big brother around. He found it futile to address this error for fear of sounding petulant.

Gavin guffawed. *"Come now, we are all friends here. Let us celebrate this joyous occasion."*

"Aye!" said Lord Baudry. The people resumed their revelry, much to the dislike of Lord Franklin. As the Franklins made their way to the center of the hall several said praises to Gavin while pretending Lord Franklin didn't exist, at least that is the way Lord Franklin saw it. He wondered who these people were, a sea of unfamiliar faces; he never saw these people on the field of battle. Throwing coin in war was not the same as serving in it. These people did not deserve to celebrate. They risked nothing, while men of lower status risked everything. This made him livid, but what angered him more was the way his brother would grovel for coin. Did he have no shame? Pretending these people are friends; how pitiful.

Scurrying behind the Franklins were four knights, the Franklin's security. They seemed to have slight trouble moving through the crowd, being harassed by the bibulous and unruly. The Franklins made their way to the center table where Lord Baudry stood. He was 65 at the time, white hair, a kempt beard and olive skin. Standing adjacent to Lord Baudry, on his right, were his sons Borin, Sadon, Fendrel, and Roger. To his left, his only daughter Elizabeth and his wife Levina. Elizabeth caught Gavin's eye and curtseyed. *"Your Grace,"* she said with a coquettish grin. She would have been twenty-six at the time. Long, flowing blond hair and a thin frame. Despite her meek gesture, she exuded confidence. This was evident in her eyes, pale green and impish. She knew something the Franklins didn't, and she wanted them to know with her not-so-subtle smirk directed at Gavin.

Lord Franklin looked at Lady Baudry, whose eyes were glued to the table. She had a slight frame, straight shoulder length black hair tied back in a conservative ponytail. Her posture was tense and she was trembling ever so slightly, diametrically opposite to the rest of her family. It was as if she anticipated, or rather knew something horrible was going to happen. She looked at Gavin briefly, then Lord Franklin and said in a low muted tone, *"Your grace, Lord Franklin."* She curtseyed, then resume her rigid posture and avoided eye contact. Both Franklins acknowledged the greeting, but unlike Gavin, Lord Franklin's eyes remained on Lady Baudry for a while. It concerned him that she would be terrified in her own home. Was she being abused? His thoughts were interrupted by Gavin's hearty laughter. At this point, it was difficult to tell whether it was genuine or not. Gavin was always keeping up appearances. That was not Lord Franklin's concern as he was there to discuss the debt they acquired from the Baudrys. *"Hadrian, you look well!"* said Gavin. *"As do you, your*

Grace!" replied Lord Baudry. Before the two could continue with idle chit chat. Lord Franklin interrupted. *"We'd like to discuss the debt owed to you Lord Baudry, not to celebrate."* Lord Baudry was slightly taken aback by Lord Franklin's direct tone but masked it with a smile. *"Then we shall discuss."* All parties sat down at the table. Lord Franklin spoke first, not wanting his brother to engage in frivolous talk and be further swindled by the Baudrys.

"How much does my brother owe?"

"Two million Tatums (one gold bar), "said Lord Baudry. Lord Franklin shot a foul glance at Gavin. He knew his brother could not be trusted with money. Why had Gavin not consulted him first before borrowing coin from the Baudrys?

Gavin sunk lower into his chair as though trying to avoid his brother's disapproving look. Lord Franklin groaned. *"We can't afford that. It is too high."*

"Well, wars are costly. Those Northern barbarians did a number on us," said Lord Baudry nonchalantly.

"I know. I was there," Lord Franklin said scathingly. Lord Baudry's eyes narrowed as he glared at Lord Franklin. Lord Franklin's features remained resolute. He meant what he said and how it was to be received.

To alleviate the tension. Gavin said, *"Lord Hadrian Baudry, we thank you for the service you provided. It was essential to our victory."*

Lord Baudry, while still looking at Lord Franklin smirked. *"Thank you, your Grace. It seems your brother doesn't understand war is expensive."*

"As are lives," retorted Lord Franklin.

Lord Baudry laughed raucously, which made the Franklins uncomfortable. *"I didn't peg you as the sentimentalist, but still a king must pay his debt."*

"You are right, and might I suggest we pay in increments. Wealth will come in time once word gets round that Iiadec is free of invaders, the neighboring lands would have to trade with us," said Gavin. Lord Franklin found this groveling repulsive and beneath a King.

"You've already been granted a Lordship, is that not payment enough?" asked Lord Franklin sharply.

Lord Baudry smiled mischievously. *"That is exactly what I wanted to discuss."* The Franklins were bemused, causing Lord Baudry to elucidate. *"I'm willing to absolve all debts the crown has to house Baudry."*

The Franklins paused for a moment. They were suspicious of his intentions, especially Lord Franklin. *"And what does house Baudry want in return for their generosity?"* asked Lord Franklin incredulously.

Lord Baudry turned to Elizabeth and smiled. *"King Gavin is a bachelor and needs a queen."*

Before Lord Franklin could respond, Gavin said, *"Then it's settled. Elizabeth shall be my bride."*

Lord Franklin thought Gavin was being impetuous. Marrying into this family could be trouble. Hadrian in particularly vexed him. The way he carried himself with an air of superciliousness. This machination of his was deliberate. Hadrian was ambitious, there was no telling what he would do to succeed. Lord Franklin's thoughts were drowned out by the sound of mirth and festivity. Over the noise, he could see Lady Baudry's piercing blue eyes staring at him.

He stared back, much to his surprise she did not avert her gaze. Her bottom lip trembled as though she wanted to say something, possibly warn him. As she slowly opened her mouth, she was interrupted by a seemingly overjoyed Lord Baudry. He clasped her shoulder. Startled stiff, Lord Franklin could see the color drain from her face.

"Levina, our daughter is to be queen," said Lord Baudry ecstatically. *"Yes milord."* Her voice quavered and she smiled weakly. He kissed her forehead. She remained stiff, like a mouse immobilized by the venom of an adder. Lord Baudry either did not notice or didn't care. This vexed Lord Franklin. What was she trying to tell him? Maybe it was nothing, he may never know.

Gavin was dancing in the center of the great hall with his soon to be bride. While her brothers drank wine. Lord Baudry, however, was alert observing the whole scene. He stood there as though anticipating. Suddenly, six figures entered the great hall. As they stepped into the light, one could see four knights dragging two men by the arms to the center of the hall. The knights were from house Baudry. This was indicated by the winged quarter note engraved on the center of their chest plate. It was a relatively new vigil at the time. It represented Lord Baudry's fascination with angels and music.

Several gasped, and the celebrations ceased as the conditions of the two men were revealed. There was a sea of several shocked onlookers, including the Franklins, as the men were dragged toward the center of the hall. Their faces were indiscernible. Much of the flesh on both men had been removed, they had been flayed. It was a marvel they were even alive. All four limbs amputated, severed below the elbow and knee joints. The wounds had been cauterized to prevent hemorrhaging. These men weren't cut by a mere butcher but a skilled surgeon. This was beyond cruel. It was pernicious and that wasn't even the worst part. One of the men was completely missing his lower jaw. His tongue dangling limply like a hungry hound.

Lord Baudry, who looked rather impassive, said nonchalantly, *"Traitors against the crown."*

"How so, did they intend to stage a coup? Are there others?" Gavin asked eagerly.

Lord Franklin closely awaited Lord Baudry's response. The actual words did not concern him, but rather the expression that came with them. It disturbed Lord Franklin that Lord Baudry seemed so aloof when discussing the men he had so violently tortured.

"They spoke ill of you, your grace, and of you milord." Lord Franklin was taken aback by Lord Baudry's indifference.

"Who gave you the authority to torture these men? If they committed a crime, then they should've been brought to the crown. This type of recklessness cannot be tolerated!" Lord Franklin said.

"Brother!" Gavin said sternly. Lord Franklin became silent but still angry and glowered at Lord Baudry, who seemed unaffected by his menace.

Gavin turned to Lord Baudry. *"Who were these men?"*

"Oh, nobody, from what we gathered. Bastards they go by Nash and Cooper."

"And for that you had them flayed," Lord Franklin retorted.

Lord Baudry was slightly irritated by Lord Franklin's words, and it became evident in his voice which became slightly strained as he said, *"We were gathering information."*

"On what exactly?" Lord Franklin said angrily.

Lord Baudry sighed. He was choosing his words carefully. He did not want to give in to Lord Franklin's provocations. *"The seeds of rebellion are like an ailment. If you don't end it before it manifests into something more virulent it might be too late."* His words were ominous and precise with an air of coldness to them. This had been intentional. It was Lord Baudry's subtle way of telling Lord Franklin to back off. The message had been received, but not without resistance.

"What did you find out?" asked Gavin.

"Sedition, your Grace, the two seemed to be acting on their own from what we gathered."

"What did they say?" Lord Franklin demanded.

"I believe it was somewhere along the lines of the Franklins always cause war. I don't care who's in charge, I just want peace. I believe that was Nash and Cooper agreed with him."

"That's it, that hardly qualifies as sedition. It shows our people are tired," Lord Franklin said bluntly.

"Tired or disillusioned? The crown needs to show strength, show the people who's in charge."

"And who's in charge?" Lord Franklin responded, almost daring Lord Baudry to respond. Lord Baudry smirked and chuckled slightly. Lord Franklin found his smugness abhorrent. *"It was only friendly advice."*

"Don't be angry dear brother, Father was only trying to help," said Elizabeth. She tried to appear as innocuous as possible, but Lord Franklin saw through her façade. It vexed him so that she was already referring to him as brother, only moments after Gavin agreed to marry. He was beginning to unravel the unscrupulous nature of this family and now that they would become his family, trouble was sure to brew. Gavin was but a fly stuck on the web of Baudry's machinations. By agreeing to marry Elizabeth, the Baudry's were liquefying his insides. There was no escape. Lord Franklin wondered if it would have been better to pay off the debt. Only time would tell. But Lord Franklin knew that if he wasn't careful, he and his brother might end up like the flayed men who entered here.

The knights holding the prisoners remained motionless at the center of the hall. The perplexed onlookers wondered what they were supposed to do while the knights awaited instruction. Curious onlookers pointed and murmured, but none bothered to speak out against such cruelty. Lord Baudry must've had them under his thumb, thought Lord Franklin. *"Take them to the dungeon. There they can await execution. Now, everyone, resume the celebration. King Gavin is to be wedded to my daughter!"* Lord Baudry instructed.

There was a loud cheer from the crowd. It was almost as if they had been oblivious to the flayed men. Were these people so callous or was something more nefarious going on? The amount of power Lord Baudry had over the highborn was disturbing, but the most puzzling question of Lord Baudry's wealth came up again in Lord Franklin's mind. Whenever he'd asked Gavin, he would simply give an ambiguous answer such as trade. Trade was such a nebulous thing to him, and the inner mechanisms eluded him, but he had a sneaking suspicion it involved piracy. He doubted Lord Baudry would ever divulge such information willingly, hence there was no point in asking. But there was another way. As the prisoners were carted out of the great hall, Lord Franklin said, *"I wish to speak to them!"*

"Them? Only one of them will be speaking. Eigil made sure of that," Borin snickered.

"The torturer I presume?" asked Lord Franklin.

"He's from the North, served on our side during the war. Got a lot of information for us" replied Sadon.

"So, this Eigil is the one with the surgical skills?" said Lord Franklin.

"It's an art form really. You can't just go breaking bone and tearing away at flesh. The victim will die. The human body is unfortunately rather delicate.... You sort of have to develop a mastery of it," said Roger, his eyes were somewhere else and there was a twinkle in them, a sadistic smile was on his face as he lingered on the word mastery. It could only be described as ecstasy and Lord Franklin found his demeanor repulsive. Nonetheless, he wanted to know what sort of character he was dealing with, hence he continued conversing.

"And Eigil is a master?"

"Precisely," Roger replied rather reflexively.

Lord Franklin studied Roger's features. He was nearly as tall as Gavin but lanky, his head narrow and his lips thin, his hair blonde like his sisters only much less so. Parted at the center with the sides tucked behind his ears, cut neatly just above the base of the neck. The most vexing thing about his profile were his eyes: they lacked something or rather several things. Fear, emotion, compassion, and most of all, empathy. It was also evident in the way he talked unfiltered, with a complete lack or regard for social norms. The unnerving confidence of the father. Suddenly, Lord Franklin found the whole environment unsettling.

Roger muttered under his breath. *"If you'd like Eigil's services, perhaps I could arrange something."*

Lord Franklin was appalled and tried desperately to hide it, for he feared an outright rebuke would further arouse Roger's interest, thus encouraging him to speak in an even more deplorable nature. Lord Franklin sensed Roger was the type that reveled in being detested. *"No, that won't be necessary."*

"Are you sure, milord? You never know when you'll need information. Life is, well... strange," Roger said with a fiendish smile.

Elizabeth caught him grinning and directed a glare at him. It was her way of reprimanding him. *"Oh, I see now, she oversaw keeping up appearances and keeping her sadistic brother in line... this doesn't mean she was absolved of all iniquity, only that she had further ambitions that were beyond causing pain.... Power,"* thought Lord Franklin. Roger, however, seemed unconcerned, and he had moved on from torturing Lord Franklin and became lost in his thoughts. His eyes deviated to the left as though he was remembering something, then a smile formed on his face. Lord Franklin didn't bother trying to analyze what Roger was thinking. He didn't want to know the malicious extent of his mind. Lord Franklin's attention was instead directed toward Lord Baudry.

He nodded his head and Lord Baudry said, *"Very well."* He ordered the Knights to bring the prisoners so that Lord Franklin could inspect them. They were brought before Lord Franklin. Although the flesh had been torn from their faces, one could still see the despair in their eyes.

Lord Franklin looked into the eyes of the one that still had a jaw. *"Are you Nash or Cooper?"*

The man lowered his head. He was slow to respond, and the anticipation made Lord Franklin uncomfortable. He thought he should repeat what he said, but the man spoke, rather listlessly, *"I'm called Cooper milord."*

"And what came you this predicament?" asked Lord Franklin. He studied the man's eyes. They appeared lifeless and defeated. They revealed nothing other than he had been tortured to the brink of death. He and his comrade were probably longing for it by now. To be displayed in front of a crowd in such a state of indignation. It was cruel of him to subject them to this, but he needed to be sure... of the malice of the Baudry's. Lord Franklin thought perhaps it was foolish of him to interrogate these men. He wasn't going to get the truth and even if he did, he probably already knew it. This man would say anything to end his suffering... no, he would say anything because he already suffered. It suddenly occurred to Lord Franklin that this Eigil might've been overzealous and broken these men beyond repair, perhaps that was the point. Nonetheless it was an oversight because they no longer needed to be compliant. They had nothing left to lose. He would say anything. But perhaps this had been wishful thinking. What good would it do, exposing the Baudry's now that their house was joined with the crown? People would deny it or simply ignore it. Lord Baudry has a hold on these people, they would not dare betray him. Most probably owe him money. Conceivably, the reason Lord Baudry even entertained this in the first place, was he knew nothing would come of it regardless of the result. More of that unnerving confidence. He had been foolish for even letting Gavin speak or borrow money from these people. The whole thing had been a mistake.

"I have nothing to give these men but mercy," Lord Franklin thought.

Cooper spoke in a low monotone and with his eyes glued to the ground. *"I believe the crime was sedition, milord."*

"What did you and your comrade say?" asked Lord Franklin. Cooper said, almost rather irritated, *"Does it matter?"* *"Answer him, prisoner!"* said one of Baudry's knights.

19

Cooper seemed unfazed by the knight's hostility. Instead his eyes wandered into the distance. "*You can do me no harm anymore.*" He looked at Lord Franklin directly for the first time since he arrived in the great hall. *"A man can die two deaths—the first being more significant, then the second a mere formality of nature... it is the way of things. The first death, however, is entirely avoidable but like all death it is liberating."* Cooper smiled. *"There's nothing you can do for me now. I've already died... those who seek status above living will always die avoidable deaths. I understand that, now soon will you."*

"*Madness,*" Lord Baudry spoke plainly.

But Lord Franklin was not convinced. He didn't understand Cooper's cryptic message, and yet he did. It felt like a warning and Cooper's words haunt him to this day. Afterwards the celebration and merriment continued as though the two men never existed and Lord Franklin had only but one word: callousness. He wondered why Lord Baudry had brought these men here. Was it to show loyalty to Gavin? Or a subtle warning never to cross them? Lord Franklin guessed the latter. One day he was going to have to end the Baudry's and the stranglehold they had on the crown. He couldn't trust Gavin to do it, he lacked the wit. He would have to do it himself. He was going to have to quell the flames before they spread into a conflagration, sooner rather than later. The question remained: How soon?

That was nearly fifteen years ago, yet Lord Franklin remembered it vividly. The Baudry's had not been stopped since then. Their influence has instead expanded greatly and now one of his finest knights, someone he trusted, was a Baudry. Not only did he feel despondent, but also foolish. How could he have not foreseen this?

He didn't want to discuss such sensitive matters with his knights. He turned to one of the men. "Avery, take the men to explore the area. There could be others like him."

Sir Avery was hesitant to perform such a task, for it put his Lord at great risk. "Milord is that wise-".

"Don't worry. I'll have the commander and Sir Ulric will be by my side." Sir Avery was still. He clearly expressed demur from this directive and so did the other men.

Lord Franklin motioned Sir Avery to come near. He whispered in his ear, "It is more strategic this way. The creature seems more comfortable spreading lies and misinformation to an audience. He is preying on your fears and ignorance. Don't worry, this imposter cannot escape Ulric's grasp." Avery nodded his head and sent the men to explore the rest of the area while making sure they were not out of sight.

When the men were out of earshot, Lord Franklin asked bluntly, "Are you a spy for Hadrian Baudry?"

"Of course not, milord. I abandoned the Baudrys a long time ago. I'm not like them."

Lord Franklin gave him a piercing glance. He studied his companion's features although in brevity it was enough to make Sir Cedric Baudry uneasy as well as Sir Ulric. Lord Franklin wasn't sure whether to be more concerned that the creature's information was correct or the fact that Sir Cedric Baudry had deceived him for so long.

"How old were you when you left the Baudrys?" Lord Franklin interrogated.

"Nineteen," said Cedric Baudry.

Lord Franklin was now angered by this confession, but did his best to conceal it. In a low menacing yet subtle voice, Lord Franklin said, "We will discuss this later."

Sir Cedric Baudry picked up on the subtlety of his foreboding tone and thought it best to explain himself, for he feared severe punishment afterwards. "Uh. Milord-"

"I said later," said Lord Franklin more aggressively. He was not interested in what Sir Cedric Baudry had to say and was clearly too angered by what he deemed betrayal to listen. Nonetheless, Sir Cedric Baudry persisted against the nonverbal advice of Sir Ulric. Meanwhile Kraag remained still. He seemed completely subdued, not making any comments or antagonizing anyone, just simply observing and there was something ominous about that.

"My Lord, I feel it's important that you hear the nature in which I left the Baudrys," Sir Cedric Baudry said forcibly.

"Could not the nature of your dealings with them wait?" Lord Franklin said with an air of distrust that wounded Sir Cedric Baudry. Lord Franklin was angered and, although hesitant, Sir Cedric Baudry continued. There was too much at stake, his life, his reputation and honor. "I fear the longer the information ruminates in your mind, the less you will be partial to my testimony," said Sir Cedric Baudry. "Do you not trust my judgment?!" Lord Franklin snapped.

"I do my Lord and I know I should not be doubting you... I have given you good reason to doubt me."

"It would be unwise to reveal sensitive information in front of an unsavory character," said Sir Ulric while glaring at Kraag. Kraag simply responded by smiling. This was unnerving for Ulric.

"He's observing us. That's how he gather's information," Lord Franklin growled.

"I have an idea, milord," said Sir Ulric.

Lord Franklin and Sir Cedric Baudry looked at Sir Ulric in anticipation.

"There is a way we can speak freely without him hearing, taking away his advantage."

"More magic? Is that not taxing to the body?" asked Lord Franklin. "This is a rather simple spell."

"Alright," said Lord Franklin.

"*Uthra Phisiu*," said Sir Ulric. Suddenly, the three of them were surrounded in a transparent bubble.

"Now we can speak freely, we can hear him, he can't hear us." Both Sir Cedric Baudry and Lord Franklin were bemused. "I'll show you. AAAAAAAAAh!" Sir Ulric shouted.

Both Sir Cedric Baudry and Lord Franklin covered their ears. "A little warning Ulric!" shouted Lord Franklin.

"Er Sorry milord," said Sir Ulric.

Sir Cedric Baudry observed the surroundings, neither Kraag nor the knights reacted to Sir Ulric's screams. Lord Franklin noticed this as well. He turned to Sir Cedric Baudry. "Very well, you may speak, but make it brief Sir Ulric needs his energy for that other spell."

Sir Cedric Baudry nodded. He began to recount his tale as best he could. It had been nearly two decades since his departure from the Baudry's house. He had been nineteen when he left. He packed only a few things. A long sword, the tunic on his back, a dagger and three bars of gold, which he placed in a satchel he slung over his shoulders. He got on his steed, grey with black spots. Grabbing the reins, he said, "*C'mon Onyx.*" The beast stepped forward lethargically. He was a lazy horse and behaved more like a mule.

Sir Cedric Baudry bumped the steed a little harder. "*C'mon!*" he said irritably. Onyx moved forward, albeit at a slow pace. Sir Cedric Baudry sighed. This was the best he was going to get with this horse. Sir Cedric Baudry peered into the sky. It would be night soon. He had left abruptly, forgetting to take supplies, food, and clothing. But he couldn't turn back... he wouldn't turn back. Hopefully Tybalt would have those things. After all he did have the gold. He felt uneasy as he ventured towards the woods. Was this the right decision? Had he been too rash, had he been followed? Suddenly he heard what he thought were the snapping of twigs and the trotting of hooves. He immediately stopped and turned around, only to see nothing. It had only been his imagination. He bumped Oynx a little harder and the horse reluctantly increased the pace.

The woods were not completely barren, there were some houses along the way, which made sense there was a town, but not nearby, and that would take another day to reach, two days on Oynx, besides nightfall had already engulfed the remaining daylight eclipsing it in total darkness.

He could barely see anything and he regretted not bringing a lantern or at least a torch. Perhaps it was better this way. The darkness would conceal him. And besides, he knew the way. The only dirt road in the densely forested woods only lead to one place: Tybalt's brothel.

He followed the winding path until it led to the medium-sized brick house with a thatched roof. The brothel was too small to house that many whores and it was a modest abode compared to other brothels. But it was strategically placed. There was no other for miles and it was the largest structure in the woods before one could reach a village. It was like a beacon for wayward travelers who often lost their way. Business was good for Tybalt, considering how little competition he had. Still, Tybalt aspired to be greater. Other brothels had notoriety that he wished he had. It was the scandalous nature that made these types of establishments profitable. They brought customers and they paid extra for confidentiality.

He was a man in his sixties, potbellied and with long, thinning gray hair. He stood outside the brothel with a lit torch. A wide, toothy grin was on his face as he saw Sir Cedric Baudry. Sir Cedric Baudry found this odd and slightly vexing. *"Why was he smiling? Did he know I would come? Does he know something I don't?"* he thought.

"I thought you might need it, considering how late it is," Tybalt said, referring to the torch. He gestured for Sir Cedric Baudry to come in, but Sir Cedric Baudry resisted. Tybalt furrowed his brow and stared at Sir Cedric Baudry briefly.

"Is something the matter?"

"Did you know I was coming?" Sir Cedric Baudry interrogated. Tybalt laughed in his husky voice. *"I knew you would come eventually, Milord, you couldn't resist that old whore Mary. It's the way you stare too. I'd say its love,"* he teased.

"Shut up!" Sir Cedric Baudry shouted angrily. He sighed. He had lost his temper.

Tybalt waited before speaking, then he said plainly, *"Why don't we go inside milord."* He appeared sympathetic, this seemed to placate Sir Cedric Baudry. He dismounted from Oynx and he proceeded to tie him to a nearby tree. He then followed Tybalt inside. Sir Cedric Baudry looked around. He was puzzled as the place was empty. I guess this made sense. It was late but was it too late for business?

He asked rather curiously, *"Did you clear the place?"*

"It's dark, even brothel owners must sleep. The whores are in their beds. I'll go wake her," he, said nonchalantly. His demeanor was too casual, it was almost rehearsed, like he was calming himself, but perhaps it was nothing. Perhaps it was just nerves.

Tybalt disappeared into a room and retrieved a weary-eyed Mary. She was raven haired, fair skinned, brown eyes. Sir Cedric Baudry stared, and he thought her beautiful. Mary was perplexed. She didn't know why this younger man looked at her in such a way as though he knew her.

"Do you know who this man is?"

"I've seen him round 'ere from time to time. He never pays, just watches…" She lingered on the word watches. There was something familiar about him she couldn't quite put her finger on it.

"This is-" Tybalt said before he was interrupted by Sir Cedric Baudry.

"Privacy, ahem. I wish to talk to her alone." Tybalt led them to a private room and closed the door behind him.

Mary, now rather suspicious, said bluntly, *"Who are you and why do you look at me so?"*

He hesitated before speaking. She studied his face and said, *"I know you, don't I?"*

He took a deep breath in before saying, *"I'm the bastard son of Lord Hadrian Baudry… I'm your son."*

Her eyes widened and she began to tremble. *"What-what do you want?"* Her voice quavered; she was frightened. Sir Cedric Baudry was wounded by her accusatory tone, but soon realized his blunder hence, he attempted to assuage her fears.

"No, no I'm not like them. I came to set you free." He opened his satchel, revealing three gold bars. *"I left them. I'm on my own now"*

"No one leaves the Baudry's without a trip to the grave!" she snapped.

"You did!" Sir Cedric Baudry retorted. *"Well, you're here,"* she said harshly. *"My name is Cedric,"* he sighed.

"They don't know about you. There is a village nearby, you could start a new life."

Mary reached for the satchel and quickly closed it. *"You must leave this place… please Cedric, go."*

"Take the gold, it's not from them," said Sir Cedric Baudry.

"I- I know I- uh . . ." Her eyes fell from his and gravitated toward the ground. She sighed. She looked at him again. Her eyes watery as she said, *"I prayed this day would come, but not like this."* She caressed his cheek and smiled. *"My son."*

Tears began to fall from Sir Cedric Baudry's face. They touched foreheads and he whispered, *"I remember you,"* and she replied, *"As do I"*

"We shan't see each other again," her voice quavered.

"Only god knows," said Sir Cedric Baudry.

Suddenly, the door flung open. Sir Cedric Baudry immediately drew his blade. Mary stood behind him.

Four figures emerged from the doorway. Sadon, Fendrel, Roger and Borin. Roger entered first with a mischievous grin. *"Bastard. Did you really think you could hide from us?"*

"Tybalt," Sir Cedric Baudry growled under his breath.

"Sorry Milord, they were willing to pay double," Tybalt said nonchalantly. His apology disingenuous and he exuded an air of indifference. This did not surprise Sir Cedric Baudry, he was a brothel owner, a detestable one, for sure. It vexed him that he did not account for this betrayal. He should've known the Baudry's influence knew no bounds.

Roger and his brothers drew further into the room. Sir Cedric Baudry threatened them with the point of his blade. *"Stay back. I'm warning you!"*

Sadon snickered. *"Stay back he says."*

"You can't take us all on, brother," said Roger condescendingly. When he was in striking distance, Sir Cedric delivered a thrust from long point guard that grazed Roger's cheek. Roger stumbled backwards. He smiled, wiped the blood from his cheek and said, *"Fine, have it your way."*

He drew his long sword, as did his brothers. Tybalt, witnessing the whole scene, said, *"Milords, perhaps it would be better if you took this quarrel outside. It's bad for business."*

Fendrel groaned, *"Will pay triple if you keep your mouth shut and make sure she doesn't escape."* Tybalt obeyed and seized Mary by the arm.

"Don't you touch her!" shouted Sir Cedric Baudry. He was interrupted by Roger delivering a descending cut from high guard. Sir Cedric Baudry narrowly parried it. And so the first engagement began. Soon all brothers were upon him. He desperately tried to fend them off, but he was outnumbered. He soon resorted to wide cuts to lengthen the distance between him and his adversaries. They delivered some wrath cuts in quick succession. He relied very little on thrust, given he was facing several opponents, it seemed unwise. He managed to wound Fendrel in the shoulder with a rising cut from fool's guard. The other brothers still pursued him. Over the melee, Mary desperately searched for means of escape. Her eyes gravitated towards the window. The other whores had awakened from all the raucous.

"Borin, make sure no one leaves," said Roger. Borin obeyed and blocked the exits. The other three whores were subdued. Mary thought to make a run for it. She bit into Tybalt's hand, leaving the indentation of tooth

marks and drawing blood and with that, he released his grasp. *"Ow, you savage bitch!"*

Before Mary could get away, Tybalt struck her in the face, knocking her unconscious.

During the fight, Sir Cedric Baudry managed to disarm Fendrel. He grabbed a hold of him from behind and placed his sword on Fendrel's throat. This seemed to halt the pursuit. *"Leave this place or I swear I'll kill him!"*

The brothers were silent. Fendrel began to sweat profusely, then a smirk began to form at the corners of Roger's mouth.

"Go ahead."

"Stop bluffing Roger, I know you don't want him to die," shouted Sir Cedric Baudry.

"I don't happen to care but I wonder how father would feel if his bastard killed his legitimate son… there'd be nowhere to run. He'll drum up a punishment even beyond my imagination. You see, either way, you and your mother are fucked. Father said you will pay and there's no getting out of this."

"You betrayed us Cedric, that cannot go unpunished," said Sadon.

"Betray? How? By saying I want nothing to do with father and his machinations or for choosing freedom over slavery?" Sir Cedric Baudry sneered. Sadon scowled.

"He gave you a name and you spat in his face. By rejecting it, you're rejecting us." Sir Cedric Baudry chuckled with a mad fervor.

"You all can go to hell cause no matter what happens here, my conscience is clear. Tell father he can't defy God for long." He raised his blade slightly closer to Fendrel's throat, but suddenly he felt a sharp pain at the side of his neck. It felt like a needle entering his skin. His limbs felt numb, and he lost consciousness.

He awoke to the sound of Tybalt screaming, *"What have you done to my whores! That wasn't part of the bloody plan!"*

Sir Cedric Baudry fully opened his eyes and found himself tied to a chair with rope. He could see blood all over the floor and the fresh corpses of three women. They had been butchered from the looks of it and by a longsword. One had her throat slit, the other ran through while the last one was bludgeoned with the pommel. Tybalt was shaking with rage.

"You'll pay for this. I'll see to it- ack-" Fendrel had slit his throat with a dagger. Tybalt keeled over and choked to death on his own blood, much to the brother's amusement. Sadon said, *"He was quite a nuisance."* Sir Cedric Baudry began shaking franticly in his chair, trying to escape the restraints. His eyes darted across the room in search of his mother. Maybe she'd escaped, maybe… Suddenly, he felt disheartened when he heard her stifled muted cry from the backroom. He had not seen Borin… Borin had been in the room.

Roger's eyes gravitated toward him. He said with fake concern, *"Oh brother, you're awake. I thought the sedative Tybalt gave you would've woken you up sooner. It's cove needle, it's from Yetic."*

Sir Cedric Baudry growled, *"What have you done to her?"*

Roger chuckled derisively. *"Oh I think you know, but I'll tell you anyway because it amuses me, your mother is quite beauteous by the way."*

Sir Cedric Baudry attempted to lunge at Roger but was still confined to the chair. Roger smiled as he drew closer to Sir Cedric Baudry and whispered in his ear. *"We each took a turn. We roughed her up a little, Borin's in there right now."*

"God will punish you," Sir Cedric Baudry snarled.

"Hmmph, if God was real, you wouldn't be in this predicament and someone like me would not be permitted to exist," said Roger ominously.

Borin left the room and pulled up his pants. Sir Cedric Baudry was repulsed. *"What's should we do next?"*

"We've been through this. We're going to torch the place," said Sadon irritably.

"Not yet… I've got a better idea," said Roger. He turned to Sir Cedric Baudry and smiled fiendishly.

"Untie him."

"What are you playing at!" shouted Fendrel while tending to his shoulder.

"Stop being such a baby. He's unarmed. Besides it was only a flesh wound," said Sadon.

"Well, I'm not doing it," Fendrel said petulantly. Roger groaned as he drew his dagger and began slowly cutting away at Sir Cedric Baudry's restraints.

"You know I feel terrible that you missed the festivities," he said mockingly.

"You're sick," Sir Cedric Baudry retorted. Roger ignored him.

"But I have remedied that." He drew nearer and whispered in Sir Cedric Baudry's ear, *"I want you to fuck her like you do your wife."* Sir Baudry's eyes widened.

They knew about Helena, so this was it, he was truly subdued. Sir Baudry's reaction aroused Roger; you could tell by the way his eyes lit up; it was repugnant. The other brothers snickered, which eventually progressed into cackles. They too knew. He had been foolish. This whole thing was a mistake. Sir Cedric Baudry hung his head low in despondence. He said in a low voice, *"How do I know you won't have them both killed?"* *"You don't, but if you don't comply, it will be your fault... You see brother, you can't hide anything from us. There are consequences for betraying family. Borin, bring her out!"* said Roger.

Her hair was disheveled, she had a bruise under her eye and a bloody nose. They locked eyes in brevity, but the exchange felt like a lifetime. He couldn't bear to look at her for it was because of him she was even in this predicament. He wanted to say it, but his lips refused to move. But he had the feeling she knew what he was going to say. *"I'm sorry,"* he thought.

After the deed was done, they burned down Tybalt's Brothel. Leaving the three women and Tybalt's corpses inside, Oynx had been beheaded. Mary was nowhere to be found until several months later. Her body nailed to a cross with the words incestuous whore etched on her forehead. Incest was a crime punishable by death. But Sir Cedric Baudry somehow suspected that this was the work of his father and brothers rather than the authorities. As for Helena, she was found weeks prior, in pieces dispersed all over his house.

The others stood aghast after hearing that harrowing tale, including Lord Franklin, whose features softened after hearing it. He was quite embarrassed for his temper.

"Please forgive me for my ignorance. You have given me no reason to mistrust you," said Lord Franklin. Lord Franklin put his hand on Cedric Baudry's shoulder and said solemnly, "We will avenge them, when I am king, that I promise you."

"First, we have to deal with this monster in front of us. We must not let him get inside our heads, he means to divide us then attack when we're most vulnerable," said Sir Ulric. He was watching Kraag as he said this. He was watching Kraag the whole time and it disturbed him that the being remained completely still. He made no attempt to escape, nor did he care that they had disappeared. *Just who exactly was he?* he thought. "You're right, Sir Ulric," said Lord Franklin. He turned to Sir Ulric, who dissolved the bubble. Lord Franklin then turned to Kraag with a defiant look on his face. "Kraag your attempt to turn us against each other has failed, such a stratagem is often used by a weaker force seeking to dominant a stronger force but once the stronger force gets wind of the scheme the weaker force is usually annihilated, you're outnumbered and outmatched. Surrender and release Tristian or die," said Lord Franklin.

"You are lecturing me about war. You have no idea how amusing that is. Anyway, I have no intention to start a fight so there is no need for me to surrender," said Kraag.

With a smile he said, "I'm already yours."

"Then release Tristian immediately," Lord Franklin demanded.

"I'm curious. Aren't you curious, Albert? Don't you have more pressing matters to attend to like who is responsible for the bodies on the ground or whether the Horridus are connected to Hector or why Ulric clings on to the sacred text so tightly?" Kraag whispered, "He has a secret."

"Or perhaps you would like to know your future, how you will die, who will betray you, how you lose this war. I know these are your fears because I can sense it inside you."

"Enough!" Lord Franklin shouted. "You are a clever one there is no doubt, but your lies and deceit end here devil for if you won't release Tristian, we will extract you from him ourselves," said Lord Franklin.

"An exorcism." Kraag guffawed. "That's not going to work." "Sir Ulric do it!" said Lord Franklin.

"Yes, milord," said Sir Ulric.

Ulric was speaking the old tongue. The old tongue is believed to be the oldest language. It is said to have some interesting properties, such as warding off evil spirits and purifying infected souls. It is also believed that all races spoke the old tongue as their initial language before branching off into their own tongues.

"*Um ne tensai bilurd relissimo.*" [release the devil/demon] Nothing happened. Kraag began to laugh raucously.

"I told you that wouldn't work on me!" he said. Sir Ulric ignored Kraag and continued to repeat the phrase.

"Um ne tensai bilurd relissimo." "Um ne tensai bilurd relissimo!" "Um ne tensai bilurd relissimo!!" "Um ne tensai bilurd relissimo!!!"

"UM NE TENSAI BILURD RELISSIMO!"

Sir Ulric's face was red with fatigue. He was panting and struggled to retrieve his breath. His forehead was sweating profusely, and he was bent over with hands planted firmly on his thighs. He sighed because he knew all his effort was to no avail. Kraag was still cackling.

"What's so funny devil? You think because we failed in this instance we will give up? We will stop you, I swear. I will tear your essence from Tristian's body even if it involves prying it apart with my bare hands!" said Lord Franklin angrily.

"What's amazing about you humans and other races like yours is that you have the uncanny ability to not realize when you're outmatched.

You're convinced surrender is weakness and martyrdom is some holy attainment. So, there is a senseless bravado of reaching for things beyond your limits. This insidious idea stems from a deep feeling of worthlessness, so you look to the sky and hope that you somehow matter, that there is a purpose to your existence, but you don't matter in the grand scheme of things, you are a speck of dust on the cog of a machine that is life.

"Insignificant and of no consequence dead or alive to the entire system. Deep down your kind is aware of its irrelevance, but the harsh reality that comes with it is too much to bear, so you construct lies upon lies until they resemble truth. Religion is the focal point of this deception. With religion you can make yourself matter, you can aspire to reach for the heavens. With religion there is an afterlife where you can achieve absolute bliss in paradise. The mendacity of the religion allows one to create a God born from a lie and this lie is told to the people who believe it to be truth. Even though they have never seen or heard of this God, they will still claim to know definitively things about this false God. For example, you claim to know a God that is not only personally invested in your welfare but one who is merciful. You claim to know everything about this God, his will, how long it took for him to build all of existence, and how he likes to be worshiped. You give it a gender you say you were made in his image; you give it a name, you call him Arda. Someone makes up a book of sacred text that detail on how to worship their false idea of God. He calls himself a prophet and people believe it after several hundred years. The propaganda spreads to the next generations who follow it devoutly. And that is how a lie becomes accepted as truth."

Sir Ulric said, angrily, "The sacred text is real, you lying Devil! Noga is a—"

"Noga was a lying rapist, a manipulator and murderer. He is said to have raped over four hundred women claiming to be purifying their souls. Those who tried to stand up to him where labeled sinners to be burned alive on a pyre," said Kraag.

"How dare you speak of Noga that way, you foul, deceitful creature. Why I—"

"Silence mortal!" said Kraag sternly. Sir Ulric tried to move his mouth, but it was sewn shut. He could not say anything intelligible he could only move his body and make noise.

"What have you done with Sir Ulric?" said Lord Franklin.

"I simply prevented Sir Ulric from saying something sanctimonious," said Kraag. "Don't you ever wonder why Sir Ulric is so pious in the first place?"

"Enough monster, your attempts to divide us have failed before and they will fail again. You said you had a message for us. You best deliver it before we extract you from Tristian's body," said Lord Franklin.

"The old tongue won't work on me for it is the tongue of the Horridus, and as for message I suppose I should deliver it. I digressed enough. I'm here along with the other Horridus to carry out the eradication of all intelligent life forms from this world," said Kraag.

"But why? I thought we were unimportant, *a speck of dust on the cog of a machine that is life. Insignificant and is no consequence dead or alive to the entire system,*" said Lord Franklin sarcastically.

"In truth, we're doing it because we abhor your kind. Your species may be irrelevant, but that doesn't make you any less vexing. The problem is that your species and like have a tendency to destroy everything in its path, including each other. You are a plague and plagues must be dealt with through eradication of the source and that source is you," said Kraag. "And what makes you think we'd stand idly by as you attempt to eradicate us?" said Lord Franklin sternly.

"Oh, you can't possibly hope to stop us. We have been responsible for the extinction of hundreds of species. Do not fret, every species meets its end. You see, your bodies don't belong to you. They're made of borrowed materials from the void and this very rock you stand on, hence it will return to the void from whence it came for the cycle of life and destruction to repeat itself. It is what every organism that ever existed has experienced; a cycle, death of what is old and a rebirth of something new, just think the environment will be so much purer with your kind gone, it will be a noble sacrifice redeeming your wretched kind," said Kraag.

"Are you asking us to be grateful for our possible annihilation?" Lord Franklin said angrily.

"No, I'm asking you to accept your deaths and surrender quietly," said Kraag.

"Bwah ha ha ha," Lord Franklin laughed. "You're not familiar with mankind are you? We don't just surrender on a whim, we don't submit to tyranny we will never succumb to monsters and demons and I certainly won't be fooled by a manifestation created by Hector and his sorcerers." "Oh, you all will submit and die even if I have to break each and every one of you and if you think this is about Hector, perhaps I shall show you how they died," said Kraag referring to the heap of dead bodies behind him.

"It starts with this vessel." Kraag managed to escape from his chains rather easily and pulled a dagger out from his waist and placed it on his throat. Lord Franklin's eyes widened and Sir Ulric and Sir Cedric Baudry looked equally as horrified, but before anyone could do anything Kraag slit his own throat. Suddenly Tristian returned to his body and the black eyes and essence of Kraag left. Lord Franklin attempted to use his hand to stop the bleeding, but it was to no avail, for Tristian's warm blood was already slipping through Lord Franklin's fingers. Tristian gazed upwards as though there was something in that vicinity. His skin was pale from the blood lost and the light was fading from his eyes with his last breath he smiled and said, "Thank you Kraag, thank you for showing mercy. I will be with the void now, oh and Lord Franklin tell my wife Janet that I love her."

Lord Franklin clasped Tristian palm with both his hands and said sincerely, "the message will be delivered." The light completely escaped his eyes, and he rested his head on the grass. Lord Franklin let go of his hand and Tristian lay dead at his feet.

"Kraag, show yourself!" Lord Franklin said with his sword drawn and looking around for any trace of Kraag. Sir Ulric was horrified by what he witnessed. Lord Franklin and Sir Cedric Baudry were not particularly versed in magic, so they weren't aware of the gravity of the situation. The Manaca-la hex is considered the most powerful binding spell known to magic wielders. It is used to restrain giants and can even bind ghosts. The spell requires a significant amount of soul manifest, hence not many magic wielders can perform this spell. Of the 36 in Arcadiem known to be able to perform this spell, 30 have died due to overexerting soul energy.

"I said show yourself!" shouted Lord Franklin.

"Over here!" said several voices in unison. Lord Franklin turned around and to his bewilderment the bodies were now reanimated with black eyes, for Kraag had possessed all the corpses. Upon seeing this, Sir Avery and the men came rushing towards Lord Franklin's side. They were shocked at what they had just witnessed and not sure what to do. No one uttered a word. Finally, Kraag broke the silence.

"I know what you're thinking, multiple possession impossible, especially from corpses, but that's the power of the Horridus."

"You think this changes anything? You don't scare us. Stop your tricks and show your real self and let us see what steel does to your flesh," said Lord Franklin.

"Oh, Albert, since you were a boy you have denied what did not make sense to you for reason and logic, well there are other forces in this world that cannot be explained by logic. Will you deny them too? For if you do, it will be your downfall," said Kraag.

"You claim to know me and my men, you claim to be greater than God, you even claim to be clairvoyant. With all that power, how come you can't smite us all here and now? Why do you have to rely on pathetic tricks such as possession? Also where is your army? You keep saying we referring to the Horridus but we've only heard from you, why is that?" asked Lord Franklin.

"You still deny our power after what you have seen? You're a foolish man whose only concern is with your little insignificant war. We slaughtered your men not Hector, for we are your true enemy, one you cannot hope to defeat, that's why I've stressed your surrender," said Kraag. "Say I believe you, tell me this what good is surrender if you're just going to kill us anyway?" said Lord Franklin.

"It can be the difference between a painless death and an agonizing one," said Kraag.

"Death is death whether painless or not and I fear neither death nor pain," said Lord Franklin.

"But what about your wife, Rose, or sons Edmund, William and John, do they fear death? Do they fear torture? Will they scream as I peel the flesh from their bones? Or perhaps they'll scream while being burned alive?" said Kraag menacingly.

"If you harm my family in any way-"

"You'll do what? Kill us, make us suffer? Don't make me laugh, we cannot be defeated, we cannot be harmed, and can never die but if you wish to test the truth in my words you're welcome to try," Kraag said sardonically, the undead suddenly drew their blades and readied their steeds. Lord Franklin and his calvary did the same. "Tell me Albert, how do you expect to defeat an army of the undead?" Kraag said mockingly.

"Never you mind that monster, you will meet death soon enough." As the two armies where about to collide Kraag utter the word Oblis, (translation: unknown) and the undead army stopped in their tracks.

"What's the matter monster, giving up so soon?" said Lord Franklin mockingly.

"I just realized it is not your time to die, but don't worry, we will meet again for I'm already inside you and death is near, but for now this is goodbye." The essence of Kraag disappeared and the reanimated became lifeless corpses.

Sir Ulric regained his ability to talk. "Ha, I can talk again," Sir Ulric said panting. "What do we do now?" asked Ulric but Lord Franklin was distracted, his gaze was fixated in the distance where Kraag disappeared, his thoughts raced, he wondered what Kraag meant by *I'm already inside you*, or *who will betray you* and even *it's not your time to die.*

"Milord are you ok?" said Sir Cedric Baudry.

33

"Eh yes, I'm fine," Lord Franklin responded halfheartedly. Sir Cedric Baudry sensed that something was vexing Lord Franklin. Perhaps he was affected by Kraag's words. Whatever the reason, Sir Cedric Baudry decided that it would be wise not to press the matter.

"Where do we go from here, my lord?" asked Sir Ulric.

Lord Franklin said, "We burn the bodies to prevent Kraag from possessing them."

"What about Tristian? Shouldn't we send his wife Janet his body and tell her what happened?" asked Sir Ulric.

"No! We can't do that. It will only cause mass panic and hysteria. Besides, do you want to deliver a reanimated corpse to his wife?" Lord Franklin said sternly.

"Kraag can possess virtually anything from what I observed, milord. He has powers beyond imagination and threatened to destroy all intelligent life in the world. We must tell someone what we witnessed," said Sir Ulric.

"Tell them what exactly? That a monster or monsters that cannot be seen, only heard, killed over a hundred men then possessed their dead bodies? They'll think us mad!" Lord Franklin said derisively. "This was all probably an elaborate stunt from Hector. All we need to focus on is Hector and winning this war."

"Hector had nothing to do with Kraag. After all we've seen, do you really think Hector and his men are capable of such complex sorcery?" said Sir Ulric with frustration in his voice.

"Don't underestimate the shrewdness of Hector," said Lord Franklin. "Alright, even if this is all Hector's doing, these things, whatever they are, are dangerous. Allow me to contact Mirama," said Sir Ulric.

"I understand you have a relationship with the holy city given the title knight and Cleric, but you underestimate your influence over them. They will think we are dealing in hokraft. We must deal with this as discreetly as possible. This is between the three of us and the calvary. No need to tell anyone at Corithni (Kore-rith-Nye) not even my sons or wife agreed?" said Lord Franklin.

"Yes, milord," both Sir Cedric Baudry and Sir Ulric said in unison. The knights agreed as well. However, Sir Ulric said it reluctantly because he was certain that this was a bad idea. So, they burned the bodies, the putrid smell of the burning corpses lingered in the air, it was hard to bear. So much, in fact, that Lord Franklin, Sir Cedric Baudry and Sir Ulric and several members of the calvary covered their mouths to avoid the stench. The embers from the flames rose into the sky along with the smoke. When the bodies were burned to a crisp, Lord Franklin and company headed to Corithni.

CHAPTER TWO

CORITHNI AND THE BLACK-EYED WOLF-BEASTS

Corithni was a robust castle. The curtain wall stood 44 feet high with a breadth of 15 feet while the tallest tower, being the watch tower, stood 55 feet. The keep was 48 feet. The castle was a total of 319,322 square feet, with each floor 10,000 square feet.

The walls were heavily battlemented and contained crenulations with arrow slits. Corithni was built with mostly white stone from Isial (Isle) lake and mortar. The lake is said to have magical properties such as causing any debris (inanimate objects only) that gets swept up in the lake to completely harden. Because of this belief, black smiths often forged swords and armor using water from Isial lake. Isial lake surrounds the land Corithni is built on. Corithni was strategically built on a hill to protect against sieges from enemies. Corithni is a 223-year old fortress and has never been conquered partially due to the rocky terrain and alleged hardened white stone. Some locals at Corithni believe the white stone to be a lucky artifact. It is believed to be a gift from Arda, his blessing; because of this, white stone is a hot commodity. Fortunately, it is abundant. White stone is used and made into several things, for instance it is made into talismans, it is placed on graves, and it is placed on the doors of houses. Despite all this, there is little factual evidence that links white stone to any of its suggested properties, it may very well just be a stone but to some people in Corithni white stone is a symbol of holiness with its ethereal craftsmanship and perfectly symmetrical surface, to some this indicated that it was engineered by a God.

The practice of placing high value on inanimate objects or worshiping a God or Gods is not a new concept, but what is rarely inquired is how these concepts came about. Religion is practiced around the world. People even based their government on religion. So, what makes religion so special? Why is the concept of a God or gods so widely accepted? Because if religious texts are how one is supposed to live their life, then freedom is being sacrificed for piety and we have a right to be free. So why would people sacrifice freedom for a dogmatic set of laws? The answer is fear of the unknown, the realization of purposelessness of existence, knowing one will die alone, the fear of there being nothing after death, the awareness that there is no reason to follow a moral code and that everything one does is pointless, making life and death unrecognizable from one another. Even the most sanguine of individuals knows this reality is bleak in the slightest. People cling to a higher power or higher powers because it gives them hope, even though hope is an illusion, but that's for another discussion, people hang on to religion because it gives them a purpose, additionally it tells them what to do with the promise of an afterlife and a reward for good deeds.

People who follow a religion or a higher power or both are not naïve nor dim-witted, on the contrary. You see this life is not an easy one. It's not your friend nor your mother, it will not support you, it will not cuddle you. Instead it will pummel you to the ground until your mangled body is rendered near lifeless only to repeat the process again and if you have aspirations of reaching the sky, then those aspirations will always be thwarted and struck back down with such ferocity that any thought of reaching the sky again will be torn from your consciousness. But if somehow you persist and stand up to the insurmountable obstacle that is life and somehow you slip past its defenses and meet your creator, you start to think maybe this is a dream but you reassure yourself that it doesn't matter, it's a victory nonetheless for you have met the creator and he exists in some reality and that's all a dream is, an alternate reality. You're beaming with excitement. You're about to talk to your creator, but suddenly you're lost for words. A disturbing thought enters your mind and you're full of rage. You think why your creator abandoned you, why is he causing so much suffering, so you go and ask these questions and he has an apathetic look on his face as he utters the phrase, "it was never about you." Then he dissolves, and you fall into the abyss back in the same pit that whence you came. You lie there looking at the sky with no more thoughts of glory and you let life pummel you to the ground because you know it won't matter if you fight back, the result will be the same. The God you met either does not exist or doesn't care. This may sound depressing, but it's an ugly possibility that everyone knows even though some seek to deny it. Those that have faith know this but cannot bring themselves to believe it because the thought would drive them to suicide. So, they use faith to protect themselves from the grim possibility. It's an ingenious strategy, it's a coping mechanism for life. And those without faith use escapism, such as the arts. Religion gives people purpose in a seemingly purposeless world. It is crucial to hang on to some sort of meaning in life, even though life is inherently meaningless. Paradoxical I know, but one must create meaning in life by switching modalities. Essentially deciding what's important to you and let that anchor you. That way, there is no fear of being wrong because the meaning of life becomes subjective. This existential process is essential in navigating your way through life regardless of your personal beliefs. It is the remedy to nihilism; it is essentially how to be.

Lord Franklin headed toward the castle with some 200 men. They were near the portcullis when they were suddenly met by archers, about 10 on the ramparts of the barbican with their bows readied.

"Who goes there?" said one of the archers.

To which Lord Franklin retorted, "Are you thick boy? Don't you recognize your Lord? Do you not see our banners? Open the bloody gate or I swear by Arda I shall have you flogged."

The archers looked at each other with fearful expressions on their faces as they contemplated letting Lord Franklin in. One of them whispered to another archer, "Ralf, if you don't let them in, we will be flogged, you heard Lor—".

"How do we know that's the real Lord Franklin and not the shapeshifter disguised as him, huh what's that? No answer? Gilbert, I thought so, now shut up and let me handle this," Ralf said acerbically.

"You're going to get us killed, you idiot!" said Gilbert in a forceful whisper.

Before Ralf could respond, Sir Cedric Baudry interrupted. "I'm sorry did you say shapeshifter, nonmagical?" Sir Cedric Baudry said with bewilderment.

"Don't suppose how he could've been magical given Corithni's resistance, eh," said Ralf.

Gilbert frowned. "That's only within the castle, you dullard." "Whatever I saw him change, I could hear his bones. It's like they were breaking, it didn't sound like magic," retorted Ralf.

"There hasn't been a record of a nonmagical form of shapeshifter in over 1000 years. It is believed that they got wiped out by the plague of Albedasis," said Sir Cedric Baudry.

"The shapeshifter is not the only thing," said Ralf as he dropped down what looked like the decapitated head of a lycanthrope. Sir Cedric

Baudry caught the object. He examined the lycanthrope's decapitated head by running his fingers through its scalp, checking for the shape. Typically, lycanthropes have human scalps on a wolf's head hence, there is no split in the middle like one would see with a regular wolf. Sir Cedric Baudry then inspected the fur to see if it was authentic by pulling on some strands. Next, he turned the head towards himself and pried open the mouth, allowing him to see a set of sharp teeth, larger than any human or wolf.

"Well, is it a lycanthrope?" Lord Franklin asked impatiently. "Yes, it's definitely a lycanthrope," answered Sir Cedric Baudry.

"Great, more problems for me to deal with," said Lord Franklin in a frustrated voice. Sir Cedric craned his neck upwards, his gaze directed toward the top of the castle

"How did it scale that wall?" Sir Cedric Baudry muttered under his breath.

"Huh?" asked Sir Ulric.

"Uh, the beast, how could it have climbed the castle's stone curtain?" explained Sir Cedric Baudry.

"Maybe someone let it in, that someone could have been the shapeshifter, then I suppose the beast could have transformed inside," said Sir Ulric.

"I thought lycanthropes only transformed during the full moon and there hasn't been a full moon in days," said Sir Cedric Baudry.

"The term lycanthropes implies being able to freely transform into a wolf beast man hybrid or werewolf for short, willingly. There are even werecat," said Sir Ulric, but before he could say more, Lord Franklin interrupted him.

"We should focus more on getting into the castle and winning this war rather than blabbering on about mindless beasts," Lord Franklin said brusquely. His gaze now directed at Ralf.

"You there, you are called Ralf, yes?" Lord Franklin asked. But Ralf did not respond he looked petrified, his face turned pale, and his pupils were dilated. He opened his mouth but nothing intelligible came out instead he just stammered, moreover the rest of the archers looked just as frightened, to which Lord Franklin responded with a puzzled look on his face. He looked around at his comrades who were adjacent to him, Sir Ulric to the right and Sir Cedric Baudry to the left. They were equally perplexed.

"Will someone speak, damn it!" Lord Franklin said crossly.

Finally, one of the archers by the name of Bryce broke the silence with a loud cry. "Wolf beasts!" he bellowed.

Lord Franklin quickly turned around. What he saw shocked him, an army of lycanthropes, about a thousand approaching from behind. They crept steadily and methodically. The beasts stood an average height of 10 feet tall when on hind legs but in this instance they were on all fours. Their fur was disheveled, and they looked rabid, this was further made evident by the irregular growls and snarls that came from the beasts. As their approach continued, the growls and snarls intensified. Lord Franklin and his men unsheathed their blades, and the archers readied their bows. Lord Franklin turned around slightly so that his gaze met the archers near the parapet.

"On my signal fire!" bellowed Lord Franklin.

"Should we trust him? What do you think, Gil?" asked Ralf.

Gilbert responded with a scowl and said, "Now you heed my advice, before it was all *Shut up and let me handle this* and my name is not Gil, it's Gilbert!"

Ralph furrowed his brow. Slightly annoyed with Gilbert's response, he retorted with one of his own by saying, "This is why I don't ask for your input."

"Wha—my input? Let me tell you something, I have put up with your insolence for too long. The next time that you cross me I will—"

"Will you two shut up already? That is Lord Franklin you see down there." The archer pointed his index finger toward Lord Franklin on horseback near the portcullis, in addition, he placed an emphasis on the word there. "Otherwise, why would the beast be after him and his party, so straighten up, ready your bows, and be prepared to serve your king!" said Bryce.

There was an awkward silence. The reason is a result of Bryce's rank. You see, Ralf considered himself a self-appointed position of head archer and he considered Gilbert to be second in command, again a self-appointed position that they often quarreled about. As you could imagine, they were surprised to have a recent recruit, and might I add a usually timid person in general, yell at them like that. Bryce was the first to break the silence. "Uh sorry," he said in a low, barely audible voice. He was quite embarrassed and lowered his head in shame. "Don't be. You're right, our squabble was meaningless," said Ralf.

"He should have been head archer," said Gilbert contemptuously. Ralf gave Gilbert a menacing scowl, to which Gilbert responded with a nervous smile. "Heh, heh. I was only joking," said Gilbert.

The beasts were approaching. As they came closer to the castle, the men grew restless and more fearful after every passing moment, but Lord Franklin kept his hand in the air with his palm open, signaling halt. "Steady, steady," he said meticulously. When the beasts came within arms distance of the calvary, Lord Franklin froze, and the beasts stopped drawing near. Both Sir Ulric and Sir Cedric Baudry looked at Lord Franklin with a worried expression. Lord Franklin looked pale. His pupils were dilated, there were beads of sweat on his forehead, and he was as stiff as a corpse. What could he have possibly seen that initiated a reaction like that? As both Sir Ulric and Sir Cedric Baudry turned their heads away from Lord Franklin and to the lycanthropes, they too had the same reaction.

"My lord, should we fire?" shouted Ralf from above the roof of the castle.

"Hold your fire!" Lord Franklin shouted from below.

The calvary was taken aback, by what they just saw, they attempted to steady their horses, who were just as spooked. And what scared them you might ask? These beasts had black eyes. "It-it-it's-him... er... I mean them, Kraaag!" stammered a member of the calvary, who went by the name of Sir Thomas. He was visibly frightened. You could see him shaking in his armor, and he was not the only one. Almost everyone was frightened, even Lord Franklin. When the archers caught wind of what was happening, there was mass panic amongst them.

"Wolves!"

"Black eyed wolf beast, the end is nigh!" cried one of the archers by the name of Zane.

"This is the work of Ulid," said a member of the calvary named Sir Merek.

By now you've heard of the Arda myth, how he created the nothingness as a template to create life, well within the void the first thing Arda created was himself. An exact clone. For the most part during the early age (before humans and their like, although it is not clear if humans were the first of the races) they got along cordially. But soon tensions boiled. You see, when Arda investigated the void, he saw his own reflection. He animated that reflection, and that reflection was an exact duplicate of the original Arda.

That Arda was deemed ewn-Arda (*ewn* is old tongue for *copy*). As a result of this, there was confusion between which Arda was the real Arda. Ewn-Arda became upset. He did not want to be considered Ewn-Arda because he thought he was more than some clone. He believed that he was an equal. Arda did not like this thinking at all, he believed he was the original. Arda was a God and Ewn Arda was his creation meant only to serve him. You can imagine how conflict arose. Near the end of the early age, Arda and Ewn-Arda engaged in a battle for the title Arda the one true God. It is believed that the original Arda defeated Ewn Arda and placed him in the deepest most dark part of the void thus granted Ewn-Arda the name Ulid *meaning origins of the deep void*. It is said that Arda chained Ulid to a rock at the very center of the void, in pure isolation and darkness. Ulid's influences however, does not end here, it is believed that he cries from the very bottom of the void and his screams travel to the surface, to the light where humans and their like live. As the screams travelled they become faint whispers and they whisper, *"I am your true God. Obey me."* Whispers they may be, but they are loud enough to whisper into the hearts and minds of unsuspecting victims, convincing them to betray Arda for this false messiah.

You may be wondering how does this happen? Well, when one responds to the whisper, a seed will be planted in their head, which matures into the poison fruit of rebellion, a rebellion against the true God. But there is another theory out there, one that states that Arda is the one in chains. The reason being is that Arda and Ulid are indistinguishable from each other, so in other words there is no way of knowing which Arda was placed in the void. So according to this theory, Arda is Ulid and Ewn Arda is the true God. These theorists are known as second wave Arda worshipers, although Ardinians considered them Ulid worshipers or devil worshipers.

Herein lies the question if God (the Abrahamic God) created us in his image, then did he also create the devil in his image as well? What is the devil, anyway? He has been associated with the ultimate form of evil; he has been called several names just like God, these names include Lucifer, Satan, the devil, Iblis and several more, and all are associated with one thing, an opponent to God. Let's pretend evil is a concrete concept. If the devil is evil at least partially, then God made him that way on purpose. Why would God create evil, anyway? And why is the devil considered evil? For defying God and is defying God evil? Even when God tells you to commit an act you know is malevolent, like murdering your own son just to prove loyalty. That seems something an oppressive tyrant would do, not a supposed just and merciful God. All these questions have ambiguous or no answers, but that is because religion is so convoluted. So, let's simplify things. God is omnificent, and he modeled his creations after himself. This includes the devil, evil, good, the universe, human beings and like beings; this would create the image of God as this constantly dynamic being switching form, mood, and action. Furthermore, if God created everything, then God is everything and is everywhere and so are his creations. Because God is part of everything. Which means there is God in us all, it also means we've got the devil in us as well, which means we are both God and the devil. This is the only way to make sense of the Abrahamic religion's idea of God. But even if we depart from the world of fantasy and mysticism, you will realize that the Bible, the Quran, the Torah, are all written by man. Because of this, our thoughts and influence are written down in the holy books. All our faults and desires, things we covet like an afterlife, and things we fear like damnation in the fire. The idea of God was created to give people hope and protection from uncertainty and the unknown. God gave people a purpose. But instead of God creating us humans in his image, we created him in ours. That's why God is considered a male, at least in Abrahamic religions, as the majority of societies are patriarchal. We made the devil that way as well. Everything we fear is in the devil. The devil is a consequence of bad behavior the Lucifer myth is an example, he defied God, so he was punished severely with hellfire. Like someone who defies some government, consequences are met with either jail, banishment, even death. We are our creations, like an author who writes a novel. Every bit of his or her personality bleeds unto the page. So, in the case of God and the devil we wrote these tales, so the tales reflect ourselves. That means we are both God and the devil, both good and evil, vengeance and mercy, seemingly contradictory ideas coalesced into one idea and that one idea is an individual.

"Everyone, calm down!" Lord Franklin shouted. All the men stopped talking; Lord Franklin turned his gaze toward his men while turning his steed in that direction as well.

"This is clearly the work of Hector. He summoned these creatures with the aid of his magic wielders to frighten us, well I am not frightened. I simply will not let Hector and his cronies intimidate us. This is a sign of weakness on his part. He has gotten desperate, so he uses the dark arts, demons, monsters and lies. Are you not men? Did you not pledge to follow me, your king to the death against whatever perils Hector throws at us?

"Show me your might against the forces of evil, show me your conviction, show me your pride, your perseverance. Let me feel the fire in your souls, let me see the flames of passion in your eyes and let me hear the bravery of your pulsating hearts. Now is not the time for trepidation, now's the time to fight and fight we shall, onward my brothers!" Lord Franklin raised his arming sword to the sky. His buckler was in his left arm securely attached to his forearm.

The men raised their swords as well and all shouted in unison, "Lord Franklin is our king!" several times. In general, the speech seemed to boost morale among the men. I say in general because not everyone was so moved by Lord Franklin's words. Particularly Sir Cedric Baudry and Sir Ulric. They were concerned about Kraag's words, *"I'm here along with the other Horridus to carry out the eradication of all intelligent life forms from this world".* Sir Cedric Baudry thought, *"If Kraag wanted to eradicate all intelligent life forms from this world, he or they certainly have the tools to do it. I've experienced firsthand what Kraag was capable of, and with the possession of wolf beasts, werewolves, lycanthropes or whatever they are called, we would need more than an army of men to stop him or them."*

Sir Ulric thought, *"How did Kraag know so much about us, our names, our relationships, and now he is at our doorsteps with an army of monsters? He knows all our secrets, including mine. He knows about her. If Lord Franklin finds out, this could ruin me."* Sir Ulric, unbeknownst to him, was clenching his jaw.

"Are you alright? Sir Ulric, you looked troubled," said Sir Merek. "Uh I'm fine, just a little headache," said Sir Ulric in a quavering voice. Sir Merek responded with a concern expression on his face, he did not believe Sir Ulric but did not want to pry any longer, so he said, "It is good to have a man of the cloth on our side." He smiled and patted Sir Ulric on the back affectionately.

Although his intentions were good, Sir Merek inadvertently made things worse for Sir Ulric, for his words filled Sir Ulric with guilt. Sir Ulric thought to himself, *"I'm not worthy of that title."*

"Those are venerable words fit for a king. They are sure to lift your men's spirits, but they will not save you," said a divine sounding voice, it was like a polyphony of sounds played by an orchestra from heaven. The sound was so infectious that the men stood there in awe, so soothing was the sound that it could only be described as angelic, and it was female.

"Who said that?!" Lord Franklin shouted.

A lycanthrope stepped up with light brown fur and said telepathically, "It is I, Fragaa (FRA-GA)." Lord Franklin craned forward so that his gaze could meet this creature. He furrowed his brow. He made it clear based on the expression on his face that he was distrustful of the creature. "My apologies allow me to introduce myself I-," said Fragaa.

"No need, let me guess, you are the original beings, the darkness, the void, coming to destroy all intelligent life forms. I've heard it all before and we will not allow it," Lord Franklin interrupted.

"Am I to believe you met Kraag, as he is called?"

"Oh, aren't you the clever one," Lord Franklin said sarcastically. Detecting Lord Franklin's sardonic tone, Fragaa spoke methodically, "We are not your enemy, Lord Franklin. We come in peace."

"Ha, you come in peace, do you think me stupid? You bring a bloody army of possessed lycanthropes to our gates, have a shapeshifter attack our people and you let another one of your beasts inside to slaughter more," said Lord Franklin irately.

"I can see you're upset and I am sorry for that, but we are not responsible for the deaths of your comrades. I have no knowledge of this shapeshifter nor this lone lycanthrope. I assure you all my lycanthropes are under my control," said Fragaa.

"If you are not responsible for their deaths then who is, and how do we know you're telling the truth?" said Lord Franklin solemnly.

"To be frank, you don't and as for who is responsible, I don't have the slightest clue," said Fragaa.

Lord Franklin was still distrustful of the creature, but he didn't know what to make of the situation, so he turned to Sir Cedric Baudry to see what he was thinking. Sir Cedric Baudry, catching Lord Franklin's glance, asked bluntly, "What is your purpose here, Fragaa?"

"To warn you about the coming days," said Fragaa.

"Warn us by possessing lycanthropes?" Lord Franklin said acerbically.

"If this form does not please you, I can use another," said Fragaa.

Then suddenly, she and all the lycanthropes turned into their human form while still possessing those infamous black eyes. They were completely naked. The men stood in awe. Not because of the transformation but because it was so seamless, usually lycanthrope transformation involved more agonizing pain, bones breaking and contorting to align with the skeleton of the beast, skin shredding, organs bursting and reforming, this along with psychological trauma.

Despite the fact that they are lycanthropes, they usually suffer the same pain as werewolves. It is also important to note that werewolves can often become lycanthropes through rigorous training. Also, there are not any visible characteristics to distinguish werewolves from lycanthropes.

"How did you do that? Are you some type of spirit?" said a bowman named Zane. He was so mystified at what he had just seen that he lowered his bow slightly. Others stood in awe at what they had witnessed. A naked voluptuous woman with long straight blond hair stepped forward from the crowd of the undressed. When she was near Lord Franklin, the archers aimed their bows at her and two large heavily armored polearm bearers on horseback, adjacent to Lord Franklin with one positioned at his right and the other to his left, aimed their lances about six inches from her face. She was not fazed by this blatant display of hostility.

Lord Franklin, sensing no danger, raised his hand, signaling his men to stop. When she was about arm's distance from Lord Franklin and his steed, she stared directly into his eyes like she was looking into his soul, staring with those black eyes, those same eyes of Kraag. This vexed Lord Franklin because he believed she knew what he was thinking, and this disturbed him because he was terrified, terrified by the lycanthropes, Kraag and Hector. He had to put on a successful front for his men, but this being saw right through his facade. She averted her gaze and instead redirected it toward Lord Franklin's horse. She seemed fascinated by it. She reached out her arm and began gently rubbing the horse's snout. At the corner of her mouth, a smile began to manifest. In addition, it was evident that she was elated because she began to chuckle almost inaudibly, with her body twitching ever so slightly; it was apparent that her attempt to contain her amusement was failing. The steed seemed not to mind her presence. While still petting the horse, she said, "I am Fragaa and I am something very old, something you cannot fathom; as for my abilities, they are the result of very old magic, possibly the earliest and purest form of magic." The rest of the black-eyed humans stood in place like statues.

Sir Cedric Baudry looked at them uneasily. He thought they would attack at any moment, but for now they stood dormant. Overcoming his fear, he asked, "Why the wolf beast?"

"They are called lycanthropes, and they came to me willingly. They offered their bodies to me in exchange for a painless existence."

"Wait, they agreed to be possessed by you after they made a deal, that would mean you're a dev—," said Sir Ulric, but he was interrupted by Fragaa.

She turned away from the horse and directed her gaze toward Sir Ulric. She scowled at him, and this startled Sir Ulric. She then said, "I am not a devil."

The term *devil*, not to be confused with The Devil (Ulid), is a colloquial term that usually applies to those with infected souls who exchange in the unscrupulous practice of soul exchange for their own benefit. What this means is that someone is tricked into selling his or her soul for anything the soul dealer, as they are accurately called, can provide. It is important to note that a being cannot live long without a soul, so when the soul dealer collects a soul, he replaces that individual's soul with another one; most likely an animal soul. What do the infected need with souls? Well, the infected need the souls to repair their own souls. It's not an exact science but there have been cases in which it works. Other times it leads to catastrophe such as creating a true demon.

The infected often dwell in soul dealing because it hurts to be infected. In other words, the unstable soul is so erratic that it attempts to flee the body, but it cannot do so. Instead, it imbues the body with harmful energy that attacks the body relentlessly, the pain is excruciating, and this is done in an attempt for the soul to escape the body by destroying it. Sometimes the body explodes but others are not so lucky. For the infected, living is agonizingly painful due to soul sickness, and it is for the most part constant and permanent. The infected cannot relieve themselves of life either because if a soul cannot escape the body, then that individual with the soul cannot die. They can only die if they are killed through extreme and unnatural means.

Sir Cedric Baudry wanted to shift the conversation to something of relevance and simply asked, "What of the coming days?"

"Ah yes," she said. She turned to Lord Franklin and said solemnly, "You're going to lose this war."

"And you know this how?" Sir Cedric Baudry asked. "I have the ability of foresight," said Fragaa.

Lord Franklin rolled his eyes. Fragaa, taking notice, said, "You still don't believe after all you have seen? You are an incorrigible man."

"I'm not incorrigible, just cynical. You and your kind seem to come out of nowhere claiming to know the future, claiming to be around for thousands of years, claiming that it's imperative that me and my men should listen. If you and Kraag are so bloody magnificent then where have you been all our lives?" said Lord Franklin.

"You're right," said Fragaa.

Lord Franklin was taken aback by this response, he assumed that she would dance her way around the question using flowery language.

"You're right in assuming that I and Kraag are like kind. We are a race known as the avalenth (*ava-length*). Although Kraag and his minions call themselves Horridus, they foolishly believe that they are greater than God. As for why we have not been around all your lives, it is because we were ordered not to interfere with the lives of mortals," said Fragaa.

"Ordered by whom?" asked Sir Cedric Baudry. "You wouldn't understand," said Fragaa.

"Try me," said Lord Franklin candidly.

Fragaa sighed and said, "Very well, the avalenth are a race of beings, ancient beings tasked with protecting all of existence from forthcoming threats. These threats are cataclysmic in nature and the events that led up to your war with Hector are particularly alarming."

"How so?" asked Sir Cedric Baudry.

"You see, if you don't come to an accord with Hector, a lot of people will die," Fragaa said seriously.

There was a long silence as the three men contemplated their situation, *to come to an accord with Hector or face possible death*. Lord Franklin thought, *"How do we know we can even trust Fragaa's information? Maybe she is some devil conjured up by Hector to distract us, it is pretty convenient that she comes at such an hour telling us this nonsense of armistice."*

Sir Cedric Baudry thought, *"This being seems to display a level of prowess not like anything displayed by Hector at least at the battle of Rilek. In the swamp, from what could be gathered, Hector only had a few sorcerers in his garrison, not nearly enough to conjure an army of a thousand lycanthropes, Hector simply did not have the manpower, so there was no way this Fragaa and her lycanthropes were conjured by Hector and it is unlikely that the two are in cahoots with one another because what would a being so powerful need Hector for? However, that did not mean she was telling the truth, caution should be advised,"*

Sir Ulric thought, *"None of this makes any sense. Why would this being come to us now predicting the future? And what was so important about our conflict with Hector? Didn't she say that she was not to get involved yet she is meddling in our affairs?"*

Finally, Lord Franklin broke the silence. "What happens if we don't come to an accord?"

"It's better if I show you. Dismount from your horse and be seated on the ground," said Fragaa.

Lord Franklin thought about it for a moment and against his better judgment he felt compelled to do as she commanded. There was something beguiling about her tone. He looked at her eyes which were now teal and alluring, her features were stunning. Lord Franklin wondered if this clandestine creature came from the heavens. She smiled with restraint, so she didn't appear too elated but not too restrained that she didn't appear apprehensive or unsure of herself. The result was a happy medium between inviting and regal. This made Lord Franklin feel like she was enticing him to come forth. He felt compelled to come partly because of curiosity and partly because he believed this information was too valuable to slip through his fingers.

As Lord Franklin was about to dismount, Sir Ulric said, "Milord is this wise? We don't even know who this woman really is."

Lord Franklin replied, "We are given an opportunity here that nullifies any risk taken and should trouble arrive, I trust you to get me out of it."

"B-But perhaps this is an unnecessary risk," said Sir Ulric. There was agitation in his voice.

"You can't win a war without taking a few risks. It's clear our enemy has taken some already," said Lord Franklin.

"It could be a trap," said Ulric.

"Only one way to find out, and it's like I said, that's why you're here," said Lord Franklin.

Sir Ulric was worried, he feared Lord Franklin overestimated his abilities, he was quite defenseless against Kraag. He was unsure how he would fare against Fragaa. Lord Franklin whispered into Sir Ulric's ear. Sir Ulric's eyes widened, and his face went pale. He was against Lord Franklin possibly doing something so dangerous, but felt it unwise to challenge his Lord's authority.

Fragaa, noticing Sir Ulric's expression, looked directly at him. "Do not worry. I will not harm your Lord for he did not harm me. The favor shall be returned."

Sir Ulric did not know what to make of that statement but surely, she wasn't talking about the two men on horseback wielding lances. When Fragaa looked at him, the first thing he observed was her eyes were different. Fragaa saw Sir Ulric staring and said, "Ah, you've noticed my eyes. I've change them. Do you like them?"

Sir Ulric said nothing, but this did not deter her from speaking. "I've changed them because your kind are wary of black eyes and equate them with the infected or possession. To us, it's a sign of acquiring otherworldly knowledge."

Sir Ulric was not convinced by her explanation but decided not to pry. Sensing Sir Ulric's suspicion of her, Fragaa sighed and said rather listlessly, "In time, your kind will know I'm not an enemy."

Lord Franklin dismounted from his steed, much to everyone's surprise, and walked toward Fragaa. Fragaa and Lord Franklin sat facing each other. The men stared at the pair, half worried, half intrigued. She placed both her index and middle fingers exactly on Lord Franklin's temples and then calmly said, "Close your eyes and you will see what I see."

He did just that. Suddenly, he was transported to a different place and there was nothing but white surrounding him.

"Where am I?" he asked, rather startled.

"Right now, your body exists simultaneously between two planes of existence, your reality, the present, and an alternate reality, the potential future. This alternate reality can be averted, but it reveals what's to happen should you fail to heed my words," Fragaa said.

Lord Franklin could hear Fragaa's voice but could not see her.

"Where are you?" Lord Franklin asked.

"I'm on the other side watching over your body."

"Watching over my body?" asked Lord Franklin, perplexed by the notion.

"Yes, you see your body is now in a dormant and vulnerable state presently while your mind has traveled to another plane."

"Why have you brought me here? I can see nothing but white."

She chuckled slightly and then said, "Open your eyes in the real world. Only then can you truly see. Focus on any point and your eyes will be able to see everything."

Meanwhile, in the present, the men watched in horror as Lord Franklin's eyes turned black. "She means to turn him into a demon!" shouted Sir Merek. He drew his blade and others followed. The archers behind the parapet readied their bows.

"Kill the demon witch!" shouted one of the Calvary by the name Sir Althalos.

"Yeah, kill her!" cried another by the name of Sir Stuart.

"Kill the demon witch," the men started chanting as they brandished their weapons in the air. Fragaa, who was fully conscious, did not move or even utter a sound, her fingers still planted on Lord Franklin's temples. Sir Ulric placed himself between the men and Fraaga and said, "Please stop. Be reasonable."

"We are being reasonable. This she-devil is possessing Lord Franklin yet here you are standing in between us and that thing. I'm sure when Lord Franklin hears of your treachery, he will have you hanged," said Sir Althalos.

"Treachery? How dare you. I am the advisor to Lord Franklin. I am his most revered friend. He trusts me with his life. You are just an imbecile who occasionally waves a sword around," Sir Ulric said angrily. Sir Althalos laughed mockingly. "An imbecile who waves a sword around am I? Tell me something, oh great Sir Ulric, what kind of knight barely raises a sword? I mean, how long has your blade been safely tucked away in your scabbard? Have you even fought in any battles? Have you ever stared into the eyes of a man and watched as the light escaped them with your sword plunged into his gut?" asked Sir Althalos.

"That's enough!" Sir Merek said sternly. "Sir Ulric is an advisor to Lord Franklin, which means he is second in command. We need to listen to him while Lord Franklin is incapacitated."

Sir Althalos and Sir Ulric were still glaring at each other. "Thank you, Sir Merek," Sir Ulric said through gritted teeth.

Sir Cedric Baudry came in between them. "Commander," said Sir Merek while bowing his head slightly.

"Sir Merek," Sir Cedric Baudry said, acknowledging Sir Merek's greeting. He then turned his eyes to Sir Althalos, who gave him a fuming look.

Sir Cedric Baudry ignored this and said, "Everyone calm down. There will be no killing of Fragaa," said Sir Cedric Baudry.

"You keep referring to her like she is a person. She is a vile demon and a deceiver. Her duplicitous nature may have fooled you two simpletons but not me. I say kill the demon witch!" said Sir Althalos. Several of the men chanted, "Kill the demon witch!"

"Halt! Halt!" Sir Cedric Baudry shouted; the men stopped.

"What do you think you're doing, Sir Althalos? Are you trying to incite a riot?" said Sir Cedric Baudry.

"I'm trying to save our Lord," Sir Althalos retorted.

"Lord Franklin's wellbeing is a concern to all of us but he's not in any immediate danger as yet," said Sir Cedric Baudry.

"Not in any immediate danger. Are you mad? Can't you see his eyes are black? Do you even know what she is?!" said Sir Althalos emphatically. "Look, even if we attack the dormant army, the shape shifting wolves will tear us limb from limb," said Sir Cedric Baudry.

"We can take them along with the witch, but you seem too concerned with your own life than the wellbeing of Lord Franklin. Typical cowardice," said Sir Althalos sneeringly

"That's enough, Sir Althalos, you can't talk to our commander like that!" shouted Sir Merek.

"Or what?" Sir Althalos said contemptuously.

"I'm warning you, if you continue with this insolence, I shall be forced to take action, and you know very well the punishment for disrespecting your commander," said Sir Merek.

"The obedient dog. One moment he is with us on our quest to smite this fiend, the next his tail is between his legs, and he is licking the commander's boots." Sir Althalos laughed sardonically along with some of the other members of the calvary. Some of them even made derisive dog sounds.

"I bet he does more than lick. He'll suck as well," Sir Stuart said while making an obscene jester mimicking fellatio.

"Tell us, what does a middle-aged man, unmarried, do with his free time? Does he pleasure himself all day or does he spend it fucking his squire?!" said Sir Althalos.

Sir Merek was taken aback.

"What was his name? Lief, how old is he? Nineteen, Twenty? That would make him almost a knight, well, not any more. As soon as Lord

Franklin hears of this, he'll strip you and your lover of your titles," said Sir Althalos.

"Sir Merek is no deviant, now I'd watch my tongue if I were you. Such salacious allegations against another knight warrants punishment," said Sir Ulric.

Sir Althalos had a defiant look in his eyes. He looked like he was about to say something but held his tongue. The jeers died down.

"Disobeying your commander, questioning his judgment, antagonizing another knight of the same order, and speaking ill of your commander, all crimes are punishable by death," said Sir Ulric.

The calvary members involved in the jeering had frightened expressions on their faces at the notion of being put to death. Sir Merek was still angered by the indignation he faced under Sir Althalos and Sir Althalos was still infuriated that he had to serve under someone who he deemed as unworthy as Sir Cedric Baudry. One of the calvary members by the name of Sir Favian, spoke up. "It was Sir Althalos. He started the whole thing; he plans to start a mutiny he—"

"Shut up, you fucking spineless oaf!" said Sir Althalos harshly. "Is it true?" asked Sir Cedric Baudry.

"Is what true?" Sir Althalos said irreverently.

"Don't be coy," Sir Cedric Baudry said sternly to which Sir Althalos reluctantly responded, "Yes, it's true."

"Why?" asked Sir Cedric Baudry.

"Does it matter?" Sir Althalos responded. "Yes, yes it does," said Sir Cedric Baudry.

"Because I think you're an ineffective twat undeserved of the title of commander."

"How many?" said Sir Cedric Baudry.

"If you think I'm going to tell you that, then you're more of a cretin than I thought."

"You will answer the commander, you insolent little maggot!" Sir Merek said irately.

"I've had enough of you, boy lover, and I won't answer to you, that bastard or the fat sycophant," said Sir Althalos while looking at Sir Merek, Sir Cedric Baudry, and Sir Ulric respectively.

"So, you choose death?" Sir Cedric Baudry said solemnly.

There was a pause before Sir Althalos spoke. Then he grinned. Looking directly at Sir Cedric Baudry he said, "You can't kill me, my father Lord Cornelius Fowler of Eredith (*e-re-dith*) provides Corithni with half of its supplies, food, weapons and coin. How is it going to look murdering his only living heir?"

"It wouldn't be murder," Sir Cedric Baudry said gravely.

"You'd kill me knowing who my father is, despite his connection to Lord Franklin, for the rules of some bloody order?!" Sir Althalos Fowler scowled as he said this, his face turned red with rage but beneath that rage there was fear, fear of actual execution. He started to think perhaps he overplayed his hand.

"That bloody order is our order. You know, the one you swore to protect and uphold!" Sir Cedric Baudry said angrily. There was a slight pause before anybody said anything. Finally, Sir Cedric Baudry broke the silence.

"Your crime is mutiny. I'll drop the other charges out of mercy, but the charge mutiny remains."

Sir Althalos Fowler had a worried expression on his face although he tried to mask it with an expression of contempt for his superior, but his eyes betrayed him, and Sir Cedric Baudry could see right through Sir Althalos Fowler's façade. As a result, Sir Cedric Baudry decided it was best to show mercy hence, he said, "But you will not be put to death, no, instead you will be stripped of your title and leave effectively by nightfall."

Even though the charges were punishable by death, it was up to the commander to decide a punishment he deemed fit for the offense. In addition, various methods of punishment can be substituted, such as flogging, torture and imprisonment.

"You want me to give up my position!" said Sir Althalos Fowler, almost perplexed. He was thinking, *Why that fucking former lowborn cunt spared his life, if he wanted something in return, he would be sorely mistaken, just because that former lowborn chose not to kill him didn't mean that they were friends."*

"Yes," said Sir Cedric Baudry.

"Why are you sparing my life?" Sir Althalos Fowler asked candidly. "Because in spite of yourself, I think you're a good knight with potential to be greater. Go and serve in your father's garrison. I'm sure you'll do well there," said Cedric Baudry genuinely.

Sir Althalos Fowler chuckled derisively. He couldn't contain his laughter. As he laughed and spoke simultaneously, he said, "You truly are a weak commander. Everyone knows you're only doing this because of my father. You think this will change anything? I still think you're undeserving of the title of commander."

"Shut up you supercilious cunt, you're lucky to be alive. You should be grateful to the commander," said Sir Merek.

Sir Althalos Fowler did something peculiar and uncharacteristic of him. He hung his head low in what appeared to be shame and said very sincerely, "You're right, my behavior toward the commander, Sir Ulric and to you, Sir Merek has been inexcusable, irreverent, and mean spirited and I like to thank the commander for showing me mercy even though I don't deserve it."

Sir Cedric Baudry was taken aback by Sir Althalos' sudden change in demeanor and simply said, "Well, I'm glad you came to your senses." "I guess this means I no longer serve under you nor adhere to your rules," said Sir Althalos Fowler.

"The rules of the order and what are you insinuating?" Sir Cedric Baudry said sternly.

"Nothing commander. Uh may I speak to Sir Merek? I'd like to apologize for my behavior," said Sir Althalos Fowler.

"You may," said Sir Cedric Baudry, still put off by Sir Althalos Fowler's sudden shift in character. Sir Merek gave Sir Althalos Fowler a suspicious look. *What was he playing at? What was this sudden change in character that somehow allowed him to act diametrically opposite to his usual revolting, malicious and condescending self?*

As Sir Althalos Fowler drew closer. Sir Merek could see a sinister smile begin to manifest on his face unbeknownst to Sir Ulric and Sir Cedric Baudry. And that's when it happened, when Sir Althalos Fowler was in arm's distance from Sir Merek, the scoundrel spit on Sir Merek whose visor was open at the time. Sir Althalos did this with the intention of provoking Sir Merek. The projectile of saliva hit Sir Merek in his right eye. Sir Merek was livid. Before anyone could act, Sir Merek drew his long sword. He delivered a horizontal strike at Sir Althalos Fowler. Sir Althalos Fowler parried the attack by holding his long sword vertically but was sent flying off his horse with his sword flung from his hand due to the fall.

Sir Merek dismounted from his steed and charged at Sir Althalos Fowler with his sword in hand. Sir Althalos Fowler was sprawled out on the floor. The men wrestled a bit with Sir Althalos Fowler, attempting to wrench the blade free from Sir Merek's grasp but to no avail. Sir Merek, the much larger man, gained the upper hand. Sir Althalos was placed on his back with Sir Merek on top of him and the tip of his blade pressed against Sir Althalos Fowler's throat.

"Stop this immediately!" said Sir Cedric Baudry. But Sir Merek did not move. He glared intensely at Sir Althalos Fowler. Sweat dripped down his brow, his hands were shaking as he contemplated killing Sir Althalos Fowler. Sir Cedric Baudry and Sir Ulric were screaming for him to stop, but Sir Merek heard none of their cries. It was like he was in some type of trance, a rage in which he could not escape. Sir Althalos Fowler started laughing and this caused Sir Merek to loosen his scowl and replaced it with an expression of slight confusion. *Why was Sir Althalos Fowler laughing? Had he finally gone mad or was it just to vex him, but what would be the point of vexing a man who had his life in your hands? Then a revelation came to his head. He realized he had lost; he gave in to rage, like a mere animal. Once Lord Cornelius Fowler gets wind of this, he will be hung for sure.*

Sir Althalos Fowler kept laughing and this only made Sir Merek more enraged. *He had already lost, his fate was sealed, but there was still one thing he could do, kill the cunt with his bare hands. If he was going to the afterlife, he was going to take Sir Althalos Fowler with him and make him suffer.*

Sir Althalos craned his neck and looked up at Sir Merek and with a big toothy grin he said, "What, do you want to kiss me?" in a derisive tone, that was the breaking point. Sir Merek threw aside his sword with a loud yell and cast aside his gauntlets. He then proceeded to beat Sir Althalos Fowler in a mad frenzy until there was blood on his knuckles. Three knights had to pull him off.

"Let me go. I'll kill him, I'll kill him, gah!" said Sir Merek.

"If you kill him, you'll be put to death," said one of the knights. "I don't care!" screamed Sir Merek.

"You still have time to plead mercy from Lord Fowler," said one of the knights.

Meanwhile, Sir Althalos Fowler was dragged away by one knight. He suffered some bruises on his face, his upper lip was swollen, his left eye was temporarily sealed shut from the swelling and he had a gash on his cheek with blood dripping from his mouth. He managed to say, "You're a dead man. I'll see you at the gallows ha ha ha!"

"Shut up," said the knight that dragged him away.

CHAPTER 3

ANOTHER EXISTENCE?

Lord Franklin felt uneasy, like a disembodied spirit or an astral projection floating aimlessly against his will, shifting in and out of time and space. When he finally opened his eyes, he could see Corithni castle, to his horror it was on fire. A great conflagration, embers of fire lit up the sky, tendrils of smoke formed a noxious gas cloud. He could hear the blood-curdling screams of his brethren. He turned around to see Hector leading the charge. He was a massive man, standing at 6-foot-5 with broad shoulders, long brown hair and a stern, clean-shaven face. He wore plated armor with chainmail underneath. The plate armor was red and the chain-mail black. On his chest plate was an insignia of House Everard. The crest was a black, three-pronged trident or pitchfork depending on who you ask. The trident or pitchfork was engulfed in flame. The trident or pitchfork represented the people, common folk. It is thought that a trident or pitchfork were tools of common folk, for fishing and collecting hay, respectively. The fire represented the soul.

Together, the symbols represented the soul of the people. (It is believed by some people in Mirthadine that the soul takes the shape of fire.)

What surprised Lord Franklin was the crown on Hector's head. It was made of some type of metal. It was not ornate nor ostentatious. In fact, it was simple, almost rough in design. It was riddled with scraps and cuts. The crown had sixteen spikes with a vacant space on the top. The spikes were poorly designed, they were varied sizes, and some were bent. Another feature of the crown was a rose-colored jewel in the center.

Hector was on his steed, an armored black horse, when he yelled "charge". Hector's army was massive. It was about 5000 men compared to Lord Franklin's 1000. *"How in all of creation did Hector manage to raise an army that large? His numbers weren't this large at the battle of*

Rilek,"thought Lord Franklin. The army looked like a rag-tag group. Many of the men did not have plated armor, some wore just chainmail, some wore only gambesons, a few wore leather armor, particularly buff coats, while others had nothing at all but tunics. However, there were a select few soldiers fully armored and positioned in front of the less armored troops to either make his army look more intimidating or make sure the fully armored troops breached the wall first.

The men were armed with polearms such as lances, poleaxes, halberds and glaives. In addition, there were only 50 men on horseback including Hector, compared to Lord Franklin's 200. Nonetheless, this was a formidable force and more than a match for Lord Franklin's forces.

As Hector and his army charged toward the burning castle, they were hit with a flurry of arrows from the opposition and about 70 of his men perished. Still, this did not deter Hector. "Storm the castle!" he bellowed. The men followed him. As they advanced forward, they were hit by another barrage of arrows, this time killing 100 men. The east section stone curtain was severely burnt, as was the watch tower, chapel, and the adjacent second knights garrison (not the one in the keep). Water elementals did their best to quell the flames, their efforts were somewhat successful. They managed to stop the flames on the wall. However, the chapel and knights garrison could not be saved, and the watch tower's structural integrity was compromised. Furthermore, sections of the wall were now in an enfeebled state. There were several fissures along the wall and there was one crevice large enough that it permitted enough space for a single person to go through. Most of the knights within the garrison were unharmed because they were stationed outside prior to the siege.

After sacrificing several men, mostly mercenaries, Hector's army was able to scale the hill that Corithni stood on and wheel a siege engine, a battering ram, within proximity to the eastern stone curtain. The ram itself was made from a broad 150ft tree trunk that was placed in a wagon suspended by ropes. The wagon had a triangular roof that was made of wood and sinewy animal hides to protect the ones operating it from arrows and fire.

The infantry and archers did their best to keep the invaders at bay, but with the compromised wall and sheer multitude of attackers armed with a battering ram it meant the eastern wall was going to collapse if something was not done.

Corithni archers were able to pick off some would be assailants. They fired from the ramparts with their powerful longbows, with average draw weights of 120lbs. The arrows from these self-bows were able to pierce mail armor. Several of Hector's men were felled, but this did not deter his forces. The truth was, Corithni was overwhelmed. Not only did they have to deal with the aggressor on the east, but there were also attacks from the north. The enemy also had two colossal siege engines; two trebuchets named Blood Bringer and the Defiler, with counterweights of 13,228lbs each, they were filled with a combination of stone dirt and sand. The trebuchets had several 250lbs round stone balls that could be hurled from a distance of 600 feet at a max height of 315 feet at an angle of 38 degrees. The trebuchets themselves without the sling stood a whopping 300ft tall. Despite such formidable catapults, the projectiles could never seem to sail over the walls of Corithni. Instead, the heavy rocks would hit the hill Corithni resided on which stood 200 ft tall, or the lower portions of the walls that guarded the castle. But the point was not to have these boulders hit the towers but rather destroy the walls, particularly the ones making up the barbican because the trebuchets were positioned in the front of the castle at a distance of 600 feet. [When it comes to these types of calculations, you have to remember Mirthadine has five times the gravity of Earth, but for simplicity purposes we shall be using earth's gravity. Remember this for future calculations.]

The constant barrage of missiles was also used to decrease morale amongst Corithni soldiers. Hector's men also did this by hurling the corpses of Corithni soldiers at the castle as a sort of scare tactic. It was also Hector's attempt at disease warfare. There was a fire that started in the lower bailey. It rose to be 15-feet high, forming fronds of smoke and fire spiraling in the air. It was such an unusual happening, especially since Hector did not fire any incendiary missiles and even if he had, they could not possibly fly over the castle battlements. A team of about 15 water elementals attempted to subdue the inferno, but their efforts proved minimal. The team had been spread sparsely due to putting out other fires in the castle. In addition, many of them were exhausted and were running out of halo-soul manifest (See prologue for definition). The squad's numbers dwindled because of conditions of the siege. They mostly died from starvation, dysentery, and poison due to consuming contaminated water.

It is generally believed by the people of Corithni that the water was polluted four weeks ago by Hector's men. After all, they did place corpses of the fallen into Isial lake. However, contrary to popular belief, it is rare that dead bodies breed diseases, and the polluted water was likely due to an unknown pathogen, most likely fecal matter. The infection took a mere five days to take effect, taking 20 water elementals in the process. The siege affected all that dwelled in Corithni, despite it only being three weeks, over 80 civilians perished. Most of the noncombatants and injured (from the current siege or the previous battle in Mydra woodlands) were in the keep. The defenders had done their best to fight off the invaders. They mainly relied on archers but also resorted to tactics such as hurling debris over the battlements like stones, boiling water, hot sand, or quicklime. Corithni forces also successfully set a siege engine on fire, thus thwarting an attempt to impregnate the castle's northwestern gate house. As a result, the enemy had to refocus their efforts on the barbican in the north and eastern wall.

In addition, the defenders also foiled an espionage tactic from their adversaries. There was a traitor amongst Corithni ranks. A soldier by the name of Bancroft attempted to let the besiegers in through the postern gate at the dead of night. Bancroft was caught and swiftly beheaded. However, despite the efforts of the defenders by the third week, the besiegers had already gained significant ground. They were able to scale the hill and still had three siege engines left. It was no secret that Corithni was well fortified, but with the sheer masses Hector had amounted, and no relief force in sight, things were looking dire for the defenders. All the horses had been evacuated sometime during the siege, making the Corithni calvary ineffective. Catapults and battering rams were not the only destructive weapons of war at Hector's disposal.

"What could have caused the blaze in the lower bailey? There is no way *Hector's army alone, as formidable as they may be, could have caused such a fire on their own. It must have been something from the sky*," Lord Franklin thought. Lord Franklin looked up into the sky and what he saw shocked him. A dragon was looming in the distant sky. It was an enormous beast, navy blue in color with a massive wingspan. Its eyes were completely black. The poor beast was being controlled by Hector, but that was impossible, at least not with magic. The dragon flew erratically in the sky as if it were resisting Hector's control. The beast let out a loud, shrill screech before spewing auburn flames into the sky. The dragon continued spewing flames inside the castle while Hector's troops proceeded to advance on the north and east sides of the castle. With this three-pronged assault, Hector's army was gaining traction despite initial difficulties in scaling the castle. It was a battle of three fronts. Archers on the ground relentlessly pelted the dragon with arrows but alas, it was futile as none of the arrows where able to pierce its scaly hide. The remaining infantry focused on putting out whatever fires they could. Two men operating a ballista fired several bolts at the dragon, but the dragon evaded the bolts effortlessly. It retaliated by burning the ballista to ash and dust. The two men barely evaded the devastating attack while others were not so fortunate. The dragon burned several archers to a crisp. There were cries of anguish and many men tried to flee but there was ultimately nowhere to run, thus they were consumed by the flame. Over the melee, Lord Franklin could hear someone cry, "Hold your fire, save your arrows for Hector and his horde. This beast is a master of the skies. Nothing you throw at it will subdue it!" The voice came from a knight. The knight removed his helmet. It was heavily damaged from dragon fire, hence he removed it to prevent the sparks from singeing his face. The knight went by the name of Sir Peter Branson.

Branson was a man of 30 with short blonde hair. He was clean shaven with blue eyes. He stood about five-feet-eleven, with an athletic build. He had a stern countenance about him and was a serious man who dedicated years of his life to the discipline of swordsmanship. You see, Branson was considered by many to be one of the greatest swordsmen in Corithni, possibly in all of Arcadiem. Amongst the swordsmen that cannot use elementals, magic or any other abilities besides basic soul manipulation, that is.

"What do you suggest, sir?" said one of the archers. "Where are the elementals?" asked Sir Peter.

"Some are at the battlements with Sir Ulric, Commander Oak, and Lord Franklin fending off Hector's army. Others are attempting to extinguish the fire in the lower bailey and other parts of the castle," said the bowman.

"Curses," Sir Peter muttered.

"Are you alright sir?" said the same bowman.

"I'm fine, but I fear the castle will not hold such an assault for much longer," answered Sir Peter dejectedly.

"Aye, we're goners for sure. Those cowards at the battlements left us here to die. They should be defending the castle against the dragon that already breached our walls. Instead they focus on Hector's men," said one of the men who operated the now destroyed Ballista.

"If all the men left their post, Hector's army would overrun the castle. Lord Franklin has to be careful about how he delegates his forces," said an infantryman.

"But how does he expect 30 something archers, 6 crossbowmen, and a paltry 20 infantry men to fight a dragon? The flying fucker's terrorizing the castle and the only weapon we had against it was destroyed," said the same man who operated the ballista. He sighed and said, "I'm afraid we are reaching our end." Many were in acquiescence with this sentiment but refused to admit it. The silence that followed, though ephemeral, felt eternal.

To the warrior, death is always a possibility, and one could say they are somewhat prepared for it. However, when the penultimate hour approaches, no amount of conditioning can prepare one for death and its impending certainty. The same logic can be applied for misery, when something terrible is suspected to happen that is inevitable, we often, partly as a defense mechanism partly as a coping strategy, suppress happiness and release sadness as an attempt to lessen the emotional blow of the foreboding news or circumstance. In our naivety, and in the guise of acceptance, we forsake ourselves. Individuals who do this claim they are realist and that they are simply accepting the reality of the situation. This is not acceptance, this is pessimism. Pessimism is a disease that deceives the mind by obfuscating the difference between what is certain and what is possible, thus the individual is led to believe that a negative outcome to a situation is the only outcome. Furthermore, they believe the only way to mitigate the consequences of such an outcome is to become negative. This, however, is quite counterproductive because being pessimistic increases the very odds of an undesirable outcome. That begs the question, if the individual comes to the realization that pessimism is virulent to their well-being, would they rebuke its principles? The answer is no, a diametrically opposing answer to what would be expected. The reason is humans are part of the kingdom animalia. In layman terms, we are animals, hence, we covet routine as opposed to change, even if said routine is harmful. The only way to escape the shackles of pessimism is to realize that everything is fleeting, emotions, physical states, and situations. In other words, we must be dynamic in a very dynamic world because if we are not, we will surely not survive.

Then the silence was broken, and the transitory feeling of misery seemed to evanesce when a young archer said, "Even if we die, we've already won."

The men all looked at him with a mixture of awe and confusion. Despite being uncomfortable with the new-founded attention, he continued speaking. "Lord Franklin entrusted us to defend the castle against a fire-breathing dragon. If we perish, people will say it was a noble sacrifice of men who refused to give in against all odds, but if we succeed, we'll be legends. We mustn't give up hope. Besides Sir Peter here has a plan, right?" The young bowman placed an emphasis on the word right as he turned to Sir Peter. His visage and words had an auspicious quality to them. This seemed to lift Sir Peter's spirits along with the other men. "Martin's right, first we'll deal with the menace in the sky then we assist Lord Franklin," said Sir Peter as his eyes fixated on the colossal dragon in the sky whose tumultuous temperament seemed to calm. It no longer sent balls of fire raining down, instead it was high in the sky encircling the clouds, methodically, as though it was planning its next assault. The dragon's demeanor disturbed Sir Peter, who thought that it was imperative that he devise a plan as urgently as possible, given the situation.

"How the hell do we deal with the dragon?" said one of the archers emphatically.

"We use the elementals. Ask one of them to create several lightning bolts to strike the beast from above so the attack will be unsuspecting, it will be stunned. Then as it descends, fire crossbow bolts at its wings, so it can't fly away," said Sir Peter.

"Alright, but how do you propose we deal with the fire breathing lizard once it's on the ground? I'm sure it's not gonna be happy now that you're thinking of blasting it with lightning bolts, not to mention how are we going to avoid being roasted alive?" said that same archer.

Sir Peter could hear the frustration in his voice. He had a point. The plan was flawed but Sir Peter was desperate. Something had to be done about this dragon.

"You mustn't be so harsh Bate, Sir Peter is only trying to help!" snapped Martin.

"It's of no consequence, Martin, he was simply being practical. We all want to survive this siege, tensions are high." Sir Peter looked around, a large pavise caught his eye, it had engravings on it, withered from scorched marks, but still visible. The shield had an insignia in the center of it. The symbol on the battle-hardened shield was that of a single red flame against a black background with ornately decorated blue borders. This meant that the shield was somehow flame-resistant.

"Tomlin, Ives!" said Sir Peter, referring to the two men who operated the ballista.

"Yes?" Tomlin and Ives said in unison.

"Is that shield still serviceable?" asked Sir Peter, referring to the pavise behind him.

"Uh yes, but that shield is only meant for one person," responded Tomlin.

"Never mind that! Do you think it can withstand the impact of dragon fire?" asked Sir Peter.

"It's hard to say. The pavise is made with reinforced leather and white stone from Isial lake, both materials should quell dragon fire for a little while but given the condition of the shield and the intensity of the flames, I'd say it will barely hold up," said Ives.

"Barely is good enough," said Sir Peter.

"But these materials have their limits. Over exposure to flames will render the shield useless. It will burn up just like the watchtower," said Tomlin.

"Then we will make this quick," said Sir Peter.

He clasped his hands together and turned to the group of archers and crossbowmen and asked, "Alright, do any of you think you can pierce the dragon from here?"

"Our arrows just aren't strong enough to impale its flesh, the draw weights on both the crossbows and long bows are too small. The only thing with enough power to kill the dragon was the ballista," said Tomlin.

"Not to worry. Look what I've got," said Ives with a toothy grin on his face. In his hands was a windlass crossbow with a draw weight of 1250lbs and one bolt.

Bewildered, Tomlin asked, "Where did you get that from?"

"Nicked it from under the ballista just before the dragon burned it to bits."

Tomlin chuckled and said, "Charlie Ives, you're one lucky fucker." Ives smiled and said, "I'm glad you're in such good spirits, my friend, because you're going to be the one to aim it."

Tomlin's expression quickly turned into distress. "Wha-wha, me-me, wait no, no," he stammered.

"No need to be modest. Tomlin here can shoot a squirrel in the eye with a cross bolt from twenty meters! He once shot the wings off a dragonfly," said Martin with a jolt of elation in his voice. He was about to continue his encomium about his comrade's dexterity with the crossbow when Tomlin stopped him abruptly.

"Will you shut up, boy?! Do you want to get me killed? I'm not about to be paraded in front of a dragon, like a puppet, with my only protection a shabby shield!"

"If you don't, we'll all be killed," said Ives gravely. The austere nature of Ives's words seemed to quash Tomlin's querulousness.

Sir Peter put a reassuring hand on Tomlin's shoulder and said, "I shall tell Lord Franklin tales of your bravery and heroism if you do this. Can you do this? Will you do this for me, friend?"

"Oh, for God's sake, don't beg! If I am to go along with your foolhardy plan, I want Lord Franklin to know that I want a promotion, a castle with a moat, lots of horses and a nice pretty maiden to keep me company till the end of my days," said Tomlin.

A smile began to spring from Sir Peter's face, and he slapped Tomlin's shoulder playfully and said, "And you shall have it, my friend. I am sure Lord Franklin will be overjoyed once he hears the tales of Tomlin the dragon slayer," said Sir Peter with emphasis on the word's dragon slayer. "Tomlin the dragon slayer… that has a nice ring to it. Now tell me this plan of yours and please tell me it does not involve me getting killed," said Tomlin.

"Well, if all goes well, you will be protected by the shield. You can use it to ward off dragon fire. Once that happens, you can shoot the beast in the eye. If that does not work or you miss, the rest of us will rush in and slay it while you draw its fire," said Sir Peter.

"That sounds like a grand plan in all, but we need something to draw the beast's attention. Our arrows can't seem to do the trick. The dragon either evades them or flies too high in the sky for them to reach it," said Martin.

"A shot to the face should do it," said Ives.

"But we still need an elemental to blast it, and in case you haven't noticed they are all at the battlements," said Bate, the only one who seemed to express demur with the plan.

"Not all of them," said a voice.

Sir peter turned around to see a boy about thirteen years of age with curly brown hair and sapphire blue eyes. The boy wore a brown tunic with a mysterious, ornately crafted dagger attached to a silver chain around his neck. He also had a long sword securely attached to his waist by a sword belt within a black scabbard.

"Godfrey! What are you doing here? You should be at the keep. Where is Elysant (wife of Sir Peter)?" said Sir Peter.

"She's tending to the wounded, so I thought I should help fight. You know, do something useful," said Godfrey.

"Godfrey, go back to the keep," said Sir Peter sternly.

"But I can help. You need an elemental, and Lady Branson's been teaching me how to create lightning bolts from the sky and—"

"Enough, Godfrey! Go to Lady Branson and do not leave her side," Sir Peter interrupted.

Godfrey scowled at Sir Peter, "I can fight, and I can manipulate fire and lightning and—"

"Godfrey, I don't have time for this. Listen to me and do as you're told!" said Sir Peter harshly.

Godfrey glared at Sir Peter defiantly and said, "I should be out there fighting alongside you, not confined in the walls of the castle like a bloody coward!"

Sir Peter sighed and he placed both hands on Godfrey's shoulders affectionately and said as gently as he could, "Godfrey, you are very dear to me. You are like the son I can never have (Lady Branson cannot bear children, but Sir Peter refused to remarry because he loved her too much). Elysant and I love you dearly. If anything were to happen to you, I couldn't forgive myself. I know you want to help, but it's too dangerous. Please go back to the keep."

Sir Peter's words seemed to calm Godfrey down as he was about to head back to the keep.

Ives shouted, "Wait! Sir Peter, perhaps you should reconsider given our current quandary."

"What are you saying?" asked Sir Peter.

"Look I know the lad is very special to you but he may be our only chance and besides, I distinctly remember you and your younger brother Heggr, fighting alongside your father Brandr, when you were his age during the fifth Mylec marauder war (1518-1533 NEEOT)."

The word Mylec refers to the Northern territories of Arcadiem. The people who reside there are often called northerners, northern barbarians, northern raiders, or marauders by their southern neighbors in the country of Iiadec (the country that Corithni resides in. The province that Corithni exists in is known as Mydra. Iiadec is home to several provinces and at the center is the aforementioned Mydra. To the east is Rilek, further east is Agor, to the northwest is Eredith, and west of that is Etlio. There are also territories that belong to the dwarfs, elves, rhodeac and sison separately) mainly because they don't practice the Ardinian religion and because they have a history of raiding and pillaging Iiadec for its resources that dates back centuries. Of course, not everyone in this region is a raider.

The Mylecans have a rich culture with many advancements. They unfortunately have limited natural resources. This does not stop southerners from calling them barbarians. During the fifth Mylec war, there was a dispute between two Mylecan leaders, Guthroth the bold and Hakon Serksson. The quarrel was about the continued use of raiding of the southern territories which Hakon wanted to outlaw. This eventually led to war, and Hakon enlisted help from the southern armies of Iiadec. Guthroth was defeated and the treaty of Hakon was signed in the year 1536 (NEEOT). The treaty basically stated that the Mylecan territories would no longer raid the provinces of Iiadec. Some of the Mylecans that serve under Hakon settled in Iiadec and assimilated, even going as far as converting to Ardiniaism or becoming knights.

"That was a different time," Sir Peter protested.

"Was it?" asked Ives incredulously. "Look, all I'm saying is you trained him, and he is the only one who can help us right now." Godfrey looked at Sir Peter with eager eyes.

"Alright," Sir Peter groaned, "but you have to do as I say, is that clear?" Sir Peter warned Godfrey.

"Clear, so what's the plan?" Godfrey said struggling to contain his excitement.

The men relayed the details of the plan to Godfrey. "So, can you do it boy?" asked Bate.

"Of course I can," responded Godfrey. "We're saved!" said Martin rather ecstatically.

"Let's not get ahead of ourselves. We have not done the deed yet. Are you ready Godfrey?" said Sir Peter.

"Ready," said Godfrey unwaveringly. Godfrey raised his right arm, which was emitting sparks of electricity, and summoned a great thunderbolt from the sky that struck the dragon with such ferocity that it sent it careening downwards. The dragon struggled to regain its coordination as it was struck with five more successive thunderbolts, each bolt about five seconds apart. The strident noise of the thunder and raucous screams from the dragon was cause for alarm and individuals observing from the keep watched nervously as the beast struggled to evade the oncoming blast. Beads of sweat began to trickle down Godfrey's forehead and he began to breathe heavily. Sir Peter gave him a concerned look. The men watched the sky, anxiously waiting for the barrage of thunderbolts to subdue the beast.

"Careful not to produce too many of those things. You'll burn yourself out, and make sure you don't miss, you'll cause more fire," said Bate. "You're not helping!" Tomlin said angrily.

"Sorry," said Bate.

"Perhaps we should strike it with our arrows to help ease the stress from the young lad," said Ives.

"No, that would only be a waste. Our arrows won't reach that far in the sky. We must trust that Godfrey can subdue the beast," said Sir Peter. "Almost got it," Godfrey said through gritted teeth. Another thunderbolt struck the dragon in the back. This knocked the dragon unconscious and it swerved, spiraling upside down with its belly facing the sky. It was descending quickly. "Everyone move!" Sir Peter shouted.

The group did as they were told. The dragon crash landed on the wall separating the main bailey from the lower bailey. The impact completely shattered that section of the wall. Debris flew everywhere. Godfrey let out a sigh of relief. He bent forward with fatigue and placed his hands firmly on his thighs. The electricity that had surrounded his hands began to wane.

"You did good, lad," said Ives. The dragon lay motionless on the ground, curled up on its side amongst a massive pile of rubble.

"Egad, I think he killed it!" said Martin. "Shh," said Sir Peter.

The group drew nearer to the beast cautiously. Sir Peter unsheathed his blade. It was a longsword of the Mylecan variety, with a brass hilt and a lobed pommel. The archers readied their bows. Sir Peter motioned Godfrey to get behind him. Tomlin carried the pavise with him as he crept along with the others towards the beast.

"I guess there is no need to shoot its wings or eye for that matter. The beast is slain," said Ives.

"We can't be so sure. If it's alive, we can't let it escape because if it does, it will burn down all of Corithni. We must end this now and here," said Sir Peter as he channeled soul manifest into his blade. The blade glowed with a whitish hue and a sword shaped aura encased the weapon except for the hilt. The aura extended the blade's length to at least five inches. As they moved closer, the dragon began to move ever so slightly.

"It's alive!" said Martin with a forceful whisper.

The dragon opened its eyes, which were no longer black but a typical reptilian yellow, with a narrow slit for its pupil. Thus, indicating whatever hex was placed on it was broken.

Everyone stopped in their tracks. The dragon raised its head languidly, as though waking from a long slumber. As the dragon opened its mouth, to presumably yawn, Tomlin, who stood behind the pavise, misconstrued this innocuous display as a sign of aggression, hence he fired a crossbow bolt at the dragon's eye. The dragon acting quickly blocked the bolt with its massive bat-like wings. The thick bolt was able to pierce the dragon's wing and nearly gouged its right eye.

"Ow! Why you, infernal human, you nearly took out my eye! I shall roast all of you for disturbing my slumber!" The dragon's voice was harsh and gruff as you'd expect from a giant fire breathing lizard but surprisingly humanlike. Everyone was taken aback by the fact that the dragon was speaking the tongue of man. (There are some beasts in Mirthadine that are intelligent and capable of comprehending and speaking languages that do not have a humanoid form, but they are rare. They are known as Orthrya Vepid—old tongue for big, brained animal).

"It speaks, and we can understand it!" Martin uttered.

"It!" bellowed the dragon. "How dare you, insolent maggot. Can't you tell I'm male? Just look at my glorious spikes, my hardened midsection, and massive wings. I am a specimen of masculinity, you damn fool!" (The dragon was referring to the spikes that were all over his body except his stomach, female dragons have smaller and less sharp spikes, the aggregate of scaly skin and muscle is protecting its thorax.)

"All impressive features, but I still don't see a——" said Martin. "Will you shut up you ninny!" interrupted Tomlin angrily.

"Dragon. We mean you no harm. Just tell us how you came to this position," said Sir Peter.

"Oh, how judicious of you. First you attack me, and now you tell me you mean no harm with weapons in your hands. You must be the leader of this deplorable group. I suspect you and your group of insects share half a brain since you have the audacity to attack a fully grown dragon," the dragon said sarcastically.

Sensing the dragon's acerbic tone and not wanting to further anger the beast, Sir Peter spoke slowly and calmly. "Dragon, you were not well. We believe you were in some type of trance."

"Dragon! I have a name you know, its Mavid (*mah-vid*) son of Aglar the great and King of the Beladaric (*bell-la-darick*) dragons (Beladar is a region in the Mylecan territories where alleged talking dragons live in caves.) Mavid's eyes were now drawn to Sir Peter's glowing blade. The blade caused him to scowl. "And I will not be treated with such disrespect, Agnarr son of Brandr." The dragon's voice raised in volume and his temperament was that of anger. He stood straighter on his front legs, puffing out his chest, and began growling and gnashing his teeth. Tendrils of smoke began to appear in King Mavid's nostrils.

Several of the men slowly retreated, but Sir Peter, whose eyes widened at the mention of his name, stood his ground and said, "I go by Peter now."

"Of course, you converted after you met that woman. Even cut your hair and beard, but you're still a Mylecan, and a raider," said the dragon, lingering on the word raider.

Sir Peter scowled slightly at the word raider but deflected by asking, "How do you know my father?"

"I'd recognized the foul blade anywhere. Reforged, it maybe, I still recognize its power. It was used by your treacherous father to murder my grandfather, Gyabolt. He even had the nerve to call the blade dragon cutter. The villain said that Gyabolt's hide would serve as great armor for his sons, who were off fighting some war. But I can see by your countenance that you were not aware of this. Very well, Peter, son of Brandr, how will you atone for your father's treachery?" said Mavid. As Mavid reared his head back, about to speak again, Bate fired an arrow at the dragon and shouted, "Die you foul beast!" The arrow whizzed past Mavid, narrowly missing his head.

"So, this is how you treat a king. This is the second attempt on my life, and I assure you there won't be a third. You shall pay with your lives for such insolence!"

The dragon fired flames at the group. Everyone dispersed except for Tomlin, who hid behind the pavise. The shield was able to withstand the barrage of fire. As Tomlin reached for another bolt, he realized he was out. Before he could react, Mavid whirled his massive tail around, knocking the pavise into the air. Tomlin struggled to maintain his balance as he was sent hurtling backwards. Mavid flew two feet into the air, still injured from the wound Tomlin had given him previously. He struggled to maintain flight, for the bolt was still lodged in his wing. Mavid relied mostly on his uninjured wing to stay suspended in the air. He shot a fiery blast at the unsuspecting Tomlin. Tomlin, now on his back, closed his eyes and used his arms in a futile attempt to shield himself from Mavid's flames. Tomlin screamed, but to his surprise, he was completely unscathed. When Tomlin opened his eyes, he saw, to his astonishment, Godfrey standing in front of him with his arms outstretched diverting the flames away from Tomlin. Godfrey could somehow part the flames, so they would not harm himself or Tomlin.

"Godfrey!" shouted Sir Peter.

"I'm all right, and so is Tomlin," said Godfrey.

"Impressive feat for such a young boy," said Mavid, as the flames extinguished.

"I see you're an elemental. You could dispatch dragon fire with such haste, few can do that."

"DRAGON!" shouted Sir Peter. Enraged, he charged at Mavid with his glowing sword, holding the blade in both hands. He delivered a cut that was angled upwards in the air. The cut formed a projection from his soul manifest creating an energy strike with the whitest hue. It cut through the air with such ferocity, being an extension of his sword swing, it sliced through the air the same way. Mavid just narrowly dodged the attack that was aimed at his midsection. Sir Peter delivered three more attacks. The first attack was an upward diagonal cut from the right, the next was an upward diagonal cut from the left. The two strikes formed an x pattern in the air. The strikes grazed Mavid on his right thigh. This caused the dragon to buckle slightly. Taking advantage of the opening, Sir Peter delivered his final blow. A horizontal cut from the left that struck Mavid square in the chest leaving a nasty cut that oozed blood. Bleeding profusely, Mavid was launched into the air and fell flat on his back. As Sir Peter advanced forward, the archers fired their arrows. Mavid responded by burning them up as they flew through the air. Next, he shot a fiery blast directly at Sir Peter. Sir Peter reacted quickly and ducked behind the pavise.

Over the tumult, Godfrey shouted, "Enough!"

Everyone ceased fighting. Even Mavid stopped spewing fire at Sir Peter. "Don't you see? King Mavid is not our enemy. Hector was controlling him against his will."

"Excuse me, but who is Hector? And no amount of magic can control a dragon. We're invulnerable to spells and hexes and what not," said Mavid.

"So, you admit to attacking Corithni on purpose, you wretched beast!" said Bate furiously.

"Shut up! Bate, this is all your fault. If you hadn't been overzealous, none of this would have happened. We were making headway with the dragon," said Ives crossly.

"Overzealous! This bloody monster nearly burnt down the castle and threatened Sir Peter. Besides, it admits it can't be controlled, so the monster acted on its own accord!" retorted Bate.

"Monster? Please refrain from using such language, Bate. We are in the presence of a King," said Tomlin angrily.

"Are you seriously that stupid? The dragon just tried to kill you. If it wasn't for that boy, you'd be burnt to bits."

"Both of you silence. We needn't quarrel amongst ourselves. This is obviously a ploy by Hector to divide us and it nearly worked," said Sir Peter. He turned to Mavid, who was breathing heavily, still recovering from the wound that Sir Peter had given him. "I am truly sorry for my actions and the actions of my men and for any injuries we may have inflicted upon you, both physical and mental."

"No need for that. I haven't had a fight like that in ages. You truly live up to your reputation, Peter, son of Brandr," said Mavid with a raucous laugh.

"I saw the way you charged at me in a mad frenzy after I nearly killed that boy. You looked at me with those eyes, the type of eyes only a concerned father has when he is protecting his seed. Is he yours?"

"Not by blood."

"Hmm, but I can see you care deeply for him. He is like your son; I have two of my own. Twin babes really, only 200 years old."

"Wait. 200 years old? Then how old are you and why don't you have more children?"

"3956, and what do you mean why I don't have more children? Unlike your kind, we dragons don't spend most of our existence fornicating," Mavid responded sharply.

(Dragons of all types, even the basic animal types, can live for a long time. Some are even deemed to be immortal but there is no proof of this. In fact, many reliable texts say most lived a max of 6000-7000 years. In addition, this is not to suggest every dragon possesses such longevity. Some dragons can only live regular life spans of 60 to 100 years. These dragons are usually, but not always, members of the splythe family.)

"And to think, he was gonna kill us for insolence, now he talks of children and fornication. Oh, has this been a strange day, talking dragons and all," Ives muttered under his breath.

"King Mavid, do you remember what happen to you before the events of today?" asked Godfrey.

The dragon gave Godfrey a bewildered look, then said, "Why, I was sleeping in the caves of Beladar when I awoke to aching pains in my back in a castle I didn't recognize surrounded by your kind."

"So, you don't remember terrorizing the castle and its inhabitants with dragon fire?" Godfrey asked.

"What, terrorizing a castle? I only started breathing fire upon you and your kind when *that one* shot an arrow at my head. Come to think of it, I've had—" The dragon coughed violently, spitting copious amount of blood on the ground.

"You're wounded," said Sir Peter.

"It's nothing but a flesh wound. I've had worse," said Mavid. "Anyway, I know what you're suggesting, and like I said before, a dragon cannot be controlled by magic."

"Then why don't you remember coming here?" asked Martin. "Well... well... I... I..." stammered Mavid.

"When I wake up in places I don't recognize, it's usually the result of too much ale," said a bowman by the name Robin.

"Maybe if you'd spend less time drinking and more time shooting, you'd be half the archer I am," said another bowman by the name of Robert.

"That's rich coming from you, who spends his waking hours in taverns lying with whores," retorted Robin.

"First of all—" Mavid was coughing up blood more rapidly which seemed to stop the quarrel between Robin and Robert.

"We need to get a healer to King Mavid," said Godfrey. "My grandmother is a healer, she's in the keep," said Martin.

"You mean Olga? The mad witch that talks to chickens? Do you think she will actually be able to heal a dragon? No, I think we need a real healer," said Tomlin.

"Olga is a real healer, and she's not mad, I can assure you," said Martin sullenly.

"Oh, that's comforting because if she's anything like you, then King Mavid's in trouble," said Tomlin. Martin shot Tomlin an angry glance.

"Hush you two. Now's not the time to argue. Martin, send for Olga and make haste. I fear Mavid does not have much time. Besides, if a king dies in our presence, it could mean all-out war," said Ives sternly.

"Wait," said Robert. Martin stopped and turned around to look at Robert. "Why don't we get Lady Branson? She's also a healer?"

"No, this is not Elysant's area of expertise. She is only used to human patients. We need Olga and her *unconventional* methods," said Sir Peter. "You mean hokraft," said Robin, giving Sir Peter a look of disapproval. "Look, if the dragon dies here, it will mean war. We are already in a war with Hector. We cannot afford another one."

"Alright, but this is a dangerous game to use such magic," said Robin gravely.

"I told you, magic will not work on a dragon and besides, I'm fine," said Mavid feebly.

"You are not fine, and you are in no position to argue. You will stay put and Olga will heal you and that's final," said Sir Peter firmly.

"Humph, a mere human bossing around a king dragon. This is a first, I guess I will abide for now, but I'm telling you it's futile," said Mavid.

"Let me be the judge of that," said Sir Peter.

"You are an officious one. I'm sure you'd make a great king of men someday, Peter, son of Brandr," replied Mavid.

Sir Peter said, "I have no interest in such things right now. I'm only trying to ensure your survival."

"Do you hear yourselves? You're talking about saving the dragon, the same dragon that killed Fredrick, Cleon, Pip, and seventeen of our best men," said Bate.

"Listen, Bate," said Ives.

"No, you listen! I don't care if it was under some spell. My friends are dead, a price must be paid in blood!" interrupted Bate.

Several of the men agreed and chanted "death to the dragon!" in unison.

"Bate, enough! Have you lost your mind?" said Sir Peter.

"Have you lost yours? What if it had been your boy? Would you be so willing to save the dragon, then?" retorted Bate.

"Calm yourself, Bate. Killing the dragon will solve nothing," said Sir Peter.

"It will satisfy the need for vengeance," said Bate.

Vengeance is a volatile thing that stems from the fragility of the human mind and its inability to cope with violent change, the type of change that imbues an affliction inside, resulting in shock from an unjustified wrong received by the individual. On the rudimentary level, vengeance does not seem like such a quandary and in many instances it can seem justifiable. Therein lies the problem: justice is not a universal concept. In fact, there is no such thing as a universal concept. Everything is relative to a situation and so too is vengeance. An individual may feel they are wronged and may seek to correct that wrong through any means necessary, even if that means becoming the very wrong one seeks to correct. In a sense, destruction and vengeance are not divorced from one another, at least not entirely. You see, the act of vengeance is like setting fire to weeds in a garden. The fire initially kills the parasitic plants but spreads and destroys the garden in the process. Of course, it would require great hubris to ignore the naturalistic and emotional impact revenge has on humans and many could argue as a result biochemically humans cannot resist the temptation of such defensible ire. Emotions are the force that drives us to perform seemingly involuntary action to initiate the change we believe is owed to us. In other words, we just feel it, so we do it and don't know why, but it feels right. Vengeance is fueled by emotion no different from love. This is why people speak with such vehemence when describing it. They say things such as *he'll get what he deserves,* or *you can't escape my wrath.* These phrases do not originate from wickedness or malice, but from pain and vengeance as their catharsis. This release of pain and confusion can alleviate stress on the mind and body, hence cure the individual of an invisible yet deadly malady. This is an ingenious stratagem for coping with pain, but it requires a certain amount of obliviousness to reality. The universe did not present you with pain to give you an opponent that you can act revenge on, but rather because you were in the way. So, the question remains, is vengeance simply a tool for cosmic destruction or is it the remedy for agony caused by a muddled and indifferent universe?

"Your vengeance is unfounded," said Ives.

"My vengeance? They were your comrades too! Or have you forgotten them?" said Bate angrily.

"I have not forgotten them and how dare you suggest that?" said Ives sharply.

"Look, we are all upset about the deaths of our comrades but that doesn't mean we should act irrationally. The dragon is most likely not responsible for its actions. He says he does not even recall coming here," said Robin.

"And how do we know that? For all we know, the beast could be telling lies," said Bate.

"Everyone calm down. We've all lost someone dear to us in this war, but we must stick together during such calamity. Like I said before, this is what Hector wants. He seeks to divide us," said Sir Peter vehemently.

An archer stepped forward from the unruly crowd and said, "Pip was my baby brother. He was only sixteen, just experiencing the world, until your dragon snuffed him out of existence. The dragon killed him, not Hector," said the archer, struggling to fight back tears.

"Timon, I am truly sorry for your loss, but now is not the time to grieve. We must cast our emotions aside and act rationally. Mavid is not our enemy," said Sir Peter.

"Says the man that nearly killed him," sneered Bate. "We all saw the way you charged at him. Were you casting your emotions aside then?" he added derisively.

"That was a mistake," Sir Peter frowned at Bate.

"All this squabbling is pointless. We don't have time for this. We should concentrate our efforts on aiding Lord Franklin or assisting Sir Merek and the troops at the gate. I say let the beast die. That way it will be out of our hands as to what happens to it," said a pikeman.

"How cold of you, Odo. We can't let the beast suffer a prolonged death, especially since it may be our fault," said another pikeman.

Odo rolled his eyes and said, "You're too sensitive, Jupp. This is war. Calculated decisions must be made, and time is of the essence. Hector is nearly at our gates!"

"This is getting tiresome. Listen everyone, we can trial the dragon later. Right now we need a healer. Martin, get your grandmother from the keep, you six to the battlements and you four protect the gate and make sure Hector and his men don't get in," said Sir Peter. The men did as they were commanded. Martin was about to head to the keep when he was stopped by Bate. Bate was standing menacingly in front of Martin, glowering.

"Get out of my way, Bate," said Martin. Bate remained still.

"Step aside, Bate," said Sir Peter sternly. Bate's countenance changed from that of ire to seriousness.

Bate spoke, his voice could only be described as fervent. "Fredrick Gifford, father of three twenty-five years old, Cleon Heron, son of a Yeoman Arthur Heron, was to be betrothed to Sabine Woeder, he was only eighteen. Pip Folet, brother to Timon Folet and son of Philip Folet and aspiring knight, he was just sixteen years old [the minimum age to join the army in Corithni]. Piers Mauntell, grandfather of four, he served under Lord Franklin for twenty years fighting in two wars and was looking forward to retiring to be with his grandchildren. He was on his 59th year. Bawden James volunteered to fight in Lord Franklin's army in his campaign against Hector at seventeen. He was an exceptional archer and skilled warrior. His father, Leonard James perished fighting gallantly alongside Lord Franklin in the battle of Wymer creek (1532 NEEOT) leaving Bawden to care for his widowed mother and two sisters at only thirteen. He was just 29 years old. There are others too numerous to state, but no less important. You may not remember them, but I do, and their deaths will be in vain if you let this creature live."

"Do not make the mistake of believing that you are the only one who cares. Now stand aside and let Martin through," demanded Sir Peter. But Bate remained unmoved. When Sir Peter came nearer, Bate gripped the hilt of his blade. Sir Peter looked at Bate with slight surprise. His countenance quickly changed to that of anger as Bate steadily continued to unsheathe his blade.

Before Bate completely drew his blade, he heard another blade being drawn. This cause Bate to stop and look. His gaze met a figure behind Sir Peter, for it was the boy, Godfrey. Godfrey's blade was nearly out of its scabbard when Sir Peter motioned for Godfrey to stop. Godfrey slowly put his sword back in its scabbard, but his eyes were still fixated on Bate. Bate gripped his blade tightly, he was anxious, his muscles stiff, and he was sweating. Sensing his would-be opponent's apprehension, Sir Peter encircled Bate slowly with his hands loosely gripping his blade and his fingers tapping ever so slightly on the grip. Bate's eyes cautiously followed while circling Sir Peter in the opposite direction. The men watched in awe at the proceeding conflict, and they surrounded the two figures in anticipation. Sir Peter's calm demeanor was in sharp contrast to his own. This vexed Bate. *"How dare he, he won't even draw his blade when challenged. How can he stand there so nonchalantly? Does he take me for some novice?"* thought Bate.

Sir Peter suddenly stopped, all his fingers now placed firmly on the grip of his weapon, but his sword still was not drawn. He looked fiercely into the eyes of Bate, as though prepared for any oncoming assault. His posture was fully erect, with his right foot behind him and his left foot to the front. He could see fear in Bate's eyes, but also misplaced anger.

Still, Bate did a good job of masking these emotions under the façade of coolness.

"If you should attempt to strike me, it will be your folly," said Sir Peter. Bate's face contorted into an intense scowl, lines on his brow aggregated and the veins on his forehead began to protrude. His blood boiled, for Sir Peter's words were an insult to him. *"How dare he talk to me in such a manner! As though I am a mere child. Does he think me wrong and he right? Such knavery, yes knave indeed, defending a dragon while our brothers lie burnt to ashes. He thinks because he has won a few battles, he is peerless. I will not listen to this marauder. I'll show him, I'll show them all!"* thought Bate. He drew his arming sword and held it in the air with both hands. He shouted madly as he charged at Sir Peter. He didn't get far. Before he could deliver a single blow, Bate was struck soundly from behind at the base of the neck just above the collarbone by the wooden shaft of a polearm rendering him unconscious. The figure that stood over him with a spear in both hands was Robin. "What'd you do that for?" cried Martin. "I was saving his life," responded Robin.

"He was engaged in single combat; you know better than to interrupt a person engaged in single combat. Those are the rules," said Tomlin. (There is an unwritten rule in Mirthadine that when an individual is engaged in single combat, others are not to intervene. Who came up with this rule nobody knows, but it is usually respected by all types of warriors except for pirates. This unnamed rule can occur when two opponents indicated that they want to challenge each other through words or body language.)

"Oh, for fuck's sake, those rules are ancient and besides, what sense does killing each other make? You'd only be doing Hector's job for him. You two pick this stupid git up."

One of the men asked, "Is he alive?"

Robin responded, "I think so, but he'll be in quite a lot of pain when he wakes up." Robin guffawed at his own words but stopped abruptly when he noticed others weren't laughing. Slightly embarrassed due to the judgmental onlookers, Robin diverted their attention by removing a leather bottle filled with ale from his belt. It was attached by a black leather strap. He poured all its contents down his throat in one sitting. The men were visibly vexed, especially Robert, but they said nothing.

"Brother, I hope you know what you did was highly—" "Relax Robert. I know where I hit him."

Robin turned back to the two infantrymen and said, "Take him to the keep." He grabbed one of the men by the crook of his arm and whispered, "Best not mention this to Lady Branson. If she asks, he hit his head. Hopefully she'll believe it. Bate's pretty clumsy."

The infantry man nearest Robin had a perplexed look on his face and, with hesitation, said, "What if he wakes up?"

"I dun know. I reckon he forgets everything anyway, seeing as he was knocked out and all," said Robin.

The infantry man said, "I don't think that's how it works." "Never mind, just go," Robin said crossly.

"Concerned about your neck, are you?" said Tomlin playfully. Robin was not amused. He scowled at Tomlin and said, "Piss off!"

The two infantry men dragged Bate's unconscious body to the keep. Martin was at the entrance of the keep, when to his surprise an old woman of 98, suddenly appeared before him. She had teleported from inside the keep. The woman had a hunched over appearance and stood no more than five feet tall. She had long white hair, wore a ragged black dress and had a peculiar silver ring on her left ring finger that looked ancient in design, it might've been older than the woman herself. It had several scuff marks and strange engravings on it, a series of symbols that could have been some language or code one that was not old tongue.

"Grandmother, how did you—" said Martin.

"Hush my child, it was the chicken's that told me," interrupted Olga. "There she goes again with the chickens," said Tomlin, rolling his eyes. "Olga, can you heal him?" asked Sir Peter desperately.

"Peter, you should be ashamed of yourself for attacking such a majestic beast as Mavid, King of the Dragons of Beladar son of Aglar the great," said Olga. Everyone was taken aback by her words, except for Martin.

"Woman, how do you know my name, my title, and my father?" demanded Mavid.

"She knows things," said Martin sheepishly.

"Let me guess, the chickens," said Tomlin. Martin scowled at Tomlin. "You mustn't let your temper get the best of you," said Olga.

"You are right, Olga, I shall try to do better in the future, but now I need your help. Can you use your magic to heal King Mavid?" said Sir Peter.

"Oh, healing a dragon is quite a feat. Most conventional forms of magic won't work on them," said Olga.

"Then can you use more unconventional methods?" Sir Peter asked with emphasis on the word unconventional, as though trying to obscure the word from his comrades.

"What you mean hokraft? Ha-ha! I do not think that is necessary!" Olga laughed boisterously.

"I guess you're right," Sir Peter said contritely. "I will see what I can do," said Olga.

"Thank you," replied Sir Peter.

Olga stepped toward King Mavid. Her gaze was directed towards Mavid's wing and the injury he received from Tomlin's cross bolt.

"Oh, we have to remove that, lend me your wing Mavid," the Dragon lowered his injured wing so that it was at eye level with the diminutive woman. She abruptly pulled out the bolt.

"Ow! Woman, you could have warned me before you so viciously removed the large projectile in my wing," said Mavid.

"Are you sure she's a healer?" Mavid said while looking at Martin. "Yeah, I mean I think so. She's not traditional, though."

Mavid groaned. To which Martin attempted to mollify his concerns by saying, "She's amazing with the chickens."

"I am not a chicken!" said Mavid angrily. "Well, you're not that far off," said Robin. "What?!" exclaimed Mavid.

"Look. I meant no disrespect, your grace. It's just you have similar structures like wings, claws," said Robin. Robert groaned.

"Do I look like a chicken?!" shouted Mavid.

"Don't be such a baby, Mavy. That was just a minor wound. Now for the hard part…"

"Mavy? No one has called me that in ages. Who is this woman?" asked Mavid.

"Like I said, she knows things," said Martin sheepishly

Olga's attention was now directed towards the massive wound in the center of Mavid's chest. "Oh, this is a serious injury. If you hadn't called for me, he might have perished."

"But you can fix it, right, grandmother?" asked Martin.

"Hmm… I'll try, but the wound is deep. It seems to have cut through bone and struck vitals, causing massive bleeding."

Olga began to tinker with the ring on her finger by rotating it counterclockwise, clockwise, then counterclockwise again. She was synchronizing it to the words she was muttering under her breath, which were inaudible to the individuals surrounding her. Her eyes were closed. She suddenly became progressively louder, and her words became perceptible. The words she muttered were unrecognizable, for they were not old tongue.

"Karos maros centharos, karos maros centharos, karos maros centharos."

Olga's voice became more sonorous, and she tinkered with the ring more intensely.

"Karos maros centharos! Karos maros centharos!"

A surge of wind manifested beneath her feet as she uttered the words. It caused her hair and clothing to thrash about wildly. She opened her eyes. They had become completely green. A greenish hue surrounded her entire body as it expanded into the air at least three feet.

The men were frightened by Olga's sudden change in appearance. Some even stepped back to avoid the gust of wind and green aura she was generating. Olga's voice also altered. In fact, there were two sounds that were being reverberated. The first sound could barely be discriminated from the second. This lesser sound was Olga's original voice. The second more domineering sound was unnaturally deep in pitch and bordering deafening. Olga stuck her right arm towards Mavid's wound with an open palm while simultaneously screaming the incantation. The ring on her ring finger rotated in the same direction she was rotating initially — counterclockwise, clockwise, then counterclockwise again.

"*KAROS MAROS CENTHAROS! KAROS MAROS CENTHAROS! KAROS MAROS CENTHAROS!*"

Mavid's wound gradually healed until it completely disappeared. Several men gasped.

"How are you feeling, King Mavid?" said Sir Peter.

But Mavid did not hear Sir Peter, for he was distracted. He stared at the now weary Olga and thought, "*Who and what is this woman? She's no ordinary witch. This power that resides within her is unlike any I've seen, but with such power there was surely a price to pay. The question remains who or whom, is paying that price?*"

Mavid was not the only one who Olga had invoked interest; the boy Godfrey was drawn to Olga's ring which, even after the spell, continued to gyrate, albeit at a reduced rate. "*It's so familiar yet I've never seen it. It's like a dream that you swear is real, but you wake up and realize it isn't. Then you start to question why you believed it so adamantly to begin with. Maybe this whole world's a dream.*"

The motion of the ring seemed to place Godfrey in a type of trance. His thoughts became mired by ones that were not his own and yet those same thoughts seemed to come out of his head without any known antecedent. "*What are we doing or perhaps we're not doing anything? Maybe there isn't a 'we'.*" As Godfrey pondered existence, he simultaneously began, unbeknownst to him, whispering, "*eso taren damen.*"

"Huh, did you say something, Godfrey?" asked Robert.

Godfrey abruptly woke from his trance said, "Huh? Wha—erm… no." "Huh, I must be hearing things," said Robert. "King Mavid!" Sir Peter repeated.

Mavid, startled, got up on all fours and said, "Oh, I've never felt better. Your healer is quite remarkable."

"Thank you, Mavy, but my work is not done. There's still the wound on your belly," said Olga.

"Oh, that won't be necessary. You see that was there before. It's an old battle wound back when I fought in the Mygar wars some 500 years ago. You see I took a nasty hit—"

As Mavid was speaking Olga collapsed. Fortunately, Martin was there to break her fall.

"Grandma, grandma!" said Martin.

"Take her to the keep, boy. She seems quite fatigued from all the... errrm... whatever that was," said Ives. Martin did as he was told.

When Martin came back, Sir Peter devised a plan. "The east wall is on the verge of being breached and the enemy has two dastardly siege engines at the barbican. It won't hold if we don't do something," said Sir Peter.

"Allow me to assist. It's the least I could do after all the damage I've done," Mavid said.

"Very well, King Mavid. You take out those siege engines. Martin and the other archers climb up the eastern wall. From the ramparts, concentrate your fire on the battering ram. Those in the infantry, come with me and guard the crack along the east wall. If any soul should breach it, see to it that they are slain. Those with crossbows, stay on the ground near the wall. Bolts are hard to come by. You can't afford to miss."

Godfrey was about to head towards the eastern wall with the other men when Sir Peter asked sternly, "Where are you going?"

"But you said—"

Godfrey was interrupted by Sir Peter. "No, Godfrey, you've done enough. Now return to Elysant."

"Have I not proven my worth?" Godfrey asked angrily.

"I don't have time to argue," said Sir Peter. Noticing Sir Peter's serious tone, Godfrey became more suppliant in his attempts to persuade Sir Peter.

"Come on, I can be of use. Look, look, there's still a fire in the lower bailey. I can help put it out."

Sir Peter sighed. He was ambivalent on letting Godfrey go, but realized it was a necessity. Godfrey had proven himself a formidable elemental against King Mavid, and Sir Peter could think of no other available that could fight the fire in the lower bailey.

Elemental manipulation entails a lot of things. One of which is canceling or dampening, as it is more accurately called. Dampening is simply reducing an element (we are not talking about elements in the periodic table but what is thought to be elements on Mirthadine, such as fire, terrain, water, wind, et cetera) in its natural state. For instance, in the case of fire, a fire elemental can lessen a blaze because of fire being the same element that said elemental manipulates.

"Okay, but return to the keep once you're done. Oh, and Godfrey, be careful."

Godfrey hugged Sir Peter and said, "You too."

By this time, the men were heading to their position when a tempest was brewing. Martin looked up at the sky. He heard the crackling of thunder and saw the flashes of lightening with mild precipitation. He rejoiced and the sudden surge of merriment caused him to laugh ecstatically. He pointed at the sky and said, "Look, it's a miracle from Arda." (Lightning elementals' powers are amplified during a storm.)

CHAPTER FOUR

BLOOD OF THE MASTER BUILDER

[moments earlier]

The keep was heavily machicolated and was on the southwestern section of the lower bailey. The atmosphere was that of panic, understandably so as both the watch tower and chapel had been set on fire and now there was a blaze in the lower bailey 15 feet from the keep. Several inside watched in horror as the flames engulfed the castle. Those inside the keep were mostly women and children and the wounded from either the current battle or a previous one. The keep had five floors, the first floor being a type of undercroft and storage room. It's also where the dungeon was. The second floor was the garrison, the injured both combative and noncombative were in here. They were attended to by healers and the Archiater who oversaw them. The Archiater was ordered by Lady Rose Franklin (Lord Franklin's wife) to attend the wounded. The Archiater, a man by the name of Giles Baker, was an elderly man in his eighties who had been Lord Franklin's physician since he was a boy. Lady Rose Franklin, or Lady Franklin as she was often called, was in the great hall which took up the third and fourth floors. She was with other civilians, both lowborn and high born. There was much tumult on the second floor. You see, it had become a sort of makeshift hospital. With the injured crying in agony, blood plastered over the floor, entrails desperately being held in place by healers and several panicking persons all cumulated by the impending sense of doom due to the fire-breathing dragon. In the pandemonium, there was a woman with long curly dark brown hair tied into a bun who was tending to the wounded. She was about thirty-four and had kind green eyes.

"Lady Branson, you should be in the great hall with the other ladies. This is no place for you," said the Archiater sternly.

"My services are needed here. Thank you very much for your concern, Archiater," Lady Branson said firmly. Her hands were covered in blood. She was preventing massive hemorrhaging of an injured soldier who received a nasty cut to the abdomen. She then cauterized the cut with flame manifest (another term for fire elemental type).

Giles grabbed her arm and said, "I don't want my granddaughter surrounded by death and misery!"

"Death and misery are all around! I'm doing my best to make sure it doesn't consume us all!" retorted Lady Branson.

Giles placed two hands on Lady Branson's shoulders and looked directly into her eyes and said, earnestly, "Elysant, you don't belong here." "Grandfather, this is where my heart lies and there's nothing you can do to stop me because God forbid Peter comes through these doors. I have to save him!" said Lady Branson vehemently.

Giles sighed. "My apologies, Lady Branson, you may remain." "Thank you," replied Lady Branson.

Giles smiled at Lady Branson and said, "You know you've become very stubborn."

"I get it from you, you old curmudgeon," Lady Branson teased. "Bakers can be quite tenacious, just like your father. You have his eyes and his skill."

He hugged her and kissed her on the forehead. "Just promise me you'll be careful," he said.

"I will, grandfather," said Lady Branson. Their embrace was interrupted by another healer grumbling about there being too many bodies and not enough beds to treat them. When the woman saw Giles and Lady Branson, her cantankerous mood shifted to awkwardness and embarrassment.

"Oh, Archiater, Lady Branson…" She did her best to avoid direct eye contact.

"Is there something troubling you, Clara?" asked Giles.

"Oh nothing," she said, laughing nervously. Her features betrayed her though. You could tell by her eyes that she was quite fatigued and under much stress.

"Clara," Giles said slowly and methodically, as though anticipating another lie.

"Oh, it's just that I don't understand why Lord Franklin has all the injured soldiers here. Surely, they should be in a hospital better suited for their injuries?"

"The nearest hospital is in Eredith. That's several days journey and men will have to accompany the wounded. Those same men would be better allocated defending the castle," said Giles. Clara still looked puzzled.

So Lady Branson stepped in and said, "Lord Franklin ordered all women, children, healers, and injured in here because Hector's forces are outside our walls, the keep is the safest place to be right now."

"How come Lord Franklin didn't move them before the siege?" asked Clara.

"I think you have quite a tactical mind, Clara, maybe even worthy of a commander. Perhaps it's because no place outside Corithni is safe from Hector's grasp. In other words, there's simply nowhere to go," said Giles. More bickering occurred amongst the people in the barracks and morale was decreasing. In addition, there were several shrieks and cries from men recounting what they saw in battle. One man, with three broken ribs and a shattered right arm that had to be hoisted by a sling, kept quarreling with a female healer.

"I'm telling you, the keep won't hold," said the man.

"It will hold, now enough of that talk; you need to focus on resting," said the woman.

"What's the point that blaze outside will spread and consume us all," said the man.

"The men are doing their best to fend off the dragon. They even have some giant contraption that fires heavy bolts," said the woman.

"Oh yeah, and what the bloody hell is one measly catapult going to do against a flying fire-breathing dragon? It'll just burn it up like it did the chapel"

"Ow!" The man attempted to sit up, but his injuries prevented him. The woman helped him lay back down. The healer woman noticed the man's breathing was irregular. His left pectoral was barely moving, and his right was moving quite rapidly. This seemed to suggest that the man had a collapsed lung. His breathing was shallow.

"You need to sit up. It'll help your breathing," said the woman. "Wha- but you just said I need to rest," said the man.

"That was before I saw you breathing. Did you receive a blow to the chest?" ask the woman.

"Yes, I did. Some big fucker hit me square in the chest with a mace, nearly knocked my breast plate off. I'm telling you; this man was at least nine feet tall."

The woman shot him an incredulous look. Realizing his hyperbole and irritated by the woman's skepticism he said, "okay, maybe not that big, but he was strong, hit me once and I was unhorsed. I tried to brace my fall, but that's when I broke my arm, my ribs from the initial blow." The woman then looked at the man inquisitively, analyzing all his injuries. The man also looked at the woman intensely, studying her face for any inclination of emotion either good or bad, but the woman remained stoic. The man's patience was wearing thin, so he asked blatantly, "Am I going to die?"

"I don't know. I am not a soothsayer," she teased.

"That's not what I meant," the man said rather peevishly by what he deemed an insensitive response.

The woman, embarrassed by her words, said rather quickly, "Sorry." She attempted to avoid eye contact as she said, "I was only trying to add some levity to the situation with a joke, good sir."

"It was a horrid joke," said the man brusquely.

"I know and I'm so sorry, good sir. I——" She was interrupted by the injured man guffawing so raucously that it drew the attention of others in the barracks. His laughter was quite infectious because the female healer was also chuckling.

"You see, you don't like those types of jokes either," the man said, half laughing, half speaking. Then he felt a sharp pain in his fifth and sixth ribs that stemmed from laughing too hard. The man let out a stifled cry. "Ow!"

"Are you alright? Sir, you mustn't strain yourself, here let me help you." She fluffed his pillow and fashioned his bed into a recliner. "Better, sir?" asked the woman. "No sir, just Colin."

"You're not a knight?" the woman asked, slightly surprised.

"Don't be too surprised. This war has made your Lord Franklin desperate. Hector's not the only one hiring sell-swords," said Colin. Sensing the woman's uneasiness with this new revelation Colin decided to explain.

"Look, I'm not some random bloody cutthroat. I'm part of the free company known as the Rilek Herons. Long story short, we owe Lord Franklin a great debt after saving our arses a while back."

"Maybe he'll knight you afterwards," said the woman. "Sure, if I don't die first," said Colin sarcastically.

"I don't think you're going to die," said the woman.

"Oh, so you are a soothsayer?" Colin teased. The woman rolled her eyes, giving the illusion that she was annoyed but that was a façade. She was really quite enjoying Colin's company.

"At least not from your injuries, whether you die stubbing your toe is unbeknownst to me," said the woman.

Colin laughed boisterously. "You're quite a woman." "This woman has a name. It's Sarah."

The distinct sound of flapping wings was outside the keep. Several people moved toward the window, thereby obscuring the view, but one could hear the screeching of the dragon and the searing of flesh below. The sizzling of flame was accompanied by the excruciating cries of soldiers below. It was a sordid affair. Hector using a beast of such caliber to kill his foes. But then again, war itself was a sordid affair. Nonetheless, very few have used dragons as effectively as Hector had during the siege. They are not exactly domesticated creatures. The idea of being burned alive was horrifying enough to most and yet the greater terror was the tedium that came anticipating the expiry of fear. The absence of fear is the acceptance of death. Those sentiments were shared by the defenders in Corithni.

The dragon mercilessly burned anyone it came into contact with, and yet it stayed clear of the keep. This was not the only peculiarity in the dragon's behavior. No, the beast did not haphazardly scorch the castle. It instead seemed to be deliberately targeting certain sections. It was as though the dragon was looking for something or clearing the way for Hector. The methodical nature of the beast seemed to suggest that Hector's goal was much more than taking the castle, but rather taking something from it.

"Fools! Fools! Get away from the window. It has eyes, you oafs," shouted Giles angrily. The people crowding the window dispersed and went about their duties, but they were still petrified. This was the closest the dragon had been to the keep since the fire in the lower bailey. It was close enough that one could hear its breath. Lady Branson looked at Giles, struggling to fight back tears. She reached her hand out and Giles held it. They closed their eyes and prayed. Others joined in. The dragon eventually flew off into the sky away from the keep, but in that allotted time there was utter silence.

"Are you all right, Colin?" Sarah whispered.

He did not respond. Instead, he gazed off into the distance, his pupils dilated, and he started gasping rapidly. His body was trembling, and beads of sweat aggregated on his forehead. Many in the barracks had the same reaction.

"Colin, it's gone," said Sarah.

"I need to get outta here," Colin said as he struggled to get to his feet and winced in pain as he took his first step.

Sarah stepped in front of him and attempted to prevent him from leaving. She placed her hand on his good arm and said, "Wait, you're not fit to leave yet."

"Well, I can't stay here. There's a bloody dragon outside," said Colin. Colin tried to sidestep her, but she blocked his way again. Colin sighed and said tenderly, "The keep won't hold. I have to leave now. Come with me."

"I-I-I can't and besides, where would we go? Hector's men are outside. How's an injured man and a maiden going to slip past them unnoticed? Colin, we'll be killed," Sarah said.

"I'd rather be hacked to pieces by Hector's men than burned alive by the dragon!" said Colin angrily.

"There's no need to throw your life away. The keep will hold," insisted Sarah.

"Just like the chapel and watch tower? Sarah, we must leave this place," argued Colin.

"The keep is reinforced with white stone from Isial Lake as is most of Corithni. White stone is flame resistant and hard enough to withstand many blows. Why do you think the dragon has not burst through our gates? It's because it would most likely break its neck on impact."

Colin studied Sarah's face. She was quite genuine in her countenance and there was no dishonesty in her delivery. Yet, Colin asked rather dubiously, "How do you know all this?"

"This castle is over 200 years old, but the keep has been rebuilt three times. Its most recent iteration is just 25 years old. My father was the main builder who helped design the new keep. He told me everything about it. I trust his judgment; do you trust mine?" asked Sarah.

"I do," said Colin solemnly. He went back to his bed and laid down on his recliner, then looked at Sarah and said, "The truth is, I'm frightened. Everything has its limits, even the castle if the dragon sets its eyes here."

"Then we'll pray to Arda that doesn't happen," Sarah interrupted.

In another section of the barracks, there was a male healer who was approaching old age and he was in his 57th year. Given his demeanor and dismissive attitude towards other healers, it was safe to assume he was senior in position and had been there for some time.

"Pay attention Leanne!" Leanne, who wasn't daydreaming, often saw visions and heard voices that other people did not. She kept this to herself, though most people in Hilag (a town southeast of Corithni) were aware of her apparent condition and did their best to avoid her. Some, even believing her to be possessed, attributed her demeanor to madness. When Lord Fowler moved some of his people from Athamar to Corithni before the siege, Lady Fowler was so vexed by Leanne's behavior that she refused to allow her entry into the great hall. She was so adamant about this that Lady Franklin had to comply and suggest that Leanne go to the barracks. Her mind was never idle, which disturbed her as this meant she was never at rest. This was apparent in her physical appearance. Her eyes were often bloodshot and had bags underneath them as a result of several bouts with insomnia. Due to her visions, which some deemed hallucinations, she could never really tell if she was dreaming or awake.

"Did you hear me, girl?" said the man. "Uh-uh. Yes, Swithin," replied Leanne.

Swithin gave her an incredulous look. "Then what did I just say?" "Uh-Uh-uh, bodies, bodies too much… eh, I don't know?"

Swithin scowled at her. "Useless, scatterbrained girl. That's what we get for bringing people over from outside Corithni. They have no work ethic."

Swithin noticed that Leanne was not looking him in the eye, and this infuriated him, for he saw this as a sign of disrespect. The truth of the matter was that Leanne rarely looked people in the eye because eye contact, along with a myriad of other things too lengthy to mention, scared her. Despite this, she was more afraid of her own mind than any external stimuli.

Swithin grabbed her chin and said, "Look at me when I'm talking to you, scatterbrain!"

Leanne started to tremble. This further vexed Swithin as he considered it a sign of weakness. He released her.

"Ugh, I am only going to say this once. There're too many dead bodies in the barracks. The place is really starting to reek." He pointed to the dead body next to her.

"Take that one out back, will you? And make haste. I don't want to catch the bloody plague." Swithin left to another corner of the garrison. Leanne turned to the recently deceased body of a soldier. From the looks of it, he had been impaled in the chest by some type of polearm, most likely a halberd. She attempted to cover the body with a white cloth, as was standard in the barracks. She immediately halted when the dead man's eyes opened. They were an atypical color with his irises being blood red. They rotated in a familiar and hypnotic pattern, counterclockwise, clockwise, then counterclockwise again. This oddly synchronized pattern was made apparent because the iris varied in intensity of color, interchanging between bold and dim, like a river if blood was sloshing about in a circle with tides coming and receding on the surface.

Before Leanne could scream and run for help, the undead man seized her by the wrist and pinned her to the wall of the barracks. He placed his hand on her mouth so she could not scream. She tried to resist his grasp, but he restrained her. Her nostrils flared. She was quite terrified given she was looking into the eyes of this stranger who sprung to life with such immediacy. Unaware of his intentions, she panicked and breathed deep audible breaths in rapid succession.

"Do not scream for they cannot hear nor see like you and I. There are forces at play controlling things. These invaders are from the Outer realm. They seek to harm us by corrupting your leaders and setting them against each other. This war, this conflict, it's only the beginning, an advent, an advent of fire. Your lords, your king, your God will fail you. You must warn them Leanne before it's too late for you are the—"

The man suddenly disappeared and reappeared in his spot on the bed, eyes closed and dead. Leanne found herself with her hand over her own mouth, her back against the wall of the barracks. Swithin returned and saw her in this position and was infuriated.

"For God's sake, scatterbrain, what are you doing mewling in the corner like a babe? This can't be your first corpse. The body's still warm. Useless girl, get outta here. I'll do it myself!"

Leanne scurried in a fright to another part of the garrison. Swithin muttered underneath his breath, "Stupid girl, what's she doing in the bloody barracks if she can't even stomach a corpse?"

"AAARGH, GET BACK DEVILS!" screamed a man with a mutilated arm and several lacerations on his torso.

"Help, help, they're after me!"

Two male healers attempted to restrain him, but the man flailed about and was able to wrench free by striking one of the healers in the face, thus sending him flat on his back. The clearly distressed man attempted to flee, but his gammy leg gave in, and he collapsed on the floor. At this moment, he realized his left arm was missing just below the elbow. He gazed in horror. His lips quivered, the lines on his brow arched upwards and his eyes widened. He began twitching slightly, uttering something unintelligible. Then, in a moment of brevity, he was virtually transfixed by his missing limb. Afterwards, he began to scream like a newborn infant. "AAAAAAAAAH!"

He quickly lost consciousness and the two male healers hoisted him up and gently placed him in his bed. Of course, this whole scene caught the attention of Giles, Lady Branson, and several of the healers.

"What happened to him?" asked Lady Branson.

"He's a survivor of the battle of Eredith, the only survivor," said Giles.

Lady Branson's eyes widen.

"His wounds are severe. I don't believe he'll make it. We did our best. We even amputated his arm to prevent the spread of infection, but he has lost too much blood," said one of the male healers.

Noticing the two were quite fatigued and frankly overworked, Giles said, "Thank you, Tim, and Alywin. Lady Branson and I will take it from here."

"Yes, Archiater," the two said in unison, then they departed. Lady Branson studied the man as he lay there unconscious. He looked anemic and was quite pale.

"What do you think?" asked Giles.

"Well, we will see," said Lady Branson as she removed the cloth that obscured the man's injuries. It was then she realized the extent of his injuries. They were quite serious and odd in that they seemed to have been made by a beast. There were claw marks on his chest and arm. Given their direction, diagonally downward and elongated toward the ends, thus leaving a trail, it suggested that whatever was trying to attack him was attempting to draw the man closer, and as macabre as it sounded, devour him. This was further indicated by bite wounds on his neck. Of course, it was not all claw marks. It was clear that he was impaled several times as well. Once in both kidneys, thrice in the liver and twice in the gut. This seemed to imply that whatever was pursuing this man either worked in cahoots with the beast, or the more likely scenario was the beast was intelligent enough to wield blades ergonomic to their palms.

The question now remained, what had caused the infection that led to this man's right arm to be hacked off? Poison, maybe, or perhaps the man broke his own arm in multiple places to escape the grasp of his assailants, thus resulting in a dead arm. Lady Branson gazed directed towards the man's right leg. It was broken, but comparative to his other injuries, it seemed benign. The reason being was there were no grazes or contusions on his leg besides the ones at the site of impact. Given the nature of the injury, it was heavily implied that he broke it falling off something, maybe a tree. There are woodland in Mydra (the region Corithni resides in) and Eredith. It was quite possible he attempted to escape within the trees then jumped down, thus breaking his leg.

"How long has this man been here?" Lady Branson asked. "Tim says he has been here for weeks," said Giles.

"That's impossible. With his injuries, he should have died ages ago," said Lady Branson.

"Consider him fortunate then," said Giles.

"Or cursed. Whatever is prolonging his life?" asked Lady Branson. "Whatever it is, it seems to be wearing out. His injuries are beyond our capabilities. Perhaps he would have fared better at a hospital," said Giles. "Don't you think he needs a holy man? I mean, he's practically a corpse already," said a voice from behind.

Giles and Lady Branson turned around slowly. Slightly startled, they saw a stout woman with a freckled face, brown eyes, and short russet hair. She was wearing a white laced bonnet.

"Ah, Eva, a pleasure to see you," said Giles. "You as well Giles," Eva grinned.

"Giles?" whispered Lady Branson as she looked at Giles suspiciously, yet playfully.

Giles caught her glance and blushed. "So, have you met my granddaughter Elysant?" asked Giles.

"I don't believe I've had the pleasure. How do you do, Elysant?" "Very well, thank you."

Eva studied Lady Branson's face for a moment. Then she became ecstatic. "Wait, you're the wife of the famous swordsman, Sir Peter Branson," Eva chuckled.

"Forgive me for not recognizing you. I'm from Eredith," said Eva. "It's quite alright," said Lady Branson.

"Eva, what are you doing in the barracks, my dear? You should be in the great hall," said Giles.

"Oh, Giles, I couldn't be cooped up there with all those fancy ladies twiddling my thumbs and doing absolutely nothing. I figured I'm more needed down here. Besides, I am no lady, just a cook," said Eva nonchalantly.

Lady Branson quickly changed the subject to more pertinent matters and asked, "Eva, you said you're from Eredith. Do you know if there is a relief force coming?"

"Sorry. I'm afraid I do not. I came to Mydra before the siege." Lady Branson struggled to hide her disappointment.

"If it's any consolation, Eredith always comes through for its allies," said Eva.

Suddenly, the man regained consciousness and seized Lady Branson's arm tightly. She tried to wrench free from his grasp, but it was to no avail.

Eva screamed. Panicking, she yelled, "Somebody help!"

Giles desperately tried to free Lady Branson, but his efforts were futile. It was as if this man had possessed some supernatural strength. He drew Lady Branson near. She was close enough to see her own frightened reflection in his eyes and feel his warm breath on her skin as he said, "Don't venture to Eredith. It's wrought with demons, monsters!"

Before he could say more, Tim and Alywin pulled the man off Lady Branson.

"Step back, milady," demanded Alywin. Tim called four other male healers to restrain him. The man writhed about in agony while wailing ambiguous sounds. All that could be made out was, "no, no, no, get away, get away!"

Seeing his pain and empathizing with him, Lady Branson said, "stop, stop, can't you see you're hurting him?!"

"But milady, he just tried to attack you," replied Tim.

Then Lady Branson said in a more authoritative way. "As wife of Sir Peter and granddaughter of the Archiater, I demand that you release this man immediately!"

"Yes, milady," the men said in unison. They stepped away from the man but stood close to Lady Branson. "Sorry, milady. I should have warned you that he can often get violent. I thought he was unconscious. I should've-," said Alywin.

"It's alright, you mustn't blame yourself," interrupted Lady Branson. The man's deportment changed drastically when he was released. He looked around the room and for once seemed present. He looked at Lady Branson as though he recognized her. Lady Branson was uncomfortable. The man took this as a sign that he was making her uncomfortable. This was further made apparent to him when she averted his gaze. The man gravitated his gaze towards the floor to appear less threatening.

"I do apologize in advance, but I do not recall the manner in which I came into these barracks. Can any of you kind souls explain it to me?" said the man.

The erudite nature of the way he spoke implied he was a knight of high status. The healers stood there aghast by the man's diametrical change in behavior. He went from deranged, speaking only in fragments, to the pinnacle of cordiality and refinement.

Attempting to ease the tension in the room, the man introduced some levity in what he believed to be a banal joke. "You all look like sentinels standing there, intimidating like, just for one man. It's quite ludicrous, don't you think?" the man chuckled.

"You punched me, attacked Lady Branson and had to be restrained," Tim said curtly.

"He was not himself," retorted Lady Branson. "What?" the man said, bemused by the accusation.

"I'm sorry, but I do not recall doing anything of the sort," said the man. "Your memory seems to be quite befogged. You are in the barracks of Corithni keep. We have been treating your injuries for weeks," said Giles. The man looked around, studying the layout of the barracks from the ceiling to the walls to the floor beneath him, but as much as he tried, he could not recollect his surroundings.

He furrowed his brow. He seemed quite irked by this. "None of this seems familiar, does it?" Giles said, as though anticipating the man's response.

"No," the man sighed. He attempted to rub his face with both palms out of frustration when he noticed his missing appendage. He looked deeply saddened.

"We had to sever it. It was dead when you got here and infected," said Alywin.

"Very well. I'm sure you did your best," said the man struggling to subdue his sadness.

Endeavoring to change the subject, Lady Branson asked, "What do you remember, good sir?"

"I remember that I am Sir Richard Brickenden of Etlio woods (ITHLEO) a province just west of Eredith," said Sir Richard.

"That's good. Your memory is returning," said Giles.

Sir Richard looked at Lady Branson again and said, "Forgive me my lady, but I seem to recall your likeness. Are you not Lady Branson, the wife of the famed swordsmen Sir Peter Branson?"

"Yes," Lady Branson replied.

"I remember you in the crowd when your now husband unhorsed me during a joust in the tournament of roses thirteen years ago at Eredith. I was knocked unconscious for the rest of the tournament, you seem distressed by the whole affair," said Sir Richard.

"Yes, I was. I don't particularly like violence, especially unnecessary violence."

"Ha ha," Sir Richard guffawed. "Tournaments are harmless blunt weapons and all," he said.

"I find nothing harmless in charging at one another at great speeds, lances in hand, to expect nothing short of injury is folly," said Lady Branson.

"I suppose you're right, but it makes for good sport," said Sir Richard. "But my days of fighting in tournaments are over," Sir Richard added rather miserably while looking at his missing appendage.

"Don't feel so bad. You're quite lucky to be alive, especially with the injuries you sustained," said Giles.

"What do you mean?" Sir Richard asked.

"Well, your injuries there—" Giles was about to continue when Sir Richard lifted his tunic and saw bandages wrapped around his mid-section and wounded leg. Blood was seeping through the bandages in the gut region, and it felt warm.

"You were stabbed multiple times. Frankly, I don't know how you even survived given how long it's been and the nature of the wounds. You should have perished a long time ago," said Lady Branson.

"How long has it been?" Sir Richard asked. "It's been roughly four weeks," said Alywin.

Sir Richard gasped and ran his hand through his hair. "Oh my God, they've turn me into them," said Sir Richard, his eyes widened and he panted. He rocked back and forth, nervously repeating the words, "Demons. Eredith, they have changed me."

"Who has changed you? What are they?" asked Giles, but Sir Richard kept repeating himself, saying, "They've changed me!"

The others around him grew anxious at Sir Richard's second mood swing. They feared he was going mad. A male healer stepped towards Sir Richard, but Lady Branson motioned him to stop. Eva was tugging at Giles to move away but Giles kept pressing Sir Richard for answers, but Sir Richard kept repeating what Giles perceived as drivel about demons and monsters. (Demons, monsters and the supernatural do exist but because of their absence for over a millennium due to the plague of Albedasis, it has caused many to become doubtful of their existence. This is especially apparent amongst humans that reside in Iiadec. Regions outside of Iiadec are aware of the supernatural. Thus, out of hubris, humans have lessened their defenses against the supernatural and are not prepared for what awaits them in the shadows.)

Before Sir Richard could continue to speak, Lady Branson said cogently, "You are Sir Richard Brickenden of Etlio woods. You are yourself, they could not have changed you because you are here now talking to us." She knelt beside him and took a softer tone and called out his name. "Sir Richard, Sir Richard." She gently turned his face towards hers. Sir Richard looked into her eyes. He was distraught at first but then he seemed captivated by the delicate features of her face and the kind aura she had been emanating. She said, "Sometimes, Arda performs miracles. That's why I believe he has brought you here. But in order for him to heal your mind as well as your soul you must please tell us everything."

"All right, but my memory is befuddled," Sir Richard said. "Understood. Just tell us what you can recall," said Giles.

"As you may know, I am from Etlio wood. Lord Anselm Blakeslee pledged a measly 105 troops to fight Lord Franklin's cause. He had little faith in your Lord's cause. Nonetheless, we successfully drew back Hector's forces at the battle of Rilek. After Rilek, we split up forces. I was tasked with going to Eredith with a few sell-swords and the remaining Etlio forces. That is where Hector's army had scattered off to after their defeat, after we chased them, of course. We were on their heels, and they were on enemy territory and, with the aid of Eredith, victory seemed all but assured. But we did not realize what evils were in store for us. Eredith forces preceded us, scouting for the enemy, I presume. We arrived to complete carnage. Eredith's army was massacred, the corpses were mutilated, mangled, impaled, and torn apart in ways no man or beast was capable of. Blood stained the foliage of Eredith that day. Hector's men were also part of the fallen.

Before we could escape the whole morbid scene, that's when they came. They came from the undergrowth, hiding, waiting to ambush us. And that's when I realized this was not the work of Hector but someone else, or rather, something else. Beasts sprung in the hundreds. They wore armor and wielded weapons, war bows, maces, swords, and several others. These fiends had great agility and strength. Additionally, they possessed claws and teeth sharp enough to tear through flesh. This hybrid species had the strength of beasts and the intelligence of man. I mean, the way they moved, it was coordinated, planned, and executed by a skilled tactician. We didn't see them coming.

The villains' features were so varied that they each could be considered a separate species. Some had horns on their heads like bulls, while others looked like what was discharged during an afterbirth. Others had multiple limbs, eyes, even heads. The ghastliest part was, they had faces. Human faces amalgamated with hideous features such as gelatinous skin and tusks. I get the feeling that they were parasites, because some took over reanimated corpses of the fallen and began to merge with them, but the unholy union was imperfect. This became apparent as you could see their organs and flesh rotting from the inside.

The whole thing was putrid. But taking over corpses was not the only thing they could do. They could regenerate and even take the appearance of anything they desire, like shapeshifters."

"That's how they were able to wield swords?" asked Lady Branson. "Yes, they could transform the shape of their hands at will so that they could better optimize weapon usage."

Richard continued his tale: "Soon they began slaughtering us like flies. There was nothing we could do to defend against such beasts. I ran several through to no avail. They killed our horses and ate them before our very eyes. Three tried to devour me, but I escaped into the trees but not before they started clawing and biting me first. I had to break free, so in the struggle I broke my own arm in several places. I fell from the tree to escape and landed on my leg. As they drew closer to my shock, they spoke the language of man, saying things like, *"This one's slippery,"* *"Let's change him."* I raised my blade. To my surprise the beast bowed not to me but to their master whom they referred to as Kraag.

I turned around to see Lord Anselm Blakeslee, all his features intact, his large coat made of animal hide, his enormous white beard and long balding hair. It was his visage alright except for one crucial detail. His eyes were completely black. The demon known as Kraag had possessed our Lord. Kraag spoke through Lord Anselm in an unnaturally harsh voice that almost sounded human but not quite, this invoked unease and revulsions because I could still hear Lord Anselm's stifled voice under Kraag's deeper more domineering one. Kraag said nonchalantly, *"We should at least tell them why they are dying."* He went on a tirade about humans and like kind being despicable and how they must be eradicated apparently. He used the same rhetoric on Lord Franklin saying so himself. Lord Franklin knew of their kind and said nothing. He could have prevented so much bloodshed. Why did he remain silent?" There was an inflection of anger in his voice as he spoke of Lord Franklin. Sir Richard got back to his harrowing tale. "Kraag said man's time and like kind was up."

"How did you escape?" inquired Giles.

"Kraag ordered the Horridus to leave the dead. He wanted people to know what happened there, so I played dead. But I think he knew because he looked right at me and said you will lose."

"How did you know they, eh, I mean Horridus were demons? You referred to this Kraag as the demon," asked Tim.

"Ehm, I don't really know. I guess I just assumed as they had such revolting appearances. What difference does it make?"

"Well demons have certain attributes. For instance they have poisonous auras that are highly contagious. It would certainly explain surviving such wounds," said Tim.

"Relax, Tim. I don't believe this man to be suffering from soul sickness. He didn't show any signs and demons are erratic, mindless forms of energy, the word is infected," said Giles.

"Do you think I'm turning into one of those infected? Is soul sickness even a thing? Could I infect everyone? By Arda, that must be why he let me go!" Sir Richard said fretfully.

"You're not an infected," said Alywin tersely. "Well, no need to be curt. Tell us why," said Tim.

Alywin sighed as though he regretted speaking then he said dejectedly, "My father was an infected, that's how I know."

"I apologize Alywin and to you, good sir, for troubling you with this infected business," said Tim.

"No need Tim, you were only being cautious," said Sir Richard.

Alywin with his head still down said, "I watched him suffer, it was agonizing. It was like every fiber of his being was destroying him from the inside. He begged for death but there was nothing I could do. Infected souls cannot die on their own without special equipment or extensive knowledge of hokraft. None of which are guaranteed and besides, I possessed neither; so instead, I had to watch his very soul kill him." Alywin concluded his unfortunate account.

"Did you not tell anyone of your misfortune?" asked Eva.

"I went straight to Sir Ulric, master of all things strange and otherworldly. I figured he would know what to do with my father's affliction. But he chalked it up as nonsense and told me not to bother Lord Franklin with it."

"The fool," Alywin said angrily through gritted teeth.

"The only one who wanted to help was the old woman Olga, but that was the year Lord Franklin placed a ban on hokraft. Anyone seen practicing it or even attempting it would be hung from the neck until dead. Look, I know few of you believe in omens, monsters, or demons. I mean, why would you? They're stuff of legends written in books before Mydra was considered Mydra, but two years ago there has been a resurgence of the supernatural that fit the description of these books. That's what I tried to warn Sir Ulric about, but I think he was more concerned with maintaining his position than listening to the ramblings of me and my mad father." Alywin placed emphasis on the word mad to describe to others how flippant Sir Ulric had been by describing Alywin's father as mad instead of in pain.

"My uncle has traveled outside of Arcadiem. He is a merchant, he said, in the far east. Infected are more common but there has been an increase in the presence of the supernatural overall. We Iiadecans live in isolation. The world is bigger and scarier than we once believed," said Tim. "You know somewhere in his diatribe of the human character, Kraag mentioned something. Monsters of old. Does that mean anything to you?" asked Sir Richard.

"I've heard some ramblings about them in the sacred text. It said they are the harbingers of the end of days and the end of humanity and like kind, but I didn't bother with it as they are only mentioned in brevity in the book of Noga and besides religion is a fickle thing, riddled with inconsistencies. It's not a reliable source of information," said Alywin.

"These monsters of old, as they're called, are real. I saw them with my own eyes. Our Lords ignored the signs out of hubris," said Sir Richard.

"Now perhaps our enemy is playing into our fears, after all Hector may have several castors at his disposal. They could be using faux magic," said Tim.

"This was not the work of some mere conjurer. Lord Anselm fell to darkness as will Lord Franklin if we're not careful," said Sir Richard vehemently.

He sighed then said, "I know what I saw. These creatures were real, Kraag was real. You doubt what you have not seen. Lord Anselm eyes were black, wrought with possession no amount of faux magic could have caused that."

"So, Hector either has powerful enough magic wielders to summon creatures such as these or the monsters of old are indeed real. Either way this war is lost," said Tim.

"If Sir Richard is right, then this war is the least of our worries. With the monsters of old, the fate of the whole world is at stake and if what Kraag says is true, we are destined to lose," said Giles.

There was a demoralizing mood in the barracks, and suddenly their efforts seemed futile in the grand scheme of things. This shared sense of melancholia manifested itself in the form of discomfited silence, the type of silence that can occur during bereavement. Because emotions and cathartic reactions are looked at as less than and frankly quite useless when the object of one's reactions cannot be change say impending doom. Inevitabilities are rare in most realities. Certainly, the only ones conceivable are death and pain other than that, nothing is set in stone as the adage goes. However, the paroxysm of pessimism may spread the falsehood that certain things are inevitable when they are not. Even those who claim to be ardent defenders of veracity fall into the pitfall of misconstruing what is factual from predictions. To understand the difference between the two, we must first determine what is fact and what is a prediction. This may seem like an obtuse semantic exercise, but it will make things easier down the line. Facts are analogous with truths, things that cannot be refuted. Pardon this digression reader but I ask you to temporarily abandon the philosophy that our perception of reality is ultimately unclear and that only one's own mind is certain otherwise known as solipsism. Additionally, we are only dealing with the corporeality hence, we must be very secular in our diction and descriptions. I am not suggesting that these philosophies are somehow irrelevant or incorrect, just that for one to define something, we must first supplant doubt with certainty. Forgive me for the verbosity, but explanations are in order when disputing fallacies. A prediction is foretelling something based on observations hence, it can be refuted. I can say with great certainty that nothing is inevitable but death, therefore there is no excuse for negativity, just because a predicted outcome looks grim, because the reality is there are two options in this paradigm, inaction, and action. Neither option has guaranteed results. However, action may lead to a more favorable outcome. Based on observation, doing something usually results in something whereas not doing something does not. When comparing action to inaction, the superlative option seems obvious, but to a pessimist the latter is the more favorable option. The reason being is that for a pessimist misery has become so palpable that any other feeling is muted. Hence misery is the dominating emotion and it's hidden under the guise of logic when it is diametrically opposite. This deception runs so deep that the pessimist refuses to accept anything positive even if it's presented in a logical manner. Pessimism equals inaction and a refusal to do anything about a situation. Life is a game of chance. If you refuse to play the game, you might lose dearly as opposed to playing it.

Finally, Lady Branson broke the silence partly to make herself feel better and partly to increase morale in the barracks since the misery had become so palpable, she said, "Kraag cannot be greater than Arda, so he cannot know things that Arda does not. If we trust in Arda, then all will be well in the end, just as it's always been."

"I wish I had your faith milady, but I fear Arda abandoned us long ago and let darkness seep in," said Sir Richard to which Lady Branson responded, "*Thou must not deviate from the path of righteousness at the very sign of trouble* (reciting a line from sacred text). Arda does not want us to falter at the sign of darkness, if we trust in our God then we will be victorious. Even in death our spirits (In Mirthadine spirits existence is not proven) will transcends into the great heavens where Kraag can never harm us, but that can only happen if we believe, believe in our God, and nothing can harm us. Even if Kraag is responsible for our end in this world, know this, this world is not the end of everything as long as we believe that we cannot lose not to Kraag not to Hector nor anyone else. We must stand tall and face evil at all costs. We owe it to the brave souls fighting outside to be strong because as long as we show resolve against malice, we will receive Arda's blessing and that is the greatest reward anyone could ask for."

"You speak like a cleric milady. I must confess my spirits are quite invigorated now," said Sir Richard.

"Agreed. Such eloquence, milady. You have a knack for orating," said Tim.

"Thank you," Lady Branson blushed.

"Yes, Elysant is quite the speaker, just like her mother," said Giles while smiling at Lady Branson.

Amidst the renewed merriment there was one person that remained silent, not in sadness but penetrating contemplation. This prompted Tim to ask, "Are you all right Alywin?"

Alywin ignored the question and said, "Kraag could be telling a lie just to scare us."

"What do you mean?" asked Giles.

"Don't you find it convenient that he references holy text from the Arcadiem continent? There are other holy books around the world. Why pick the book of Noga?"

"You bring up a good point, especially since some religions have multiple deities and no tales about the end of days," said Eva.

"Exactly. Kraag could be an infected and not this insurmountable force destined to kill us all. I believe he is deceiving us," said Alywin.

"And he's using the war as a distraction. If we survive this, we must tell Lord Franklin," said Tim.

"Lord Franklin already knows didn't you hear Sir Richard?" Alywin said brusquely.

"But we must tell someone. This is bigger than all of us," insisted Tim. "You're right. If we survive this battle, someone must warn Steward King Godwin Ackles at Mirama," said Giles. (City in the Wood, Mirama, is a city located in Mydra and where the true king of Iiadec is crowned. Godwin acted as steward king after King Gavin Franklin died. He is believed to act impartially and crown the person who is victorious in war as king.)

Then Sir Richard said anemically, "I believe my time is up in this world, but I still feel Arda's blessing thanks to you milady, and I thank all of you for staying with me, but I'm afraid I must go." Richard said this as copious amounts of blood seeped through his bandages. The wounds on his kidneys and gut had reopened. He lay on his back, barely breathing. Lady Branson and others rushed toward his side. Lady Branson placed both hands on Richard's wound in order to clot it, but it was to no avail. The warm blood oozed through her fingers. Others did the same with Sir Richard's other wounds, but they were met with equal results. Sir Richard looked at Giles and said, "Looks like my luck is running out."

"Stay strong," said Giles.

Sir Richard smiled faintly and said, "At least we can rule out soul sickness. The pain is not so much."

"Stay with me, Richard," Lady Branson said, her voice quavered, and others fought back tears. Eva cried profusely.

Sir Richard touched Lady Branson's hand, then wiped away a tear forming on her face. Lady Branson was shaking until Sir Richard calmed her down with his voice. "Hey, hey, you did everything you could. All of you have. I commend you all, but I will not survive, but I know you all will survive."

When Sir Richard began to stabilize, he said, "I want to give you something. It was in my bag, err." Before Sir Richard could continue, Tim brought him a brown leather bag. Sir Richard opened the bag and within its contents were some incendiaries and a map of Corithni castle plans.

"My plan was to hand this over to Lord Franklin before I was attacked by Kraag's minions. It was intercepted and taken from one of Hector's soldiers at the battle of Rilek. My guess is that the enemy was trying to undermine the castle," said Sir Richard.

"By God, why didn't you mention this before? Hector's army could be building tunnels right now!" said Tim.

Lady Branson gave Tim a fierce scowl, to which Tim responded saying rather ashamedly, "Er, Sorry."

"No, the fault was mine. I was not of the right mind and lost track of time," said Sir Richard.

"That's quite alright. I don't think Hector would risk mining. The archers would see his men digging from the ramparts," said Alywin. He looked at the plans and he furrowed his brow while observing them. "These plans are dated too, and the usage of incendiaries could quickly be extinguished by water. This was a poor attempt to storm Corithni," said Alywin.

"Still, these types of explosives could start quite a blaze," said Tim as he opened a spherical container of one of the incendiaries that contained a liquid mixture of pine resin, napatha, quicklime and other combustible materials.

"The castle will most likely get overrun. I thought this could be a means of escape. Lord Anselm told me about the tunnels constructed by the builders beneath this very keep. The explosives would be used as a distraction for the besiegers while the innocent could escape," said Sir Richard. (Terrestrial manipulation involves the ability to manipulate the terrain around oneself. However, not all terrain can be manipulated land that is claimed by a seal cannot be manipulated. Such seals are often placed on castles and other large landmarks where people reside. These seals are created by the blood of the master builder, the main architect of the castle or structure. Other seals can be placed on a structure by other builders. However, those seals only work if they have permission from the master builder. The master builder seal will always override any other seal. The term builder refers to a type of terrestrial manipulator that is responsible for the construction of a castle or structure. The seals of the master builder or builders can only be temporarily broken by those sharing blood with the original master builder of the structure or castle. In addition, immovable terrain can only be manipulated if one shares blood with the individual or individuals whom place the seal.)

"Even if that were possible, we know no one who knows of the alleged tunnels under the keep or anyone who is kin to the master builder of Corithni castle. The castle is over 200 years old," said Alywin.

"Um, excuse me. I believe I can help," said a voice. The group turned around to see Sarah, who looked quite embarrassed to have been eavesdropping on their conversation. She then cleared her throat and said, "I am kin to the master builder. My name is Sarah Mason."

CHAPTER FIVE

BROTHERS

[*moments earlier*]

The dragon evaded some projectiles and others, that struck the dragon's skin, were deflected by its muscular body. It whizzed past the battlements but then it stopped abruptly mid-flight. It slowly turned around and looked directly towards three individuals standing on the ramparts in a crowd of archers on the eastern wall.

"Edmund, it's looking right at us!" said one of the figures, a tall young man about age eighteen. He was frightened, but did not falter in movement or speech. He wore plated armor with chain mail and an arming doublet underneath. The doublet acted as a shield for the recent cold front that had mysteriously shrouded Mydra. It was not yet winter (seasons in Mirthadine resemble our own) yet the artic chill was already here. This was peculiar because no snow fell from the sky yet temperatures where at times below freezing, naturally things did not bode well for the besiegers who had to stand about meandering in the cold. Whereas the defenders had the privilege of staying warm within the confines of the castle walls. Nonetheless, many within the castle took the early onset cold as a bad omen of unfortunate things to come. Some defenders wore on their chest plates the engraved Franklin's house vigil. Most of them, however, wore only chain mail and gambesons, with archers having the vigil engraved on their helms. Most of the knights wore full plated armor. The one known as Edmund was a ginger who stood about 6-foot-2.

He had a muscular build and had features that greatly resembled his late uncle Gavin Franklin. He was twenty-five. Edmund readied his bow. The dragon opened its mouth in response. You could hear the crackling of a combustive force within its throat along with the sound of the beast inhaling.

"Now!" said one of the men standing next to him. He had long black hair tied in a ponytail. He resembled Albert Franklin, and he was in his early twenties and stood 5-foot-10. All the archers, including Edmund, concentrated fire on the dragon's mouth and eyes. Arrows sailed into the air towards the dragon, but the dragon evaded them by flying further above.

Edmund bombarded the dragon with missiles as did the other archers, but the projectiles did little more than agitate the dragon. Some of the barbs even broke off on impact.

"Aim for the eyes!" said the man with the likeness to Albert Franklin. "We are aiming for the eyes, John. The blasted thing's moving too fast," said Edmund frustratedly.

"Maybe we should try lightning," said the tall, slim young man standing next to Edmund. He stood about 6-foot-5 and had shaven blonde hair.

"That's a good idea, William. It may be the only weapon we have strong enough to pierce its hardened exterior," said John.

"And it's a lot easier to land a lightning shot than a trick shot to the eye on a moving target," said Edmund.

"Alright men, brace yourselves. When the dragon comes towards us, fire lightning bolts at it. Make sure you don't miss. We don't want to add any damage to the castle because of recklessness," said John.

Before he could finish speaking, the dragon swooped down and breathed fire upon them. "Everyone, find cover!" screamed Edmund. The men were panic-stricken and several attempted to flee down the steps of the battlements where they perished in flame. Edmund, William, and John hid behind the merlons of the crenulated wall. Where they retaliated by firing lightning bolts through arrow slits.

The dragon once again evaded the lightning bolts. (It is important to note that most individuals cannot manifest lightning faster than the speed of sound like normal lightning that requires a considerable amount of practice and a specific technique) William poked his head above the merlon. "The dragon's gone to the keep!" shouted William.

"Damn!" Edmund responded.

"Archers, split your forces. Some of you focus your fire on the besiegers to the east wall. The rest of you distract that dragon and make sure at all costs it doesn't attack the keep," said John.

"Yes, milord," said the archers.

Then suddenly an assailant arrow whizzed over the wall with the barb striking John's temple. He fell to the floor.

"John!!" Edmund and William said in unison. Four more arrows came over the wall. The men all dove behind the merlons of the parapet wall. Edmund drew his blade and yelled fire. There was a multitude of projectiles being exchanged between the besiegers and the defenders. Over the melee, John shouted, "This is all a distraction!" He had just regained consciousness and was tending to the fresh wound on his temple where the barb had grazed him.

"John, you're alive!" Edmund said ecstatically. "Praise Arda," said William.

"Tame your mirth if this is (John pointing to his wound) any indication then we have been quite careless. The enemy is using the dragon as a distraction, so its forces can draw near the weakened wall," said John.

"Their archers have advanced considerably. They're now about 70 feet from the castle, within killing range milord," said a bow man. The exchange of arrow fire dialed down as the defenders hid behind the merlons and besiegers deemed it unwise to waste artillery. Hence, they refocused efforts on the battering ram.

"What do we do then? We can't just let the dragon burn down the keep," said Edmund.

"Well, we only need two people distracting the dragon, Carac here's the best Archer in Corithni," said William.

Edmund, perplexed, asked, "I'm not following. What exactly are you suggesting?"

"He's saying we carry out with the original plan only instead of splitting our forces we simply use Carac to concentrate fire on the dragon while I blind it with light," said John.

"Why not lightning? It's more effective against the dragon," asked Edmund.

"It's proven time and time again that despite its size, it's surprisingly agile and a stray bolt could set the keep on fire. Isial rock is only so fire resistant, it's not worth the risk," said William.

"Alright, fight this war on two fronts. Carac, ready your bow. Make sure you hit your target. You're not expected to fell the dragon, but if you can, do it. Archers, concentrate your fire on that battering ram, there are pesky archers out there so make sure you're shielded behind the wall," said Edmund with authority.

The men did as they were told. They aimed their bows downward, slaying twenty infantrymen on the besieger's side. The defenders also hurled down stones over the crenels of the battlements. At least two stones struck the assailants below enough to incapacitate them. The bowmen rained down arrows at those wheeling the battering ram, but the siege engine was protected by a triangular roof made of animal hide and wood. The defenders tossed stones at the siege engine, they managed to damage the roof slightly, but the siege engine was still fully operational. The defenders had trouble aiming their bows at a downward angle into the wagon, especially with the limitations of the arrow slits now that the invaders were clinging to the castle wall to avoid arrow fire from above. At this point in time, it was more effective to throw down debris than hail arrow fire. The silver lining was that the besiegers where too busy trying to cover their heads than break down the eastern wall. This did not, however, mean that tensions were eased. The battle for the eastern wall was a deadly game of anticipation. The besiegers had the numbers, but the defenders were protected behind the castle walls. They knew that even if they managed to break down the wall, they would still have to navigate through the rubble and there was no way Lord Franklin's army would stand idly by as Hector's forces entered the castle. There were probably dozens of pike men, swordsmen, archers, and crossbowmen behind the walls. The besiegers were hoping the dragon would either dispatch most of Lord Franklin's forces from the inside or distract the defenders long enough to enter through the wall.

Several of the defenders attempted to fire arrows down at the besiegers, especially the ones operating the siege engine, but exposed themselves to enemy fire because they were aiming from the crenels. As a result, twelve souls were felled. Carac drew his bowstring and released it. The arrow whizzed though the air and narrowly missed the dragon's eye. Carac shot six more arrows at the dragon. Three hit its tail, two hit its midsection, and the last sailed past its wings. The dragon did not even flinch but drew closer towards the keep.

"Aim for its face. We need to draw its attention, hurry," said John.

Carac fired an arrow that grazed the dragon's nostrils. This caused it to flail its head about in irritation. Next, John summoned some light energy to directly obscure the dragon's vision. The dragon was visibly vexed. Carac fired four more arrows at the dragon while it was distracted. The dragon evaded the projectiles and moved away from the keep and up into the sky, where it was out of range and seemingly out of sight. Carac readied his bow at the beast's silhouette. But was stopped by John.

"Don't bother. It's out of range. No need to waste artillery, save it for the eastern wall," said John.

"Yes, milord. Erm milord?" John turned to Carac. "Don't you think it's strange the dragon didn't burn down more of the castle?"

"Yes," said John. This time, staring at the silhouette of the dragon in the sky John said.

"It's like the beast is looking for something and we're just in the way. Although I don't think it's acting on its own accord." "Do you think it's found it?" asked Carac.

"I don't know and I'm not sure I want to," said John. He stood still, preoccupied with the dragon in the sky.

"Milord, look out!" Carac shoved John to the ground and used his body as a shield to protect John from enemy fire. It was a fire-hex that would have struck John in the head had Carac not intervened. Both Carac and John ducked behind the merlons.

"John!" screamed Edmund.

"I'm all right, thanks to Carac," said John. "Whew, almost lost you twice," said William.

Then there was the deafening sound of solid wood hitting the stone curtain on the eastern wall below. The wall was breaking, and the enemy was gaining ground. "What are we going to do about that, though?" asked John.

"Don't worry. I've got a plan," said William. William grabbed a spear from the ramparts. He touched the metal tip and imbued it with electricity. He then quickly hurled it over the battlements towards the siege engine. The spear struck one of the besiegers operating the battering ram in the skull, killing him instantly. As the spear tip went through the roof of the battering ram with electricity still on its tip, William was able to amplify the current, killing the remaining men inside. (This technique is known as the phantom touch. In order for an elemental to channel electricity through an object, that object must be a good conductor. Secondly, in order for the elemental to manipulate the electricity channeled into the object, the object and the elemental must not be parted for more than 30 seconds. The time elapsed for the object to be active is known as the phantom touch. Phantom touch is an extremely rare technique and difficult to master given its nature.)

Suddenly an aggregate of magic wielders appeared in the distance, along with a 500 strong new mercenary army. They seemed to come out of thin air, simultaneously, which would have been impossible because kiklu transportation, as it is known in Mirthadine, is limited to only two objects at the same time. William looked at the figures in the distance. From what he could make out, the group wore long robes and golden masks, concealing their faces.

"Who are they?" William asked himself under his breath.

About a quarter of them dissipated into black mist along with half the army adjacent to the mysterious cloaked figures. They reappeared at the wall at such an overwhelming ferocity that they caught the defenders by surprise. A flurry of spells was hurled at the defenders. Hexes ranging from very basic fire charms such as the charm Fithra (old tongue for fire) to concentrated beams of light such as the spell Anlaga (old tongue for compressed energy). The men at the ramparts did their best to fend off the magic wielders and Hector's reinforcements, who were now using siege ladders. The besiegers used sorcerer fire to help traverse the eastern wall. (The siege ladders were part of the things teleported by the magic wielders.)

"Aim for the castors," bellowed John as he kicked down a siege ladder, killing four besiegers in the process. Several besiegers were able to scale the wall and were locked in combat with the defenders. It was hard to make sense of what was going on over the melee. All that could be heard was the raucous clanging of swords and other metallic weapons. It was also difficult to see as both the defenders and the besiegers were packed together like sardines. Several fell from the battlements. Because of this, the besiegers, amidst the brawl, divided their forces. Half attempted to hex the weakened wall while the remaining attacked the defenders, all while keeping their distance to avoid arrow fire. Not that it mattered. The bowmen were too preoccupied with being attacked to be concerned with other approaching threats. As you can imagine, the ramparts were particularly crowded, hence, there was a lot of half-swording.

Edmund fought several besiegers. One attempted to strike him with a vertical cut but Edmund struck him in the face with the pommel of his blade. The besieger staggered and attempted to re-align his helmet, given Edmund apt time to kick him over the battlements. Another attempted to strike Edmund from behind. Edmund narrowly evaded the attack, the besieger then delivered a down cut which Edmund parried by holding his blade horizontally with his right hand firmly grasping his grip and his left hand on the blade. The force of the blow caused Edmund to stumble slightly, so he rested his weight on his back foot to account for the change in balance. Unbeknownst to him, another assailant charged at him from the right. Before the assailant could act, he was struck in the back with a battle-axe. His lifeless body hit the floor with blood seeping through his armor.

William, holding the battle-axe, said, "We're overrun, what should we do?"

"Just keep fighting. I'm sure John will think of something," shouted Edmund. He struck his opponent with the pommel of his sword by grabbing the blade of his long sword with both hands and swinging it like a baseball bat. The would-be attacker collapsed on the floor instantly. Meanwhile, Carac and John fought side by side, half-swording their way through the throng of soldiers. Carac was teetering precariously over the battlements as he had been fighting a foe. Both had been somehow disarmed, so they resorted to grappling. That was when Carac's opponent gained the upper hand and pushed Carac towards the edge. Fortunately for Carac, John pulled the foe off him and he regained his footing. John then proceeded to stab the assailant in the eye slit of his helmet with a dagger. The attacker groaned in pain before perishing from the wound. John handed Carac back his sword.

"Thank you, milord," said Carac.

"Don't mention it. The castors (a colloquial term for magic wielders) have concentrated their efforts on the wall. It has relieved the pressure off the ramparts," said John.

"Well, I reckon they don't want to strike their own men," said Carac, his voice strained from struggling to kick a besieger over the ramparts.

"We must get to the castors before they breech the wall!" screamed John. He, too, was engaged in combat with several besiegers. One assailant delivered a thrust directed at John's neck all while half-swording. But John deflected and responded by striking the attacker in the chest plate with the cross guard of his sword, hitting the surface of his enemies' armor. This caused a noticeable dent in the armor and the assailant stumbled backward. John had aimed for his opponent's head, but the strike seemed to be effective nonetheless. Before John could deliver a fatal blow, he was quickly pursued by two other assailants. This type of close quarter combat skirmish was common in the ramparts. Both parties fought relentlessly until they were stricken with fatigue and even then, they did not give in entirely. Because forfeiting such a stronghold such as the eastern wall would be folly. It was the turning point in the war for the besiegers. Losing it would be loss of ground that they desperately needed to be able to penetrate the supposed impregnable Corithni and, for the defenders, loss of the eastern wall would be the end of Corithni as they knew it. Things were looking dire for the defenders. Several of their numbers were depleting and the besiegers were approaching in the multitudes. On the eastern wall, the besiegers had abandoned siege ladder tactics and refocused their efforts in assisting the magic wielders along the crevice in the wall, for the magic wielders had summoned another, albeit smaller and less protected, battering ram. The new siege engine was 100ft long and, like the old one, had a triangular roof made of wood and animal hide. The wood was made of much weaker material and the animal hide was less condensed than the last. (It also operated on wheels.) But given the time constraints, it was still an impressive siege engine.

There were sixteen besiegers left on the eastern ramparts and ten defenders. There had previously been 56 and 43, respectively. Edmund, Carac, John and William, along with six other defenders, stood back-to-back as the approaching besiegers surrounded them. There was a drawn out tension and an eerie silence before one of the besiegers yelled "charge!" Edmund shot a lightning bolt at the man leading the charge, but he evaded the attack. John fired another bolt at the charger, but he simply evaded that attack as well. (The brothers had previously not resorted to lightning attacks for fear of hitting their own men.) Before Edmund or John could manifest more lightning, they were in arm's distance of their opponents. There was a clashing clanging of swords, axes, and war hammers. One could hear the metallic sounds of long swords pummels hitting helmets, axes hitting breast plates and hammers denting plated armor and the groans of the felled warriors. Only six defenders remained, including the Franklin brothers and Carac. There was something admirable about the way they fought. They were like a well-organized machine, not wasting a single strike nor wasting any opportunity to strike their enemies. The same could not be said about their adversaries, for what they had in numbers they lacked in discipline. As a result, the defenders slew many of their foes until their numbers nearly matched the enemy.

There were now nine besiegers and six defenders on the battlements. Seeing their fallen brethren caused the besiegers to approach more cautiously. Being impetuous would mean certain death for they no longer had the number advantage. And despite being primarily archers, apart from the Franklin brothers, the defenders had proven to be adept enough with melee weapons. It was as if they were prepared for armored foes scaling the wall. This was something a besieger would expect from shrewd Lord Franklin. Nonetheless, Lord Franklin's resources were sparse. Etlio, Eredith, and the other regions only provided so much. This was evident in the armor the defenders wore. It was outdated and tatty, most likely passed down from generations. The situation was exacerbated by a severe lack of blacksmiths. It seemed many of the defenders, apart from the archer units and knights, did not even wear helmets. (The archers wore archer's helms/kettle helmets.) Which was peculiar because the archers usually would not see close quarter combat. So that begged the question, why would Lord Franklin allocate his resources in such a way? Perhaps it was because of arrogance, honestly believing Corithni to be impregnable or maybe he tactically predicted the archers would be attacked first, hence they needed the bulk of the resources since they were the first line of defense.

The latter was probably the most likely reason. The few who wore helmets that weren't knights mostly had the spectacle type often worn by Mylecan warriors. They were nasal helmets that provided very little protection of the face, unlike a great helm or a bascinet. To be fair, these nasal helmets were reinforced with mail coifs and provided a greater field of vision. Still, the defenders had proven their worth during this siege, underestimating them would be erred. Especially since the Franklin boys were elementals and now had space to attack without fear of killing their comrades since many of them were deceased. The besiegers crept forward slowly.

Carac whispered, "Why don't we use soul weapons? We can cut through their armor."

"Their armor is made from Anactuken (*anak-tooken*) steel, designed to cancel out most halo-soul energy. That's the reason the enemy has not resorted to such attacks. (Anactuken steel only cancels out external halo-soul energy that comes in direct contact with the metal. Additionally, Anactuken steel cannot cancel out soul manifest once it's been fully transformed into an element. Furthermore, the steel only cancels out halo-soul manifest. Additionally, it shows resistance against standard magical attacks, although not totally impervious). But we can still use elemental attacks. Everyone get behind me and my brothers," said John. Edmund looked at John and said, "So we're doing this?" "Yeah," John replied.

"Okay then," Edmund said. Sparks of electricity appeared on his free hand (left hand). (The process of converting soul manifest into an element occurs in the blink of an eye. There are very few that can see the transition.)

William also harnessed electrical energy from his free hand while John's left hand was glowing with bright light. (Channeling soul energy through inorganic objects is quite difficult, hence people usually use their bodies, particularly the hands. Additionally, the more solid and object is, the more difficult it is for soul energy to travel through it due to the arrangement of the molecules within said object. That is why it is more difficult to channel soul energy with a clenched fist than an open palm. It is important to note that it's not impossible to channel and distribute soul energy in inorganic objects. Several in history have accomplish such a feat but it's not a simple endeavor and it drains soul energy.)

John stuck his left hand out towards the approaching assailants, an intense bright light emitted from his hand. The besiegers shielded their eyes. William and Edmund fired several lightning bolts at the besiegers. Two were struck in the chest and died instantly. Four others were struck in the head and perished. The other besiegers evaded their strikes. The remaining three besiegers charged at the defenders.

One of the besiegers said, "I can't see where they are," to which another responded, "It doesn't matter. We know they're in front of us."

"Maybe we should retreat," said another besieger.

"There's no fucking where to go, you stupid git. Just avert your eyes and fight. I, for one, am not going to stand here and wait to be fried by fucking lightning bolts." (The besiegers had this conversation while evading lightning bolts). As the assailants approached, William and Edmund fired more lightning bolts. The attackers evaded the bolts as they advanced. One besieger came close to striking John, and he was later poleaxed by Carac. The other two besiegers were quickly cut down by Carac.

"Well, that's the last of them," said one of the defenders who wielded a war hammer.

"It's not over yet. We still need archers on the ramparts to defend the wall," responded John.

"Carac, call for reinforcements," said John. "Yes milord," replied Carac. Before Carac could turn around, a masked figure appeared, surrounded by tendrils of black smoke. The figure appeared male, judging from the physique. The individual stood about 6 feet tall; the mask was gold, ornately decorated with multiple spirals.

He wore chain mail with a longsword attached to his sword belt. The sword was securely placed in the scabbard. Outside the scabbard was a small leather pocket in which a wooden wand was placed. The man's eyes were crimson and his irises kept rotating, counterclockwise, clockwise, and then counterclockwise again. The men stood, transfixed at the sight that beheld insomuch that they were motionless. Then, within the blink of an eye, the mysterious figure vanished and simultaneously fifty more besiegers appeared on the battlements, all clad in plated armor from head to toe, wielding an assortment of weapons from spiked maces and battleaxes to halberds. The Franklin brothers looked at each other in disbelief, shocked by what they had just witnessed. The new assailants had special engravings on the armor and weapons that resembled some sort of language or code, unbeknownst to the defenders. The six defenders looked at each other in acquiescence. It was time. Their enemies had made them desperate. It was the 11th hour, a pinnacle moment in the entirety of the war. The Franklins realized that the odds were against them, and that this final technique would mean that they would forfeit their lives, but they had no choice. Their lives were forfeit, anyway. They knew they could not face the might of fifty armed besiegers without resorting to some extreme.

"If we are to die, so be it. But know this, we will never surrender Corithni!" shouted Edmund to the besiegers.

"Pride is one of the greatest maladies of man and like kind, stupidity disguised as bravery. You have lost. Surrender the castle and you can have your lives, for if you don't, it will be no quarter," said a besieger holding a halberd, presumably the leader of this particular group.

"You speak diplomacy now when your people have a dragon attacking my people!" said, Edmund angrily.

"You must be Edmund son of Albert Franklin. You have a likeness to your uncle Gavin, they told me about you, stubborn like his father. It's one thing to sacrifice oneself for a cause but to sacrifice your people is selfish," said the besieger.

"I will not mince words with my enemies. My father is the rightful king and, as for my people, they would rather die than kneel before a scoundrel and deceiver, but I wouldn't expect you to understand. Your kind fights only for coin," said Edmund.

"You are sending them to their graves. I know what you and your brothers are planning, and it will only result in senseless death. You can end this right now. Nobody has to die."

The besieger opened the visor of his bascinet helmet. He had the face of a middle-aged man, and a vertical facial scar that intersected his eyebrow eyelid and cheek. It was an old wound from the looks of it. His right eye was clouded implying it was no longer functional because of scar tissue. "I am Terrowin commander of the red vultures."

"You choose a scavenger as a vigil?" asked Edmund.

"Vultures are necessary just like us. They devour the things other animals are unwilling to consume, thus relieving nature of harmful impurities. Like the vulture, we do things that others are unwilling to do. We are necessary," said Terrowin, lingering on the word necessary for a second time.

The repetitive hypnotic nature in which he uttered the word made Edmund particularly uneasy. Edmund studied the face of this enigmatic stranger. Their countenances were diametrically opposite. Terrowin was one of lucidity and calmness, whereas Edmund's countenance was one of perplexity and agitation.

"I tell you this to show you that I'm not a monster. When I was a young man-"

Terrowin was interrupted by John.

"Spare us the useless parables. My brother cannot yield the eastern wall, and do not play coy, for I am no dullard. What is it you truly want?" Terrowin was not fazed by such blatant hostility. He smiled, not in a condescending way, but like he had genuine respect for his enemy. "The blood of the father runs deep, but the river is shallow," said Terrowin. "Your words are of no consequence, and I care not their meaning. Now what do you want?" John said firmly with emphasis on the word want. "I desire nothing. I speak only of Lord Hector's will. He insists that you yield the castle in order to avoid further bloodshed," said Terrowin. "Terrowin, we are the wrong ones to ask this of and if you think we would undermine our father, you are sorely mistaken. Our resolve is just as potent. We will never waver, even at the cost of our lives," said William. Suddenly, the Franklin brothers started to radiate with blue light (blue light is the most common aura color). Because of incandescence, there was a strong hot gust of wind that came from the brothers, which caused individuals near them to brace themselves. In addition, there were sparks of electricity in the air, most likely from free roaming electrons now in an excited state due to the abrupt change in energy levels. To the observer, the Franklin brothers appeared to be obscured in luminous blue light. There was also the smell of sulfur in the air.

During both the usage of core and halo-soul manifest, light energy is emitted because the soul becomes excited, hence the warm wind gust and sparks of electricity. During the use of soul manifest, the soul heats up and releases energy. That energy appears as light energy. The reason the individual harnessing this energy does not burn is because inert gases are released from the body and air such as argon, krypton, and nitrogen to prevent the combustion of oxygen, similar to a filament in a light bulb. For instance, without the assistance of the inert gases, heat from an excited soul can reach 3000K and even higher depending on the soul. There is a period just before the usage of the core-soul manifest known as the intermediary. During this period, soul energy may glow and emit heat. Also, the smell of Sulphur indicates the total depletion of halo-soul manifest. When core-manifest is used, gas aggregates and slowly encircles the vessel. This gas forms during halo-soul manifest, but it does not surround the vessel (the person harnessing soul energy) but can appear in close proximity, said gas can be used to create concentrated energy beams by converting gas to plasma. Additionally, during halo-soul manifest, very little light is emitted. The gas produced in core-soul manifest is translucent in nature and glows. This gas is made up of a combination of unknown elements found only in Mirthadine. It is different from the inert gases used to protect the vessel from excitation. To simplify things, the usage halo-soul manifest involves little to no glowing because the light energy is not as visible. Core-soul manifest involves lots of glowing and gas surrounds the vessel.

Seeing such a raw display of defiance and power slightly vexed Terrowin, but he maintained his calm demeanor. He said, "very well" and closed his visor.

The besiegers charged at the defenders, but the defenders stood their ground. Edmund muttered something under his breath that was inaudible to everyone but him. He raised his sword in the air, grasping the hilt with both hands. It was immersed in electricity. Flashes of blue lightning surrounded the Franklin brothers. The scintillating display from the electrical discharge started to dissipate from John when he saw the platoon of 50 defenders armored from head to toe with the Franklin house crest engraved on their chest plates. Their armor was newly forged and burnished. They wore basinet helmets; it was quite a rare sight to see such pristine armor on the battlefield. Judging from the appearance of these heavily armed warriors, they were knights that serve under Lord Albert Franklin. They most likely traveled on foot from the barbican and northern wall. They wielded a variety of weapons, the longsword, which was standard for every knight in Iiadec, several melee weapons, mostly of the trauma variety, which included, but were not limited to, clubs, maces, war hammers and battleaxes. They also wielded pole arms such as poleaxes, spears, glaives, and halberds.

Edmund and William saw the knights approaching and their electrical fields started to dissipate as well. The knights positioned themselves in front of the previous six defenders. This halted the advance of both the defenders and besiegers on the eastern ramparts. One of the knights turned around and lifted his visor while the other knights prevented the besiegers from attacking with their formidable presence alone. The knight had a youthful face. Judging from his features, he was probably not much older than Edmund. He had short, wavy, sandy-brown hair and a shaven face.

Knights that served under Lord Albert Franklin are required to cut their hair (no longer than neck length) and keep shaven or short facial hair. Of course, there are exceptions to the rule. A knight who has served a certain number of years or knights who have accomplished great feats can grow out their hair, provided it's well-groomed.

"My lords, are you alright?!" said the young knight. "We're fine, Sir Avery, but where is Sir Peter?" said John.

"He went to deal with the dragon with some infantrymen and archers; a bit of a maverick, that one," replied Sir Avery.

Sir Avery looked at the Franklin brothers. He saw they were quite fatigued. There was a deep look of concern on his face, this concern intensified when he smelt the Sulphur in the air. Sir Avery's eyes widened, and before he could speak, Edmund stopped him.

"Don't worry, we didn't go through with it."

Sir Avery sighed with relief. "But you're still out of soul energy, here." He first extended his forearm out to Edmund. Edmund was hesitant to grab it, but eventually held it. John held Edmund's forearm and William held Johns. There was a transfer of ATP, which was converted to soul energy. This exchange of energy lasted a matter of seconds, but the impact was significant. Sir Avery was visibly fatigued but endured, and the Franklin brothers regained their energy.

Sir Avery removed his helmet and gave it to Edmund. "I couldn't," said Edmund.

"You're going to need it my lord, if you're going to take on the dragon," said Sir Avery.

"How did you know?" asked Edmund.

"We've known you, my lords, for a long time," said a tall knight with his visor open. He held two bascinet helms in his hands and handed them to William and John respectively. "These are for you."

"Thank you, Sir Baret," said John. "May Arda bless you all," said Edmund.

"May his blessings extend to you as well (referring to the Franklin brothers). Now go. We will be fine here," said Sir Avery.

The Franklin brothers put on their helmets. When they turned around, they faced the three original comrades that were with them during the first attack on the ramparts. Before any of them could protest, Carac said sternly, "We're going with you, milords!"

"Aye!" said the other two defenders.

"Okay, but take your bows with you," said John.

The six comrades preceded down the staircase of the battlements and headed towards the bailey where the dragon was. Edmund peered off into the distance and saw quite a lot of destruction. The wall separating the main and lower bailey was destroyed and the fire in the main bailey was nearly extinguished. To his dismay, the dragon was nowhere in sight.

There was a lone figure in the distance dampening the anemic flames in the center of a pile of ash. Edmund peered and craned his neck to better see this figure. He could make out a boy about the age of thirteen with curly brown hair and a brown tunic.

"Godfrey?" Edmund said.

Godfrey turned around and caught Edmund's gaze. The Franklin brothers lifted their visors.

"M-Milords," Godfrey said.

"Godfrey, what are you doing here? You're supposed to be at the keep. Lady Branson must be worried sick," said John.

"So how did you escape?" said William playfully.

"Well, I slipped past—" said Godfrey before he was interrupted by John, who scowled at William and said, "Don't encourage him!"

"Where are the dragon and Sir Peter?" Edmund asked. Godfrey relayed the details of his account with King Mavid.

"You fought a fully grown dragon!" said William, not even attempting to contain his excitement.

"William, focus! Its clear Hector is using some advanced Hokraft. Dragons can't be hexed so easily, especially an Orthrya Vepid. We should tread carefully," said John.

"You know you don't have to make up words to make yourself seem more intelligent," teased William. John rolled his eyes in response.

Edmund's thoughts were racing. He thought of Giselle, a low-born woman, about twenty-two, whom Edmund had impregnated. His father was unaware, but his mother knew. He could not be with a lowborn. Albert Franklin would not allow it, and he didn't want his seed to be terminated or risk the health of Giselle. Hence, Edmund's mother Rose concocted a lie that Giselle was impregnated by another lowborn. This, however, did not sit well with Edmund, for he thought he should one day tell his father, but his seed would be a bastard. This was not the only thing troubling Edmund; he was already in love with a married woman. "Are you alright, Edmund? Don't tell me Edmund the great is frightened," said William. Edmund burst into laughter.

"Edmund the Great, please don't remind me," said Edmund, struggling to regain his laughter.

"Remind you of what, milord?" asked Godfrey. "Let's just say it involves a girl from Etlio and—"

John interrupted William and said, "Now's not the time. We have a child here." To which Godfrey protested, "I'm almost a man!"

"This almost man, reeks of Sulphur. Come on, let's get you back to Lady Branson. You've given her enough stress for one day," said John.

"I don't need escorts. I can go by myself," said Godfrey slightly piqued. John shot Godfrey an incredulous glance. Godfrey groaned.

"Wait. Is my mother and the others in the keep alright?" said Edmund. "Very much so," Godfrey responded.

"Alright, Godfrey's right. He doesn't need escorts," said Edmund. "Yes," Godfrey said under his breath.

"That's why I will be escorting Godfrey alone," said Edmund.

Godfrey groaned again, realizing he celebrated too early. "And don't bother arguing. You'll find I am not as easily swayed as Sir Peter. As for my brothers reconvene with the others, I will join you shortly."

CHAPTER SIX

WHAT IS REAL, WHAT IS ILLUSION?

Mavid was furious but he had to be methodical in his approach, for his enemies were clearly cunning. He was still perplexed about how he was hexed in the first place. From everything he was told, winged dragons (colloquial name for Arcadiem dragons) could not be hexed, especially a Beladaric dragon because of their magic-resistant hides. He flew over the barbican and into the field where there were a multitude of besiegers. It was there he saw the two gargantuan trebuchets—the defiler and blood bringer.

Mavid was about to dive down and set the two deadly siege engines ablaze, but something stopped him. He could sense something was awry. Mavid thought it was odd that he flew over these meager humans without any of them reacting to his presence. What was even more perplexing was none of the humans seemed to be reacting to anything, in fact it was like they were frozen in place, frozen in time.

In all his years of existence, he had never seen something like this. Mavid's thoughts raced. *What sort of sorcery is this?* Then Mavid remembered and the thought horrified him. *It can't be. It was only myth, this power it's… it's—* Suddenly Mavid's wings became numb, and he was unable to move them. He descended rapidly. He flailed about wildly in the sky, trying desperately to stay suspended in the air, but it was to no avail. As he was falling, he could see the beings below him start to move again. However, this was not a return to normalcy, they moved in an unnatural fashion like automatons. In addition, they did not move their limbs instead, they seemed to slide about like chest pieces being moved by an invisible hand. The frozen humans cleared the path for Mavid, leaving a large circle on the ground. Mavid braced himself for impact by curling himself into a ball.

He hit the ground with a loud thud, debris flew everywhere. Mavid was now in a completely paralytic state. He wondered if it was the result of the fall or because of... No; he didn't dare ponder it because, if what they said was true, thinking about it too much would only make things worse. There was a cacophony of noise that irritated Mavid's ears. At first it seemed unintelligible, but then the sounds started to coalesce into a type of chant. When the chanting became unencumbered by extraneous sound, it became apparent that they were intoning his name but in tones of his mother's voice. This greatly disturbed him because his mother, Myaga, had died 250 years ago. Mavid, now panic-stricken, tried to move, but his efforts were futile for he could only move his eyes. They continued chanting his name, with each successive word gradually becoming louder.

"Mavid! Mavid! Mavid! MAVID! MAVID! MAVID! MAVID!

The chants eventually stopped and only one voice remained; the voice of Myaga and she spoke in the tongue of the dragons.

"*Crak da cree sait hrgh blz pfz ough krz hur rh.*" [My son you have failed your mission/quest, you will be unborn.]

Suddenly the immobilized people moved freely again, but they did not seem to be acting on their own accord. The subsequent events that had befallen Mavid are graphic in nature and difficult to explain, for this is one of several parts of Fragaa's vision that cannot be seen by Lord Franklin. Reader, in case you were wondering, Lord Franklin cannot read the minds of the individuals within this alternate reality.

The humans approached Mavid, only this time their eyes were crimson, and their irises rotated counterclockwise, clockwise, then counterclockwise again. This was unsettling for Mavid because he continued to hear his mother's voice as the multitudes came towards him ominously. She kept repeating the phrase "*krz hur rh*" (you will be unborn.) As the masses came closer to Mavid, they too joined in the chant but spoke the tongue of man reciting the phrase "You will be unborn" repeatedly. Suddenly, they started sprinting towards him with unnatural vigor, all while screaming, "YOU WILL BE UNBORN! YOU WILL BE UNBORN! YOU WILL BE UNBORN! YOU WILL BE UNBORN!"

Myaga's voice was still present during all the tumult, thus adding to the disconcerting atmosphere. What occurred next could only be described as macabre. The humans piled on top of Mavid and began to slowly tear him apart with their bare hands. He screamed in agony internally as they ripped off his wings, tore out his tongue and flayed his scaly hide. The torture didn't stop there. They gouged out his eyes and took out his entrails. The humans continued to dig into his flesh, taking out several organs including, but not limited to, his heart, lungs and liver. Mavid was eventually reduced to a pile of flesh, tissue, and bloody innards spread out across the ground and the chanting stopped. The gory scene was appalling, but what was truly shocking was throughout the entire ordeal, Mavid was still alive. His corporal self was destroyed, but he somehow existed in some sort of ethereal plane where everything seemed airy, and he felt no pain. This feeling was ephemeral, however, and in stark contrast to what happened next.

Mavid became hyperaware to the extent that he could hear his own heartbeat and the blood traveling through his veins, yet he could not see, and he could not breathe. He seemed to be trapped in a confined space that might have been some type of egg. He was submerged in a type of liquid that might have been amniotic fluid. He tried to free himself from his prison, but the task was proving difficult. His limbs felt anemic, and his bones felt brittle. This began to change as his body started to increase in size and maturation rapidly. His eyesight returned to him and he saw he was inside a liquid that was tinted yellow. He looked at his wings, they were much smaller. In fact, his entire body resembled a newborn.

Mavid's eyes widened when he came to the realization that he was inside his own egg. Upon such a discovery, Mavid began to writhe about in distress. He eventually freed himself from the egg, and his body and physique returned to normal size. When Mavid escaped from the egg, he was in an entirely different location. One that he did not recognize. He was surrounded by nothing but a field of grass. Mavid had trouble processing what had happened, and he began to hyperventilate. Even though he was whole again, he could still feel the sensation of literally being torn limb from limb and being reborn in his egg. The pain and shock were so debilitating that Mavid lost consciousness. He awoke again. To his surprise, he was within the castle walls of Corithni. He was in the main bailey.

Reader, what happened next is difficult to elucidate because it doesn't have a single answer. You see, Mavid had no memory of the ordeal he went through, either because he suppressed it, or it faded from his memory. Even if he could recall it, he would most likely attribute it to a dream.

Reality, or should I say realities, are complicated. In fact, it may be the most difficult thing to explain in all of existence. A bold claim indeed, but it may be the closest thing to absolute truth in this world. Solipsism basically states only the self is known to exist. In other words, the only thing that is certain is that you are real. "Cogito ergo sum" Rene Descartes. I am not making a gnostic claim that only the self-exist nor am I rejecting realism without digressing too much into semantics the word known suggests sureness and the antithesis of the word is uncertainty which leaves us with a quandary. That the reality experienced outside of oneself has a probability of being artificial but also a chance of being authentic. Things start to get befuddling when one adds perspective into the equation and purports that reality is relative. Since our senses are flawed, how we perceive the world is in turn flawed. Hence, we cannot even determine if the self is real, which seemingly contradicts the very tenants of solipsism or at least questions it. Let me elucidate, if we take the creationist argument that we were somehow engineered by a higher power or powers, then everything we do is predetermined hence free-will is an illusion. If one postulates that a creator exists, it may suggest that we do not. An analog would be a simulation. What comes to mind is an avatar in a video game. That avatar has a predetermined set of actions and behaviors that are determined by a programmer or creator. Their fate is determined by a script, but for all intents and purposes, they believe they are real and have free will. They are oblivious to the fact that they are in a simulation. Now, the questions I leave you with reader are: are we really humans or simply avatars? If the very tools we used to interpret reality are inaccurate, then how can we discriminate between what is real and what is false? How can we say what is certain when certainty is uncertain? Eight defenders were passing by when they caught sight of Mavid.

Frightened expressions manifested on their faces. One defender pointed and shouted, "DRAGON!" Then, like a chain reaction, several pikemen, bowmen, infantry, and crossbow men stood in front of Mavid. None of the defenders attempted to flee but one could tell from their visage that they were terrified. Several of the pikemen were shaking with pikes in hand. Mavid did not recognize these faces but assumed everyone was under the command of Sir Peter.

"You humans, where is the one known as Peter?"

The defenders were dumbfounded. One of the men was about to speak, "It-it" when Mavid interrupted him.

"Yes, I know I can speak, that's not important. Just tell me where Peter is. Your lives depend on it," said Mavid impatiently. Mavid looked at a sea of perplexed and terrified onlookers. Then one of the pikemen said, "There is no one by that name here," then another man said, "There is a Peter." Mavid's ears perked up and his spirits lifted "Blonde, blue eyes-"

"Yes, yes," said Mavid impatiently.

The man continued, "…and he was born yesterday." Mavid groaned. "No, no, I mean Peter, son of Brandr, also known as Agnarr," said Mavid, his patience growing thin. The men noticed his increasing irritability and tightened their formation and became more hostile in their demeanor.

"For the last time, no one goes here by that name. Now state your purpose and how you got here," said a bowman, with his bow aimed at Mavid's head. In fact, all the men were on high alert with their weapons drawn. Mavid could see the frightened looks on their faces and attempted to alleviate the tension by speaking as calmly and methodically as he possibly could.

"I am called Mavid son of Aglar, and the great King of the Beladaric Dragons. I was somehow hexed by the villain you know as Hector, or at least someone in his camp. The reason evades me. I crash landed on this very spot where I convened with some of your comrades led by the one called Peter and devised a plan to exact revenge on the one called Hector and his dastardly legions. The exact plan I can't recount the details of."

His explanation seemed to ease the tensions amongst the defenders and himself. Their once terrified faces were now replaced with ones of general confusion. Which was understandable as most of the defenders had difficulty wrapping their heads around the fact that dragons could talk much less convene with humans, but still the beast was apparently an enemy of Hector, which in turn meant they were allies. This sentiment was not shared amongst all the men. Many were suspicious of Mavid believing him to be the result of hokraft and weren't going to be cajoled into revealing secrets to the enemy. Others believed the dragon to be mad. Nonetheless, it seemed unwise to provoke a fully grown dragon, so many of the men decided to tread lightly.

"Errm, your grace, I don't believe you crash landed. You more so appeared out of thin air," said the defender who initially spotted Mavid. "What? That's preposterous! I landed right here, see the wall collapsed—" Mavid was shocked, for when he turned around, he could see the wall separating the main bailey from the lower bailey completely intact.

"Impossible... that... that's impossible," Mavid stammered. *Was this some sort of dream, or had he lost his senses?* he thought. This whole day had been quite strange for Mavid. First he woke up in a place he did not recognize, then he started to imagine things that were not there. Mavid accepted that he was not in his prime, but he was still far from old age and an addled mind that often came with it, perhaps too many battles, and the head trauma that accompanied it was finally starting to take its toll. Mavid expelled such thoughts from his mind and regained his resolve. *I am King Mavid, not some weak-minded simpleton. This is a feeble attempt by my enemies to harm me, but I will not meet my end at the hands of those meddling with hokraft. To my adversaries, whoever and whatever they may be, I congratulate you all, for you have done the impossible, jinxing a Dragon of Beladar's bloodline, but know this you have also made a costly mistake. I know this is an illusion, but the pain I'll inflict on you once I escape will not be.*

Mavid closed his eyes and waited for what he believed to be the false reality to dissolve into nothingness. He concentrated on the images of Sir Peter, the debris from the smashed wall, and Godfrey. The men watched in awe as this majestic beast stood completely still in a meditative state. Many of them had never even seen a dragon before. When Mavid opened his eyes, he was surrounded by darkness, devoid of any light. There was no solid ground, and he seemed to be floating aimlessly in this endless void. Then a single entity appeared in the distance, emitting light. Naturally, Mavid gravitated towards it. As he got closer to the entity, he could start to make out its image. What he saw horrified him. Before he could speak or react there was a flash of white light and then there was nothing.

Sir Peter felt something was off. He had been running towards the eastern wall with the other defenders, but they somehow did not seem to cover any ground. They were still in what could be interpreted as the main bailey. It seemed illogical, but it was like time itself was being warped. A type of time dilation. A journey that should have taken a few minutes felt like hours. Sir Peter started to worry about Godfrey. He was a good boy but reckless and very eager to fight just like his father. This scared Sir Peter, which was why he was initially hesitant to train him. Nonetheless, he loved Godfrey and truly believed he had a good heart, but even good hearts can be corrupted without proper guidance.

The feeling that time was being dilated was really vexing to Sir Peter. What also had him piqued was the fact his men, usually a loquacious bunch, seem oddly quiet. This could easily be attributed to the siege, but it was still odd. Sir Peter finally just turned around to inquire about his comrades and their silence when he realized they were nowhere to be found. Sir Peter stopped to look at his surroundings. The castle was completely empty.

"Tomlin! Ives! Martin! Robin! Robert! Jupp! Odo!" He called their names multiple times, but they did not answer. "Is anybody there?" No one responded. Sir Peter soon grew weary of shouting and became restless. *Hokraft, but how? I made no deals, no blood oaths; was this some sort of illusion? Faux magic, perhaps? After all, Hector did have castors at his disposal. It still doesn't make any sense. I'm no expert in magic, but I believe to jinx someone requires some sort of direct contact, whether being eye contact (for faux magic) or a bodily sample (hokraft),* thought Sir Peter. He continued to ruminate on the matter. He wondered if he had any contact with any magic-wielder who might have cursed him. He could think of none now, but then someone came to mind. Aslaug Heggr's mother, but that seemed unlikely. Although, Aslaug abhorred him, she had been dead for over fifteen years and, as far as Sir Peter knew, curses do not last that long. So, he figured this illusion must have been created recently.

Sir Peter could smell an acrid scent in the air that made him somewhat nauseous. The repugnant festering smell only grew more potent as time passed. A single droplet from the sky landed on his forehead. The fluid like substance did not feel like normal precipitation, it was thicker than water, less dense than snow. Sir Peter touched his brow with his index and middle finger. He looked at the tips of his digits and what he saw had him bemused. He could not believe what he saw. There was blood on his fingertips, and it reeked. More blood began to cumulate on him as it poured profusely from the sky and soon, he was drenched in copious amounts of it. As irrational as it sounded, it appeared the sky was raining blood.

"What in God's name is this?" Sir Peter said out loud. Sir Peter was understandably terrified. His fear only heighten when he heard a whisper of a familiar sounding voice but one he could not identify entirely. It whispered "murderer".

Sir Peter unsheathed his blade. "Who goes there, what is this place?" The same familiar voice responded, "Agnarr, son of Brandr, you can't fight your way through this. That blade was forged by two, but it doesn't change what's within you, murderer (whispers)."

"What? I don't get your meaning. Explain yourself," said Sir Peter. The mysterious voice instead only kept whispering the word "Murderer". This single voice eventually became multiple voices that whispered in unison like a harmonious chorus. Then the voices quickly became more discordant as murmurs became shouts. "MURDERER! MURDERER! MURDERER!"

The voices kept screaming and Sir Peter attempted to desperately locate the source of the screams. He stared at the floor, transfixed by what he had seen. The blood had reached his knees. The rain was flooding the castle. Sir Peter sprinted and attempted to find higher ground. He intended to climb up the battlements of the eastern wall, but he felt something seize his ankle.

"Traaaitor," a voice groaned. This voice silenced the other voices. The elongated hollow wraithlike nature of the voice did not impede Sir Peter's ability to recognize it. In fact, it was unmistakable to him who this voice belonged to. The hairs on his neck stood on up. His breaths became shallow and rapid. Petrified, Sir Peter uttered, "Father?" He turned around only to see the emaciated corpse of a large man. The undead man's head and torso were the only thing visible to Sir Peter.

Presumably the corpse's lower half was in a portal in the ground obscured by tenebrific tendrils of smoke and ash. Even with the decay, Sir Peter could identify this reanimated cadaver based on its visage alone because the face was better preserved than the body. This was no doubt Brandr. Sir Peter made several attempts to wrench himself free, but Brandr's grasp was too strong.

He finally swung his sword downward at Brandr's wrist. Instead of severing Brandr's hand, which would free him, the blade shattered into several pieces leaving Sir Peter with nothing but a lobed pommel. Sir Peter couldn't believe it. The legendary glowing blade Seggr forged twice, once with Mylecan steel, second with both Iiadecan and Mylecan steel was so easily broken.

The blood now reached his navel and Brandr had not loosened this grip. "My son, you cannot escape your fate, but do not fret. Your deaths will be memorable."

"I did what I had to father," said Sir Peter with conviction.

"Despite everything, I loved you," said Sir Peter in a much more somber tone with an emphasis on the words loved. Brandr released his grip on Sir Peter's ankle and the blood stopped rising. Brandr stood up revealing his massive stature. Even with the emaciation he was still intimidating, standing at a whopping seven feet six inches. The portal in which he came from dissipated.

"Mawkishness is unbecoming of you." This provoked ire in Sir Peter, which he struggled to contain.

"You are not my father! My father is dead! You are an aberration conjured up by the twisted minds of hokraft castors and I rebuke you in the name of Arda!"

Brandr started to laugh derisively then he sneered and said, "What do you know about what is real, you of all people?" Sir Peter could hear a plethora of voices in the distance of varied pitch. Some laughing while others jeered. "There he is, the mad marauder," said a voice.

"Oh, its bloody locks," said another. Several other derogatory epithets and insults were thrown in his direction until Brandr shouted, "Enough!" The jeers ceased. Brandr turned to Sir Peter with a mixture of anger and hurt he said, "You, were Agnarr the Merciless."

Sir Peters smirked and replied, "Now who's being mawkish." Brandr scowled at Sir Peter in response. "I no longer walk that path, imposter. That was my father's path, a path I couldn't follow. No, a path I wouldn't follow," said Sir Peter gravely.

"And yet you bare my name," said Brandr as his body completely decomposed before Sir Peter's very eyes. Sir Peter was dumbfounded, but he did not have time to contemplate what happened. The blood was rising rapidly. Sir Peter quickly started to take off his plated armor until he was only left with chainmail, which he wore under a red tunic, and black trousers. The castle was severely flooded now, and the rotten blood had submerged several parts of the castle, including the chapel and most of the keep. Sir Peter struggled to stay afloat, which seemed odd given the viscosity of blood compared to water, and yet he could still feel something pulling him down.

He looked down briefly only to see his own face, except from fifteen years ago, with all the typical features that came with adolescence. The younger Sir Peter had shoulder length, disheveled hair, light facial hair (a couple of strands of hair that aggregated on his chin) and a wild look in his eyes. Before Sir Peter could react, the younger Sir Peter drew the originally forged glowing Seggr, a one handed Mylecan sword with the same lobed pommel as the current two-handed Seggr with his right hand. With his left hand he grabbed Sir Peter's leg. Sir Peter attempted to free himself, but his younger self ran him through twice. Once in the chest and another through the stomach. The adolescent Sir Peter disappeared, and the acrid blood that flooded the castle gradually began to diminish.

When it completely dissolved, Sir Peter was on his back sprawled on the floor in a pool of his own blood, too weary to even tend his wounds. He closed his eyes. When he awoke, he was in a place he did not recognize. A seemingly boundless field of grass with no wildflowers in sight. In this strange place, the sun was out, and the weather was mild. He could hear laughter in the distance. Reader, like Mavid, Sir Peter had no memory of previous events. Sir Peter no longer had fatal wounds nor was he drenched in blood, neither the repugnant kind nor the fresh kind. He saw two figures running up to him. The images became clearer as these people drew nearer. These figures stood over him. Sir Peter smiled at the familiar faces, for they were the faces of the two people he loved the most: Godfrey and Lady Branson. They, however, were not smiling. Godfrey had Seggr two in both hands, the blade pointed directly at Sir Peter's heart. The light from Seggr two seemed to disappear in Godfrey's hands. Godfrey was on the verge of tears when he said, "You did this. You had no right to judge me!"

"Godfrey! Elysant!" Sir Peter screamed. Lady Branson turned to him, her eyes impenetrable and her countenance emotionless. She asked, "Did you love her more than me?"

"What?" Sir Peter asked, dumbfounded by the question. To which she responded, "She was with child." Before Sir Peter could respond. Godfrey dove Seggr two through his chest.

"AAAAAAARGH!" Sir Peter screamed and everything faded to dark. Sir Peter found himself naked, manacled, and fettered to a circular stone slab that was suspended in the air. His hair was now shoulder length, and he had a long beard. Two figures loomed over him. They seemed slightly spectral; their gigantic bodies stared at Sir Peter. The apparition to his right resembled an elderly man missing his left eye. He did not wear any form of eye covering, so there was just a vacant space where his eye should have been. This figure wore long black robes.

The being next to him resembled a muscular man with long red hair and a large beard of the same color. The being held a hammer in his right hand. It looked ceremonial. It had raised golden engravings and an overall black finish. The handle was equally bedecked with gold. It was short, meaning it could only be wielded with one hand, at least by this being, remember the descriptions are proportional to their sizes. The being was adorned in typical Mylecan warrior attire. This meant he was equipped with a large round shield at his back, chain mail armor with a brown tunic on top, and white trousers. Both figures' feet were obscured in darkness, and they were generally semitransparent. This gave them an otherworldly look, thus making it difficult to determine their true size or exact location.

The elderly figure said bluntly, "You know who we are, or rather what we are, so there is no point in introductions. We are here to tell you, all of you, that you pray to a false God, and you will be punished for it. You will be unborn." The elderly man looked at the red-haired man as though signaling something. The red-haired man raised his decorative hammer in the air and started muttering something in a language that was not even native to Mirthadine.

Ekrah ash hal ebah kroat lish beih. The hammer became encased in copious amounts of electricity and the gold engravings became red. They began to radiate light, like an incandescent metal on the forge. There was a loud clanging of thunder and lightning.

Sir Peter was bewildered. *"That hammer that must mean—"* His thoughts were interrupted when the two apparitions disappeared. Then something appeared before him. It was the most horrifying, indescribable thing he had ever seen in his life. Before he could speak or react, there was a flash of white light and then there was nothing.

***

Lady Branson along with Eva and Giles were tending to the ailing Sir Richard. While Alywin and Tim discussed Sir Richard's plan. They were asked to give Sir Richard some space and talk amongst themselves. Giles' words. He felt they were aggravating Sir Richard's condition by badgering him with questions.

Tim and Alywin were quarreling in another section of the garrison. "Wait, we can't just move people into tunnels in a middle of a bloody siege. It will cause chaos. It will never work," said Alywin.

"We have a guide now," said Tim, referring to Sarah.

Alywin was quite vexed by this response. "Are we really going to risk the lives of so many innocents, not to mention Lady Franklin, on some woman we don't even know?"

"I know her well," said Tim.

"Is that what this is about?" Alywin said.

Not liking what he was insinuating, Tim said, "It's not like that." "It's not like what?" asked Sarah.

"Erm, nothing?" Tim said nervously. Tim and Alywin continued to argue.

"Um, I've been here for weeks now," said Sarah as she stood there awkwardly between them as they continued to quarrel.

"Alywin, when did you lose your senses? Sarah's our best option of getting everyone out alive. That includes us," Tim replied angrily while lingering on the word us.

This only further infuriated Alywin. He said, "I am one of the few people who seems to still have his senses. We can't risk people's lives meandering underground like a bloody mole. We don't even know where this labyrinth leads."

Alywin sighed. "Look, it's obvious you care dearly for these people, but it's too much of a risk. We're better off in the keep riding out the siege. Even if Hector breaches these walls, we'll just have to agree to his terms. Such is standard in siege warfare."

"You're truly delusional if you think Hector is going to allow us to live," said Tim.

"Why wouldn't he? There is a reason the dragon hasn't attacked the keep," said Alywin.

"Then why did the dragon burn down the chapel killing several clerics?" said Tim.

"The chapel caught fire after the fire in the inner bailey," replied Alywin angrily.

"How did we know that wasn't intentional?"

"Hey, hey," Sarah whispered while gesticulating awkwardly to garner attention towards herself. Despite her timid and subdued behavior, she was successful at getting both men's attention.

Both men looked at her, their brows still furrowed from their heated argument. This made Sarah uncomfortable, hence she averted her gaze and directed it toward the ground. She swayed back and forth slightly as a means of calming herself down. "Erm this plan of ours is a hypothetical, if the siege is successful in the way of the defenders, then we can stay put. If it is not, then we have a means of escape. But I agree the plan is risky. That's why someone needs to go down and check if it's safe enough to transport everyone. Since I am the only one here that can access the tunnels, I volunteer myself."

Alywin was ambivalent about the prospect of this plan, but saw no reason to protest. Tim was about to discuss his demur with the plan when Sarah's attention was directed toward someone else.

"Colin you're up, you mustn't strain yourself," she said.

"Don't think you're clever. I saw you slip off somewhere, tired of my company already?" Colin said in a light-hearted manner.

Alywin rolled his eyes in response, finding Colin's statement pedestrian believing his motives were transparent. Tim, however, found Colin's actions to be far less benign and saw him as a possible threat, thus watched him closely.

"Nonsense, I just wanted to give you some much needed rest," said Sarah.

Colin saw the concerned look on Sarah's face and said, "I'm fine. I promise I won't strain myself too much. I'm actually more concerned about you. What's this talk about going into tunnels?"

"So, you heard?" said Sarah.

Colin, who now had a worried countenance, said slowly, "Sarah, this is dangerous. If this place is as old as you say it is, then the tunnels are old too. Old and unsupervised, old enough to collapse."

"I know, which is why I am the right person for the job. I'm a terrestrial manipulator. I can maneuver around shoddy tunnels."

"Sarah, something could be living down there. Something unfriendly," said Colin. Tim thought he might redirect attention by dismissing Colin's claims with a joke.

"What? Giant spiders?" Tim said while bursting into laughter. None of his comrades were amused. Embarrassed from their reactions, Tim made a poor attempt to explain himself. "Ahem. You know, because it's ridiculous, giant spiders." Alywin groaned in response. Colin and Sarah continued their conversation as though nothing had occurred.

"Colin, I can take care of myself. Besides, I don't have a choice. These people need a means of escape in case Corithni falls. I'm sorry, but there's no other way," said Sarah emphatically.

"But what if there was?" said Colin. "Sarah, listen carefully, I know Lord Hector Franklin."

"Is that what he's calling himself?" Alywin said under his breath. "Even if you escape through these tunnels, he will still find you and he'll probably torture, kill or maim you. Lord Hector Franklin—" "Hector!" the three said in unison, thus interrupting Colin.

"Hector is a cruel man, but he is reasonable. He will not kill those who did not actively fight against him as long as they submit of their own will. This means the women, children, healers, the clerics; all of you. Leave the soldiers and one sell-sword behind. We're as good as dead."

"That's not an option. I won't leave you or anyone else behind and that's final," Sarah said firmly.

There was a brief silence between the two, but even in brevity the exchange of communication was potent. They studied each other's faces. Sarah had childlike features that juxtaposed her attempt at a stern countenance. Judging from her overall appearance, she couldn't have been more than twenty-five.

Colin was more focused on her eyes; central heterochromatic, with each eye having two rings that made up the iris with the inner wider ring being turquoise and outer thinner royal blue. A feature that could only be noticed upon close inspection. Sarah sported a crown braid which, in itself, wasn't anything unusual. Plenty of women sported that hairstyle in Iiedec. (Hairstyles are not prohibited for certain classes like other regions, at least not during this current age.) What was peculiar was the ornately decorated silver pin in her blonde hair; it was in the shape of angel wings and looked like some sort of emblem. The way the metal glistened in the light was like no other metal Colin had ever seen. This was a strange thing to have for a lowborn woman (in Mydra, builders are considered lowborn). As Colin was examining Sarah, she did the same to him. Judging from his visage, he was about 27. He wasn't particularly handsome but far from hideous, he had a look about him that suggested gregariousness. Despite this, he was not particularly smiling at the moment. He instead seemed curious. His gray eyes peered into hers as the two drew closer towards each other. Colin was the first to disengage. He sighed and ran his hand through his dark brown hair.

"Colin, are you alright?" asked Sarah.

Tim, who had been looking at Colin suspiciously during his interaction with Sarah, said rather brusquely, "Colin is it? Care to tell us how you know Lord Hector Franklin?" He placed emphasis on the name and title Lord Hector Franklin.

Colin, visibly angered at what Tim was insinuating, said, "I am no friend of Hector."

"Why is that?" asked Tim, not fazed by Colin's hostility.

Sarah, sensing tension between the two, said, "That's enough Tim. Colin is not our enemy. Now let's all calm down."

But Tim did not seem to heed her words and pressed Colin further. "How do we know you're not just another Bancroft?"

"I don't know who that is," said Colin.

"Don't play coy. He was executed three weeks ago," said Tim angrily.

"He was brought here two days ago," Sarah retorted.

"That doesn't mean he wasn't conspiring with Bancroft beforehand," Tim responded.

"Enough, Tim. You're being obstinate. He and Bancroft are not cohorts. Lord Franklin is no fool. He wouldn't make the same mistake twice," said Alywin.

"He is a sell-sword he admitted it himself, they fight for the highest of coin," said Tim rather angrily.

"Yes, I know what a sell-sword is thank you, but this is war. Everyone's hiring sell-swords. Don't be so naïve. Besides you and I have no right to judge people," said Alywin under his breath so Sarah wouldn't hear.

"That was different. We were just trying to survive," said Tim before realizing the hypocrisy of his words. One could tell the point at which he came to this realization by the way he uttered the word survive, subdued and of low volume, in stark contrast to his overall tone. Nonetheless, Tim was persistent and would not take this indignation lightly. He attempted to further scrutinize Colin's motives which only appeared as senseless bravado to the others. To Tim, however, it was appropriate he did not trust this outsider, especially how he behaved around Sarah. The way she fell for the charms of this stranger vexed him.

"This still doesn't change the fact that this man has a relationship with Hector and even refers to him as Lord Hector Franklin and talks now of submitting to his Lord. He sounds like a spy," said Tim.

"Tim, Colin is not a spy," Sarah said sternly.

Before she could say more in defense of Colin, he stopped her, and said, "It's alright. I suppose I owe you all an explanation. I am Colin, the bastard son of Galeran Harlow, former knight of Agor. He used to serve under late Lord Rowan Everard. My father left the position of commander for unknown reasons and settled in Rilek where he later formed the free company known as the Rilek Herons. Several years later, Hector hires the Rilek Herons to fight in his war with Albert Franklin. Father was hesitant at first to take the job, but Hector offered so much gold and his army was massive. It was during the first battle of the war you all know as the battle of Daggard castle in Etlio (1536 NEEOT). The battle went in our favor. I know because I was there, thirteen, spear in hand and fighting alongside my brothers. But Hector refused to pay what was owed, kept saying we'll get our due after the war is won. Father explained to him that that's not how free companies work. You pay per battle. Anyway, father was royally pissed when he found out that the other free companies Hector employed were paid a fat sum, especially the red vultures. Naturally, Father told Hector to fuck off and he wasn't working for him anymore unless he received payment. Hector had him executed, torn apart by horses while me and my brothers watched. Since then, we've been revolting against Hector as much as we can, but Hector has reduced our numbers on his quest to hunt us down."

The group took time to digest the tale presented before them, hence, the delayed response. That made Colin slightly apprehensive since he just confessed to them. Finally, Sarah broke the silence.

"I'm sorry about your father Colin," said Sarah sincerely as she placed a hand on his uninjured shoulder.

"Thank you," Colin replied.

"If you don't mind me asking, how did you come to know Lord Franklin?" asked Alywin.

"We met at the battle of Rilek (1548 NEEOT). The Rilek Herons launched a surprise attack on Hector and his men, but we underestimated their numbers. I thought we were fucked until Lord Franklin and his calvary came. I knew that day, Lord Franklin had power on his side when this one knight came in riding a one-eyed steed and carrying a strange glowing sword. Lobed pommel, like the Mylecans but it was a longsword. This crazy fucker killed twenty people without using soul energy or elemental energy," said Colin. He was quite excited when describing the account of this knight.

"That crazy fucker is Lady Branson's husband, Sir Peter. Speaking of Lady Branson, we should probably inform her and the Archiater of this plan," said Tim.

"What's an Ack-cheeter?" asked Colin.

"It's Archiater and he's basically the head healer. I'll admit it's an unusual term. It was used during the wild era in one of the old empires. He and Lady Branson are our superiors," said Sarah.

Colin was quite impressed by Lord Albert Franklin's organized medical unit and the fact they had a hierarchy. The Rilek Herons just licked their own wounds and hoped for the best. If someone was severely injured, they were left for dead. He was equally impressed by Sarah's overall knowledge of things. *How can a lowborn girl know the origins of the word Archiater?* he thought. This also made him feel quite small. He was amongst learned folks, lowborn or not. It didn't make him feel any less insecure and out of place. These people could perform surgeries while he could barely read. What Albert Franklin lacked in numbers he more than made up for in skill, and this was a comforting thought to Colin.

Tim was quite irritated. He could not figure out why his comrades were so enamored by a turncoat. He hoped Lady Branson or the Archiater would put an end to this nonsense and expel him from the barracks, but he knew this was wishful thinking. Lady Branson was too kind a soul. She would never turn away an injured person. In fact, he suspected if Hector himself came to the barracks mortally wounded, she would probably still heal him. *I'll just have to keep an eye on this ruffian and make sure he doesn't try anything,* Tim thought.

"You can't go by yourself," Colin said unexpectantly and abruptly. "Colin," Sarah said, quite flattered by the fact that he wanted to protect her, yet sympathetic to the fact that he knew he couldn't.

Colin anticipated what she was going to say. "I know, I know you've made up your mind, but going into tunnels in the dark is just plain reckless. I know I can't obviously go with you, but please just take someone along."

"I'll go," Tim said without hesitation.

Sarah looked at Tim. She was quite surprised by Tim's declaration. She expressed her gratitude by smiling and saying, "Thank you, Tim."

Tim blushed as he smiled back. He tried to appear nonchalant but instead he looked nervous as he said, "No problem."

"Thanks, mate. Take my sword and bow with you. They're underneath my bed along with other armaments you may need," said Colin.

"What do you expect him to do with the bow? He is a notoriously bad archer, almost as bad as Sir Peter," said Alywin bluntly.

"You know, Alywin, Sir Peter is a nice person, but I'm sure he wouldn't want you talking about his inefficiencies with a bow and besides, I'm not that bad," replied Tim.

Alywin rested his hand on Tim's shoulder and said, "Yes, you are. I guess what I'm saying is I'm going as well. Just so we're clear, I still think this is a bad plan."

"Thanks, friend," Tim said sincerely. Tim went to retrieve the weapons underneath Colin's bed. When he returned, three figures came into view from across the garrison. The figures were Giles, Eva and Lady Branson, their faces saddened and their heads low. They were recently bereft.

Sarah asked, "How is he?" knowing full well by their demeanor that the news would not be good, yet a part of her still hoped she was wrong. Giles spoke first. "Sir Richard Brickenden has passed."

CHAPTER SEVEN

MEMORIES AND SECRETS

Sir Richard's death was not surprising, but it still had an impact, especially on those he interacted with. Lady Branson took it the hardest. Giles tried his best to console her, to no avail, not that he thought he'd be successful in his attempt, but he wanted to try, nonetheless. Lady Branson had been a healer for nearly twenty years, but she never got used to the death that accompanied it. She was just that kind of person. She wanted to save every patient, and took it as a personal failure when she could not. She saw people she cared about in every patient. Sir Peter, Godfrey, Giles, Tim, Alywin, Clara and several others, so naturally, it affected her when someone died. Sir Richard's death, however, was quite different because he brought with him bad news.

This plan to burn down the keep and escape through the tunnels was a desperate one. Not only that... it spelt doom for the defenders. It was as though Sir Richard had it on good authority that the defenders would lose, or perhaps it was just a contingency plan. Either way, it was impossible to know now. She couldn't stop thinking about Sir Peter. She knew he could handle himself. He had been fighting since he was five years of age, but even seasoned warriors can fall. Lady Branson knew it was expected that knights might die in battle, but she could not bear losing Sir Peter. He was such a good man; he was so good to her and Godfrey and had come so far. She prayed Arda would protect him from harm every day he put on the armor. She even closed her eyes during the tournament of roses (1535 NEEOT) because she couldn't bear to see Sir Peter hurt. Of course, Sir Peter wasn't Sir Peter then. He was still Agnarr, and Lady Branson was still Lady Baker. Furthermore, Sir Peter was betrothed to another woman from Etlio, named Faye. All she remembered about this woman was that she was beautiful and died suddenly a week later of some unknown sickness. Lady Branson had only known Sir Peter tangentially, but she didn't like the thought of this seventeen-year-old boy possibly getting injured in what she deemed a senseless act of barbarism. Sir Peter eventually went on to win the tournament. This upset several Iiadecan knights who did not like losing to an adolescent from Mylec, who wasn't even a knight. Although, he fought alongside Iiadec during the fifth Mylec Marauder war (1518-1533 NEEOT). Many Iiadecans still saw Mylecans as the enemy due to previous wars and conflicts before Sir Peter's time. It didn't help that Sir Peter was involved with the Etlio/ Tegr (TEGER) conflict (1534 NEEOT).

A series of skirmishes between Mylecans, who served under Brandr, and some rebel Iiedecans, who served under Wade Brown. Wade believed the Iiadecans were entitled to Mylecan land after Guthroth was defeated. To prevent another war, King Gavin bought Tegr from Brandr and decreed that no Iiadecan could lay claims to any remaining Mylecan lands. He also had Wade and his followers swiftly executed, thus ending the conflict. There were many Wade sympathizers at the time, so naturally, Sir Peter acquired some enemies.

There were several jeers and boos from the crowd as Sir Peter went to collect his prize, which was four boxes of gold and a painted metal sculpture that resembled a bouquet of flowers of the same type. The flowers were a depiction of Linnea Borealis or Twinflower. A pink bell-like flower that grew in pairs in Yelithr (*yewl-lith-thur*), the region in Mylec where Sir Peter was born.

Amid the uproar, Lady Branson stood up and lambasted the crowd. She called the men cowards and the women imbeciles. She pointed out that if it were not for the bravery of Sir Peter, many of them would not be sitting where they were sitting. *"At thirteen, this boy who stands before you, fought against Guthroth's fiercest hordes while the brave men of Iiadec fled from battle. Some of those men are sitting in this very crowd and you have the audacity to boo your champion?"* (The battle Lady Branson was referring to is the battle at Moran-Ure (YORE) or, as it is known by the Mylecans, the battle of the flying Iiadecans. It was said, during this battle, Guthroth, who was not present, sent a legion of 4000 to fight against Hakon, who was also not present. Hakon's troops measured 1000 and they were aided by an additional 1500 Iiadecans. During the battle, the Iiadecan forces were overwhelmed and so half of them retreated, leaving the remaining Mylecans and Iiadecans to fight Guthroth's forces. They fought valiantly and were able to fight to a standstill, despite having the disadvantage in numbers.)

Lady Branson's outburst caused quite a stir in the crowd, but all she noticed was Sir Peter staring at her. As they locked eyes, she studied his face. It did not look like the face of some savage killer from Mylec, as he was sometimes called, but rather an innocuous child that desperately needed companionship, at least at the moment. It was almost as if he just needed to be told that he was more than what society said he was.

Before they could exchange words, Giles pulled Lady Branson to her seat. He didn't want to make a scene, but at the time, Giles did not approve of Sir Peter. He would say things like, *"We are only here to tend to the wounded. If you see that boy, you are not to speak to him. He's dangerous,"* or *"He's already betrothed. You are not even to look at him,"* and finally *"He's a marauder. It doesn't matter what side he fought on"*. Lady Branson told Giles he was being a bigot, but Giles was convinced that he was protecting his granddaughter from this foreign threat. And that was the sentiment of many in Iiadec at the time. They still feared Mylecans due to previous wars. Lady Branson was different. She saw something in Sir Peter that most didn't; she saw a victim of duty. She believed he did things out of obligation and that his heart was somewhere else. Only she didn't quite know where that was, and she had the feeling neither did he. Identity is a complicated term that encompasses several things, hence it can be quite ambiguous. Identity is, however, most definable by one term, and that is self. *Self*, in its simplest terms, is everything that makes you uniquely you. The caveat is that self involves a single entity. In other words, every essential article that makes up the individual must coalesce into that one individual. There is certainly evidence of self in nature and the stipulation of uniqueness in nature. No two snowflakes are exactly alike or that even identical twins are not completely identical. But these examples, however, are a microcosm of a much larger universe. We cannot simply prove self-existence because according to our definitions, uniqueness is a core tenant and if uniqueness does not exist anywhere within the universe on a macroscale then neither does self. Of course, there is another theory. If we postulate self-existence as a single entity, then we can deduce that no two things are alike for the reason of environmental factors. All things react to the environment differently therefore, the twin example is relevant. Assuming the universe is not unilateral, there is a sort of randomness that occurs, a type of entropy and since no two objects can occupy space at the same time, one can assume most objects are affected differently by this randomness. Hence, uniqueness and, in turn, self is at least probable if not entirely proven. Now that we've discussed the legitimacy of self, we can further discuss why self is often difficult to identify even to the individual from which it spawns. The reason is individuals are quite complicated. Oneself could be compared to a Rubik's cube with the different colors representing the different components of self and the ability to change color represents the reaction to external stimuli. In other words, what makes up oneself can be attributed to how they react to circumstances based on the tools they already have in their arsenal/colors. The question of who am I is a difficult question to ponder and no one expects an exact breakdown. However, there are individuals who struggle to answer this question even at the surface level. The reason is they put other people, other obligations, and other ideas above themselves until they no longer recognize themselves. When the individual, who is befogged about the self, asks themselves "Who am I?" they have no answer, but the individual that is in tune with oneself will say "many things too numerous to detail but at its core I am me."

She remembered talking to Sir Peter directly after slipping past Giles, of course. She introduced herself as Elysant Baker, to which he responded, "I am called Agnarr, son of Brandr, but you probably already knew that." Sir Peter smiled nervously. He was quite embarrassed because they announced his name at the beginning and ending of the tournament. He was introduced as Agnarr Branson, the savage from Mylec. Lady Branson chuckled as did Sir Peter.

"I was beginning to think you were incapable of smiling." Lady Branson's eyes gravitated towards the metal bouquet that Sir Peter was holding. "It's beautiful. Is it for your betrothed?" Lady Branson asked.

"Huh, yeah, I made it for her," said Sir Peter.

"You made it?" asked Lady Branson quite surprised. Slightly startled by her sudden enthusiasm towards him, Sir Peter felt he should qualify, "Well, I had help from a Mylecan blacksmith."

Her eyes widened and she whispered, *"Is this made of the legendary Mylecan steel?"*

"We call them Modith (*mode-ith*) cores, and yes, it is," whispered Sir Peter. (Modith is the Mylecan God of metallurgy. Modith cores are metal cores found deep within the ground they are a type of unrefined steel alloy sometimes known as Mylecan steel.)

Lady Branson grinned and struggled to contain her excitement. Sir Peter placed his hands on her shoulders and said seriously, "Can you please keep this between us?"

Lady Branson was distracted by Sir Peter's warm touch and got lost in the intense sea of blue that was his eyes. Sir Peter felt he had been overstepping boundaries by touching her, yet he felt a sort of spark. He found something tantalizing about her green eyes and found her face alluring. But he thought of Faye and immediately removed his hands.

Lady Branson picked up on this and averted her gaze briefly. Slightly embarrassed, she said, "Eh, yeah, sure, I mean, of course. I swear I won't tell a soul."

"Good," said Sir Peter. "Erm, might I ask why?"

Sir Peter was hesitant to speak. Seeing this, Lady Branson said, "You don't have to tell me."

He responded, "No, no, I'm already trusting you with sensitive information. I should probably tell you why you're keeping it secret. The truth is, Modith cores are extremely rare, even in Mylec. If someone found out this bouquet was made from Modith cores, well, I fear it would draw some unwanted attention."

"Right, but how did it get here?" asked Lady Branson.

"It's a long story. You see, the blacksmith that helped me forge it sold it."

"Oh, dear, how awful," Lady Branson responded, genuinely empathizing with him.

"Yeah, apparently, he sold it to some Iiadecan. A Lord Humphrey something," said Sir Peter.

"Lord Humphrey Blakewood. He runs the tournaments in Iiadec, especially after wars," said Lady Branson.

"So you know him?" asked Sir Peter.

"Not personally, but several people have described him as an arrogant old fart." Sir Peter smiled at the mention of the word *fart*.

"What? I don't have to act ladylike all the time. I'm much more than that, you know," Lady Branson said, while chuckling.

"Aye, you're quite brave. Some of the toughest shield maidens would not speak with Agnarr the Mad," said Sir Peter.

"Well, I am sure it can't be all bad. You managed to find yourself somebody you love dearly, that's more than most people," she said.

Sir Peter looked into her eyes, quite moved by what she had just said. "Thank you."

"For what?" Lady Branson asked.

"For standing up for me during the tournament when the crowd hurled their insults. You are truly Brave Lady Elysant Baker," said Sir Peter. "Please call me Elysant. Oh, please forgive me, I've gone and interrupted your story," said Lady Branson.

"It's quite alright. I've forgotten where I was," said Sir Peter.

"Erm, Lord Humphrey Blakewood, I think," responded Lady Branson.

"Ah yes, he asked for an exorbitant prize that I could not afford, nor was I willing to pay for. If I did, he would've suspected it was made of Modith cores and might never sell it. He gave me an alternative. He said I could win it back in the tournament, so I entered," said Sir Peter.

Lady Branson smiled and her eyes narrowed as they often did when she smiled. "Wow, that's rather noble of you. So tell me about it, it must have a story.

Sir Peter replied, "Modith cores are nigh indestructible when fully forged. They will never rust nor dull just like my love for her. The flowers are twin flowers from my homeland of Yelithr. They remind her that I am a part of her now."

"You're quite the romantic, Agnarr Branson. It's Faye that you're betrothed to?" she asked.

Sir Peter was quite surprised she knew her name.

Sensing this, Lady Branson quickly said, "I saw her once before. You were calling her name the last time you were at Corithni during the treaty signing. She's quite beautiful." (Treaty of Etlio was signed in 1535 at Corithni. It ended the skirmishes during the Etlio/Tegr conflict.)

"Yes, she is. But she can be quite troublesome. She insisted I bring her along, then wandered off. I thought I'd lost her," said Sir Peter.

"Well, it seems you really care. I'm sure she was thrilled with her gift," said Lady Branson.

"Well... she never saw it and she doesn't even know I'm here," said Sir Peter.

"Well, I'm sure she'll love her gift enough to forgive your deception," said Lady Branson.

Sir Peter was taken aback by the word deception. He laughed nervously "Wha—he-he! I would hardly call it deception."

Lady Branson shot Sir Peter a playfully incredulous look. "Really? What would you call it?"

Sir Peter sighed as though admitting a wrong "deception".

Lady Branson laughed. "You don't have to sound so defeated. Are you always this serious?" Sir Peter smiled.

"You sound like my younger brother, Heggr. He's quite the talker, silver tongue that one."

Then suddenly, Sir Peter grew suspicious of Lady Branson. He seemed to think she had been interrogating him the whole time without him noticing until now. His brow furrowed and his eyes narrowed slightly as he studied her face, looking for any signs of deception.

Lady Branson's eyes widened in response. She was startled by his change in demeanor. "Are you alright, Agnarr?"

Ignoring her, Sir Peter continued to peer into her eyes, searching for any dishonesty. Lady Branson felt uncomfortable, but felt it unnecessary to leave or cry for help.

"Agnarr," she called out in an attempt to get his attention.

Instead, Sir Peter said, "Heggr once told me information is like a weapon. Be careful who you sell it to as they may use it against you. So tell me, Lady Elysant Baker, who has the pleasure of owing the information of the mad marauder?"

Lady Branson was highly offended by the accusation but maintained her composure. "I'm sorry that you feel that way and you have every right to be suspicious. The people in Iiadec have not been so welcoming to you, but I am no spy. I just felt compelled to show you that we are not all bigots. Our kingdoms can coexist. If I was lying, why would I defend you at the tournament? Look into my eyes Agnarr, no falsehood lies within them." Her face displayed no signs of treachery as far as Sir Peter could tell, and her words seemed to placate him.

Sir Peter's gaze gravitated towards the ground and his head hung low, quite ashamed of his accusation. "I'm sorry… it's just, well, you see, there was this man in a black hood. I couldn't see his face, but he kept looking during the tournament. I don't know what he wanted. Anyway, I thought you were spying for him. I know it's quite stupid. Again, I'm sorry."

Lady Branson placed her hand on Sir Peter's shoulder and looked directly into his eyes. "You have nothing to apologize for. You had the misfortune of experiencing war at a young age. Naturally, it's made you suspicious of other people, but know this, there are those in Iiadec who appreciated all that you sacrificed and are aware of your bravery. We are and I am truly in debt to you Agnarr, son of Brandr, you may not be a knight, but you truly embody what it means to be one."

Sir Peter placed his hand on hers and said, "Thank you Elysant."

"Elysant! Elysant!" cried a voice.

"Grandfather!" Lady Branson said. She removed her hand from Sir Peter's shoulder and said, "Erm, I'm sorry, but I've got to go." She smiled. "It was nice meeting you officially."

Sir Peter smiled back and said, "Likewise." The two waved to each other as Lady Branson sprinted away to find Giles.

***

Back at the barracks, tensions were high. The news of Sir Richard's plan had spread like wildfire and people were in desperate need of leadership. Giles tried to calm people down, telling them to trust in

Lord Franklin, but that didn't seem to work. People only grew more agitated. Several within the barracks were ambivalent about the prospect of escaping, especially by such drastic means. Some thought escape was futile, and they should remain and negotiate with the enemy, while others believed escape was the only means of survival.

Meanwhile, Lady Branson was alone with the recently deceased Sir Richard. She was praying to Arda for Sir Richard's soul to reach paradise and for Arda to forgive his sins as she often did for the deceased. She recited some verses from the book of Noga and sat down in a chair, lamenting. She stared at the ceiling and wondered why Arda placed them in this predicament. Hector was most likely going to breech the walls and, even if they escaped, they would leave so many behind only to be pursued later. She started asking Arda questions in her mind like *"Why did this need to happen? Haven't the people at Corithni suffered enough from one war? Why did there need to be another in such a short time span? Why did Hector have to contest for the throne? Why did King Gavin have to die? Please Arda, protect us all and bring reason to Hector's heart so there can be peace."* Tears streamed down her face as she cried silently. Unbeknownst to her, Alywin was watching her.

She eventually caught him staring and she quickly wiped the tears from her eyes. "Erm… I'm sorry, did you need something?" she asked.

"Milady, it's the others. They want to know our next course of action given the circumstances," said Alywin.

"Oh, right, I'll get back to them once I've finished up here," Lady Branson said, as she averted her gaze. His eyes were filled with deep-seated concern for her. This was made apparent to Lady Branson. She responded by smiling artificially. "I'm fine, really."

But Alywin saw past her façade. "Are you? Because it's alright not to be, especially given everything going on."

Alywin anticipated a different reaction, one where Lady Branson attempted to further mask her emotions, but instead it was diametrically opposite. Lady Branson burst into tears in a full-blown catharsis. She started saying unintelligible babble but from what Alywin could make out, it had something to do about priorities, death, and not being able to save people in need. He thought it was best to console her by hugging her. He was hesitant to perform such an action initially, for a lowborn man to hug a highborn lady was deemed inappropriate in many respects but ultimately, he realized it was the right thing to do for she was in distress after all. This seemed to calm her, and her crying was subdued. During their embrace, in an attempt to soothe her, Alywin kept saying, "Let it out, let it out."

When they finally separated, Lady Branson asked, "Can I ask you a personal question?"

"Sure, milady" replied Alywin.

In a quavery voice and with watery eyes she asked, "How is it you always have it together despite your lack of faith when I'm barely hanging on with it?"

Alywin sighed heavily. "The truth is I don't always have it together. I simply rely on other people like Tim, the Archiater, you."

"You don't have to be nice to me just because I sullied your clothes with my tears. I know you're not really like that, Alywin," she said.

Alywin frowned. "I'm not mean. I just have a strong distaste for nonsense and stupidity." After a brief silence, they both laughed. "You know just because I don't have faith doesn't mean I don't have faith, just not in God. My faith lies in principles created by man—honesty, empathy, and friendship—and I will follow anyone who embodies that, which is why I follow you."

Lady Branson was left speechless by his words. Alywin, who was disheartened by her response, or lack thereof, laughed nervously. "Heh-heh, sorry for making you uncomfortable. I didn't mean to imply... I'm mean... I didn't... I'm sorry I'll be on my way." Feeling quite ashamed of himself, Alywin was about to turn around to leave when Lady Branson stopped him.

"No, please stay."

Alywin turned to Lady Branson, and they stared at each other in brevity. Her words had a resounding effect on him, as he was not expecting them.

Lady Branson cleared her throat. "*Ahem*, I'm truly honored that you have faith in me. It's just with Sir Richard's plan, well there is no guarantee I'll successfully execute it."

"Aye, but I know you'll try," said Alywin.

"Alywin, I think your faith in me is misplaced," said Lady Branson. "Do you remember how we met, milady?"

"Yes, it was quite eventful," she said.

"Tim and I were mere thieves from the wretched town of Garla, when you spotted us at your chambers. When Sir Peter and the knights barged in, demanding to know who we were, you simply said we were weary travelers in desperate need of work. You saved our lives that day. We would have been executed. I can't tell you how grateful I am to you, milady. You have a kind heart; you care for people. A hallmark of a great leader. Something I dare say Lord Franklin could learn from. You're capable. One man's death shouldn't change that."

Garla is a town that many considered to be the slums of Eredith. It is filled with unsavory sorts and the downtrodden.

Lady Branson hugged Alywin. "Oh, thank you, Alywin. You have lifted my spirits. You are truly a good friend."

Eva walked in on them. "Oh, was I interrupting something?"

The two quickly separated. "No, no," said Alywin and Lady Branson in unison.

"Good," Eva smiled. "Giles asked me to check on you. Are you alright, milady?"

"I'm fine, thank you," replied Lady Branson.

"That's good, erm, could I maybe ask you a favor?" asked Eva. "Sure," replied Lady Branson.

"You see, Giles is having trouble with the people here. Many feel agitated, given the news. I was hoping you could assist him in calming them down," said Eva.

"I was just getting to that," said Lady Branson.

Eva sighed a heavy sigh of relief. "Oh, thank heavens, thank you, milady." She returned to Giles and whispered something in his ear. Giles looked at Lady Branson, trying to determine whether she was ready. She nodded her head in response. Giles then turned to the people in the garrison, who eagerly awaited an update on their situation.

"People, people, please calm yourselves. As I said before, we must be patient and trust in the might of the defenders and the strength of Corithni castle walls. However, if a situation should arise in which they fall, and the castle walls are breeched, a plan has been devised to protect everyone in the keep."

Giles motioned his hand towards Lady Branson. "My granddaughter, Lady Branson, will explain the details of this plan."

Lady Branson stood at the center of the garrison, where all eyes were on her. Keep in mind, reader, all the healers are still attending to the injured while Lady Branson addressed the crowd. "As you already know, the late Sir Richard Brickenden of Etlio found a plan of escape. This plan is quite drastic and would be a last resort. To be frank, I'm hesitant to go along with it myself, but we don't seem to have another option if Hector's men do, in fact, breech the walls. Even under the unlikely scenario Hector listens to reason and spares our lives, there is no telling what the dragon will do if it's still alive by the end of the siege. Hector has not specified his demands other than taking the castle, but I think we can assume that given the casualties he suffered, he will not be so kind to us if he does."

An elderly man who had recently lost an eye and had a bandage wrapped around his head interrupted. "It will be no quarter. Lord Franklin had his chance to surrender during the siege and he refused. There is only so much we could expect Hector to do."

A young man with a missing hand scowled at the one-eyed man. "You know, it's almost like you're blaming Lord Franklin for not yielding the castle because only a traitor would do something like that."

"Careful, boy. I've fought in several battles and lost so much. I know enough about war to know it's about compromise, not blind loyalty to Lords," said the one-eyed man.

The young man's face reddened with anger. "You talk of lost, old man, like I am unfamiliar with it. How dare you!" the young man said through gritted teeth.

The one-eyed man seemed unfazed and nonchalantly said, "I don't expect you to understand you're just a—"

"A what? A lowborn? We lowborns have done more for Lord Franklin than you knights ever have. We're on the frontlines. We're the pikemen, the archers, the infantry. I may have not fought in as many battles as you, but I know loss. This proves it," the young man pointed to the stump that was his right hand. "And I'd rather die than submit to the enemy." Several cheered him on.

The one-eyed man sighed. "The Lords don't care about the people who serve under them, lowborn or highborn. Trust me, I served under both Gavin and Albert Franklin. The Lords have their own agendas, and their needs will always take precedent over ours. That's a simple fact." The one-eyed man's voice raised with an inflection of anger. "You think Lord Franklin or Hector give a damn how many people die in their war? Your naivety is appalling."

The young man was about to lunge at the one-eyed man, but he was restrained by a male healer. "Calm down, Addy. Sir Wybert's mind has been addled with old age and injury."

"Oh, my mind is intact. This fool, on the other hand, I am not so sure," said Sir Wybert.

Addy, not heeding the healer's warning, blurted out, "You call yourself a knight? You swore allegiance to house Franklin, yet you speak so ill of them!"

Sir Wybert, speaking to the healer, said, "Let him go. I'd wager my one eye to his one hand any day."

Addy growled and broke free of the healers' grasp. He struck Sir Wybert in the mouth, causing his lip to bleed. Sir Wybert wiped the blood from his lips and said, "Well, you've got heart, but lack reason. You just made a costly mistake."

"Enough!" Lady Branson screamed, and the two stopped and looked at Lady Branson, quite surprised by her sense of control over the situation. "You've made your point, but this isn't about classes, the agendas of the powers at be, or even the war. This is about survival. We shouldn't be arguing amongst each other because senseless arguments lead us nowhere. People, the stakes are higher than they've ever been. We need to do this together because if we don't and the defenders fall, we will die."

Addy and Sir Wybert's demeanor changed, and they both calmed themselves.

Sir Wybert even asked, "What do you suggest we do, milady?" "First, we must get an account of everyone in the keep before we speak of escape through the tunnels."

"Perhaps I can be of assistance, milady. I have been keeping track of who has entered the keep," said one of the male healers.

"Thank you, Clifford."

"You are most welcome, milady. I shall start in this very garrison," said Clifford, quite eager to perform such a task.

"Oh, I'd like to help as well, if you'll have me. We'll cover more ground," said Clara.

"Very well," said Lady Branson.

"Lady Branson, we have a plan for the tunnels," said Sarah, who was referring to Tim and Alywin.

Sarah relayed the plan to Lady Branson. "Be careful and report back immediately at any sign of danger," she said.

"Don't worry, milady. I'll have these two with me," said Sarah, nodding to Alywin and Tim.

"Then I leave it in your capable hands," said Lady Branson.

Alywin whispered to Tim under his breath. "She's placed a lot of faith in us. I just hope, for all our sakes, she knows what she's doing."

Tim responded by whispering, "Oh, hush up now. She's kin to the bloody master builder. Of course she knows what she's doing. If you didn't want to go, why'd you volunteer?"

Lady Branson heard some rumblings of noise from Tim and asked, "Is something wrong?"

"Nothing," Tim and Alywin said in unison.

Colin approached Lady Branson and Giles. He bowed his head awkwardly. He was unfamiliar with the customs of the lowborn and highborn, as he had been a sell-sword most of his life.

"Hello, I am Colin of the Rilek Herons," said Colin.

Giles gave Colin a suspicious look. "Yes, you're part of the mercenary group Lord Franklin hired," said Giles.

"We prefer the term free company," he responded.

Giles, very wary of Colin, said, "I'm sorry, what was it you wanted?" Sensing Giles' uneasiness towards him, Colin was rather vexed by his attitude but instead of being reactionary he decided to let it go. "Sorry, it was nothing."

Colin was about to turn around when Lady Branson stopped him. "Wait, please. You seem worried. Is something the matter?"

Giles frowned at Lady Branson, she frowned back. They seemed to have a nonverbal disagreement over how to deal with Colin. Unbeknownst to them, this was obvious to Colin.

"No, really, it's nothing. I wouldn't want to bother you with trivialities," said Colin.

"Nonsense, forgive my grandfather for his rudeness. His senses have dulled due to age," said Lady Branson.

To which Giles responded quite angered, "Young lady!"

Completely ignoring Giles, Lady Branson asked, "You said you were part of the Rilek Herons. You must have fought in the battle of Rilek?"

Colin, quite surprised and yet impressed by her knowledge, said, "You really know your battles, milady, no doubt the result of your husband, Sir Peter."

"I make it a habit of knowing as much about battles as I can, so I know where we stand, and I think it is important for everyone to know the cruel reality of war, so they are less eager to wage it. So many people risk their lives, minds, and souls to protect our freedom. The least we could do is not let them die in vain. Whether they be knights, lowborn, or sell sword, each has a story, and that story should be told."

Colin was quite moved by her words, and before he could speak, Giles interrupted. "Forgive my granddaughter. She can be quite mawkish. No doubt a result of being a young woman in such troubling times."

Lady Branson scowled at him. Unmoved by her glare, Giles continued by saying, "Anyway, I'm sure you have more pertinent matters to attend to, otherwise we'll be on our way."

Colin worked up the courage to say it. "Actually, something has been troubling me. You see, there should be a relief force arriving from Eredith. My brothers Edric and Thorley Harlow traveled with a band of knights from Etlio, but we received no word."

Lady Branson and Giles looked at each other, wondering if they should tell Colin the unfortunate news and which one of them would tell him. Giles finally broke the silence. "There were no survivors in the battle of Eredith."

Colin's eyes widened. "Wha-What... that doesn't make any sense. Edric said Hector's forces were all but defeated."

Both Lady Branson and Giles had their heads down and they contemplated whether telling him more.

Before either of them could speak, Colin spoke, "Your silence says it all. They were ambushed. God, that fucking cunt Hector."

"I'm truly sorry, Colin," said Lady Branson.

Colin sighed and said in a low, menacing voice, "I swear I will kill him, for my father and my brothers, even if we lose the war, he'll die for this." "In order to do that, you'll still have to survive first," said Lady Branson.

Colin nodded his head, indicating he understood, and he went back to his elevated bed Sarah fixed for him, thinking of ways to extract his revenge on Hector.

Giles and Lady Branson watched as he went. When he was out of range, Lady Branson asked, "Are we sure it was the best idea not telling him about Kraag?"

Giles responded by saying, "No need to decrease morale even more by mentioning the monsters of old."

"So you believe Sir Richard?" asked Lady Branson.

"I don't know what I believe anymore," said Giles despondently.

He kept a wary eye on Colin, who was muttering something under his breath while shaking a clenched fist. "Be careful with that one and his type," said Giles. Lady Branson responded by rolling her eyes.

"I'm serious Elysant. Men like that are very dangerous," said Giles. "You are aware my husband was a former raider from Mylec?" retorted Lady Branson.

"That's different," Giles protested.

"Really? You didn't seem to think so back then," responded Lady Branson.

Giles groaned. "Must you always fight me?"

"Only when you're wrong." Lady Branson smiled, and Giles smiled back.

"I love you, Elysant."

"I love you too, Grandfather," said Lady Branson.

"Remember, Lady Franklin ordered us to treat all allies of House Franklin," said Lady Branson.

"Yes, I remember, but that doesn't mean I have to trust them," said Giles.

"If Lord Franklin trusts them, then we should, as well. Besides, you heard Colin, it's not just about money for him, it's personal," said Lady Branson.

Giles wasn't paying attention. Instead he looked at Lady Branson affectionately. This prompted Lady Branson to ask, "Grandfather, are you alright?"

Tears streamed down his face as he said, "Oh my Elysant. How you have grown over the years. Both your mother and father would be proud. I really hope the hands of fate don't separate us prematurely and I pray the defenders are successful in their efforts because I don't see a future for us if Hector wins. Even if we escape, we'd always be running. I don't fear dying. I lived to see many seasons, but the thought of you perishing, I just couldn't bear."

"No one here is going to die as long as we stick together. Even if the defenders should fall, we can flee to Mirama. There is no way the Steward King and the kingmakers will allow us to be executed. Do you remember what you said? We still need to go there anyway to discuss Kraag, so we need to survive for the sake of everyone in Mirthadine. Grandfather, I know this is overwhelming. It is for all of us, but we must remain strong for each other sakes," said Lady Branson. She held Giles shoulders. "I know we can survive this siege. As long as we have faith in each other and God we have everything."

Giles hugged Lady Branson and kissed her forehead, tears still streaming down his face. He said, "Bless you, child. You are a beacon of hope in these dark times."

Some semblances of order were returned to the barracks. Clifford checked the garrison to see if everyone was accounted for, and Clara ascended the stairs to the Great Hall to embark on her mission. The Great Hall was in turmoil. Several people were panicking with others pacing about nervously, and children crying. A woman in her forties was at the center of the hall on the fourth floor. She looked quite regal, wearing a black cloak on top of a black and red gown with golden trimmings embroidered with images of flowers. She had the hood of her cloak lowered, revealing long red hair with a smidge of gray. Her hair was ornately tied into a long, loose braid with hair trinkets conservatively placed throughout the braid.

There was another woman panicking. She shouted up and down the Great Hall. She paced back and forth shouting, "He's gone! I can't find him anywhere." The woman started hyperventilating under stress.

A small infant girl started tugging at her dress. "Mummy, mummy, let's play a game. I'm bored."

The mother was trying her best to calm down by breathing in deeply. "Not now, Jetta. Mummy is quite busy now."

The regal-looking woman walked up to them. "Who is it you're looking for, Hollis?"

Hollis bowed her head before speaking. "Lady Franklin, it's Godfrey. Lady Branson told me to watch him, but I can't find him anywhere." "He could not have gone far. We'll search the other floors," said Lady Franklin.

Clara overheard their conversation. She gasped. *"Oh, no. Godfrey's missing. Lady Branson will be horrified."*

Lady Franklin heard Clara gasp. "Clara, what are you doing up here?"

Clara bowed. "Milady, I was asked to take account of everyone in the keep."

"And you wouldn't happen to have seen Godfrey?" asked Lady Franklin. Clara shook her head.

"Oh heavens," Hollis groaned.

"He could not have gone far," said a voice. It came from a young pregnant woman.

"Giselle, you should be resting in the chambers," said Lady Franklin. "I'm sorry, milady, but I tried really, but there is so much tumult outside. I just couldn't-"

"It's quite alright. Just be careful for your child's sake," said Lady Franklin. Lady Franklin and Giselle exchanged looks as though they were communicating something in secrecy. Clara took notice of this peculiarity but chose to say nothing.

"Er right, milady," said Giselle.

Hollis, quite panic-stricken, asked, "Where could he have gone? I searched everywhere…. Huh what, what if he escaped the keep? Oh, my God. There's a dragon out there!"

Lady Franklin attempted to calm her distressed comrade. "He couldn't have escaped without anyone noticing," said Hollis.

Lady Franklin caught the eye of a very shamefaced looking boy, who was standing close to Hollis. He appeared to be the age of five. "You wouldn't happen to know where Godfrey went, do you Haywood?"

Haywood hesitated to respond. "Speak boy!" cried Hollis. "I dun-I dun know anything," stammered Haywood.

"Haywood, if you don't speak truth, right now by Arda I will-" Lady Franklin, seeing his mortified expression, interrupted Hollis.

She smiled at Haywood and knelt to his level. "Haywood, I know you're a good boy, yes?" Haywood did not answer. Instead, he stared at Lady Franklin, unsure how best to answer the question.

"Answer Lady Franklin, Haywood," said Hollis sternly.

To which Haywood, visibly frightened, responded, "Yes! Milady." "That's good. Now I know you and Godfrey are friends," said Lady Franklin.

"The best," Haywood qualified while smiling.

"Oh, I see, well you know that friends must always look after each other. Right now, Godfrey is missing. I would like it very much if you'd help us find him," said Lady Franklin.

Haywood was on the verge of tears as he said in a quavering voice, "But-but he made me promise. He said he'd make me his squire when he became a knight."

"It's alright, child. Did he say where he went?" asked Lady Franklin. "He said he went to fight the dragon and that he'd be right back," said Haywood.

Hollis gasped and started breathing heavily. Giselle, Clara, and Lady Franklin tried to calm her down. "You must calm yourself. Hope is not lost. Godfrey will return to us," said Lady Franklin.

"Yes, there is still time. We can send out a search party to bring him back to the keep," said Giselle.

A middle-aged, highborn woman eavesdropped on their conversation. "A search party for a mere child, Lady Franklin? Surely, you're not seriously suggesting it?"

"Godfrey is like a son to Sir Peter and Lady Branson. They love him dearly. I cannot allow him to perish."

Haywood's ears perked up at the mention of the word perish and asked, "Is Godfrey going to die?"

To which Lady Franklin replied, "No, no child. Why don't you and your sister run along and play with the other children. Remember, do not stray too far from Lady Uptone." The two children went to another section of the Great Hall.

The highborn woman waited until they were out of earshot before speaking again. "There is no point in lying to them. This Godfrey is as good as dead. The boy was eager to meet his own demise. His death is probably a good thing, given who his father was."

Lady Franklin scowled at the woman. "I implore you next time to not be so loose of tongue. You forget yourself, Lady Fowler."

Lady Fowler was frightened by Lady Franklin's demeanor and quickly said, "Apologies for my tactlessness but, need I remind you of our situation? Daggard has been recaptured, Lord Blakeslee is nowhere to be found. There is no word on Athamar, only rumblings from that god-forsaken town Garla that monsters have run amok, but I believe it's just

Hector playing a trick. The point is, there are few places safe in Iiadec. It would be folly to risk our survival on a boy."

"Our survival is already at great risk, regardless. Maybe that's what prompted Godfrey to behave so recklessly in the first place," said Lady Franklin.

"Reckless indeed," said a voice. The group of women turned around to see a woman in her mid-thirties wearing typical lowborn garb, a wimple to cover her hair and a long gown of unremarkable design.

"Lodema, shouldn't you be attending to Bernia? She must be distraught, well, with all the noise," asked Lady Franklin.

"Oh Bernia. She's fine now. Probably counting the tiles on the ceiling or the steps of the keep."

Giselle frowned at Lodema, to which Lodema responded, rather peeved, "What? I can't be expected to take care of my husband's—ugh, if I can call him that—wayward sister along with his two children from a previous marriage."

Giselle said, "She needs to be taken care of, for if Robert or Robin were here, they'd both be furious."

Lodema sighed while rolling her eyes. "Robert and that drunkard can go to hell for all I care. Did you know, before the siege, Robert came home smelling of different women every night? I mean, where does an archer get the coin to spend on whores? I bet yours doesn't come home smelling of whores, does he? After all, Martin's a sweet boy."

Giselle said, "Um, yes, he is," rather nervously and desperate to change the subject.

"Where are the twins now?" asked Hollis, rather concerned given the situation.

"Relax, they're with Lady Uptone. They're not as clever as Godfrey. They're Robert's children after all. That boy Godfrey used the commotion with the dragon and little Haywood faking a fainting spell to escape through the window of the keep. A plan like that takes dedication, luck, or both. Of course, I don't blame him for escaping. It's rather dreary and boring in here," said Lodema.

Lady Fowler, rather annoyed with Lodema for butting into her conversation with Lady Franklin, said curtly, "Is there something you wish to contribute? Otherwise, cease your incessant babbling."

Lodema was taken aback by such rudeness and was about to speak her mind, as she often did. Such a catastrophe was averted when Giselle signaled to Lodema by shaking her head, thus indicating to Lodema that it would be unwise to lash out at Lady Fowler. Hence, Lodema instead decided to let her anger go. She gave Lady Fowler an artificial smile and said, "My point, milady, is that Godfrey's hardly defenseless. One more year and he would have been Sir Peter's squire, and my husband, that buffoon Robert and his drunk of a brother Robin, are excellent archers in spite of themselves. I believe they've already subdued or killed the dragon. I haven't heard any of its movements since. Therefore, there is no need to dispatch such a large force to find Godfrey. One person could do the task."

Clara, who had been busy trying to keep track of everyone in the keep, was jotting names down on parchment and said, "A quiet dragon is not the same as a dead one. I think we should be cautious. It could simply be a standoff."

"Which is why it is important we send as few people out there to avoid alerting it. Now, if we could only see what we're up against," said Lodema, her gaze directed towards the northernmost keep window.

Clara saw her looking at the window. "No. Lord Franklin said *not to vex the dragon in any way.*"

"Ah, come on. I've never seen a dragon. I'm sure a peek won't hurt," said Lodema.

"I think we should be cautious about this," said Hollis.

The others, too, were wary of this prospect. Lady Fowler was quite vexed by Lodema. "Your Lord has forbidden you from looking at the beast. Please cease such insolence."

"Forgive me, milady, but those words came from Robert, who is an oaf and quite unreliable. Who knows what Lord Franklin really said and secondly, the words were *not to vex the dragon in any way.* That could mean anything. How do we know a harmless look will vex the dragon? We can't be in the dark forever," said Lodema.

"Can you believe such utter disrespect, milady? What do you have to say to this?" said Lady Fowler.

Lady Franklin responded in a calm manner, a sharp contrast to Lady Fowler. "I don't see it as disrespect but rather concern for our wellbeing and yet I am ambivalent at the notion of looking through the window at the beast." She turned to Clara and asked, "What do you think? You know the most about dragons and these sort of things."

Lady Fowler was upset that Lady Franklin placed so much trust in a lowborn. It was making her judgment questionable. She thought, *"Imagine, in the middle of a siege she talks to these lowborn like they're members of counsel and she wants to use our limited resources to save a boy. No wonder we're losing the war. Perhaps things would have been better if House Fowler had sided with that brute Hector, but I'm sure it's much too late for that now."*

Clara spoke. "Dragons, at least those that reside in Arcadiem, are sensitive creatures according to the literature. Eye contact may aggravate them. Robert said the beast had black eyes which shouldn't be possible, unless…"

"Unless what?" demanded Lady Fowler.

"We may be dealing with something that goes beyond our understanding, at least within Arcadiem. If Hector could possess a dragon, there is no telling what power he holds," said Clara. The others were quite horrified by the revelation including Lady Franklin, but she maintained her composure for the sake of the others.

"Then it's decided. We will dispatch a small team to stealthily get Godfrey back to the keep and we won't do anything to provoke the dragon, hence no looking at it as if it looks back, there is no telling what will happen."

"Forgive me for asking, Milady, but how do we even know they're alive?" said Hollis despondently.

Lodema frowned at Hollis. "Don't talk like that Hollis."

"But it's what everyone's thinking. If Hector has that type of power on his side, how can Godfrey survive? How can any of us?" said Hollis.

There was silence, in which all the women contemplated the gravity of their situation. Clara finally broke the silence. "Sir Peter's with them."

"What?" said Lady Fowler.

"One of the injured in the garrison said he went to help some archers and infantrymen deal with the dragon," said Clara.

"He abandoned his post?" said Lady Fowler.

"Well, he's no good with a bow, so the walls aren't an option, and his people are renown for dragon slaying," responded Clara.

"His people are savages. They barely kept any records, and the ones they do have are unreliable, shrouded in mythical tales and fiction," Lady Fowler said. She was quite dismissive of Clara's claims.

"There's nothing fictional about Sir Peter's feats and he wields the legendary blade Seggr that glows," said Giselle.

In Mirthadine, objects that glow, resonant, or emit heat on their own contain hidden potent power. The reason is unknown, but many believe that those objects have a soul within them. The other women found it peculiar that she knew so much about Sir Peter's blade. Especially since Sir Peter was such a private person. Sensing this Giselle, simply said, "Martin told me. He's practically obsessed with him, as are most people in Iiadec are, probably outside of Iiadec as well."

Lady Fowler, quickly changing the subject, said, "Even if this Sir Peter is as amazing as everyone says, one man alone can't change the tide of battle."

"That is true, Lady Fowler, but it does make our prospects more favorable, especially when dealing with the dragon," said Lady Franklin. "Then he's alive. Sir Peter wouldn't let him die, whew," Hollis said.

She then exhaled in relief before saying, "Oh, thank God."

"We must still be cautious if we are going to retrieve him. They're about twelve capable men in the barracks that have all but healed. They can defend the keep, if need be," said Clara.

"That seems a bit unnecessary, and besides, wouldn't that many people just provoke the dragon?" Lodema asked.

"Then what do you suggest?" asked Clara.

Lodema was cautious when laying out her proposition because she knew they would consider it preposterous. "Well, I could—"

Lady Franklin interrupted for she already knew what Lodema was about to suggest. "Out of the question. Is that clear, Lodema?" she said sternly.

"Yes, milady," said Lodema.

"Good. We will be sending ten men to defend the keep while two go out and retrieve Godfrey. If the dragon is vexed, make sure the men keep it away from the keep. Clara will go to the barracks and inform the Archiater and Lady Branson of the plan. Clara makes sure to deliver the news to Lady Branson as delicately as possible."

"Yes, milady," said Clara.

As she was about to head back towards the barracks, Giselle said, "Wait, milady. Clara still hasn't accounted for everyone in the Great Hall. There may still be people missing."

Seizing an opportunity to escape what she deemed the dreary hall, Lodema said, "Might I suggest that I talk to Lady Branson instead?"

Lady Franklin was unsure of this, but she felt she had no other choice. "Fine. But you are not to leave the keep under any circumstances. Understood?"

Lodema, struggling to contain her excitement over being given a task, replied, "Yes, milady."

Hollis sighed, "That woman."

Noticing her frustration, Giselle said, "It can be boring being a woman in these times, especially during war. Historically, we're mostly just used as leverage for the men."

"We all have our roles, and no role is insignificant," said Lady Franklin.

"Forgive me, milady, for sounding despondent just now. It may help better raise my spirits if I help out with menial tasks, such as helping Clara." Anticipating resistance, Giselle assured Lady Franklin that she would not strain herself too much. Lady Franklin eventually gave in.

"You can assist as long as Clara believes it to be medically advisable, Clara?" Clara was too busy looking at Giselle to notice her name was being called. She was curious what sort of scheme Giselle was hatching. Giselle looked back at Clara as though telling her to play along.

"Clara?" Lady Franklin repeated.

"Er… yes milady, it's quite fine. A bit of exercise could be good for the baby," responded Clara.

The group soon departed to go their separate ways. Hollis went to look after her children. Lady Franklin and Lady Fowler went to calm everyone down in the hall. And, of course, Lodema went to the Barracks to tell Lady Branson the situation on Godfrey.

When the other women were out of earshot, Giselle whispered, "What's really going on down there?"

Hesitant to tell her the truth, for fear of spreading more panic amongst the people, Clara replied, "I don't know. What do you mean?" in a very disingenuous tone.

Irritated by this, Giselle whispered, "Don't play coy, Clara. I know you know more than you're letting on."

Angered by Giselle's tone, Clara responded, "You think because you somehow have the ear of Lady Franklin, you can simply make demands of me? You're not a highborn, you know."

"I'm sorry, it's just that you never used to keep secrets from me." Put off by what she deemed hypocrisy, Clara said curtly, "Well, it seems I'm not the only one keeping secrets." Her gaze was directed towards Giselle's belly.

Giselle's eyes widened, and her skin paled. It was at that moment, Giselle realized Clara knew something, but she didn't know how much she knew. "Might we speak somewhere more private?" Giselle said.

"I'm afraid I must decline. I have a task to do." Before she could leave, Giselle grabbed her hand and squeezed it gently and said, "Please." The two ascended to the private chambers. Giselle removed a key she placed on her breast and locked the door behind her.

"How did you know?" she asked bluntly.

"It was pretty obvious. I mean Martin really, he barely even knows you and he is not your type," said Clara.

There was a brief silence between the two, with Giselle trying to figure out what to say and Clara reminiscing about their past. Clara finally broke the silence. "So, who else knows besides the father, obviously?"

"Just Lady Franklin," Giselle replied.

"Ah, that makes sense. It explains why she is treating you so nicely. So I'm guessing it's one of the Lords. Which one?"

Giselle sighed. "Does it really even matter?" "It matters to me," said Clara.

"Fine, if you must know, it's Edmund," said Giselle.

Clara did not respond immediately. The emotional blow made her numb. This prompted Giselle to say, "It just sorta happened I—"

"Do you love him?" Clara interrupted. She looked at Giselle. "You do. I can see it in your eyes."

Clara turned away from her in a desperate attempt to obscure her tears from Giselle, but Giselle noticed. Giselle placed her hand on Clara's shoulder. "I'm sorry, but what we had, it just wasn't proper, we simply couldn't be. We were only pretending. It simply wouldn't work, but know this, Clara. I will always value our friendship."

This made Clara furious. She turned around and displayed her full range of emotions. "I don't need your friendship! We fucked, and it was your idea... You said you loved me. Did that mean anything to you?" Clara felt a lump in her throat and found it difficult to talk. Her tears were on full display. She looked at Giselle and said, "How could you?"

"Clara, please. It had to be so. Try to understand there comes a point where a woman has to settle down, have children and find a man," Giselle wiped the tears from Clara's cheeks and she then moved some loose strands of curly, raven dark hair from Clara's forehead and tucked it behind Clara's ears. "Eventually, you'll find a husband."

"I don't want to find a man. I don't like men like that. I'm not like you. I don't have the luxury of choosing," said Clara. Clara turned away from Giselle again. "Did you really mean it when you said it?"

"Clara, will you please just look at me?" said Giselle.

Clara turned around and took a good look at Giselle. She had a lightly freckled face with the freckles being more pronounced on her left cheek than her right. Long, light brown hair that curled at the ends and green eyes. Clara found her beautiful. Giselle placed both hands on Clara's cheeks and looked directly into Clara's grey eyes and said, "I will always love you, but we simply cannot be."

"We could run away. I hear the snake people are more accepting of people like us," said Clara.

"We would be foreigners, and persecuted for being human, also we would have to pass through Agor, enemy territory, just to get to Silas-Dor," said Giselle.

(Sison land in Iiadec is landlocked and is encircled by Agor.) "You can use your magic to take us there," said Clara.

"I've never been to Silas-Dor. I cannot simply transport there and how will we live there? We don't even know the language," said Giselle.

"We'll learn together and then we'll disguise ourselves as snake-people if need be. Surely, making fork tongues out of magic shouldn't be too difficult for you," said Clara.

"For how long? We cannot mask our appearance forever. Spells don't last that long. Clara, you're dreaming," said Giselle.

"So, we'll assimilate into their society and as for moving there, there are people who are light of feet that may be able to travel with objects, even people, in an instant," said Clara.

"Clara, those are only stories and even if true, those people would be rare and why would they want to help us?" said Giselle.

"I'm not giving up on this. I'm not giving up on us. So just say you'll run away with me, say you want this, please?" pleaded Clara.

Giselle did not respond immediately, which was nerve-racking for Clara. She finally said very somberly, "Clara, I'm sorry, but I don't want this."

The emotional blow was felt. Clara was clearly distraught, but she tried to mask it by smiling and chuckling. "He he. I'm sorry, that was a silly thing to ask, so stupid of me."

Giselle saw through her façade because tears were streaming down Clara's face, which Clara did her best to wipe away.

"Clara I—"

"No, no, it's my fault. I should've known you didn't feel the same way," Clara interrupted. What vexed Clara the most was Giselle's pitying eyes. She felt so humiliated by them, and she began to wonder, *how can something so beautiful be so cruel?*

Clara said, "Um, I should be going."

"Clara, wait!" Giselle called, but Clara had already slammed the door behind her. When Clara stepped outside the chamber, she nearly bumped into another woman. The woman was heavy set and had several children with her.

"Lady Uptone. I'm so sorry I—"

"No, no, the fault is mine. I can be quite clumsy." Lady Uptone studied Clara's face and noticed the tears that were in her eyes. "Oh, dear. Are those tears? Are you alright?"

"I'm fine, just water in my eyes."

Lady Uptone was not convinced. "These are stressful times. It's alright to talk about it sometimes. We must lean on each other if we're going to overcome adversity. When I lost my husband and sons to that brute Hector during the third battle of Daggard Castle in 1545, I thought I'd lost everything, but then you, Giselle, Lady Franklin, and everyone else in Corithni treated me so warmly. I am forever in your debt. Just know, whatever it is, as long as we hang on to the ones that we love, we'll be alright."

"Right, milady, er, if you don't mind me asking, where is Bernia?" asked Clara.

"Oh, she's with Hollis. The little ones were disturbing her, so I figured I'd take them somewhere else. Is Giselle in there? I didn't mean to disturb her. Is she feeling alright?" asked Lady Uptone.

"Um, she's just fine, just needing her rest," replied Clara.

Haywood, one of the children with Lady Uptone, studied Clara's face as children often do when curious. "Is Clara sad because of the dragon outside? Don't worry, Clara. Godfrey and Sir Peter will slay the Dragon."

Clara giggled. "No. I'm not sad and I'm sure they will." Haywood smiled back.

"The little ones give us hope in such times. That's why it's our duty to keep them safe," said Lady Uptone.

"They are the future," replied Clara.

The door opened from behind them. Giselle peeked her head out from behind. She appeared ill, but Clara knew better. This ruse seemed to fool Lady Uptone.

"Oh, dear, you look terrible. You should get some rest."

Giselle winced. "I'm fine, really. It's just pregnancy pains. I'd actually like it if Clara would assist, if that's alright with her?"

Clara said, "Of course." She was just keeping up appearances, but Giselle seemed genuinely happy with this response.

"Well, I'll leave you two to it. If you need any help, we'll be somewhere in the Great hall. Come on, little ones." Lady Uptone descended the stairs with the other children. They were all holding hands.

Clara entered the chambers, quite furious.

"Giselle. Oh, why do you torture me so? I thought it was obvious that I wanted to be left alone."

"I know, but just listen to me, Clara, please," said Giselle.

"No! You're always pleading, never listening. Haven't you humiliated me enough? I'm not your fucking pet to be summoned at will!" Clara headed for the door, but Giselle blocked the door.

"Move Giselle."

"I won't until you listen to what I have to say."

"You're so manipulative. Is that how you got Edmund? By tricking him into loving you, then you spread your legs like a common whore, just to increase your status?" Clara saw the look of hurt on Giselle's face that Giselle tried her best to subdue.

"I'm sorry. I shouldn't have said that. I didn't mean it," said Clara. "No, no, you're angry with me and you have every right to be. I was dismissive of what we are, where we stand, and I'm sorry for that," said Giselle.

"Is that all? Or are you more concerned with me revealing your secrets?" asked Clara.

"Clara, have I hurt you so much that you think so lowly of me?" asked Giselle rather defensively.

"I'm sorry," said Clara.

Giselle sighed. "Truth be told, Clara, I want things to go back to the way they once were."

"You made it clear that we simply couldn't be," replied Clara. "You know what I meant," said Giselle.

"Did I?" retorted Clara.

"You've made your point, Clara. I'm a horrible person and you hate me for hurting you," said Giselle.

"I don't hate you. I love you, it's just—"

"It's Edmund, isn't it? You never liked him. Clara, I love him, and I know it pains you, it pains me as well, but I do. I know you think I planned it, but I didn't."

"I'm sure you didn't summon me again to discuss Edmund, so what is it you truly want?" said Clara.

Giselle's reaction was unexpected. She burst into tears. "Hey, hey. I'm sorry, Giselle. What's wrong?"

To Clara's surprise, Giselle ran into Clara's arms. They held each other, and Giselle said with tears in her eyes, "I just need you to be there for me like when we were children."

"I'll always be," responded Clara.

"I'm frightened. It's the baby. I… I don't feel it anymore. It's been 20 weeks," Giselle said in a quavering voice before crying again. Clara held her closer and dried her tears.

"Look at me, Giselle." Giselle did just that. "We will get through this, just like we always have."

"But if Edmund dies, I'll be a widow. Husbandless and childless."

"Your child won't die, God willing, and as for Edmund, we will have to have faith that he and the others will prevail," said Clara.

Giselle was silent as she was contemplating telling Clara. "What is it?" Sensing her hesitation Clara said, "You can tell me. You can trust me."

Then Giselle said, very seriously, "I'll tell you, but you have to swear not to tell another living soul."

"I swear," Clara said unwaveringly.

Giselle looked truly terrified. Her eyes became watery, and tears began to manifest on her face again. She cried, "Oh Clara. I've done something horrible, and I can't reverse it."

Clara, now apprehensive, asked, "Giselle, what is it you think you've done?"

"I jinxed the baby with hokraft." Clara's eyes widened, and she was utterly shocked by what she had just heard.

"You did what?!"

"I was desperate. The baby wasn't kicking," Giselle wailed. "Giselle, hokraft is—"

"Forbidden and punishable by death, I know. The worst part is, I don't even think it worked. I still feel nothing," Giselle interrupted.

"How did you even learn this?"

Giselle removed the key she used to lock the chamber doors from her breast. On that key was another key. She used it to unlock draws revealing a spherical translucent object that appeared to be made out of glass. Giselle held it out in her hands.

Clara looked at it, bewildered. "What is it?"

"Motharya's (moth-tha-rye-ya) eye. It lets you communicate with people, beings from a long distance, as long as they have one themselves. The eye becomes completely transparent when activated," said Giselle. (Motharya's eye is a magical invention made by a sison sorcerer by the name of Motharya Llaws in 1062 NEEOT.)

"Who gave you this?" Clara asked.

"I found it," Giselle said. Clara was not satisfied with that answer, but decided not to press her too much on it. She instead asked her another question. "Who were you contacting?"

"A witch from Mylec," said Giselle. "What is her name?" asked Clara. "Aslaug," replied Giselle.

CHAPTER EIGHT
REALITIES

Tensions were high. The people of Corithni felt uncomfortable with Fragaa's army, but many were in acquiescence with Sir Cedric Baudry's thinking. It would be unwise to provoke her. She had powerful magic they had never seen before. An army that could turn into lycanthropes in an instant at her command. It was heresy for anyone in Iiadec to think about, but Fragaa was making them question their beliefs. Many wondered if Fragaa was a goddess, while many others believed she was some type of archdemon. (Demons are often erroneously confused with infected, so an archdemon would be considered a powerful infected by most.) Sir Cedric Baudry looked at Lord Franklin, who was still sitting on the ground motionless with Fragaa's fingers on his temples. Lord Franklin's eyes were still black, which vexed onlookers including Sir Cedric Baudry. Many were wondering why Lord Franklin agreed to this. Perhaps it was curiosity, but that wasn't like Lord Franklin. So maybe he was bewitched from the moment he laid eyes on her. A third option was that Lord Franklin had no choice and did as he was bid, realizing he was outnumbered. Lord Franklin had been in this meditative state for only a few minutes, but it was enough to draw concern from the other men.

Time passed slower in Lord Franklin's current state.

"What do you make of it, commander? It's nothing like we've ever seen," said a knight. His visor had been opened, revealing a youthful face. "We must tread with caution, Sir Avery," Sir Cedric Baudry said while looking at Fragaa's massive army. "She definitely planned for resistance, and we are massively outnumbered."

"Then what should we do?" asked Sir Avery.

Sir Cedric Baudry stared directly at the black-eyed Lord Franklin. He furrowed his brow. Something about this scene did not make any sense to him. He wondered who this enigmatic figure truly was. She called herself Fragaa, but was that really the truth? Kraag made his intentions clear. Her motives, however, are unknown. Then there's the matter of what Fragaa is doing to Lord Franklin. The only other being that had magic like that was Kraag. She claimed all avalenth had black eyes, but was her word to be trusted? But as far as he knew, black eyes could only mean possession or turning into a demon. But was such a thing possible? Regardless, there was not much they could do but wait. Lord Franklin made the decision to communicate with this being and only time will tell whether she is friend or foe.

"We wait," Sir Cedric Baudry responded.

Sir Cedric Baudry noticed something that disturbed him. Lord Franklin was disappearing and reappearing in flashes of light. It didn't take long for everyone to notice the oddity. Naturally, it caused upheaval. "What's going on?" Zane asked. The other archers were equally terrified. Fragaa, who remained in the same position, was sweating profusely and she had a look of concentration on her face as though she were struggling to maintain Lord Franklin's essence.

"What did you do to him?!" Sir Baret shouted angrily.

Fragaa did not respond. This further aggravated Sir Baret to the point where he drew his sword, and several of the knights followed suit. The archers also readied their bows. Some of the knights said that Athalos was right and were about to attack Fragaa, when Sir Cedric Baudry shouted, "Halt!"

The knights stopped in their tracks. "Why have we stopped? The witch clearly means to kill—" said Sir Baret before being interrupted by Sir Ulric.

"Look around." Sir Baret did just that and to his surprise, Fragaa's army had turned back into lycanthropes. Some were growling while others were on all fours preparing for an attack. This was exactly what Sir Cedric Baudry had feared. An organized Lycan assault led by a powerful sorceress would spell the end for the knights, especially since they did not have Sir Peter with them. He began to regret sending him home early after the battle of Rilek (1548). But Sir Cedric Baudry figured word would get around how powerful he is, and it would naturally attract powerful enemies. In addition, there were rumors that Hector was planning an assault on Corithni. Which was why Sir Cedric Baudry had split up the forces after the battle of Rilek. A decision he was beginning to regret, for he had not anticipated being mauled to death by lycanthropes. If what they said about these beasts were true, the only ways to kill them is to behead them using steel equal to or greater than in sharpness—to

Mylecan steel. The only person with a blade that sharp was Sir Peter. Surely, Sir Peter and the other knights would hear the commotion and try to rescue their comrades from peril. But that was just wishful thinking. The reality was by the time Sir Peter and the other knights get wind of what happened they would already be ripped to shreds.

Much to his surprise, a beastly voice that was male said, "Calm yourselves. Their primitive weapons cannot harm her."

The lycanthropes did as they were told. A lycanthrope with a greyish hide stepped forth amongst the crowd. He looked directly at Sir Cedric Baudry. "You are wise not to attack for you and your people would have met your end. I am called Euthma (e-youth-ma), Fragaa's emissary. I was once a lowly farmer, a werewolf named Wesley, until I was liberated by Fragaa." Euthma was a particularly large lycanthrope. On his hind legs he stood twelve feet tall, and he was quite brawny when compared to the already massive bunch of lycanthropes. It was hard to believe he was simply just an emissary. He had several lacerations all over his body. Two pronounced ones on his Snout and two x shape scars on his chest. These wounds were old. However, they indicated that he was no stranger to combat and from the looks in their eyes, none of the lycanthropes were. Sir Cedric Baudry looked back at Euthma. He was quite intimidated, but stood his ground. "I am called Cedric, commander of these men and humble servant to Albert Franklin. I thank you, Euthma, for not attacking us, but our people are concerned with the status of our Lord Albert Franklin."

Everyone was speechless and some wondered how Sir Cedric Baudry could communicate with this beast so cordially. Surely, they were the enemy. While others believed this to be a necessary form of high stakes diplomacy for these other worldly figures. Behaving reverently was the key to getting their Lord back, and many knew Sir Cedric Baudry must choose his words carefully or risk dooming them all. It was a nail-biting experience for the onlookers, one that posed more questions than answers. Euthma responded by saying, "I don't profess to know how Fragaa's magic works entirely, but I can tell you this. She does not intend to harm your Lord. What is happening to him is a result of his own doing." "How so?" asked Sir Cedric Baudry.

"Like I said, I do not completely understand her magic. All I know is that it acts as an entity on its own. You must accept it as such or suffer the consequences," explained Euthma.

"Forgive me, but I do not understand," said Sir Cedric Baudry.

"If your Lord doesn't accept her powers as truth, then he will experience pain," said Euthma, emphasizing on the word pain. Sir Cedric Baudry's eyes widened.

***

The figures in the alternate reality became silent and the image of the world around Lord Franklin began to dissipate and he was surrounded by whiteness. He was staring directly at Fragaa, whose eyes were black again and looming over him.

"What happened? Is that it? It doesn't make any sense. That girl said she had been communicating with Aslaug, but Aslaug is long dead and where is Sir Peter and the men? They should have met up with William and John. What happened to the dragon? Why are there things I cannot see?" These were several questions Lord Franklin had for Fragaa.

"I pulled you out prematurely. It was for your own good and as for your other questions, I can only show you the future. I did not create it. I do not know why things are so and there are even some things I cannot see or understand." Lord Franklin noticed Fragaa's eyes and Fragaa saw him looking at them.

"My eyes cannot retain the disguise here. I'm sorry if that displeases you."

"Where's here, anyway?" asked Lord Franklin.

"Here is no different from anywhere in a sense that it is a place, and all places are connected," said Fragaa.

"More secrets," Lord Franklin said under his breath.

Fragaa heard him and scowled. "Your doubt and distrust nearly led to your downfall. If I hadn't saved you, you would have surely suffered. You should have more faith in my powers," Fragaa said.

"I don't even know if I have faith in Arda and besides, how do you expect me to take you seriously when you're completely naked?" responded Lord Franklin.

"Is this not the natural state of humans? Why are you so afraid of bodily flesh? Perhaps I should resort back to my beast form?" asked Fragaa "No, no, that won't be necessary. I was just suggesting you put on some clothes. That way you will be less distracting," said Lord Franklin placing emphasis on the word distracting.

Fragaa chuckled. "You know, for such a bold and arrogant race, you humans are quite bashful when it comes to your bodies. Always concealing the flesh with dead flesh. It is quite amusing. Anyway, I digress. I shall wear these clothes as you say, but just keep in mind the more I alter my appearance, the less potent my magic will be."

A fur coat made of animal hide manifested around Fragaa that she used to barely conceal her privates. Lord Franklin looked at her incredulously, like he was certain these were not the best clothes she could muster.

"What? It is not as though I am an expert on human garments. You are truly an incorrigible man," said Fragaa, rather peeved.

Lord Franklin chuckled. "You know, for a powerful being, you're quite easily vexed. I guess the avalenth are not that different from humans."

Fragaa's demeanor changed, and she did not seem angered by what Lord Franklin suggested, but she did not agree with his assessment. Her countenance changed to that of seriousness. "I believe we are completely different. That's why I am here."

Her words perplexed Lord Franklin greatly, but he decided not to press her on their meaning, for he had an agenda that was more important than needless philosophical debate.

"Lord Albert Franklin, I have not been entirely truthful to you and I apologize for that. Henceforth, I shall be as frank as I possibly can. For one, I was not sent here by anyone or anything. I sought this place out. The other avalenth wanted to leave things to Alar, our God, but I knew better."

"So, you have doubts about the existence of your God too?" asked Lord Franklin.

"Well, I have never seen it nor heard it, but other avalenth say it exists and even claim to have communicated with it. Of course, I have no way of determining the legitimacy of their claims."

Lord Franklin stood up from the spot whence he was once sitting and look directly at Fragaa and asked bluntly, "Why have you come here, truthfully?"

"It's like I said previously. I aim to prevent catastrophe. There are parallel realities that are nigh infinite in number. For the most part they are similar, however, there are rare occurrences in which something drastic happens that can alter the very fabric of all realities."

"Like my conflict with Hector," replied Lord Franklin. "Precisely," said Fragaa.

All this talk of parallel realities was making Lord Franklin's head spin. "And what catastrophic event occurs between Hector and I that causes these changes in all realities?" asked Lord Franklin emphasizing the words *all realities*.

"If I tell you through this medium, it will surely come to fruition again, and this time spread to all of existence."

"Wait what, this has already happened?" asked Lord Franklin rather dumbfounded.

"No, reality is false only separate from one another. There are living, breathing beings in each reality, just like you and me, that simply experience things differently," replied Fragaa.

"So, where are you from? Erm, I mean which reality?" asked Lord Franklin.

"Our realities are not parallel, and my world is far from yours. I am from a place called the Outer realm."

Lord Franklin tried to digest the information he had just received. It was clear this Fragaa was knowledgeable and quite powerful but it didn't mean that she was telling the truth. But still, he was almost sure that her knowledge was beyond Hector's. Thus, it was unlikely Hector was using her to trick him. The missing piece of the puzzle was Kraag. What role did he play in all this?

He finally asked, "Who is Kraag and does he really mean as he says?" Fragaa took her time responding, like she was pondering the most appropriate way to answer that question. She finally said, "He is an enemy to humanity and like kind, for reasons I don't know. In fact, many things about him are unknown to me except that he despises the avalenth for cursing him and his followers, the Horridus. Some believe he is a zealot of the old religion that believes in the inevitable cycle of birth and destruction.

"Now that can't be right. When me and my men met him, he heavily criticized religion. He called it deception, not your typical zealot and that's not all. He knew things about me and my family and said he'd been watching me."

There was a worrisome look on Fragaa's face. "I've been fortunate enough not to have ever met this fiend, but I fear the rumors about him may be true. He goes by many names: the cursed one, the great influencer, the deceiver, the fallen, the corrupter. Some believe that he has transcended and become a god of Chaos. Some individuals also believe him to be over a hundred thousand years old. Even for an avalenth, that's unnaturally long. But as you know from my statement before, many claims about him might be inaccurate with even some doubting his existence, thinking him to be some sort of boogeyman."

Lord Franklin studied her face. "But you don't believe that, do you? You have the look of someone who is worried and fearful. Your brow tells it all."

"It seems it is quite obvious that I am afraid. That's because I believe Kraag is real, though all the stories about him may not be," said Fragaa.

"What if he has influenced Hector?" asked Lord Franklin.

"I believe he already has, though I think Hector is unaware of his presence. I suspect he is slowly guiding you two into a drawn-out conflict. A voice whispering from the shadows," said Fragaa.

"He certainly was not in the shadows when he revealed himself to me," said Lord Franklin.

"Perhaps he sensed you were someone with an iron will, who cannot be so easily swayed, thus he decided to use a more direct method," replied Fragaa.

Lord Franklin smiled briefly at what he saw as a compliment. Fragaa smiled back, indicating that she did intend her comment to be received as a compliment. Lord Franklin still wasn't sure if he should trust her, which is why he had a contingency plan at hand just in case something should go awry. He did not know whether she could read minds, otherwise she would know his true intention. He didn't bother to ask her because if she could, she would probably deny it. Despite all his suspicions, he was doubting that she had any ulterior motives. Still, there was one barrier of entry that prevented him from believing her entirely. "Why are you being so open all of a sudden? Last we spoke, you were so enigmatic."

"Quite perceptive. I needed to eliminate any doubts you had about me. My powers require the elimination of doubt. If you continue to doubt my intentions or what you see in any way, you will enter a state of unbearable pain."

Lord Franklin stroked his chin several times as he contemplated her words. *"If you continue to doubt my intentions or what you see in any way, you will enter a state of unbearable pain."* He found it rather convenient that she would ask him to abandon all doubt. That meant she could control him without any resistance henceforth and he did not like that. Not being able to raise an objection to her intentions was an abuse of power. As for this unbearable pain that he would feel. He was inclined to believe this was a fabrication or at least a hyperbole because he had been having doubts since he entered this state, and he wasn't in any pain. Suddenly, his distrust of Fragaa was beginning to increase again.

This being may not be working with Hector, but she wanted complete subjugation over him without any concrete reason why, like a God. Lord Franklin wasn't even sure God deserved to have that sort of control. And yet she could be a powerful ally in his fight against his enemies. The gift of foresight was not a trivial one. With such abilities at his disposal, the possibilities were endless. Lord Franklin became enamored with the idea, but he thought it was best not to show any sign of outward elation. For Fragaa would suspect that he had ulterior motives. He thought it was best to keep his intentions hidden and play along with Fragaa's demands for the time being.

Blind faith in anything is unnatural. It's normal for humans to be suspicious about the ways of the world. So, when religions tell people to believe in an unseeing God without an iota of reliable evidence, naturally it will procure doubts, even some outright objections. Such is expected from human beings, though limited in our scope of knowledge, we have the most advanced mental faculties on the planet. Other species pale in comparison. But reader, you don't need me to tell you that the fact that you're reading this, comprehending, and criticizing this amalgamation of irregular shapes that coalesces into an article of writing is a testament to human intelligence. We have developed through natural selection, evolution, and mutation, minds that allow us to naturally be curious. It is not in our nature to just accept things without significant evidence presented before us and even then; we don't accept such things as fact, at least not entirely. So why then, does most of the population follow religious dogma that tells them that God or Gods are fact and not theory? The oldest religion is approximately 4000 years old and yet humans have been around for roughly 200,000 years. To put things in perspective, religion has been around for 2 percent of our existence, yet it dictates how we live our lives. The answer is introspection and the fear that comes along with it. As I said before, we humans possess advanced mental faculties, and one of those faculties is introspection. It allows us to self-examine ourselves and when we do that, we realize how alone and insignificant we are and, ultimately, how much we don't know about the universe and ourselves. This breeds fear, and fear breeds madness. Religion preys on this cycle by offering answers to these questions without any evidence. Because the masses are so desperate to relieve themselves of fear, they abandon their reason so they can feel comfortable.

Don't misconstrue me, I do not mean to suggest religion or dogma is entirely bad and I must profess I do not know the major tenants of every religion on the planet; hence I apologize in advance for generalizing. I'm simply arguing that anything telling one to abandon doubts for beliefs can be harmful. It takes a lot of conviction to believe in something and it can be quite admirable. However, believing something without evidence is harmful and quite dangerous. For instance, not knowing what you stand for but devoting yourself to a cause anyway can give way to fanaticism and even madness. This is because doubt is a form of reason. It's your mind trying to make sense of the stimuli it's reacting to rather than simply accepting it. Now, reader, I'm not suggesting that you doubt everything that can be harmful as well. Just make sure you believe you have the necessary evidence to eliminate your doubt next time you want to believe in something. It is also important to allow oneself to doubt in the first place. Question everything. There's no guarantee you will find the answer, but you'll be more knowledgeable than you were before.

Before Lord Franklin could utter a word in response, Fragaa suddenly fell to her knees. She was sweating profusely, breathing heavily. With genuine concern, Lord Franklin exclaimed, "Fragaa, what's the matter?!" Fragaa struggled to her feet, relying on Lord Franklin to help her up.

This was the first time he had touched her. Her skin felt so humanlike it was quite fascinating how a being so powerful could seem so corporeal during a moment of weakness. He held her up as she struggled to remain on her feet.

"Fragaa, are you alright?"

"No, I am not. My power is waning. I cannot hold you here forever." She was quite fatigued, but mustered the strength to seize Lord Franklin's shoulders. She looked him directly in the eyes and said seriously, "You must believe!"

"Alright, I believe!" Franklin exclaimed. "Good." Fragaa grinned weakly.

He could feel her grasp gradually lessen to which he compensated by holding on to her tighter. Fragaa eventually completely collapsed. Lord Franklin broke her fall. He didn't know if she was alive or dead, for she had stopped breathing. Lord Franklin checked her pulse but felt none. "Fragaa, Fragaa!" He shook her in an attempt to revive her, but it was to no avail. Before Lord Franklin could do anything more, he heard a thunderous noise. Lord Franklin placed Fragaa gently on the ground. He then proceeded to unsheathe his blade and had his buckler in his other hand.

"Who or what goes there and are you friend or foe?"

Six more deafening sounds proceeded. Suddenly, all the light from the space from which they resided dissipated until it was engulfed in darkness. Despite less light, the heat intensified to the point where Lord Franklin felt his flesh was a degree away from melting. Things were even more arduous for Lord Franklin as he felt lightheaded as the oxygen in the space he resided, had depleted to dangerously low levels. There was a crackling sound of what appeared to be electricity, and then flashes of bright light manifested out of thin air. Lord Franklin shielded his eyes. The light began to formulate into what seemed to be six large erratic balls of gaseous energy, with each being roughly the size of a cow. They resembled translucent clouds that were imbued in a strange aura. These balls of energy were floating in the air and had an orange hue to them.

Lord Franklin could feel the hot gusts of wind that they emitted on his body. Upon further inspection, he could see what was within one of these large orbs; they projected some sort of image. The image horrified him. Several flayed, mutilated bodies with entrails stuffed in most of their orifices. Some had maggots coming from their eyelids while others had their eyes gouged out or sewn shut. Their skin coated crimson with fresh blood, yet their bodies were emaciated. They were fused together in a spiral pattern. The most disturbing part of it all was that the poor souls were still alive during the whole ordeal, which should have been impossible given the nature of the wounds they received. He could hear them cry out in agony, the unnatural sound of their cries disturbed him, and the repugnant scene he had just witnessed was making him nauseous. The erratic spheres drew closer and then the cries strengthened. Lord Franklin fell to his knees and covered his ears. There was nowhere to go, no way to escape from whatever these things were. There was only one option, and that was to fight.

Lord Franklin rose to his feet and channeled electricity through his left hand, his buckler hand, and fired a lightning bolt at the orb nearest to him. The orb began to spin rapidly and radiated with energy. It elongated, then contorted until it eventually sprouted several misshapen appendages, all while increasing in size. The newly shaped monstrosity resembled some sort of arachnid. Its color had changed to a bright yellow. The being had no hide nor defined body, so it resembled the essence of a beast. The remaining five gaseous spheres orbited the being. The entity stood on solid ground and, despite taking up so much space, it was still not very dense, most likely attributed to it being mostly gaseous. It moved toward Lord Franklin but collapsed, falling because some of its appendages became entangled within each other. The aberration struggled to its feet, but Lord Franklin did not wait for it to regain its footing. He figured his electricity might have caused this metamorphosis, hence, he decided to rely on soul energy alone. A spear formed entirely out of soul manifest formed in his hand and he hurled it at the abomination before him. The spear struck the monstrosity in what would have been its head. It seemed to be subdued for the moment. Lord Franklin sighed with relief, but he soon realized he had celebrated too early. There was a penetrating blue light that was being emitted from the aberration and a gust of wind that sent Lord Franklin careening backwards. By the time he was able to get back upon his feet, the aberration was already upon him. It formed a mouth with the intention of devouring Lord Franklin. The aberration was only just three inches from his face when he heard Fragaa shout, "*Recmium!*"

The aberration was repelled several feet backwards. It was clearly disoriented from the blow as were the five other orbs. Light was restored to the area they were confined to. Fragaa, who was still visibly enfeebled, said, "We don't have much time, come hither quickly."

Lord Franklin did as he was told. Fragaa placed a magic shield with a reddish hue around them. "Wha… What is that? What are those things?" Lord Franklin stammered.

Fragaa was breathing heavily. It became apparent that she was exhausted. "They're demons. A side effect of dimension-hopping. They're mindless and only desire to become stable. They feed on most forms of energy, even psychic."

"Wait, dimension what?" asked Lord Franklin.

Fragaa, who was clearly irritated with his constant questioning, seized Lord Franklin by the shoulders. "Listen to me. I don't have the power to vanquish them. I have to enchant your blade so you can smite them. Can you do this?"

Lord Franklin was terrified; the demons were certainly intimidating with their gargantuan size and the grotesque images inside them, but this was not the time for fear. Their survival depended on him completing this task. "Yes, I can,"

"I will be with you every step of the way. Oh, and you must not let them touch you. If you do, you will become an infected or worst they will consume your essence." Her last words did not help to quell his fear, but instead he masked it.

"How do we do this?"

"Raise your sword in the air."

Lord Franklin did as such. Fragaa began to mutter some incantations in a tongue Lord Franklin did not recognize. When she was done, his sword glowed a whitish hue, just like Seggr. Lord Franklin felt a sensation in his body that overwhelmed him. It was as if something new was coursing through his veins. *What is this indescribable feeling of power?* he thought. He felt a sense of vigor that he had not even felt in his youth.

"Do not be alarmed. The power of the sword is being transferred to your body. It is for your hands alone. Only you can wield it in its proper state," said Fragaa.

"How long will it last?" asked Lord Franklin.

"The connection will dissolve when you eventually pass on."

Lord Franklin was dumfounded upon hearing such information. He had never heard of spells lasting that long before. He had no time to contemplate the possibilities of such potent magic as he heard the raucous noise of the demons. From the crackling of electricity to the roaring sound of footsteps of the arachnid type demon. The larger aberration charged headfirst into the shield Fragaa created, cracking it slightly. The other five propelled themselves upon the shield like missiles. The demons did this repeatedly, thus further weakening the integrity of the shield. Over the tumult, Lord Franklin pointed his blade at the demons and abruptly they stopped assaulting the shield.

While maintaining his stance, and without looking at Fragaa, he asked, "What's going on? They've stopped."

Fragaa responded, "The energy that flows through that blade repels them because they cannot absorb it and it will not make them stable. As long as the blade is unsheathed, it will repel them."

"Then we're safe as long as I have this?" Lord Franklin said, referring to his newly enchanted blade. He could tell by Fragaa's expression that they were not, in fact, safe.

"It's only temporary. Soon they will notice that one of us does not bear repellent energy and will attack relentlessly," said Fragaa.

"How long do we have?" "Not long," replied Fragaa. "Very well. Dissolve the shield," said Lord Franklin.

"What? Are you mad? Did you hear what I just said?" asked Fragaa, shocked by what she deemed such a ludicrous suggestion.

"We don't have time to argue. You're barely hanging on. You were dead temporarily only moments before. If you keep using your magic, you'll be dead permanently," said Lord Franklin.

"How dare you? I am not some mere subject of yours to command. Besides, I have a plan. I'll shape shift into a lycanthrope. They have an aura that is unaffected by demons," said Fragaa.

"No transformation, no more magic. I'll protect you from now on," demanded Lord Franklin.

"You underestimate my abilities, but I wouldn't expect—" Fragaa began coughing up blood, and she tried to conceal it, but Lord Franklin saw.

"So her kind bleeds," he thought.

Fragaa felt dizzy and stumbled. To maintain her balance, she supported her weight on her hands and knees. She took time to catch her breath. "I'm not going to die here."

Lord Franklin knelt beside her. "And you shan't as long as you place your faith in me." Before she could protest, Lord Franklin said, "You are unwell and in no condition to cast. Please dissolve the shield."

Fragaa groaned. "Very well, but know this. I cannot protect you once the shield is down. If the demons touch you—"

"Yes, I know," Lord Franklin interrupted. Fragaa looked at him incredulously. Lord Franklin responded by saying, "Do you trust me?" Fragaa did not respond. "Your survival is crucial to me getting out of here. I am not about to let you die if that doesn't convince you then—"

"I trust you," Fragaa interrupted. Suddenly they could hear the crackling of electricity resume. The arachnid demon was still immobilized.

"Looks like they've awoken from their trance," said Lord Franklin. "Are you ready?" asked Fragaa.

"Yeah."

Fragaa raised her open palm in the air and said, "*Erkma!*"

The shield completely disintegrated. The first floating demon flew toward Fragaa at great speed. In the nick of time, Lord Franklin struck it with his sword, and it disappeared immediately.

"Get behind me!" Lord Franklin shouted.

Fragaa did just that. The other four floating demons encircled them. Lord Franklin took a swipe at one of them, but it evaded his attack. Another came dangerously close to Fragaa, but Lord Franklin impaled it and the demon disappeared into thin air. Three more floating demons remained. Two charged toward them. Lord Franklin delivered a strike that struck both demons. A single floating demon remained. Lord Franklin took many swipes at it, but it evaded like an annoying house fly. Lord Franklin swung at it relentlessly as it loomed precariously over Fragaa's head. The demon eventually retreated and began orbiting around the arachnid demon. This caused the arachnid demon to awaken from its trance.

"Run! Go! I've got a plan!" screamed Lord Franklin and Fragaa sprinted as fast as she could.

The arachnid demon had her in its sights. Lord Franklin removed his buckler and channeled lightning through it. He then hurled the buckler in the opposite direction in which Fragaa was running. The arachnid demon stopped and then eventually headed for the buckler. The buckler was still brimming with electricity as a result of phantom touch. The arachnid demon opened its grotesque mouth and was about to swallow the buckler when the floating demon flew toward the buckler. The arachnid demon then struck the floating demon with its appendage. The floating demon then consecutively rammed into the arachnid demon. The arachnid demon did not retaliate.

"They're fighting over it," said Lord Franklin.

"No, they are not," said Fragaa. She startled Lord Franklin.

"What the? I thought I told you to run. How long have you been standing there?"

"Not long," Fragaa said nonchalantly. Lord Franklin scowled at her. She anticipated what he was going to say.

"Forgive me for my sudden apparent aloofness. Your plan was quite ingenious. They should be preoccupied for some time and before you ask, I did run, far in fact, but it seems in this place, no matter where you run to, you are eventually transported back to your original position."

Lord Franklin furrowed his brow, befuddled. She either did not know where they were or did not properly inspect the place. He said rather critically, "Fragaa, you are truly reckless. Do you even have a plan? Or do you just do things on a whim?"

Fragaa was offended. "How dare you? Of course, I have a plan. I just can't account for every obstacle life throws at me. You should be grateful, since this is all your fault. All you had to do was just trust me!"

"My fault. If you had been more forthright, we wouldn't be in this predicament!"

"There are certain things I can't reveal, for the stability of all of space-time is at stake," said Fragaa.

"I don't even know what that means," Lord Franklin said frustratedly. "It's hard to explain but—"

"Enough! I think you're deceiving me, and I will not be made a fool. This quest of yours was probably forbidden by the other avalenth, seeing as it's riddled with danger. That's why they most likely refused to help. But given the way you haphazardly involved me in this and traveled through realities just to get here, must mean that you're either desperate or insane," said Lord Franklin angrily.

Fragaa was silent for a moment. She bowed her head and lowered her eyes, ashamedly. "You are not wrong. I am desperate. Everyone's future is at stake, and I've nearly damned us all by taking such a risk."

Believing himself to be too harsh, he softened his features. He looked at Fragaa and said softly, "Just tell me everything and I'll help you."

With tears in her eyes, Fragaa said, "We are from different worlds, different realities. There is much you do not understand, and I wish I could tell you everything, but I just can't. I won't, because it could mean the death of us all."

Before Lord Franklin could respond, he fell to the floor. He was in excruciating pain and the veins on his neck and face began to protrude as he started flailing about uncontrollably and he cried in agony. He had trouble controlling his limbs, which were behaving erratically, like they were being doused in quicklime. His flesh felt the sensation of being scorched by dragon fire and his bones ached like they were being shattered repeatedly. He felt like he was impaled by a thousand spears, all while his wounds were sewn shut with salt. The process repeated itself with each successive sensation, becoming more unbearable than the next. Fragaa tried to calm him, but he just kept thrashing about.

"Albert! Albert! Listen to me. You need to calm your mind and accept. Albert, do you hear me?!"

Lord Franklin's vision became blurry, and he looked up at Fragaa and from what he could make out, she wasn't there anymore. She had been replaced by a familiar face. Same blond hair, but the features of her face were different, and her eyes were teal. The pain was subsiding as well.

"Mother?" Lord Franklin asked. "No, it's me Fragaa."

Lord Franklin's eyes rolled at the back of his head, and he lost consciousness. Fragaa shook him to wake him, but it was no use. This was bad. She did not come this far to watch him perish, but things were looking dire. The body has a pain threshold. If it should exceed that threshold, it will relieve itself of pain permanently. Lord Franklin slipped into a dreamlike state. He entered into what seemed to be a particularly traumatic memory of his childhood. Only he couldn't recall it entirely before, at that moment it seemed so clear. He was a small child, no more than five, with long raven black hair. His mother let him keep it long. She even tied it in a ponytail for him. Little Albert was sprawled out on the ground and unresponsive. His brother Gavin looking down on him from the watchtower of Corithni.

"Albert?" He was petrified and assumed the worst. Gavin screamed, "Albert! Albert! Somebody, help!"

The knights came rushing towards the scene with King Aiken Franklin and Queen Alice Franklin. When Queen Alice saw her son on the ground, she became hysterical. She was crying, and she ran up to little Albert and held him.

"Oh, Arda, save my child." King Aiken looked up at Gavin, who was terrified. "Gavin, what happened?"

"He fell. He must've followed me. I swear I didn't see him." Gavin began sobbing profusely.

"Sssh… that's enough, my child. Just come down from there using the *staircase*." King Aiken placed emphasis on using the staircase. Gavin did as he was told. King Aiken turned to one of the knights. "Get a healer and make haste!"

"Yes, your grace."

The knight returned with a tall, slim man with short sandy brown hair. "You called for me, your grace?" said the man.

"Yes, it's my son. He has fallen from the watchtower."

The man examined little Albert. "Speak truth, Healer, will he make it?" asked King Aiken candidly. The healer placed his ear on the boy's chest. "I do not hear a heartbeat."

"Oh, God!" exclaimed Queen Alice as she fell into her husband's arms. "But I can attempt to start his heart again," said the healer. "Through Magic?" asked King Aiken, perplexed.

"No, through healing," the healer said. He then began to do something the onlookers deemed unusual. He performed chest compressions on little Albert until little Albert became responsive and began to cough.

Queen Alice hugged Little Albert. "Oh, Thank Arda, my little one is alive!"

"Healer, what do they call you?" "Giles Baker, your grace." "Henceforth, you shall be known as Lord Giles Baker. You have saved my child's life. I am forever grateful." "Thank you, your Grace." "Albert! Albert!" Fragaa screamed. Lord Franklin slowly regained

consciousness. As you could imagine, he was a bit disoriented. "Wha… What was that?"

"My powers are rejecting you. They see you as a threat. They're trying to eliminate you, similar to how an immune system attacks a foreign body."

"What does that mean?" asked Franklin, perplexed by what she just said.

"It senses the conflict, negative psychic energy, between us and believes you are a threat."

"Arrrgh!" The pain returned to Lord Franklin. Fragaa hovered her hands over him and began muttering incantations. Before she could continue, Lord Franklin grabbed her hand tightly. He said through labored breaths,

"No more magic. I believe for real this time." There was genuine elation on Fragaa's face. She laughed and cried tears of joy as she helped Lord Franklin up. The pain Lord Franklin felt gradually subsided. He was quite fatigued and placed his hands on his knees and began breathing heavily.

"Are you alright?" Fragaa asked.

"I'm just tired." Lord Franklin stood erect and began stretching his back and limbs to alleviate tension in his bones and joints.

He turned to Fragaa and said, "So, what do we do about them?"

The demons were still distracted. "We wait until I have the strength to vanquish them."

"And how long will that take?" asked Lord Franklin.

"Not long. I can already feel my power returning," she said while looking at her palms and moving her fingers ever so slightly.

"How long is not long? I feel like we've been here for quite some time," Lord Franklin said while pacing back and forth.

"You fear for your men, I understand, but the lycanthropes won't harm them. Do not fret. The passage of time is faster in here than where your physical body is. A year here is roughly a day out there."

Lord Franklin furrowed his brow.

"Time does not affect all of existence uniformly even in one reality," said Fragaa.

"So, you do know where we are?"

Fragaa sighed. "Not exactly. I know what this place is, not where it is exactly."

"Let's not get caught up in semantics and just tell me what you know of this place," said Lord Franklin.

Fragaa groaned. "We both almost died because of this line of questioning. It seems unwise to bring it up again."

"If you don't tell me I'll think it and this place, urm, your powers will attack me anyway," replied Lord Franklin.

Fragaa frowned at him. "You're incorrigible."

"Yes. Yes, you said that already," said Lord Franklin.

"It's a fitting description," she retorted. "Very well. I shall tell you, but I doubt you'll understand." Fragaa took in a deep breath. "There is something called space-time, that's the space in which everything inhabits. Sometimes space-time folds and entangles. This warped space-time makes sections unobservable to beings who live in a more uniform part of it. Sections that are there, but just hard to see and hard to get to." "And that's where we are? In warped space-time that exists in my reality?" Lord Franklin said.

"Precisely. It seems I've underestimated you," said Fragaa.

"That doesn't explain how you knew the time difference between here and the outside," said Lord Franklin.

"As I said before, time does not affect everything uniformly. In the warped space, time passes much faster than it does on the outside. I know this because I've traveled to warp space before, just not in this reality. Are you satisfied?" said Fragaa, placing emphasis on the word satisfied. She was quite peeved, but this did not deter Lord Franklin.

"Actually, no. If you want me to aid you in your quest, I want you to tell me everything you can tell me without endangering all of existence. I at least deserve that."

Fragaa hesitated to respond. "That's a lot of information."

"And we have the time, now do we have an accord?" asked Lord Franklin.

"Only if I get to ask you questions as well," said Fragaa. "You have my word," he said.

Lord Franklin was sweating profusely. He had been since the demons arrived. He wiped some sweat from his face. "It's uncomfortably hot here." "As long as they're here, it will remain that way. They emit energy in the form of heat. I'd advise you to remove your armor," said Fragaa.

Lord Franklin did just that, starting with his gauntlets and eventually working his way to his breastplate. When he was down to a tunic and pants, he sat down. Fragaa sat down facing him. "What is it you desire to know?"

"For one, what are they doing?" asked Lord Franklin. Fragaa turned to the demons.

"They are attempting to fuse, but such a thing is impossible. Demons cannot absorb demons. They do this because they believe the kinetic energy they generate from constant collisions can be absorbed."

"You know you speak the tongue of man, yet your words are so foreign to me. Where did you acquire such knowledge?" Lord Franklin asked.

"My kind has existed for an unfathomably long time, hence, we've procured knowledge that has advanced us."

"I suppose to you my kind might seem primitive," said Lord Franklin. "Ignorant, maybe, but I see great potential for usefulness," replied Fragaa.

Lord Franklin sighed. "I guess the rumors are true about there being other worlds."

Quite surprised by his statement, Fragaa asked, "You've heard of beings like me?"

"Just ramblings from outside of Arcadiem. Talk of beings coming from an Outer realm, traveling to my world, ingraining themselves into society. I believe the words otherworldly interlopers were used," said Lord Franklin.

Upon hearing this, Fragaa experienced a mixture of emotions, mostly panic and shock. *So they have been contacted before. I didn't account for such variables. I wonder how deep an influence these interlopers had on them. It is now more important than ever that I stick to the plan.*

"What else have you'd heard about other worlds or other realities?" asked Fragaa, eagerly trying her best to mask her emotions.

Surprised by her sudden interest, Lord Franklin responded with a slight delay "…Well, when you talked about warped space-time, there are tales that such a thing exists. The philosophers call it by several names—the hidden passage, a back doorway through time, a secret bridge between time and the eternal plane (Mirthadinelings' primitive concept of universe), an ethereal road that can only be seen and ventured by those capable. Travelers who can essentially bend time to their will, covering great distances at preternatural speed. Some even say these travelers take energy from the ethereal road and some say they receive it, suggesting it's alive somehow. They say sections of the ethereal road exist in Mirthadine," said Lord Franklin.

"And you believe these tales?" Fragaa asked.

"I didn't until I met you," responded Lord Franklin. He looked at Fragaa and, choosing his words carefully, asked, "Are you one of these travelers?"

"I don't believe so; such a thing sounds—" "Impossible," Lord Franklin interrupted. "You sound disappointed," said Fragaa.

"I wouldn't expect you to understand. The Avalenth are practically immortal, humans and like kind live short lives. Time is not a luxury for us. We will never get to experience the things your kind has, even if it took five lifetimes. An ethereal road would have changed that."

"Fragaa, I'm not a young man. I spent the majority of my existence in my brother's shadow and lived a pretty uneventful life because of it. I need to make my mark on the world before time catches up with me," said Lord Franklin.

"You have already experienced plenty. For instance, you're probably the first man from Mirthadine to encounter someone from another world. The first to see an actual demon and the first to slay one. If we are successful in our endeavors, you'll be a hero to the entire worlds."

"And if I die?" said Lord Franklin.

"Then people will remember your noble sacrifice because it helped lay the groundwork for others who came after," replied Fragaa. She drew nearer to Lord Franklin.

"I empathize with you. I know you think I don't, but I do. Time is an enemy to us all, and I am no exception."

"What are you talking about?" asked Lord Franklin. "It's my heart." "What?"

Fragaa placed Lord Franklin's hand on the center of her chest. He felt an abnormal heartbeat. Lord Franklin's eyes widened. "Is this normal for your kind?"

"No, it will stop beating in three months' time," said Fragaa despondently.

"Fragaa," said Lord Franklin.

She smiled. "Don't fret. Up until now, I have lived an uneventful life and I doubted my existence impacted anyone up until you."

Lord Franklin did not respond. He did not know what to say and was overwhelmed with guilt.

"Say something please," Fragaa said, as tears began streaming down her face.

"Fragaa… I-I-I-I."

Fragaa dried the tears from her eyes. "Oh, never mind. I have embarrassed myself enough today. Spare me further indignation by remaining silent. I shall rest until my powers return." She turned away from Lord Franklin.

Lord Franklin touched her shoulder affectionately. She was shaking, for she had been weeping silently to herself.

"Fragaa. You are a child, a child of royalty, I presumed, who's overwhelmed because you're in another world very different from your own and you're afraid to die prematurely."

"How could you be so callous?" asked Fragaa.

"I mean no offense, but your actions and demeanor make it obvious," said Lord Franklin.

"I suppose you're not entirely wrong," she said.

Lord Franklin gently turned Fragaa around to face him. Then he said sincerely, "You have shown to me how little I know about the way of things. You have also shown me the many possibilities that life offers. You are a powerful being who's travelled all this way with the gift of foresight. You may yet be able to save yourself and if you cannot alone, we will find a way."

"Thank you for your kind words, but it's inevitable," said Fragaa.

Lord Franklin wiped a tear from Fragaa's eye. "That just means you haven't found a solution. You need to dig deeper," said Lord Franklin.

Fragaa smiled. "I'll try."

"Good. Now you need to get some rest if you want to be strong enough to smite some demons," said Lord Franklin.

"What about your questions?" said Fragaa.

"That'll have to wait for later. Right now, I'll watch out for the demons," said Lord Franklin.

Fragaa looked at Lord Franklin and he looked back. There was no exchange of words and it was hard to tell what Fragaa was thinking due to her black eyes, but Lord Franklin suspected she was admiring him. At least, that's what he wanted to believe.

She finally broke the silence. "Albert Franklin." "Yes?"

Fragaa's head hung low, and she was hesitant to speak. She believed she could alter the fabric of reality and time with her words if she was not careful.

Sensing her inhibition, Lord Franklin asked, "What is it?"

She looked up. "You're an admirable man. Do not deviate from that path... A defining moment for most cultures was the advent of fire. The fire spelt many things, development of cooking and the hearth, but it also expedited war and destruction. The fire itself is not evil, nor is it good. It is simply a tool and tools can be abused in the wrong hands. Fire is knowledge. Do not abuse it lest you be consumed by it." Such a cryptic message left Lord Franklin feeling uneasy for he didn't bother to ask the meaning, for he feared he might already know.

Fragaa eventually slept and Lord Franklin fell asleep as well. He fought to stay awake, but he succumbed to fatigue. Fragaa awoken to the signs of faint electrical buzzing. She opened her eyes only to see the arachnid demon and the flying demon looming over them.

"Demons!" she gasped. She then realized that they were moving very little and emitted less electricity than before. This could only mean three things: they were running low on energy, hence dying, they reached a temporary catatonic state, or they were simply resting. She moved as quietly as she possibly could to not alert them. The demons reacted slightly to her movements through sound and electrical discharges. This indicated they were resting. She tapped Lord Franklin's shoulder and he woke up immediately. He was completely flustered and disoriented.

"Huh, hah, demons!"

Fragaa quickly put her hand over his mouth. "Ssssh. They're not awake." She removed her hand and pointed to the flying demon.

Lord Franklin peered through its translucent coat and saw no images. This was the same for the arachnid demon as well. "These things sleep?" Lord Franklin whispered.

"Yes, but as long as they live, they never stop moving, so let's leave before they fully awaken."

"No, now's the perfect time to strike now that they're immobilized." Lord Franklin drew his sword. "You leave. I'll finish what we started." Anticipating protest, Lord Franklin said, "You entrusted me with the power to vanquish them. Let me do that."

Fragaa nodded in silent acquiescence. Fragaa crept away to be out of sight but close enough to see Lord Franklin and assist him if need be. Lord Franklin drew closer to the hovering demon until he was within arm's distance from it. He delivered an angled thrust that pierced through the demon's coat and center. The demon disappeared. The strange thing about these beings was they seemed wraithlike, yet he could feel their heft on his blade and when he cut through them, it felt like he was cutting through human flesh. Despite all this, they were clearly not entirely corporeal beings because they left no blood or flesh behind. When killed, they just dematerialized.

Lord Franklin was relieved as to what he just accomplished, but he soon realized he celebrated too early. For the arachnid demon had fully awakened. He could tell by the electricity that surrounded it. The demon had Fragaa in its sights and chased her relentlessly. Lord Franklin chased after it, but the demon eventually caught up. It was dangerously close to her. It attempted to grab at her with one of its spindly limbs. Fragaa evaded by rolling out of the way and crawling underneath the demon. It soon became disoriented, not realizing Fragaa was behind it, and began to spin around aimlessly. It eventually regained focus and continued the pursuit. Fragaa ran as fast as she could, but the demon was at her heels. Lord Franklin fired several lightning bolts into the air. He had his sword in its sheathe so the repellent energy imbued within it wouldn't stop the demon. The demon was seconds from devouring Fragaa when it turned around and started charging at Lord Franklin. It did not take long before it was upon him.

Lord Franklin delivered two horizontal cuts with one hand, each going in the opposite direction, striking the two front legs of the demon. The appendages dematerialized instantly. The demon lost its balance and began to flail about on its side. Lord Franklin was about to smite it when one of the demon's legs knocked his sword out of his hand. The sword spiraled through the air and landed with a metallic thud. The demon thrashed about wildly until it regained its footing. It turned its head 180 degrees so that its back was now its front. It dragged its back across the floor because its hind legs were missing. The demon charged at Lord Franklin. He tried to reach for the sword, but the demon blocked his path. It took a horizontal swing at him. This might have been a clumsy attempt to grab him. Lord Franklin dodged the swipe by leaping to the floor and laying as low as possible. The demon then franticly used its appendages to thrust downward at Lord Franklin. Lord Franklin rolled over multiple times to avoid being impaled or crushed to death. Over the melee, he could see his sword, the Great Divider enhanced with repellent energy glowing a whitish hue. He stumbled to his feet and went for the sword. The demon followed him. Lord Franklin was just inches from the hilt. Unbeknownst to him, the demon was close to impaling him. Lord Franklin grabbed the blade. When he turned around to face the demon, he heard Fraaga yell, *"Citaroba!"*

The demon's coat slowly began to disintegrate until there was nothing left but a translucent sphere that resembled a lens. Fragaa breathed heavily as she hunched over with her hands at her thighs. As she was trying to recuperate, she noticed Lord Franklin was drawn to this object. Lord Franklin stared at the sphere as it suddenly became transparent. He saw the same horrible images of the spiral made of live, emaciated human bodies. Only this time, he saw a severed head at the center. The head was emaciated, but its features were unmistakable. For he was staring at his own head. Shocked beyond reason, beads of sweat began to form on his forehead and his heart began to pound.

Before he could speak or react, the head opened its eyes. It was still alive. It looked directly at Lord Franklin and said, "She lies. The path she leads you down will result in your death. You will fail just like the others. You are weak, but it doesn't have to be so. There is an alternative I can show you; I can give you what you truly desire. Just take the sphere and you shall have control of your destiny." The voice of the head was not his own. It belonged to someone, or rather, something else. It was imposing and unsettlingly deep, yet Lord Franklin was enquiring towards it. The head kept repeating the phrase "take the sphere".

Lord Franklin dropped his blade and drew nearer. Fragaa ran towards Lord Franklin, screaming. But Lord Franklin did not hear her. He seemed to be in some type of trance. All he could hear was "take the sphere" and the voice got progressively louder. "Take the sphere! Take the sphere! TAKE THE SPHERE!"

Lord Franklin reached out his hand to grab it, but it started crackling along the surface. Lord Franklin looked at Fragaa. He couldn't hear her, but it looked like she was mouthing the words to destroy it. The sphere eventually shattered into several pieces. This broke Lord Franklin completely out of his stupor. Then the light in the space they resided restored completely. Fragaa protected Lord Franklin from the shrapnel with a magical shield that surrounded him. When no foreseeable shards of glass flew in the air, Fragaa caused the shield to dissipate. She ran up to Lord Franklin and started roughly inspecting his body, even attempting to take his tunic off.

"Stop that! What are you doing?" He grabbed her hands, preventing her from taking off his tunic.

"Ugh. I'm trying to see if the demon shards touched you," she said.

"Thank you, but I can do that myself."

"Don't be ridiculous. Take those garments off and let me inspect you," she said.

"I'm perfectly capable of examining myself. I'm not a child," Lord Franklin said, quite peeved.

"Fine. If you insist on being obstinate, go ahead," said Fragga.

Lord Franklin inspected himself for loose shards. When he was done, Fragaa scowled at him. "Care to explain your antics? Or are you usually this oblivious to commands?"

Lord Franklin expected as much as he had behaved rather foolishly, and he wasn't sure why. "Did you not hear it?"

"Hear what?" asked Fragaa.

"The demon spoke to me," Lord Franklin responded.

Fragaa was perplexed. "Demons don't speak. They don't think. They don't even see."

Lord Franklin came closer to Fragaa and looked directly into her eyes. "I speak the truth. I know what I heard."

Fragaa couldn't believe what she was hearing. Talking demons? Such a thing was absurd, but she didn't suspect any sort of deception from Lord Franklin. This could only mean that there were more forces at play than she anticipated. She turned away from Lord Franklin and ran her hand through her hair and started pacing back and forth.

"That doesn't make any sense."

Unbeknownst to her, Lord Franklin was watching her suspiciously. "That's not all. I saw something within the sphere." Lord Franklin told her about the spiral of bodies with his severed head at the center, but omitted what the head said.

Fragaa was still pacing, trying to figure out what this meant. "It's some type of omen, right?"

"I don't know," Fragaa said.

Lord Franklin was hesitant to ask but asked anyway. "How many others?"

"I don't know what you're talking about," said Fragaa.

"The demon said there were others. How many?" Lord Franklin said sternly.

"It's hard to explain... you wouldn't understand." "Try me," Lord Franklin demanded.

"I've had nine champions. They all failed... I've made mistakes, but things have changed."

"You saw my victory."

"No, but I didn't see failure. I have to believe... I want to believe. That means something," Fragaa said vehemently.

"What did the future reveal to you?" Lord Franklin said eagerly. "Despite what you think of me, I cannot tell the future and I don't think any living being can. The future isn't written down on parchment hence, it cannot be foretold. What I see are glimpses of different realities that have already occurred or are occurring. I am able to transport myself to different realities and warn others of past events that have befallen," explained Fragaa.

"Thereby, averting a crisis in the future," said Lord Franklin.

"Not exactly. You see, there are many factors at hand. For one, my very presence. Telling you all this information may alter an outcome. Secondly, just because an event happened in one reality, does not mean it will ever occur in another reality, even if that said reality is parallel," said Fragaa.

"It seems predicting the future is not an exact process," said Lord Franklin.

"Hence they call it predicting," replied Fragaa.

Lord Franklin furrowed his brow and scratched his head. "So you don't even know if this cataclysmic event will come to pass?"

"That may be so, but I can't take that risk," said Fragaa.

"You're not the only one taking a risk. You said yourself your presence may alter the outcome… you may be making things worse… maybe it's best to let events run their natural course," said Lord Franklin.

"Do you doubt me?" Fragaa said. She was wounded by Lord Franklin's words.

Feeling guilty about what he said, Lord Franklin attempted to explain himself. "No, no. That's not what I meant. It's just this is all too confusing to me. Demons, multiple realities, dimensions, space-time, is all too much for my mortal mind."

"And you no longer want to help based on what you thought a demon said?" Fragaa retorted.

"I am not so easily swayed, you know that," protested Lord Franklin. "You don't need to justify yourself. I never formally asked for your help… I don't know why I thought things would be different," Fragaa said rather despondently. "Fragaa I-"

"Why did you agree to let me show you the parallel reality?" Fragaa asked bluntly.

"What?"

"You didn't resist, even though all your men were distrustful," said Fragaa.

"I don't know. I suppose I was curious. The way you appeared unexpectedly, I thought you were some type of goddess. Such beauty, such grace, erm, I mean that hair, those eyes you had at the time, reminded me of my mother."

"Your mother?"

"Yes" Lord Franklin replied, quite embarrassed. "Mother was the only person I completely trusted, so you resembling her made me, in a way, trust you."

"I understand. How do you feel about me now that you've met me? Do you still trust me?" asked Fragaa.

"Of course I do. I owe you my life… now that I've met you, you seem humanlike," said Lord Franklin.

"I am not human," said Fragaa.

"Clearly. But what I mean is you're more relatable. You're desperate to complete a quest as I am. You told me everything you could, despite the risk, because you knew it would make me understand. Now I understand you." He held out his hand to Fragaa, and she looked at it, unsure of the meaning of such a gesture.

"You must shake. It is a symbol my people use when they have an understanding," said Lord Franklin.

Fragaa was confused. "Like an agreement?" "Exactly." "What are we agreeing on?" asked Fragaa.

"I'm agreeing to help you" Lord Franklin chuckled.

"Well, didn't you agree to do that before? What difference does this handshake make this time?" Fragaa asked.

"Well, now it's official," he said.

Fragaa looked at Lord Franklin incredulously.

"Just shake it. Nothing will happen. It's not magic. It's more ceremonial," said Lord Franklin.

"And everyone from your world does this?"

"Probably not everyone. It means different things to different people," replied Lord Franklin.

"They probably have good reason not to. It's odd," she said.

"Odd? You're fine with stark nakedness, but not handshakes? Oh, you'll fit in fine with the snake people."

"You didn't mind the first time we met. What were your exact words *such beauty, such grace?*" Fragaa laughed.

Lord Franklin was not amused. "Alright, enough of that."

Fragaa stopped laughing and started violently coughing. Blood stained her palm. She exhaled deeply and rested on one knee. Lord Franklin was about to move toward her, but she signaled him to stop. "I'm fine. There's nothing you can do now. I just need some rest."

"You've overexerted yourself again," said Lord Franklin. He handed her a handkerchief to wipe her hand. She wiped her nose and hands with it. "Thank you, but I'll be better soon, I promise. Please sit. This is a long process."

Lord Franklin did just that.

"May I ask a question?" Fragaa asked. "Sure," replied Lord Franklin. "You referred to me as a child. Why?"

"Um, well, I didn't mean child. I meant someone in their youth. You may be long lived, but you still exhibit traits of someone youthful," said Lord Franklin.

"Such as?" asked Fragaa

"Your appearance, your propensity for recklessness, and your over emotionality," said Lord Franklin.

"Were you always this insolent, or is that something that comes with age?" Fragaa teased.

"Now who's being insolent" Lord Franklin replied playfully.

Fragaa smiled. "And what of your appearance? Were you always this hairless?"

Lord Franklin guffawed at the remark and Fragaa laughed as well. "No, no. I had a lot of hair when I was younger. In fact, as much as yours." "What color?" Fragaa asked eagerly. "Black," Lord Franklin replied.

"I like black hair on men."

"Well, when we get back to my world, you can change my hair color and, while you're at it, give me back some of the hair time has robbed from me," said Lord Franklin.

Fragaa chuckled. "That seems unwise given your kind are so easily frighten."

"So, how did a royal get mixed up with mortals from other worlds? What do your parents—" said Lord Franklin.

"I'd rather not," Fragaa interrupted, and her demeanor changed to that of somberness.

"Apologies. I understand if you do not wish to tell me," said Lord Franklin.

Fragaa turned away from him and made her animal hide coat into a makeshift blanket. "Let's just get some rest," she said.

Lord Franklin laid on his back, and he wondered whether Fragaa was a typical avalenth or was she special? And if so, were more coming besides her and Kraag? Who were her parents? He did not really believe she came here without help. She had an army of lycanthropes with her. Surely, that took a considerable amount of organizing. This worried him because he knew this type of thinking could be dangerous in a place like this, but he could not help it. One thing he was pleased about was that he had a considerable amount of power on his side for the time being. Though he was not sure about this Kraag business. He did not see him and Hector coming to an accord to help defeat Kraag. And even if they did, what would happen afterwards? He was not about to let Hector receive all the knowledge Fragaa showed him. No matter what Fragaa said, that would certainly be folly.

Then there was also the issue of Fragaa living on borrowed time.

He wanted to know more of her secrets. The possibilities were endless, and he could imagine expanding the kingdom of Iiadec to the other continents, to the other worlds, to the Outer realm. However, none of this will be possible if Fragaa remained fixated on her quest to prevent a catastrophe that may not happen. He must obtain crucial information from her about how to expand his future empire and he can't do that if he has such limited time with her.

"Damn," Lord Franklin said under his breath.

Unbeknownst to him, Fragaa heard. "It's cruel, isn't it? Someone from the ethereal plane telling you your conflicts and ambitions are unimportant. To have them meddling in your affairs, telling you what to do and for that, I'm sorry. But I wouldn't be here if I didn't believe in averting this crisis," she said.

"Why me? Why did you choose me as your champion?" asked Lord Franklin.

"You command legions of men who respect you, your word, and authority," replied Fragaa.

Lord Franklin was not satisfied with that answer. "There are other kingdoms in Mirthadine. Why not one of them?"

"I believe fate brought me to you," said Fragaa.

Lord Franklin was skeptical of that remark. "More like chance." "Fate, chance, it doesn't make it any less special if God exists, I believe it is cruel and uncaring, but what if sometimes it's not? What if divine intervention is at play and looks favorable on one? Call that chance, if you like, but I will always seize an opportunity when it presents itself. Like I said, before I saw no failure here, I presumed that had something to do with you, the rightful King of Iiadec," she explained.

"So, you're here because you have feelings that things will turn out successful," said Lord Franklin, placing emphasis on the word feeling.

"I am here because I believe," said Fragaa. "In God?" asked Lord Franklin.

"In you," said Fragaa.

Fragaa stood up and extended her hand. "Now c'mon, your grace. It's time to return to the parallel reality."

CHAPTER NINE

TUNNELS

"Are you sure you're strong enough?" said Lord Franklin. "Yes, my powers have returned now. Shake my hand so that I can performed that strange ritual of yours." Lord Franklin shook her hand. Fragaa had a disappointed look on her face.

"Nothing happened."

"What did you expect? I told you it wasn't magic," said Lord Franklin. "Well, I shan't be doing that again. Anyway, I assume you are familiar with the procedures by now."

"Yes," said Lord Franklin. "Good. Be seated now."

Lord Franklin sat down, and Fragaa placed her fingertips on his temples. Lord Franklin closed his eyes and when he opened them, he saw three figures with rushlights approaching. The figures looked around. They seemed unaware of their surroundings. One figure was constantly turning around. He looked to be a young man with short blond hair who was showing early signs of balding. Lord Franklin could see, upon closer inspection that this was Tim.

"Will you stop spinning around, it's disorienting!" exclaimed a tall, very muscular, intimidating-looking male with an annoyed countenance. From the looks of him, he was not much older than Tim. He had short, dark brown hair. Lord Franklin recognized this young man as Alywin.

"I'm trying to see where we are," said Tim.

"We're in a dungeon. That's where we are, Tim," said Alywin. "Thank you for your astute analysis," said Tim sarcastically. Alywin scowled at him. "Will you two stop bickering? We're almost there," said a petite blonde woman holding a map. Lord Franklin recognized this woman as Sarah. "You said that before," groaned Alywin.

The three continued down the dark corridor. "How do we even know that map will lead us to wherever it is we're going? I mentioned before, it's quite old and they definitely might have shifted around a few things," said Alywin.

"Well, we will just have to hope the builders didn't change too much in the dungeon. Now c'mon, let's go," said Sarah.

"I agree with Sarah. We should press on and hope for the best," said Tim.

"Of course you do," Alywin sneered. "Shut up, Alywin," Tim said angrily.

"You're so transparent," Alywin retorted. Sarah was unaware of their conversation, for she was preoccupied with finding the opening for the entrance of the tunnel.

"Shh, this is it."

The others stopped talking and Sarah put her rush light in front of a cell door. It had rusted metal bars and an overall weathered look.

"It looks like no one's been here in ages," said Tim. "How do we get in?" said Alywin.

Sarah, slightly using her free arm while leaning most her body on the wall next to the cell door, pushed the door. It opened

She looked at Alywin and Tim. "It's unlocked." "We should be careful," said Alywin.

Sarah nodded her head.

"It's possible someone's been here recently, so I'll go in first, then you two rush in," said Alywin.

All three agreed. Alywin drew Colin's bow, and he leaned on the wall adjacent to the cell door. He craned his neck to see through the doorway. "There are lit torches in there," he whispered. Tim gripped Colin's blade hilt tightly.

"Whoever's in there, we mean you no harm, but it would be folly to challenge us. We are heavily armed," said Alywin.

There was no response. Tim and Sarah looked at Alywin. Alywin nodded his head. He kicked the door wide open and slowly entered the cell. Tim followed with Colin's sword completely unsheathed and lastly, Sarah, with a dagger in hand that she always carried in case of emergency. The room was filled with skeletons. There were various torture devices, such as a fully operational iron maiden, a torture rack, and a breaking wheel. There were also several utensils on a wooden table, such as several knives, cleavers, and tweezers.

Alywin examined the room. "Well, whoever was here left. I doubt they knew we were here."

Tim and Sarah looked visibly horrified and repulsed. Alywin looked at their terrified faces. It suddenly occurred to him they most likely had never seen skeletal human remains. "Hey, they died long before we were here. They can't harm us."

This seemed to calm his comrades.

"Wha-what do you suppose someone would want down here?" asked Sarah.

"Same as us, I suppose or…" Alywin studied the room and observed the position of the lit torches. They were all around the room.

"Or what, Alywin?" Tim asked impatiently. "Witches," Alywin said. "Witches like Olga?" responded Tim.

"No, you fool. I'm talking about the ones who eat flesh and devour organs."

Sarah grimaced at the words *devour organs*. She generally felt queasy, and Alywin's incessant babbling did not help.

"That's probably what the witch or witches are feasting on; human remains to satiate their hunger. They're probably grinding the bones with their sharp teeth," said Alywin.

Tim, who was disgusted by the image Alywin placed in his head, said, "Alywin. Please, just stop."

The two suddenly heard vomiting. Sarah was hunched over with a pool of vomit at her feet.

"For God's sake, Alywin. Look what you've done."

Tim and Alywin walked over to Sarah. "Are you alright, Sarah?" Tim said while placing a hand on her back affectionately.

"I'm fine. I just feel a bit humiliated, like I let Lady Branson down. I volunteered for this task, and I can't even stomach some bloody skeletons."

"Most people can't," said Alywin. "How do you?" asked Sarah. "Father used to be a grave digger or grave robber. Come to think of it, he didn't specify which, anyway, we'd exhume a lot of corpses." "I don't envy you," said Sarah as she got to her feet.

"Still, this is quite undignified. I'm a healer. I've seen dead bodies before."

"Sure, when they're warm and not in the ground, feasted upon by maggots. You're new, anyway. Lady Branson has you working with mostly live bodies," said Alywin.

"And if it's any consolation, I find this whole room quite repugnant," said Tim.

"Thank you both. You have lifted my spirits," she said.

"And that's not all. The witches will most likely not eat you because of the putrid smell," said Alywin.

"Alywin!" said Tim.

Sarah laughed. "Seriously, Alywin. Do you really believe the person or persons here were witches?"

"This is certainly a great set up for hokraft," said Alywin.

"Women aren't the only ones who practice hokraft. Historically, there are more male practitioners," said Sarah.

"Regardless of gender, a person or persons was here, most likely possessing magic. How did they get in?" asked Tim.

"Who's saying they got in? Maybe they were here all along within the castle," said Alywin.

"There are only two known castors in Corithni. Olga and-," said Sarah. "Ulric. There's no way this is that fat fuck's secret hokraft chamber. He is the one who was so adamant about banning hokraft," said Alywin angrily.

Sarah was perplexed as to why Alywin had such harsh words for Sir Ulric. Tim looked at her and said, "It's a long story."

"Then that leaves Olga," said Sarah.

"Wait, we're forgetting something; Sir Richard said the map was taken off one of Hector's men, who had to have stolen it or received it from someone within Corithni," said Tim.

"Are you suggesting we have another traitor in our mist," said Alywin. "It's possible," replied Tim.

"Or maybe it's the same person. Bancroft may have had a contingency plan," said Sarah.

"He could have let Hector's men in," said Alywin. "How could he let them in undetected?" asked Tim.

"Castors have their ways. Some can change appearance and even shape shift into animals," said Alywin.

"White stone is magic resistance," explained Sarah.

"Resistant not impervious. That implies limitations. We've already seen evidence of this with Olga," said Alywin.

"That means Hector has already infiltrated the castle," said Tim.

Tim saw a rat that was unnaturally still. He looked at Alywin, who understood. Tim unsheathed the blade. Alywin readied the bow. Sarah held her dagger up. They crept closer to the rodent. When they were in arm's distance the rodent scurried off. Alywin's eyes widened for he knew something was afoot, but before he could react, a large burly man tackled him to the ground, knocking the bow from his hands.

Tim was about to swing his sword when another equally large man punched him in the face. The sword was knocked out of his hands and Tim fell to the floor. The man was about to pursue Tim further when

Sarah stabbed him in the chest with her dagger. The man winced in pain and pulled the dagger from his chest.

"You fucking bitch," he said, before striking her across the face with his back hand. She fell to the floor. The man moved toward Sarah with the dagger in hand. Before she could react, the man grabbed her by the hair. During the struggle, her crown braid came loose. Tim, who was disoriented, attempted to free Sarah from the man's grasp. He wrestled the man to the floor and fought for possession of the dagger. The man gained the upper hand and pointed the dagger dangerously close to Tim's throat. Tim struggled to keep the tip from puncturing his throat.

Suddenly Sarah jumped on the man and dug her teeth into the side of his neck drawing blood. The man screamed. Tim took the opportunity to wrench himself free. The man turned to Sarah and looked at her menacingly. Before he could react, Tim grabbed a skull and smashed it on the man's head. This caused the man to drop the dagger. Sarah went for it first but was punched in the face and knocked unconscious. Meanwhile, Alywin managed to get back on his feet where he and the other man traded blows. They were evenly matched in strength, but Alywin edged him out slightly in skill getting in several jabs to the face and body. The man who initially attacked Alywin, however, was not too deterred. He seemed to have weathered the pain for now.

Tim, who was preoccupied with the assailant who had concussed Sarah, dove for the dagger as did the man. They grappled for the dagger but the man overpowered Tim. The man was about to drive the dagger into Tim's chest, when Alywin stood up with the other assailant he was fighting. That other man was barely conscious. Alywin pointed a single arrow at his juggler. The other man was severely beaten with many bruises on his face. Alywin had managed to break through his defenses when they were fighting, and his opponent could no longer withstand Alywin's relentless attacks and superior skill. Alywin had taken advantage of the man's weakened state during their fight and grabbed an arrow with the intention of slaying the man but after seeing Tim in peril, he thought it was best to utilize other methods.

"Drop the dagger, or I'll end this fucker!" said Alywin. The man was still with the dagger in his hand. "I said drop it, you stupid git!" insisted Alywin.

"Are you alright there, Benton?" said the man.

"Just a little banged up. Nothing I can't handle. Been through worse…" Benton lost consciousness.

Alywin responded by gripping him tighter. "I'll kill him!" Alywin insisted.

"Go ahead," said the man. He laughed derisively. "You have no leverage. Kill Benton and I kill her and him. That leaves you. Now, I'll admit you've proven to be a formidable fighter. Not many could best Benton. But you've overexerted yourself, holding that arrow awkwardly with your left hand. I can only assume you injured your dominant hand in the fight. You wouldn't last long against me."

Tim and Alywin looked at each other. He knew what Tim was thinking, but he could not allow it. It was too risky. Trying to take the dagger from the man while he was distracted seemed erred especially since that same dagger was near the center of Tim's chest. Hence, Alywin signaled with his eyes a resounding no.

"If you truly care nothing for this man, you wouldn't be talking to me. I can still kill him, injured hand or not," said Alywin.

"Don't test me or perhaps you'd like to see what the inside of his throat looks like" The man raised Tim up and placed the dagger to his throat.

"What do you want?" Alywin asked. "For now, drop the arrow." Alywin did not respond.

"Alright. I confess. I'd rather you not kill the oaf, but make no mistake, I do not care for him as much as you care for them. I can see it in your eyes," said the man.

"If I do that, you'll just kill them both," said Alywin.

"I'll cut you a deal. If you all shut your fucking gobs, we'll pretend none of this ever happened and nobody has to die," replied the man.

"I'll keep quiet as long as you drop the dagger first," said Alywin.

The man scowled menacingly. "You're really trying my patience. I'm just going to kill him, kill her, then you." He pressed the dagger tighter against Tim's throat. "I am going to give you to the count of three to change your decision."

"One, two…"

Alywin lowered his hand slightly at two.

Before the man could say three, a voice said, "Stop." The man froze. A haggardly looking woman appeared before them with disheveled hair and raggedy garments. From the looks of it, she was middle-aged. She had tan skin, long unkempt black hair, an aquiline face, and hazel eyes. But perhaps the most unusual thing about this woman was that she was levitating a few inches above the ground. She slowly descended upon the ground.

"Knox, you've gone and fucked things up again. Drop the bloody dagger you stupid oaf!"

"Watch your tongue, hag, these people saw us. They can't be allowed to live!" said Knox.

"Drop the dagger, Knox. We need them alive." "We or you?" retorted Knox.

The woman scowled at Knox. "Have you forgotten your oath?" said the woman.

"Listen, you—ack." Knox grabbed his throat as though an invisible hand was strangling him, thus dropping the dagger.

The woman was holding some sort of doll that crudely resembled him. It had a rope around its neck that the woman tightened. Knox stared at it as he was choking.

"A trinket from another land," she said, referring to the effigy.

Knox gasped for breath, barely breathing. His face turned red and veins protruded on his face. She eventually released the string on the doll's throat. Knox took some time to catch his breath. Tim took the opportunity to seize the dagger and sword from the ground. He pointed the sword at the strange woman and placed the dagger in his belt.

"What do you people want?"

"You don't get to ask questions," said the woman.

"Answer him!" Alywin shouted, while still holding an unconscious Benton.

The woman looked at Alywin briefly, then said, referring to Benton. "Would you kindly step away from that man."

"You must think I'm stupid, I—" said Alywin. "*Uthra Fithra.*" Upon hearing the hex, Alywin immediately jumped out of the way.

Benton was left to be scorched by flame. He awoke to the sight of his flesh being seared. Crying out in agony, Benton flailed about, attempting to extinguish the flames. As he moved, the flames rose.

"Benton!" Knox cried.

Knox was about to aid his comrade when the woman placed the doll in front of his face. "Not a muscle."

Knox stopped in his tracks. Benton rose to his feet. He picked up a cleaver while still on fire and he then charged at the woman.

"*Uthra Hyga.*" [summon weapon] The cleaver disappeared from Benton's hand and reappeared in the woman's hand. She then struck Benton in the forehead with it. He collapsed on the floor. His lifeless body continued to be engulfed by flame. The woman stared into the flames for a moment, then said, "*Kargama.*" [return] The flames extinguished, leaving Benton's freshly charred corpse behind.

Knox looked horrified. "You killed him!" screamed Knox.

"Of course I did. He stole from me," said the woman nonchalantly. She retrieved a necklace with a blue crystal attached from Benton's corpse and placed it around her neck.

Sarah had awoken and she was disoriented. She saw Alywin on the floor looking terrified and Tim pointing the sword at a woman. His eyes stared curiously at the blue crystal around her neck. Sarah's eyes gravitated towards Knox, and she gasped.

"Don't worry, dearie. He won't harm you. He's learned his lesson," said the woman.

Sarah saw the remains of Benton on the ground and concluded that the woman was a witch.

"What do you people want?!" shouted Tim.

The woman walked towards Tim. His heart began to beat rapidly, and hands began to shake. "Stay right there!"

The woman stopped and smiled. "Aw, you're trembling. You're right to fear me, but I won't harm you, not yet," the woman said. She then proceeded to walk towards Tim.

"Witch, stop right there, don't try anything!" said Alywin.

Sarah looked at the ground, then at the witch. She had never done it before in the castle and was not sure that she could. The witch looked at her curiously. Sarah extended her hand toward the ground, her palm open. The floor started to vibrate slightly.

"I wouldn't. I'm a seasoned castor. Best not to test your luck," said the witch.

Sarah stared at the witch. She contemplated moving a stone from the ground and striking the witch using elemental manipulation.

"You are a terrain manipulator. You will be of use," said the witch.

"Whatever it is, I won't do it," said Sarah.

"I was hoping you wouldn't say that."

There was a sound of rattling bones. Alywin turned around to see reanimated corpses. The skeletal figures, at least the ones with missing bones, fused spare bones together to become whole. There were about 30 reanimated corpses in the room. Before anyone had time to react, the skeletons piled up on Tim and Alywin and seized their weapons. They then pulled them to their feet and restrained them.

"Arrgh, get off," said Tim.

The woman walked up to Tim and waved the cleaver in front of his face and watched his expression. He was frightened but he did his best not to show it. She intended to do the same to Alywin but when the witch drew closer to Alywin, Sarah said, "Stop it!"

The witch looked at her and said, "Sure, but first I need you to do something for me."

"What is it?" asked Sarah.

"Look upon the floor and you shall see an entrance." Sarah was perplexed. The skeletons pointed to the spot on the ground where there was a fissure. Sarah looked at it.

"Good. Now I want you to open it," said the witch.

Sarah slowly knelt beside the crack. Upon further inspection, she saw engravings on the ground of symbols she did not recognize, but she figured this must be the symbols of the other builders, including the sign of the Masons. She placed her hands on the crack and the symbols lit up in a bluish hue. The signs started to appear on the back of her hands. One symbol in particular, an upside down, double-sided hammer with a dots next to each side of its head, began to burn into the back of her right hand like a brand mark. She winced in pain as the ground shook. It gradually began to separate until a staircase revealed itself.

A skeleton then seized Sarah. She struggled, but to no avail. "I did what you asked. Now, let us go!"

"Descend the steps and take us to him. The girl will lead the way," said the witch.

"Where are you taking us?" asked Tim.

The witch did not respond. Instead, the skeletons brought their captors down the staircase. The witch then turned to Knox, who was still in mourning, and said, "Will you behave now?"

Defeated and despondent, he nodded his head in acquiescence.

They descended the steps until they came upon a tunnel with six unlit candles within wall mounted sconces.

"Uthra Fithra," said the woman. Suddenly, the candles were lit. They continued north until they reached a wall of solid stone. The witch hastily grabbed Sarah's hand and looked at the markings on the back of it. They were glowing blue. The witch smiled. "We're here."

The skeleton restraining Sarah released her and pushed her to the floor. The witch stood above her and said, "Open it."

Sarah did not respond.

"I know you're a Mason. Do not play coy. Open it," said the witch.

"Will you just let them go?" Sarah pleaded.

The witch looked at Sarah for a moment then whispered in her ear, "I know you care for them deeply, but if you don't do what I say, you'll be weeping for them."

Startled by her words, Sarah stepped forward and placed her hand on the wall. It began to vibrate, and an unnaturally straight line divided the wall into two equal parts, vertically. Those parts separated, revealing a large room. The witch's eyes widened. Sarah looked at her.

"Enter... all of you," said the witch.

They entered the room. It was dark and hard to see, but one could hear something gnawing at bone, the smell so putrid that it attacked the nostrils.

"Gytha," said a thunderous voice that did not seem entirely human.

The witch looked startled, as did everyone else in the room. "I brought gifts, my master."

This creature, who had been resting on a pile of corpses, stood on its hind legs, revealing a silhouette of a massive rodent. "I've not seen light in ages, Gytha. Let my eyes look upon you, for I cannot see."

"Yes, my master, *Uthra Fithra*," said Gytha.

The candles on the wall lit, illuminating a circular room made of stone. It also revealed dozens of corpses and a mound of feces. The light from the candles revealed the creature's true form. A form of a giant black rat. Everyone stood aghast, with the exception of Gytha.

"This is madness," said Knox.

The others were lost for words. "I have not fed on human flesh in over 150 years. I have grown thin and weak. I fear the light will leave my eyes soon," said the creature.

"Fret not, my master. I have brought you sustenance. Bring him here."

The skeletons seized Knox. He resisted. "What is the meaning of this? Arrgh! Let me go, you fucking bitch, you'll pay for this!"

The skeletons brought Knox to the beast, who proceeded to gobble him whole. The crunching of bone and flesh made the others wince. They heard him cry out in agony. It was a moment in brevity, but it would be forever ingrained in their memories.

"I am not yet satiated. Bring me more," said the creature. Gytha looked at Sarah, then Alywin, and lastly, Tim. Her gaze suddenly gravitated towards Alywin. The reanimated skeletons grabbed Alywin. He struggled, but there were too many of them.

"Alywin!" Tim screamed.

"Wait, wait, I'm a Mason!" Sarah shouted.

The skeletons stopped, and the creature looked at her curiously. "A Mason?"

"Yes-yes, see." Sarah revealed the mark on her right hand.

The creature's eyes widened. "Mason, the master builder of this very castle... my prison," said the creature.

"Yes, yes, and I can help you escape," said Sarah.

"She speaks lies, for this is your home. Where else would you live?" said Gytha.

"There is a whole world out there full of tasty humans and I can show you, if you promise not to eat my friends!" said Sarah.

"She lies. She doesn't love you like I do. If you go out there, the hunters, they will kill you!"

Tears started streaming down Gytha's face. "I don't know what I'd do without you!"

"Don't listen to her. She wants to keep you here in the dark, lonely, emaciated, and depraved in a cage like some pet!" said Sarah.

"Shut up. Shut up, you filthy wench!" Gytha slapped Sarah across the face. She then brought the cleaver to Sarah's face, causing Sarah to wince. She whispered, "Master does not need you alive to eat you. In fact, he prefers his meat chopped up into bits. He finds it's easier to chew that way." She slid the cleaver down Sarah's face toward her foot. She was gentle enough not to leave a mark.

"We'll start with the foot," she said.

"Enough! Gytha, you are not to harm the Mason or her comrades. It is time I left this horrid place. I've grown weary of the company of corpses," said the creature.

"But master, she lies. If you go out, they'll kill you. Please don't leave me, she doesn't love you like I do!" Tears continued to fall down her face. "Silence woman. I have decided you and your undead will accompany us incase anything goes awry." "Yes, master," said Gytha. "Lead the way, Mason." Sarah nodded.

"What do you think you're doing?" whispered Alywin. "Saving us. Trust me. I have a plan," whispered Sarah. Alywin looked at her incredulously.

"Don't look at me like that," said Sarah.

"We're about to be eaten by a giant fucking rat, aren't we?" whispered Alywin.

"What did you say?" asked Gytha.

Before Alywin could respond, Sarah quickly interjected. "Nothing. We said nothing."

Gytha furrowed her brow and peered into Sarah's eyes. "I saw your lips move. Speak the truth or you shall suffer the consequences." Glowering at Sarah, she was about to mutter something under her breath when Tim interrupted.

"I believe no harm was to befall upon us."

She turned to Tim and pointed menacingly at him. "You listen and listen well I—"

"Gytha! Enough squabbling and let us proceed," said the creature. "But they are planning something. They mean to harm you. I only wish to protect you. Please let me destroy them," Gytha said, emphasizing the words destroy them.

"No! I am the great Salkar, and I am no fool. Now stop your tantrums. You will not be warned again." "Yes, master," said Gytha.

They proceeded outside the room. Sarah looked at the ceiling, then at her hand. The mark still burned. How was she going to get herself, Alywin, and Tim out of here? She thought of manipulating the stone that made up the tunnel, but that was something she never really practiced at such a scale. Terrain manipulation is often considered to be the hardest form of elemental manipulation. Furthermore, her hands were restrained. She looked at the ground. This was her only chance, and she prayed silently that this would work. She stomped her left foot down hard on the ground. A mound of stone surged from the ground and destroyed the skeletons restraining her. Breaking them apart. Those skeletons appeared to be deactivated due to the impact. Sarah, with her hands now free, placed her hands on the floor and pillars of stone rose from the ground destroying the skeletons restraining Alywin and Tim.

"You could do that the whole time!" exclaimed Alywin.

Tim seized the bow, quiver, dagger, and sword that was resting on a pile of broken bones. He gave the dagger, bow, and quiver to Alywin, who took it with his left hand.

"Seize them master, they deceived us. They shall pay for such insolence!" said Gytha.

"AAArgh! You wretched maggots. You've just sealed your fates!" bellowed Salkar.

"Run!" screamed Sarah.

The three sprinted from the remaining mob of skeletons, as well as Salkar and Gytha. Gytha hurled several hexes at them.

"Uthra Thragaa!" she said.

The lightning nearly struck Sarah, but Tim pushed her out of the way. He himself was grazed in the shoulder blade in the process. This caused him to wince in pain and buckle his legs slightly.

"Tim! Are you alright?" asked Sarah. "I'm fine, it's just a scratch," replied Tim.

"Trying to play tough, are we?" said Alywin. "Now's not the time, Alywin," Tim said angrily.

"Right." Alywin turned to Sarah. "Sarah, you know that thing you did earlier. Could you like do it again, please?"

Sarah sighed with exhaustion, she was not accustomed to this level of terrain manipulation, and it was taking its toll on her body. She felt perhaps she did not possess enough soul manifest, or perhaps she did not know how to fully optimize her abilities.

"You two go ahead. I'll stop them," said Sarah.

"We're not leaving you behind," Alywin and Tim said in unison. "This isn't up for debate. I am not that skilled a terrain manipulator.

I cannot run and alter the ground at the same time I—"

"Were not leaving you and that's final. We will protect you while you're stationary," said Alywin.

"Alywin," she said.

"We don't have time to argue. Now do your thing," Alywin interrupted.

Sarah acquiesced. She raised her hands to the ceiling, and it began to slowly crack.

"She means to seal us in. Quick after them," said Gytha.

Salkar was right behind her with more skeletons. "Gytha. I grow weary of this foolishness. This girl and her subordinates have proven quite troublesome, and you brought them here. End them before I entertain the notion that you conspired with them to destroy me!"

"No. No, master I would never—" "Silence! Kill them!" "Yes, master," said Gytha.

Gytha saw Sarah standing with her arms to the ceiling, with Tim and Alywin next to her. Alywin had a bow in hand, using his teeth to hold the string.

"Uthra ack."

Alywin had already released the string that sent the arrow whizzing through the air and it lodged its way in Gytha's throat. After an unsuccessful attempt to apply pressure on the wound, she collapsed on the floor and died. The skeletons that followed her command crumbled to the ground.

"Gytha. You fool. You've gotten yourself killed!" Salkar charged at Sarah.

Tim helped Alywin place another arrow in the string of the bow. Alywin fired three shots at Salkar. Two entered his left shoulder and the third pierced his head. Much to Alywin's dismay, as well as the others, this did not impede the beast in the slightest. Salkar came charging in with an arrow in his skull. When he was within arm's distance from Sarah, the ceiling collapsed, and rubble fell on top of Salkar. Sarah sighed in relief. Before she could celebrate, Salkar's head popped out from the rubble. Sarah screamed and Alywin stumbled backwards.

"I am the great Salkar. You cannot kill me, I am in—"

Tim immediately dove Colin's sword into Salkar's skull, and the light went out of Salkar's eyes. Tim pulled it out, and he breathed heavily.

"Is he dead?" asked Alywin. "I think so," said Tim. "Well, go on. Check, just in case," Alywin demanded.

Tim was slightly vexed by his comrade and replied, "I drove a bloody sword into his head. I'm pretty sure he's dead."

"He's a giant fucking talking rat. He probably has supernatural powers or something," said Alywin.

"Do you hear yourself? Sarah just dropped the ceiling on him. You shot it in the head with an arrow, and I stabbed it in the head with a sword. I'm pretty sure it's dead," retorted Tim.

"Is it so crazy to believe this fucker's still alive? Some deranged bitch resurrected the dead. Anything is possible now," said Alywin.

While they were arguing, Sarah took a large rock and repeatedly bashed it onto Salkar's lifeless head until brain matter came out of his now crushed skull. Alywin and Tim watched in disbelief.

Sarah then turned to them. "Is he dead now?" "Definitely dead," Tim and Alywin said in unison.

The three looked at each other for a moment, trying to recuperate from their whole ordeal. Tim finally broke the silence.

"Well, what do we do now?"

"We report back to Lady Branson," said Sarah.

Alywin walked toward what remained of Salkar's head. He used the dagger to begin cutting away at Salkar's ear.

"Uh, what are you doing?" asked Sarah.

Alywin finished cutting Salkar's ear and held it in his hand.

"She'll never believe us unless we've got proof. Now, the question is, who's gonna hold it?"

Both Sarah and Tim looked disgusted and reluctant.

"Come on Tim. You slew it. Why don't you do the honors," said Alywin.

"No way, Alywin. I don't wanna get sick or worst cursed. Besides, why don't you hold it?" said Tim.

"I can only hold so many things with my hand and all," replied Alywin. Tim, who was visibly irritated, said, "The answer is no, Alywin." "You're such a baby. What about you, Sarah?" said Alywin.

"Er, I don't think so. Uh, that's a no for me, as well," she said. Alywin groaned.

"Tell you what. I'll take back my dagger and you can hold the disgusting rat ear," Sarah said while slowly taking back her dagger. Alywin suddenly felt foolish.

Tim looked at Sarah. "We should probably check the other tunnels and see if they lead to the outside."

"Are you mad? We almost got killed. It isn't safe. Who knows what's out there?" said Alywin.

"We can't tell Lady Branson we failed. If there is a way out of the castle through the tunnels, we should at least try to find it," said Tim.

He looked at Sarah for some support. She was reluctant but eventually said, "He's right, Alywin. If Hector's army invades, we need an escape."

Alywin groaned. "Alright, lead the way."

The three walked through a labyrinth of tunnels, which were mostly vacated.

"Where are we going? We've been walking for a while," said Alywin impatiently.

"We are following the map. Let's see, we go left, no right..." said Sarah. "So, in other words, we're lost," said Alywin.

Sarah frowned. Tim looked around at the tunnels they resided in. He found it peculiar that the walls of the tunnels were so ornately crafted, as were the wall mounted sconces that contained candles that were somehow still lit. Was this magic? Gytha had lit up the candles on the walls when entering what appeared to be Salkar's domain, so maybe all the candles lit up with that one spell. Tim was beginning to ponder how long Gytha had been living here.

Sarah noticed Tim was deep in thought. "Tim, are you alright?" "Don't you find it odd? It's like someone wanted us to come here," said Tim.

"You think it's a trap?" said Alywin.

Tim sighed. "I don't know, but I feel like something's been watching us?"

The three heard a squeaky sound and they turned around, startled. Tim drew Colin's sword. A creature stepped out of the shadows. It was a ground squirrel holding an acorn. It stood there and seemed quite perplexed to see three humans underground.

Alywin looked at the others. "Another witch?" Before they could respond, the squirrel left.

"After it!" said Sarah, who was already running after the squirrel. Tim and Alywin were hesitant to follow. "Sarah, it could be another trap!" exclaimed Tim.

"It's already seen us. We must capture it before it informs its allies," she explained.

The trio ran through the tunnels; there were five pathways. One pathway was already sealed when Sarah collapsed the ceiling on Salkar. They were traveling through the northern pathway. The squirrel eventually led them to a dead end. The three cornered the squirrel, who surprisingly did not move. They crept closer and still the creature did not move.

Growing impatient Alywin shouted, "Alright who are you? What do you want?!"

There was no response.

Alywin looked at Tim. Tim shrugged. "Maybe it's just a squirrel." "Let's kill it just in case," Alywin seized the squirrel. It writhed in his hand. Alywin was about to crush the creature to death, when suddenly it sprung from his hand and transformed into a human male.

Tim pointed the blade at the man's throat. "Who are you? Where are the others?!" shouted Alywin.

The man, trembling, looked at Sarah, who was ambivalent of Tim and Alywin's method of interrogation. Tim caught his gaze and shouted, "Speak!"

The man was quite gaunt, possibly malnourished. He was clothed in rags, had a scraggily beard and long, disheveled dirty blonde hair. "I am called Leland, and I mean you no harm."

"Why should we believe you?" Tim scowled and pressed the blade further upon Leland's throat. Leland's eyes gazed upwards, as though recalling something. Then he did something quite strange. He began to sing.

"You don't need to cry, For I am by your side.

You'll grow big and strong, If you move along.

Be brave day by day and the pain will go away."

Sarah's eyes widened and Tim and Alywin were befuddled by her reaction to the tune. Several thoughts went through her head. How did this stranger know the song her mother and father used to sing to her when she was just a babe? Why did he lead us here if his intentions were an ambush? None of this made any sense.

"Sarah, are you alright? You look like you've seen a ghost," said Tim. "Let him go," said Sarah.

"What?" said Alywin.

"He can't speak comfortably with a sword at his throat. Any answers he will give will be irrelevant because he will say anything to save his own life," replied Sarah.

Tim and Alywin released Leland, but they kept their eyes on him. "Who are you exactly?" asked Sarah.

Leland stared at Sarah for a moment. "You have his likeness." "Whose likeness?" she asked.

"Your ancestor, Landyn Mason."

Sarah was confused as to how he knew this.

Leland suspected this and explained. "I knew you were a Mason because of the mark on your hand."

Sarah looked at the mark on the back of her right hand. She had not spent time to analyze her natural tattoo due to the ordeal she experienced.

Leland looked at the ground at Salkar's ear. Alywin had dropped it when he grabbed Leland in squirrel form.

"I take it Gytha is dead along with the beast?" asked Leland. "We're asking the questions here," said Tim.

"Right sorry," said Leland.

"How do you know that lullaby?" asked Sarah.

"I taught it to Landyn years ago. He was looking for a way to calm his daughter during the cold winter nights. Apparently, it worked so well that he swore to use it for all Mason children and their descendants.

Sarah furrowed her brow. "Landyn Mason was born—"

"256 years ago. I know because we were only seasons apart. I considered him a dear friend," Leland interrupted.

Sarah was surprised that he knew the exact number. Leland anticipated such a reaction.

"One remembers such things after spending years in isolation and having the misfortune of being granted a prolonged life of suffering. Counting, remembering when things weren't so, is the only way to stay sane," Leland said dejectedly.

Sarah looked into Leland's woeful eyes and began to empathize with him, much to the concern of Tim and Alywin.

"What happened to you?" she asked with genuine concern. "I was cursed for something I did," he replied.

"For over 200 years?" Alywin said skeptically.

"I admit it sounds ludicrous and I wish it wasn't so, but there are forces at play that go beyond reason."

"Hokraft," said Tim.

Alywin remained distrustful of Leland and believed Sarah, and now Tim, had fallen prey to his deception. He did not know Leland's angle, but he was not about to wait to fall into a trap.

"What are you playing at?" he asked.

Leland looked confused, and this angered Alywin.

"Look, this may be the end for us. Your cronies may come out of thin air or from Ulid's fucking arsehole. I don't care. Just know this, if you don't start speaking straight soon, I will personally see to it that you'll meet your end before they get here!"

Leland was frightened, and Sarah and Tim were alarmed. Leland looked at Alywin's injured right hand. Alywin noticed this and smirked.

"That's good. You're thinking of ending your fucking charade and want to take your chances, so go ahead, take a shot, but make no mistake.

I only need one arm to kill you." Leland began retreating from Alywin. "Alywin, stop. Can't you see you're scaring him?" said Tim.

"He is a fucking liar. He's probably one of Gytha's associates. How else does he know that name? Am I the only one with any bloody sense around here?" said Alywin.

"Alywin," said Sarah.

Alywin, still fuming, replied, "What?!"

Sarah was startled by this response. Upon seeing her frightened countenance, his features soften. He sighed as he felt ashamed for losing his temper.

Sarah changed to a stern expression. "You're scaring him."

Alywin was about to protest when Sarah interrupted him. "You're scaring us."

He turned to Tim, who had a concerned look on his face. Alywin turned away from them, feeling humiliated and defeated.

"Do you really think he is a victim of some centuries old curse?"

"We'll never know unless we ask him," said Sarah.

"Fine," groaned Alywin.

"Thank you, Alywin," Sarah said softly.

Tim looked at Leland, who was cowering in the corner. He looked quite wretched. His response to Alywin suggested he was someone who knew abuse which he might have suffered under Gytha, if he was to be believed. It did not help that Alywin was a much larger, more imposing man, by comparison.

"Forgive my friend. He really is a good lad. Well, most of the time, it's just that... how can I say this?"

"Gytha," Leland interrupted.

That was not what Tim was going to say, but he went along to get the conversation going.

"Yes, Gytha. She's quite something. Her antics have taken a toll on my poor friend," said Tim.

Alywin rolled his eyes, and he muttered under his breath. "If this fucker attacks us, I'm blaming you two idiots."

Sarah overheard and shot Alywin a foul glance that Alywin ignored, as though protesting at Sarah nonverbally reprimanding him. Quite vexed that Alywin was ignoring her, Sarah attempted to gain his attention.

"Ahem, Alywin, don't you have something to say to Leland?" "I don't believe I do," Alywin said rather curtly.

"Really? Ugh," said Sarah.

"You see, my friend lived a hard life and has trouble expressing his emotions. He's usually a lot friendlier."

"Fuck off, Tim!" Alywin said angrily. "You're not helping," said Tim.

Sarah was growing ever so impatient. "For God's sakes, Alywin. You threatened to kill the man. You must apologize!"

Alywin and Tim were quite taken aback by Sarah's outburst. She sighed. "Just apologize."

"No," Alywin replied.

Angered by the response, she said, "Excuse me?"

"Spear me the dramatics. I don't feel like getting into a quarrel with you," Alywin said rather dismissively

"Oh, you're so infuriating," said Sarah. Mocking Alywin, she puffed out her chest and gave an exaggerated and highly inaccurate impersonation of the male voice. "Oh, I'm a big bad man from Garla. That means I have to act tough all the time and treat others poorly because I'm a bloody killer."

Alywin was surprised she knew he was from Garla. He had never told her. When he realized how she possibly knew this, he groaned, and he looked at Tim, who began to laugh nervously. That confirmed his suspicions.

"Tim, when are you going to learn to shut your fucking gob?" "Don't speak to him that way. He's no longer your lackey," said Sarah.

Alywin turned back to Sarah. "I'm sorry, is your name Albert Franklin?" Alywin said sarcastically.

Sarah scowled. Taking advantage of her silence, Alywin said, "Didn't think so, 'cause I don't take orders from diminutive, self-absorbed, petulant girls!"

"Diminutive?!" Sarah exclaimed.

"Oh, please. You're a few inches shy of being a dwarf," Alywin retorted.

Tim, looking to deescalate the situation, said, "But dwarves are a whole separate race and beards, yeah beards."

"Shut up, Tim!" they said in unison.

Tim looked at Leland who was quite confused by what he was witnessing.

"They're usually not like this," said Tim.

"Ugh. You're so stubborn. Why can't you just behave like a normal person?" said Sarah.

"Against my better judgment, I agreed to listen to the ramblings of someone who is either clearly mad or deceiving us, and now you want me to apologize like some subservient, weak-willed, sorry excuse for a human being. You must be joking," said Alywin.

"Is that what this is about? You have an image to maintain?" retorted Sarah.

"You're the one barking orders like some bloody royal. You think you're better, but your lowborn shit like the rest of us," retorted Alywin. "You don't even know me," said Sarah. "And I don't want to,"

Alywin replied.

There was a brief silence between the two. Alywin realized his criticism had been too harsh and unwarranted and his features softened. He sighed, and he was about to say something when Tim interrupted.

"Alywin!"

"I know. I should not have said that. I didn't really mean it, I just—"

"No, that's not it. He's gone!"

"What?!" Sarah said. She looked at Alywin, who, in turn, looked at her. They were thinking the same thing,

"Oh fuck," they said in unison. Sarah paced back and forth.

"Wait. How did this happen? Weren't you watching him?" she said, referring to Tim.

"Don't blame him. This is your fault. I told you he was playing us. He's a bloody castor. He's probably warning his mates," said Alywin. "My fault? If you hadn't scared him away, none of this would have happened," said Sarah.

Tim, believing this to be a senseless quarrel, shouted, "For the love of Arda, both of you, please shut up!"

Both Sarah and Alywin remained silent.

"Alywin, Sarah saved our lives with Salkar. We should be grateful and trust her judgment. Sarah, Alywin defended us against Gytha's subordinates and even managed to kill her. In other words, you two are some of the smartest and bravest people I know, so quick bickering and let's figure this out. We are here for one reason: to find an escape route just in case the war does not go in our favor."

Realizing their foolishness after being reprimanded, both Alywin and Sarah stared at the floor ashamedly. Sarah eventually broke the silence.

"He could be anywhere now."

"Not necessarily." Sarah and Tim looked at Alywin, quite intrigued by his words. "From what I know about castors from my time in Garla, they can only transport themselves to places they have been prior. If we are to believe Leland is a castor, which he most likely is, his physique would suggest he has not seen the surface in a while," deduced Alywin.

"The surface has changed significantly over the years, particular Corithni Castle, which means he won't be able to transport there. Hence, he is confined to the tunnels, in theory," said Sarah.

"There are four remaining pathways. He has to be in one of them," said Tim.

"We can't just go poking around. There could be others like Gytha lurking about," said Alywin.

"Hmmm." Tim had a pensive look on his face. "What is it?" said Alywin.

Tim turned to Alywin and said, "What if I go alone?" "Don't be stupid," said Alywin.

"What choice do we have? We have to make sure the tunnels are safe for the others, anyway, and I'm the best man for the job," said Tim.

"Have you gone mad? You're not going by yourself. I won't let you," said Alywin.

"You can barely use your right hand," said Tim.

"I can do plenty with my left. Killed the bitch with it, didn't I?" said Alywin.

"Stop acting tough. That was a lucky shot, and you know it," said Tim angrily.

"And what about me? Do you expect me to just leave you here? Do you think me so callous?" said Sarah.

Tim sighed. "Sarah, you're our only way out of here. You've got the mark that can open pathways in stone. You're simply too valuable. If you die, we are trapped here forever."

Sarah and Alywin expressed demur with the idea, but they did not see an alternative.

"I'll be careful, but if I do not return, warn the others that it is not safe down here."

As Tim was about to leave, Alywin said, "Tim, that shot was not luck, and I couldn't live with myself if I let you die down here. It doesn't matter if we both meet our ends, as long as we do it together."

"Alywin," said Tim.

"Please don't say anything too mawkish. I'm already uncomfortable. Just lead the way," said Alywin.

Tim smiled. "You're a good friend."

"What did I just say!" replied Alywin. Tim chuckled. Sarah looked at the two with admiration.

She had known Tim for a few weeks now. He had introduced her to the Archiater's healer program. She recalled when they met. She was in the bailey of Corithni. It was her first time there. She was originally from a neighboring village of Sigate, southeast of Isial Lake. The villagers were relocated partly because Lord Franklin and the powers at be thought Hector might attack and partly to recruit more soldiers. She saw Tim and another non-armored male carrying a severely injured soldier into the keep. She was quite surprised to see noncombative males somehow aiding soldiers. She had never seen such a thing. She noticed Tim because he nearly dropped the man.

"You bloody idiot, Tim, you nearly dropped him!" *"S-ssorry, Swithin."* *"S-sss shut-up, you mangey git."*

The two continued towards the keep. *"Wait, wait. What are you doing? This bloke needs to be elevated. That's the whole point of both of us carrying him. You can't just hoist him about, you brainless oaf,"* said Swithin.

It was then that Tim caught a glimpse of Sarah for the first time, along with the other women from Sigate. The men were being armed for battle. Swithin caught his gaze.

"They're from Sigate. Lord Franklin relocated them here. Now come on. We don't have all day," said Swithin. The two entered the keep barracks.

"I think that's all we can take," Swithin sighed. He looked at the man who was now on a bed. The man was mortally wounded. *"This fucker's not gonna make it,"* Swithin turned to Tim. *"Why don't you make yourself useful and look for more injured? This one won't need a bed."* Tim nodded and left the keep.

He was in the lower bailey where Sarah and the women of Sigate were. *"Excuse me, Tim, is it? Are we supposed to be let in or…"* Sarah asked. *"Er, right, come in,"* said Tim.

Neither Sarah nor the other Sigate women moved. Sarah broke the awkward silence.

"It's just we were expecting a highborn to let us in… you don't particularly strike me as highborn." Immediately regretting her words, she attempted to correct this by saying, *"I'm sorry. I didn't mean to say that it's just Lord Franklin's men practically forced us out of our homes. We don't want to get into trouble."*

"I'll get someone," said Tim.

"Thank you," Sarah replied.

Tim came back with an elderly man who called himself Giles.

"Are you a Lord?" said one of the women.

"Well, yes, but titles are more loose here in Corithni. So, you don't need to trouble yourselves with formalities. You are guests here. Please come in," said Giles.

Sarah and the other women were a little hesitant to comply. The way they were so briskly carted away from their homes and how their men were forced to fight, they did not feel like guests; more like captives. Eventually, they followed Giles and Tim. They were led up to the first floor of the Great Hall, where they saw others. Women and children. Giles showed them around and explained why they were here.

He ended by saying, *"You're safe here."*

The words resonated with a few, but Sarah was still ambivalent. Giles and Tim were about to go to the barracks when Sarah said, *"Wait. Can I come with you, er, milord?"*

Giles turned to her. *"The barracks are not a place for the faint of heart."* *"Umm, Archiater,"* said Tim.

Giles turned to Tim. *"Yes?"*

"She is willing. It would be unwise to push her away," said Tim.

"Hmm, fine, but you will guide her," replied Giles.

The three entered the barracks. Sarah saw all the injured people being attended to by both men and women. She was quite befuddled by the scene. She took some time to get adjusted to her new environment. In that time, Giles disappeared in the shuffle of cries and commotion. Sarah, feeling out of place, asked, *"What is going on?"*

Tim, seeing the dumbfounded expression on her face, said, *"This is, uh, a typical day in the barracks... uh, hey, what'd you say your name was?"*

"Sarah," she said.

"There's no shame in feeling overwhelmed," said Tim.

"Can I ask you something, Tim?" said Sarah.

"Sure," Tim replied.

"You seem able, young. How come you're not fighting like the rest of the men?"

"I uh, well, you see, I'm not much of a fighter," replied Tim. *"Neither is my brother, yet they put a spear in his hand,"* she said. *"I'm sorry, but I don't decide—"*

"Who lives and who dies?" Sarah interrupted.

Tim was starting to feel uncomfortable. He knew he had to choose his next words carefully. *"In Corithni, we do things differently. This is the healer's program. It ensures that wounded warriors live to fight another day. It's more efficient than sending people out in the field of battle who have no experience."*

"Says your boss," Sarah replied.

"Ah, the Archiater," said Tim.

He saw that she was confused. *"It's an old term from the old empires. Basically, he's been Lord Franklin's personal physician since he was a boy."* *"So, who decides who gets to be a healer? Is it the Archiater?"* asked Sarah. *"Not exactly. Although his opinion is important in the decision process. Instead, Lord Franklin or the knights have the final say in such matters."*

Sarah looked around. Despite the commotion, there was a reliable system in place.

"All this was set-up for one battle?" Sarah asked.

"Actually, the program was planned in advance. Lady Branson, the Archiater's granddaughter, suggested it a year ago, but she and her grandfather had been training people four years prior."

"People like you," said Sarah.

"You could say that," Tim replied.

Sarah was silent, and she was looking quite dispirited.

"You're worried about your brother." He looked at her brooding eyes, attempting to read her face. He knew he was right, but he suspected there was something else bothering her.

"It's not easy, you know, watching other men die when you know you escaped that fate on a whim. I confess, I'm grateful I don't have to be out there, but I also feel a sense of overwhelming guilt because I know others are not so fortunate as I. I know it pains you to see me here while your brother's out there, so I can understand if you think me a coward."

Sarah turned to look at Tim. She must've been moved by his words because she gave him a sympathetic look. *"Hey, I don't think you're a coward. We're all doing what we can. That's all we can do. It's not for mortals to question the will of fate. I believe God wants you here."*

Tim stared at her for a moment. He admired her strength and was surprised by her response. Before he could say anything, Tim heard someone call his name. It was Clara.

"Tim, can you get that useless oaf Alywin?"

Tim scanned the room and he saw Alywin was busy with a patient. *"Alywin's busy at the moment, but I can help."*

Clara was hesitant. *"Oh, it's just that I need someone strong."* *"Very funny,"* said Tim sarcastically.

Clara's eyes gravitated towards Sarah. *"Who's this, Tim? I don't recognize her. I recognize everyone."*

"Oh, this is Sarah from Sigate. Giles said she can help," replied Tim.

Clara looked at Tim incredulously. *"What? It's true,"* said Tim defiantly.

"Fine, Sarah. Do you have any experience as a healer?" Clara asked.

"Only with animals," Sarah responded.

Clara had a dubious look on her face. *"Well, I guess that'll do. Now come on. You two help me hold him down."* Clara was referring to the nearly unconscious patient on the bed adjacent to her.

"Sssh, not too loud. We are going to have to be careful what we say around him. We need to be subtle, as he's barely awake."

"May I ask why?" whispered Sarah.

"Because we're going to need to chop his right leg off," replied Clara. The man heard Clara. *"What?!"*

"Real subtle," said Tim sarcastically.

"Just shut up and help me," retorted Clara.

Sarah and Tim restrained the man while Clara severed his leg above the knee, the extent of the infection, with a large hand saw blade. Clara wiped the sweat off her brow. *"Whew, that was something, huh? So, Sarah, how'd you like your first time here in the barracks?"*

"Well, there never seems to be a dull moment," she laughed nervously.

Clara smiled. *"Good because, from now on, you're going to have to do things like this until the war ends."*

"Clara, your assistance is needed," said a voice.

"Oh, that's Lady Branson. I should be going. I trust you two to patch him up."

Clara went to assist Lady Branson and Giles in dealing with a patient.

"She's quite interesting," said Sarah.

"More like a pain in the arse. She watches everyone like a hawk. It's quite irritating," said Tim.

Clara, who was not entirely out of earshot, said, *"I heard that. You ought to have more respect for your elders."*

"You're only two years my senior," retorted Tim. *"I'm still older,"* she replied.

"Will you two stop squabbling and focus?" Giles said angrily.

"Yes, Archiater," they said in unison.

Sarah could not help but chuckle. She found this banter quite amusing. Tim noticed her laughing.

"It's good to see you smile. Hopefully I, er, I mean, we can make you do it more often. I know it sounds silly, but by allowing yourself to feel joy, no matter how fleeting it may be, is essential to living a fulfilling life because, during times of darkness, it's important to remember you were once happy. You can't stop the pain from coming, but you don't have to give it all your attention."

"That's beautiful," said Sarah.

Tim blushed and he pretended to scratch the back of his neck. *"I'm no bard, but I sometimes think about things too deeply, heh heh. I'm rambling, sorry, eh, so anyway, how do you really feel about this place and your newly appointed position as healer?"*

"Well, it's a bit overwhelming. Calf legs are certainly different from humans, that's for sure, but I think I could get used to this," said Sarah.

"You'll find we're like a big family here. Albeit dysfunctional, obnoxious, and not to mention loud, but everyone loves each other. We'll always be there for you, as long as you'll have us, and now, I am officially welcoming you to the healer's program."

Sarah giggled. Tim smiled. *"You're thinking I've outdone myself as welcoming goes. This is probably the best one you've had."*

"Well, you certainly have a way with words, but everyone loves each other? What about that gruff looking man you walked in with?" said Sarah *"Ah, you're referring to the ole curmudgeon known as Swithin. He is actually really nice most of the time, but sometimes he can behave like a mean ole-"*

Unbeknownst to Tim, Swithin was right behind him. *"Hi, Swithin you look—"*

"Don't even, boy. Lady Branson wants us to find more of the injured and bring them here. Do me a favor. Quit talking to girlie here and make yourself useful," said Swithin.

"He sounds really nice," Sarah said sarcastically. *"Shut up,"* Tim said with a smile on his face. Sarah smiled as well.

Tim and Swithin exited the keep to search for more of the wounded. Over the following days, she got used to the routine and continued bonding with Tim. He revealed more about himself. He even revealed both he and Alywin tried to steal from Lady Branson and would've been executed if it had not been for her kindness. He explained that those who were accepted, be it women or males, had a history of healing and they were usually vetted by Giles. Tim had no experience of healing. Alywin had been healing since he was a child and was skilled at it under no tutelage, of course. They were the only males that were not cross-examined for the program by either Lord Franklin or Giles, because Lady Branson highly recommended them, despite not knowing their propensity for healing.

She did not know much about Alywin, except that he had a troubled past. Despite this, he and Tim were close. Tim even said he was like a brother to him, partly due to the fact that Alywin protected him for years when they lived in Garla. Though Sarah suspected Alywin might have drawn Tim to criminality, even though Tim never suggested this. Sarah noticed, as time passed, Tim began to express subtle feelings of jealousy towards Alywin. He would often complain that he was stuck with grunt work with Swithin while Alywin was busy performing complex surgeries on patients. Tim also pointed out that Alywin seemed to be working with Lady Branson and Giles a lot. He joked that Alywin was so busy, he did not even notice them, which was at least partially true.

***

Sarah saw the two men before her. They surpassed her expectations. They were, somehow, even braver than she thought they already were.

She could not see herself going on this journey without them. She turned to Tim and said, "You are no coward. You have to believe that. You're kind, with a blessed heart." She turned to Alywin.

"Don't worry. I won't let this fool die, so spare us the eulogy," said Alywin.

"I was going to say I'm sorry. I've misjudged you. You are not the insensitive ruffian I believed you to be. Everything you did was for us, you were protecting us, and I truly apologize for not recognizing that. Just know that your efforts will not be underappreciated," said Sarah.

This line of speaking was making Alywin uncomfortable. "Woman, would you just quit it?"

Sarah smiled. "Under that hardened exterior is a sensitive man."

"Don't push it," Alywin said. Tim chuckled, as did Sarah.

Sarah suddenly looked at Tim and said sincerely, "I want you to have something." She removed her angel wing pin and placed it in Tim's open palm.

"But this is—" said Tim.

"It belonged to my mother. Before she passed, she said it would bring luck and good fortune to its wearer. I want you to have it," said Sarah.

"I can't accept this. It belongs in your family. It's wasted on me. I—" said Tim.

Sarah calmly interrupted. "You can return it when you've come back."

Tim received the message. Sarah hugged them both. "May Arda bless you both."

When they separated, Alywin said, "We will be back. Also, don't lose that ear. I don't want anyone on the surface calling me a fucking liar."

"It shall not leave my sight," Sarah said playfully.

Tim placed the pin on his tunic. Tim and Alywin departed and ventured into the uncharted tunnels. They explored the southernmost tunnel. As they were walking through the tunnels, Alywin turned to Tim and asked unexpectedly, "Are we really the bravest and smartest people you've met?"

"Well, you make it seem ridiculous when you say it like that," replied Tim.

"That's because it is," replied Alywin.

"You know, most people don't criticize the very people speaking well of them," retorted Tim.

"Forgive me, you're certainly the expert on most people. Given that you've only lived here and Garla," said Alywin.

Tim sighed in annoyance. Alywin did not seem to notice. "Still, if what you said is to be believed, it can only mean one thing?"

"What's that?" Tim said eagerly. "You need to get out more."

Tim rolled his eyes. "I'll be sure to take note of that when I'm not underground, running from giant rats or a deranged witch."

"I meant after the war is over. I told you my uncle's a merchant. He works for a company known as *the windy gulls*. He travels all over the world trading commodities like spices and textiles. I'm sure he'll give us work, honest work, too. The company was sanctioned by King Gavin, so no looting involved. I can send him a letter for him to meet us at Gasco port just north of Etlio. I'll introduce you. He goes by the name of Captain Winthrop Morgan," said Alywin. He was quite serious.

"You really thought this through Alywin, but what will the Archiater say if his best healer left?" Tim teased.

"I'm sure Clara would be more than happy to fill that position and besides, no one else really likes me here except you, Sarah, Leanne, the Archiater, and Lady Branson, and she likes everyone, so it doesn't count." "Well, for what is worth, I think you're more liked than you know. I might even dare say loved," said Tim.

Alywin's eyes widened and Tim placed his hand on Alywin's shoulder affectionately. "My best friend, if you think it's a good idea to be a world traveling merchant, then I suppose it's worth looking into."

Alywin smiled, but was slightly disappointed. "Thanks."

Suddenly, the flames from the wall mounted candle holders that lit up the tunnel flickered on and off. This caught their attention, and Tim drew Colin's blade. Alywin looked around. He studied meticulously the rate at which the flames were forming and dissipating. It was quite an unnatural occurrence and was most likely attributed to one thing: magic.

"He's near. Keep your guard up," said Alywin. Tim nodded.

They crept toward what look like an exit. They peered and saw a figure in the distance bearing a rushlight. The figure walked toward them and, upon further inspection, they could make out his features.

"Leland?" asked Tim. The figure came into full view, and it was, in fact, Leland.

CHAPTER TEN

THE CURSE

Leland approached the two. He was about to speak when Tim pointed the sword at his throat.

"Don't move."

"You're not going to kill me. I'm your only way out of here," said Leland.

"Don't test me," retorted Tim as he pressed the blade further on to Leland's throat.

"Look. I'm not a castor," said Leland.

"Really? Then what explains the disappearing act?" asked Tim. "Where are the others?" asked Alywin bluntly.

"Who? Benton and Knox? I assumed you took care of them." Seeing their confusion, Leland said, "This scene is getting strangely familiar. Why don't we start over?"

Tim looked at Alywin, who nodded his head. Tim then removed the sword from Leland's throat.

"Look into his eyes. If he is a castor, his pupils will dilate three times before a spell is cast. If you see this, run him through immediately," said Alywin. (This is an unconfirmed theory in Mirthadine, but many believe it is known as the darks of the eye theory. It states that before a magic wielder can cast a traditional spell, hokraft not included, the darks of their eyes will expand, then shrink back to normal in rapid succession at least three times before a spell is cast.)

Tim did just that. "Is this really necessary? I don't like being stared at," said Leland.

"Would you rather be without a head?" asked Tim.

Leland was silent for a moment. He eventually spoke, referring to Alywin, he said, "So you're the one who slayed the beast?

Before Alywin could respond, Tim interrupted. "Actually, it was me." Leland looked at him incredulously. "Really?"

"What do you mean really? It was me! Ugh, why am I explaining myself to you?" said Tim, feeling insulted.

"The Mason, where is she?" asked Leland. "Not your concern," said Alywin.

"Look. I'm not your enemy and I swear I'm not a castor. I want what you want. To get out of here," Leland said.

"Why should we believe you, just because you know a lullaby?" asked Alywin.

The man removed what was left of his rags. It was a ghastly sight. An emaciated figure stood before them with several lacerations and contusions on his arms and torso. He turned around to reveal that he had been flayed and the majority of the skin on his back had been removed. He pointed to his back. "Courtesy of Gytha's ancestors, so you see I'm not her underling."

Tim and Alywin were repulsed by Leland's wounds, as one could imagine they were hard to look at, but that was Leland's intention, to make them uncomfortable. Leland put back on his ragged tunic and turned away from them.

"I used to be a knight.... A long time ago, under King Leofric Franklin. We were tasked with clearing the land for the construction of a castle that would later be known as Corithni. The land belonged to a castor family from Elpica. They were known as the Baltierra's. Gytha is their descendent. It is said they were banished from Elpica because of their abuse of hokraft. No one really knows why they settled in Iiadec. Possibly because they worshiped an ancient beast known as Salkar, who is believed to live in Iiadec."

"Is that the same beast Gytha called master?" asked Tim.

"I don't believe so. Salkar is a mythical beast of an old religion. According to lore, he'd be over hundreds of thousands of years old, not even Orthtya Vepids live that long. I doubt he even exists," said Leland.

"But if he's a God, he would be immortal," said Tim.

"Even if gods exist, I doubt they would be killed so easily," said Alywin. "The beast you're referring to most likely deceived Gytha. Actually, now that you mentioned it, Landyn did say he found a talking rat while laying down the stone for Corithni. I didn't believe him at the time," said Leland.

"Pardon me for the digression. As you can imagine, the Baltierra's were not happy to give up their land. A battle ensued and the knights, well, we, I... killed the patriarch and I, along with the other knights, killed most of the men in their garrison. The Baltierra's were forced off the land and we burnt down Talama castle, their home, because King Leofric wanted a castle built with stone blessed by Isial Lake," said Leland. He let out a heavy sigh. "I truly regret that decision. A part of me believes I deserve all the suffering I endured. It must be Arda's way of punishing me for my sin."

Feeling sympathetic to Leland's plight, Alywin said, "You couldn't have ignored the orders of a king," said Alywin.

Leland looked at Alywin, his eyes watery and his voice quavered. "Leofric never said to kill them." He fought back tears and struggled to compose himself. He laughed to mask his pain as he said, "I thought he was going to attack the commander and I reacted poorly... I, uh, shot Lord Bernaldo Baltierra with an arrow to the chest because he raised his hand to my commander. He was signaling him to stop, but I thought he was casting a spell. I disobeyed direct orders. Leofric said we were to negotiate a price. The knights were just there to protect them in the relocation process. *"Relocate and negotiate"* is how he put it. Instead of punishing me for my blunder, the commander, Osgar Howard, congratulated me. He said, *"foreign blood should have no place owning Iiadec land, let alone be granted the title of Lord, it's despicable really, Great King Tatum Franklin,* (A legendary figure shrouded in mystery existed during the first Mylec Marauder war, 1032-1066 NEEOT. It is said he was crucial in stopping the Mylec invasion of Iiadec, a feat that would grant him the title of Great King, thus cementing the Franklin line as royalty. He is often considered the major reason Iiadec has never been fully conquered. Although historical evidence is sparse, he was believed to most likely have been a farmer before his military campaign. Because of this his story is seen by many as the classic rags to riches tale. The legend of the Great King often galvanizes the masses, especially the lowborn who aspire to become something more. The story of the Great King is used as propaganda to encourage military service, especially amongst lowborn.) *would be spinning in his grave if he knew foreigners soiled his lands. You did the right thing, Leland. They weren't going to give up the land".*

The family said their grievances to the King, hoping to be compensated for the destruction by the knights, but they mostly sought my head. Osgar spun the story that they had refused to comply with our very reasonable offers and that Bernaldo had attacked him. I went along with it. The king took our side and stripped the Baltierra's of their title. The family soon relocated to Garla to plan their revenge. They killed the knights that were responsible for their pain. For me, they had greater plans. They had me beaten and tortured mercilessly. Leofric retaliated by sending more knights after The Baltierra's. The knights killed all of them except the eldest daughter, Godina, who went into hiding. They searched for me, but Godina hid me underground in this very tunnel."

"I thought Landyn built these tunnels," said Tim. "He did, but not of his own free will."

"She threatened him with magic?" asked Alywin.

"Worse. She cursed him with one of the deadliest curses known to man and like kind, yet few know of its existence. It is known as karasa mollo (MOE-LOW) (old tongue for death of the mind. An ancient curse that is not considered hokraft, it is a type of mind control that allows the spell castor to gradually hijack the mind, initially making the victim believe their thoughts are their own. The curse becomes more harmful as time passes. The mind eventually degenerates, sometimes causing psychosis, but more often one's sense of self deteriorates, and they become little more than puppets for the spell castor. There are other mind control spells, but they are less potent and their effects are almost always temporary. With karasa mollo, eventually the victim becomes so dependent on the spell castor that they must be commanded to perform basic bodily functions like breathing. Death follows shortly at that point because the victims do not perceive themselves to be alive but rather an inanimate object for its master. It is then that the brain expires). She tricked him into falling in love with her. By the time she was done with him, he was no more than an empty husk, no will of his own.

As for me, Godina cursed me with prolonged life and eternal hunger to never be satiated like a blood sucker. Sustenance provides no nourishment. My body will decay till the point of death, but death has eluded me up until now. She confined my body to that of a squirrel. Only by her will alone, could I change to a human. Everyone thought I was dead… even my wife, Kaelyn, stopped searching."

This tale was taking its toll on Leland emotionally. That part was obvious. Alywin and Tim allowed him to compose himself. Tim eventually asked, "How did the curse last so long?"

"It was renewed through blood magic and human sacrifice," said Leland. (Blood magic is an umbrella term for hokraft that involves the use of blood. In the case of Godina's curse, a descendant of the Baltierra bloodline would have to renew the curse by donating blood and performing ritual sacrifice.)

"The corpses in the torture room," said Alywin. "Yes," replied Leland. "But the curse is broken now. Gytha's dead. She's the last of the Baltierra's. No one is left to renew the curse, right?" asked Tim.

Leland was silent. His silence made Alywin and Tim feel uneasy. "There are others?" asked Tim, fearing Leland's answer.

With a frightened expression on his face, Leland said, "I don't know."

This was somehow even worse than a confirmation. Tim and Alywin stepped away, attempting to stay out of earshot of Leland.

"Where are you going?" Leland asked.

"We need to think. Just stay there and don't follow us," said Alywin sternly. Alywin ruffled his hand through his hair, and he had a worried look on his face. "This is bad, Tim. This whole fucking place might be cursed."

"Alywin, the curse has been lifted. Gytha's dead. Even if there are others, they would have to come down here to renew the curse," said Tim, attempting to calm his comrade.

"It doesn't make any sense, Tim. His whole story is odd," said Alywin. "You still don't believe him, even after we've seen the scars," said Tim. "It's not that I don't believe him. I just doubt Godina and her descendants would spend all their efforts on one man. Think about it. This fucker's been in this state for over 200 years. Does that make sense to you? And why did she need a vast underground lair just to torture someone?" asked Alywin.

"What are you saying, Alywin?" asked Tim.

Alywin exhaled. "I'm saying there's more going on here than we know and I'm not ashamed to admit it's got me proper scared."

"Alywin, whatever happened down here is in the past and does not concern us. We are only concerned with granting our people safe passage. Alywin, look around. This place is dilapidated. It's been abandoned. Any hokraft experiments performed down here have been disbanded. There is no need to worry," said Tim.

Alywin was not convinced. "How did she get here?" he muttered to himself.

"What?" Tim asked.

"Gytha. She knew her way around. She's been down here before. How did she get here the first time without Sarah's mark?" said Alywin. "Alywin, you're torturing yourself. Look, none of that matters. He's alone. He is no threat to us," said Tim.

Leland, who had been listening to their conversation, said, "She got here using Landyn's preserved hand with the mark of the Mason still intact, but after repeated uses, its potency diminished until it was eventually useless."

Leland had startled the two. "What the—I thought I told you to stay put," said Alywin.

"I've stayed put for 219 years. I will not do it anymore," said Leland gravely.

Alywin peered into Leland's eyes, attempting to read him. "What do you want, Leland?"

"To die," replied Leland.

Tim and Alywin were at a loss for words upon hearing this, though in some ways it was to be expected, but this didn't make Leland's words less disturbing. "I've suffered for a long time. It's time for that suffering to end. Although the curse is lifted, I am still here. With my fleeting time, I'd like to help you and the Mason on your quest whichever way I can."

"How do you know the curse is lifted? I mean, like you said, you're still here," asked Alywin. "Because I died," said Leland.

"You mean you disappeared, then reappeared through magic?" said Alywin.

"I didn't disappear. I stopped existing temporarily," explained Leland.

Both Alywin and Tim were perplexed by such a revelation. Tim especially. He massaged his temples. "That doesn't make any sense."

"The curse is tied to the castor's physical body, not soul. Hence, it's called blood magic. Nevertheless, its power diminishes when the castor is dead. In other words, since Gytha's body is still warm, there are residual effects," explained Leland.

"Hokraft is more dangerous than I thought. No wonder Lord Franklin banned its practice," said Tim.

Leland looked at Tim, perplexed upon hearing that name. "Lord Franklin not King Franklin?"

Tim contemplated telling Leland about their current predicament, but he decided against it. "It's a long story. You said you were going to help us. C'mon, let's find Sarah. She must be worried sick."

The flames in the tunnels flickered again. "What was that?" asked Tim. "We're running out of time. Let's make haste," said Leland. "That's happened before. Why?" asked Tim.

"It's tied to her magic, isn't it?" said Alywin.

Leland did not respond. This confirmed Alywin's suspicions. Tim, who was feeling apprehensive, said, "Let's just go to Sarah and make sure she's safe."

The two agreed, then walked to the northernmost tunnel where Sarah was staying. She was on her knees in a praying position with her eyes closed, muttering some verses from the book of Noga.

"Sarah," Tim said gently.

Sarah slowly opened her eyes. When she saw Tim and Alywin, she was elated. "Oh, thank Arda, you've returned."

Tim removed the pin from his tunic and handed it to Sarah. "This belongs to you."

"Thank you," Sarah said, and she placed the pin back in her hair. Her eyes gravitated towards Leland, who averted her gaze. She turned to Alywin. "Is he?"

"He's with us now. He is here to help." "Oh, good," she replied.

She hugged Tim, then Alywin. She noticed Alywin was being distant and had a troubled look on his face. "Alywin, is something the matter?"

Alywin looked at Tim, who shook his head, signaling Alywin not to mention anything. Sarah immediately took notice. She turned to Tim.

"Tim!"

Tim laughed nervously. "Well, you see, it's a bit ridiculous, but Alywin believes this place is cursed."

"What?!" Sarah shouted in disbelief.

"No need to panic. Alywin's just a little frightened because of things said," said Tim.

Sarah scowled at him. "You tell me what he said right this instant!" "Um, uh, it's sort of a horrible story. You wouldn't like it," said Tim. "I don't care. Tell me now. I mean it. You don't want to cross me," she said sternly.

"Right sorry," said Tim.

Tim relayed Leland's harrowing tale to Sarah and included Alywin's thoughts on the tale. Sarah was dumbfounded upon hearing this.

"This... that's—"

"Terrifying," Alywin interrupted her.

Tim felt he needed to calm his comrades. "We are grossly overcomplicating things. Corithni has been around for nearly two centuries and nothing bad has happened."

"Yet," Alywin retorted.

"Whatever evil magic that existed during the castle's construction is most likely gone," said Tim.

In frustration, Alywin said, "You're doing what you always do in a crisis... convince yourself everything is fine when it's clearly not. Can't you see we are all fucked if we keep this to ourselves?"

Tim, feeling insulted and angered, said, "And what good would that do Alywin? Our people are already scared to death of Hector's army. For God's sake, there's a bloody dragon on the surface. Do you really think telling them is in their best interest? We are at war. If this information spreads, our enemies will surely take advantage of it."

Alywin, seeing Tim's point, remained silent. Sarah broke the silence. "We wouldn't just tell anyone... Lord Franklin would know what to do."

Tim sighed. "You haven't lived here long enough; Lord Franklin would most likely have our heads at the mere mention of hokraft."

Sarah's eyes narrowed; she was perplexed.

"You don't believe the rightful king of Iiadec would help us?"

Tim did not speak. He regretted his statement. He feared Sarah might judge him if he didn't choose his next words carefully. For speaking ill of the rightful king could be considered sedition. A crime punishable by death. Tim could not find intelligent words to escape his predicament.

"I… uh, I… uh…"

Alywin, seeing his friend struggling, said, "What he means is Lord Franklin is probably too preoccupied with fighting and planning battles to be caught up in this."

Tim sighed with relief, and he was grateful to Alywin for rescuing him from his blunder. Sarah did not seem to notice Tim's anxiety. She had not asked the question with ill intent. She was generally curious about Tim's seemingly unprecedented criticism of Lord Franklin. As a result, she completely moved on, oblivious to the crime Tim almost committed.

"Lady Branson, then?"

"We can't involve her in this. She's dealing with enough already," said Alywin.

"She's already involved. She's the one who sent us down here," said Sarah.

"We volunteered," retorted Alywin.

"Look. I realize she is beloved by everyone in Corithni and rightfully so. She has a pure heart. I could tell, even without knowing her as long as you two. But that's the exact reason we need to tell her. We owe her the truth. Besides, she is no fool. She will suspect something went awry. Can you honestly tell me you could stand before her and look into her eyes and lie?" asked Sarah.

Tim and Alywin realized Sarah had made a compelling argument that they could not refute.

"You're right," said Tim.

"I know. I usually am," said Sarah with a smile. "So, humble," Alywin teased.

Leland was silent during the whole conversation but was listening intently. Sarah turned to him, and he tried to redirect his gaze.

"Leland, it's alright. You will find peace. I am truly sorry for what happened to you."

Leland began to weep. "No. It is me who is sorry. I caused all this through my stupidity… I can't even look at you. You resemble Landyn too much. It's a reminder… He was innocent. I can't help but think, if not for me, he would not have suffered."

"Hey, hey, Leland. You mustn't punish yourself for mistakes you made in the past. If you truly want to make amends, you will help us," said Sarah.

Leland looked at Sarah, tears still streaming down his face. "I will try," he replied.

Leland revealed the reason Tim, Alywin, and Sarah had got lost in the first place. He stated that the map Sarah was using was designed prior to construction of the castle. The position of the tunnels was changed when construction began.

"Leland, are there any other exits? And if so, where do they lead?" asked Sarah.

"There are three other exits. They lead to parts of Mydra woods, with one leading directly to Mirama. The other adjacent tunnel leading to a castle west of Mydra wood," explained Leland.

"Lord Baudry's castle near Hilag?" said Tim.

"I do not know of this Hilag you speak of, but Dae le Maut was nearing completion when I was still a knight. The master builder boasted it was even more impressive than Corithni," said Leland.

"Where's the nearest exit?" asked Sarah.

"Behind you," said Leland, referring to the wall of stone behind Sarah. The wall seemed organic and did not have any of the strange markings that she had seen on other areas she had opened with the mark. Naturally,

Sarah was confused, as were Alywin and Tim.

"Touch it. The mark of the Mason will allow you to open it."

Sarah did just that. The mark on her hand glowed again, and the stone wall split into vertical pieces, revealing a staircase.

"The exit was right behinds us the whole time. You could have told us that in the beginning. Might've saved us time," said Alywin.

To which Leland replied, "I was too busy being threatened by a certain person."

"You've made your point," Alywin groaned.

"Leland, do you think these tunnels are now safe for people to travel?" asked Sarah.

"Gytha, her cronies, and the beast are dead. We are the only ones here, so there is no threat," responded Leland.

"Other than a possible curse," Alywin chimed in. "Which we don't know exists," said Tim.

Alywin rolled his eyes.

"Our people won't be down here for long. If at all, if the battle goes in our favor, As long as the tunnels lead to Mirama, we should be fine," said Sarah.

She looked at Leland. There was kindness in her eyes. "Thank you for helping us. I guess this is where we say goodbye. I believe you'll move on soon. Is there anything we can do for you?"

"I would like to see the outside world before I die," said Leland. "We will make sure that happens," said Sarah.

"We will have to burn the body first," said Leland.

"I'll get the body. I remember the way. After all, I'm the one who killed her," said Alywin. He navigated to the site where Gytha and the beast were slain. He pulled her body from the rubble and hoisted her over his shoulder. He returned to his comrades. He looked at them. "Are we ready?"

They nodded. The four ascended the staircase. There was a ceiling that blocked access to the outside. Sarah used the Mark, and the ceiling opened. They were outside. Leland took time to observe the scenery.

He could see Mirama in the distance. It was not far. It was a grand city, but not a fortress. The walls were too low, and it lacked certain defensive structures. It could easily be taken over with a sizeable army. It was designed more for its aesthetic rather than its function. It made sense, as Mirama was considered a holy city built to appease Jaynor, the human embodiment of Arda. Readers, according to Ardinians, Jaynor and Arda are one and the same. Jaynor was just Arda posing as a man so he could walk amongst mortals without terrifying them. It would be sacrilegious for any Ardinian to attack the city.

Tim and Alywin went to fetch some firewood to fashion a torch. When they returned, they spotted Sarah and Leland just looking off into the distance.

Leland turned to Sarah. "Sarah, if you or your people are lost, just follow the mark of the Mason. Close your eyes, imagine where you want to go, and it will appear in your mind." His eyes were watery. "I'm truly venturing into the unknown now. I spent most of my existence as a bloody squirrel. Ahem, uh, Sarah, this is quite embarrassing, but could you—"

Sarah knew exactly what he was talking about. She sang for him. "You don't need to cry,

For I am by your side. You'll grow big and strong, If you move along. Be brave day by day, and the pain will go away."

He looked at Tim, who was holding the torch. Leland nodded, signaling for Tim to proceed. Tim lit Gytha's body on fire. When the flames completely consumed Gytha, Leland disappeared.

"I hope he will find peace in the afterlife," said Sarah. "We know that his suffering has ended," said Alywin.

The three went back into the tunnels to return to Corithni castle.

CHAPTER ELEVEN

MAKING SENSE OF THINGS

"He did what?!" Lady Branson shouted.

"That boy!" shouted Giles.

Lodema, realizing she might've been the wrong person to deliver the news, was beginning to panic. Lady Branson was hyperventilating as she feared the worst for Godfrey. Giles tried to calm her down to no avail. "Elysant, breathe, breathe!"

"Oh God, Oh God, please don't take him!" exclaimed Lady Branson. Lodema did not know what to say and was desperate to fix the situation.

"You know, dragons don't usually eat children so Godfrey should be alright… unless of course, he's burned alive."

Giles shot Lodema a menacing scowl and he was about to say something when Lodema interrupted. "Not helping, got it. I'll get Clara." Lodema sprinted towards the staircase leading to the first floor of the Great Hall. She nearly knocked over a female healer on her way there.

Before she could reenter the Great Hall, Lodema spotted Clara on the staircase. She was walking with Giselle.

"Clara, oh praise Arda, you're here. Listen. I talked to Lady Branson and things did not go over well so I need you to—" Lodema stopped talking as she had just realized Giselle was present.

"What are you doing here?"

Giselle looked at Clara for help, but Clara appeared too distraught to notice she then said, "I, uh… I, uh, wanted to see other parts of the castle and where Clara worked."

Lodema looked at her incredulously. "Really?"

"Alright, I confess. The truth is I've grown weary of the constant mewling and squabbling of women and children," said Giselle.

"You're sure to make a great mother then," Lodema said sarcastically. "Oh, shut up," replied Giselle.

"Anyway, we need all the help we can get. Lady Branson is in a bad shape."

Lodema noticed Clara seemed distressed. "Clara are you alright? You look pale, paler than usual that is," said Lodema.

"I'm fine. Let's just help Lady Branson," said Clara.

The three descended from the staircase. Once they were in the garrison, they approached the distressed Lady Branson. Lodema said, "Don't fret milady, Clara and Giselle are here to fix everything."

Lady Branson's ears perked up upon hearing Clara's name. "Clara, is everyone else accounted for?"

"Yes, milady." Clara spoke methodically and gently in order to calm Lady Branson.

"Lady Franklin said we should deploy two capable men to retrieve Godfrey and ten to guard the keep. All you have to do is give the order." "I can do that. Just be strong, Elysant. God willing, that troublesome boy will return to us," said Giles.

He went on to gather capable men in the barracks whose injuries have all but healed. Many were more than willing to help.

"She patched me up pretty well. I thought I was a goner for sure. I owe that woman my life. I will make sure her boy is returned to her," said one of the men.

While others were hesitant. "Damn that boy. Why do I have to risk my neck for some meddlesome child? I mean, I almost bloody died for God's sake," said another man.

Eventually all twelve agreed to partake in a perilous quest. Lady Branson had calmed down a little since initially hearing the news, but she was still panic-stricken. She was shaking and started talking rapidly. "Is twelve really enough? It is a dragon after all, what if they're unsuccessful? What if—"

"That's not going to happen. Your husband is with him along with several other brave men. Lodema confirmed this," said Clara.

"Right," said Lodema.

Lady Branson did not seem convinced. "These men, do they have weapons? I'm sorry, that's a silly question. This is a knights' garrison, I should be out there searching."

"That won't do us any good, milady, you're needed here in the barracks," said Giselle.

"Of course, you're right," said Lady Branson.

In an attempt to calm herself, Lady Branson changed the subject. "So, Giselle how's the baby?"

Both Clara and Giselle had frightened looks on their faces and did not respond immediately, making it obvious to Lady Branson that something might be troubling them.

"By Arda, is something wrong?"

Looking very anxious, Clara was about the say something when Giselle interrupted her.

"No, no, nothing you need to worry about milady, honestly everything's fine." Giselle smiled. It was disingenuous, but it threw Lady Branson off her scent. This made Clara feel uneasy because it suddenly occurred to her how much better at lying Giselle was than she was.

Giles returned with the fully armored soldiers. Giles looked at Lady Branson and touched her shoulder affectionately. "We will bring him back."

Giles looked at the men. "Is everyone ready?" "Yes, Lord Baker," said the men in unison.

One man said, "Let's go slay a dragon." Some of the other men cheered.

Giles said, "Your goal is to retrieve the boy. Let Sir Peter and the others deal with the dragon."

"Why does he always have all the fun?" said the same man. The men were about to exit the keep, when Edmund and Godfrey entered the barracks. Lady Branson immediately ran to Godfrey and hugged him, tears streaming down her face.

"Oh, thank Arda, you've returned to me."

When she released Godfrey from her embrace, she started touching him in random places looking for signs of injury. "Are you alright, are you injured?"

Godfrey was visibly irritated by this and said, "I'm fine. Elite warriors, such as myself, don't need their mums licking their wounds all the time." Lady Branson was silent upon hearing this. Godfrey, fearing he'd said something wrong said, "Er, I mean Lady Bransons, their Lady Branson's."

Tears of joy came down Lady Branson's face. "Did you just call me mum?"

"It slipped out. I—" She hugged him again.

This moment was the first time Godfrey had ever referred to Lady Branson as mum since his infancy. There was a collective "Awwwwww" in the barracks. Lady Branson turned to Edmund and hugged him.

"And you returned him to me. Thank you, Edmund."

Edmund felt at peace from her embrace. He felt like suddenly all his problems disappeared. Unfortunately, this moment of bliss was short-

237

lived when Lady Branson quickly disengaged, realizing her blunder. She felt embarrassed by letting herself be overcome with emotion. Edmund saw this as rejection and it wounded him. Lady Branson tried to correct her faux pas by being as formal as possible.

"Sorry milord, that was very careless of me. It shan't happen again." She bowed her head slightly.

"No, no, it's quite alright. I like hugs," said Edmund.

"I am eternally grateful to you, milord, for risking your life for Godfrey," said Lady Branson.

"Well, I didn't really do much. It was mostly Godfrey and Sir Peter. Anyway, it's easy to do things for someone you love."

There was a silence between them, and Lady Branson had a bewildered look on her face as did others, including Godfrey. Giselle, who was initially elated to see Edmund, was devastated upon hearing these words. Clara did not like seeing Giselle like this, though a part of her was relieved, because, in her mind, it meant Giselle would stop obsessing over Edmund, now that she knew his true nature.

Edmund felt humiliated and attempted to fix his slip of the tongue. "Er, I mean, ahem, I meant people, people you love in a strictly non corporal spiritual type of love, not a romantic type of love, like you and Sir Peter that would be silly heh, heh, heh. I, um, actually love everyone that way, like Godfrey, my dad, my mum, my brothers, Sir Peter, the knights, uh, uh." Edmund's eyes gravitated towards Swithin. He pointed to him. "This man, uh, uh, I'm sorry what's your name?"

"It's Swithin, milord."

"Right! Swithin. I love you, Swithin."

Swithin was quite insulted but because of Edmund's status, held his tongue. "Thank you, milord." He muttered something under his breath, making sure no one could hear. It went along the lines of, "Been here forty-five fucking years and they still don't know my name."

"Anyway, I should be going now." Edmund was on his way out when Lodema said, "We'd like to know how the battles going, if that's alright with you, milord."

"Lodema, I don't think that's really necessary. I'm sure Lord Edmund is busy," said Lady Branson.

"It's alright. I bring good news," said Edmund.

As he came back into the barracks, he saw Giselle looking rather despondent. She was on the verge of tears but maintained her composure.

"Milord."

Edmund, in turn, greeted her. "Giselle." He knew she was upset; he had known her long enough. She usually was quite adept at masking her emotions, but this recent emotional blow caught her off guard.

"I'd like to be excused now, if that's alright with you, milord." "Uh, yeah, sure," said Edmund.

Giselle scurried off, averting her eyes from Edmund so he would not see her cry. Clara noticed, and said, "Uh, I better follow her, milord, it could be illness from the pregnancy."

Edmund nodded his head. So Clara ran after Giselle as they exited the Barracks. Edmund was aware he had caused Giselle so much pain and deeply regretted his slip of the tongue. Because of this, he was a bit flustered.

Godfrey noticed, so to alleviate tension, he joked, "milord, aren't you going to tell them the tale of my unwavering courage, unmatched skill and unsurpassed determination?"

"I'll be sure to tell them of your undying humility, as well," Edmund teased. Godfrey smiled.

Giles was not amused. "Wipe that grin off your face, boy. Do you have any idea the horror you put Lady Branson through? What you put us through? Yet you saunter in here, nonchalantly, making light of our situation. We are at war. The enemy is at our gates. This is serious. What you did was not only reckless and stupid, it was selfish. You put good men's lives at risk. What do you have to say for yourself, child?"

Godfrey had his eyes glued to the floor and had his head down. "Apologies, Lord Baker."

"It's not only me you've offended, child."

Godfrey looked at Lady Branson. "Apologies, Lady Branson." Lady Branson smiled. "I'm just glad you're alright."

"And another thing—" said Giles.

"I think he's learned his lesson now. You can spare the speech," interrupted Lady Branson.

Giles groaned. "Elysant, you're too soft on him. The boy needs discipline. Treating him like a babe will only mean his troublesome behavior will get worse—" Giles noticed she was not looking at him as she had been kissing Godfrey's forehead and muttering prayers from the book of Noga. This vexed Giles.

"Elysant, are you even listening?"

Startled, Lady Branson said, "Er, um, yes."

Giles looked at her incredulously. "Then what did I just say?"

Lady Branson laughed nervously. "Heh heh." She quickly changed the subject. "Lord Edmund had something to say to us."

"Right," said Edmund.

Edmund recounted the tale of King Mavid in the bailey with Godfrey adding in sometimes to emphasize his participation and contribution. Godfrey would say things like, "You'll notice there is no longer a fire in the bailey. You're welcome". Edmund also talked about the dangerous magic wielders they encountered on the ramparts. When he was done, several people in the garrison cheered. Others asked questions like, "An Orthrya Vepid in the castle?" or "There is such a thing as a king dragon?" "Dragons can be affected by magic?" Sarah, Tim and Alywin entered the Barracks. They had troubled looks on their faces.

Lady Branson noticed this immediately. "What happened down there? Are you alright?"

They did not respond immediately. Lady Branson noticed Alywin's hand was injured and Sarah had a bruise under her eye from being attack by Knox.

"Alywin your hand and Sarah your eye!"

"Milady. I think its best we discuss this some place more private," said Alywin.

Before she could respond, Edmund looked at Alywin and said, "Alywin? Wait! You're Alywin Bears Bane?"

Alywin sighed. He was uncomfortable with that name. "I prefer simply Alywin, milord."

Sarah was bemused by the revelation. "Bears Bane?" A smile began to manifest of Edmund's face.

"I can't believe you're him. Sir Avery told me you rescued him from a bear with nothing but your bare hands."

Alywin, feeling rather embarrassed qualified by saying. "I had a stone, milord."

"You saved his life that day. It was during the battle at Mydra wood, along the outskirts of Sigate (1547 NEEOT). They say that after you fought the bear, you carried an injured Avery back to the keep. I don't know why father has not knighted you already," said Edmund.

"Not to sound arrogant, but I'm pretty sure fighting a dragon is more impressive; they should call me Godfrey Dragons' Bane."

"Will you stop!" said Giles angrily. "Sorry, Lord Baker," said Godfrey. "Wait! You fought the dragon?" Tim said quite surprised.

"Yes, and don't worry. He's on our side now. A couple of lightning bolts shook him out of his bewitchment that had caused him to attack the castle in the first place."

"Dragons can't be bewitched," said Tim.

"That's essentially what he said, but when asked how he got here, he said he couldn't recall," said Godfrey.

"Karasa Mollo," Alywin whispered under his breath unknowingly. He suddenly became more terrified upon hearing this little detail. Though he did well to mask his fear, it slowly became more apparent on his face. Godfrey had heard him.

"Kara what?" said Godfrey.

"Nothing. I said nothing," said Alywin.

Lady Branson was able to detect the subtleties in Alywin's expression that suggested that he was feeling uneasy. Edmund, who was completely wrapped up in Alywin's feats, forgot to ask what happened to them. He eventually noticed Alywin's hand.

"Alywin, I know Lady Branson already asked. How did you injure your hand? Don't suppose you've been fighting more bears in the woods," Edmund chuckled.

Alywin was too preoccupied with racing thoughts to receive the joke. "I... I... uh."

Tim jumped in before Alywin could concoct a story. "We were in the dungeon milord," said Tim.

"Doing what exactly?" Edmund asked. He found it peculiar because, as far as he knew, no one had been in the dungeon in ages.

"Uh, well, you see, milord," said Tim.

Lady Branson intervened. "We discovered from Sir Richard that there are tunnels underground that we could use as a possible escape route, in case the castle was overtaken."

She purposely left out the part about Kraag and his minions attacking. "He survived the battle of Eredith?" asked Edmund. He was surprised to hear this information because he initially believed there were no survivors. "He did, but he later passed. His injuries were too severe, and I couldn't save him," said Lady Branson despondently.

"Oh, I am sorry to hear that. I'm sure you did the best you could," said Edmund.

Edmund turned to Tim, who was sweating profusely. "These tunnels, are they dangerous?"

"Nope," Tim answered rather quickly and in a high pitch sound, a nervous tick of his and often an indication that he was lying. His voice dropped to his normal volume. "Nope, ahem, no, just regular old tunnels. Nothing strange. Nothing out of the ordinary."

"Then what explains your injuries?" asked Edmund.

Tim started to laugh nervously, his sweating increased, another nervous tick of his. "Ha ha ha. It's actually rather a funny story, milord.

You see, tunnels are really dark, but you already knew that, never mind. Anyway, Alywin, he-he-he, couldn't see behind him because it was dark, but he heard footsteps. He thought someone was chasing him again, because it was dark and he, uh, punched that person and injured his hand. Because it was dark. I—I, uh, already said that three bloody times, so I'm sure you know what I'm getting at. That person was Sarah." Tim began to exhale heavily. He was exhausted from concocting such a lie.

"Well, didn't you have rushlights?" said a female healer. "Well, Alywin dropped his?" replied Tim.

"Why?" said the same healer.

"Er, I dunno, Wilona, maybe Alywin is clumsy?"

"But you had your rushlight, right? You would have seen Sarah and told Alywin," said Wilona.

"We, uh. We, uh, shared a rushlight and Alywin was holding it."
"You shared a rush light?" Wilona asked innocently.

"Yes," Tim replied. He stressed the word and was becoming increasingly agitated by her questions.

"Why did you do that?" Wilona asked.

"Eergh, because it's easier that way. You can carry more things when one person carries the rush light. Besides, if there were three rushlights, and they all fell down, there'd be a big fire and the whole bloody castle would burn down," said Tim.

"The castle is made of stone and granite. It takes more than three rush lights to burn it down," said Wilona. "And also, why was Sarah walking behind him when you came in together, especially since you all shared a rush light? You should have been standing shoulder to shoulder."
"Well, we're dullards. Just three dullards who traversed underground tunnels," said Tim, at this point very irritated. "Even if that's true, that still doesn't explain—"

"Wilona, for the love of Arda, will you please stop asking questions?!"

Everyone was silent. It was uncharacteristic for Tim to lose his temper to this extreme. That was more akin to Alywin.

Wilona, completely taken aback by what she deemed unprovoked aggression, said, with a completely innocuous expression on her face, "Are you angry with me, Tim?"

Tim sighed. "No, Wilona, er, sorry, really sorry. I'm just feeling unwell." Quite alarmed to hear, and misconstruing his words as Wilona often did, she had a limited understanding of social cues and often took things literally, she asked, "You're sick? Is it contagious? Is it the plague? Did you catch it down there?!"

"No, no, no. That's not what he meant. He meant emotionally, you know, with work and the war and dealing with his own personal demons," said Sarah.

Wilona's eyes widened upon hearing demons. "Demons!"

Sarah quickly responded by saying, "Metaphorical demons, metaphorical demons, of course! Heh, heh, such as feelings of inadequacy, hopelessness, alienation all stemming from an unfair class structure."

Alywin and Tim were horrified upon hearing this. Their fear was exacerbated by the fact that Edmund tilted his head slightly and said, "Huh?" It was an utterance of bemusement rather than scathing disapproval, but Alywin and Tim feared and assumed the worst.

"We're fucking dead," Tim muttered under his breath. "Did you say something, Tim?" asked Edmund.

"Uh, uh," Tim stammered.

Sarah intervened. "It's, uh, affecting him physically as well, causing sweating, unintelligible speech, uh, uh, hair loss."

"What? I'm not losing my hair," said Tim.

"Oh, so you cut it that way on purpose," said Sarah.

Before Tim could respond, Wilona intervened. "I have a solution. Why don't you just wear a hat?"

"I don't need a hat, Wilona, because I am not losing my hair," Tim said, rather irritated.

"But you are losing your mind" Godfrey snickered. Giles shot Godfrey a foul glance. Godfrey immediately stopped laughing and remained silent.

"This is all a misunderstanding. Look, war is bad and during war tensions are high. Sometimes people lose their tempers when other people won't stop asking them bloody questions, or people say misinformed things about other people's hair based on preconceive notions about how regular hair is supposed to be styled and sometimes people punch other people in the dark when they're scared," explained Tim.

Alywin whispered in Tim's ear, "Tim, please stop talking." Feeling humiliated, Tim replied, "Right."

Edmund, who was baffled by the whole scene, said, "Is he usually like this? Last time we met, he seemed so meek and quiet."

To which Godfrey said, "It's always the quiet ones."

Edmund turned to Lady Branson and said, "Maybe you're overworking them. Little breaks are important."

Lady Branson laughed nervously. "I'll be sure to take that into consideration when next assigning tasks."

"Forgive me, milord, but if anything, they need more work. That Tim especially is lazy and is always fraternizing with the female healers. I keep telling him this place is not his own personal fucking harem and girlie has been here only a few weeks and I catch her seducing a bloody sell sword. Alywin, that fucker, is a regular maverick. Comes and goes as he pleases," Swithin said.

"Watch it, old man," Alywin warned Swithin. "Swithin. I think you've said enough," warned Giles.

Swithin ignored the warnings. "Thinks he is too good to treat certain patients whose injuries he deemed benign. Arrogant shit. I know his type. Acts like a purebred but is really just a cur."

Alywin was livid and lost his temper.

"Just ignore him, Alywin. He's a mad old fool." Tim tried his best to stop Alywin, but Alywin was a much larger male and he easily broke through Tim's hold.

"Calm yourself, Alywin," said Giles.

But Alywin was too angered to listen to reason. "Why don't you say that to my face, you fucking old cunt, 'cause I have no problem pommeling you until you're shitting your own blood!"

"Alywin, enough!" said Lady Branson.

Alywin immediately regained his composure. "Sorry, milady."

Edmund was impressed with her sense of authority. This Alywin had ignored Lord Baker but was completely subservient to Lady Branson. The amount of power she had over the people here was fascinating. Edmund also suspected that she was most likely unaware of this power. As she was not abusive, her concern was probably in keeping Alywin out of trouble. He thought such talent was fit for a queen.

Lady Branson turned to Edmund. "I'm sorry, milord, he's usually not like this—"

"It's alright. Tensions are high. The war has done a number on us, myself included. Everyone loses their temper from time to time. Even the knights get into squabbles. Just ask commander Oak. In fact, there was an incident when Sir Avery threw a buckler at Sir Ryder just because he believed Sir Ryder ate his meal. Next, they got into a full-on fist fight. It would have been bad if commander Oak hadn't stepped in."

Godfrey, who was intrigued by the whole story, asked, "Who was the victor?"

"That's not important. I believe what Lord Edmund is trying to say is we all have lapses in judgment. That's what makes us human, after all," said Giles.

"Speaking of lapses in judgment. Alywin really striking tiny maidens?" said Godfrey.

"It was dark!" shouted Tim.

"And I'm not that tiny, child," retorted Sarah.

"No, I suppose you're regular sized for a female dwarf."

Edmund could not contain his laughter. Sarah suppressed her anger as she said through gritted teeth, "What a wonderful child."

Giles, however, was fed up with Godfrey's antics. "I will teach you the meaning of respect, boy!" He raised his hand in the air, ready to strike, but stopped when Lady Branson stood between them with a scowl on her face.

"You shall not harm my child!"

"But he is being insolent," replied Giles. "I do not care," said Lady Branson.

Lodema, watching all this, was quite giddy. "Things are way more exciting here than in the Great Hall."

Colin was pretending to sleep during the whole debacle, but heard every word. He thought he should see if Sarah and her friends were alright. He approached the group, and he pretended to just be waking up from a long slumber. Sarah noticed him first.

"Colin. I hope we didn't disturb you?"

Colin yawned. "It was hard to sleep with all the noise, but I think I managed."

Colin's eyes gravitated towards Edmund. He had never met Edmund in person up until now, but he fit the description from Dale, one of the Herons. "*Big fucking ginger*" Dale was not one with words. Colin assumed he must be Edmund and he was adorned in what he deemed fancy armor that bore the Franklin crest.

"You must be Prince Edmund."

"Er, actually, it's just Edmund, not a prince yet. I, uh, don't believe we've met."

"No, we haven't, but I met your father on the battlefield in Rilek. I'm Colin, bastard son of the late Galeran Harlow."

Edmund took a moment to put the pieces together. "Galeran Harlow, the man who rebelled against Hector. Your people assisted us during the battle of Rilek. For that, I'm grateful."

"More like your father and his army saved our sorry arses," said Colin. "Nonetheless, your service will not be forgotten," said Edmund.

"Oh, how rude of me. I haven't greeted you all," said Colin.

He looked at Lady Branson and said, "Milady." He looked at Giles and said, "Milord." He looked at Godfrey and said, "Little lord."

"I'm not a lord, but I'll soon be a knight," said Godfrey. Colin smiled and said, "So little Sir, then."

Godfrey smiled. "Why'd you think I was a lord?" "I dunno, fancy garments?"

Godfrey furrowed his brow. "Fancy?"

"I'm a bastard from Rilek. Any garments that aren't riddled with moth holes are considered fancy," said Colin.

Giles was growing increasingly apprehensive. He did not like the idea of a sell sword becoming friendly with Godfrey. "I'm sure Colin is quite busy and does not have time for idle chat with troublesome youths."

To which Godfrey responded, "Busy with what? It's not as if he could enter the field of battle with those injuries."

"Busy with healing. Godfrey," Giles retorted.

"The best remedy for broken bones is exercise," replied Godfrey. "Godfrey, will you stop bothering the man? He needs to heal," said Giles frustratedly.

"Lord Baker is actually right. Sorry, little Sir, I actually wanted to see Sarah. I was wondering if she could help me with my injuries. I've started to develop some new pains that I feel only Sarah, with her expertise, can address."

Sarah was surprised and it showed as she looked at Colin and whispered, "What are you doing?"

Colin whispered back, "Rescuing you."

"Uh, uh, fine. That's fine. I'll take a look, but first I—I, uh, am going to require two capable healers to assist me in this, uh, very serious endeavor. Alywin, Tim."

She motioned her hand for them to follow. They did just that. The four traveled to an unoccupied corner of the barracks. They placed a veil covering themselves from others.

"Colin, what did you want to tell us?" asked Sarah.

"Actually, it's you who needs to tell me something. What really happened down there?"

The three remained silent. Tim spoke first. "You see, Alywin—"

Colin interrupted. "Please Tim, don't tell me it was dark. I may be barely literate but I'm not an imbecile."

"So, you heard," said Sarah.

"Every word, even the part when you mentioned the unfair class system in front of the future prince. Now, I'm not too familiar with Iiadecan law, but that sounds like something that will get your pretty little head chopped off."

Sarah smiled. "You think I'm pretty?" "Sarah!" Tim shouted angrily.

"Sorry." Sarah, rather embarrassed, said, "I—I didn't know what I was thinking."

"You weren't thinking. You could've gotten us bloody executed," said Alywin.

"Well, you were no bloody help, standing there like a fucking log whilst Tim and I humiliated ourselves in front of Lord Edmund," retorted Sarah.

"Sssh, keep it down. Someone might hear us," said Colin.

Suddenly, they saw a shadowy figure behind the curtain. The figure peeked its head out. It was Wilona with her large, curious brown eyes, blank expression and curly multicolored hair, a mixture of light brown with blondish streaks sprinkled randomly in between.

"So, this is where you've run off to. And you've built a fort too!" The four stared at her in bewilderment.

"What, did I do something wrong?" she asked.

Sarah was the first to respond. "No, no, Wilona, it's just that we need some privacy."

Wilona then asked, rather bluntly, "Why?"

Tim quickly said, "It's men's issues, personal men's issues." "Then why is Sarah here?" asked Wilona.

"Uh, well, he trusts her. She has experience dealing with said issues. She has lots of brothers," said Tim.

"Oh, what kind of issues?" asked Wilona, rather innocuously.

"Uh, uh." Colin and Alywin were stammering, trying to figure out a way out of this line of questioning. When suddenly Tim blurted out, "It's his cock."

Alywin, Colin, and Sarah looked at Tim like he had lost his mind.

Wilona seemed oblivious to this and said, "What's wrong with it?"

Colin was about to speak when Tim interrupted. "It's broken. He uh fell whilst he was sleeping."

"That's sounds horrible," said Wilona.

"Yeah. He's putting on a brave front, but he is in agony," said Tim. "Oh," said Wilona.

"So if you don't mind, could you give us some privacy?" said Tim. "Of course," she muttered under her breath.

"I'm glad I don't have a cock. That sounds painful."

As she turned to leave, Tim said, "Oh, and Wilona, could you do us a favor? Colin's really embarrassed about all this. He'd prefer it if no one knows about this."

"You mean like a secret?" she asked.

"Exactly, can you do that? Keep this a secret?" asked Tim. "I think so," said Wilona.

"Good. Remember, don't tell anyone," said Tim.

Wilona nodded. She was about to leave, but turned around and looked at Tim with a worried expression.

"Tim, you're not still angry with me? I don't know what I'd do if you were still angry with me."

Tim replied, "No, I never was."

Her countenance changed to that of elation. "That's wonderful. Oh, and Colin, I hope your cock feels better." She left into another area of the barracks.

When she was out of earshot, Colin said, "My cock, really?" "I panicked. Besides, none of you came up with anything."

"I swear, the pair of you (Colin referring to Sarah and Tim) are the worst liars I've ever met."

"I'm sorry we didn't grow up as sell swords in fucking Rilek, mastering the art of deception."

"Easy Tim," Alywin said, in an attempt to defuse the situation.

Tim sighed. "I'm sorry, uh, here's your sword." Tim held the blade out to Colin. "Alywin, give him his bow."

As Alywin was about to give Colin the bow with the quiver, Colin said, "Keep em for now. There's not much I can do with them in this condition, anyway." He pointed to his broken arm. "This is my sword arm."

"But the blade belongs to you," said Tim.

Colin studied the blade closely. It did not look particularly special, but that was to be expected. Long gone are the days of unique blades which are now relegated to ceremonial use. Modern blades have a streamline design because of blacksmiths discovering the most efficient design for cutting and thrusting. For longswords, that meant a basic cruciform hilt with a two-handed grip measuring 6 to 11 inches, the blade straight and double-edged measured 33 to 43 inches. Of course, there were subtle variations in blade design, depending on where it was forged or things such as the size and shape of the pommel. Some blades had slight curvatures on the cross guard and different textured grips usually made out of leather or wood. Often, but not always, longswords had a fuller or fullers. There are several types of swords manufactured all over Mirthadine longswords, great swords, rapiers, claymores, scimitars, katanas falchion, messers, cutlasses and countless others, yet despite the variety in type, the variation within each specific type is minimal. Colin's sword had one fuller that tapered off roughly halfway through the length of the blade and a blade measuring 36 inches with a 7.5-inch hilt. A leather grip with three distinctive horizontal depressions equidistant apart on the upper portion of the grip. The three isolated depressions on the leather seemed to serve no functional purpose and might have been purely aesthetic. Nonetheless, a grip of this type was certainly unique.

Colin looked at Tim. "The thing is, it's not even my blade. Nicked it off a corpse."

Tim was surprised to hear this, given that the blade was in such good condition. In fact, one could say, apart from the grip, it appeared newly forged.

"You found a blade in this condition just lying around?" said Tim. "Well, you have a good eye for that sort of thing. Anyway, it wasn't in that condition when I found it. I had to reforge it."

"You're a blacksmith," Sarah said, quite impressed upon hearing this. "Not officially, but I have tempered a few blades and pieces of armor here and there. When you're in Rilek, you can't afford to pay people to do things for you, so you have to be self-reliant."

Sarah was enamored by Colin's words. Tim saw the look in her eyes as she stared at Colin and it vexed him.

Alywin said, rather bluntly, "So, you killed a man and stole his sword." "Alywin!" Sarah exclaimed.

"Hey, I'm not the one on trial here, and besides, he was already dead. Now speak the truth, again what really happen in the tunnels?" asked Colin.

The three remained silent. Sarah was the first to break the silence. "We don't want to involve you."

Colin smirked. "That's just a gentle way of saying you don't trust me." "No, that's not it at all…" replied Sarah.

"Then what is it? Look, I'm already involved, so is everyone in the castle. The boy may have tamed the dragon, but Hector's army may breech these walls. The tunnels may be these people's only option. They are going to ask questions." Colin sighed. "I know you don't want to spread panic and cause chaos, but I can keep a secret and I can help if you let me."

The three looked at each other and, based on their expressions, Tim was clearly against the idea. Sarah was for it and Alywin was ambivalent. This man was still a stranger from Rilek and a sell sword for that matter. Alywin had run into people affiliated from free companies in Garla. He was approached by one free company at the time known as the White Steeds. They were based in Eredith and, as far as he knew, had since disbanded. The deal did not fall through. The White Steeds were concerned with

Alywin's family name. Although not much is known about the Morgan name outside of Garla, they are infamous in certain parts of the town. There are several who associate the Morgans with crime, mostly theft, but many within their circle know them for more heinous things. Alywin, himself, had committed several thefts, even robbing people at knife or fist point. He also partook in usury, mostly intimidating people into paying their debts. He was never caught with such crimes up until the Corithni incident. His uncle, Winthrop, was often accused of associating with pirates at Gasco port. All these factors led to the White Steeds rejecting him. They never officially said this, but it was ultimately his loyalty that was in question. They feared he would only end up stealing from them, and the pirate association meant he had no semblance of code. (In Iiadec, Pirates are considered some of the worst criminals out there, completely lawless and irredeemable).

Colin was a sell sword which meant he worked for coin and had more allegiance to the Herons than Lord Franklin. Nonetheless, if his story is to be believed, he had a vendetta against Hector and his allies. In other words, he was unlikely to betray the only people that could grant him reprisal. This is further solidified with his interaction with Lord Edmund and his mentioning of this figure, Galeran Harlow. The way Colin said, *"I am Colin, bastard son of Galeran Harlow"* suggested he wore it as a badge of honor. In Iiadec, most people do not admit they are bastards. It is a form of social suicide, unless they truly revered their father. In addition, the way Lord Edmund said, *"The man who rebelled against Hector"* like he was some type of martyr. Several signs pointed to Colin being an ally, at least for now. But there was still the lingering detail that Colin was initially hesitant to reveal this information to three lowborn but willing to reveal this potentially damaging information without being asked to Lord Edmund, of all people. Perhaps they were a test to see how his background would be received. Perhaps he wanted Lord Edmund to know he was on his side.

Alywin was about to speak, when Tim shook his head.

Alywin ignored Tim's warning and discussed what happened in the tunnels with Sarah, sometimes adding details that Alywin missed out. Colin listened without interrupting, right up until the part when they mentioned the Othrya Vepid posing as Salkar.

"Wait. A giant fucking rat?" he asked in disbelief. "Sarah, show him the ear," Alywin said impatiently.

"Alright, alright calm down Alywin," Sarah removed the ear from the upper portion of her dress.

Alywin grimaced. "You put it there? You wouldn't hold it, but you'd put it there next to your, your, woman parts?"

"You said not to lose it, and where else was I supposed to put it?" asked Sarah.

"Oh, I dunno, the same place where you kept the bloody dagger?" retorted Alywin.

"My leg? That's too close to my—"

"That's highly irrelevant information and private, heh heh," Tim said interrupting Sarah.

Colin looked at the ear. "May I?"

Sarah handed him the massive rat ear. He turned it around a few times and felt the texture, then bit it. All three of them recoiled in disgust. Colin, who either did not seem to notice or was not concerned, said, rather excitedly, "Holy fuck, by Arda's cock, it's real."

Tim, feeling uncomfortable with Colin's vernacular, said, "Please don't say that, it's quite sacrilegious."

Colin was too fascinated with the ear to hear Tim out. "I bet the giant fucker could feed a family of 20 for a year. My God, it's fucking massive." All three of them winced upon hearing such a repugnant statement.

Sarah wondered whether Colin was accustomed to eating rat meat, but was too repulsed to ask.

After settling down, they continued their story. Colin was surprisingly calm upon hearing their harrowing tale. Even when hearing about Leland and Godina. This alarmed the three to the point when Sarah had to say, "Colin, you're taking this rather well, especially given the nature of the information."

"Yeah, it's scary how calm you are about all this. What gives?" asked Tim.

Colin smiled. "Look, hokraft has been practiced for ages. Way before your Lord Franklin banned it and it will continue to be practiced well after he dies. I reckon if you look under any castle in Iiadec it would reek with remnants of hokraft."

"So basically, we're fucked and this whole fucking land is cursed," said Alywin.

Colin laughed. "You all need to relax. The effects of hokraft have been greatly exaggerated. First of all, you can't curse a whole land, hokraft only works on living things, or things that were once alive. You've got nothing to worry about in terms of a cursed castle, unless you consider stone and mortar to be amongst the living."

Tim was not convinced that there was not a threat. "Maybe not castles, but plants and trees are certainly living. Trees, especially, are used to build scaffolding for castles."

"When I said living things, I meant ones bearing a soul. Last time I checked, trees don't have souls," said Colin.

"But animals do. That would explain where lycos come from," replied Tim.

"Yeah, but no one has seen one of those things in ages," responded Colin.

There was still something troubling Tim. "You know a lot about hokraft."

"Eh, I ran into a couple of castors who knew the craft. Killed some of them, rival free companies. Know your enemy and all. You'd be surprised how many castors join free companies. They are a highly sought after bunch. Anyway, not all the castors were bad. I even shared a few glasses of ale with some of them. You won't believe how much information one could reveal in a drunken stupor."

He said this so nonchalantly that it made Sarah and Tim uneasy. Alywin, however, wasn't concerned, for he had been in similar situations in the past, so he was a bit desensitized. Colin saw the uncomfortable looks on Tim and Sarah's faces when reacting to his anecdote.

He looked at Sarah. "Those enemy castors were terrible bloody cannibals, rapists, and unsavory sorts."

Sarah was relieved to hear this. Tim, however, was not convinced. "As for the dragon connection to this spell. I highly doubt there is one. This spell, from the way you've described it, seems like traditional magic, not hokraft. It's pretty obvious dragons can't be affected by normal hexes, no matter how potent they may be. Their hides are too thick," explained Colin.

"So, you're telling me we shouldn't be concerned about anything?" asked Alywin.

Colin said, with a pensive look on his face, "I wouldn't say that entirely."

The three's interest piqued upon hearing this. "I dunno. It's kinda odd the whole Mason bit innit? You said this rat referred to Sarah as *the Mason*, not the Mason girl, right?"

"Yes," said Sarah.

"That's sounds more like a title than a name, don't you think?" said Colin.

Before any of them could respond, Colin turned to Sarah. "You said you had a mark that helped open a secret passageway."

Sarah had been concealing her mark ever since she reached the surface. She was hesitant, but eventually held out her hand, revealing the mark of the Mason. Colin held it and studied this almost organic looking tattoo.

"Did you show this to anyone else?" Colin said gravely.

Sarah, taken aback by Colin's sudden change in demeanor, replied, "No."

Quite alarmed Tim asked, "Why? What's wrong?"

Colin looked around, making certain no one was watching. "I've seen marks like these on pagans. The Church in Mirama executes pagans, but you didn't hear that from me."

"People in the city of Mirama executed? That's pure nonsense. It's a neutral body. It's a holy city with houses of worship," said Tim.

"Neutrality is a rare thing in war. Everyone usually plays their part, whether active or passive," said Colin gravely.

"You actually think Mirama is secretly supporting Hector? Are you mad?" asked Tim.

"You know what's mad? The fact that Hector has managed to amass an army that dwarfs your Lord Franklin's army and got nearly every free company in Rilek working for him. Free companies require coin. Lots of it. So where is Hector getting the funding?" asked Colin.

"I dunno. Maybe he raised it on his own. Maybe foreign ties?" retorted Tim.

Alywin remained silent. He was processing the information while Tim and Colin argued over the legitimacy of Colin's claims. Sarah tried to calm them down.

"He's proper mad. How does a sell sword enter the holy city of Mirama, anyway?" asked Tim.

"Tim, keep your voice down," Sarah said in a loud whisper.

"There is much you don't understand. You've lived in isolation here. There is a whole other world out there that extends beyond our borders. Several forces are at play here," said Colin.

"So now the whole bloody world is involved?" Tim retorted. "Tim!" said Sarah.

"What?!" Tim sighed. "Sorry, but this whole thing is ridiculous. Right, Alywin? Alywin?"

Alywin did not respond; he was in deep thought. If what Colin was saying was true, then they were in bigger trouble than he thought. And just when he thought they'd escaped one danger, another one might rear its ugly head. If Colin was to be believed and Hector has the might of Mirama, then the war was already lost.

Alywin looked at Tim. "Alywin, surely you're not seriously entertaining this ridiculous idea?"

Alywin did not respond.

"Really, Alywin. It's the holy city. They don't take sides!"

"Yeah, but what if he's right? I mean, it wouldn't be the first time the powers at the top have been swayed by monetary gain, especially during times of war."

Tim looked at Alywin in utter disbelief. "Are you suggesting Mirama placed coin before God?"

"God is ethereal, coin is tangible and feeds bellies," responded Alywin.

Tim scowled. "Of course you would say that. You don't have any faith."

"This isn't about me, Mirama, or God, but something tangible— Lives. If we go to Mirama, our lives, and the lives of many, maybe forfeit."

All four were silent, contemplating Alywin's words.

Tim rubbed his face with both his hands, a clear sign of stress. "Let's entertain this theory that Mirama is secretly supporting Hector. The question remains, why? His claim to the throne is obviously illegitimate."

"Well, there is that rumor," said Sarah.

"That's entirely a fabrication. Lord Franklin was cleared of the charge in the very courts of Mirama," Tim said forcibly.

"I'm not saying I believe it, but there may be others that do. It's quite damaging," replied Sarah.

"The deceased Lord Rowan Everard has paid handsome sums to Mirama in the past. Even helped with the construction of their walls," said Alywin.

"That doesn't prove anything. All major Lords pay tithe to Mirama," said Tim.

"It's optional and only 10 percent," replied Alywin.

"You all are determined for this to be true!" exclaimed Tim.

"And you're determined for this not to be!" exclaimed Alywin. "Open your eyes. There is a possibility that this might be true. In the event that we lose the war, which we most likely will, we need to make sure where we go is safe."

"Why are you certain we are going to lose the war? Did you not hear Godfrey and Edmund? Hector's main weapon is now on our side," said Tim.

"We have everything to lose in this battle. Corithni is one of the last strongholds that support Lord Franklin's claim. It doesn't matter how many sell swords perish, Hector will come back with more from Rilek or

Agor or somewhere else. He has the numbers, so he has nothing to lose," said Alywin.

"Except his life," said Colin. All eyes were on Colin. "What are you getting at?" asked Tim.

"If Hector dies, then regardless of if Mirama is treacherous, they would have to support Lord Franklin's claim. Lord Franklin and his men don't have to defeat an army, they just have to kill one man," said Colin. "Easier said than done. He's not going to just challenge Lord Franklin to an outright duel for the throne. Besides, he's surrounded by legions," said Alywin.

"I didn't say it would be easy, but there are still Herons and other sell swords loyal to Galeran Harlow scattered around Rilek, even reaching as far as Agor. Given Hector lost control of the dragon, he may be forced to retreat. That should give us a couple of weeks to contact an admittingly ragtag band of sell swords and assassins all who want Hector dead. If I can't kill him myself, then I'll revel in orchestrating his death and avenging my father and brothers," said Colin.

Those last words eliminated any doubts in their heads of Colin's true intentions. He may not have been completely loyal to the Franklins, but he certainly was not a friend to Hector. It was hard to refute this when every time he mentioned Hector's name or anything relating to Hector, his jaw tightened and his brow contorted, forming visible lines on his forehead. This was a bit peculiar, since Colin did not display such emotions initially when describing Hector, even when describing his father's death. The three attributed this to his discovery that his brothers had fallen at Eredith, thus renewing his ire toward Hector.

Sarah sympathized with Colin. He had recently lost his brothers because of the actions of the same man responsible for his father's death. He clearly desired reprisal but must have felt so powerless confined to a bed and in no condition to fight, knowing full well his enemies were outside these walls. She hesitated, but eventually summoned the courage to extend her hand out and touch his good shoulder.

"I'm sorry for your loss."

Colin did not respond. Instead, he studied the mark on the back of her hand again. Sarah was about to pull away when Colin held her hand gently, tracing his index finger along the mark on Sarah's hand. (The hammer section of the mark was raised like a burn mark or imbedded tattoo.) Sarah was quite enamored by the tactile sensation. It was apparent by the rose color her cheeks turned as Colin touched her hand. This vexed Tim, but he remained silent. Alywin was bemused and wondered what Colin was doing. He anticipated an explanation for such odd behavior.

After a few minutes, he got one. "The mark is raised in the center. It's almost as if you have been branded. Did it hurt when it happened?" asked Colin.

Sarah, quite distracted, responded, "Huh? I mean no, maybe a little. Not as much as I thought."

Colin had a pensive look on his face. "Hmm." "What does it mean?" said Alywin eagerly.

"I don't know. But marks like these often attract negative attention. They are often associated with paganism or Ulid. We'll have to remove it," responded Colin.

"We will do no such thing. It's just a bloody tattoo. People have tattoos," Tim responded immediately.

"Pirates. The mere suspicion of piracy is punishable by death. Mirama considers them irredeemable miscreants," replied Alywin.

Tim was about to protest when Colin said, "We don't have to remove it now. The scar will draw as much attention as the mark itself. No, we need more sophisticated equipment than daggers. We need capable hands to make it look natural, to avoid suspicion, for now." Colin attempted to remove his leather archers' glove with his teeth. He struggled.

Sarah saw this and said, "Here. Let me help." But as she reached for the glove, Colin said, "No, I'll never heal if you're always helping me, but thank you."

Sarah smiled. Colin eventually managed to remove the glove and placed it on Sarah's hand with her assistance. The glove was too large for her hand, but it concealed the mark and had a buckled wrist strap to adjust for size.

Sarah looked at Colin with a concerned look. Something was troubling her. "Colin, what if your plan fails? Or Hector takes the castle?" "If you really believe surrender is not an option, then you must flee as far away from here as possible," said Colin.

Sarah looked in his eyes then said, "We must flee."

"Where would we go if Mirama is compromised? The situation in Eredith is unclear, so what other place is safe?" asked Alywin.

They pondered this question for a moment, until Sarah said, "Dae le Maut, the home of Lord Hadrian Baudry."

CHAPTER TWELVE
BATTLES

Sir Peter was unconscious on the floor near the remains that separated the lower and main bailey. His men stood around him.

"Is he dead?" asked Robert.

"Only one way to find out," said Robin. He gave Sir Peter a sharp kick to the side.

Sir Peter immediately sat up. "OW!" As you could imagine, he was quite disoriented.

"Brother, have you lost your mind? He is a fucking knight!" said Robert.

"It worked, didn't it?" retorted Robin, as he took another sip of ale from his leather bottle.

Sir Peter was breathing heavily. He asked, "What—what happened?" The men looked at each other and were unsure how to respond.

Martin spoke first.

"Well, we were discussing battle plans and... um, you fainted." "What?!" said Sir Peter in disbelief. He had never fainted in his life before and he didn't remember feeling light-headed.

"Maybe you overexerted yourself with all the fighting and all?" said Ives.

Sir Peter shook his head slightly and furrowed his brow. He couldn't believe what he was hearing. "No, no, that doesn't make any sense. It's almost like I was... somewhere else."

"Maybe you were drunk," said Robin bluntly. Martin and the other men shot Robin a foul glance, to which Robin simply responded, "What?" while taking another sip of ale. Although it was a ridiculous suggestion, Robin's assertion did lead the way to a more credible one.

Tomlin was afraid to ask this of Sir Peter and attempted to say it in the most delicate way possible. "Maybe it's a reaction to all the *plants y*ou used to take when you were a raider in Mylec."

Sir Peter knew what plant Tomlin was referring to, but was surprised Tomlin knew this. The plant is known as the Irakorthar (old tongue for rage inducing) plant, and it grows in certain parts of Mylec. It is known to cause hallucinations and fits of rage. Although it can be used as an anesthetic, it is highly addictive. The closest earthly equivalent would be Henbane (*Hyoscyamus niger*) with the addictive properties of cocaine. The more Sir Peter thought about it, the less it surprised him that Tomlin knew this information about him. When you fight in so many battles, word gets around. Additionally, the symptoms of the Irakorthar plant were blatantly obvious to onlookers, dilated pupils, agitation and, as you can imagine, a quickness to anger. Iiadecans were especially good at keeping tabs on their enemies or anyone they deemed a threat, and someone in Mylec was bound to let some information slip.

Sir Peter had been abusing the plant since he was eight years old, when Brandr first introduced it to him. Brandr told him it would make him more powerful and make killing things easier. The latter was true. In fits of rage, it was certainly easier to disembowel your enemy because one is freed from most inhibitions that would impede such an act, like the burden of conscience, at least for the time being. The prior was most certainly a fabrication. There was very little evidence that Irakorthar increased power in any way, shape, or form. Despite this, Brandr did not intentionally deceive, for he was also an abuser, and it is ultimately believed to be the cause of his death, though this is uncertain. Brandr genuinely believed in the plant's alleged properties, as did other Mylecans. Heggr never took part in such activities. Aslaug made sure of it through her many machinations. Brandr never pressed her on it, believing Heggr to be too weak to reap the benefits of the plant, anyway. Sir Peter did not stop using the plant until his marriage to Lady Branson, who helped wane him off it.

Sir Peter looked at Tomlin and said, "No, I don't think so. I haven't meddled with such things in ages. Besides, Elysant would be devastated if I was still using the plant. I couldn't bear that and trust me she'd know. Besides this is different. It's like a portion of my recollection has been removed… Or maybe it wasn't entirely mine to begin with, yet I still felt it. It's almost like a collective experience of something so horrifying, but I have no memory of it, yet the feeling remains… Ugh, I'm not making any sense."

"No, I feel the same way, minus the whole horrible experience bit," said a young pike man with thick, curly red hair that was somewhat rounded and loosely resembled an afro. He had brown eyes, and freckles. He was lanky and couldn't have been more than sixteen.

Robin studied the boy's visage as though he were seeing him for the first time. Robin peered at the boy, making him uncomfortable. He then said, rather brusquely, "Who the hell is he?"

Sir Peter sighed. Robert scowled at Robin. "He's the new recruit from Sigate. He's been with us the whole bloody time!"

"Really?" Robin was genuinely surprised by this. "Ugh, you're hopeless," said Robert.

"It's quite alright. I'm not that memorable. This is my first war and all, heh heh. Anyway, sorry for the rambling. I'm Kamden, er… Kamden Mason," said Kamden.

"Well, no one needs to know your last name. It's not like you're a bloody Lord, otherwise you wouldn't be sulking around with this lot. Besides, what kind of name is Mason? It's weird. I'd keep it to myself, if I were you, er… er," said Robin.

"Kamden!" Sir Peter said frustratedly. "Right, I was going to say that," said Robin.

Ives shook his head in disapproval, to which Robin replied, "What? I was!"

"You were saying, Kamden?" said Ives.

"Uh, right, well, it's difficult to explain, but it almost feels like we had a discussion at this very spot doing something. I dunno, it all feels strange, like we were going somewhere, but I don't know where," said Kamden.

"I, too, feel out of sorts, like we were somewhere else, now where here," said Martin. The other men felt the same sense of bemusement.

"It's great to philosophize about why we're here, but who's going to wake up the dragon," said Robin.

Sir Peter's eyes widened. "Mavid! Where is he?" Sir Peter rose to his feet. Robin pointed behind Sir Peter. Sir Peter turned around to see the unconscious dragon laying down on a pile of rubble. Sir Peter looked at his men and said, rather half heartily, "Any volunteers?" Knowing full well there would be none. None of the men responded. Sir Peter looked at Tomlin. "Nope, it's bad luck to wake a sleeping dragon. Besides, he likes you," said Tomlin.

Sir Peter approached. "Mavid. King Mavid. Ahem, King Mavid!"

Mavid did not respond. Sir Peter moved closer. When he was in arm's distance, Mavid suddenly awoke from his slumber. He was quite disoriented, much like Sir Peter had been. He roused onto all fours with a bewildered look in his eyes. He stared at the surrounding men, who were slowly stepping away, unsure if Mavid was himself. He said something in what could only be assumed as dragon. "*Carg zzit malza dak.*" [where is this place?] His eyes gravitated to Sir Peter. "Brandr?" He peered at Sir Peter again. "No, no, much too small, Agnarr?"

"It's Peter, remember?" Sir Peter said.

Mavid had a befuddled expression on his face but then said, "Aye, yes, uh, where's the boy?"

Before he could respond, he saw John and William approaching with Carac, Berold and Heward from the eastern wall. John had an angry look on his face which, of course, amused William.

"Uh-oh, it's the mean Franklin," said Robin, referring to John and did his best to appear sober. He turned to Kamden. "Psst, hey Cadwallon."

"Actually, it's Kamden," said Kamden.

"Whatever, I need you to hold something for me before—" "Is that ale?" John interrupted.

"Nope!" Robin said quickly. John gave him an incredulous look, then he turned to Sir Peter and said, "You let him drink alcohol in the middle of a bloody siege?"

"I—uh, I—uh," Sir Peter stammered.

"It's not ale! It's, uh, water. A bowman's got to stay quenched, milord," said Robin.

"Really? Hand it over," said John sternly. "What?" asked Robin. "You heard. Your lord is thirsty. He would like a drink of water," said John, placing emphasis on *water*.

Robin gulped. "Milord, as soon as I—" Robin quickly drank all the contents of the leather bottle, then let out a relieved sighed. John frowned at Robin. Robin laughed nervously.

"Heh-heh, it had maggots. You wouldn't have liked the taste." He then turned to Kamden and whispered, "Thanks for nothing, Cadwell. You really let me down." To which Kamden responded, "Uh, never mind." William found the banter to be quite amusing and struggled to contain his laughter. John turned to William. "I'm glad you find this funny, William. We're in the middle of a siege and our defenders are engaging in idle chit-chat and what I can only assume is drunkenness." He turned to Sir Peter. "Where were you? We searched the entire bailey and suddenly you appear out of nowhere in the same spot we searched."

Before he could respond, Mavid said, "You humans seem to enjoy incessant babbling."

William immediately stopped laughing. His eyes widened and his face lost color.

"By Arda's fucking cock, it talks!"

John rolled his eyes. "Did you not even hear Godfrey?"

"Yeah, but I didn't believe him, at least not that part. Imagine, a talking dragon!"

Mavid was vexed by being referred to as the dragon.

"The dragon has a name and title. It's Mavid, son of Aglar, King of the Beladaric Dragons." He turned to Sir Peter. "Are humans usually this irreverent and, well, stupid?"

This infuriated John, for he felt the creature was being dismissive of him by turning to Sir Peter. "Hey dragon, I'm in charge here. I'm the second son of Lord Albert Franklin, rightful King of Iiadec. Tatum Franklin's sacred blood runs through my veins. Now, I suggest you show me some respect or—"

"See. I'm going to stop you right there, oh sacred second son, before you say whatever it is I think you're going to say. I need you to understand I am a very large, fire-breathing dragon with claws, teeth and scales as hard as breast plates."

John was subdued. "Good point."

After an awkward silence, William said, "So, King Mavid, is it? King. I would assume that would make you male right... so, where's your cock?" There was a collective groan amongst the men apart from Martin. "Ah c'mon. I can't be the only one thinking that?" said William.

Martin said rather timidly, "I thought the same thing, milord, but Tomlin criticized me."

"What should we do now, milord?" asked Carac.

"We wait for Edmund to return from the keep and resume our assault," said John.

"He's been there for a while," said Berold.

"He's probably with Lady Branson," William said jokingly. John was not amused by what William was insinuating and gave him a look of serious disapproval. The grin on William's face vanished rather quickly as a result. Sir Peter was initially bemused by the joke, but did not take too long to connect the dots, though he was not as angered by William's comments as John, mainly because he felt no reason to be worried.

Edmund approached them from the keep. "Took you long enough," said John.

"Err, sorry. Our people had a lot of questions, mostly about the war front."

"Is everyone alright, milord?" asked Ives.

"Oh, yeah. They're naturally scared, but that's to be expected. But Lady Branson and Lord Baker have done well to calm them down, but

I've only been in the barracks. I'm not sure of the situation in the Great Hall," said Edmund.

"Yeah, but mother's with them. They should be fine," said William. "If you don't mind me asking, milord, how are Elysant and Godfrey?" asked Sir Peter.

"Uh, they are very much fine. She was very happy to be reunited with him," said Edmund. This answer pleased Sir Peter.

Edmund realized he forgot to mention something. "Oh, in the Barracks they've found a tunnel system that leads outside the castle."

"An escape route?" asked Heward. "Uh, I think so," said Edmund. "Hopefully they'll never have to use it?" said Ives.

"And they won't have to if we launch a counterattack and end Hector once and for all," replied John.

"Oh, oh, milord, perhaps we should introduce Lord Edmund to King Mavid," said Martin.

"Uh, that's not necessary. We've already met. We, uh, tried to kill each other earlier," said Edmund.

"You can't really hold that against me. I wasn't myself," responded Mavid.

"Yeah, milord, he was drunk," said Robin.

Edmund was confused and was not sure if Robin was being serious when providing such a ludicrous defense.

"You're not helping," said Robert.

"So, what's the plan, oh second son?" said William. "Oh, shut up," retorted John.

After a few moments of deliberating, they came up with a cohesive plan. The men gathered around John.

"King Mavid, you will take out the siege engines outside the castle. They should be close to the barbican that's near the northern wall by now. See to it that they do not come any closer. Once you have completed the task, I want you to defend the keep."

Mavid was befuddled upon hearing this. "Why return to the keep when I could just burn all of Hector's forces to crisp and be done with it?" "Because we don't want to lose our main weapon to a volley of arrow fire. As big and mighty as you might be, Hector still has legions out there and besides, if they discover you have been released from whatever spell they placed you under, you can be sure Hector has a contingency plan. We can't risk you getting close to Hector," said John. He continued speaking, "The bowman among you, you are to take on a more immediate problem."

He turned to Robin. "Are you sober enough to use a bow?"

Before Robin could respond, Robert said, "As sober as he's going to get."

John did not like this answer but realize there was no time to argue given they didn't have the luxury of time. After all, Robin was almost as renowned for his drunkenness as Sir Peter was for his swordsmanship. Robin was also renowned for his skill with a bow, something his drunkenness did not impede, apparently. It was frustrating to John because he believed Robin would be an even better archer, warrior, and soldier if he was not inebriated all the time. A fact that everyone else in Corithni seemed to ignore.

"I guess I'll take it. Anyway, you'll oversee defending the castle from the horde on the eastern wall. Kill as many invaders as you can. Some have reached the ramparts. But fear not, you will be assisted by brave knights. Take the crossbow men with you. Clearing the ramparts will impede Hector's assault but not stop it entirely. He still has masses taking advantage of the weakness in the wall. We need infantrymen to prevent an assault in case they breech the wall. Jupp, Odo. Gather half the pikemen and other infantry to assist you in the task."

"Aye, milord," they said in unison.

"The rest of you will be tasked with defending the keep, in case things don't go our way."

"But, milord, surely Lord Franklin needs assistance at the barbican or northern walls? I may not be skilled with a bow, but I can still use soul manifest techniques that have a range of three hundred feet," said Sir Peter.

John turned to Sir Peter.

"You are the greatest swordsman in Arcadiem. There is no other more capable of defending the keep from my enemies than you. It is where my mother, your wife, your boy, our friends, and many others we hold dear, currently reside," said John.

"And I will defend it with my life."

John placed a hand on Sir Peter's shoulder and said, "I know you will."

With that, the group parted ways with the Franklin brothers heading to the barbican to assist their father along with Carac, Berold and Heward. There was a blackbird perched on top of the keep. It remained oddly still. No one else seemed to notice it. It was hard to tell how long it had been there.

***

There was intense fighting between the knights led by Sir Avery and the Red Vultures, a group of sell swords led by the enigmatic Terrowin. Terrowin's band of sell swords were not like other sell swords in Iiadec. They were in full plate armor and wielded various weapons. Both their weapons and armor were in excellent condition, given the circumstances. They looked newly forged by skilled blacksmiths using advanced techniques. This was quite different from the Rilek Herons, who often went into battle with nothing more than gambesons and wielded weapons that were in poor condition. The full plated armor that the Red Vultures wore was black and had a symbol on it. It appeared to be a silhouette of what could be presumed to be a blood red vulture at the center of the breastplate.

The defenders were on one side in amalgamated rows within the ramparts. With the first rows filled with knights, who were bearing mostly polearms, such as poleaxes, glaives, spears, and halberds. The back rows contained knights wielding shorter length melee weapons of the trauma inducing kind. In other words, weapons whose purpose was to concuss the opponent and later finished them off. Each knight was equipped with a rondel dagger, a dagger designed to be slipped through the gaps in plate armor and chainmail, they were also equipped with a standard longsword with a blade of thirty-six inches with a reinforced tip designed for piercing through chainmail. The Vultures had similar weapons and a similar formation.

The knights and the Vultures were just shy of striking distance from each other, with several on each side feinting thrusts to keep the other at bay. This intense standoff would have to end as Sir Avery, leading the knights wielding a poleaxe, led the charge against the Vultures. Terrowin retaliated by leading his own charge on the side of the Vultures. The two groups collided in a violent melee. Several knights and Vultures were slain in the clash. The various polearms crashed into each other, causing them to point in various directions. Some skyward or angled slightly, while others pointed at their respected targets. There was a cornucopia of weapons being utilized. As mentioned previously, polearm weapons such as spears with various sized and shape heads, to halberds, to bills, to glaives, poleaxes and shorter melee weapons such as spiked clubs, maces, battleaxes, longswords, and war hammers. Polearm bearers were more restricted in movement due to the limited size of the ramparts and being so close to the enemy. In addition, they were in close proximity to their allies, so they were limited to mostly thrusting motions. This meant very little cutting with the spear or not being able to utilize the full swing of a halberd or bill. This is where those with melee weapons came in handy, taking advantage of the fact that they were able to maneuver around in tight spaces, such as on the ramparts. Several knights and Vultures resorted to half-swording. While others resorted to using blunt force weapons. At this point, the formation between the Vultures and defenders were blurred and they coalesced into a ferocious brawl. This meant some people were cut off from support of their allies, leaving them exposed and vulnerable to enemy attacks.

Amongst such people was Sir Ryder. One of the Red Vultures had struck Sir Ryder in the head with a war hammer. The blow severely damaged his helmet, resulting in a sizable dent to the side of it. But that was the least of his worries. The blow nearly knocked him unconscious as he was sent to his knees. Another knight attempted to come to his aide, but was quickly struck down with a battle axe to the neck. As for Sir Ryder, he met a gruesome end, repeatedly struck in the chest by the back end of a hammer in quick succession by his aggressor until it tore through his chest plate, piercing through his mail, arming doublet and eventually his flesh. The sharp end of the weapon reached his heart, but not before shattering his sternum and ribcage. Before Sir Ryder could even react, the aggressor pulled the war hammer from his chest by placing his foot on Sir Ryder's chest plate and using both hands to wrench the hammer free. Sir Ryder collapsed on the ground, surrounded by a pool of his own blood. This besieger with the war hammer walked over Sir Ryder's lifeless body and towards Sir Avery, who was engaged in close combat with Terrowin in the center of the ramparts, with both the knights and Red Vultures aiding their respective leaders. This Vulture was planning a surprise attack on Sir Avery, who was unaware he was behind him. When he was within striking distance, he raised his war hammer and brought it down hard. It hit something else, however. The blade of Sir Baret. Sir Baret pushed his opponent's weapon forward.

"Coward," Sir Baret said. The Vulture's balance shifted slightly because of the counter strike, and Sir Baret took advantage of the opening. Striking with the cross guard, he delivered a horizontal blow to the side of the Vulture's head. The Vulture stumbled backwards. Sir Baret pursued him but was struck in the back with a flanged mace. The Vulture wielding the war hammer retreated into the crowd.

Sir Baret could feel the blunt impact force affecting his internal organs, yet he did not flinch. Before he could retaliate, he found himself broken off from his group, surrounded by the Vultures. There were four of them. Two wielding battleaxes and the other two wielding flanged maces. Sir Baret had his back facing a crenel of the battlements adjacent to the staircase that would have given access to the bailey. These besiegers were not concerned with killing him but would not hesitate to if they had to. No, instead they intended to breach the castle walls. He could see this in their eyes. Sir Baret could not allow this, and he intended to defend the walls from these besiegers even if it cost him his life. The four besiegers charged at Sir Baret. Sir Baret performed a murder stroke on one besieger, this resulted in a sizeable dent in the opponent's head causing the assailant to concuss and drop his mace. Unfortunately, for Sir Baret, half the cross guard on his longsword was damaged from performing the technique too many times on his previous opponents. Meaning, if he wanted to perform another murder stroke, he would have to rely on the pommel or other sections of the hilt that were not damaged.

Other assailants attacked Sir Baret simultaneously. Sir Baret did his best to parry their attacks, using his sword to shield his head from cuts and swings. Additionally, he guarded the gaps in his armor. His armor prevented serious injury from most of their attacks, but that defense was waning and it had taken quite a beating. Sir Baret managed to stab one of his overzealous aggressors in the neck, through a gap between the armor. Although the Vultures and knights wore plate armor, the gaps in the armor, which made them particularly vulnerable, were being protected by mostly mail. The chainmail attached to the pig- faced bascinets (the helms worn by both the knights and the Vultures) offered limited protection in the way of the throat, neck and parts of the shoulders. This was most likely a design choice to support mobility, which would be crucial on the battlefield when encountering magic wielders and elementals. If you're wondering why the knights don't use more advanced helmets, like the sallet or an armet, since those helmets offer better protection and come with better neck protection in the form of a bevor or a gorget respectively, the reason is those helms and armors are relatively new inventions, although used more prevalently in other parts of Arcadiem. In addition, very few have been tested in the field of battle like the bascinet chainmail combo. (A gorget could be used with a bascinet, but it would prove cumbersome to the wearer, adding heft to an already weighty helm. And then there's the issue of mass production. New designs required greater fees because not many blacksmiths in Iiadec knew how to make those new helms.)

He quickly pulled his blade out of the Vulture's throat. It was not long before his other pursuers were on him, attacking relentlessly to avenge their fallen comrade. The two besiegers swung at him with their battle axes. Sir Baret, half-swording, assumed a high guard to parry the oncoming attack. Then from the bind, he quickly pulled out and switch to low guard to parry the other attack. His enemies kept him playing defense, constantly blocking their attacks, and returning very few of his own.

Either through carelessness or fatigue, most likely the latter, one of his axe wielding adversaries was able to place a well time chop to Sir Baret's helmet as he parried late. Given the nature of the swing, in other words, it being a straight chop instead of a slicing cut as battle axes are designed to be most effective at slicing cut, the axe only left a superficial scratch on the helm, but it was enough to disorient Sir Baret. His opponents took advantage of this and they delivered several cuts to his torso and chest, which Sir Baret did his best to avoid by parrying and dodging. Unfortunately for him, there was little space in which to perform these actions effectively. As a result, he found himself losing footing and teetering over the battlements and was about to fall on the staircase below. He dug the heel of his back foot into the ground and stood firm. He was in a precarious position for he was one of the few things that stood between the battlements and the inner castle. Other besiegers had joined in the effort to displace Sir Baret, along with the besieger that he had previously knocked down. It was possible they had caught wind of what their allies were doing. The knights soon came to Sir Baret's aid. They fought valiantly to keep the besiegers away. One knight, in particular, hit the besiegers attacking Sir Baret in the base of the skull with a mace. The two besiegers collapsed. The knight didn't have time to finish them off before he himself was struck in the face with a war hammer. The war hammer was wielded by the same Vulture that Sir Baret had initially pursued for attempting to attack Sir Avery.

The blow from the hammer was so powerful it caused the knights visor to open momentarily. The Vulture attacked the knight again. This time the knight was ready for him and defended with his mace. Sir Baret tried to intervene but was grazed in the neck by a spear thrust and was forced into combat with other Vultures crowding that section of the ramparts. He was, of course, aided by the other knights who helped diminish the enemy efforts.

The hammer wielding Vulture managed to disarm the knight, catching him off guard by hitting the knight's gauntlet, forcing the knight to drop his weapon. The Vulture saw an opening and swung his war hammer down at the knight. The knight was not completely defenseless and he acted quickly. He stopped the blow midway by grabbing his aggressor's arm and using his free hand to pull out his rondel. With the dagger the knight stabbed the Vulture in the armpit and twisted the blade so that it would puncture his enemy's heart. The knight then pried the war hammer from his recently slain adversary's dead hands. He then proceeded to slay six more Vultures with his newly acquired weapon and the assistance of other knights. He did this through a combination of concussing his opponents with the war hammer and quickly finishing them off with his rondel through a gap in the neck or armpit. He managed to even puncture through one of his opponent's armor with the spiked part of the hammer. Something he did sparingly to avoid the weapon getting stuck. The knight mostly used the hammer face of the weapon to attack the joints in his opponents' armor to impede movement. He saw who he assumed was Sir Baret, (not many knights were 6-foot-8) with several other knights struggling with a group of besiegers. Sir Baret was half-swording against several of his foes. His longsword was his only weapon besides a rondel. The sword looked damaged, particularly the hilt.

Many of the other knights were aggregated at the center of the amparts fighting Terrowin's forces. The knight went to readjust his visor, since it was slightly misaligned from the blow from the war hammer and was negatively affecting his vision. Then in that split second, he heard Sir Baret scream his name, "Audley!"

Almost instinctively, Sir Audley ducked, and he narrowly escaped a blow from a mace. Sir Audley turned around to face his opponent. They traded blows for a moment until Sir Audley was able to hook his opponent's arm with the spike part of the hammer to bring it down. Then, while holding his opponent's arm in place, he delivered a quick thrust of the hammer. It struck his opponent in the throat. He wasted no time; he twisted his aggressor's arm in a way that exposed the inner elbow. He then used his knee to strike his opponent's outer elbow, causing the joint to overextend, resulting in the Vulture dropping his mace. Sir Audley then proceeded to strike with the sharp part of the war hammer to puncture his opponent's inner elbow. After a brief struggle, his opponent was able to break free of his grasp.

The Vulture took out his longsword, which he could only wield with one hand due to severely injuring his arm. With his blade inverted, he delivered a languid downward vertical cut; he was exhausted from loss of blood which Sir Audley took advantage of. Sir Audley easily evaded the attack and his opponent collapsed on the ground. Sir Audley removed his adversary's visor and stabbed him in the face with his rondel. He turned to Sir Baret, who was standing with the other knights over several slain Vultures. Sir Baret had acquired a new longsword from one of his fallen foes. They looked towards the center of the ramparts where Sir Avery and the other knights fought tirelessly against the Vultures. Neither side was letting up. Sir Baret and Sir Audley nodded to each other. Sir Audley placed his war hammer on his belt and unsheathed his longsword. He figured, given the nature of the melee, it would be more beneficial to have a weapon that had more reach and could compete with all the polearms. Sir Baret and Sir Audley half-sworded their way through the ramparts with the assistance of the other knights. When they got to the center, they saw Sir Avery. They recognized him because he was not wearing a helmet, because he had previously given it to Edmund. Whether it was a testament to his skill or luck, he had not been impaled in the face. Several polearms were used to push unsuspecting Vultures over the battlements to their deaths by thrusting diagonally. The Vultures utilized similar tactics.

Reader, as you can imagine from the usage of pole weapons, the two opposing forces had returned to their formation, at least partially, for they knew veering away too much would most likely result in more death. They were in striking range of each other, however.

Sir Avery was at the center of the brawl, fighting with what could be assumed to be Terrowin and his men. Assumed because Sir Avery called his name out before the second clash. He most likely saw Terrowin's cloudy eye through Terrowin's visor. Sir Avery directed several thrusts at Terrowin, which Terrowin expertly parried with his halberd.

There was an exchange of thrusts and parries between the knights and the Vultures. No sweeping cuts due to the limited space every warrior was given. This repetitive cycle was broken when one of the knights was impaled in the gut by a halberd. The weapon penetrated through the armor before getting stuck. It was able to get pass mail and gambeson and critically injured the knight, but the weapon remained stuck in the knight's armor, leaving the assailant open to attack. The assailant was stabbed in the neck by a spear with a reinforced head. He eventually perished, but his death set off a chain reaction of events. Several knights and Vultures were knocked down by polearms. Some were slain. One knight, with several thrusts of his spear, pushed a Vulture over the battlements. That Vulture fell to his death. Several were impaled in armpits, necks, and sections of the shoulders. As serious as these injuries may seem, keep in mind most of the polearm's thrusts were halted by the plate armor. Nonetheless, they helped to impede each other's advancements.

The knights and Vultures, at least the ones that were still standing, got into a sparring match. At the center of it were Terrowin and Sir Avery. While they were fighting, each of their allies on respective sides prevented each other from intervening by deflecting any stray thrusts or attacks from coming in the way of their leaders. Sir Avery and Terrowin also parried other attacks directed at them, while mainly focusing on each other. Terrowin and Sir Avery were in measure, as you can imagine.

Sir Avery thrusted his poleaxe at Terrowin, which Terrowin set aside with his halberd. Sir Avery, with his poleaxe tucked in the armpit, thrust anew from the bind at his opponent's mail protected armpit. Terrowin got wise to what Sir Avery was attempting and quickly switched to a low guard, thereby protected his once exposed armpit.

Sir Avery's attack landed on Terrowin's plate protected shoulder. To prevent his weapon from completely veering off, Sir Avery grasped his weapon tightly and redirected his weapon towards his opponent. Naturally, he found himself in a bind to which he performed a circular disengagement. He then performed a thrust toward Terrowin's mail protected neck, which Terrowin blocked by performing a high guard. Sir Avery responded by attacking with the handle of his weapon, causing Terrowin to stumble slightly. Taking advantage of this, Sir Avery quickly swung his poleaxe around and delivered a vertical cut while Terrowin was still in high guard. The blow broke Terrowin's guard and struck him in the helmet, leaving a scratch on the canonical part of the helm. Terrowin, still holding his weapon, was forced into a low guard, where the axe part of his halberd was right behind Sir Avery's front foot. Before Sir Avery could deliver the killing blow, Terrowin hooked Sir Avery's leg, causing him to lose balance and fall on his back and at the mercy of his enemy. His other allies were unable to help him due to being preoccupied with their own battles.

You see, during the second skirmish, lines were broken a second time. The Vultures advanced forward and slew several knights. Especially the ones in close proximity to Sir Avery. In other words, Sir Avery was surrounded by Vultures and blocked off from his allies. Sir Audley, Sir Baret, and several other knights were blocked off by a wall of Vultures, as well. One particular Vulture, wielding a bill, had single-handedly killed seven knights, hence the other knights were hesitant to approach him.

Terrowin looked at Sir Avery and said, "You should have worn a helmet." Terrowin had barely moved an inch when he felt a sharp pain in his armpit. The pain caused him to immediately drop his halberd. He observed the wound. It was from a longbow arrow. Blood oozed from the wound, and Terrowin found himself unable to utilize his injured arm. The arrow came from below. Shot by Robin the bowman, accompanied by twenty-nine other bowmen and six crossbow men.

Before the besiegers could respond, a barrage of arrows ascended upon them. Their helmets were designed to repel arrows, hence the conical shape, and the arrows did not have the penetrative power to pierce plate armor, but they did manage to startle the besiegers enough for Sir Avery to escape and for the knights to regroup.

As Robin and his companions ascended the staircase of the wall. Robin slung his longbow across his shoulders diagonally, similar to a rifle. He pulled out his buckler in his left hand and arming sword in his right which he inverted. The other bowmen did the same, though some wielded different melee weapons, mostly battle axes and war hammers, with occasional bastard swords or maces. The six-crossbow men left their crossbows at the bottom of the stairs and equipped their melee weapons. All the men were armed with a bollock dagger. When they got to the stairs, they found the besiegers were retreating slightly, despite having nowhere to go. This, of course, made sense since their numbers had dwindled down to a mere seventeen. And the remaining twenty-two knights had gained thirty-five reinforcements.

"They're retreating," said Martin.

"Yeah, but we must be vigilant. We can't allow them to enter the castle," said Ives.

The two forces collided once again. The knights, with their reinforcements, overwhelmed the Vultures. This did not, however, completely stop the Vultures who took advantage of the fact that the bowmen and arbalist did not wear plate armor and most weren't as skilled in close quarter combat as the knights. As a result, the Vultures slew several of them. The Vultures also shielded their ailing leader from the approaching knights and their reinforcements. Most of the Vultures bearing polearms had been slain except for the infamous Vulture wielding a bill, who managed to kill five bowmen and injure two knights. The others, bearing polearms, were defending Terrowin.

Tomlin, who wielded a war hammer, found himself at odds with a rather large besieger wielding a spike club. The besieger swung relentlessly at him. Tomlin did his best to parry the attacks, but he was clearly outmatched. Then, out of some stroke of luck, the sharp part of the war hammer got stuck on the spikes of the club. Tomlin was able to wrench the club from his unsuspected opponent's hand. Before he could respond with an attack of his own, the besieger front kicked him in the stomach, which sent him on his back and nearly knock the wind out of him. The besieger quickly pulled out his longsword, ready to finish the disoriented Tomlin off. Martin came to his aid and hit the besieger in his mail protected neck with the thin side of his buckler, nearly smashing the besieger's Adam's apple. The besieger stumbled backwards, struggling to maintain his already low oxygen levels due to fighting in armor. The besieger was still in range of Tomlin's war hammer. Tomlin, who was still on the ground, struck the besieger in the groin with the spike side of the hammer. Before the besieger could even cry out in agony, he was shoved by Martin and hurled over the battlements to his death.

Robin fought with his brother Robert, with the aid of Sir Baret and Sir Audley, against the bill man and other besiegers wielding melee weapons. Robert had been wounded by the bill man. The polearm had grazed his side. This was not enough to impede Robert. The bill man thrusted downward at Robert from a high guard. Robert set the attack aside with his buckler. The bill man quickly pulled out to thrust anew. The thrust was aimed at Robert's chest. Robert quickly grabbed the weapon and fastened it tightly under his armpit, narrowly avoiding the blade. The bill man could not wrench his weapon free. While the bill man was temporarily immobilized, Robin stabbed him in the neck with his bollock dagger. The dagger was stuck between the rings of his opponent's chainmail; hence, Robin did not bother trying to pull it out. Instead, he focused his attention on other enemies. The besieger released his grasp on his weapon and fell to his knees. Much to Robin's surprise, and the surprise of the other defenders, the besieger was not dead. With the dagger still lodged in his neck, he sprung to his feet with surprising vigor and flailed his arms about wildly, knocking Robin over. He drew his longsword but before he could attack Sir Baret, half-swording, hit the besieger in the head with the pommel of his longsword by performing a murder stroke. The besieger stumbled backwards, tripping over Robin. He fell from the battlements to his apparent death.

Although the defenders had lost many, they were able to dwindle the besieger's forces to seven, including the injured Terrowin. The defenders now had a total of forty men. Sir Avery and the other knights were able to slay the remaining Vultures guarding Terrowin. It was shocking that Terrowin was even still alive, given the duration of the fighting and the nature of the injury he received. Nonetheless, Terrowin persevered, holding his longsword in his left hand while his right arm remained limp from the blood loss.

"You've fought valiantly, now drop your blade and I shall give you a swift death," said Sir Avery.

Terrowin removed his helmet. "A soldier, a warrior, a knight, a sell sword is no different from a blade. A tool that is used to serve the desire of its master."

"And Hector is your master?" Sir Avery retorted. Terrowin did not answer Sir Avery's question and instead answered another one.

"When the blade has served its purpose, becomes dulled or shattered, it can be reforged, or it can die. Which one is up to the will of its creator," "Do not mince words with this deceiver. End him now," said Sir Baret.

Sir Avery walked towards Terrowin to do just that. Then suddenly the man with the spiral mask appeared from out of thin air, same eye color, same rotating irises. He stood between Terrowin and the defenders.

"An enemy castor," said Sir Audley, the, bowmen readied their bows, and the knights unsheathe their weapons. The masked man pulled out his wand attached to his sword scabbard. But before he could draw, Robin shot the weapon out of his hand. Several other archers shot upon this enigmatic figure, but it was to no avail, for the arrows were simply replaced by roses when reaching what appeared to be his body. This is a magic wielder technique in traditional magic (not hokraft, or faux magic but standard magic) known as Biligas (*bill-li-gas*), which is old tongue for replacement or substitution. It usually involves replacing an object with another while occupying the replaced object's space. Biligas technique usually involves immobile, inorganic objects. That is precisely why it is so unusual that this magic wielder was able to replace several arrows at once, given the speed with which they were traveling, with an organic object. It was a testament to his skill. Because such a feat should be nearly impossible, requiring impeccably quick thinking and timing, factoring in the complexity of the technique.

The men were dumbfounded by what they observed. They had never seen magic used in such a way. From their perspective, the masked man turned their arrows into roses. The masked man suddenly created what appeared to be twenty versions of himself, with his exact likeness instantaneously. The archers shot arrows at the duplicates, but all their projectiles went right through them.

"Wraiths, we need Ulric. We mustn't engage them any longer, for we may get cursed!" cried Sir Baret.

"We cannot afford to yield the wall if the castor summoned them. We'll just have to find him, kill him, and relinquish them. C'mon, there are still plenty of men left charge!" said Sir Avery.

Before most of the defenders could attack, a one-handed battle-axe flew through the air and struck the masked man square in the chest. All the duplicates vanished, and he collapsed on the floor motionless and presumably dead. The other defenders were shocked. Not that an axe was thrown, but that it actually hit its intended target and that it was Martin who threw it.

Sir Avery looked at Martin, quite perplexed. "How did you—" "Faux magic, Sir. Even wraiths cast shadows. Grandma once told me shadows are difficult for a castor to replicate when performing faux magic because of their dynamic nature. In the end, it was an amateur mistake that did him in. The only shadow cast was his own. That gave everything away," Martin interrupted.

"But why the axe?" asked Sir Audley.

"Well, I figured since the arrows didn't work, then why not try an axe? Plus, he didn't expect it. Nobody did, really," replied Martin.

"Wow, you're quite the warrior, Martin," said Tomlin. Martin smiled. "Thanks."

Sir Avery shifted his focus towards Terrowin. "No more tricks, this is the end for you," said Sir Avery.

"It is the end for all of us," replied Terrowin.

With a vertical cut from his longsword. Sir Avery slew Terrowin. Suddenly the defenders felt uneasy. A sensation that permeated the battlements which they occupied, but they did not have time to fully register Terrowin's words, yet they somehow thought they were more than just nonsense; they had a deeper meaning.

"Archers, arbalist, assume positions!" shouted Sir Avery. They did just that, with the crossbow men retrieving their weapons at the bottom of the staircase. The bowmen peered over the battlements only to see a siege engine was close to breaching the wall.

"Fire upon that siege engine. It must not break through our defenses. One opening for the enemy could mean certain doom for us!" cried Sir Avery.

The bowmen and crossbow men rained a volley of arrows on the battering ram while avoiding fire from enemy archers. The roof of the battering ram shielded those it housed from arrows. The knights hurled down enemy soldiers at the siege engine. Still, that did not deter the enemy. While firing his crossbow, Tomlin said, "If only we could set the blasted thing on fire. Where's an elemental when you need one?"

***

The infantrymen consisted of mostly pike men, waiting anxiously by the eastern wall while it continued to crack gradually.

"The wall won't hold!" shouted Kamden.

"I can see that!" retorted Jupp. There was a loud thud. It was the sound of the battering ram hitting the wall and it was cracking. The men braced themselves upon hearing this.

"I think I can fix it!" said Kamden.

"What!" Jupp shouted over the raucous noise.

"I said, I think I can fix the wall!" Kamden replied.

"How? Castles can't be manipulated, even by elementals. Unless you have enough rocks from the outside to reseal the wall, there's no fixing it. We'll have to fight and hope for the best!" shouted Jupp.

Before Kamden could respond, Odo interrupted. "I think we better call Sir Peter and the rest of them; things are looking dire."

"We are the first line of defense between the castle and the enemy. If we abandon the wall, they will slip through, and the castle will be overrun!" replied Jupp.

After successive banging sounds, the eastern wall finally gave in. It was only a narrow opening, obscured mostly by piles of rubble, but it was enough for the besiegers to slip through. The pikemen slaughtered anyone who slipped through the narrow opening, but the enemy was relentless and came in the multitudes. Even though besiegers were blocked by debris, they did their best to scour through stone and gravel to get to the other side. Suddenly, some of the debris on the ground was suspended in the air. The men were surprised to see Kamden's pike on the floor with his hands on the ground.

"Get back!" He told the infantry men. They understood and did as they were told. Kamden proceeded to pelt the enemy with the rocks. The flying debris pelted the besiegers with several of them slain due to being to hit by high velocity stone projectiles. This was not the end of Kamden's assault on the besiegers. He clumped large amounts of debris together and began repairing the wall. In the process, several of the besiegers were crushed to death by big stone boulders. The crack in the wall was eventually sealed by Kamden's makeshift wall, and many of the besiegers that initially breached the wall were either killed or trapped behind mountains of rubble.

The men were bewildered by what they had just witnessed. Jupp turned to Kamden, who was quite fatigued.

"How the hell did you do that?"

Kamden sighed with exhaustion. "My ancestors helped build this castle. They were part of the builder pack."

This answer did not suffice, but Jupp did not want to press Kamden any further. (A builder's pack consists of the owner of a property, usually meaning a castle though not always, and a group of architects, colloquial name builders. These individuals place a seal on the castle or building that requires all the individuals or descendants involved to remove. The seal is in place to prevent any terrestrial manipulator from destroying or drastically altering the castle. The reason Kamden's, and by extension Sarah's, terrestrial manipulation only involves one party, one builder to break the seal, is because they are a descendent of the master builder. If you have the seal for the master builder, you can unlock all other seals.)

"I'm not sure what that means, but if you have more tricks like that up your sleeve then maybe we aren't entirely fucked," said Odo as he placed a hand on Kamden's shoulder.

"Were do we go from here?" asked one of the pikemen.

"No use standing idly by. Let's report back to the keep and explain the situation," said Odo.

Jupp's eyes gravitated toward the remains of the broken siege engine buried under a pile of rubble.

"No, we shall remain here. I heard the enemy castors summoned that contraption (referring to the siege engine) close to our walls. If they do it again, we must be prepared," said Jupp.

Odo looked at Kamden, concerned. He whispered to Jupp. "I don't think the boy will be doing that trick again. Moving all those rocks seems to have taken a lot out of him."

"Then we'll have to rely on more traditional methods of attack," replied Jupp.

Kamden was out of earshot, but he could tell the men were talking about him. It was clear that it was likely due to his involvement in the events that had just transpired. What was unclear was if what he had done was wrong. Had the others never heard of a builder's pack? Kamden doubted his prowess with terrestrial manipulation was anything of note. After all, he was not as good as his sister. Maybe due to having less skill or less soul manifest. Upon pondering such information, Kamden felt a sharp pain on the back of his hand, like something was being etched on the back of his right hand. He removed his leather glove, and that is when he saw it. The mark. His eyes widened.

"This must be the mark of the Mason," he whispered.

This rumored mark is bore by every Mason and is activated when breaking a builder's pack seal. His ailing mother told him this before she passed. She was quite delirious at the time of her death, so Kamden did not know what to make of the information. His mother, Fleta Mason, claimed his father, Dean Mason, was a renowned builder who traveled the world and had to leave the family for undisclosed reasons. Kamden always took this as his father not wanting a family. Kamden did not remember his father. When he would ask Sarah, she would say her memory of him was quite scant. She only remembers her father singing her a lullaby and her mother would chime in from time to time.

Unbeknownst to Kamden, Jupp and Odo approached him. Upon seeing them, Kamden was startled and quickly put his glove back on, thus concealing the mark.

"Kamden, I trust you're in good spirits after defeating so many foes single handedly? And repairing the eastern wall," said Jupp.

Kamden, still flustered, answered, "Uh, yeah, sure. Uh, I mean—" "No need to explain yourself. Listen, we were deliberating with some of the men, and we've decided it would be best if you explained the situation at the eastern wall to Sir Peter," interrupted Odo.

"Wait, what? I... I don't think that's a good idea," replied Kamden. "There's no need to be bashful. Tell him of your heroism and there's a good chance you might be promoted to knight," said Jupp.

The color suddenly went from Kamden's face upon hearing the word knight. The last thing he wanted to do was any more fighting, something he typically detested. Additionally, he didn't know how to explain how he repaired the wall using terrestrial manipulations without getting disconcerting looks from the men like he was getting now. Jupp placed his hand on Kamden's shoulder.

"Whatever it is you did, you saved us and because of your actions, we might survive this siege. Your deeds deserve to be noticed."

Kamden nodded and picked up his pike from the floor and went to deliver the message.

When Kamden was out of earshot Odo said, "That was definitely hokraft. Did you see the strange mark that appeared on his hand? No way that's normal."

"How do you think Sir Peter will take it?" asked Odo.

"He'll probably spin the story in the boy's favor, make him look less guilty. Ah, he'll know what lie to spin to keep the boy safe," replied Jupp. "He didn't seem to know he was performing hokraft," said Odo. "He's from Sigate. They're a farming village. They are ignorant of many of the laws of Corithni and still, I don't think Lord Franklin will punish him for saving lives, including our own," said Jupp. "But will never know for sure," replied Odo.

[*Outside the Northern walls of the castle in the battlefield a few moments earlier*]

Mavid flew over the barbican at a breakneck pace. This startled the individuals within the barbican. This included Lord Franklin (The one in the vision), Sir Ulric, Sir Cedric Baudry, Sir Merek, and others. He soared to the battlefield burning many besiegers on the way. As he approached The Defiler, he was met with some resistance, but nothing he could not handle. He faced a volley of arrows, which he easily evaded. Next, the ones operating the defiler started firing several rounded stone projectiles at Mavid. After six attempts to hit him, that Mavid easily evaded. He eventually set the siege engine and its operators on fire. Mavid flew over to Blood bringer after raining fire on several besiegers on the way. What he saw bemused him.

The besiegers operating the trebuchet were in full plate armor, so were the men operating the six ballistae adjacent to the siege engine. It was almost like Hector was prepared for Mavid's assault, but how could this be? He thought. Should they not be more concerned with storming the castle, rather than making a contingency plan for him? Furthermore, the question remained, how did Hector's forces prepare a stratagem like this in such a short time? He couldn't imagine they were just carrying six ballistae in the midst of battle, just in case his supposed hex backfired. That would be counterintuitive. Then it occurred to him that those blasted castors were summoning objects of war to the battlefield. Before Mavid had time to contemplate more on his surroundings, a round projectile narrowly missed his head. He flew higher into the sky to avoid the upcoming projectiles from the ballistae. It had steel tipped bodkin-type, ten-pound arrows. The besiegers aimed for the shallow parts of Mavid's skin, such as the nostrils, the eyes, the inner ears, and the wings.

A ballista bolt grazed past Mavid's neck. Mavid did not flinch, and the projectile did not even leave a mark. Mavid soared higher into the sky and set all the approaching projectiles ablaze. He set his eyes on the besiegers operating the siege engine. With his nostrils flaring, he reared his head back and spewed a great flame of a bluish hue. The flame was so intense that it caused the steel armor that the besiegers were wearing to melt and attach to their skin. They screamed in horror as they were burnt to a pile of metallic ash. Blood bringer met its end in the blaze as well. Mavid also set the ballistae on fire, along with their operators. Upon seeing such a display, many of the infantry ran for their lives.

Since fewer projectiles were flying, other than from a few pesky long bowmen, which Mavid dispatched quickly before descending slightly from the sky, he was able to navigate the skies more easily. He peered into the battlefield, searching for any signs of castors. He knew very little about magic wielders, but what he did know was that when they summoned something, they usually had to remain still and would stay in close proximity to the location of the object's designated summoning area. Though it was possible they fled as soon as they'd figured out he had awakened from his trance and was after them. There was very little a castor could do against a winged dragon, especially one from Beldar.

Hector's forces, while initially fleeing, did not entirely retreat. But why was this? Mavid thought. Surely, the war was lost on Hector's part. They had lost several men and two crucial Siege engines and not to mention they have to deal with him. A logical thing to do would be to retreat and gather more forces to retake the castle and yet his men, though cowering, did not retreat. Mavid wondered what kind of hold Hector had over them. Mavid did not see any form of summoning on the battlefield, which either meant the castors had given up summoning or they were hiding and trying to be more discrete.

Mavid was several feet in the air but noticed the men were no longer attacking him, but instead appeared to be anticipating something. Mavid descended slightly to see eight magic wielders placing their hands on the ground like they were summoning something. Something large.

"Castors!" exclaimed Mavid.

He did not wait for them to summon whatever they were summoning. He swooped down and cast orange fire upon the castors and the men that surrounded them. A great conflagration ensued, and embers of smoke soared in the sky. When the flames eventually dissipated, smoke gradually took its place. The smoke slowly receded, revealing a monstrous figure. A giant winged black dog beast with red eyes and three heads, almost as large as Mavid. A dog that large could only mean hokraft was somehow involved, and now the beast was bound to the magic wielders either through soul exchange or blood (This bond involves sacrificing the soul of either the wielder or the beast, hence they will share a soul, which usually involves a stronger, longer lasting bond, or blood sacrifice—a constant blood donation to keep the dark beast subservient. Keep in mind, reader, as aforementioned in the prologue, this is considered a form of hokraft).

Much to Mavid's surprise, the beast remained unscathed by Mavid's flames, as did the magic wielders it shielded.

Mavid gasped. "A Hellhound. I haven't seen one of those things in ages." (Hellhound is a colloquial and somewhat erroneous term. The reason being is that they don't necessarily come from hell, not that such a place has been confirmed to exist. Though there have been several artificial places created that fit a similar description. Nonetheless, hellhounds are not demons, they are sentient. Their origins are unknown, although there are several theories, most of which claim they are the result of powerful hokraft and soul sickness.)

The beast looked directly at Mavid. Then it became invisible. This made Mavid uneasy. Unaware when and where his enemy was, he looked around aimlessly. Suddenly, he felt a sharp pain in his tail, like a bite.

Mavid looked down to see the three headed beast. Its center head had its teeth clenched tightly on to Mavid's tail. Mavid struggled to maintain the weight of the beast. He flapped his wings upward, but the beast was determined to drag him down. After an intense struggle, Mavid eventually clawed at the beast's face with his hind legs. The other heads of the beast thrashed about wildly. This proved useful, as Mavid was able to wrench his tail free, this, however, was not the end of their violent conflict. When they were separated, Mavid took the opportunity to breathe blue flame upon the beast. The beast narrowly evaded the flames with a few embers singeing a small section of its wing. It was more of minor agitation than serious injury. Mavid breathed more blue flames into the sky. The beast again evaded the flames by swirling underneath them. The creature once again turned invisible.

"Not again," Mavid said frustratedly. Before Mavid could react, the beast was upon him. Sprawled on his back, the beast's claws and teeth had dug into his wings and back. Mavid flailed about wildly, trying to shake the troublesome beast off. One of the heads took a chunk out of Mavid's neck and drew blood. Mavid swung his head about wildly and roared in response. He eventually shook the beast off him. The beast was propelled forward and spiraled through the air. Mavid delivered a devastating claw strike to the creature, permanently blinding one of the heads and severely injuring the other two. The creature retreated and turned invisible again. Mavid was prepared, however, his ears perked up as he would now rely on sound rather than sight to detect the movements of his adversary. The beast came at him, attempting to strike from above, but Mavid could hear the flapping of its wings and dodged the oncoming attack. The beast gave up on hiding and all three heads were visibly frustrated with nostrils flaring. The creature decided to use a more direct approach. It quickly flew toward Mavid, roaring ferociously. Mavid spewed blue flames directly at the creature. The beast was engulfed in flames for a moment. Yet, much to Mavid's surprise, it had not turned into a pile of ashes. Instead, the creature rose from the flame with minor but visible injuries, particularly on its torso and faces.

The creature, while escaping the flames, delivered a vertical claw strike to Mavid's snout. This caused Mavid to wince. With his eyes temporarily closed, the enemy pursued Mavid, but he was prepared. He deflected two oncoming strikes with his front legs. The two titans then proceeded to exchange blows, with Mavid eventually gaining the upper hand. He grabbed a hold of his opponent by sinking his teeth into one of its necks. He then proceeded to take a large bite out of his adversary. He drew copious amounts of blood as he pierced the jugular vein.

The beast recoiled in anguish, screaming, "Oh, master, I have failed you for I—" That head of the beast soon succumbed to his wounds.

The other heads pulled away from Mavid's grasp and retreated into the distance with their lifeless kin. Two heads remained, the blind head and the troublesome center head.

"You've killed our brother, you supercilious lizard. You'll surely pay," said the center head.

"Supercilious? I didn't know your kind knew such words," Mavid teased.

"Do not mock me, dragon. You claimed to be a king, but I know beasts cannot be king. Only man and like kind can be king," retorted the center head.

"Who told you that? The one called Hector?" said Mavid.

The center head seemed perplexed upon hearing that name. This reaction also bemused Mavid. Mavid was beginning to think that perhaps this creature was under a similar hex that had befallen him. It clearly was unaware of Hector's influence. Before Mavid could contemplate further, the blind head interrupted.

"Brother, we don't mince words with the enemy. It is not the hellhound way. Have you forgotten what he has done to me? What he has done to Ceratith (CERA-TITHE)?!"

The nostrils of the beast flared. Mavid could see that they would not listen to reason, which was understandable given the injuries he had inflicted on them.

The beast charged at Mavid, no longer relying on tricks but a direct approach that involved close quarter combat. Which, for quadrupedal beasts flying in the air, means tooth and claw. The beast was relentless, clawing and biting at any opening it could find from Mavid's neck, torso, face and wings. Mavid tried to retaliate but most of his strikes missed or were partial hits, equally as ineffective. The beast was being more aggressive but fighting smarter than before and Mavid was getting tired and sloppy from prolonged combat. He knew he had to end the fight now, not just for his sake but for the castle as well. The more time he spent up here the more time the besiegers had time to find a way to advance upon the castle. But with very little hope of his enemy letting up, things where not looking good for Mavid.

He had several lacerations to his torso and while his wings were obviously still operational, due to wounds inflicted on them, it pained him to move them. Furthermore, his enemy was fighting at a renewed intensity now that Mavid had slain its brother. Fortune, however, would aide Mavid, for his adversary made a costly mistake. They lunged at Mavid and, for some reason, he anticipated it; for Mavid, the attack was almost telegraphed. Mavid soared upward slightly to avoid the blow. With the creature's wings precariously close to his mouth, he took advantage of this position and dug his back and front claws into the creatures back for stabilization purposes. He then proceeded to chomp down on the upper portion of his opponent's wing. He chewed and gnawed at the wing and he was able to pry it off piece by piece. The creature rapidly descended and attempted to fly with one wing but, as you can imagine, it was quite futile. As it fell into open space, it caught hold on to Mavid's tail. Sinking its teeth into it and clinging on for dear life. This vexed Mavid, who swung his tail about wildly along with his body. After a lengthy struggle, Mavid was freed, and the creature was sent careening down below.

It landed with a loud deafening sound. The impact caused a large indentation in the group. Several rocks were propelled into the air. The weight of the beast crushed several besiegers to death, who were either to slow to move out the way or oblivious to the large object falling out of the sky. The beast lay sprawled on the ground surrounded by its own blood. The center head gravitated to one of the besiegers.

"I have failed my master. A slave whose failed his master has no purpose."

The other besiegers were dumbfounded that the creature was still alive and that it talked. The besieger, the creature was looking at, remained calm, despite the reaction of his comrades. He wore chainmail adorned with a tunic bearing the Everard crest. So, despite his lack of armament, he must have been high ranking enough in position to be gifted that tunic with fancy embroidery. The majority of Hector's men usually brought their own clothing and armament to battle. The man looked to be in his thirties, had medium length brown hair and a stubble beard. He had a blank expression on his face as he said rather listlessly, "Maybe your purpose was to die."

The ailing creature guffawed. "You amuse me man creature with such a preposterous notion."

The man smirked. "Maybe as preposterous as purpose itself."

The eyeless head chuckled. "Brother, I think we know very little about the way of things. It took death for us to figure that out." And with those last words, the creature died.

[*At the barbican a few moments later*]

Lord Franklin stood on the barbican peering off into the distance with his sons at his side and several knights, lightning manipulators, and some bowmen. He stared at the dragon, who was way up in the sky. Mavid looked to be scrutinizing the battlefield. The besiegers were oddly enough not attacking him. It was almost as if they were trying to trap him. Lord Franklin could make out, in the distance, a wall made out of what resembled hardened clay. This substance would be akin to high grade refractory fire clays that could withstand temperatures up to 3227 degrees Fahrenheit. Enough to quell blue dragon flame. The wall was reinforced with dirt and stone raised from the ground by terrestrial manipulators. It was mostly a monolithic structure coated again with fire clay. However, there were some sections connected with cement-based mortar, such mortar would have been rare in such a region and time. It was thought that such masonry techniques were lost for hundreds of years in Arcadiem. For comparison's sake, the mortar used in castles, including Corithni, was lime mortar.

The structure had an indentation which encompassed a group of individuals which, to the best of Lord Franklin's knowledge, housed Hector and his cronies. He also suspected that they could seal that opening in the wall if they were under heavy fire. The structure itself was comprised of an organic concrete equivalent, with the surface coated entirely with fire clay. Lord Franklin didn't know what sort of machinations they were conjuring up, but it made him uneasy. He looked at the remains of the hellhound and wondered, *"What sort of magic is Hector dealing with to summon a hellhound, temporarily bewitch a dragon, and summon objects as large as this with such immediacy and accuracy? This is truly baffling. Why were all these castors so loyal to him?"*

War is a dynamic concept, which means it is nearly impossible to accurately predict the outcomes of a particular battle, let alone the war in its entirety. But reader, I don't need to tell you that. Chances are you've either heard of or even experienced war to come up with your own conclusions. If we were to define war in its most ambiguous simplistic form, I think I could safely deduce that most of us would center around the word conflict. Conflict is the root of all wars, which is why war often seems inevitable and ubiquitous. But I'm not here to discuss the unavoidability of conflict and, by extension, war. Perhaps I'll save that discussion for another time. I simply want to discuss the very nature of conflict. When entering any type of altercation often preparedness is often emphasized. Yet, preparedness does not guarantee a favorable outcome nor lessen an unfavorable one. Such a notion would be ludicrous. This does not suggest that preparedness is futile in all forms of conflict, but rather it is easier to "expect the unexpected". A paradoxical idea, but it is essential for handling a conflict. We can postulate certain things about an outcome of any event or events based on details provided to us, and this has its merits. It can mean that we have a plan and plans are more often linked to success than no plan. However, these are still just assumptions. Randomness plays a role in predicting an outcome and an outcome is just that; a possibility of something occurring. No amount of preparation can account for chaos because it cannot be controlled.

Another issue with a plan is it is often created without knowledge of a situation. In other words, there are hidden factors, outside influences that grossly impact the outcome of any battle and might have been overlooked by the plan. Such an oversight is hardly negligible. The way we interpret reality is flawed, that much is known and many debate whether we are at the whims of fate or whether choice itself is irrelevant due to the sheer amount of randomness that appears in nature.

So where does that leave the individual? Well, the answer is not that simple. In fact, we may not ever find an answer, but that does not stop one from theorizing. One thing is true: "For every action, there is an equal and opposite reaction": Newton's third law. We are reacting to our environment, our surroundings, our universe. This is evident because we breathe, we consume, we excrete. We're born, we grow, we die. The universe is reacting to our actions in a systematic way, meaning there is at least some semblance of order in the madness. One can never completely control the outcome of a conflict, but can control their reaction to one. A great boxer reacts to the punch as it's being thrown rather than anticipating one that has not been.

"What's it doing, erm, what's he doing?" asked Sir Merek.

"My guess waiting. Waiting for Hector's men to attack or for him to come out of that structure his terrestrial elementals constructed," said a young man of about 19, standing next to Sir Merek. He had his visor up, revealing a youthful face, hazel eyes and long dark brown hair.

Sir Merek looked at this individual. "Lief, if you're going to be a knight, you should probably cut all that hair. It's a miracle you can even see out of that helmet."

"You have a beard," Lief retorted.

"Yes, but it's trimmed and groomed. Also, beards don't get in the way when fighting. Besides, I've earned my right to have one."

Lief smiled. "Because of your many feats during the Mylec marauder war that you don't stop reminding us of."

Sir Merek frowned. "You may jest, but if it weren't for my bravery, things would have been a lot different around here. You should be grateful."

Lief looked at Sir Merek affectionately. He smiled. "I am grateful to stand beside you. There's no place I'd rather be... and who knows, maybe one day, I'll have some feats of my own and I'll get to keep my hair. They say it helps provide extra padding in helmets."

Sir Merek's features softened as he looked at Lief with a sense of both guilt and care. Lief noticed the change in Sir Merek's expression.

"Hey, it's alright. I chose this. I chose this. I wasn't going to leave you by yourself, especially after everything you've done for me. I am a foreigner from Mylec, of all places, yet you made me your squire. You've done more for me than anyone has and if we die here, we die together." Sir Merek placed an affectionate hand on his squire's shoulder. "If we survive this, maybe we could do that thing that we always promised we do."

Lief 's eyes widened. "Do you really mean it?" Sir Merek smiled, "Yes." Sir Ulric and Sir Cedric Baudry stood beside each other. "Our enemy is relying heavily on castors and is obviously using hokraft, and it doesn't look like Hector and his associates are planning to step out of their cocoon anytime soon. I reckon he's biding time in order to launch an offensive," said Sir Cedric Baudry.

Sir Ulric had a pensive look on his face. "How could he be so prepared when things don't go his way? Seems like he has a contingency plan for every crisis. How do we even know it's Hector over there? Maybe it's all some type of ploy."

"It's him alright," said Lord Franklin. He furrowed his brow as he stared off into the distance. "We can't just stand here and wait... He's taken heavy losses. Now's the time to attack before he can recuperate." "But father, we should exercise caution. It could be a trap to draw us out," said John.

"It is most likely a trap, but what choice do we have? If we wait, Hector will just retreat and come back with more men or he'll muster up enough magic to summon another hellhound or worse, find some way to repossess the dragon. Time is of the essence. Our very future is at stake," replied Lord Franklin.

Edmund looked at his father with a concerned look. "What do you suggest we do, father?"

On the battlefield, Hector was accompanied by others in the terrestrial structure. He looked at the castle.

"Should we retreat? We've lost so many," said a man standing next to Hector.

This man was equal to Hector in stature and physique. He was in full plate armor. He lifted his visor as he spoke to Hector. He was a man in his forties, clean shaven, with short dirty blond hair and blue eyes.

"Vagabonds, dead weights, rapist, cutthroats, thieves the lot of them," said Hector.

"That maybe so, but this continued sacrifice of our forces is unwise. The invasion of Corithni has failed. We should retreat and proceed anew, milord," said the man.

Hector looked up at the sky. There was a copious amount of rain and the crackling of thunder. The man was slightly perturbed that Hector didn't seem to be paying attention to him. "Milord?"

"I heard you, Kelton, but we've come too far to go back," said Hector. "It seems unwise to risk a one-on-one duel with the Lightning bringer. Why not used the castors to strike him from a distance?" said Sir Kelton. "We don't have many castors left. Hexes don't travel that far and the few castors that remain would have to move closer to the castle, hence, we would have to launch another assault which would not bode well for us," said Hector.

"Milord, then what should we do?" asked Sir Kelton.

Hector sighed. "The weather is not on our side. To strike a lightning bringer during a tempest would be folly. Especially since Albert Franklin is not the only one. With their combined might, they could even control the skies."

"I don't think they would risk it with that technique and possibly destroy half their forces. Albert Franklin is too attached to his men," said Sir Kelton.

"Even so, desperation combined with recklessness could nullify morality and reason," replied Hector.

A bowman, standing adjacent to Sir Kelton, said, "We still have archers, milord. We can keep them away from the walls so we can launch another attack. We still have the numbers."

"If we leave our position, Albert will cast lightning upon us. He knows this. He is waiting for us," replied Hector.

"He won't wait forever. He is at the height of his power. There is a storm and he now has a dragon for an ally. He'll want to take advantage of the current situation. We are powerless against him," said an elderly man, possibly in his seventies.

Hector turned to this man; his eyes narrowed. "Do you doubt your king, Lord Hildred Everard?"

Hildred turned to Hector rather vexed by the suggestion, yet his face remained unreadable. "You are not king yet. You have to take Corithni first."

"And so I shall. You forget the power that I have on my side," said Hector.

"How are you so sure it belongs to you?" replied Hildred.

A black bird suddenly appeared and transformed into a man. The man was thin and pale. He had long black robes, brown eyes, and fine neck length platinum blonde hair.

"Eardwulf, any word?" asked Hector.

"Yes milord. The hex on the dragon has broken and it has sided with the defenders," said Eardwulf.

"That much is obvious. Tell us something relevant," said Sir Kelton, rather annoyed by Eardwulf's foolishness.

"Er, sorry," replied Eardwulf.

"Does the dragon recall anything about how he was bewitched?" said Hector eagerly.

"I don't believe so, but some of the defenders believe you are responsible for the bewitchment. They have not pieced together how," said Eardwulf.

"Things would have been easier if the former raider had simply slain it. All traces of our plan would be gone. Now they suspect something. We can't have them on our tail, especially not now," said Hector.

"He was about to slay it, milord, when a boy intervened." Hector gave Eardwulf a puzzled look. "A boy?"

"Yes, milord. He is an elemental called Godfrey," replied Eardwulf. Hector's eyes widened upon hearing that name.

"It seems there was a fight between the defenders and the dragon," said Eardwulf.

"No doubt that Sir Peter was involved," said Hildred.

Eardwulf continued. "Yes. During the fight, the dragon was severely injured and was healed by the old hag and, uh…"

"And what?" Sir Kelton asked impatiently.

"Well, I, uh, lost track of them," said Eardwulf nervously. "You lost track of them?" Sir Kelton said incredulously.

Hector furrowed his brow. "What exactly do you mean, lost track?" "I dunno. They just disappeared then reappeared when the Franklin brothers arrived. They seemed disoriented."

"Could they have gone somewhere through the use of castors, maybe?" asked Hildred.

"Unlikely. The Franklins don't know how magic works. The only one with a working knowledge of spells is that old woman, and she's half mad. I reckon Eardwulf here fucked up the transformation and switched the bird brain with his human brain and went off scavenging for worms or something," said Sir Kelton.

"Is such a thing possible?" asked Hildred.

"Uh, I suppose so, but I don't think—" said Eardwulf. Suddenly, a man appeared in a heap of black smoke. "Oswin," said Hector.

Oswin was a man of short stature and stocky build. He had medium length black hair that greyed on the sides, a goatee and green eyes.

"I see you spent your time avoiding battle, as usual," said Sir Kelton.

Oswin smirked. "It's always a pleasure, Sir Kelton." "Where were you, Oswin?" said Sir Kelton.

"If you must know, I was concerning myself with preparations."

Rather vexed with Oswin's dismissive tone, Sir Kelton said, "You didn't answer my question."

"Didn't know I answered to the likes of you," Oswin retorted.

Sir Kelton frowned at Oswin. He knew exactly what Oswin was trying to do and refused to engage.

"The dragon is released from the hex, so your preparations are for naught."

"Hmm," said Oswin nonchalantly.

Oswin's indifference angered Sir Kelton. "Does this not concern you? The dragon is no longer under our control. Half our forces are gone, and we've lost several castors. You have failed us."

"Huh, that's interesting," Oswin said sarcastically. "You had the numbers, the tools. A bloody dragon. And yet you still managed to mess things up. Your shoddy work as commander led to this predicament," he continued.

Sir Kelton scowled at Oswin. "You have no idea how war works. The castle was beleaguered until you lost control of the dragon."

Oswin rolled his eyes. "Spells don't last forever. It shouldn't have even worked, but I wouldn't expect you to understand."

Sir Kelton frowned in response. Oswin gave him a wry smile. "I mean no offense, of course, but had your men attacked earlier, we could've averted such circumstances."

"I find your scathing criticism of me cowardly, especially because you stand amongst us while not participating in battle. I have proven my merit. Can you say the same?"

Hildred groaned. "Enough. I've grown weary of your constant verbal sparring."

"Lord Hildred is right. We cannot waste our time bickering. Eardwulf, did they find it?" Hector asked eagerly.

"No, milord, I don't think they even know to look for it," Eardwulf said. Hector sighed with relief.

"But what if they find it, milord?" said Sir Kelton apprehensively.

"They don't know what it is or even how to control it. Very few do," said Oswin dismissively.

"Do we?" Sir Kelton retorted.

Oswin was taken aback by this line of questioning, but before he could respond, Hector said, "There is no need to be concerned. This has been in the making for a long time. Nothing has changed."

Hildred looked up at the sky at the great beast, Mavid. "The dragon is aware something is up. That's why it does not approach."

Sir Kelton grabbed the hilt of his blade. "Then we shall meet it in battle and slay it."

"That would be unwise. Did you not see that infernal beast slayed the hellhound and is responsible for the deaths of many of our men?" said Hildred.

"Forgive me, Lord Hildred, but I see no other way. The creature will not remain fixated in the sky indefinitely. It is planning an attack. We must respond," said Sir Kelton.

"He will attack," said Hector. All eyes were on Hector. He had a pensive look on his face. "But not right away. He will not risk it. Mavid knows we have powerful magic. He most likely knows that if he could be controlled before, it can happen again, and he no doubt recognized the content of this structure. He knows he cannot burn down the fire clay."

"Then what's he doing?" asked Hildred.

"Reconnaissance for the Franklins. This clay may quell dragon flame, but it is defenseless against lightning." He turned to Oswin. "How good are dragon ears?"

"About as good as dog ears, milord," replied Oswin. "Can he hear us?" asked Hector.

"Not from this distance," said Oswin. "How about the eyes?" asked Hector.

"For comparison's sake, slightly better than a hawk," replied Oswin. "So, he's trying to gage the distance it will take for the Franklins to launch an attack, but do we still think he will try it?" said Kelton. "I don't know, but we must be prepared," said Hector.

"And prepared we shall be, milord. You still have it," said Oswin.

Sir Kelton was wary of this situation. The use of such magic, if you could even call it that, was sure to have some detrimental effects. "Milord, is this even safe and, most of all, is it necessary?"

"Albert Franklin leaves us no choice," replied Hector.

"That's what the wizard would have you believe. We've defeated many of Albert Franklin's allies. A loss will not tarnish our reputation. We don't need this godforsaken relic. We can retreat and—"

"There will be no retreat," Hector said sternly. He sighed. "We do this now or we don't do this at all. A lost here would be devastating. They will spin the narrative and say that Corithni stood against overwhelming odds. Thousands will flock to their cause."

Hildred looked bemused by Hector's statement. "Forgive me, milord. Are you suggesting that Albert Franklin would seek foreign aid? That seems risky and it would put the sovereignty of Iiadec in jeopardy."

"He's desperate. The self-righteous fuck would rather see Iiadec burned to the ground than watch me sit on the throne," said Hector.

"He is a bit of a stubborn arse, but he would not stoop so low as to desecrate the sanctity of this land by perverting it with foreign influences," said Hildred.

"He let a Mylecan become a knight. He doesn't give a shit about sanctity and let's stop pretending we're any different. War itself is perversion. It's a game of who wants the bitch called power more. Who's willing to go farther, who's more ruthless. Morality is for the victor to decide. When the war is won, the minds of the masses will be like clay, free to mold into any shape one desires. They will back anyone who puts food in their bellies and a roof over their heads, as long as these conditions are fulfilled, the people will forever remain indifferent to the atrocities committed by either side because they are not players but merely pieces."

Eardwulf had an uncomfortable look on his face, as did Hildred, but Hector paid no heed. He was too concerned with victory to notice the discontent amongst his men.

Sir Kelton turned to Hector, looking quite apprehensive. "Milord, this thing, whatever it is, allegedly could alter the fabric of reality. Supposedly, that would make its wielder—"

"A God amongst men," said Hector. "Or a demon," Sir Kelton said gravely.

"What are you insinuating, Sir Kelton?" said Oswin, rather vexed by the statement.

Sir Kelton scowled at Oswin and said candidly, "Very well, Oswin, you've forced my hand. I don't trust you and I think you endanger the lives of others, especially our Lord, with use of hokraft disguised as ancient relics."

"Have I not provided the future king with the weapon?"

"Yes, but what have you to gain out of this? You're going to let our Lord wield the ultimate power," said Sir Kelton.

The others awaited a response. Oswin removed his tunic, revealing several scars and lesions all over his body. From the looks of it, they appeared to be magical injuries. The other men gasped, but Hector was not fazed.

"I cannot wield it, it rejects me. It requires a more capable master. It's one and only true master is our king, our messiah, our father the reincarnated Arda himself." said Oswin.

"That's utter nonsense. It will be your head if—" said Sir Kelton. "Enough," said Hector. "Oswin, is this witch woman old enough to recall its properties?"

"She cannot wield it. Only you can wield it. I just merely awakened it. If the enemy discovers it... Well then, I guess you'll have to destroy them with its power," Oswin said.

Hector had a stoic look on his face. "Will have to destroy loose ends if things get hairy, but for now, we will resort to less drastic measures. Eardwulf, see to it that this old witch is silenced."

"What about the dragon, milord?" asked Eardwulf.

"I'll deal with the dragon. After all, even dragons can die of mortal wounds."

Eardwulf transformed into a blackbird and headed for the castle keep. Hector looked out into the distance, first at Mavid, then at the defenders. He placed a rose-colored crystal in the center of a vacant spot on his crown.

***

"Certainly, you don't mean that technique, father," said Edmund gravely.

"What technique?" John asked, knowing exactly what his father was talking about, but was hoping he was wrong.

Lord Franklin sighed and there was brief silence, as, by this time, everyone there knew what Lord Franklin was planning and all eyes were on him.

"Look, the longer we wait here, discussing what to do next, our enemies will be planning their next offensive. We do not have time to lose," he said impatiently. He looked around for any form of agreement, but received nothing but looks of concern and general fear. Lord Franklin furrowed his brow and tried a more direct approach. "I'm performing the technique whether you like it or not."

"But, milord," said Carac.

"Enough. I need to finish this once and for all."

Lord Franklin was about to unsheathe his sword when Edmund grabbed his forearm.

"Father, this is dangerous."

Lord Franklin turned to his son in an attempt to be reassuring. "Do not fret, my son. I've done this before."

Before he could proceed, John said, "We know. We were there…"

A surprised look appeared on Lord Franklin's face, to which John responded. "It was a long time ago, but that doesn't matter now. I've studied up on Hakaneira (HAKA-NEARA, old tongue for travel by lightning.)"

(The Hakaneira is an ancient elemental technique. Its origins are unknown and there are many that doubt its existence. It does, however, exist and, if done successfully, it allows the user to travel an unspecified distance at the speed of lightning, that is roughly 1/3 the speed of light. Although, the percentages are not entirely accurate because few have tried such a technique. However, the current data would suggest Hakaneira has a 98% mortality rate on anyone even attempting it. Some attributed this to genetics, and they claimed only rare breed lightning elementals can perform such a feat. Other scholars say that it is a lack of knowledge of such a difficult technique. The reason for this is that the technique often involves shooting lightning into the sky, often with a lightning rod or metallic object, though neither is necessary. They just make the technique easier. A lightning storm is also advantageous. Without a storm, the user must incite a storm which takes more energy. The idea is to have natural lightning from the sky connect with electricity generated by the user. At this point, the user is supposed to become electricity and travel in the direction of the lightning. Where they go is limited to places they can recall, if a user cannot recall a place, they will die. Turning into electricity, let alone lightning, is a difficult feat and it is a requirement for Hakaneira. It is also something that the elemental needs to do nearly instantaneously to work. During this process, many individuals perish as the electricity imbued in their cells often becomes lethal. With the intensity of the lightning in the sky and the electricity coming from the individual, a user is effectively electrocuted if an attempt is unsuccessful.)

"And I've discovered that it requires accuracy, like to a tee, anything less would be a catastrophe," said John.

"That much is known," said Lord Franklin impatiently.

John continued. "Even if you're successful in the initial transportation and transformation, you can't account for distance because you don't know where Hector is exactly. Entering the battlefield in an unknown location would be folly and Hector's men would most likely kill you before you can take his life."

Lord Franklin looked uneasy as he leaned on the parapeted wall and exhaled. "The shockwave will kill everyone in his vicinity."

"It won't take out the whole army. You'll still be in danger," said William gravely.

"Then what do you suggest?" Lord Franklin sighed. "Look, we don't have the luxury of time. Hector summoned a bloody hellhound. One can only imagine what other dark, twisted creatures he can summon if given the time."

"There's another way," said John.

Lord Franklin had a befuddled expression on his face. John looked at his brothers and Lord Franklin's eyes widened. "No, I forbid it."

Carac, who immediately understood, said, "Milords, that would be madness."

"Look. Let's think of this rationally. Three lightning elementals are better than one, and we all know the technique," said William.

"Yes, but have any of you actually performed it? There is a difference between knowing of it and performing it," said Lord Franklin.

"We are your blood. We should be able to do it," said John. "Should is not a guarantee," said Lord Franklin.

"Father, it's like you said. There are no guarantees in this world except death and failure as the result of inaction," said Edmund.

"Milords, if all of you die—" said Carac.

"Then we won't die and if the event should occur, I trust our people would choose a new king to continue the cause," interrupted William.

"Besides, if we're not willing to die for the throne, then we don't deserve to have it," said Edmund.

There was a flapping of wings. "With words like that, Hector does not stand a chance."

The men turned around to see Mavid above them. Quite startled, William said, "Bloody hell, were you there the whole time?"

"Pretty much," said Mavid.

"But—but how?" William stammered. "You're so massive. Surely someone would have heard you?"

"I suppose you were too busy discussing a suicide mission," said Mavid bluntly.

"So, you've heard of Hakaneira," said Lord Franklin.

"I've heard some rumors. Never really believed them. I mean, it is a bit ridiculous, traveling by lightning bolt, but then you were so willing to go out there, I figured it must be true."

"You don't believe we will survive the transportation?" Edmund asked.

"That's not the issue. You don't know where Hector is exactly, which

293

I believe is crucial when attempting to kill him and since human eyes are known for being shit, you'll probably mess up on the location when you land. In other words, you'll most likely be surrounded by Hector's army. All in all, shit plan," said Mavid.

Lord Franklin massaged his chin and furrowed his brow. "You make a good point, dragon, but time is of the essence. There is no other option."

"There is an alternative," said Mavid.

Lord Franklin had a curious look on his face.

"My eyes are much better than yours," said Mavid.

"King Mavid, you can't go near Hector," Edmund said gravely. Mavid had an irritated look on his face. "Here's the thing. I am a king.

I do not take orders from would-be princes, or humans, for that matter." "I'm sorry. I meant no offence," said Edmund.

Mavid sighed. "Look. We all want the same thing: Hector dead. This is the only way. It's like your father said, we don't have the luxury of time. I've lived many years, fought many battles, seen many things, and for the first time in a long time, I am frightened."

John furrowed his brow. "Do you know what type of power he possesses?"

"That's just it. I don't. And that is precisely what terrifies me. We cannot allow him to continue his machinations. Not just for the sake of Corithni, but the world," said Mavid.

"Then it's settled. We will proceed with your plan, dragon," said Lord Franklin.

"Right. Eh, what exactly is that plan again?" said William.

John groaned. William looked at Carac. "Seriously. Did you hear any plan being discussed?" Carac shook his head.

"Quit kidding around. Mavid is going to take us close enough to Hector so we can transport and kill him."

"He never said any of that," said William.

John groaned. "It was implied. Honestly, you need to start paying more attention."

"We don't have time for this. Let's move," said Edmund.

"Wait, milords, at least take some of us with you," said Sir Cedric Baudry.

"We are not experts on the Hakaneira. We are barely capable of transporting an individual successfully, let alone a group. If you should perish during the application of the technique, it would greatly diminish our efforts thus far. You are much needed here in case things don't go our way," said John.

"Understood," the men said in unison. "Now that's settled. Hop on," Mavid said.

Edmund, Lord Franklin, and John hoisted themselves onto Mavid's back. Only William remained looking nervous.

"William, will you hurry up and get on!" John said impatiently. Yet William remained.

Edmund said more calmly, "What's the matter?"

"It's just I've never ridden a dragon before. I don't even know what to hold on to," replied William.

"I suppose it's not too different from riding a wild horse," said Edmund. "I am not a horse!" Mavid said angrily.

"Sorry, it was just an analogy," said Edmund.

"A poor analogy. Horses don't have bloody wings or fly thousands of feet in the air. Seriously, Edmund, you're not being considerate of my predicament," said William.

Edmund rolled his eyes. "You know you're starting to sound like John."

"Hey, what does that mean?!" said John. William gasped. "How dare you!"

"Enough! The three of you cease your bickering and William, get on the bloody dragon! Do I make myself clear?" asked Lord Franklin angrily. "Yes, father," the brothers said in unison. William got onto Mavid's back and the five headed towards Hector. "Er, King Mavid?" asked William. "Yes?" Mavid replied.

"You have done this before, right?" "Done what?" Mavid asked. "You know. Carry human passengers on your back," said William.

"Can't say I have. Being a royal, I'm not really responsible for transporting things, especially humans, but hey, first time for everything, eh?" explained Mavid.

William's eyes widened. "What if you swerve and we lose our grip?" he said nervously.

Mavid smiled. "Then what's your human expression? Oh yeah, you're fucked."

William was horrified by what he had just heard.

"Oh, c'mon. It was a joke and besides, it's not like your lot lives that long anyway," said Mavid.

"I'm glad you're enjoying yourself at our expense. Real mature for a roughly 4000 year old dragon," John said sarcastically.

"How did you know how old I am?" asked Mavid.

"It's quite obvious. Your physique, especially the thorax, indicates middle age and all the reliable literature on winged dragons suggest they live 6000-8000 years and reach peak physical shape approximately half their life span."

"Do you spend a lot of time researching trivial facts on creatures?"

"One can never be too prepared, and I don't like what you're insinuating," replied John.

"I'm not insinuating anything. I just think it's pretty clear you don't attract many maidens."

Edmund burst out laughing. William had a massive grin on his face. "He does not."

"Shut up, William!" shouted John.

"Sssh. We're close. I can see Hector and his cronies near that monolith up ahead," said Mavid.

John looked down and saw several besiegers. They did not seem to react to their presence.

"Why are they not attacking?" asked John.

"Maybe they can't see us from this height," said Edmund.

"Not likely. They'd be sure to see a massive silhouette in the sky. King Mavid, can you see their eyes?" asked John.

Mavid peered down at the battlefield. "Barely, but what I can make out is that they're definitely staring at us"

"Hector does not want to destroy his biggest asset. He seeks to reclaim you. We must proceed with caution," said John.

Mavid was bemused. "That's rather odd, considering he tried to kill me with the hellhound."

"That didn't go according to plan, so he forged a new plan. He is waiting for us to get close," said Lord Franklin.

"There is some good news to this. It means Hector no longer has any more tricks up his sleeves," said John.

"It also means Hector knows what we're planning, and this is likely a trap," said Lord Franklin gravely.

"Well, we're already here," said William.

"There he is. You can transport from here," said Mavid.

"King Mavid, we are not experts at the technique. The lightning may strike you in the process," said John.

"That's alright. I've been electrocuted before. I can handle it. Now hurry up. I'll take care of the enemies on the ground," said Mavid.

"King Mavid, make sure you stay out of Hector's sight," said John.

"Right," Mavid replied.

The Franklins pointed their swords in the air (The swords act as a lightning rod).

"Ready, on my count one, two, three."

With a bright flash of light, they disappeared into the lightning and reappeared near the stone structure Hector and his men were inhabiting.

The shockwaves and stray electricity killed the surrounding besiegers, but the structure remained. The Franklins were two feet away from Hector and his men. With blades drawn, the Franklins made their intentions clear. They approached with caution; their enemy was ready for them. Except for Hector, most of the men in the stone structure had their weapons drawn. Hector's right hand was loosely grasping his longsword. He looked directly at Lord Franklin and said rather smugly,

"Hello, Uncle."

CHAPTER THIRTEEN

THE INTRUDER

Eardwulf rested on the roof of the keep in bird form. He carefully analyzed his surroundings. There were several guards outside, amongst them was Sir Peter. Eardwulf recognized him from the battle of Rilek, where the former raider slew many of Hector's men with his glowing sword. He couldn't risk walking through the front door, that would be folly, yet he couldn't remain a bird forever. Even magic has its limits. He knew he had to find a way in somehow. He heard them say "take her to the keep" so he knew he was in the right place. The problem was the old woman was most likely surrounded by other people. Killing her would attract too much attention. Corithni was said to be magically resistant. Apparently, this did not include transformation but then again, magic from the Holme bloodline was not typical magic.

Reader, there are often claims made that fortresses are magic proof, but nothing ever really is. Fortresses are not made unilaterally. Some of the architects responsible for magic proofing, using magic repellent materials, which in the case of Corithni is white stone, don't always agree which amount is sufficient for repelling magic. The literature on such things is rather ambiguous. Furthermore, it is expensive and laborious to build a structure entirely of stone. Especially white stone, which is hard to mold due to it being hardened by Isial Lake. In other words, wood and other regular materials would have to be used as well. Hence, a fortress cannot be completely impervious to magic or anything for that matter. This does not even consider the fact that the foundation of Corithni was not built with white stone, nor the tunnels underground. It is important to remember, when it comes to magic resistant objects, there is a limit to their resistance.

Eardwulf was contemplating how to successfully infiltrate the keep when Sir Peter looked up and spotted him. Acting quickly, Eardwulf flew to the backside of the keep where he was out of site. It was there he noticed a sizeable window, more than large enough for him to fit through. Instead of entering, he perched himself on the window and listened in to the conversation Sir Peter was having with the other men.

"Is something the matter?" asked one of the men.

"It's probably nothing, but something feels off," said Sir Peter. "Off?" asked the same man.

"Ugh I can't explain it, but something doesn't seem quite right. I feel like something terrible is about to happen and we're not prepared for it" "Other than Hector?" asked the same man. "Perhaps, Brock," said Sir Peter.

"I feel the same way. Hector has a massive army that he seemed to raise from thin air and where does he get the money to support sell-swords and castors? Especially ones practicing hokraft, cause loyalty ain't cheap and Everard's aren't that wealthy. He's most likely working with dark forces beyond our understanding. Then there's the issue of why Mirama won't intervene. Anyone with half a brain knows Hector's claim to the throne is horseshit. Godwin could end this whole fucking war in a heartbeat, yet he stands idly by and lets this potential usurper gallivant about Iiadec proclaiming to be a bloody Franklin," said another guard.

"Blake, I've had enough of your bloody conspiracy theories. Now's not the time to be inciting panic. We've got enough to deal with already," said another guard.

"Fine, Cordell, remain ignorant while the truth is so blatantly in front of you, you fucking dullard," Blake retorted.

Cordell was visibly angered by the insult but before he could respond, Brock intervened, attempting to deescalate the situation. "No need for name calling. We're all in this together. Besides, even if what Blake says is true, once Hector is dead, all his machinations and dealings will die with him. Don't you see? We're winning. We need not worry," said Brock.

Sir Peter was not convinced but remained silent. Blake, however, was vocal about his disagreement of Brock's analysis of their situation and said, "Your naivety is appalling."

Cordell groaned. "You're hopeless."

Eardwulf took in what he could from their brief conversation. From what he could gather, the people of Corithni were beginning to suspect Hector had greater motives beyond seizing the throne. Perhaps his lordship had been too reckless in jinxing the dragon. Eardwulf decided that it was unwise to remain in the same position, for it might breed suspicion, especially since Sir Peter and the one called Blake were already suspecting something. Fortunately for him, no one in Corithni seemed to know exactly what was going on, only theories. The Olga woman was, of course, an exception. He didn't know her personally, but she had been described as *a woman who knows things*, something that could be particularly troublesome for Hector and his plans. As far as Eardwulf knew, Hector, nor any of his cohorts, knew what the old hag knew, but they weren't taking any chances. That's why he was instructed to assassinate her. Eardwulf, however, couldn't help but think that she was more valuable alive. A sorceress of such old age is bound to have some secrets under her belt. But it was not up to him. He was instructed with a task, and he intended to complete it.

He flew through the window and rested himself on one of the arches on the slightly vaulted ceiling. He seemed to be in the Great Hall full of many people. None seemed to have noticed him apart from one little girl. The little girl who spotted him was with, what Eardwulf assumed to be, her mother and a little boy not much older than her. Possibly a sibling. At first the little girl stared at him. Eardwulf did not know whether he should move or not for fear of drawing unwanted attention.

The girl pointed, then said, "Look, look, Haywood, it's a bird on the roof."

That was his signal. Eardwulf flew out of sight. He could feel exhaustion start to kick in. Constant transformations were beginning to take its toll. If he was not careful, he would turn back into a human soon and that would be his undoing. *"Damn. I should not have been so reckless with my powers, but now's not the time to dwell on such things. I need to find out where this woman is."*

"Where Jetta? I don't see no bird," said Haywood.

"It's right behind the—" said Jetta. Before she could say more the mother took both of them by the hand.

"Come on little ones. Let's move along and get you to Lady Uptone so you can play with the other children."

"But, but, the bird," said Jetta.

The mother was bemused. "Bird?" She looked around at the ceiling, but she did not see Eardwulf. "Well, Jetta, it's gone now. Let's hurry along. We don't want to keep Lady Uptone waiting."

Three other women entered the Hall. These women were Giselle, Lodema, and Clara.

"Is Godfrey alright?" asked the mother.

"Yeah, sure, he's fine. Practically saved the war effort," said the one called Lodema nonchalantly.

"Oh, thank God. Well, did you report back to Lady Franklin?" asked the mother.

"Of course, we're not complete idiots. We told her on our way up here. We figured we might as well tell you, Hollis, since we knew you'd be worried sick and, well, you lost him in the first place," said Lodema.

Hollis frowned upon hearing this.

"What? It's true. Lady Branson entrusted you to watch him and you—" "Lodema, that's enough. We talked about this, remember?" said the one called Clara.

"I was just being honest. Whatever, that's not important. Hollis, you should have been at the barracks. It's an absolute madhouse. The healers are a funny bunch." Lodema recounted her time in the barracks. Lodema was quite talkative, and her eyes lit up when describing the events that had occurred.

While Lodema was rambling, Hollis's attention was instead drawn to Clara and Giselle, who were aberrantly quiet. She turned to them as Giselle hung her head low and was looking rather despondent. Clara was looking equally dejected.

"Is something the matter?"

"Uh, it's nothing really," said Clara.

Hollis was not convinced. "You've both been awfully quiet since you've got here. Are you sure everything's alright?"

"You know it's rude to interrupt one's story. I was just getting to the good part," said Lodema irritably. Tears formed on Giselle's face. "What? Was it something I said?" asked Lodema.

Clara did her best to console Giselle.

"Giselle, what's wrong?" Hollis said softly. Giselle struggled to get her words out.

"It-It's—it's Martin. It's just I worry about him constantly. When I saw all the injured and dying in the barracks... Oh, I couldn't bear the thought that he might be amongst them. I-I-I." She began sobbing profusely into Clara's arms.

Both Clara and Hollis began soothing her.

"Great job, midwife. Sending her to the barracks when she clearly couldn't stomach it," Lodema said sarcastically.

"I am not a midwife. I am a healer. And I didn't force her to enter the barracks," Clara said, trying her best to suppress her anger, but Lodema was making it difficult.

"Midwife, healer, they're essentially the same thing. Besides, that's not the point. You should've had better judgment, Clara."

"Enough, Lodema!" Hollis said sternly.

302

Lodema remained silent briefly. Hollis turned to Giselle. "I'm sure Martin is fine, but I don't blame you for being worried. The castle is beleaguered, everyone is afraid. But we must remember that hope is more powerful than fear, and as long as we trust in Arda, we cannot lose, even in death."

Giselle smiled and she dried her tears. "Thank you, Hollis."

"Love is the strongest force in the mortal realm. It does not discriminate between race, gender, creed, or class. It comes in many forms, all of which are wonderful. To simply love someone is enough to satiate us till the end of days. So long as we keep it in our hearts and minds, we will remain at peace and the ones we love will never die."

Giselle and Clara looked at each other. Clara smiled. "You're going to be just fine. I'll take care of you."

Giselle embraced her warmly.

"I have some good news, Giselle. Before I was rudely interrupted…" said Lodema, as Hollis rolled her eyes. "I was going to say Martin's fine. He was with Sir Peter and the others while fighting the dragon. Lord Edmund and Godfrey said so and don't worry, the dragon didn't harm Martin. Godfrey says it was in a trance. Oh, and Olga was taken to the barracks by Martin."

Eardwulf's ears perked up upon hearing the location of his target. He listened in closer. Lodema recounted Godfrey's tale of how Olga came to be fatigued. Eardwulf was growing impatient because he already knew this information and did not have the luxury of time.

Giselle turned to Clara. "Will she be alright?"

"She's in good hands. She's with Wilona." Giselle gave her an incredulous look. "Oh, don't give me that look. Despite her oddities, Wilona is an excellent healer. Besides, she didn't suffer any injuries, just fatigue. She just needed rest."

Giselle sighed in relief.

Eardwulf had discovered the location of his target and her caretaker. A plan was starting to form in his head, but it was too risky to move. He had already been spotted once, he would not risk it again. He had to be meticulous about his next move.

Lodema looked at both Jetta and Haywood, who were playing some sort of game that involved gestures. Quill, parchment, and stone was its name.

"Erm, Hollis?" asked Clara. "Yes?" replied Hollis. "Where's Bernia?" asked Clara.

Hollis's eyes widened. "Oh God, she's wandered off again, hasn't she?" "You know, you have a knack for losing people," said Lodema. "Don't start with me, Lodema," Hollis said angrily.

"She couldn't have gone far. We'll help look for her," said Giselle. "No, Giselle, you need to rest. You've had enough adventures for today," said Hollis.

Before Giselle could protest, Hollis turned to Clara. "See to it that she is well rested." Clara nodded and escorted Giselle to the chambers.

Hollis turned to Lodema. "Well, don't just stand there. Make yourself useful and help me search for her."

"What? Why me? You're the one who lost her," retorted Lodema. "For God's sakes, Lodema, she's your sister."

"Only by marriage," replied Lodema.

"Ugh. I don't have time for this. I'm going to take my children to Lady Uptone. You search the lower floor," said Hollis.

"Alright, fine," Lodema groaned.

The two parted ways. Which gave Eardwulf ample time to make his move as everyone seemed to be preoccupied in the Great Hall. Eardwulf did not bother to listen in anymore. But if he could guess, it was about the war front and their chances of surviving the siege. Eardwulf proceeded to the barracks. He avoided being spotted by employing the same strategy he utilized before, that being clinging to the ceiling arches. When he got to the staircase leading to the garrison. He remembered the one called Clara. He had studied her physique, clothing, voice, and face. He was an expert in this by now and could recall a person's look as though they were right in front of him even after only observing them in brevity. Some have called it a gift.

He carefully descended from the ceiling to the floor. He clung to the wall and made sure no one was watching before transforming into a figure that greatly resembled Clara. Eardwulf made his way through the barracks where there was several injured and ailing with healers both male and female attending to them. There were mostly female healers which in itself was surprising. In fact, this had been the first time Eardwulf had even seen a female healer. What was more surprising was that some seemingly capable men were in here instead of out on the battlefield. Corithni was quite an odd place. He did not have time to ponder. He was on a mission.

Eardwulf looked around for someone to help him locate Olga and her caretaker Wilona. His eyes gravitated to a gregarious looking male. He appeared to be in his twenties.

"Hey, hey, you come over here," said Eardwulf.

The man walked towards Eardwulf. He had curly black hair and blue eyes.

He smiled. "Very funny, Clara. I know I haven't been here long, but you should know my name by now."

Eardwulf did not respond and had a blank expression. The man was quite embarrassed by such a response.

"Oh right, you really don't. Not that I'd expect you too. I'm not that memorable. It's Aldway, by the way." He laughed nervously.

Eardwulf noticed Aldway's hands were shaking. Not from nervousness or embarrassment but rather from some type of uncontrolled tremor. Aldway realized what Eardwulf was looking at. He quickly put his affected hands behind his back.

"It's nothing, really. I get occasional shakes. Erm, what did you want exactly, Clara?"

Eardwulf asked rather bluntly, "Where's Wilona?"

"Uh, she's in the back attending to Olga," said Aldway, as he pointed towards a bed shielded by a makeshift curtain.

Eardwulf was about to head in that direction when he heard a man say, "Where do you think you're going Clara?"

Eardwulf stopped and turned around to see a man in his fifties with an angry countenance. "I've been looking for you all day."

"I-I-uh," Eardwulf stammered, struggling to think of something feasible to say.

"Never mind that, girl. Lady Branson needs you. Come along," the man interrupted.

"Uh, actually, I was instructed to look after Olga. Wilona can be a bit absentminded at times," said Eardwulf.

The man was perplexed. "But she told me—"

"She must've forgotten to tell you. I'm sure she's really busy," said Eardwulf trying to sound as convincing as he could.

"Right, you lazy lot are working er too hard. Anyway, make sure you keep an eye on Wilona, the senseless girl built a curtain around Olga. Waste of bloody resources if ye ask me. She says she got the idea from Alywin, Tim, and the new one, Sarah. An unscrupulous bunch. Dem is clearly lying about something. That Alywin is the worse of them, fucking cunt threatened to kill me and all I've ever done is mind my business not antagonizing anyone. That fucker belongs in a cage or better yet at the gallows awaiting death. Who does he think he is? I served in two wars. Why, if I were a younger man—"

Eardwulf was growing impatient with this man's incessant rambling. "Uh I think I should be going now, don't want to keep Olga waiting," Eardwulf interrupted.

"Right, on you go," said the man. Eardwulf walked toward Olga's bed. As he walked, he could hear the man speaking rather rudely to Aldway. "Hey, shakes, help me dispose of these beds. They're filthy and unusable."

"Er, Swithin, I can do more than lift empty beds," said Aldway. "Well, I can't have you lifting the injured and ill not with those shaky hands. As long as I'm here, lifting beds is all you're ever going to be doing. You must think me mad if you think I'm going to let you do anything else," said Swithin.

Aldway, looking uncharacteristically despondent, replied, "Right, sorry, Swithin."

"Come on then," Swithin said impatiently.

Eardwulf approached the bed and he drew back the curtain. He saw who he assumed was Olga resting on the bed, eyes shut but very much alive. Standing adjacent to her was who he assumed was Wilona. Wilona turned around to look at Clara and a smile began to manifest itself on her face. She had an innocuous childlike energy and seem oblivious to Eardwulf's ill intentions.

"Oh, hello Clara. Do you like our fortress?"

Eardwulf smiled disingenuously, but Wilona didn't seem to notice. "I was inspired by Tim, Alywin, and Sarah's one," she said. Then, dropping her voice to a whisper added, "They're helping the poor man with his cock. He needed some privacy." Wilona then groaned. "Shoot. I wasn't supposed to say anything. Tim will definitely be angry with me now. Clara, promise you won't tell anyone? Tim said that was supposed to be a secret."

Eardwulf smiled. "Your secret is safe with me."

"Oh, thank you, Clara," said Wilona. It was evident in the inflection of her voice that she was relieved.

"Erm, Wilona, Lady Branson is asking for you. I'll stay here and watch over Olga," said Eardwulf, trying his best not to draw suspicion.

"Why would she send you to watch Olga? She's just sleeping. She's quite fine. Honest, I've checked. You're one of the best healers here, rivaling only Alywin, the Archiater, and Lady Branson herself. Such a task seems beneath you, don't you think?" asked Wilona.

"Uh, Lady Branson's orders. I wouldn't question it if I were you," said Eardwulf nervously.

Wilona was quite bemused by this. "That doesn't sound like her at all." Eardwulf was getting apprehensive. This girl was beginning to suspect something. He had to think of something fast. "Er, I just meant she's under a lot of stress and could use someone like you to help her like you helped Olga."

Still perplexed, Wilona asked bluntly, "Why me?"

Eardwulf was getting increasingly vexed by this line of questioning, but he did his best to contain his frustration. "It's because you're amicable and charming. You're like a ray of light that illuminates the darkness." Eardwulf gently held Wilona's hands, looked directly in her eyes and said, "Please Wilona, she needs you."

Wilona was flustered by the apparent gravity of Eardwulf's words. She had no idea that Lady Branson depended on her so deeply for emotional support. She was not aware they had that type of bond. But she didn't bother to question it. She must attend to Lady Branson with immediacy and care.

"Right, I'll go right away. Uh, where is she?"

Eardwulf gently pushed out from behind the curtain to look around. "Ask around. I know you'll find a way to her."

"Uh right" With those words, Wilona disappeared into the crowd in search of Lady Branson.

Now, with the girl gone, Eardwulf had to act quickly. He hastily and quietly made his way to Olga, who appeared to be in a deep sleep. He reached for the pillow Olga rested her head upon and meticulously removed it from underneath the old woman. Eardwulf held the pillow in both hands and brought it closer to Olga's face. With the pillow just inches from her face, Olga's eyes opened, and Eardwulf was instantly immobilized.

"What? I can't move… Is this an immobilizing spell? That's impossible. That type of magic shouldn't work here!" "Ediac," (Old tongue for reveal) said Olga.

Eardwulf could see his hands getting bigger and more masculine, he felt his spine getting longer and his shoulders become broader. His physical appearance was returning and, because he was changing against his will, the transformation was excruciating. He felt his body contort and twisting back into place. Eardwulf felt like screaming and writhing about, but he was limited in movement to his internal organs and eyes. Additionally, as you could imagine, it would be unwise to draw further attention to himself. Eardwulf had underestimated this woman. She clearly possessed magic potent enough to overcome the magic resistant barriers constructed throughout the castle and because of this costly mistake, he found himself in a precarious situation. He was in enemy territory, isolated from his allies, and at the mercy of a powerful witch.

"A Holme so far away from home, a bird so far away from the nest."

Completely taken aback by what he had just heard, he thought to himself, *"How does she know my family's name? How does she—"*

Then Eardwulf noticed sweat propagate on Olga's forehead. She was breathing heavily. Eardwulf felt his fortunes returning. He managed to smile as he could feel the power over him waning. She could not sustain this power in her current state. All he had to do was be patient and the spell would wear off. Olga eventually gave in to fatigue. Her eyes rolled back and she lost consciousness.

"Whomever you are, Olga, your secrets die with you," said Eardwulf quietly as he prepared to assassinate her.

Unbeknownst to Eardwulf, the curtain was drawn back, and Wilona was right behind him. "AAAAAAAAH!" she screamed.

Eardwulf turned around and acting quickly, he struck Wilona in the face, knocking her unconscious. He was careful to catch her before she hit the ground and placed her at the foot of the bed. He used the curtain to obscure what was happening from everyone.

In the bed nearest were Tim, Alywin, Sarah, and Colin. "Did you hear that?" asked Sarah.

Tim's eyes widened. "Wilona!"

He ran toward Wilona and Alywin and Sarah followed, as did others. Tim drew back the curtain. He found Wilona unconscious. Eardwulf had placed a dagger to her throat as he held her limp body up. Olga was still on the bed.

"Don't move any closer or I'll cut her fucking throat!" screamed Eardwulf.

Everyone did as they were commanded. Wilona regained consciousness and naturally, she was frightened by all the commotion. Tim was the first face she gravitated towards. He made her feel comfortable. He made her feel safe, especially in her anxiety inducing predicament.

"Tim, I'm scared," Wilona said, trembling. "You'll be alright, just stay still," Tim said slowly. Wilona nodded while whimpering.

"Easy mate, ye don't wanna do this," said Alywin, slowly inching towards Eardwulf.

Eardwulf, stepping back slightly, noticed Alywin moving towards him. "Stay back, I'm warning all of you."

Eardwulf was panicking. That dastardly woman's spell had not completely worn off. He could not revert back to bird form and that was his only feasible means of escape. No doubt walking out the front door, even with the girl, would result in him being cut to pieces by Sir Peter and his men, who were most likely listening after all the raucous going on inside.

This assassination attempt was a failure. His main goal now was escape and this girl was going to bide him time before his powers returned.

"We are not combatants. Please let her go and I can assure no harm will come to you," said a woman.

Eardwulf looked at her. He thought he had seen her likeness before, maybe at the tournament of roses long ago. Then it occurred to him she was, in fact, Elysant Baker, the one who defended Agnarr, now known as Sir Peter. From there, Eardwulf was able to draw a conclusion. Standing next to her was the boy called Godfrey. It seemed he had invoked ire in the child. Eardwulf had witnessed firsthand what the boy was capable of when he fought the dragon. Eardwulf had to be careful. Killing this girl would most likely cause an uproar, resulting in him being killed or worst, being captured. Keeping Wilona alive and threatening to kill her would give him leverage. Even if they suspected that he was bluffing, they would not risk testing him. He could tell the girl was too dear to them, otherwise Sir Peter and his men would have stormed the garrison already. Eardwulf turned to the woman that just spoke. "Are you Lady Branson, the wife of Sir Peter?"

"Yes," she replied.

"Then your words are worthless, as is this maiden." Eardwulf pressed the blade closer to Wilona's throat.

Wilona began to snivel. Several gasped.

"No, no, please we can help you," Lady Branson pleaded. "Horseshit! Do you expect me to believe you? Your husband's a fucking raider, cuts down his foes without batting an eye," retorted Eardwulf. "It's not hard to see why, when there're people like you, threatening the lives of an old woman and a defenseless maiden. What a big fucking man you are," said a furious Godfrey.

Eardwulf saw electricity emerging from Godfrey's hands. Eardwulf pulled Wilona closer to him and tightened his grasp on her. "Don't try it, boy," Eardwulf said through gritted teeth.

The electricity on Godfrey's hands dissipated but Godfrey still scowled at Eardwulf defiantly. This vexed Eardwulf, so he said rather sternly, "Turn around, boy." Godfrey remain still. "I said turn around now!" Eardwulf demanded.

Lady Branson was frightened but kept her composure. She looked at Godfrey. "Godfrey turn around please." Godfrey did just that. (The reason Eardwulf told Godfrey to turn around was that most lightning or electrical manipulation attacks required some semblance of eye contact with the target (peripheral vision is included). There are some exceptions, like the previously mentioned Hakaneira and Tithonite (TITHE-ON-NITE) (old tongue for release of electricity from body), but they are too few in number. Other types of elemental manipulation have their limitations as well, but that will be discussed another time.)

Eardwulf was growing more suspicious of the crowd by the moment. He had not thought this all the way through. In addition, his powers had not returned. He knew because he could not feel the sensations that beings who wielded magic often felt when their powers are active. This sensation is indescribable. One only knows the feeling when they have lost it. Eardwulf realized he was in a dire situation if his magic did not return in time. How long before the desperate crowd turned into an angry mob? Or Sir Peter and the others come bursting in? And it may all be for nothing. This Olga woman may already be dead from overexerting herself. A possibility he had not entertained till now. She was incapacitated but he wasn't sure if she was dead. He didn't dare turn his back to see, for fear of being attacked by someone in the crowd. He thought of a plan for when his magic returned. He would take the maiden to the staircase, order everyone to stay put, and then escape from the window whence he came. For now, he had to stall by changing his demeanor.

"It seems like you people aren't taking me seriously. I mean what I said. Anyone trying to be a fucking hero will have her death on their hands!" "Hey, we're all taking you seriously. You just haven't given us any demands yet," said Alywin.

"I want you all to stay put." Eardwulf saw Sarah bending slightly forward. He wasn't sure what she was attempting, but wasn't taking any chances. "I said don't fucking move!"

Sarah froze.

"No one is moving. You're in charge here, but if you want us to continue to comply, you have to ensure she's safe," said Tim.

Eardwulf was about to respond when he heard a knock on the door. "Do not enter. I have a hostage and I'll fucking kill her if any one of you dumb fuckers out there so much as move.

There was a brief silence before the voice of Sir Peter said, "May I speak, then?"

Taken aback by Sir Peter's polite manner, Eardwulf waited slightly before responding. "Your words are futile at this point. Just do as you're told."

To which Sir Peter replied, "Words are the only thing that can help you now."

Eardwulf remained silent.

"Look, the more you drag this out, the worse it will get for you," Sir Peter continued.

"It can't get any worse," retorted Eardwulf.

"Oh, but it can. Trust me, I know… You've already made a mistake by coming here. Do not make another by murdering an innocent," said Sir Peter.

"Death is imminent for me, anyway. Why not kill her and take my chances?" said Eardwulf as he inched toward the staircase.

Several onlookers gasped.

"That would be a mistake that would cost you dearly. Listen to me and listen to me closely. If she is harmed in any way, I will personally make sure you will suffer a painful death," said Sir Peter sternly.

Eardwulf gulped, but he put on a façade to appear menacing. "You don't get to make threats. I'll kill this bitch just to make you all suffer, and whatever death or torture that comes with it will be worth it."

"This is not what you want… You're not some martyr. You're somebody who's in over his head, who got roped into the machinations of a cruel lord. Who is overall indifferent to your existence and now your only instinct is to survive. Well, I can make sure you survive if you let her go," Sir Peter said emphatically.

"Horseshit, you don't know who I am," retorted Eardwulf.

"I don't, but I'm willing to spin whatever story I have to when my superiors return. So will the men outside with me. You could be the villain or victim. You decide, you only have to let her go," said Sir Peter. Eardwulf was silent briefly.

"So, do we have an accord stranger?"

Eardwulf lowered the dagger slightly. But then he began to chuckle as he felt his powers returning to him. He had stalled long enough to plan an escape. "Mercy from my enemies, I think I'd rather die," said Eardwulf as he brought the blade closer to Wilona's throat, presumably to slit it.

Suddenly, Olga leapt from her bed with the vigor of a jungle cat and pounced on Eardulf, biting his neck and cheeks. She was able to draw blood and tear off some flesh. Eardwulf cried out. He was in excruciating pain and he dropped the dagger. This allowed ample time for Wilona to escape. She kicked the dagger away from Eardwulf. It slid across the floor in Sarah's direction. Sarah quickly picked it up. Tim extended his arms out to Wilona and she ran into them, nearly knocking him over. She dove her face into his chest and began sobbing profusely.

Eardwulf was able to wrestle Olga off his back. She fell back on the bed and then, enraged, Eardwulf clasped his hands on her throat and began strangling her. Alywin quickly came to her rescue, pulling Eardwulf off her. Eardwulf threw several punches at Alywin, which Alywin evaded. Alywin then struck Eardwulf in the face with his uninjured hand. Eardwulf, quite disoriented, fell to his knees. Before Eardwulf could get back up, Aldway jumped on top of him. They grappled for a bit, but eventually Aldway was successfully able to pin Eardwulf to the ground.

"Sir Peter. He's dropped the dagger. Wilona's safe you can enter now!" screamed Aldway.

Sir Peter and some infantrymen burst the door open. Before they could respond, Eardwulf had escaped Aldway's grasp and turned into a black bird. He flew towards the staircase.

"Quick. Don't let him get away!" cried Swithin.

Eardwulf reached the staircase when he was struck with a single lightning bolt. His lifeless body fell to the ground. It gradually reverted to human form.

Standing over his body was Godfrey, still with electricity emanating from his hands.

"Everyone, move!" said Sir Peter and the crowd cleared a path that led to Godfrey and the recently slain Eardwulf. Sir Peter made his way towards him so did a few other infantrymen.

Blake, one of the men, checked the deceased Eardwulf's pulse. He confirmed to Sir Peter that Eardwulf was dead.

Sir Peter knelt beside Godfrey and said gently. "Godfrey, are you alright?"

Godfrey turned to Sir Peter. Godfrey's face expressed a mixture of guilt and fear. As if he thought Sir Peter would disapprove of his actions. He became anxious and it showed as he spoke. "I'm sorry. I had to. He was going to... I-I couldn't let—"

"I know. You're not to blame. He forced your hand," said Sir Peter as he hugged Godfrey.

"But-but all the things you said out there," said Godfrey.

"Sssh, never mind that. I'm just glad you're alright," Sir Peter interrupted.

Lady Branson ran up to Godfrey, her eyes watery. She hugged him immediately. "Oh, my dear, are you alright?"

Godfrey smiled weakly. "I am now."

Giles walked up to Godfrey and placed a gentle hand on his shoulder. "My boy. You saved us from a great misfortune. Heaven knows what dastardly plans the villain hatched for us."

Godfrey smirked. "A compliment from Lord Baker. Have you taken ill?"

All four of them laughed. "Now, does this mean I get to become a knight?" asked Godfrey.

"You know the rules, and besides, let's focus on winning the war," replied Sir Peter. Godfrey groaned.

"About that, things are looking grave. There are so many things we don't know. Like what the hell did the shape shifter want and how did he get in here?" said Blake.

"He tried to kill Olga," said Wilona.

She was still next to Tim, holding his hand.

"But why would someone risk going through enemy lines to kill a noncombatant?" asked Cordell.

"She's not just some noncombatant. She's a powerful witch that Hector believes possesses certain information, like how to jinx a dragon, due to her proficiency with atypical magic, something Hector would most likely want her silenced for," replied Blake.

"She rarely leaves the castle, so how would he know about that unless—" said Brock.

"He's been spying on us for who knows how long," Sir Peter interrupted.

"That means there could be others," said Blake.

Cordell was quite befuddled and frustrated. "None of this makes any sense. How could they breech castle walls? They're magic resistant."

"Olga could perform magic within the castle," said Brock. "That's different. She's a rare case," said Cordell.

"Maybe she's not," said Sir Peter, while looking at Olga, who was unconscious on her bed being attended to by Alywin.

"Er, magical shape shifting that occurs outside a contained structure cannot be nullified by White stone," said Kamden.

Some of the other infantrymen looked at him with perplexed looks, wondering how he knew such information. Kamden laugh nervously. "Heh heh, son of a builder."

Sarah's ears perked up upon hearing his voice. She could not see due to her short stature and several people obscuring her view, but she knew it was her brother speaking.

"Kamden!" she said. "Sarah!" he replied.

Sarah made her way through the crowd and eventually spotted him.

She ran towards him and hugged him. "Oh, thank God, you're alive," she said. "For now," Kamden said jokingly.

Sarah did not find the joke amusing. She said very seriously, "Don't say that."

"Right, sorry," replied Kamden.

Kamden suddenly noticed Sarah's bruised eye. "What happened to your face?"

"It's a long story," Sarah replied.

"One that you're going to tell me, eventually?" asked Kamden. "Er yeah."

Kamden shot her an incredulous glance.

"I will. It's just that now's not a good time," she said as she whispered the words, "I'll explain later."

Sarah was elated to see her brother again. "My baby brother is a proper warrior now."

Kamden blushed. "I wouldn't say all that."

"There's no need to be modest. Oh, are you hurt? Any injuries?" asked Sarah.

"Not that I know of. Just a bit tired is all. So you're a healer now?" said Kamden.

Before Sarah could respond, Swithin interrupted. "As touching as the family reunion is, we have more pressing matters to attend to." He turned to Kamden. "What did you mean contained structure?"

"Well, a solid structure, presumably made out of white stone, that encloses the magic wielder with walls and a roof like this here keep," explained Kamden.

"Does the structure have to be completely sealed?" asked Aldway. "No, just mostly sealed off," said Kamden.

"He heh, right, otherwise we couldn't breathe without windows," said Aldway rather embarrassed for asking what he deemed silly.

"White stone is a multifaceted tool, being both fire resistant and magic resistant, but it has its limits. The watch tower and the chapel are testaments to that. For optimal fire resistance, it needs to be in direct contact with flames not exceeding a certain temperature. A single wall constructed of White stone can ward off most magic up to a foot away. More complex forms of magic, such as shape shifting, as I said before, require containment within a structure, but then there are other forms of magic that are completely invulnerable to its effects," explained Kamden. Swithin groaned. "Ugh, that's just a long-winded way of saying White stone is shit at protecting us against magic and only works some of the time."

"Well, I suppose it's akin to a shield. A shield can only protect its wielder for so long until it gives in, especially if it faces a barrage of enemy fire. Hector has hundreds of castors. With their combined might, they could have weakened our defenses, right?" said Aldway.

"That's only partially correct. The castors are outside our walls and the keep was never attacked, not even by the dragon. Unless you're suggesting our would-be assassin is that powerful," said Sarah.

"It's not beyond reason. After all he did transform within the confines of the keep. Which, I'm guessing, would only be possible for a castor with extremely potent magic," said Sir Peter.

"That still doesn't explain why he didn't transform into the bird to escape straightaway. It certainly makes more sense than taking a hostage. I doubt Hector would hire an amateur assassin. So that can only mean he took Wilona hostage because he had no other option," said Alywin, as he gently massaged his injured hand, which was now in a long bandage fashioned from elastic wrap.

When he tried to wiggle his fingers, Lady Branson frowned at him and said, "Stop it. You'll only make it worse."

"Sorry, milady," he replied.

"Well, the only one who has answers to such questions is Olga. So we will have to wake her up to find out, since we can't exactly ask him," said Swithin, referring to Eardwulf's corpse.

"You have me. I'll answer any questions. After all, besides Olga, I was the first to see him," said Wilona.

Tim looked at Wilona. She did not seem quite as traumatized. "Are you sure you'll be alright?" asked Tim.

Wilona nodded.

"Well, go on then, girl, speak," Swithin said impatiently.

"Well, I think he was posing as Clara, he claimed Lady Branson needed me but when I went to her, she said she was fine and asked for Clara, when I returned to Olga, I saw him with the pillow and that's when he attacked me," explained Wilona.

"Where's Clara now?" asked Sir Peter.

"Probably off dillydallying in the Great Hall with that girl, Giselle. They're inseparable, those two. It's revolting," said Swithin.

"Great Hall. That must mean he flew in through a window at the back of the keep. It leads directly to the first floor of the Great Hall," said Godfrey.

Sir Peter's eyes widened. "Lady Franklin's chambers are only one flight up," said Sir Peter.

"You don't think..." said Brock.

"We shouldn't assume the worst," said Lady Branson. "Aye, but we must be prepared for it, milady," said Blake.

"We would have heard something; Lady Franklin is too young to die of natural causes like Olga. Other people would've noticed an assassin's dagger leaving its mark and the dead body of Lady Franklin. Even if he had some way of disposing of the body, others would search for her," explained Alywin.

"Well, you may be right, but it's been awfully quiet up there," said Blake as he looked up at the ceiling.

"We should see if everyone is alright just in case," Sir Peter said, talking to the men. "Some of you will stay down here and keep your eyes open for any sign of trouble." The men nodded.

Before they could part ways, there were footsteps descending the stairs. The people in the garrison could make out Clara's voice. "Wait, milady, we don't know if it's safe yet."

Three figures appeared in the garrison. Lady Franklin, Lady Fowler, and Clara, not too far behind. Before anyone else could speak, Lady Fowler turned to Sir Peter and said, "Did you get him?"

"He is slain, milady," replied Sir Peter.

Lady Fowler sighed in relief but then quickly became vexed. "Took you long enough. We've been waiting upstairs for ages."

"Sorry, milady. The assassin took one of our own hostage. As you can imagine, it was a delicate situation," explained Sir Peter.

"Who was taken hostage? Your wife? Lord Baker?" asked Lady Fowler. "Er no. It was a healer named Wilona," replied Sir Peter.

Lady Fowler had a look of utter disgust on her face.

"A lowborn girl? That's what all the fuss was about? I swear Corithni's obsession with lowborn wellbeing is appalling. If you had half the concern for your men, we'd have won the war by now!"

"Apologies, milady," said Sir Peter.

Completely ignoring him, Lady Fowler continued to press the matter. "And another thing, how is it that they call you the greatest swordsman in Arcadiem, yet we're still in this predicament? What the hell is the point of knighting a Northern savage if he's not going to be useful?!"

"That's enough, Lady Fowler!" said Lady Franklin. She turned to Sir Peter and said, "Apologies, Sir Peter. She has been on edge as of late. We are yet to hear any word from Athamar. It's likely she fears the worst."

"No need to apologize, milady, and Lady Fowler, I will do everything in my power to make sure Hector is stopped and, God willing, we will hear back from Athamar," said Sir Peter sincerely.

"I don't need God's will. I need my husband and son," Lady Fowler said angrily. She stormed off and headed back into the Great Hall. Lady Franklin sighed. "Please forgive her." She soon followed her.

After a few moments or so, a sense of normalcy was regained in the garrison. At least, normal for the garrison. Aldway and other healers placed the dead in a mass grave outside in the sizable section of grass outside the keep. This area was originally intended for aesthetic purposes, for growing a garden to make the keep look livelier, but now, during times of war, it functioned as a graveyard. Giles said a few brief words for the fallen before he, and the rest of the healers, went back inside. Sir Peter ordered some of his men to stand guard outside in case of any eminent threats. He himself remained inside the barracks with Kamden and others. Brock, Blake, and Cordell were in the Great Hall. They were instructed to watch over the highborn ladies, particularly Lady Franklin and Lady Fowler. Sir Peter volunteered to personally watch over Lady Franklin, but she insisted he be with his wife and boy at this time.

Clara remained in the garrison, trying to make up for lost time, but she was still worried about what Giselle told her. Jinxing a fetus to prevent stillbirth was bound to have severe complications regardless of whether it was successful or not. Clara was so preoccupied with her thoughts, she didn't notice she was wrapping a man's foot too tight in bandages.

"Ow, too tight," said the man.

"Sorry," Clara said, quite embarrassed by her blunder.

Aldway noticed Clara was a bit flustered and approached her. They had not known each other for long, but Aldway sought to change that with humor. He smiled. "You almost broke that man's foot and to think he came in with a sprained ankle!"

"Ugh, what is it you want? I am quite busy and therefore cannot tolerate your nonsense. So unless you've got something useful to say, go away and stop standing there like a fucking imbecile!"

"Yeesh, I don't think she likes you, mate," said the injured man.

Aldway ignored his remarks and said, "Clara, are you feeling alright? You're behaving—"

"Like an arsehole!" retorted Clara crossly.

"Actually, I was going to say oddly, but now that you mention it."

"Oooh!" exclaimed the man.

"Shut up!" Clara said angrily. She turned to Aldway, her expression softened. "I'm sorry."

"Just to be sure, you do know my name, right?" asked Aldway.

Clara looked both irritated and perplexed at Aldway. The brief silence between them made Aldway apprehensive. Clara quickly alleviated this tension by saying, "Of course I know your name. It's Aldway, now who's being odd?"

Aldway sighed with relief. "Oh, thank goodness."

Clara, now generally concerned, asked, "Aldway?" To which he quickly replied, "Nothing. It was something the shapeshifter said, or rather, didn't say."

Clara's eyes widened upon hearing Shapeshifter. "Shapeshifter? A bloody shapeshifter? How come no one told me the assassin was a shapeshifter? How is that even possible that he used my likeness?"

"It was really nothing. It's all taken care of," said Aldway, attempting to assuage the events that occurred.

His attempt was thwarted by the injured man, who said rather bluntly, "Like Arda's cock, it was nothing! It took three bloody people to catch him. This one was one of them," said the man. He saw Clara's curious expression upon hearing Aldway's involvement.

Aldway blushed as the man continued. "Yeah, this one tackled and pinned him to the ground until Sir Peter and the rest of dem arrived. Like I said, there were two other people involved, so he can't take all the credit. A big lad nearly knocked him unconscious, which was quite impressive since he only hit him once with one arm. His other one was injured. Eventually, Sir Peter's boy did him in with a lethal lightning strike. Of course, if I wasn't so injured, I'd have killed the ugly blighter for sure."

"I'm sure you would have and thank you so much for your account of current events, er…" Aldway said sarcastically.

Oblivious to this, the man said, "Sam, and you're welcome."

Clara took a deep breath in, trying to register all the information she had just received. "First of all, I have so many questions, like how he got past the magic proof defenses, who he was targeting, and how do we know there aren't more?" Clara asked eagerly.

Before Aldway could respond, Sam answered for him rather abruptly, "The gangly ginger pike man, I think his named was Kamden, explained that White stone is shit when up against really potent magic. That's my take, anyway. You'll have to ask him for more information. As for who he wanted, some woman named Olga. Bit of an odd name. Don't think it's Iiadecan in origin. Anyway, we pretty much don't know if there are more like him."

Clara felt uneasy about what she had just heard. "What? So you're telling me we have no fucking plan, in case of another shape shifting assassin?" Clara said emphatically.

To calm her, Aldway said, "I suppose that's what the extra security is for, and Sir Peter is asking around for any information about the assassination attempt."

"We'll all be fucking dead at that point!" she retorted.

Aldway, again, tried to mollify Clara by saying, "You're being a bit dramatic."

To which Clara responded rather aggressively, "Am I?! There was a shapeshifter here, there could be others and they could potentially look like anyone. Also, I wonder what else White stone will not protect us against?"

"The woman has a point"

Both Aldway and Clara were quite vexed by Sam constantly intruding on their conversation and looked at him with disapproval.

"What? It's not like I can go anywhere. I can hear your whole bloody conversation. Look, we're in this together now. This concerns me just as much as it does you. What are we gonna do?"

"We aren't doing anything. You stay here," she said, referring to Sam. "And you keep him company. Make sure he doesn't do anything stupid," Clara said to Aldway.

"Where are you going?" asked Aldway.

"To find some answers," replied Clara as she scurried off into the crowd.

Sam turned to Aldway. "What does she think I'm going to do? Hop about on one foot? That woman's something else."

Clara saw Kamden speaking to Sarah. She overheard their conversation, even though they were whispering.

"Sarah, you said you tell me later," said Kamden. He seemed rather annoyed with his sister.

"I know, but I didn't mean now. Besides, there's too many people around who were already spooked because of the incident," said Sarah carefully, looking around.

"You weren't this secretive back home. Also, why are you wearing one glove that is clearly oversized?" asked Kamden.

"Look. I said I'll tell you later and I'll tell you later when everything's cooled off," said Sarah.

Out of the corner of her eye, she spotted Clara listening. She turned to Clara and gave her a disingenuous smile. "I'm sorry, Clara, did you need something?"

Clara immediately knew Sarah was hiding something. "You know you two haven't mastered the art of whispering."

"I-I-I," Sarah stammered.

"Don't bother, I heard everything," said Clara.

Sarah hung her head low, ashamedly. "Oh, don't look so defeated. I haven't come to divulge your secret, at least not yet. Besides, I'm not the Archiater," said Clara nonchalantly.

Sarah had a frightened look on her face.

"He's behind me, isn't he?" asked Clara. Sarah nodded. She turned around to see a concerned Giles.

"Hi, what brings you here Archiater?" Clara smiled, saying the first thing that came to her head.

Giles, seeing through her façade, responded by saying, "You know, people have been behaving oddly, even before the incident. It's all connected to the tunnels. Something must've happened down there. I figure you might as well tell us, Sarah. Give us a proper explanation of how you got the bruise under your eye, eh?"

Sarah, unprepared for such questioning, said, "You see, it was dark and heh, heh, it's quite embarrassing. Tim, bless his heart, was trying to—"

"Don't bother concocting another lie," Giles interrupted. "Listen. I get the barracks is not the best place to discuss sensitive matters, especially given the climate, so I commend you for being wise enough to remain silent. But, Sarah, people are starting to panic. We need to reassure them they are safe. To determine that, I need to know exactly what we are dealing with, understand?"

"Yes, Archiater," said Sarah.

"Now, Clara. Gather everyone. Olga has woken. Oh, and Sarah, we will discuss the events of the tunnels later," said Giles.

"Right," replied Sarah.

Clara gathered the healers and injured around Olga. Most of the injured were already healed or in the process of healing, so this was not a difficult task. Olga's bed was in the center back of the barracks. She was sitting up and looked fatigued. Sir Peter placed a gentle hand on her shoulder. "Do you remember anything from the attack?" said Sir Peter softly.

Olga turned to Sir Peter wearily and caressed his cheek and said, "You're a good boy, Agnarr. Always remember that."

"Oh boy, she's gone again," Swithin said under his breath.

Sir Peter held her hand and he smiled. "I will, but I wanted to know if you remembered anything about the man who attacked you," said Sir Peter slowly.

Olga looked bemused for a moment, which worried everyone. Her countenance soon changed to that of lucidity. "Ah yes, he was a Holme."

"Holme?" asked Sir Peter.

"They were an old house of shapeshifters that used to live in Arglia (ARGH-LEIA)."

"So, Hector's receiving foreign aid. Is he that desperate?" Sir Peter asked.

"I don't believe this attack to reflect the sentiments of the whole nation of Arglia, but rather a solitary action from one wayward house," explained Olga.

"What do you mean, wayward?" asked Lady Branson.

"Last I remember, the Holme house had disbanded. It's believed they were betrayed and later their manor was overrun by bandits. The remaining survivors fled to other lands such as Iiadec. That's most likely where Hector met him and was so impressed with his abilities that he recruited him. You see, the Holme bloodline are magic-based shapeshifters, who can shape shift despite magic dampening material and are some of the best in their craft. That's how I knew he was a Holme; when he posed as Clara," said Olga.

"That explains how he was able to transform inside," said Kamden. "Olga, how did you know he wasn't me?" asked Clara.

Olga smiled. "My child, it was easy. Your aura is so much different from his. That is something you cannot mask."

Clara was slightly taken aback by what she had just heard. "You can sense auras without seeing them? Is this by magic?"

Olga giggled. "No, my dear, just years of meditative practice. Don't worry, dear, there is no shape shifter here. I would know."

"Uh, how exactly?" asked Tim, genuinely curious about her ambiguous explanation.

Olga looked off into the distance as though viewing something. "Patience. All will be revealed in time. When the soul bleeds, so too will the vessel and only then will it know what it means to be alive and what it means to die."

Tears began to spring from Olga's eyes as she cried softly. "What does that mean?" Lady Branson asked gently.

"It describes pain. It was my father's last words."

Lady Branson looked at Sir Peter and he looked back at her and understood.

He turned to Olga and said gently, "We can talk when you're ready. For now, you need your rest."

As he tried to put the blanket on her, she seized his arm. She looked terrified. "No, I cannot rest, for I fear... I can still be useful, uh, auras." "Alright, just remember to take your time, Olga. Don't push yourself too hard," Lady Branson said, as she held Olga's other hand affectionately.

Olga closed her eyes and took a deep breath in. After that, she seemed more present. As she spoke, she seemed more confident in herself.

"Auras are present even when invisible and each is unique in how they feel. I was able to feel that he was different from you, Clara, despite his near perfect disguise. I can tell most everyone in this room is themselves."

"Most everyone?" asked Clara.

Olga smiled. "Attentive as always. I must confess, I am not familiar with everyone's auras, but I know plenty such as yours, Peter's, Elysant's, Tim's, Alywin's, and so on. I may be old, but sensing auras is not something you forget. It's instinctual once you learn it."

"And that's the best we can hope for," Sir Peter said reassuringly.

Wilona, who was standing next to Tim, whispered in his ear, "She seemed so sad when she mentioned her father's last words. What do you suppose they meant? Her explanation was rather vague, don't you think?" "I don't know, Wilona. I suppose it tells us she has had a hard life," said Tim.

"You know, I never really thanked her for saving me. I'm going to give her a great big hug. Would that be appropriate?"

"Just be careful, she's quite fragi—"

Before Tim could finish his sentence, Wilona ran up to Olga and hugged her warmly. "Thank you," she said.

Olga giggled. "It is I who should be thanking you for taking care of an old woman." She gently ran her fingers through Wilona's hair. "You are a bundle of joy and a blessed child, Wilona."

Afterwards, Olga continued to talk about how she thwarted Eardwulf's assassination attempt and, in turn, his escape. Aldway was generally impressed by Olga's feats. "First the business with the dragon, then stopping an assassin by suppressing his magic. You're quite remarkable." "Thank you, child, but those were joint efforts. It is important to remember, in these dark times, we are stronger together."

"Everyone, the threat has been neutralized. I suggest you carry on in a normal fashion," said Giles.

He turned to Swithin and whispered, "You will be in charge for the time being. Lady Branson and I are having a meeting about the tunnels." "Where will you have this meeting?" asked Swithin. "In the dungeon," Giles replied.

Swithin gave Giles a concerned look. Giles responded by saying, "It's the only place in the keep where we can speak freely without frightening the others. And don't worry, Sir Peter will accompany me, along with others. You may inform everyone, be as delicate as you deem fit."

Swithin nodded and faced the crowd and said bluntly, "Listen up. I'm in charge. The Archiater and Lady Branson have something to do. Don't ask any stupid questions. Now carry on yer lazy good fer nothins."

No one in the garrison raised any objections. Though there were more than a few concerned faces.

Giles groaned in response. This was the farthest thing from delicate that he could imagine, but what did he expect from Swithin In another part of the garrison, Lady Branson and Sir Peter were talking. Godfrey was with Aldway.

"You know, things have really quietened down here. Maybe you could stay here and ride out the siege. From what I heard from Edmund, the war is already won. We have a dragon, thanks to you and Godfrey," said Lady Branson.

"Thanks to me he nearly died," replied Sir Peter.

"You mustn't torture yourself. You're a good man, Peter, and one I fell in love with. You have to believe that," said Lady Branson as she gently placed her hand on his cheek. She slid her hand down to the side of his neck, just behind the ear. She positioned her other hand on the opposite side. With her fingertips at the back of his neck, she gently pulled him closer. They drew nearer until their foreheads touched. They locked eyes for a moment or two, then Sir Peter said in a breathy whisper, "Oh, Elysant."

Lady Branson smiled. When they eventually separated, they began to speak casually.

"You know, Godfrey called me mum today," Lady Branson said rather excitedly.

"Did he now?" said Sir Peter.

"Yes, but I think it was an accident," she said, grinning, still quite excited to deliver the news.

Sir Peter smiled. "A victory, nonetheless."

"After the war, we can return to the manor and live in peace. No more fighting, no more wars. Just me, you, Godfrey, grandfather... Is that wishful thinking?"

"No, it is not. Even when the future seems unstable, we must cling on to hope because, apart from God, it's the only thing that keeps us going," said Sir Peter.

Lady Branson smiled. "You do pay attention when I talk." "How could I not? You're my wife," Sir Peter said.

Lady Branson giggled. "Grandfather has met someone," said Lady Branson. "Really? Who?" he asked.

"A woman named Eva from Eredith. Of course, it's nothing official, but I could see that they fancy each other. She seems lovely," said Lady Branson.

"Then I can't wait to meet her," replied Sir Peter.

"If all goes well, maybe she will come and live with us," said Lady Branson.

"I suppose so," said Sir Peter. His mind was somewhere else, and he looked off into the distance with a concerned look on his face. Lady Branson, who was looking at him, noticed he seemed troubled.

"You're worried about Godfrey, aren't you? Well, you needn't be."

"Elysant. It was his first kill, and I didn't prepare him for that," said Sir Peter.

"There's nothing you could've done to prepare him for such a thing. You just have to trust that he learned from the example you set forth," said Lady Branson.

"But am I the best example, given my own past?" said Sir Peter.

"You are the best example because of it," said Lady Branson. She looked around, making sure no one overheard, and whispered, "Godfrey is not his father."

"Yes, I know… One day we're going to have to tell him," said Sir Peter.

Lady Branson was uncomfortable about the prospect of divulging such a secret, but nodded her head, anyway.

Meanwhile, in another section of the Garrison, Aldway was talking to Godfrey, who seem annoyed by Aldway's constant questioning. Godfrey was sitting on a bed. Aldway standing next to him.

"I'm not ill. I do not need to be attended to by a healer," said Godfrey, irritated.

"There are several types of injuries beyond physical such as emotional, mental, oh, did I mention it's alright to not be alright?"

Godfrey groaned. "You won't stop mentioning it."

"Well, it is. We're in the middle of a war and are currently under siege. It's only natural that—"

"If this is about the assassin, I do not regret my decision. He was a bad man and was going to kill Olga and possibly Wilona," interrupted Godfrey. "And no one's disagreeing with you, but how did it make you feel?"

Godfrey was hesitant to respond, but Aldway waited patiently.

Godfrey's eyes were glued to the floor, and he said in a low voice, "I don't know."

It was unclear to Aldway whether this was an honest answer, but what was apparent was Godfrey was uncomfortable speaking about the subject any further and Aldway did not want to pressure him for an answer. Aldway wisely changed the subject.

"Why do you want to be a knight?"

"To protect the ones I love. A man is only as powerful as the people who love him. It is not enough to protect their corporal bodies, but their minds, hearts, and souls as well. All of which are essential principles that make up the way I choose to live my life. For, without them, I am nothing."

"That's very noble of you, Godfrey, and you think becoming a knight of Corithni will help you protect people?" asked Aldway.

"I know so," said Godfrey unwaveringly.

***

Giles was discussing with Lady Branson and Sir Peter about their potential meeting. Clara overheard them. "I'd like to come with you, if that's alright Archiater, milady, Sir Peter?"

"I think that would be wise, given that you'll eventually have to relay the information to Lady Franklin. Clara, I want you to gather the others," said Giles.

"Others?" asked Clara.

"Tim, Alywin and Sarah. They explored the tunnels before. We need to find out the truth about what happened down there," responded Giles. "Maybe we should bring Kamden. He seems to know a lot about buildings and Sarah will probably be comfortable with her brother around during the interrogation," said Sir Peter.

"It's not an interrogation. Just an informal discussion about the safety of the tunnels," said Giles angrily.

"There's nothing really informal about a dungeon, though," said Lady Branson.

Giles groaned. "It was the only place. I asked you two if you had any objections," Giles said crossly.

"And we don't. It's just we have to remember they're probably already frightened about the assassin and who knows what they discovered down there. We have to be gentle with them, and you can be a bit..." Lady Branson was hesitant to say.

"A bit what? Elysant, Elysant?" Sir Peter added, "Intimidating." "Intimidating? Do you find me intimidating?" exclaimed Giles. "No, no, not to us, er, just to other people," said Lady Branson,

deemphasizing the words other people in hopes Giles would not hear. "Nonsense!" Giles turned to Clara. "Clara, do you find me intimidating?"

"Uh, uh," stammered Clara.

"Oh, never mind. Just get the others, including Kamden, and make haste!" said Giles.

"Yes, Archiater," Clara said as she scurried off.

She found Tim, Alywin and Sarah discussing something, and she decided to listen to their conversation, unbeknownst to them.

"The Archiater wants to discuss what happened down there," Sarah whispered.

"What did you tell him?" asked Alywin. "Nothing!" Sarah exclaimed. "What are we going to say? He's most likely rounding up people who know," said Tim.

"Who else knows, Tim?" Clara blurted out.

Startled, Tim said, "Oh God, she's everywhere. Er, ahem, I mean knows what?"

Clara's eyes narrowed. "Don't play coy, Tim. You know what I mean?" "What do you want, Clara?" said Alywin brusquely.

"I demand to know the truth. Who else knows?" said Clara.

Alywin, quite vexed, said, "Last time I checked, you weren't the bloody Archiater or Lady Branson for that matter, so sod off."

"Excuse me. I'll have you know I'm fourth in command here after Swithin, and I will not be spoken to in such a manner by a brazen ruffian." "I'm sorry. I didn't realize you were highborn and not lowborn shit like the rest of us," Alywin said sarcastically.

Before Clara could respond, Tim stepped in. "Hey, hey we're all friends here. Let's just relax."

Clara looked at Alywin angrily. "I wouldn't use that term so loosely."

In an attempt to alleviate tension, or possibly simply panic, Sarah said, "Colin, he knows."

"Oh, for fuck's sake, Sarah!" said Alywin angrily. "What?! I'm sorry, she was going to find out, anyway."

Clara's eyes widened. She was in disbelief at hearing what she considered a serious blunder.

"You told the bloody sell sword?"

"Sssh, keep your voice down!" Sarah said in a loud whisper. "This man's father used to work for Hector," said Clara. "And he rebelled!" Sarah retorted angrily.

In an attempt to placate Sarah, Clara spoke slowly and methodically. "Sarah, you don't know this man. He could be dangerous. We shouldn't be giving away sensitive information to sell swords."

"I trust him, and he knows things. He can help," Sarah said defiantly. "Sarah," Clara said with a concerned look on her face.

"Look, he's involved now. There's no taking it back. If Corithni didn't trust him as well, they'd have left him to die on the battlefield. Besides, Lady Branson already told everyone about the tunnels. It's not like he wouldn't figure out how to access them should the worst-case scenario arise," said Sarah.

Clara sighed. "Fine. If you have so much faith in this sell sword, then perhaps we should take him with us. Oh, and get your brother. His knowledge may be required."

"Wait, where are we going?" asked Sarah.

"To the dungeon. The Archiater is holding a meeting."

Tim gulped. Alywin responded by saying, "Relax. It's a meeting, not the gallows."

Clara smirked. "That's the most sensible thing you've said all day, Alywin, but I suppose even you have your moments."

Alywin scowled. "You know you could've just told us this in the beginning instead of acting like a proper—"

"I don't have time to mince words with you, Alywin. Make yourself useful and retrieve the sell sword. Tim, you go with him and see to it that Alywin actually completes the task. He seems to have very little respect for his superiors." Clara interrupted

"Really?" said Alywin. He was quite annoyed with her.

"Well, what are you three just standing here for? You've been given your orders. Now, make haste, don't keep the Archiater waiting"

As the three departed, Alywin turned to Tim and said, "Who does she think she is, barking orders at us like that?"

Tim responded by saying, "Alywin, how long have you known her?" Alywin groaned.

They soon returned, and Clara led them to where Giles, Lady Branson, and Sir Peter were located.

"Clara, what took so long?" said Giles.

"I'm sorry, Archiater, they were being insolent," said Clara. "We were not!" Tim exclaimed.

"Alright, it was mainly only Alywin," clarified Clara. Alywin rolled his eyes in response.

Giles' eyes gravitated toward Colin, who made him feel uneasy.

Colin noticed this and tried to mollify him by saying as cordially as he could, "Hello, Archiater. I heard there was a meeting. I'm happy to attend, if you'll have me."

Giles looked at Clara. "They told him what happened down there, and Sarah insisted that he can be trusted."

Giles turned to Lady Branson. "If Sarah trusts him, then so do I," she said.

Giles then looked at Sir Peter. "If we can't trust our allies, who can we trust?" said Sir Peter.

Finally, he turned to Colin. "Are you sure you're fit to travel, given your injuries?"

"Eh, I'll be alright. Sarah's been taking care of me, and I promise not to stress myself too much," responded Colin nonchalantly.

"Very well, let the meeting commence," said Giles.

CHAPTER FOURTEEN

CONFESSIONS

They descended into the dungeon. The dungeon was dark because it wasn't used much, thus; the wall mounted candles were not lit. Luckily for the group, some half-used flint was on the floor. Sir Peter lit the candles, though this light was not sufficient, because the oil from the candles had nearly dissolved, thus some of them were not operational. As a result, the group relied on rush lights, with the exception of Lady Branson, who utilized fire manipulation to generate a small flame emanating from her palm.

They did not wait in the darkness for too long before Giles was the first to speak. "Let's not waste any time. I gathered you all here to find out what went down in the tunnels. This is a matter of utmost urgency. The survival of our people may depend on it. Please take that into consideration. Now that we've addressed that, does anyone volunteer to speak first? Do not fret, you may speak freely here."

Alywin spoke up because the others were reluctant. He took one deep breath in and said, "The assassin wasn't the only person to infiltrate the castle."

Clara gasped. "What?!" asked Giles. "Was it another castor?" asked Sir Peter.

"A woman and two others. I'm not sure the other two were castors, though. The woman was definitely a hokraft practitioner."

"How'd they get in?" asked Sir Peter. Alywin looked at Sarah and she nodded.

He continued. "Sarah is a Mason, which means she bears the mark of the Mason. It allows her to manipulate Corithni's castle terrain, where other terrain elementals could not."

Sarah raised her right hand and removed Colin's glove, revealing the mark etched into her skin. Upon seeing this mark, Kamden removed his glove, revealing the same mark on the back of his right hand.

Sarah and Kamden looked at each other in awe. "I got mine defending the eastern wall. They told me to come to you, Sir Peter, afterwards. I guess they figured you'd know what to do. I'm sorry I wasn't entirely truthful earlier. I told you that the rocks from the wall fell down to form an obstruction for the enemies, when truthfully, I moved the rocks to form a pile to close the crack in the wall," said Kamden.

"No need to apologize. I can't imagine how Blake and the other men would have taken it, if you had told the truth. They'd probably call you a demon," said Sir Peter. He chuckled as he said the last part of his sentence. Everyone else was not amused at what they thought he was implying.

Their faces were ripe with concern. Sarah, Tim, and Kamden looked particularly terrified. Sir Peter was quite embarrassed. These things often happened when he attempted to be humorous. He often suffered from poor timing or, in his current predicament, not being able to read the climate of the room before telling a joke. Heggr was so much better at these sorts of things.

"I'm sorry. That wasn't funny. What I meant was they wouldn't understand. You're not demons," he said, referring to Sarah and Kamden. "They're called infected, dear," corrected Lady Branson. "They're

infected?!" Tim said fearfully.

"No!" said Lady Branson and Sir Peter in unison. "Oh, thank God," said Tim, relieved.

"Those things are called curse marks," said Sir Peter. Sarah's and Kamden's eyes widened.

Tim blurted out, "That doesn't sound any better!"

Lady Branson looked at Sir Peter and said gently, "Peter, I think you're scaring them."

"That's what they're called in Mylec, not because they're cursed per se," said Sir Peter, before being interrupted by Tim.

"Per se!" his voice cracked after uttering the word. "You can't be sure of these things. After all, I don't have one."

Realizing he was making things worse, Lady Branson said more forcefully but still softly, "Peter."

Sir Peter got the hint. "Ahem, they're called curse marks because once they are activated, they can't be removed."

"Not even with magic?" asked Colin.

"Not even with magic. In fact, if you cut off the part of the body the mark formed on, it will shift to another part of the body if the bearer is still alive," explained Sir Peter.

Colin looked disheartened.

"Is there something the matter, Colin?" said Lady Branson.

Colin sighed. "What I'm about to tell you may sound like heresy, but it's true… When I was a boy, I saw members of the church of Mirama taking people, bearing curse marks like Sarah's, against their will. I recognized them by their long white clothes and the vigil at the center of their chest, a fish within two circles."

"The symbol of Jaynor," said Sir Peter.

"Yes, father said these people were pagans and that the church hated pagans well because of, uh, your people," said Colin.

"Understandable," replied Sir Peter.

Colin continued. "So anyway, father told me and my brothers not to get involved because Mirama's influence went beyond Iiadec, so meddling in the church's business would be unwise, as he put it. As I got older, I heard rumblings about Mirama. Most of it sounded like horseshit, but some of it made sense. Some claim they want to cleanse pagan influence from all of Iiadec and eventually Arcadiem. They want to forcefully unify all of Arcadiem under one banner of Arda worshiping people with themselves at the helm," said Colin.

"But there are other holy cities in Arcadiem. Won't they have competition?" said Tim.

"Some in Mirama consider them illegitimate, so I've heard," replied Colin.

"Mirama itself is illegitimate and so is the idea of holy Cities. Jaynor said, *"The ground I walk upon is sacred and so too, is everything connected to it. It should be revered, for it is a home to all."* He wasn't just talking about Mirama, he was talking about the whole world," said Alywin.

The others were surprised by Alywin's knowledge of the book of Noga. "I didn't know you read the Holy Scriptures," said Sir Peter.

"Of course I have. How else am I to disagree with it if I don't know what it says." said Alywin.

"Fair point," said Sir Peter.

"Be careful when professing your nonbelief, Alywin. You're in Corithni now, where people are liberal, but should the church ever find out, I fear they would not tolerate it," warned Giles.

"You know what's wrong? The church has too much power and influence. Why are we afraid of monks and clerics who are supposed to preach peace but instead spend their time harassing people who are different from them? Faith itself is a belief. Which means you can choose to have it or not. So why is the church set on choosing for you?" asked Alywin.

"In an ideal world, they would not have a say in your personal choice, but sometimes men pervert the words of God for their own agendas. It's hard to prepare men for battle on the premise that you should *love thy enemy*," explained Sir Peter.

"Speaking of agendas. I believe Mirama's got one. Coin. I believe Hector is financing Mirama and they, in turn, are maybe supporting him through their influence, most likely promising a couple of sell swords and castors' salvation in return for supporting Hector's claim," said Colin.

"Why would the church support a man who so brazenly uses hokraft? A practice Godwin himself rebuked?" said Clara.

"Influence is the seed of power that grows steadily under the shadow of conflict, but when it reaches maturation, it adheres to no masters, yet it controls everything whilst remaining in the shadows of obscurity forever, like a dark God you don't realize is there, but it affects every waking moment of your existence, anonymity is an asset something my dad told me long ago," said Colin.

"I didn't realize Galeran Harlow was such a philosopher," said Clara. "The free companies aren't entirely made of halfwits with swords, you know. Besides, he was a knight of Agor first," Colin said playfully.

In an attempt at self-deprecating humor, Sir Peter said, "As a halfwit with a sword, I didn't understand any of that."

Tim laughed, "Good one."

Sir Peter was quite satisfied with himself that he had told a successful joke. Heggr would be proud.

Lady Branson was not amused. "That's not funny Peter!"

"What?! I'm just saying there's a reason I'm not commander," said Sir Peter.

"When you say awful things about yourself, you're hurting me as well," said Lady Branson sternly.

"I'm sorry, Elysant," said Sir Peter.

Sarah and Tim found their banter to be both amusing and endearing. Colin was just relieved that Sir Peter was more than a merciless killer but also a genuinely kind, if not an awkward person. Colin believed he was amongst good people. He thought, maybe if the war went their way, he could stay in a place like this, and they could be his family.

Giles, who was taking everything in, turned to Colin and asked, "Are you suggesting that Mirama has fallen to corruption and desire their own self-interest above the welfare of the people?"

"At the end of the day, it's about power. They want to control things from the shadows without suffering the wrath of the people should something go wrong. That's why they are king makers and not kings. They place a king on the throne as a figurehead when the real power belongs to the church, and everyone is none the wiser. I believe this is what my father meant by influence. They seek to be invisible to people while simultaneously controlling them, making them believe that the only oppressor is the king because he's the only person they can see," said Colin.

"No, that can't be right. Godwin Ackles is a pious man whom I know personally. He wouldn't allow the church to stoop to such depravity," said Giles.

"He's only one man," Alywin responded.

Everyone had pensive looks on their faces. Lady Branson spoke up. "Even if Hector essentially bribed the church into supporting his claim, where did he get all that coin? Sure, Everard's are wealthy, but wealthier than House Fowler, Baudry, Blakeslee and Franklin combined? I don't think so."

"He could be funneling the money from other countries. That assassin had ties to Arglia. Maybe Hector co-opted others to aide him. It wouldn't be the first time a country intervened in other countries' affairs to suit their interests. We did during the fifth Mylec Marauder war," said Kamden.

"That was different, but I see your point. The question is, who would want to see Hector on the throne of Iiadec as opposed to Lord Franklin?" asked Sir Peter.

"The people of Arglia and the neighboring country Lakamo (LA-KA-MOE) used to be provinces to the crown of Iiadec up until 1246 and 1260 NEEOT, respectively. They were also conquered by the Mylecans in 867 NEEOT," said Clara.

"We don't need a history lesson, Clara," Alywin interrupted.

Clara glared at Alywin. "What I was getting at was they may have ill will toward Iiadec and could see the knighting of Sir Peter as an alliance between their former masters. They might see Hector as the more favorable option."

"I doubt it. Neither country is particularly wealthy enough, even with their combined efforts," said Sir Peter.

"If Mirama is too dangerous, then I think a safe bet would be going to Lord Baudry. If the castle should fall, that is," said Sarah.

"Forgive me for my ignorance, but where was Lord Baudry during this entire conflict?" asked Kamden.

"He provides mostly monetary support. He doesn't have an active army to dispatch. He spends most of his wealth to maintain his fortress, Dae le Maut. Its defenses are even more impressive than Corithni. It will hold if Hector's men come for us. The Baudry's have been loyal to the Franklin's for decades. After the Fowlers, they've spent the most coin on the war in favor of the Franklins," explained Sir Peter.

"We've gotten sidetracked with all this talk of Mirama. We came here to discuss the tunnels. Alywin, walk us through it," said Giles.

"Right," said Alywin.

Alywin, Tim, and Sarah continued the harrowing tale in the tunnels. When they finished, they were met initially with silence. Sarah eventually spoke up.

"I know it sounds like madness. I hardly believe it myself. A 200-year-old curse, a giant Othrya vepid rat, a mad witch with an even more demented bloodline, but it's all true. If you go down there, you'll see the beast's corpse under a pile of rubble. The others remained silent.

Kamden eventually broke the silence. "I think I speak for everyone here, with the exception of Colin. It's not that we don't believe you, it's that we don't want to."

"It's fucking disturbing, right?" said Alywin.

"It's really not that bad," said Colin, in an attempt to assuage the situation.

"Not that bad? Are you mad? Corithni was built on cursed ground. The very tunnels we're to escape through, if needed, have most likely been a sanctuary for hokraft practitioners for over 200 fucking years. Who knows what nefarious schemes this Gytha and her cronies have been hatching while we were up there as defenseless as a babe in the woods," said Clara. She began to breathe rapidly.

Tim attempted to mollify his comrade. "Clara, calm down."

Alywin however, took the opportunity to criticize. "And this is why we don't tell you things."

Sarah gave him a scathing look of disapproval before turning to Clara. "Clara, listen to me. Gytha, the last Baltierra, is dead and the curse is lifted. Leland is freed, and the beast is slain. All traces of hokraft are gone."

Clara was not convinced. "Oh yeah? What about that curse Godina placed on your ancestor, Landyn? What was it, Karasa mollo? Theoretically, any castor can learn it. How do we know one of Hector's castors didn't already use it on someone here in Corithni? Oh God, maybe that's how Hector amassed so many followers?"

"She has a point, Sarah," said Kamden.

"Great. As if I needed to be more worried," said Alywin.

"I've never heard of this spell before, and I doubt many castors have. Potent hexes like that usually require a sacrifice and it wouldn't be practical to lead an army where soldiers can't think for themselves. You have to remember, Hector can't attend every battle. His commanders are going to have to make decisions without his input," explained Sir Peter. This seemed to calm Clara. Lady Branson looked at Sir Peter and smiled. "You see, you're not a halfwit with a sword. You're a brilliant man with a sword."

"Pfft, you're swayed by the title of wife," said Sir Peter. "My title does not make my opinion any less relevant." Sir Peter smiled. "Oh, I love you, Elysant."

Before Lady Branson could respond, Giles interrupted. "Focus. We have serious matters to address!" He muttered under his breath, "I can't believe adults are behaving like a pair of adolescents."

Both Lady Branson and Sir Peter chuckled upon hearing his disapproving remark.

Colin turned to Clara. "Look. Despite what went down there, the tunnels are still the safest way out of the castle. Sarah and Kamden are the only ones who can access them, so our enemy has no way of pursuing us if we should flee."

"Not true. What about the other builders or other Masons?" said Clara.

"My father had no siblings; my brother and I are his only children and his current whereabouts are a mystery. I doubt Hector would even know where to find him. As for the other builders, they have since passed and their bloodline has ended. I checked the annals in the library in Sigate," said Sarah.

This answer seemed to satisfy Clara. Kamden was feeling slightly out of place amongst people who were well versed in what went on within the walls of Corithni.

"We're placing a lot of thought into a hypothetical. From what I can tell, in my time outside the castle, it will most likely hold, and there still might be a relief force from Eredith."

"One should never hope for the worst but always be prepared for it," said Sir Peter.

"Speaking of worse things, I fear I may have troubling news. As some of you may know, Sir Richard Brickenden has passed," said Lady Branson.

Sir Peter was visibly saddened upon hearing the news. Lady Branson placed a gentle hand on his shoulder. "We really did try to save him."

Sir Peter turned to her and said, with a rueful smile, "I know he was in good hands and paradise awaits him."

"Forgive me for being insensitive. I did not bring him up just to grieve over him. His death in itself is tragic, but it is what he said before death that I find alarming. I don't know if he is to be believed, though his injuries would suggest... he was attacked by monsters, possibly monsters of old," said Lady Branson.

"Monsters of old? He must've been mistaken. It seems a bit too early for the end of days. I mean, there would be signs. Not to belittle our predicament, but quarreling between Lords doesn't exactly spell the end of the world," said Kamden.

"Hexing a dragon is not enough?" retorted Clara.

Sarah, sensing Clara's hostility, and feeling the need to protect her brother, said, "What he means is that we Arcadiens have a very limited and cultural-biased view of what the signs are for the end of days. Most of us don't know what happens outside of Arcadiem. In fact, most of us here have never stepped foot outside Iadec. So, who's to say that hexing a dragon isn't normal someplace else?"

"Hmmm, you bring up a good point, Sarah. I know Sir Peter's travelled outside of Iiadec. Mylec obviously, and Arglia, where you attended multiple secret gatherings with other swordsmen from across the world. Perhaps he can tell us if our predicament is normal," said Clara. Sir Peter was surprised she knew such information. He didn't remember sharing it so readily. "I suppose nothing gets past you, Clara, but I would hardly call it a secret gathering. It was sanctioned by King Gavin at the time. Although Lord Albert Franklin had a hand in my attendance, he wanted me to observe what he deemed the competition and report back useful information about their respective countries. You see, we formed a group called the cutting edge, inspired by a supposed ancient brotherhood called guard. Yeah, I didn't come up with the names, anyway we were five, including me, from different lands and were considered some of the best non-elemental, non-magical swordsmen in our respective regions. I never bothered to ask about the happenings in their lands. I guess I didn't make a good spy."

"But you made friends. Oh, he's making it sound so serious. I accompanied him to Arglia on occasion. We became close with one of the swordsmen, Li-Chen, from Yetic. His wife, Lin, even helped Peter pick out my wedding ring." Lady Branson held out her hand. On her ring finger was an ornately crafted jade ring. Jade is most common in Yetic.

"That's sounds like a wonderful story, milady, don't you think Tim?" said Sarah, quite enamored by Lady Branson's anecdote.

"Yeah, sure, but also not very helpful," he replied.

Sarah shot him a foul glance. "Er, I mean, it's great you made friends from other lands, milady, really great." He smiled disingenuously. Sarah's features softened into a smile.

"You have no spine," Alywin whispered in Tim's ear.

To which Tim responded by whispering aggressively, "Shut up, Alywin."

"I'm sorry, did you say something?" asked Lady Branson. "Nope. I said nothing, milady," Tim said quickly.

Then Clara said, rather bluntly, "What did Guard do?"

"Why must you pry into this man's business? It's not even relevant," Alywin said angrily.

"It may be relevant. Maybe they knew something about all of these oddities, such as hexing dragons, curse marks, and monsters of old," retorted Clara.

"It's quite alright. I'm happy to oblige. Unfortunately, I don't have much information on Guard if it even existed. Gwydion, the founder of the Cutting Edge, said Guard was a group that was intended to defend the world against threats no one country alone could handle. It is believed that they intended to raise an army of non-magical, non-elemental warriors from different lands to do battle with what they deemed the great evils," said Sir Peter.

"Any particular reason the group is non-magical and non-elemental?" asked Clara.

"Forgive me, it was so long ago, much of Gwydion's words were lost on me and I'm not a historian, but I do recall him saying something that both elemental manipulation and all forms of magic were, in the past, considered by many to be evil practices. Apparently, wars were even fought over them," said Sir Peter.

"An army with the combined might of multiple countries united under a just cause, defending the world against great evils… That sounds like horseshit. It would never work," said Alywin.

"Can't blame you for being cynical. It sounds absurd," said Giles. "But it would be a sight to behold," said Colin.

"Ahem, now back to the matter at hand. Sir Richard was definitely attacked by something, and with his injuries he obtained in battle, he should have perished sooner. Lady Branson can attest to that," said Giles.

Lady Branson nodded her head in agreement.

"For an ailing man, he was quite strong. It took several of us to restrain him from what I assumed were bouts of delirium. Whatever attacked him really traumatized him" said Alywin.

"Where was he attacked?" asked Colin. "Eredith," replied Giles.

"Eredith? You mean during the battle of Eredith? You're sure he wasn't attacked by Hector's castors posing as monsters? Because some castors can make one see things that aren't real," said Colin.

"I am well aware of faux magic and what it does to the mind, but what Sir Richard described was vividly disturbing. Something no mere castor could conjure up. His injuries were real both of body and mind. Sir Richard also claimed Hector's men were amongst the fallen," said Giles. "You were there, milady. Is he to be believed?" asked Clara. "There was no lie in his eyes," replied Lady Branson.

"Then that means my brothers were killed by monsters instead of Hector's men?" Colin was visibly disturbed by the news.

Sarah looked at him. She wanted to say something that would comfort him, but she was lost for words. In truth, she was equally troubled by the news.

Kamden, who was distraught, said, "These monsters, defeated forces from Etlio, Eredith, and Hector's army, how are we going to survive? They've probably stormed Athamar already, which means there is no relief force coming."

"We mustn't give up hope. Lord Fowler most likely didn't send his whole army. They're probably defending the castle in case of an attack. There could still be a chance," said Sir Peter.

This seemed to calm Kamden.

"What I don't understand is, how did you know there were tunnels under Corithni?" said Colin.

"Sir Richard provided us with a map that he intercepted from the enemy," said Tim.

"A map? Who could have given them such a map?" asked Clara. "A spy," said Sir Peter gravely.

"So, there are more like Bancroft?" asked Alywin. "So, it would seem," said Sir Peter.

Clara turned to Tim. "Do you still have it?"

Sarah took out the map from her upper blouse and handed it to Clara. Alywin grimaced. "That's where you put the dirty old map?"

"Well, where else am I going to put it? It's either here or that other place," retorted Sarah.

"Ugh, I didn't need to know that," said Alywin.

"You should probably invest in some type of satchel. Putting dirty paper on flesh is bound to cause infection," said Kamden.

"Thank you, Kamden, for your advice. I didn't know you were a healer," said Sarah sarcastically. Then, feeling she had been too harsh said, "Sorry, that was unnecessary."

Clara studied the map briefly before saying, "This parchment is of poor quality. It's brittle and the ink drawn into it is faded. Given the inaccuracies of the map, I wager it was scribed before the construction of the castle."

"That certainly makes sense. Often times, builders' first drafted plans are made on cheaper quality parchment and when plans are finalized, they are moved to better quality parchment where they can be displayed," said Kamden.

"So, whoever stole this map knew about Landyn, Godina, and the Balterria curse. They probably suspected something was down there," said Alywin.

"That explains the explosives. They'd want to cover their tracks so nobody else could find whatever they thought was down there," said Tim. "But the map is over 200 years old. Who else could have known about it? I doubt Godina would have divulged her plans to just anyone who wasn't under the influence of Karasa Mollo," said Sarah. "Wait. Explosives?" asked Clara.

"Enough to start a blaze," said Tim. "Undermining," said Sir Peter.

Kamden had a befuddled expression on his face. "This is rather confusing, undermining usually involves digging tunnels underground to get to the enemy stronghold or a place to hide noncombatants. So, why then, do these besiegers need a detailed, albeit inaccurate, map of the layout of Corithni that leads to the keep? Simply getting beyond the wall would suffice."

"The dragon didn't burn down the keep for a reason. Maybe they were not concerned with transporting an army, but collecting something from the keep specifically. It's like you said, why would they need a map that reveals a network of tunnels if their only goal was to attack?" said Alywin. "I think the real question is on how they were planning on getting in or out without a Mason. It would take days to build an adjacent tunnel through solid rock, and that's not without being seen first," said Sarah.

"Maybe Gytha was supposed to let them in. You know, with Landyn's dead hand and as for the thing they were looking for, maybe it wasn't in the keep but somewhere else, maybe it was Salkar," said Tim.

"Salkar?" asked Sir Peter.

"Does that name mean anything to you? Is it pagan?" asked Giles. "No, not that I know of," said Sir Peter.

"He was the giant rat we had the unfortunate pleasure of meeting. Leland thought he was just calling himself that, though," said Alywin. "I wasn't the most devout pagan, but I think I would've remembered stories of a giant rat in the sagas," said Sir Peter.

"Sounds mad, doesn't it? Wouldn't have believed it myself if it weren't for this." said Colin.

He removed a giant rat ear from a satchel attached to his belt and displayed it to the others.

"Ugh!" said Lady Branson, Giles, and Clara in unison.

"Will you put that thing away? It's fucking repulsive!" said Clara. Colin put the ear back in his satchel.

"It was no doubt Alywin's idea to collect the ear?" said Clara derisively. "Of course it was. I can't almost die in the bloody tunnels and have people call me a liar. Also, Colin, I want my ear back," said Alywin. "But Sarah said you said I could have it," said Colin.

"That's not what I said, Sarah," Alywin said angrily. "What? You said he could have it," said Sarah.

"I said he could hold it because I didn't want you holding it and damaging its structural integrity with the oils of your contaminated body," said Alywin

"Alywin!" said Tim furiously.

"Just when I was beginning to think you weren't a complete arsehole," said Sarah.

"What were yer gonna do with it, anyway? Preserve it and put it on a shelf for public display? A fucking waste, I say," said Colin.

"Then what were you gonna do with it?" asked Alywin. "Something practical... I was going to eat it."

Lady Branson nearly vomited in her mouth. "Elysant, are you all right?" asked Sir Peter.

"What? I wasn't going to eat it raw. I was gonna fry it," said Colin. "Fry my ear and I will break your other arm," said Alywin.

"No need to be aggressive. It's a big fucking ear. We can share, see?" Colin removed the ear from his satchel again.

"Please stop," Lady Branson pleaded. She was already queasy, but they didn't seem to hear her and continued quarreling.

"Sarah, why did you tell him he could have my ear? This is why I can't trust you with things," said Alywin.

"Excuse me. Who saved your arse in the tunnels? Me! So I'd appreciate some fucking respect," said Sarah angrily.

"But what does that have to do with my ear?" retorted Alywin. "Alywin, you can take that ear and shove it up your—"

"Enough! What the fuck is the matter with you three? This is a meeting discussing sensitive matters, not a bloody market. And Colin, for the last time, put that bloody thing away. You're upsetting Lady Branson," said Clara.

"Thank you, Clara," Lady Branson said weakly. Colin put the ear back in his satchel.

"Now that everyone got that out of their system, let's proceed with our discussion," said Giles.

"Archiater, on behalf of me and my comrades, I'd like to apologize to you all for our petulant behavior. It shan't happen again," said Sarah.

"Apology accepted," said Giles.

"There's nothing petulant about discussing the importance and rarity of a rat Othrya vepid's ear. It belongs in a museum," said Alywin vehemently.

"It belongs in my belly," said Colin.

"Colin, give me the ear," demanded Sir Peter. "What? But why?" asked Colin rather querulously. "Yeah, what for?" Alywin said, equally petulant. "Give it," said Sir Peter more forcefully.

"No," said Colin.

"Give it," insisted Sir Peter. "No," Colin said again. "Give it," said Sir Peter. "No" Colin said.

"Colin," said Sir Peter.

"Alright, alright, but when do I get it back?" asked Colin as he handed Sir Peter the ear.

Sir Peter folded it and placed it in his satchel.

"You mean when do I get it back?" Alywin retorted.

"You'll get it back when you both stop acting like children," said Sir Peter.

Tim looked at Sarah and said sarcastically, "That Colin is a real mature lad, eh, isn't he, Sarah?"

"Oh, shut up Tim," Sarah retorted. Sarah turned to Giles and said, "Again, apologies, Archiater. Colin and Alywin are under a lot of stress because, uh, the war, but of course, you knew that, heh, heh, war bad, peace good. Go Arda, yay! Ahem, that was silly, sorry. I don't know why I said that. Anyway, it's, uh, lack of sleep causing their, um, well irrational behavior."

"I dunno what you're rambling on about. I slept like a babe. And irrational behavior, really? Coming from the person who coined the phrase Go Arda yay. How ridiculously asinine. Why does she think she can speak for me?" said Alywin.

Sarah was livid, and her face became red. Kamden, who had seen this look before on his sister, tried to placate her by saying. "Sarah, he didn't mean it."

"Stay out of this Kamden!" Kamden remained silent.

Tim then tried his approach. "Sarah, you can't take this sort of thing too personally. Alywin, he, uh, has a disease."

"What disease, Tim?!" Sarah demanded furiously.

Quite frightened, Tim panicked and said the first thing that came to his head, "Er, arsehole."

"I am not an arsehole. I'm just allergic to bullshit," said Alywin. "That sounds like something an arsehole would say," said Clara. "You would know," retorted Alywin.

"Fuck you, Alywin, I hope Sir Peter kicks your arse, so you can stop menacing us in the barracks," said Clara.

"Who do I menace?" asked Alywin. "Everyone. Just ask Swithin," replied Clara.

"Oh. If that old cunt said it, then it must be true," said Alywin sarcastically.

"Watch your tone, Alywin," said Giles.

But Alywin did not heed Giles' warning. He instead turned to Sarah. "You can end your tantrum. You're embarrassing yourself. Everyone knows you're not going to do anything because you're just a good little girl from Sigate."

Sarah could no longer tolerate Alywin's derisive remarks. "Alywin, don't you start with me or, so help me God, I will tear this whole fucking castle down!"

"Young lady!" Giles exclaimed. "Sorry, Archiater," said Sarah.

Colin turned to Kamden. "Is your sister usually like this in Sigate?" "Well, she's always been quick to anger," said Kamden.

"I'll be honest... I am aroused," said Colin. "Ugh, I'm standing right here!" said Kamden.

Tim looked at Colin. "Have you no respect? Are you that uncouth? Sarah is a woman who should not be sexualized by a bloody sell sword," said Tim.

"Actually, Tim, it's alright, it's kinda flattering," Sarah said. Alywin rolled his eyes and muttered, "Where's this girl's head?"

Tim was visibly angered. "Flattering? Sarah, he wanted to eat a fucking rat ear!"

"Oh, don't be so judgmental, Tim," Sarah retorted.

She looked at Colin. "Just out of curiosity—" said Sarah. "A big ole fat one," replied Colin. Sarah giggled.

"Oh my God, this is a bloody nightmare," said Tim.

Still looking at Colin, Sarah said, "Does this mean we're, er, um, lovers?"

Colin, looking nervous, said, "Well, um, I uh, it's just that, that's a bit much, don't you think?"

Clara was furious. "Colin, you lowdown, rat eating shit. Sarah is not a tavern whore!" shouted Clara.

"Mind your fucking business, Clara!" cried Alywin. "Make me!" shouted Clara.

"Enough! Anyone else who so much as utters irrelevant drivel, I will personally see to it that they are publicly flogged. Do I make myself clear?" said Giles.

"Yes, Archiater," Alywin, Tim, Sarah, and Clara said in unison.

There was someone descending from the barracks. He was average in height, but somewhat brawny.

"Aldway? What are you doing here? This is a private meeting," said Giles.

"It's just that we, uh, heard a lot of shouting. We were worried someone was being tortured. It is a dungeon and all, heh heh. Anyway, Swithin asked me to check it out."

"How much have you heard?" Giles demanded.

"Oh, nothing much. Honestly, Just the part where Alywin unfairly criticizes Clara and something about a rat ear. Yeah, not much."

"You see, he understands," said Clara.

"Then why don't you just marry him," Alywin retorted. "I mean, it's not beyond reason," said Aldway.

"She barely knows you, Aldway," said Tim.

"Yeah, that's just not happening," said Clara bluntly.

Rather embarrassed, Aldway laughed nervously. "Right. A rather silly thing to say. I was only joking, of course. Anyway, Alywin, you should go easy on Clara. She's a woman, after all."

"And what is that supposed to mean?!" Lady Branson, Sarah, and Clara exclaimed in unison.

"Uh-oh," said Sir Peter.

"Tread carefully, my boy," advised Giles.

"I uh, I uh, what I meant was at a certain time of the month—" "Get out!" shouted Clara, Sarah, and Lady Branson.

"Yes, milady." Aldway immediately returned to the barracks. "Oh, she's definitely not marrying him now," said Colin.

"Now that we've wasted enough time, does anyone have anything relevant to ask?" asked Giles.

"Er, I do actually," said Kamden. "You may proceed," said Giles. "Tim, you mentioned explosives, which are very rare in Iiadec. Do you know what type?"

"Well, Alywin opened the container, but I'm guessing it was some type of fire starter material," said Tim.

"It was some liquid stuff that smelled of resin, naphtha, and quicklime. I'm sure there was other stuff in the concoction, but I'm no expert," said Alywin.

"Liquid not black powder?" asked Sir Peter.

"Sounds like Fire of the Gods. The ancient fire starter invented by the Kolotiks (KO-LOW-TIKS)," said Kamden.

The Kolotiks were ancient people of Arcadiem, whose reign began during the wild era beginning of time and ended during the beginning of the new era, end of time 576 WEBOT-7 NEEOT. They resided in a province known as Kolotos. They are considered by many to be the bedrock of Arcadiem civilization, though many of their ancient teachings have been lost.

"I thought Fire of the Gods was a myth," said Tim.

"No, it's not. The Kolotiks were a shrewd bunch. The formula for Fire of the Gods was one of the best kept military secrets of ancient times. Gone unknown for almost 700 years. It is deadly enough to burn whole warships to ashes and hot enough to burn on water," said Colin.

"Galeran Harlow taught you this, I presume?" said Giles. "Taught me how to make it."

"Great. That's just what we need. Sell swords with deadly chemical weapons," said Tim sarcastically.

"How flammable is it? Can something in the castle ignite?" asked Giles. "Well, it's carried in containers. So unless it's smashed to bits, it won't burn. If the contents come into contact with water, it can ignite. The naphtha in it is very sticky and it can adhere to clothes and armor and be quite hard to extinguish," explained Colin.

"I don't know why Sir Richard wanted us to use fire starters just to cover an escape. Seems a bit much, burning down the whole bloody castle," said Alywin.

"Maybe it was a precaution to make sure the enemy didn't discover our secrets," said Tim.

"Where are the fire starters now?" asked Kamden.

"Well, after we buried Sir Richard outside with the others, we took his belongings to the chambers," said Lady Branson.

"It would be wise to keep it away from anything flammable, Elysant," said Giles.

"I assure you, grandfather, it's in a secure place," she replied. "Wait, hang on. Aren't we forgetting something?" said Clara.

Alywin groaned. "Ugh, what are we forgetting?" he said. "As if this meeting wasn't long enough," he added under his breath.

Clara, ignoring him, said, "I'll tell you what we're forgetting. The builders pack. How do we know they didn't have any descendants for sure? Bastards are a thing and besides, that could be where they got the map from."

"Unlikely, all the other builders were quite pious. It says so in the builders' records of Sigate. Builders are sort of revered there. The records would've kept track of any extended family."

"Sigate keeps track of all their builders and families, eh?" asked Alywin. "And?" Sarah retorted.

"Oh, nothing. It just seems a bit, eh, oppressive," said Alywin. "Oppressive? Since when is keeping records oppressive? What? They don't keep records in Garla? Oops. I'm so sorry."

Tim laughed nervously. He looked at Sarah. "Heh heh, Sarah, that was supposed to be a secret."

"Really, Sarah!" said Alywin angrily.

"I know, and I'm sorry. It just sort of came out," said Sarah.

"You're telling me this arsehole is from Garla? Well, that explains everything. The miscreant attitude, lack of respect for authority, intimidating demeanor," Clara went on with her diatribe against Alywin. Tim tried to stop her by calling her name, but she paid him no heed.

"Clara," said Tim.

"The overall hideous appearance..." Clara continued. "Clara," Tim repeated.

"...the downright unfeeling (psychotic/sociopathic) tendencies," Clara continued.

"Clara!" Tim shouted, trying to get her attention. "What?" asked Clara.

"I'm from Garla as well!"

Clara paused for a moment, then said, "Really? But you're not even remotely threatening."

"Thanks, Clara," Tim said with a mixture of sarcasm and anger. "Honestly, Clara. I'm very disappointed in you. Not everyone from

Garla is or was a criminal," said Lady Branson. "Eh," Tim and Alywin said in unison. "Apologies, milady," said Clara.

"Not to me," said Lady Branson. "But, but," stammered Clara. "Clara!" Lady Branson demanded.

Clara turned to Alywin and said reluctantly, "Sorry, Alywin," with an inflection of anger and resentment in her voice.

"Now, Alywin. Do you have anything to say to Clara?" asked Lady Branson.

"Nope," Alywin said bluntly. "Alywin," said Lady Branson.

Alywin groaned. "Fine. I'm sorry you're offended by things… that you think are related to me."

"Really? That is the most horseshit apology I have ever heard," said Clara emphatically.

"Clara, listen to me. It's the best you're gonna get. Trust me," said Tim.

Clara sighed in annoyance. "You're unbelievable, Alywin. You are such a—"

"Clara," Lady Branson warned.

"A person, such a person," Clara said through gritted teeth.

Sir Peter, who had been quietly contemplating the information he was receiving, asked, "Sarah, are you sure there aren't other Masons besides you and your brother? Others who could have borne the mark?" "Like I said, father never had any relatives, so I don't believe so," said Sarah.

"Our family tree is riddled with disease and death. The majority of the Mason bloodline perished during the Ghost fever (A type of plague that spread like wildfire during the period between 1485-1519 NEEOT, affecting mostly Arcadiem. But affecting places sporadically. Although, villages and towns were affected the hardest because of the density in population. Sigate, in particular, was the most affected village in Iiadec, with about 85% of its residents dying from it. That's why Sigate today is described as dilapidated when compared to more populous regions, such as Garla. The disease has no known origin or cure. The Sigations have a saying of unknown origin that best describes the plague's mysterious and unpredictable nature. *"We didn't cure it; it just went away… But I fear the Ghost might come back someday."* The most unsettling thing about ghost fever was that it affected people randomly of any age and gender and social status. It's called ghost fever because the victims would have skin of an ashen white hue, pallid eyes and would constantly and uncontrollably moan after losing the ability to speak) outbreak. Apart from father, we're, um, the only ones left…"

"Ahem, ghost fever is what killed the other builders as well. We're the only ones left," said Kamden. He was rather despondent but trying his best not to be, but his efforts were largely unsuccessful.

Everyone in the room could hear the pain and heartbreak in his voice when he said the words, *we're the only ones left.* Sarah had shared the same sentiments.

"Sarah, forgive me for asking, but where is your father?" asked Sir Peter.

Kamden and Sarah looked at each other with sorrowful eyes. Sarah spoke first. "He, uh, um, well, left after mum died, he just couldn't deal… I don't know where he went honestly."

"How old were you, if you don't mind me asking?" asked Clara. "I was about 11 and Kamden was 4."

Sir Peter was trying to put this as delicately as possible. "I know you were quite young, but was there anything he said that would indicate he was disillusioned with House Franklin?"

He didn't say it outright, but she knew what he was insinuating. "Um, no, actually, he was a bit of a Franklinite (a pejorative term for individuals obsessed with Tatum Franklin's blood line, even believing it to be holy)." Sarah laughed slightly, though it was hollow and filled with pain. "My mother sometimes would get angry with him and say, *"Dean, Tatum was not a God. This obsession is revolting!"*"

Alywin, attempting to be as delicate as possible with his questioning, said "Sarah, just because he was a Franklinite doesn't mean—"

"No, no, Alywin. I know what you're insinuating, but father wouldn't work with Hector. He just wouldn't. He's not a bad man, just a broken one."

Not wanting to upset her further, the inquiry about her father stopped. "Can we, uh, talk about something else?" said Sarah, eager to change the subject.

"Yeah sure," said Tim.

"Good, because there is another thing that concerns me. How is it that no one suspected, from the corpses in the woods of Eredith, that the fallen might've been slain by beasts as opposed to men? Surely such creatures would have left tracks?" asked Sarah.

"It is odd. When Sir Merek and the other knights brought Sir Richard to the barracks, he made no mention of tracks or peculiar wounds," said Clara.

"The knights are not healers. They don't share your expertise in analyzing wounds. Additionally, they wouldn't have time to examine all those bodies during times of war, at least initially," explained Sir Peter.

"Or they knew and kept quiet for us not to panic. Giving us the illusion they have everything under control," said Alywin.

"The commander would never allow something like that," said Sir Peter.

"Unless instructed to by Lord Franklin," said Alywin. Sir Peter was bemused.

"Look, Sir Richard mentioned something about him knowing about these creatures' intentions," said Alywin.

"And what were their intentions?" asked Sir Peter.

"To end man and like kind, that's why some of us liken them to the monsters of old. But I don't believe that's their true motive. I think other more human threats are behind the attacks and have summoned these monsters to frighten us. They're trying to scare us with this end of day's horseshit. That way, they can seem like an unstoppable force of nature instead of a couple of arseholes with a grudge against anything and anyone resembling authority. If anything, this is an act of terrorism, not war. And they will largely be successful in their efforts if we panic. That's probably the reason Lord Franklin didn't say anything," replied Alywin.

"So, disgruntled lowborn's with an affinity for hokraft?" asked Kamden. "Whoever this third party is, they should not be underestimated.

An enemy whose true intentions are unknown could be deadly," said Sir Peter.

"Who led the charge? The monsters themselves? They must have had some semblance of intelligence, devoid of their masters, to orchestrate such an attack on armies of men," said Colin eagerly.

"Sir Richard claimed the being known as Kraag was responsible. He believed that this Kraag took the form of Lord Anslem Blakeslee. How he did this is unclear, but Sir Richard said Anslem's eyes were black," said Giles.

"Possession," said Sir Peter.

"We are not certain, but it would seem so," said Giles.

"So Kraag is either a powerful castor or infected?" said Colin.

"Or neither. There was no trace of soul sickness or magic. Even hokraft has its limits. What Sir Richard described is no mere gathering of beasts but an army and a cunning one," said Giles.

"What would give you that impression, Archiater?" Clara asked. "They spoke the tongue of man, according to Sir Richard, and attacked in a coordinated fashion, similar to that of an ambush, using the foliage to their advantage. He said they wielded weapons such as war bows, maces, swords, and others," said Giles.

"What kind of monsters are these?" asked a surprised Kamden. "They don't sound like monsters at all," Clara added.

"They may not be. The more I think about it, the way he described them, not having a unified look, but an amalgamation of everything putrid and horrifying, yet intelligent... they could be something entirely different," said Tim.

"What?" Clara asked,

"Interlopers from the Outer realm."

There was a slight silence. The others were not sure if Tim was being serious. Then Colin burst out into laughter. "Outer realm! Oh man, that's a good one."

"He's being serious," said Alywin.

Colin immediately stopped laughing and awkwardly said, "Oh." Clara groaned. "Tim, again with this nonsense."

"What? This type of thing is described in Oaken Thragfoot's book *Beings of the Outer Realm*: '*In the Outer realm, there are strange beings that defy the laws of magic soul manipulation and much more. They are a constant reminder that we mere mortals know nothing about the way of things.*' Thragfoot's book is in print and can be found in libraries around the world," replied Tim.

"In the fiction section! Which means it's not relevant," retorted Clara. "Not relevant 'cause he's a Dwarf? Honestly Clara, that type of bigotry is beneath you," replied Tim.

"No, because he was a half mad pariah. Even the dwarven lords think so!"

Tim turned to Lady Branson. "You believe me, right, milady?"

"I-uh, I-uh, ahem. I believe that you believe what you're saying is true," she said.

"That's a very diplomatic answer and not at all indecisive," Giles said sarcastically.

"Oh, leave me alone, grandfather. I don't work well under pressure," said Lady Branson.

"Says the healer," Giles responded.

Tim got the hint and accepted that no one believed his theory. For fear of sounding insane, he decided not to push the theory further. Alywin, not comfortable seeing his friend looking so defeated, said, "Can't blame him for theorizing. None of us know what the fuck Kraag or the Horridus are or who is responsible for them. We are in the dark about so many things. All we can do is theorize, no matter how outlandish our theories may be."

"Does this mean you believe, Alywin?" asked Tim.

"Of course not, Tim. There is nothing beyond the sky but the sun, the moon, and the stars, but I don't think any less of you for thinking otherwise."

"I can live with that," said Tim.

"Alywin, you mentioned the word Horridus?" asked Sir Peter. "Yeah, it's what Sir Richard said they were called. Why, does that word mean anything to you?" asked Alywin.

"I don't know. It sounds familiar," said Sir Peter.

"I can assure you it's not old tongue. Father made us practice the language relentlessly," said Giles.

Lady Branson gave him a curious look. "Great grandfather was a sorcerer? Really? You never mention him," said Lady Branson.

"That's because, excuse my use of foul language, he was a bit of an arsehole," replied Giles.

Tim grinned. "I don't believe I've ever heard you swear before, Archiater."

"Don't get used to it. Anyway, he forced me and my brothers to learn it till we were fluent, despite us being non-magical. He believed we had some dormant ability or some such nonsense," replied Giles.

Sir Peter had a pensive look on his face as he tried to recall where he had heard that word. Then it hit him. "I remember now. It was back when I was still pagan in Mylec. We weren't very devout. I don't think mother even believed in the Gods, but occasionally, my father would read to me passages from sagas which our religion of no name was written in. Father read me the saga of the progenitor gods. Sagas, books in general, were scant in Mylec back then, due to there being no reliable means of printing at the time. This particular saga was the rarest. Only 15 copies were known to exist. Thirteen of which were altered. My father somehow got his hands on one of the original two. At the end of the saga, the progenitor Gods did battle with beings called the old ones, who were made from the ground itself. The Gods won, but the majority of them perished. Eldjor, leader of the Gods, was slain in battle. His last word was Horridus. Many scholars believe it to be a mistake, so many scribes removed it from new copies altogether, likening it to be a misspelling of a name or something unintelligible. I believed so as well until now."

"There was something else that Sir Richard mentioned, even before telling us his account in Eredith. He kept saying they have changed me, as though he believed he was becoming the creatures. I'm afraid to say there is some warrant to this theory. It would explain his strength and ability to survive mortal wounds for so long. Additionally, he even said one of the creatures said they wanted to change him," said Lady Branson. "Change? Like what blood suckers often do to their victims?" asked Colin.

"He did say they might've been parasites," said Tim.

"They're called vampires and when they convert another person, that person usually comes back nearly immediately according to reliable sources. Same with roamers, so I doubt Sir Richard was attacked by those," said Clara.

"He described the Horridus as having an amalgamation of features. The Romer parasites are uniform in appearance in that they don't drastically alter the body of the host, so I doubt they attacked Sir Richard," explained Lady Branson.

"Then what about lycos? Getting bit or scratched by one usually results in a slow, painful death and occasionally turning into one," said Colin.

"It would explain why he lasted that long, but again lycos have a similar appearance, are incapable of speech and, as far as I know, cannot grasp clubs, let alone bows, and rarely travel in packs, not to mention raving mad," said Alywin.

"You're thinking of werewolves, Alywin. But you're right. They can't be lycanthropes. There was no mention of the beasts having fur," said Giles.

Sir Peter sighed. "Then we've exhausted all theories. We don't know what these creatures were, who sent them, nor their motivation for what seems like an unprovoked attack, and we won't figure it out in one night. I suggest we focus on what we do know: the tunnels. I'll ready the men to see if they're fit for travel or if there are any enemies still lurking, so unless there's anything else, I think this meeting is adjourned," said Sir Peter.

Clara was hesitant to speak, but, as the others were about to depart, she built up the courage. "Wait!"

They all turned around towards her. This was nerve-wracking for Clara, for she faced the weighty decision of betraying someone she held dear. "There is something else...it's Giselle."

"What's wrong? Is it the baby?" Lady Branson said, now quite concerned.

Clara's breath was labored, her palms were sweaty, and she began trembling as she averted her gaze from the others.

"Clara, you're shaking," said Lady Branson. There was great concern on her face. She was not alone in her thinking; the others were equally worried.

"Clara?" asked Tim.

"I-I need you all to promise me something... not a word of this gets out to anyone, especially Lord Franklin. Please, I beg you." Slight tears formed in her eyes. She wiped them away, her voice quavered. "I'm betraying her trust by just speaking to all of you."

She began sobbing profusely. Somewhere in her muffled speech was a semblance of a start of a confession. "I wasn't supposed to tell anyone, but then we decide we'd tell you, milady, that's why she was in the barracks, but then she saw how distressed you were with Godfrey and all. I guess she decided against it. She's really scared. I-I don't know what else to do… Oh God." She covered her hands over her mouth. "I shouldn't have said anything. Forget I said anything, stupid Clara."

"Clara, you've … you've…" Clara began crying again.

Lady Branson immediately hugged her and Clara began to calm down. "It's alright. I'm here for you, you can just tell me and Peter. You don't have to tell anyone else." She looked at Giles, who understood.

"Alright, the rest of you back to the barracks. We've still got work to do. That includes you too, young man," said Giles.

"Uh, yes, milord," said Kamden.

They departed upstairs. When they were out of earshot, Clara looked at Sir Peter, ambivalent whether to divulge such damaging information to him.

Lady Branson noticed. "I tell my husband everything, but don't worry, he won't tell a soul, nor will I, swear to Arda. Right, Peter?"

"You have my word," said Sir Peter.

This seemed sufficient for Clara to begin talking. "She said she couldn't feel the baby after 20 weeks of doing so. She feared the worse, so she panicked and uh… She, uh, performed a hokraft spell on her unborn child. I don't know the details of this, but she has always been proficient at magic. Ugh, that's another secret I failed to keep," Clara said despondently.

"Hey, you're doing well, Clara. You just want the best for her, and we can help with that," assured Lady Branson.

"What's going to happen to her? Is the baby going to be alright? Is it going to be born dead?" asked Clara.

"I won't know until I've examined her," said Lady Branson.

Clara's eyes widened and the color drained from her face. "No, no, please, milady. She can't know I told you. Oh, that would—"

"Clara, if we are going to help her, we have to speak to her," Lady Branson said, slowly and calmly.

Clara looked at Sir Peter and gulped. "We?" She started breathing heavily.

"Clara, if she's in any type of trouble or connected with the wrong people, I have to know. It's the only way to help," said Sir Peter.

"We wouldn't do anything to harm her. We just want to help. Do you trust us?" said Lady Branson. Clara nodded.

When Clara was calmer, Sir Peter asked, "Where did she learn this spell? Was it from Olga?"

"No. She's been in contact with someone using a crystal ball like device called Mothrya's eye."

"Who has she been contacting?" he asked.

"A woman named Aslaug." Sir Peter's eyes widened, and he stood aghast.

"What, what? Does that name mean anything to you?" asked Clara. Sir Peter turned to Lady Branson. "Heggr's mother."

Lady Branson, equally shocked, said, "But that's impossible. She's—"

"Dead," said Sir Peter gravely.

"Maybe it's someone else named Aslaug?" said Clara nervously, in an attempt to rationalize things.

"In Mylec, Aslaug has become more of a title given to the most powerful witch, a tradition that dates back thousands of years after the very first Aslaug (278-312 NEEOT) wife of hero King Erik (266-331 NEEOT). No one is to be named Aslaug for at least 1000 years after the death of one," said Sir Peter.

"So, this person is lying, or Aslaug isn't really dead?" asked Clara.

"My father, Brandr, ran her through after he alleged she tainted his batch of Irakothar. I witnessed this myself. Because of her status, this was kept secret and she was given a proper Mylecan funeral that involves burning the body over a pyre," said Sir Peter.

"This Aslaug woman, was she dangerous?"

Sir Peter did not respond. He was trying to find a way to tell her the truth without frightening her. Unfortunately, his silence only made things worse.

"Oh, God. You think she'd hurt Giselle?" said Clara, horrified by the prospect.

"I don't know. When I knew her, she was quite unpredictable, manipulative...our family dynamic was complicated."

"How complicated?" Clara asked eagerly.

"It's hard to explain. Things were different back then. I was different. Let's just say we weren't exactly amicable," explained Sir Peter. He was more hesitant to reveal this information than he was about his time in Arglia, prompting Clara to believe he was ashamed about this part of his life.

"This woman, did she truly practice hokraft?" asked Clara.

"I suppose so, but I'm no expert. It's not like it was illegal. In Mylec, very few things are. There aren't many castors in Mylec to begin with, so the people aren't sure what real magic even looks like. That's why she was so revered," explained Sir Peter.

"So, what you're saying is she may be deceiving Giselle, or there is the possibility that the spell she taught her was real," said Clara.

"If this person even is Aslaug, it could go either way. But we won't know for sure unless we speak with Giselle. Where is she now?" asked Sir Peter.

"In the chambers," replied Clara.

CHAPTER FIFTEEN

REVELATIONS

Giselle sat in the chambers on the bed with Mothrya's eye in her hands. Her eyes were closed as she whispered, "Show me Edmund, show me Edmund Franklin."

Mothrya's eye did not react. The sphere was not transparent but rather cloudy with a greyish hue.

"Oh, curses. Why won't it work?"

Suddenly, she heard the squeaking sound of the door opening. She froze. She stared at the door for a moment. It was slightly open, and she wondered if she had imagined someone there. Perhaps Clara forgot to lock the door, or it was simply the wind. But then, terrified, she saw a face in the narrow space between the door and the opening. It was a woman, about twenty-eight. She had a countenance that would suggest stiffness. Her eyes were blue and extremely focused, hair short, not exceeding her jaw, which was an odd hairstyle in Iiadec, a place where most women kept their hair long. The color was dirty blonde, its texture wavy.

"Bernia!" exclaimed Giselle as she frantically tossed the orb to the floor and threw the bedsheet over it in a desperate attempt to conceal it. She tried her best to compose herself. "How long have you been standing there? You've startled me."

"Not long, not long. Long is subjective, subjective means relative, yes subjective means relative. If it's subjective, it can't be determined, meaning it's inconsequential. Yes, inconsequential to ask questions that aren't relevant. That's a superlative level of reasoning. Also, rude. Rude apologies required subject will take offense. So not long... not long... not long, no." Bernia rambled like this often and, to an untrained ear, it might sound like unintelligible babble, but was actually the result of

355

an overworking mind. As a result of this misconception, she was often overlooked and simply considered as not being right in the head.

Giselle knew Bernia long enough to decode her seemingly incoherent speech. "Bernia, unless there's anything else, I'd like to be left alone now." "Mothrya's Eye! Mothrya's eye! Anything else, anything else. Invented in 1062 NEEOT, 1062. By Mothrya Llaws, sison male, male, male born in 1015 NEEOT, died 1078 NEEOT, NEEOT. 65 years, 65 years, yes, 65 years. Mothrya's eye, just tool, not hokraft, not hokraft, hokraft. No need for concealment, not hokraft, not hokraft, hokraft, hokraft!"

Giselle panicked upon hearing Bernia shout hokraft repeatedly. She hastily grabbed Bernia by the arm and closed the door behind.

"AAAAAAh!" Bernia squealed, as she often did when she felt threatened. She did not like being touched. Giselle knew this, but she was desperate. Having Bernia shouting hokraft while she was in the chambers was sure to get her executed or at least garner unwanted attention and suspicion, especially since an unwanted guest arrived at the barracks, who most likely used potent magic to enter. People were already on high alert. If caught with the eye, they would claim she conspired with the enemy using hokraft.

"Danger, danger! AAAAAAh! Danger, danger!" cried Bernia.

Giselle put her hand over Bernia's mouth to silence her. Bernia was clearly agitated and frightened. She began breathing heavily into Giselle's palm. Giselle felt a sense of remorse for aggravating Bernia's condition by handling her in such a way. She gently removed her hand from Bernia's mouth. Giselle then pressed her index finger on her lips.

"That means quiet, too loud, Bernia, too loud," said Bernia. "Yes," whispered Giselle.

Bernia was still visibly frightened. Fearing she would have another panic attack, Giselle said slowly, "Bernia, I'm sorry I was rough with you, and that's not nice."

"Not nice, not nice, not very nice at all."

"I know, and I'm sorry. Can you forgive me?" asked Giselle.

Bernia did not respond. She was suspicious of Giselle's intentions and found her apology disingenuous. This was typical behavior for Bernia. She was slow to trust, especially if she felt it had been violated. Bernia's thoughts became apparent to Giselle through her expression and the tense silence that accompanied them, thus Giselle decided to pacify her further.

Giselle raised her hands in the air and said, "I won't do it again, I promise. I won't hurt you. Just please sit with me like you did before with Clara," said Giselle.

"It wasn't locked, wasn't locked, Clara forgot to lock," Bernia covered her ears. "Noisy children, noisy children."

"Yes, I know Bernia, but they're not here now. It's just you and me," said Giselle softly.

"Clara was with us, yes Clara was with us, but that, that was before, in the past, in the past where. Where's Clara? Want to talk to Clara, not, not you, sorry rude, rude."

"It's alright, Clara will be back soon. I know this because, well, Clara and I are, um, close friends. She visits me often after working in the Barracks. She'll be back. But you know what she'd want…" said Giselle.

"What?" Bernia asked eagerly.

"She'd want us to be friends too and friends protect each other," said Giselle.

"Protect?" asked Bernia.

"Yes, protect. You can do this by keeping what you saw a secret," said Giselle.

"Mothrya's eye?" asked Bernia.

"Exactly. Keep it a secret between you and me?"

"A secret. Don't tell anyone, don't tell anyone," said Bernia.

"Right," replied Giselle. "You know friends, they help each other too." Giselle reached out for Mothyra's eye under the bedsheet that was on the floor and held it in her hands in view of Bernia. "Do you know how this works?" Bernia nodded. "Remember: secret," said Giselle.

"Secret. Don't tell anyone," said Bernia.

"Bernia, I want to see something, someone. Where they are and who's there with them. Can you help me do that?" asked Giselle.

Bernia remained silent and she avoided eye contact.

"Bernia?" asked Giselle. Still, Bernia did not respond. This made Giselle anxious. She needed to be more forceful, but she knew she had to be careful. Bernia was very sensitive.

"Bernia, look at me. Look at me, this is very important. There are people out there who wish to harm us. We have to make sure the ones we love are protected."

"The ones we love?" asked Bernia. "Yes," replied Giselle.

Giselle made the mistake of moving too close to Bernia. As she tried to place Mothrya's eye in Bernia's lap, her hand touched Bernia's arm. Bernia stood up.

"Too close, too close, too close, uncomfortable, uncomfortable, don't touch! Don't touch!" shouted Bernia.

"Ssssh, Bernia, please, I'm sorry," said Giselle. Giselle placed her finger on her lips again.

"That means quiet."

"Bernia, it was an accident. I won't do it again, I swear. Just please sit with your friend. I won't touch you, c'mon," said Giselle.

"You said that before, before, before, liar, liar, liar, you said that before, you said that before."

"No, no, I'm not lying. I-I-uh, just want to talk. Can I talk to you Bernia as friends? You know, friends hel—" said Giselle.

"Stop, stop, stop patronizing! Not stupid, not stupid!"

"No, you're not. You're very intelligent," replied Giselle, trying desperately to placate Bernia.

Bernia, however, became more agitated and vexed. "Sarcasm, sarcasm, derision, lies, lies. I understand, I understand just like Lodema does, just like Lodema does." Bernia rushed towards the door.

"Wait!" Giselle exclaimed. Bernia turned around.

"Bernia, please just listen. I'm not lying, you are intelligent. That's why I'm asking you to help me. It's not sarcasm. I'm not Lodema. I'm your friend and Clara's friend. We have to help each other," said Giselle. "Friends don't hurt, friends don't hurt each other," said Bernia. "I know and I'm so sorry I hurt you, I—" said Giselle. "No," Bernia interrupted.

Giselle was perplexed; this was an oddly coherent utterance from Bernia. She wondered what she meant by such a repudiation.

"No, not me. Clara."

Giselle's eyes widened, terrified and confounded she wondered, could it be possible Bernia knew the nature of her relationship with Clara? And if so, what else did she know and dating how far back?

"Did Clara tell you this?" asked Giselle, trying her best to conceal her worry. She was largely successful in her efforts.

Bernia shook her head. "I saw her crying…when she left the chambers, when, when she left the chambers. She didn't see me, she didn't see me, no. You were the only other person, yeah, only other person, yeah. Therefore, you hurt Clara, you hurt Clara, yeah."

Bernia said this in a subtle but noticeably morose way. Giselle was surprised Bernia was capable of this level of emotion, given her condition. This made Giselle empathize with her more. She said softly, "I didn't mean to hurt her. It was a misunderstanding…a mistake and, um, people sometimes make mistakes… Clara, she, uh, means a lot to me…I would never intentionally hurt her…Do you believe me?" Giselle looked at Bernia with a pleading expression on her face. Something she did often, wheedling someone, especially Clara.

Bernia was becoming susceptible to her coaxing. Her forest-colored eyes had an endearing quality to them, as did her whole visage. Bernia found this alluring, and all her suspicions of Giselle seemingly vanished. Bernia nodded.

"Bernia, can you help me, please?" said Giselle slowly and methodically, but not too slow. She did not want to risk sounding condescending and potentially upsetting Bernia again. Bernia nodded.

"Will you sit with me and talk?" said Giselle.

"No! No, no, no sit, just talk. Just talk!" said Bernia.

Fearing another outburst, she decided not to aggravate Bernia any further by suggesting she sit.

"Alright, that's fine. Talking is fine." Giselle held up the eye again in view of Bernia, but was careful not to let it touch her.

"I'm trying to locate someone. He is someone, uh, very important to me and uh—"

"Edmund... Lord Edmund...Born 1523 NEEOT on a Sunday, yes, Sunday, eight pounds at birth. Delivered by midwife, Kestral Varnhame, died at 76. 76. Currently 25 years old, six foot two inches tall, 215 pounds. 215. Eldest, first-born son, yes son of Albert Franklin, son of Aiken Franklin, descendent, descendent, descendent of Tatum Franklin. Albert, Albert Franklin born 1485 NEEOT on Wednesday, 63 years old, younger brother to late, late, late Gavin Franklin, former King of Iiadec, 1481 NEEOT to 1536 NEEOT, born on Tuesday, yes Tuesday. At death, six foot five inches tall, 256 pounds, 256. Two—" Bernia rambled on.

Giselle realized that Bernia must be stopped, otherwise she would list Edmund's entire known lineage dating back to the wild era.

"Bernia," Giselle said forcefully, but not enough to be considered a fully-fledged shout. Nonetheless, it was effective enough to get Bernia's attention. "Bernia, erm, can you help me find Edmund using Mothrya's eye?" Giselle said softly. Bernia waited to respond. This made Giselle anxious.

Bernia finally said, with an uncharacteristically terse reply, "Impossible."

Giselle was taken aback, and she unintentionally revealed her true frustration, anxiety, and desperation. "What? What do you mean, impossible?"

Bernia slightly recoiled. Upon noticing this, Giselle regained her composure and spoke softly. "Bernia, I don't understand."

"Edmund...not magic, not magic, not magic wielder."

Giselle still had a look of bemusement on her face, which Bernia noticed. Hence, she tried to further explain herself.

"Mothrya's eye only for magic wielders, yes, magic wielders, based on ruda ruda ruda particles," said Bernia.

"Ruda particles?"

Bernia was getting noticeably frustrated by not being able to effectively communicate with Giselle. "Ruda particles are what magic wielders souls are made of, yes souls are made of, souls are made of, emit, emit energy, yes energy. Mothrya, Mothrya's eye detects. Like signal, like signal, signal more, more ruda particles wielder has, emits stronger signal then you can locate, yes then you can locate," said Bernia.

"So, you're saying, I just have to look for a magic wielder with a lot of ruda particles and then I can find Edmund that way?"

"Not, not that simple, not that simple, signal can be disrupted by many, by many wielders, yes, many wielders of magic. And the person that you, you locate is who you will follow, follow. Their point of view, yes their point of view, not Edmund, not Edmund, no."

Giselle understood it was a shot in the dark, but maybe she could latch onto these magic wielders signal and hopefully find Edmund and see if he was alright. In the event that Edmund was in danger, Giselle could aid him with magic using Mothrya's eye. Reader, you see, standard magic requires eye contact, which limits the magic wielder by how far they can see. Mothrya's eye allows one to see great distances, hence spells can be cast.

"Thank you, Bernia." Bernia blushed. "No problem, for Clara, for friends." Giselle grinned. "For friends."

Suddenly, there was a knock on the door. This startled Giselle and Bernia. Bernia ran from the door and sat in the corner of the chambers in a fetal position, something she often did when she was frightened. Giselle did her best to maintain her composure.

"Uh, coming. I'll be there in a moment!" She quickly put Mothrya's eye back in the drawer and locked it securely. She quietly and calmly opened the door to find Clara, Sir Peter, and Lady Branson standing outside with concerned looks on their faces. Giselle was worried, but did not jump to conclusions. *"It's not like Clara would ever... Just relax, they're probably here to make sure I'm alright. After all, I'm pregnant in the middle of a siege."*

"Clara, Sir Peter, milady, what brings you here?"

When Giselle made eye contact with Clara, Clara avoided her gaze. Clara had a remorseful look on her face that made Giselle nervous. "I'm sorry, is there something wrong? Was it the intruder?" asked Giselle.

"He has been dealt with," said Sir Peter. "Was anyone harmed?" asked Giselle.

"No, but the people in the Barracks are just a little shaken," he said. "Well, I'm glad to hear everyone's alright, thanks to your efforts, of course," Giselle smiled nervously.

Sir Peter did not smile back, and she found his gaze to be disquieting. He then asked, "Is anyone else here?"

"Erm, just Bernia. The noises were, um, disturbing her. I, uh, thought she should stay here, keep me company and, um, well, you know how she is. But it's perfectly fine. I'm fine, really, I am. I'm alright, so, um, you don't need to check up on me, but I am grateful that you came, uh, thank you, all of you," said Giselle. At this point, her façade of calmness was starting to dissolve, and this was apparent to the others.

"Giselle, we'd like to talk to you alone, if that's alright with you. Uh, you see we don't want to disturb Bernia… Giselle. You know you can talk to us about anything, right?" asked Lady Branson.

"Yes, milady," replied Giselle.

"And we'd never intentionally do anything to put you in danger," continued Lady Branson.

"Right, milady," said. Giselle.

"May we come in?" asked Lady Branson.

"Of course, milady?" Giselle motioned them in.

Lady Branson turned to Clara. "Clara?" She motioned her head towards Bernia.

"Yes, milady," replied Clara.

Clara walked up to Bernia and knelt beside her. "Bernia, hello," Clara smiled.

Bernia looked up at Clara and a slight smile formed on her face, which on any other person would be interpreted as a sign of uneasiness, but on Bernia it was a sign of elation. She rarely ever showed this range of expression.

"Hi Clara, hi Clara."

Clara moved closer to Bernia, who, surprisingly, did not flinch. She was comfortable enough around her not to.

"Bernia what are you doing back here Hollis and Lady Uptone will be worried," Clara said softly.

"Noise, noise, noise," said Bernia.

"I know, Bernia, but you have to go back. Giselle needs her rest." "Can't I, can't I stay here with you?" asked Bernia while looking Clara directly in the eyes, something she rarely ever did for anyone else. Clara was slightly taken aback by this abrupt shift in demeanor. Bernia's amber eyes focused and studied Clara's lineaments, searching for a reaction of acquiescence.

Clara smiled. "I'll tell you what. After we're done talking to Giselle, you can come back here, I promise," said Clara.

"Promise?" asked Bernia.

"Yes, promise," said Clara. "Now, let's get you to Lady Uptone. C'mon."

As Clara got up to lead Bernia. Bernia did something atypical from her usual behavior. She gently grasped Clara's arm. This intrigued the others and caught Clara by surprise. They began to think that maybe Bernia was not as emotionally crippled as they were led to believe. She then looked at Clara, sounding and looking completely lucid, and said, "Promise?"

"Bernia, when we go to Lady Uptone, I want you to wait there for me. Then I promise I will come back for you." This answer seemed to satisfy Bernia. Bernia slid her hand down Clara's arm until their hands touched. They interlocked fingers and departed for the Great Hall, and closed the door behind them. With just Sir Peter, Lady Branson, and Giselle in the room, there was an awkward silence. This made Giselle very uneasy, but she eventually spoke.

"Clara's really good with her. Bernia, she, um, never held my hand or anyone else's. I mean, I don't think so. But anyway, Clara has, uh, talent, uh, a gift. It's no doubt due to your tutelage, milady."

"Bernia certainly has taken a liking towards her, but I can't credit for her talent. You see, Bernia's condition is beyond my field of expertise."

"That Clara, eh? So talented, she does everything really, heh heh. So, uh, I'm sure you have some better things to do than watch after a lowborn pregnant woman, heh heh," Giselle laughed nervously.

Neither Sir Peter nor Lady Branson responded.

"So, eh, what exactly did you want to ask me? I'm not in any trouble, heh heh, am I?" said Giselle, placing emphasis on the words am I.

Lady Branson was going to say something when she saw that the mere act of opening her mouth terrified Giselle. She thought *"Oh, God they know, wait, wait, Giselle, calm down if they don't know and if this is something else, then losing your composure will surely put them on your scent."* There was a knock at the door. Desperate to change the subject,

Giselle smiled and said, "Oh, that must be Clara."

She went for the door when Sir Peter motioned her to stop. "It's alright. I'll get it."

Sir Peter opened the door and Clara entered and locked the door behind her.

"Clara, Lady Branson and Sir Peter all here to see me and keep me company. I really am grateful, but also very tired, so awfully tired, so can you all just um—" said Giselle, trying her best to conceal her fear by pretending to be excited.

"We won't be long, we just have a few questions," said Lady Branson. "Oh, I see. This is about the intruder and you're asking around to find out if anyone knows anything. Standard procedure. That's why Sir Peter is here and you're here, milady, because I, um, am pregnant and you want to make sure I'm not stressed out. Because that could affect the baby. That's alright. I welcome questions. Whatever keeps us, uh, safe from the ones who seek us harm and, um, no, I don't know anything about this intruder, sorry that I-I wasn't useful," said Giselle.

Sir Peter, no longer comfortable with the continued periphrasis said, as calmly as possible. "Giselle, we know."

Giselle's eyes widened, her skin turned pale, and she started breathing heavily. Her body stiff and her movements minimal. Petrified with fear she turned to Clara in the most unnatural of movements. Without blinking and barely moving her shoulders or neck, she kept repeating, "Clara, Clara, Clara, Clara."

"Giselle. Giselle, you're going to be alright. We're just here to help you. Everything is going to be alright."

But Giselle paid no heed on Clara's attempt to assuage her situation. "Clara, Clara, Clara," she kept repeating as the attempts to soothe her by Clara, Lady Branson, and Sir Peter were ineffective.

"Giselle, Giselle, listen to me. We just want to help you. We just want what's best for you," said Lady Branson.

"You have my word as a knight. I won't tell a living soul," said Sir Peter. The word knight made her feel worse and aggravated Giselle's already panic-stricken state. Still staring at Clara, and still not blinking, she said with watery eyes, the precursor to full-blown tears, "Clara… you have killed me."

Subsequently, she fell to her knees and began to hyperventilate. With each successive shallow breath she kept repeating the phrase, "Oh God, oh God, oh God."

"Giselle. There's no need to panic. It's going to be alright. Just listen to me, please," said Clara.

She turned to Lady Branson and Sir Peter. "Can I, uh?"

Both nodded and understood. They exited the room, making sure to lock the room behind them. Giselle stopped hyperventilating and stood unnaturally still.

"Giselle," said Clara slowly.

"I didn't know, I didn't know, I didn't know," Giselle kept repeating. "Giselle, Giselle, what didn't you know?"

Her voice quavered and filled with pain. She was on the verge of tears as she said, "That you hated me so much."

Hearing this from Giselle was like being impaled in the breast with a glaive. Clara's eyes became watery. "I... I... I don't hate you. I—"

"Love me! Horseshit!" Giselle interrupted.

"No, no, it's not horseshit. I do. I really do. More than anything in the world. That's why I told them. I'm sorry, so sorry I didn't tell you first, but I was scared you were in trouble, and I wanted to save you... I-uh, couldn't do that alone."

Clara, attempting to console Giselle, approached her but Giselle blatantly rejected her advance and shouted, "Don't you fucking touch me! Don't fucking touch me!"

She pointed at Clara, who was in tears at this point, and said, "You have no right, you have no right, no right," and began to sob profusely.

"Giselle. I'm sorry I betrayed your trust, but just let me help you, please," said Clara.

"Help me? Are you really that thick? He's a fucking knight, Clara. His sworn duty is to Lord Franklin and only Lord Franklin. You really think he is going to risk his title, life, and well-being to protect some low-born foreign bitch from Nalmia, secretly practicing hokraft? Oh, and once Lady Franklin finds out the baby is dead, she'll hang me herself. She already hates me. She's only nice to me because she thinks I'm carrying her grandchild. And then everyone will make the connection between the intruder and me," said Giselle.

"But there is no connection," Clara interrupted.

"Doesn't matter. I'm the only other person that can produce magic within castle walls besides Olga. They're going to say I let him in, foreign ties," said Giselle.

"Listen to me, Giselle. The intruder acted on his own accord and had ties to Arglia, not Nalmia. Olga said so herself. She would clear you of any wrongdoing," said Clara.

"Did you tell them about us?" said Giselle. "Of course not, I wouldn't," said Clara.

"Good, because there isn't going to be an *us* anymore. Not that it matters, because I'll be a corpse by the end of the siege."

Clara hurt by the phrase *there isn't going to be an us,* said, "Giselle, don't say that. Look, I know I hurt you, but now's not the time to be acting—"

"Irrational?" Giselle interrupted.

"I'm not trying to harm you. I would never do that. You're the love of my life. You have to believe me," pleaded Clara.

Giselle waited before she spoke. "Clara, you're not an idiot. I know you. This was not some scatterbrain mistake in an attempt to save me. This was a calculated maneuver to punish me for Edmund. Just admit you can't stand the fact that I chose him over you and you'd rather me dead than me be with him!" exclaimed Giselle.

"That's not true and you know that," Clara said, heart broken by those words.

"It doesn't even matter anyway, because Edmund doesn't want anything to do with me. He, uh, professed his love for Lady Branson in front of everybody in the Barracks. But you know that. You were there. That's why you strategically bring her here, just to relish in my pain." Giselle wiped tears from her eyes. "God, I'm so stupid. Why did I ever think he'd love me back?"

"Giselle," said Clara in an effort to comfort her.

"No, no, it was my own stupidity. I must accept it." She laughed, but it was hollow and riddled with despair.

"I mean, we only made love once and not even in a bed, in the stables next to actual horseshit… I bet it made you happy when you saw me like that. The evil witch that broke the noble Clara's heart is getting what she deserves."

"Giselle I—" said Clara.

Giselle interrupted her, regaining the appearance of slight composure. "No, it's alright. I, uh, was being a bit melodramatic… I just want you to know that I don't blame you for this. I, uh, wasn't a good friend or lover to you and I'm sorry. Heh heh, I'm always saying that and, um,

I know you don't like it but, uh, I mean it, heh heh." "Giselle," said Clara, saddened to see her in a state like this.

"Just let me finish, please, Clara. I have always taken advantage of your kindness and you're always protecting and encouraging me, even though I don't know anything. I'm not an amazing healer, nor do I have any real talent."

"Don't say that. You're beautiful, kind, smart, cool-headed, you have magic, really potent magic," said Clara.

"Oh, please, Clara. I can't even cast a simple fire spell without running the risk of burning down the entire castle," said Giselle.

Clara drew nearer to Giselle. "Look at me. I'll take care of you." Giselle moved away from Clara.

"Ahem, I have something I want to say, and I need you to hear it first, so no more interruptions, alright?"

"Alright," Clara said nervously.

"I accept my punishment. I do deserve it. Hokraft is a crime, and I knew that. It wasn't fair of me to let you harbor this ugly secret."

Clara was about to speak, but Giselle motioned her to stop. "I am not a kind person. I treat people who love me like shit. I lie. I manipulate, take advantage of people to get what I want, and, um, that has to stop." Giselle turned to Clara. "I know I'm always asking you to do things for me without giving you anything in return, but can you do one more thing for me?"

"Anything," said Clara.

"Can you kill me?" Giselle said. Clara was in utter shock and disbelief. "What!?"

"I know I've upset you, and it's not fair for me to ask, and I'd do it myself if I wasn't so scared," said Giselle.

"Stop it" Clara demanded.

While crying, Giselle said, "I don't know your intentions. Whether it be reprisal for years of abuse or maybe you're actually trying to save me, but either way, I'm still going to die."

"You don't know that!" shouted Clara.

"Clara, secrets in Corithni spread like wildfire. Even if Lady Branson and Sir Peter plead my case to the would-be king Albert Franklin, he would be pressured by Sir Ulric to execute me."

"Giselle, even if it comes to that, Sir Ulric is one man and not the king."

"Clara, he is his advisor and staunch supporter of the church of Mirama, who absolutely forbid hokraft. He is the one who pressured Lord Franklin to place the ban in the first place."

"You can't ask me to do something like this. I won't do it. Giselle, we can save you from all this. For God's sake, why the hell do you want to die?"

"I don't, believe me, I don't. But there's no other way. I don't want to be dragged kicking and screaming in front of a crowd of angry onlookers who will watch me hang. Most of whom will be people I know who will now think differently of me. Who will point the finger and say hang the foreign bitch. Some will be cheering, others praying for my damnation. Clara, I'm begging you, if I die by your hands, I can still have my dignity."

"Stop it, just please stop it!" shouted Clara.

"Clara, you don't have to worry about getting caught. Between my magic and your healing prowess, we can make it look like an accident. Pregnant women die all the time due to complications," said Giselle.

"I said stop it. This is the one thing you can't convince me to do for you! I love you. I don't know how many times I have to say that for it to sink in. Tell me what I need to say to you for you to believe that. Giselle, your pain is my pain. When you first told me, I was in distress. I couldn't think straight. I couldn't breathe. I couldn't function at all. Just the thought of you in pain brings tears to my eyes and now you have the audacity to ask me to kill you. You're a cruel woman," said Clara vehemently.

"Clara. I'm asking. I'm begging you to help me have some agency, some control, a say in how things end for me. Clara, it's my life at stake here," pleaded Giselle.

"Our life!... Because if you're executed, I'll be hanging right beside you for the crime of loving another woman."

Giselle was subdued. She burst into tears and cried in Clara's arms. "I'm so sorry, Clara. I'm so sorry," she wept.

When they finally separated, Clara said, "I'll let them know. Whenever you're ready."

"I'm ready," said Giselle.

Clara unlocked the door, and Lady Branson and Sir Peter entered, closing the door behind them. Clara and Giselle sat on the bed while Lady Branson and Sir Peter stood in front of them.

"Are you alright Giselle?" asked Lady Branson

Giselle smiled nervously. "No, not really. I'm actually quite terrified. My mind keeps telling me this is a bad idea and I'll be killed, but, uh, Clara's with me and she has convinced me otherwise and I trust her, heh heh."

"That's perfectly normal and we apologize for the intrusion and scaring you. It's just that we are a bit concerned," said Lady Branson.

"No, I understand, milady. It's, uh, not something to be taken lightly and is, um, troubling indeed," replied Giselle.

"We're here because you contacted someone calling themselves Aslaug," said Sir Peter.

"She, uh, taught me things about magic, uh, about hokraft," Giselle said ashamedly.

"Have you ever met Aslaug in person?" asked Sir Peter.

"Uh no. I just saw her through the eye. She, um, had long silver hair and wore a mask. Uh, a black leather one. It, uh, resembled a cat," said Giselle.

Silver hair was certainly one trait of the actual Aslaug, but besides that, there was nothing much to go on. It could still be an imposter. As for the cat mask, Aslaug did love cats, thought Sir Peter.

"How did you perform this spell, exactly?" asked Sir Peter.

"I, uh, didn't do much performing. I just followed Aslaug's lead. She, um, told me to say some incantations that I didn't understand. It didn't sound like old tongue... It didn't sound like a language at all."

Both Sir Peter and Lady Branson were perplexed and felt uneasy. It was certainly neither of their area of expertise, but it was, nonetheless, disturbing to hear. Magic with no articulated utterances was unheard of, be it hokraft, standard magic, or faux magic. They all require clear speech. If one pronounces a spell wrong, it will not work, or it will backfire. This was known throughout Iiadec. This was known throughout the world. If what Giselle was saying was to be believed, then this was an entirely different breed of magic that which the world had never seen before.

"Are you sure this was, uh, hokraft? It could all just be a trick.

Someone preying on your desperation?" asked Lady Branson.

"Oh, I wish it were so, milady, but I, um, saw her prowess. She, uh, was surrounded by corpses of babes, human stillborns. She shouted something that sounded like violent, animalistic chanting. She took a dagger and slaughtered three baby goats, and took their entrails to fashion herself a necklace. She then carved the heart out of one of them and, um, ate it. But the babes, the babes, uh, they, um, oh, God."

"It's alright, just take your time," said Lady Branson.

"It's just, it's madness, absolute madness. What I'm about to tell you is just mad, and I'll understand if you don't believe me because I'm just a stupid, stupid, stupid girl from another land, but the babes, the human babes, were alive again."

Everyone was dumbounded. Such a thing should not be possible, even with hokraft.

Sir Peter was about to speak, but Giselle interrupted him. "I know what you're going to say. But no, they weren't roamers or blood suckers or... or demons. They were ordinary babes—blue, green, brown-eyed babes." Giselle continued. "I-uh, followed her instructions. She held out her hands full of goat blood and transported it to me. I then smeared the blood over my belly whilst repeating the incantations. She then transported the other goat heart, which I, uh, ate." There was a tinge of pain and shame in her voice when she said the word ate.

She turned to the others, who had very concerned looks on their faces. "This is bad, isn't it? I really fucked up this time, heh heh. I-uh, understand if you think less of me now."

Clara was about to say something, but Giselle interrupted. "No, no really, because I think less of me and, um, it's perfectly reasonable if you no longer want to help me. I-uh, don't want to be a burden I—"

"Giselle, this was an act of desperation, not malice. It's only natural that a woman would do anything in her power for her baby to survive. You shan't be punished for being a loving mother. We will get through this together. We are all here for you," said Lady Branson.

"Thank you, milady," replied Giselle gratefully.

"Giselle, do you remember if Aslaug asked for anything in return for her knowledge?" asked Sir Peter.

"No, she just said *in time you will know and when it comes, I only ask of you not to waver…do not waver, my child.*"

The ambiguity in that statement troubled the others. They weren't sure what it meant, and not knowing disturbed them.

"How did you meet Aslaug?" asked Sir Peter.

"Well, she, uh, just sorta, uh, appeared to me in the eye, shortly after I, uh, stopped feeling the baby," said Giselle.

This was disconcerting because it meant this Aslaug person might have been spying on Giselle and possibly Corithni the whole time.

"If this were true, however, why Giselle?" Sir Peter thought. *"Why not Lord Franklin or the knights? It would certainly be a strategic move in winning the war. Or perhaps this Aslaug's motives were not related to the conflict between Hector and Lord Franklin. And if so, what were her motives? Most of all, was this the real Aslaug?"*

"You said she appeared in the eye, right?" asked Sir Peter. "Uh, yes," replied Giselle.

"Any chance you knew her location?" he asked.

"I, uh, don't know. I mean, the few times that we spoke, it was always dark, like she was in some type of cave, maybe?"

"Makes sense. One does not typically practice hokraft in the open," Sir Peter thought.

"Few times?" asked Sir Peter.

Giselle was frightened at her faux pas. "I-uh, I-uh, may have tried to contact her after the initial spell, but, but she, um, mostly ignored me. I-I wanted to know if it had worked but she kept saying *patience, my child,* but I still didn't feel the baby, so, eh, yeah."

"How many times?" asked Sir Peter.

"Er, um, three times in total, heh heh. I know it's, it's quite pathetic, really. I'm pathetic, heh heh. I-I, I uh, appreciate you all trying to help me, but I can tell by the looks on your faces that things are…are, well, um, a lot worse than you thought they'd be. Ahem, I just want you all to know that I'm sorry that I dragged you into this and its high time I took responsibility for my own actions for once in my life, because, let's face it, I-um, am fucked. So, I'm going to do the right thing and turn myself in after the siege," said Giselle.

"You will not!" shouted Clara.

"Clara, Clara. I made the mistake, and I don't want to see you hang for it alongside me."

Lady Branson knelt beside Giselle. She held her hands. "Listen to me, Giselle. No one is going to hang… Do you trust us? Do you trust Clara?"

Giselle looked at Clara and nodded.

"Then believe me when I say this, we will not abandon you, for you are loved."

She kissed her on her forehead, then started quietly praying for her. It was then Giselle thought, *"I now see why Edmund is so enamored with her… I couldn't possibly compete with this level of kindness. This altruism is beyond my understanding, it's otherworldly. I am insignificant in comparison, so how can I fault Edmund for loving her or anyone, really?"* Giselle cried silently.

When Giselle regained her composure, she looked at Sir Peter with a remorseful look on her face and said, "I'm sorry I lied about the nature of my conversation with Aslaug. She did tell me to be patient but, eh, um, the third time, she spoke about you, but she referred to you as your old name, Agnarr."

This news was troubling, but didn't necessarily mean he should panic. He was quite renowned in Mylec. Plenty of people knew him by that name. This didn't mean she was the real Aslaug.

"I know you're asking for trust and I'm still keeping secrets and I'm sorry, heh heh. I know you're tired of hearing that. Giselle always apologizing, but I, I wanted to soften the blow, if that makes any sense," said Giselle.

"That's alright. You're telling us now, that's what's important," said Lady Branson.

"What did she say about me?" asked Sir Peter.

"She-uh, sounded remorseful, to be honest. She mentioned your sword, Seggr, how she created it for your father Brandr," said Giselle.

This was news to Sir Peter. When Heggr gave him that sword, he said he found it during an elven raid.

Giselle continued. "She said that the sword is imbued with magic because she enchanted it."

Sir Peter found this information to conflict with what he had been told. As far as he knew, his blade was not magic, but rather the result of an advanced technology that allowed soul energy to be more easily channeled through metal. The blade glowed because the Modith cores reacted to the soul energy surging within it, not enchantment.

"Aslaug said your father couldn't wield it for some reason. It did not glow in his hands, so she gave it to Heggr. She told him to give it to you and not mention the truth of its origin. She cursed it with the intention of killing you. She was extremely adamant that Heggr was unaware of this," said Giselle.

This detail did not surprise Sir Peter. It was not the first time Aslaug had tried to kill him.

"You didn't die, obviously. She said she was regretful for her old ways and hoped you could forgive her someday," concluded Giselle.

"Now that's complete horseshit the real Aslaug regretted nothing. In fact, remorse was like a foreign concept to her," Sir Peter thought.

Lady Branson held out her hand towards Giselle's stomach. "May I?"

"Yes, milady," said Giselle.

Lady Branson gently felt her belly, and her concerned expression validated Giselle's suspicions.

"You don't feel anything either," said Giselle.

Lady Branson shook her head. In an attempt to assuage the situation Lady Branson said, "But that doesn't mean the child is dead. Sometimes this can be the result of stress. You may have been overexerting yourself."

This did not pacify Giselle, who said, "But we won't know for sure until I give birth."

"Right, but it is important to rest. Babies often kick inconsistently. It may yet happen again," Lady Branson reassured her.

"Why did this woman tell you all this?" asked Sir Peter.

"Because I asked her. Not about you, specifically, just who she was, where she came from, and why she wanted to help me, and your name came up," said Giselle.

"Why do you think she wanted to help you?" asked Sir Peter.

"She said she found me by accident. She saw another woman in pain, and she couldn't bear it. She believed helping me would be the start of her redemption," explained Giselle.

Sir Peter took some time to digest all the information he had just heard. *"Could this be Aslaug? It is a ludicrous idea but, according to Giselle's account, this woman knew things about me that would imply she was Mylecan in origin or at least familiar with the region. The trouble with her story was in the conflicting tales of the origin of Seggr. The only way to determine the legitimacy of these words is to talk to Heggr himself. But it is not like I could just sail to Mylec in the middle of a siege and even if I could, would the Mylecans even accept me? They were not too keen on me converting to Ardinianism and marrying a thrall,"* he thought.

Sir Peter asked, "May we see the eye?"

Giselle nodded. "It's in the top draw." She handed him the key.

Sir Peter held the eye in his hand. He was perplexed, as he had never seen such a device before and certainly not in the hands of Aslaug. He peered into this spherical ball and saw a thick cloud of grey.

"It won't work in non-magical hands," said Giselle. "How does it even work here?" asked Sir Peter.

"Uh, just like your sword. Very potent or old magic, I suppose," replied Giselle.

"My sword, hmm? She is still attached to the theory that it's magic. This person called Aslaug is adamant in revealing her alleged connection to me, but why?" thought Sir Peter.

"Were did you get it?" asked Sir Peter. "It was a gift from my grandmother." "Then why did you lie?" asked Clara.

"It's because of who she was, or rather, what she was associated with," said Giselle.

The others didn't understand. "I-uh, am from Nalmia, but you already knew that, but I am not a bastard like I said I was, heh heh. I know, more lies. My full name is Giselle de la Barre, the, uh, granddaughter of Marion de la Barre, Barre for short. She was the first woman in Arcadiem to be executed for hokraft."

The others were baffled by such a revelation. Marion was famous, or rather infamous, and the name Barre was practically synonymous with hokraft, even in Iiadec. Marion was an alleged seductress, who was said to have seduced over 40 men, amongst them the King of Nalmia, at the time Estienne Babineaux II (1477- 1534 NEEOT) whom she shared a blood relation. Of course, none of this was ever proven and the Nalmians didn't make much a distinction between hokraft and traditional magic. They accused many, mostly women, of communing with Ulid (the devil) and burned them alive during their infamous hokraft trials (1531- NEEOT). "You don't have any other relatives?" asked Clara, sympathizing with her. "Uh, no, you see, the, uh, Barre were all castors and, um, the king at the time, well, he didn't much like us, our power, or influence, and he pretty much considered all forms of magic to, um, be hokraft. Either out of ignorance or indifference to the distinction. So, my family were all executed and burned at stake."

Giselle saw the pitying look on Clara's face and thus averted her gaze.

"Ahem, I only survived because a stranger took pity on me and smuggled me to Iiadec. I was 5. I-uh, never saw that stranger again," said Giselle.

"This, um, eye is the only thing I have left of my family. That's why I kept it."

"You still have a family, me, mum and dad, and when this is over, we'll go back home like none of this ever happened," said Clara.

Giselle smiled weakly. She was not totally convinced but was encouraged, nonetheless.

"How come Lady Franklin never found it when looking through the drawer?" asked Sir Peter.

"When she let me inhabit the chambers, she gave me keys that she said she had never used, nor did she have a spare... She said I could put my belongings there. She trusted me... and I betrayed her," Giselle said, rather despondently.

"You are not entirely to blame, for I asked you to keep something for me and Lady Franklin wanted you to use these drawers as you deemed fit," said Lady Branson.

"The explosives?" asked Sir Peter. Lady Branson nodded.

Sir Peter gave her an incredulous look. "They're the safest place in the castle," she reassured him. She turned to Giselle. "Now, you see, you're not the only one who has taken advantage of Lady Franklin's generosity."

Giselle smiled. "She certainly likes you more than she likes me. She will like me even less if she finds out."

"Don't mistake reservedness for coldness. Lady Franklin is just slow to trust. She just needs time," Lady Branson said.

"Thank you, milady," said Giselle.

Giselle saw Sir Peter scrutinizing the eye and it made her uncomfortable. "I-uh, can show you how it works, if you like?" she smiled nervously. "It's the least I can do for all the trouble I have caused. I swear it's not hokraft. The device itself is not a product of any soul dealings, ritual sacrifice or, or anything of that nature. I-I, uh, know you don't have any reason to believe that because it's, um, coming from me, but it's true. I-I just want to, um, help any way I can, to make up for, well, everything. I mean, by God, you've all got enough to worry about already and now you're literally risking your necks for some stupid, stupid, stupid—"

"Giselle, stop. This was a mistake. It is in the past. You cannot dwell on it any longer, do you understand?" asked Clara.

Giselle nodded. Suppressing tears, Giselle looked at Sir Peter and asked, "Can I, um?" He understood. He handed her Mothrya's eye.

She held it in her hands. "You seek to communicate with this Aslaug again?" Sir Peter asked gravely.

"Well, if I could just talk to her, just convince her to remove the spell, then—"

"It is not merely a spell; its hokraft," interrupted Sir Peter. He sighed. He did not want to upset the others, but his frustration was becoming apparent. "It will take more than words to remove it. That is, if it can even be removed."

"I know it's a shot in the dark, but if it works... I-I-I have to try," said Giselle.

"This woman calling herself Aslaug is a hokraft practitioner. Most do not take kindly to the reversal of their work, there could be retaliation... She could be dangerous," explained Sir Peter.

Giselle gulped.

"What do you suggest, Sir Peter?" asked Clara.

He looked at Giselle. "Can you operate that thing without touching it and staying out of its sight?"

Giselle, slightly confused, said, "Uh, yeah, I think so. It's a simple tactile spell." (Tactile spell is a spell that allows the magic wielder to touch things without the use of their Corporal bodies through the extension of ruda particles from their soul.)

"Good. Place the eye on the bed and get behind me and make sure you're out of sight."

Giselle did as she was told. Sir Peter placed emphasis on the fact that she remain out of sight.

"Clara, Elysant. Leave this place and close the door behind you," said Sir Peter.

"I'm not leaving her," protested Clara.

"Clara, you're not helping her by staying here," replied Sir Peter.

"Peter, what is going on?" asked Lady Branson.

Sir Peter unsheathed Seggr, which was now glowing. "If my sword is magic, then it will harm her...even if not, it can repel her."

"Peter," said Lady Branson.

"This woman will most likely not let her go and if this is the real Aslaug, Giselle will almost certainly be in bondage till the day she dies, maybe even the hereafter. This is the only way she can be freed. Leave this place, both of you," he said.

Clara took Lady Branson by the arm, who was still looking at Sir Peter, and exited the room. "C'mon, milady," said Clara.

Giselle, who was frightened, cast the tactile spell. "Resalis," (extended touch) said Giselle. Tendrils of turquoise energy formed from her fingertips and latched itself on to the eye.

"Do not move," Sir Peter demanded.

Giselle stayed put. With Seggr in both hands, he pointed at the eye. The cloud in the eye dissipated, revealing an image. It was not of this woman calling herself Aslaug, and not in a cave in some foreign land, but right in Iiadec. Mydra, to be exact, not far from Corithni and Hector's army. They were just standing there. A man wearing Everad's vigil, whom Sir Peter did not recognize, was standing looking off into the distance at something that Mothrya's eye did not allow him to see. The man, for the most part, did not look particularly menacing, average height, average build. His appearance suggested he was native to Iiadec. medium length brown hair, blue eyes and a stubble beard, but there was something unsettling about him that Sir Peter could not explain. Maybe it was the lax way in which he stood, or the eerily calm expression on his face that juxtaposed the situation he was in. Another soldier walked up to him. "Sir, the hellhound has been slain, the dragon is responsible."

"Yes, I know, and it was a spectacle. I was there when the fucking thing died," the man said nonchalantly.

"But Sir, Lord Hector is surrounded by the Franklins and the dragon is in league with them," said the bewildered soldier.

"And what the fuck do you want us to do? Lord Hector Franklin or Lord Hector Everard or whatever the hell he's calling himself got himself into this shit situation. Let him get himself out. Last time I checked, I'm not exactly fireproof. Are you?" said the man.

The soldier, now angered at the man's indifference to Hector's perilous plight, said, "You fucking cunt. You bear Everad's vigil, you fight for Lord Hector. This is treason!"

"You're not particularly bright, are you we don't serve Lord Franklin hence, we don't lick Lord Hector's arse like Franklin's men do Albert Franklin. We fight for coin and that other thing...." The man lingered on the phrase, that other thing. He continued. "Lord Hector isn't honoring his end of the deal. He is not delivering what's promised... He's a bullshitter. Said he could take on Corithni says, *how are we going to lose. We have a fucking dragon and army of castors with enough magic to tear the bloody sky down,* he says."

"You're a coward and a disgrace," the soldier glowered. He gripped the hilt of his blade tightly.

"And you're an imbecile with no vision," the man retorted. "He is the rightful heir to the throne of Iiadec!"

The man laughed derisively, as did some other men surrounding him. "You really believe that horseshit? Ha ha ha. You really are unsurpassed in stupidity."

"So will you switch allegiances from Lord Hector to Lord Franklin? You think he's really going to accept a fucking turncoat? you miserable sack of shit" said the soldier.

"Fuck Hector. Fuck Albert Franklin. Fuck the throne. Mirama controls it all anyway. I've got better things to do than get involved in a squabble between royal arseholes. Let them kill each other," said the man. The soldier unsheathed his blade with fury in his eyes as he said, "You will die for this!" He charged at the man but was impaled in the chest by a glaive held by a boy of no more than thirteen. He had green eyes and medium length blonde hair. The soldier perished on the ground with his eyes still open and his blood staining the grass.

"Did you really have to humiliate him?" asked the boy.

"*Did you really have to humiliate him?* You sound like a fucking twat," the man mocked.

Ignoring the man, the boy asked, "So, how are things with the castle infiltration?"

"Not good. Those idiots got killed by a bunch of Etlians, the map is lost and so is the Fire of the Gods."

"That's not a problem. We'll just have to try again. You have me this time," said the boy.

The man turned to the boy with a serious look on his face. "You better be who you say you are or it's your arse. You understand me, you little shit?"

The boy, not fazed by such aggression, said calmly, "I am Chad, bastard son of Dean Mason and I have the mark to prove it."

Chad revealed his right hand. On it was the glowing mark of the Mason.

Sir Peter was bewildered.

The man then asked, "And what does this Chad, bastard son of Dean Mason want?"

Chad said, in a rather menacing way, "What is rightfully mine."

The man smiled. "You are a little devil." He then stopped and looked around as though something had caught his attention. He appeared to be looking right at Sir Peter when he said, "We're being watched. Someone with a Mothrya's eye."

"Mothrya? The sison shit?" asked Chad. "It appears so," replied the man.

"Well, can't you blast them from here?" asked Chad.

"You need another eye for that. I cannot see them at the moment... but I can disrupt the signal." He held out his hand, closed his eyes and muttered the words *zemar tolik* (old tongue for hide).

The eye slowly went grey again. Sir Peter stood up straight. "Can I move?" asked Giselle.

"Yes," said Sir Peter.

Giselle looked at Sir Peter. She was terrified. "We, we didn't find her. I-I-I don't understand. I envisioned the caves. Is she even alive anymore? And who was that boy and the man I heard? I don't recognize them, I swear. And Mason? That's Sarah's last name. Why, why is that so important? I-I-I lost her. Ugh, I'm such an idiot. Bernia told me it was based on something called ruda particles and the signal will latch on to the castor with the most ruda particles or something like that. But I thought, I thought I could somehow manipulate the signal to get to her. What if she never returns? God knows what will happen to me. I-I-I am damned." Giselle began sobbing profusely, and Sir Peter embraced her.

"We will find another way once we realize how to use the eye," Sir Peter reassured her.

There was a knock on the door. "May we come in?" said Lady Branson.

Sir Peter looked at Giselle. She assured him she was okay. He then opened the door. Clara rushed in and hugged Giselle.

"Are you safe? Was the spell removed?" But Clara could tell by her dispirited expression that this was not the case. Lady Branson looked at Sir Peter and he shook his head.

"So, it didn't work this time. We can try again," Clara exclaimed, trying her best to lift the mood.

"I'm afraid we have some more troubling news," said Sir Peter. "What is it, Peter?" asked Lady Branson, her eyes widened upon seeing the concerned look on his face. Sir Peter sighed as he said, "There is another of Mason blood."

CHAPTER SIXTEEN
FINAL BATTLE

The Franklins were staring down at their adversaries while Mavid loomed in the distance, presumably out of range of Hector's magic wielders. Hector's remaining forces were greatly diminished and were not eager to challenge a dragon who had slain a hellhound. Yet, despite all odds, Hector did not seem worried in the slightest. Whether this was a façade or not was yet to be known to the Franklins. Whatever it was, he was doing an excellent job of presenting himself in a way that would suggest unwavering confidence, and whether Lord Franklin wanted to admit it or not, this vexed him. The smug smile on Hector's face made him feel uneasy. Lord Franklin began to think had he made an error, or was this just bravado? Either way, Hector was getting in his head. "Hector, it's over. Your forces have dwindled, your men grow weary of fighting, and you're surrounded, hiding in a stone structure like a scared animal," said Lord Franklin.

"Hiding? Is that what I'm doing? Because from up here, it looks like I'm observing the land to find the perfect place to bury you. It's the least I can do, you know. Since we share blood," retorted Hector.

This angered Lord Franklin, and Hector reveled in it. "Struck a chord, did I? You know, Uncle, you're not as stoic as you present yourself to be," Hector chuckled.

"Hector, we don't have time to mince words with you. And if you insist on spinning this horseshit narrative, know this. I have only one question for you… How do you want to die? Because that's the only offer that's on the table, so I suggest you take it," said John menacingly.

"Hmm, tsk tsk. It is a shame, a disgrace, really. Can't even address me by my full title cousin, huh?" said Hector derisively.

"What? Lord Hector Cunt Face the Master of Bullshit?" William teased.

Instead of getting angry, Hector had a diametrically opposite reaction. He laughed heartily. "Cousin William, I didn't realize how amusing you were. I mean, it is all rather amusing, isn't it?"

Hector looked at the men in the structure and they nodded. Hector then turned to the Franklins. "But you know what I find most amusing? That you all think you're going to survive this."

"You can act tough all you want, save face in front of your men, but we all know you are pissing your undergarments right now. You are outmatched. The more you go on with this charade, the worst you'll make it for yourself, and that goes for any man that follows you... you were warned," said Edmund.

"Outmatched? There's ten of us up here and only, eh, four of you." "We have a dragon," retorted Edmund.

"Do ye?" asked Hector.

William furrowed his brow upon hearing that remark. The Franklins were nervous, but they did not show it. Hector knew what they were thinking.

"Oswin!" shouted Hector.

William shot a lightning bolt at Oswin, but it narrowly missed him as he transported somewhere across the battlefield. Hector unsheathed his blade and the others beside him drew their weapons as well. Hector's weapon was a large longsword, almost great sword length, 43 inches, with the hilt measuring 6.6 inches. This was understandable, given Hector's size. It had a reddish hue, not glowing from magic, but the actual metal was red. Which would be peculiar enough in itself if it weren't for the skull pommel. Yes, an actual skull for a pommel coated with metal in order for it to be functional.

"Done talking, huh?" said Lord Franklin with the Great Divider and buckler at hand.

"Uncle, your legacy will be about how you and your seeds died in agony as they tried to usurp the throne of Iiadec from its rightful king."

Hildred placed the one jeweled crown on Hector's head as Hector said rightful king.

"Putting a shitty crown on your head don't make you a king, it just makes you an arsehole," retorted William.

Hector smiled. The Franklins put on their visors, and with that, the two forces collided.

The Archer standing next to Sir Kelton wasted no time in shooting five incendiary tipped arrows at Lord Franklin's head. Lord Franklin evaded the first two then blocked the remaining with his buckler. Edmund retaliated by firing three successive lightning bolts at the lightly armored bowman. The bowman avoided the attacks, but the last attack grazed his shoulder, causing him to lower his bow. Lord Franklin took advantage of this and fired a lethal lightning strike at the bowman's head. He died instantly. John and Edmund were in close quarter combat with four other warriors. Two were wielding blades and the other two had polearms, one being a pike, the other being a spear. None of the four were heavily armored with Anactuken steel, so they were susceptible to elemental attacks. The polearm bearer wielding the spear delivered a thrust at John, aimed at the space in between the neck and the breastplate. John retaliated by deflecting the attack downward, thus angling his opponents' weapon to the floor. Before he could pursue his opponent, John was attacked relentlessly by a swordsman wielding a messer. The swordsman delivered five strikes in various directions while his blade inverted. John anticipated this and successfully parried all strikes. William and Lord Franklin attempted to intervene but were stopped by Hildred, who stayed back from the fighting to cast hexes at them. Hector, Sir Kelton, and another full plated armored clad knight played spectator.

Edmund was engaged in combat with the other two warriors. He narrowly evaded a thrust to the neck from the pikeman. He found it difficult to keep track of both his opponents. They were certainly not novices. He thought about striking the pikeman with a lightning bolt, but the swordsman wielding a falchion did not give him enough opportunity to channel one. The falchion wielder was quick and unyielding. He was wise to strike mostly with the pommel of his sword, only using the blade when he saw an opening. For the most part, Edmund was on the defense. Had he not been wearing armor, some of the strikes from his opponent would have resulted in mortal wounds. The pikeman was patient, but cunning. Using his comrade as a distraction, he would wait for an opening to strike. He advanced, then retreated when his attacks were ultimately thwarted by Edmund.

Hildred tried to cast a fire spell on William and Lord Franklin. He held out his hands and repeated, "Uthra Fithra, Uthra Fithra."

But William and Lord Franklin did not remain still, making hexing them difficult. Hence, the fire created by the charm kept missing. Lord Franklin hurled one lightning bolt after another at Hildred as Hildred's fire charm nearly set him a blaze. Hildred summoned a magic barrier that shielded him from the attack.

"*Uthra Aloygus ruda,*" Hildred said. He started to sweat.

William knew this was no ordinary spell. It drained soul manifest. That was the price of a near invulnerable magical shield. Hildred was suffering from fatigue. He was not a young man, nor had he ever been one for physical combat. When the magic depleted, he would be left defenseless. This was a gamble, William thought, but if successful, it could mean certain victory. William took a slight step forward. He held his sword like a spear with his index finger wrapped around the cross guard and the flat of the blade resting on the palm of his hand. He then did something unthinkable and what some would consider devoid of logic. He hurled his blade like a spear directly at Hector. The sword sailed through the air at a rapid speed, with surprising accuracy. Hector narrowly avoided the missile and with such a bewildered expression on his face, he could not even hide that he was caught off guard. The sword hit the wall behind Hector and fell to the floor adjacent to his feet.

"You missed id—"

But Hector was interrupted when a surge of electricity expelled from the blade. So much that it cracked the stone structure. The monolith crumbled to pieces, collapsing on Hector and his allies.

***

Oswin appeared in front of the men. He was not close enough to Mavid to jinx him and he had caught the king dragon's eye. Mavid flew higher in the sky to avoid him. This irritated Oswin. He didn't want to admit it, but he had used up too much soul manifest and could only afford one more transport. He was beginning to reek of Sulphur. Even if he transported, there was no guarantee where he'd land. The blasted beast kept moving. It was so infuriating. He approached a man wearing Everard's crest and a boy of no more than thirteen wielding a glaive. They seemed to be carrying about all lackadaisical, as if Hector were not in extreme peril, as did the other men. This invoked ire in Oswin.

"What the bloody hell are you doing? You're supposed to be a fucking army. Go and distract the dragon so I can claim it again. The boy and the man had indifferent looks on their faces. One sell-sword approached Oswin to present his grievances with the idea of berating Oswin.

"You are completely mad if you think we're going to challenge that fucking fire spitting demon in the sky again,"

Several of the men shared the same sentiments. He turned to the men and laughed. "Distract em, he says, for what? So you can cast spells from the distance while we burn alive?"

"You will do as you're told or suffer the wrath of Lord Hector himself," said Oswin angrily.

The man started pretending as though he was really frightened by Oswin's threat, pondering what the consequence would be of such insolence.

"Lord Hector, huh? That's quite the title, but the thing is, we don't serve titles. Not lords, not kings, not even God. The only thing we give a shit about is coin. You may think little of us for what you perceive to be such a trivial obsession. But you see, this whole ground that we stand on, this whole world we reside in…. it's all we have. Because when we die, that's it. Our corpses become food for the maggots, none of that horseshit afterlife business. Puts things into perspective, doesn't it. And suddenly coin is not so trivial. We sell swords from Agor, are immune to the great deception known as morality. I'll admit, I'm not exactly unfeeling, but I'm not what you'd call a good man. Hell, I'd murder a newborn babe for enough coin, crush its little skull under my boot for the right price. But you knew that, Oswin. We're fucking sell swords, after all."

"So why, then, desert Lord Hector now he has coin?" said Oswin.

The sell sword chuckled. "You see. Oswin. Hector's not the only one with little birdie spies like that fucking cunt Eardwulf. We got word from Agor that the Everard gold mines have run dry. And you know what happens when you don't give a sell sword from Agor his well earn coin." He drew his blade, a longsword with strange markings on it that appeared to only serve an aesthetic purpose. The other men behind him drew their weapons as well. All bearing similar marks.

Oswin appeared defeated. He hung his head low, his eyes concealed by his hair. He sighed. But he said something that would betray his apparently despondent demeanor. "Edvin, it's fitting, really. You never were one for titles, not even with your own father."

This was a revelation to some of the sell swords. "And yet I never once punished you for your irreverence, but this was a grave error."

Oswin slowly lifted his head to look at Edvin, his eyes completely black, his voice unnaturally deep as he said, "One that will cost you more than you know."

The men were astonished and afraid, for they had awakened something they should not have. The man with the Everard emblem and the boy with the glaive were not too far from this whole spectacle.

The boy, visibly frightened, said, "That's, that's impossible." And the man standing next to him said, "In my experience, when dealing with hokraft, nothing is impossible." He placed a hand on the boy's shoulder and whispered in his ear, "Chad, let's get out of here. I don't wanna wait around for this blood bath." The pair transported out of the battlefield to an unknown location.

The men that remained with Edvin readied themselves, after most deserted after seeing Oswin in this state to pursue Mavid.

"Cowards the lot of em," said Edvin in response.

He looked at his father and with his long sword in both hands, shouted, "I don't know what the hell you became, but you're still going down. There's all of us and only one of you."

Instead of responding with some threatening vernacular, Oswin hunched over and roared like some kind of feral animal. The two parties clashed, but most of the men's advances were halted, including Edvin's. They could not move, which was a precarious position to be in when dealing with an enemy magic wielder. They were in Oswin's direct line of sight. Oswin bellowed as he clenched his fist while looking directly at the sell sword next to Edvin. The sell sword collapsed and died immediately. His heart had been crushed from the inside through some type of force, an unidentifiable power. More deaths like this became prominent, with the men receiving several lacerations, some to their internal organs. They received other mortal wounds despite not being struck by any physical, magical, or soul-based energy. One man's head simply parted from his shoulders with a wound initially forming around the base of his neck and circumnavigating the entire collum, resulting in beheading. There were other bloodless, but equally macabre, fatalities such as internal decapitation. One of the men had the base of his spine spontaneously liberated from his skull. Resulting in a rather grotesque sight of his head only being attached to his body by his skin. Another man fell to his knees, screaming out in agony as his internal organs simultaneously exploded. Blood leaked out from his orifices.

During this whole ghastly scene, not one of the men managed to get within arm's distance of Oswin. Many of the men tried to flee, but they were slain by Oswin and whatever dark forces he wielded in the same violent fashion as their comrades. After every kill, Oswin would say something that would have been incoherent if one was not listening attentively. This was due to the erratic and irregular vocal patterns he had developed since entering such a state. It was but one word, claimed. When Oswin grew tired of his massacre. Several corpses remained, with surprisingly very little damage to their armor and weapons. There was so much carnage on the battlefield with heaps of bodies laid out like grains of rice. To put things into perspective, Edvin had 219 men with him. By the end of the massacre, only six remained.

Oswin stepped forward for the first time since his arrival on the battlefield. He surveyed the aftermath of the destruction he caused. His eyes still black. He walked about differently than he had done previously. Prowling like a beast, he approached the remaining survivors, most of which had received serious injuries. Amongst them was Edvin. He looked at his son, his countenance not one of disgust or pity, but of indifference. It was as though Oswin was no longer Oswin but something else entirely. "What do you want, you fucking hokraft riddled cunt?" said Edvin, bleeding internally while resting his back on his deceased comrade. He could not stand for his legs stopped working and were quickly becoming gangrenous.

"What we always wanted. To serve," said Oswin.

Edvin, in a desperate act of defiance, said, "Fuck off!" as he spit blood at Oswin's feet.

Oswin tilted his head slightly in a very unnerving and unnatural way that would provoke anxiety in the faint of heart. "He did warn you. The other one you know, your father. Now you will meet the same fate as the others," said Oswin.

The other men were trembling. One man said in desperation, "We surrender."

Oswin looked at the man directly in the eyes and said rather curtly, "We do not accept." He then roared a deafening, harsh noise, unforgiving to the ear and even more unsettling for the mind. With the exception of Edvin, the rest of the men died convulsing. Looming over Edvin, Oswin said nothing.

"I will not give you the satisfaction of watching me plead for my life… so loyal to Lord Hector, but you messed up his plans." He mustered all his energy to pick up his blade. The distinct markings on it started to glow red, and the blade started to vibrate. "We are the only ones who can vex a dragon enough so that you can claim it… That's right, father. You're not the only one who's been dealing with hokraft. This blade, and the weapons of others, can only be activated by the Ruthless Pariahs of Agor, who swore a blood oath to the corporeal devil, coin our only true master. Did you really think you claimed the king dragon by yourself? Come on, you see you need us."

Oswin, not fazed by this revelation, said bluntly, "We don't need ye, just your bodies."

Edvin immediately suffered from a stroke and collapsed on the ground where he flailed about wildly. He eventually succumbed to his affliction and perished. Then, one by one, the corpses of the fallen began to rise. Their bodies were present, but their minds were gone, skin pale, eyes cloudy and lifeless. This could only mean one thing: reanimation. They were no longer men, but an army of the undead.

Mavid was way up in the sky but had observed the horrible sight. He was beginning to understand how he had been bewitched, although he did not know all the details. From what he understood, this sorcerer, master of the dark arts, and by extension, Hector, possessed power so potent and unexplainable that it broke all the rules of what was to be considered possible. It made Mavid question reality and what it meant to comprehend certain absolute truths, things that cannot be refuted. He had been around for nearly 4000 years and had never seen anything like this. And for the first time in a long time, he was truly terrified.

His thoughts were racing, and he was beginning to panic. *"Remaining in this accursed land is unwise. Humans with the ability to bewitch dragons? Sorcerers with the ability to slaughter whole armies and then raise them from the dead? Performing incantations without uttering any language. Instead, bellowing primal sounds like some deranged hell-beast. So loud that they could be heard from the sky.* (Beings on Mirthadine have more resistant eardrums, so the pain threshold is higher*). This is absolute madness. I should probably flee to Beladar and warn the others of this human plague. But then... would my brethren suffer the same fate as those other humans? Or worse, will they be slaves forever bound to dark forces beyond my understanding? No, no. I must end this and end this now."*

Mavid headed towards the combat zone with the intention of slaying Oswin, making sure he avoided eye contact and being as stealthy as possible. He flew quickly, but quietly. He had to make haste, for a single miscalculation could cost him his life, or worse, his freedom. He viewed the area from the air. Some of the army of undead sell swords, combined with Hector's other remaining forces, were on the move. They were aggregated in a uniform formation, marching through the woods of Mydra like a large hunting party and Mavid was game. Some of them were obscured by the trees and undergrowth, but Mavid could still see them. He, however, could not spot Oswin. The enemy had renewed their assault, starting with a single archer shooting an arrow in his direction. It did not land, but dozens of others followed.

Mavid thought it was peculiar. Surely, they knew that such weak instruments could not pierce his hide? But they did not intend to wound him, did they? No, they were planning something far more insidious. They were alerting the sorcerer to his direction. He had already been high enough in the sky to touch the clouds. They must have seen his silhouette in the sky. He could not risk going any higher in an attempt to further obscure himself. Oxygen levels at that altitude were significantly depleted and he would have difficulty breathing. He peered down at the fields of Mydra, yet he still could not spot the sorcerer. He figured he must descend. It was the only way he could locate this fiendish villain and effectively end him. As he descended, he was accompanied by a volley of arrows. None of which were able to strike him. He contemplated raining down fire on his enemies, but then he would be in the sorcerer's sights, so he decided against it.

Then something peculiar happened. The army of undead raised their weapons in the air and the distinct markings on them began to turn crimson, like the color of blood. It was as though the metal that formed the weapons was bleeding. Blades and other weapons stained with blood, fresh blood. They began to vibrate at high frequency, to produce a sound that would be inaudible to a typical humanoid, but to a dragon it was excruciatingly painful. The sound was ear splitting, reaching the pain threshold. Mavid did his best to escape. Frantically flying through the air in a desperate attempt to escape the infernal sound.

"*A screamer* (A type of mutation that allows one to control sound waves primarily by screaming), *but, but, I thought they were rare, and I saw no one yelling.*" Then he remembered. "*The weapons... It must be the weapons.*"

The irritating sound suddenly stopped and dropped to a dangerously low, almost inaudible sound. Although barely audible, its presence was made apparent as it affected the internal organs. The men on the ground took ill. Some feeling nauseous, even vomiting or suffering bowl spasms, while the undead were unaffected. Mavid felt his bones rattle and had trouble breathing. His wings felt unstable and were insufficient for flight due to the adverse effects of this low sound. He found it difficult to stay suspended in the air and was slowly descending against his will. His body was acting erratically, and he felt disoriented. He spewed a great inferno into the sky, in the hope that such an action would act as a release from his agony. He could not remain in this perilous state for much longer or else run the risk of perishing. But what was he to do? He was powerless to resist. His body had betrayed him and his mind was abstracted. He felt the excruciating pain of his innards convulsing. In his befuddled state, he could only muster one coherent thought. "*Is this the end for the great dragon king of Beladar?*"

He felt his body grow cold as he slowly closed his eyes.

***

The Franklins stood over the bodies of the foes they had dispatched. They were truly dismayed at what had occurred. "William, that was truly amazing," said John. "Don't act too surprised," replied William.

"So, Hector is no more?" Edmund said, dumbfounded.

Lord Franklin remained quiet. Something made him feel uneasy, but he could not pinpoint it. Suddenly, the rock and debris from the collapsed monolith began to shake ever so slightly. A huge boulder surrounded by piles of stone began to rise, much to the surprise of the Franklins. It revealed what appeared to be Hector holding a boulder the size of an eighteen-wheeler truck over his head with apparent ease. Adjacent to him was Sir Kelton, crouching down on the ground, along with the other armored clad knight and what remained of Hildred, with his crushed body smeared in the rubble. Blood and innards sprawled over stone and dirt, but from the look on Hector's face, he did not look even remotely concerned. The right half of his face had been scorched from fire, stemming from the electrical shock he received, but he did not seem affected. The crown on his head remained intact, the rose-colored crystal glowing.

A devilish toothy grin formed on his face. He had a mad look in his eyes as he said, "Oh, Uncle, for all your shrewdness, cleverness and ability to anticipate what's next… I guarantee you did not see this coming."

He hurled the boulder at the Franklins. They would have been crushed if it were not for Lord Franklin's quick thinking. In an almost unconscious movement, simply a mere reaction to danger, a beam of soul energy sprung from the Great Divider's point. A straight and narrow but concentrated cylindrical projection, later being imbued in electricity, struck the stone. With an upward cut, Lord Franklin split the rock in two, causing it to miss the Franklins, hitting the ground with a loud thud. The Franklins shielded their eyes to the debris. Although he was successful in avoiding death with such a technique, it would later prove costly for Lord Franklin, for he was running out of soul manifest and began to reek of Sulphur.

His sons watched their father with deep concern as they heard their father's labored breaths from his helmet. Lord Franklin tried to look robust, but he began to slouch. His limbs appeared weak. This was made more apparent by the slight lowering of his sword and buckler. He did not have much energy left and the other Franklins knew it. What was even worse was that Hector was clearly more than capable of hurling large projectiles of similar size. In a moment of brief but serious contemplation, Edmund stepped forward as a blue aura surrounded his entire body. He began to glow, incased with sparks of electricity and the smell of sulfur in the air, this was the intermediary.

He turned to his brothers and said, "Get father out of here using the Hakaneira… I am going to end this."

"Edmund!" Lord Franklin, John and William screamed in unison, but he paid them no heed.

He grasped his blade tightly in both hands and said, "It's already done." And with that, the aura surrounding him nearly doubled in size as a gust of warm wind started permeating around him. His armor rattled due to the impact.

"Edmund, stop this nonsense immediately!" shouted Lord Franklin. But William and John knew he had already tapped into the core, his life force. It was too late. They seized their father, who resisted, but was ultimately overpowered, and raised their swords in the air, vanishing in a flash of lightning. Hector, Sir Kelton, and the other armored knight stood on the rubble and looked down at Edmund. Hector had looked at Edmund with a sense of reverence. He admired the fact that Edmund was willing to give his all to defeat his foe because, after all, that is the way it should be. Only the weak are unwilling to do everything necessary to win. The strong risk everything to achieve supremacy. They are a whole different breed of man and like kind. Standing on the rubble, looking down at this scintillating figure, made Hector realize Edmund was amongst this breed of man. This could not be denied, but in the end, there could only be one victor, one man standing. There can only be one God amongst men.

The men beside him drew their blades, and Hector motioned them to stop and said, "Do not interfere."

Hector and Edmund charged at each other and collided in an awesome clash.

***

Oswin was hiding somewhere on the battlefield, concealing himself with magic, making the average onlooker think him invisible. He looked up at the sky. The rain was intense, and the lightning was more unyielding than before. Whatever state Oswin was in had made him hypersensitive to his surroundings. A flash of lightning and roll of thunder would appear every 15 seconds, except for one wayward bolt. Oswin immediately thought the Franklins were fleeing to the castle. So he closed his eyes and cast the hex on the wayward bolt with his mind. The peculiarity with such a feat was Oswin's chance of locating the exact lightning bolt the

Franklin's essence were on was slim to none. He located it by chance, not with some inherent ability within him.

Somewhere, during transportation, neither John nor William could perceive the castle. Whether this was faux magic or fatigue was not relevant. If they did not perceive anything in the allotted time, they would surely perish. So, in an act of desperation, they landed somewhere in the fields of Mydra. The most tangible place they could think of. This was all done in a matter of seconds. They crash landed in the grass, feeling disoriented and sprawled on the ground from the nearly fatal Hakaneira. They looked around. The first figure they saw was a black-eyed Oswin looming over them. He was surrounded by his allies and the undead sell swords.

The Franklins quickly rose to their feet. "Don't try it," Oswin said sharply.

They were appalled by the irregularity of his speech and his eyes. "There is no point. The Hakaneira requires nearly absolute perception of one's desired location. With the hex we placed on you, you are no longer able to perceive locations beyond your current one. In other words, it would cost you your lives if you attempted to transport anywhere else. It's faux magic, of course, so it won't last, but that doesn't matter. You'll be dead by then," said Oswin.

"What do you want, demon?" Lord Franklin said through gritted teeth. "Demon? Last time we checked, demons were incapable of magic. Must be the eyes. They mean so much more than you know. As for what we want, well, we want what's best for Iiadec…We want what's best for the world," said Oswin.

"And that's a usurper sitting on the throne?" retorted John.

"No. Liberation from a corrupted system," replied Oswin. "You see, you Franklins are like a plague, infecting everyone you contact. And the best way to end a plague is to kill it with fire," he continued.

Mavid suddenly descended from the sky and landed next to Oswin. His eyes were black, wrought with possession. Unflinchingly insentient.

**

Hector delivered a diagonal cut descending from the right that met on the strong of Edmund's blade. (Strong of blade is a HEMA (Historical European Martial Art) term referring to the strong side of a sword in reference to balance. Similar terms are used such as the weak of a blade which means inversely the weak side of a blade.)

Edmund had successfully parried the attack by striking Hector's blade and rotating his hips. From his new position, he attempted to deliver a thrust to Hector's head. Hector avoided the attack by leaning back. Edmund tried to pursue him, but Hector quickly disengaged and stepped offline. This was the first engagement. Both warriors returned to guard position just out of striking distance from each other. With Hector resuming high guard and Edmund on long point guard. Edmund's aura allowed him to barely match Hector's strength, otherwise he would have surely been crushed under the weight of Hector's strikes. Edmund thought he could retaliate by delivering elemental or soul strikes. Reader, you have to understand, Anactuken armor has its limits and is completely ineffective against energy coming from the core. Given Hector's strength and Edmund's energy output, half-swording was deemed unnecessary, because a well-timed cut or thrust from either one of them would go through plated armor.

From long point guard, Edmund delivered a thrust towards Hector's torso. The attack was extended by a plasma beam emitting from Edmund's blade. The attack was blocked by Hector using the flat of his blade. The eyes of Hector's skull pommel turned red, and the energy beam Edmund hurled at him, completely dissipated.

"It won't be that easy cousin," said Hector.

Edmund scowled and renewed his assault. From wrath guard, Edmund delivered a horizontal cut from the right to which Hector responded by exchanging one of his own. From just a brief moment in the bind, Edmund could feel the impact of the force on his limbs. He did not falter, however. He quickly switched to long point again and threatened Hector with the point of his blade. Hector, choosing not to engage, stepped offline to avoid the potential thrust and delivered a descending cut aimed at Edmund's torso. It was met with an undercut. With both blades meeting at their exact center and neither gaining much of an advantage, both combatants disengaged. Hector, from high guard, delivered two quick descending cuts to Edmund's head on both his right and left side, respectively. Edmund successfully parried both attacks using ox guard. Edmund, from high guard, delivered a descending cut at Hector's head. Hector completely avoided the attack, leaving Edmund exposed due to overextending. Before Hector could take advantage of this, Edmund shot the electricity out of his sword, directed at Hector's feet. Hector was forced to defend by digging his blade into the ground so that the attack would hit his weapon, not him. The electricity was absorbed by the blade.

Edmund, wasting no time, delivered a diagonal descending cut to Hector's exposed neck. Hector, acting quickly, deflected with the strong side of his blade on the weak of Edmund's blade, thus gaining the advantage. Edmund had been overzealous hence, he made an error in judgment. Through winding, Hector was able to deliver a thrust to Edmund's head which would have been fatal if not for Edmund's helmet. The helmet cracked into pieces upon impact, exposing Edmund's face. Edmund thought he ought to be more cautious next time. His over aggression nearly cost him his life. Edmund quickly stepped offline to avoid further attacks, but Hector still pursued him, relentlessly delivering cuts with Edmund just barely parrying them.

Forced on the defense, Edmund thought Hector was getting more aggressive. He must do something. Edmund believed this new power he had tapped into was not being fully utilized. It needed to be more than a shield from Hector's immense strength. It is important to note that the soul energy Edmund imbued in only protects his body, making him more resistant to blows. It does not act as a shield unless he wills it. Soul energy is like gas. It is intangible unless intentionally altered.

Using the technique known as Tithonite, which results in massive amounts of electricity being expelled from the body, Edmund created an electrical field around himself. Hector struggled to defend himself from the barrage of electricity. He used his blade to shield himself and absorb the electricity. But this tactic was starting to diminish in effectiveness. Hector was being overwhelmed and his skull shaped pommel began to crack. Beads of sweat formed on Hector's brow as he struggled to defend himself against Edmund's constant cuts and electrical based attacks. Meanwhile, from high guard, Edmund delivered a descending cut which Hector narrowly escaped by voiding (HEMA term for dodging an attack). Hector attempted to return the attack, but it was easily deflected by Edmund.

Forced to disengage for fear of being cut, Hector side stepped and resumed high guard. He delivered another descending cut, which was met in a bind with the strong of both blades on top of each other. Edmund, acting quickly, turned his blade around, so it was underneath Hector's arms and delivered an undercut that sliced Hector's forearms. The strike cut through armor and drew blood. A flesh wound, but nonetheless, kept Hector on his toes. Hector winced and Edmund saw this slight moment of weakness and took it as a chance to engage. Edmund delivered a descending cut at Hector's face by rotating his arms into high guard and striking. Hector avoided the oncoming attack and answered with one of his own. A horizontal strike that met the strong of Edmund's blade. It was performed by holding the sword horizontally and rotating the hips. By the end of the strike, Hector's hilt was resting on his hip. Edmund disengaged, seeing no benefit in winding, for Hector's stance would not allow much wiggle room. Edmund, however, quick to attack anew, did not let Hector rest.

From high guard, he delivered four descending cuts, alternating between right, left, right, left, respectively. Hector parried the attacks successfully using ox guard. Both combatants were forced into long point guard after such a frantic exchange. Hector engaged first, delivering a thrust to Edmund's torso. It was parried by Edmund. The blades slid past each other. With the strong of Edmunds blade resting on the weak of Hector's, he lowered Hector's blade and, winding, delivered a thrust at Hector's head. Hector narrowly avoided the attack by simply tilting his head in the opposite direction. But this was a late dodge and Edmund's blade still cut Hector in the unmarred section of his face, on the left side. It was another flesh wound but the second time Edmund had drawn blood. Hector scowled. He was too reckless, and it was costing him.

After the near fatal attack from Edmund, Hector started fighting more cautiously. Edmund from wrath guard delivered a horizontal strike at Hector's torso. Hector parried the attack with his own horizontal cut. From the bind, Edmund attempted to wind his sword in such a fashion where the point was directed at Hector's head. To avoid being impaled in the face, Hector employed similar techniques. Fighting for leverage, neither combatant gave in. Although a moment of brevity, it was still one of tension because this brief exchange could determine the victor of the entire fight. One wrong move and either combatant would be slain.

Edmund gained the upper hand, his sword sliding pass Hector's in a thrusting motion, in what looked like a confirmed kill, with his point just millimeters from Hector's face, when Hector impeded the attack by delivering a sharp kick to Edmund's torso. Edmund was forced on to his back. Hector pursued him. Edmund acted quickly. From the ground, he held his sword out in front of him and directed it at Hector. As a result, Hector respected his space and Edmund got back on his feet. They were hesitant to engage each other again due to the near costly exchange.

With both men in long point guard, they slowly approached each other. Hector stepped forward and delivered a descending diagonal cut that was met at the strong of Edmund's blade. Upon contact, Hector half-sworded with the hilt of his sword resting on Edmund's inner arm just below the wrist. Hector then used his sword as a lever, pushing the blade forward towards Edmund's neck, forcing Edmund to lean forward with his sword safely away from Hector. As Hector was pushing his blade towards Edmund's neck, Edmund noticed the cracked skull shaped pommel. He knew his only option to get out of this predicament was using Tithonite. He expelled copious amounts of electricity from his body. So much that it completely shattered the skull pommel of Hector's sword. With pieces of metal and bone being shattered in the air, Edmund retreated. Hector, no longer being able to absorb the attack due to a broken pommel, was propelled several feet back and his blade parted from his hands. Hector lay on the ground, motionless.

As Edmund attempted to approach him, he was blocked by Sir Kelton and the other knight. They had their blades drawn. The other knight slowly inched toward Hector while his blade still pointed at Edmund Sir Kelton approached Edmund.

"Hector is dead. It's over," Edmund said with a labored breath. "I wouldn't be so sure about that."

Edmund was fatigued and in so much pain. Common symptoms for those who used core-soul manifest. The core of one's soul is supposed to simply provide energy to the entire body. That is why it's sometimes called a life force. When that energy is depleted, then one's survival is in jeopardy as the aforementioned energy taken from core-soul manifest cannot be regenerated. In other words, individuals taking energy from the core will suffer rapid apoptosis, central nervous system depression, organ failure, excruciating pain as the gases protecting the individual from the intense energy of the aura have long disappeared, giving one the feeling of being burned alive. The likeliest of outcomes is death. The lingering heat will eventually subside, as the energy input is no longer present. The burning sensation is also not indicative of everyone's experience as the heat ceases immediately for some people when core soul manifest is depleted or reached significantly low levels.

Edmund did not have much left in him. His vision blurred, his breathing sparse and irregular, his body ailing. He could barely stand and was reeking of sulfur. He was in so much pain, but did not have the energy to cry out in agony. He felt like his insides were burning. The aura that had surrounded him had since dissipated. Yet he persisted with only one thought in his head. *I must kill Hector before I exit this world.*

***

The Franklins were surrounded by their enemies and a possessed Mavid, bound together by magical restraints that not only inhibited movements but also soul manipulation. They were made of organic chains. It was an enchantment known as Manaca-la. Sir Ulric used it prior to bind Kraag in the other reality.

With their backs against each other, the Franklins stared at the deranged Oswin as he shouted, "MAVID! End these Franklins. End them with fire!"

But Mavid did not respond. This surprised Oswin. *Is the beast not fully claimed? It is ignoring a direct order. But that's impossible, after all. It simply couldn't be the case.... Our power is absolute.*

One of the men not amongst the undead army said, "Let's just kill them and be done with it. No need for theatrics."

Oswin quickly set him on fire with the Uthra Fithra charm. The others moved away from him, not even attempting to extinguish the fire.

"It must be dragon fire!" Oswin screamed.

John whispered to his father, "Any way we can get out of this charm?"

"Ulric said the Manaca-la is nigh impossible to escape. The only way is to kill the castor that cast it," replied Lord Franklin.

"Even if we escaped, we couldn't take out an entire army of about 200 undead, nearly 2000 living, and a possessed dragon. I don't even think Sir Peter could do that... We may be the last of the Franklins," said William, uncharacteristically despondent.

"Edmund may yet survive if he didn't use the whole core," said John.

"Even if that were so, he'd still be in a vegetative state, unfit to be king," said William.

"We are still breathing, thanks to Edmund. I will not let his sacrifice be in vain. You two will survive and carry on the bloodline," said Lord Franklin.

"Father, we cannot escape the Manaca-la you said—"

"I said nigh impossible. Everything has its limits," replied Lord Franklin.

"Edmund said the boy shocked the dragon out of possession, perhaps I can do the same."

Lord Franklin attempted to free himself by releasing enough soul manifest to overwhelm the enchantment. It was to no avail. He could not even access an iota of soul energy. After several tries, he gave up.

Mavid had still been unresponsive, even after Oswin yelled several commands. The men were getting restless. Then something peculiar happened. Mavid's eyes began flashing between the reptilian yellow to the possessed black. This brought hope to the Franklins that Mavid was somehow resisting the possession. But then Mavid began to convulse. He was reacting violently to the hokraft placed on him. He collapsed on the ground. Several men moved out of the way to avoid being crushed by the colossal beast.

Flailing and writhing on the ground, Mavid was getting flashes of images in his head, possible memories. The first was him being tied down in a ship, apparently unconscious. Large chains fit for a beast his size, most likely made from Modith cores. Bound at the neck and torso to a large wooden ship that appeared to be a Mylecan variety, but the size was almost tenfold. Long narrow shape with shallow draughts. The Long ship was traveling south to Iiadec to Agor. The second image was somewhere in the forest of Beladar. He was bound by chains, being tortured by hooded figures, presumably magic wielders. They were muttering incantations. None of which sounded like old tongue. *Where were his brethren? Why did they not come to his aid? How did fiends capture him? Was this even real?* he thought.

Mavid was on his back, writhing in pain, when a hooded figure approached. He revealed himself as Oswin.

"The wizard!" Mavid thought.

Oswin was carrying a large dragon tooth and said, *"My name is Oswin, dragon, do not resist, for you will be a vessel for the greater good. You will be the first step in the ascension of humanity."*

He plunged the tooth in the exact same spot in his abdomen where he had received a wound in the Mygar wars. What was bemusing was that there had been no wound there beforehand. Where was his wound? Then suddenly, a horrible revelation occurred to him. The Mygar wars were over 5000 years ago, not 500... that thought had been implanted. How could he be so easily deceived? After all, faux magic was not that potent. Oswin, and another hidden figure, cut open his belly, revealing his innards. They placed a device that resembled a mobius strip deep inside his intestine. Could this device be one of the reality breakers (legendary objects that are said to allow the wielder to defy the rules of reality and do things that should be impossible. No one knows the origins of these legends, but most individuals believe it to be pure fiction).

It was no wonder he was hexed. These cunning magic wielders hexed the strip so they could control him from the inside, knowing full well magic would not get through his hide. But if the device was inside of him, there must be another... Hector.

Mavid awoke from his unconscious state, lucid. His eyes were no longer black, but reptilian yellow. He looked at Oswin and said very menacingly, with smoke coming out of his nostrils, "Oswin."

William smiled as he looked at Oswin. "I think you're in trouble now." Oswin ignored him, turned to Mavid, and started muttering some incantations. Mavid did not allow him to finish, and hastily set Oswin ablaze, killing him. As a result, the Manaca-la spell was lifted, and the Franklins were freed. Most of the men had fled upon seeing Mavid had returned, but others remained to challenge him. He set many of his foes ablaze. The undead sell sword army challenged the Franklins. They became more feral. As the result of Oswin perishing, they no longer had him to command them. In other words, no brain, just a stem like ordinary roamers.

The undead Edvin was the first to attack. Growling like an animal, he dropped his weapon and started running on all fours. Soon others followed suit with only one desire: to devour. Edvin leapt into the air in an attempt to bite Lord Franklin. William decapitated Edvin with his long sword. Edvin's body still pursued the Franklins, and his decapitated head was still moving. John put an end to this by smashing Edvin's head repeatedly with the cross guard of his blade. This proved effective in halting the attack, but still there was a horde of roamers with equal vigor. The Franklins fled through the fields of Mydra while shooting thunderbolts at their undead assailants to keep them at bay. If one of the undead strayed from the pack and got too close, they were ended quickly by half-swording techniques, which primarily relied on holding the blade inverted and smashing skulls with the pommel or cross guards. For the undead wearing helmets that protected their heads, they were simply knocked down, given that there wasn't any effective way to slay them with the blade without risking getting up and personal. Remember, concussed attacks will not work against the undead. In order to effectively defeat them, one must completely smash the stem.

"They're gaining on us!" shouted John. "I can see that!" retorted Lord Franklin.

"I still have some soul manifest. C'mon, help me build a wall!" said John.

The Franklins manifested a solid wall in front of them that was bluish in color. The roamers collided with it and smashed against it with such intensity that they left cracks along the surface. Reader, objects created out of soul manifest are rarely as solid as metal or stone. This wall was more akin to plexiglass, but most objects created are much weaker. This was a temporary solution for the Franklins, not a permanent fix. The roamers did not think to walk around the wall; they were only stem without Oswin. One roamer managed to pierce right through the shield with his head. His eyes were completely clouded, indicating blindness, meaning he only got around based on sense and sound. Constantly chomping, indicating hunger, this roamer no longer resembled a man or anything of intelligence, but a flesh-eating parasite wearing a human skin cloth.

William quickly stabbed the roamer in the face and it was felled, but soon the others started to compromise the integrity of the wall by repeatedly smashing their heads against it. That eventually created a fissure along the surface that eventually turned into a narrow opening. The roamers took advantage of that and entered through this aperture. One by one they were slain by the Franklins. Two managed to enter the enclosure. They were beheaded by John and bludgeoned by William. Lord Franklin fired several lightning bolts at the oncoming horde through the fissure. Some were felled. However, most managed to get back up given their undead physiology.

As more encompassed the wall, John said, "There's too many of them. We have to use Hakaneira."

"We'll die. Oswin's spell still hasn't worn off. I can't even remember what Corithni looks like, can you?" said William.

John's silence indicated that he could not. In fact, he didn't even remember what his own living quarters looked like.

"We'll just have to wait it out," said Lord Franklin, while firing another lightning bolt.

Soon, the wall had completely collapsed under pressure. The roamers pursued them in a frantic chase. The Franklins fled through the fields of Mydra in a desperate attempt to escape the undead. But because of Oswin's spell, they didn't know where they were going.

"Curse that little shit. When I get the chance, I'm going to resurrect the cunt, then kill him again!" said William angrily.

He fired six shots at the oncoming roamers, slaying four of them with precision strikes to the head. The other two were not affected and continued on. Soon they were surrounded. Making lightning strikes an unwise option. The Franklins desperately started slashing at their adversaries, unconcerned with form or angle. They bludgeoned the ones that were heavily armored. About five roamers jumped on top of John. Attempting to bite through his basinet. Had he not been wearing one, they would have surely chewed off his face. He struggled to unsheathe a rondel from his waist, now that his sword had been flung out of his hands during the struggle. He stabbed a roamer in the eye with it and pushed it off him. He tried to regain his footing but thirty more had piled on top, scratching and biting; attempting to find a way to break through his armor. The basinet was providing excellent protection, but the weight of the roamers was beginning to take its toll and he was having trouble breathing.

William was faring no better. He was forced on to his knees as nine roamers descended upon him with several more approaching.

Lord Franklin was not even visible under the pile of nearly a hundred undead on top of him. Just as things were starting to look dire, sparks of electricity started crackling from underneath the roamers on top of Lord Franklin. The abrupt explosion of electricity caused the roamers to be propelled into the air. With Lord Franklin no longer concealed, it became apparent he was the source of this devastating attack and was emanating with electricity. Sparks flew everywhere, hitting some of the roamers. Although most were not killed by the attack, they were certainly disoriented by the noise it generated. Enough for William and John to escape.

The Franklins regrouped, standing shoulder to shoulder, weapons drawn. Lord Franklin stood tall, but he was beginning to reek. The last attack depleted his halo-soul manifest.

William turned to his father. "The Tithonite?"

"I had no choice. Unfortunately for us, I don't have enough soul energy left. The little I regained from listening to that repulsive cretin Oswin is all but depleted. I'm going to have to rely on you two for this one," replied Lord Franklin.

The remaining roamers, numbered about a hundred, began to growl restlessly.

"We're not faring much better. The Hakaneira took a lot out of us, but we'll see what we can muster," replied John.

Sparks of electricity began to emanate in both William's and John's hands. The roamers charged at them once more. The Franklins readied themselves, their visors completely closed. When the roamers were in striking distance, all of a sudden fire rained from the sky, incinerating the undead in a blaze.

Above, not too high in the sky, was Mavid.

John lifted his visor and said angrily, "Where the hell have you been? We almost died!"

"I don't know. Fighting an entire army. Do I have to do everything for you Franklins? I mean—"

Then, without warning, Mavid collapsed. He went into a dream state like before, with vivid images. He was not present in them, however. Two dragons, two ships chained to a large ship. Mylecan in origin. His sons, twins Yert and Ghew (GOO). They were unconscious. "*So they're using dragons for hokraft experiments,*" he thought. The image soon disappeared and Mavid awoken.

The Franklins stood over him. He had not been unconscious for long. "Are you alright, Mavid?" asked Lord Franklin, but Mavid was a bit disoriented.

"My sons. My sons! They've taken them. How could I have forgotten?!" "Who?!" said Lord Franklin.

"I don't know. Probably the same ones who jinxed me by placing an object in my belly... a reality breaker."

"Reality breaker?" asked Lord Franklin, completely dumbfounded. "I didn't believe it myself until I saw it in a vision. I mean, how else do you jinx a dragon?" replied Mavid.

"What is a reality breaker?" asked William.

"It means what is says. It's an ancient device, said to allow the wielder to alter certain conventions of reality in order to achieve the impossible," said Mavid.

"You said 'a reality breaker', not 'the reality breaker'. Are there more?" asked John apprehensively.

Mavid nodded.

"Does Hector have one?" asked John.

"Can't say for sure, but if Oswin had one..." said Mavid.

"The jewel on his crown. Curses. How did I not see it?!" said Lord Franklin.

Mavid was looking weary. The light from his eyes was fading. He started swaying back and forth and was having trouble standing upright. His breath was labored.

"Mavid?" asked John, concerned for his comrade.

"Whatever Oswin and his cronies put inside of me, it's... poison and it is lethal...lethal enough to kill a fully grown dragon. I don't think I was supposed to last this long. Oswin or Hector probably hexed it as an insurance policy, in case I escaped my trance."

Mavid collapsed on the ground, still fully conscious but simply too fatigued to stand. The Franklins rushed to his side.

"How-how can we fix it?" said William, his eyes watery. "I don't think you can," Mavid said anemically.

"We-we just need to remove it," said John, tears in his eyes.

"No, they most likely jinxed it with Hokraft spells that Hector most likely controls with his own reality breaker. If the poison is this lethal to a dragon, it would kill a human in an instant," replied Mavid.

"If we take the other reality breaker from Hector, we could heal you?" asked Lord Franklin.

"I suppose," said Mavid.

"Then we shall do that," said Lord Franklin.

"I'll be a corpse by then. Hector will not give up that jewel so easily… If you survive this, find my sons," said Mavid as he closed his eyes for the last time.

The rain and lightning intensified. The Franklins did not have much time to grieve the great dragon for Oswin's spell had worn off and they needed to stop Hector.

"Edmund," they said in unison.

"We only have enough soul energy left between the three of us for one more transport. Is everyone ready?" asked John.

Lord Franklin and William nodded. They raised their blades in the air and disappeared in a flash of lightning.

CHAPTER SEVENTEEN
FINAL BATTLE, PART TWO

Edmund was on the ground, barely breathing, yet he still found the energy to stand up using his longsword for support. He managed to resume his, albeit poor, fighting stance.

"How the hell is this fucker still alive?" said the armored clad knight. "Never mind that, just perform the ritual!" said Sir Kelton.

The knight lifted his visor, removed his gauntlet, took his rondel and cut his open palm. He poured the blood all over Hector's face. Edmund tried to prevent this but was stopped by Sir Kelton, who delivered a descending diagonal cut at Edmund's head. Edmund successfully parried the attack but given his anemic state, he was sent to his knees. The knight continued the ritual, muttering incantations until Hector finally opened his eyes. Except they weren't his, they were stark black.

He looked at the knight and said, "Not enough. I need the whole thing."

Unlike Oswin, Hector's voice was not altered which suggested that whatever dark power he possessed, he was more in control of it than his lackey. The knight was terrified at what Hector was suggesting. But before he could react, Hector crushed the knight's skull with his bare hands, blood oozing from the knight's helmet. The knight, was screaming in agony, one could hear bone crunching. The cries only stopped when Hector snapped his neck and the knight collapsed on the ground with blood still leaking out of his damaged helmet.

Hector rose to his feet and readjusted his crown. Sir Kelton seemed unaffected by his comrade's rather macabre demise and asked nonchalantly, "So how's things with the others?"

Hector's nostrils flared as though he were smelling something. The veins on his face began to protrude a blackish hue.

"Not well. Oswin is dead. So is the dragon. What a waste in the end. You were right, the fool could not deliver."

"What do we do with this one?" asked Sir Kelton, referring to Edmund.

"He fought valiantly; he should die valiantly." Hector picked up his blade and approached Edmund, who was on all fours, too weak to stand. Hector assumed the high guard position with the intention of delivering a downward cut.

Instantaneously, a flash of lightning appeared, and so did the other Franklins. William wasting no time delivered a vertical cut that knocked Hector's crown off his head, while Lord Franklin pulled his ailing son to safety. Sir Kelton stepped in to do battle. He crossed swords with John. Sir Kelton delivered a descending vertical strike at John's head with his blade inverted. John parried the attack through half-swording, with Sir Kelton's cross guard precariously close to his helmet. Without such a late parry, John would have surely suffered a concussion or worse.

William did battle with Hector, who was more aggressive than before. Although the crown had been removed, he had not lost all strength and still proved a formidable opponent. The crown was behind William. William did not bother picking it up for fear of being poleaxed, yet he would not let Hector get to it.

Hector from high guard, delivered a descending vertical cut that met on the strong of William's blade. Although William successfully parried the attack with ox guard, given Hector's strength, he was forced on to his knees and his blade was severely damaged. Hector attempted to deliver the killing blow but was thwarted by Lord Franklin, who ran to Hector and bashed him in the side of the head at full force with his buckler. An attack that should have knocked him unconscious, but instead, seemed to mildly irritate him. William went for the crown but was soundly kicked by Hector. William was sent sailing across the ground with three of his ribs cracked.

Meanwhile, John had gained the upper hand on Sir Kelton. He managed to thrust his blade through a chink in Sir Kelton's armor between the helmet and the breastplate through half-swording. The attack was fatal, and Sir Kelton perished. John went for the crown now that he was free of Kelton. Just as he was mere inches from getting it, his whole body felt numb, and he could not move. He fell on the ground, paralyzed.

"*Another hex?*" he thought.

This even surprised Hector, who did not realize the crown was jinxed. Hector smiled and thought, *"Hildred's doing, no doubt assisting from the grave."*

But Hector had not been paying attention, for Lord Franklin delivered two quick diagonal cuts to his head which Hector narrowly avoided. William, who had recovered but was bladeless, threw a haymaker that struck Hector in the face and forced him to his knees. The incantations were wearing off and Hector's supernatural strength was waning. Hector's eyes turned back to brown, their natural color.

Before he could raise his blade, Lord Franklin pointed the Great Divider at his throat.

"It's over Hector."

Hector smiled. "Just one last trick ani—"

Lord Franklin hastily cut off his head. Hector's body collapsed on the ground. William ran over to John, who was slowly gaining control of his body and helped him up. Along with Lord Franklin, they knelt beside their ailing brother, who was on the ground.

"You did it," he said anemically. "We did it," said John tearfully. "Eh, I didn't do much," replied Edmund.

"Nonsense. You took him on all by yourself, even without knowing about the crown," said William.

Edmund looked at his father. "Giselle's baby is… mine, not Martin's. Mother didn't want it to be a bastard. She didn't think you'd approve of me marrying a low born since she's from Nalmia and all… and tell Lady Branson I love her with all my heart."

"You will tell her yourself," said Lord Franklin.

"And it will be a very awkward conversation," said William. The Franklins laughed briefly.

Edmund sighed. He looked at his father and said, "I'm sorry. I will not be able to succeed the throne of Iiadec, but I'm sure John will make a worthy heir."

Lord Franklin wept silently.

"You may yet succeed. Before he died, Mavid said Hector's jewel is a reality breaker. Well, it means we can ignore the conventions of reality and do the impossible, like restore core soul manifest."

"No. That thing has got hokraft written all over it. Besides, it's probably still jinxed. I forbid it."

"The hexes have worn off. John's proof of that. Besides, I am the King of Iiadec now. I command you to let us heal you… I will not lose my son today," said Lord Franklin.

He walked up to the crown, but as he approached, it started shaking and the light on the surface of the jewel started to flicker.

"Another hex—"

But Lord Franklin never got to finish that thought. Because he and others within a 1.86-mile radius were incinerated by the center of the explosion. The shockwaves reached as far as 5 miles. Enough to shatter the northern walls of Corithni.